The SOUND of BOW BELLS

*

The SOUND of

*　*

BOW BELLS

*

Jerome Weidman

Random House　*New York*

FOR

Lee Wright

FROM

J. W.

"The unexamined life is not worth living."

—SOCRATES

"If you can't have what you like, you'd better like what you have."

—CLAUDE SARGENT

The SOUND of BOW BELLS

What took him by surprise was the suggestion about a telephone answering service.

"I don't see why," Rebecca Meissen had said shortly after Sam moved into 16E. "The telephone answering service was practically invented for men like you."

This struck Sam Silver as not unlike saying the Union Pacific tracks had been laid down especially for his benefit. It was true enough up to a point, but it was equally true that in the process of opening up a continent the railroad builders had managed to provide something that a great many other people found equally useful.

"I'm merely surprised to find that all of a sudden anybody should think it's an essential item in the scheme of my existence," Sam had said. "After all, I've managed to live almost thirty-six years without one."

"You didn't live those years in Sutton Crescent," said Rebecca, who, with her son Ronnie, had moved from their town house on East Sixty-first Street into the huge apartment house on the East River almost three years before Sam did. The Meissen family, meaning Rebecca's father, brothers, and uncles, had been an important name in New York building construction circles for a quarter of a century. Sutton Crescent was one of the first, and still considered one of the most desirable, of the large apartment houses that had paced the New York postwar building boom, and it was Rebecca's influence with the rental agent that had landed one of the much coveted "E" apartments for Sam in spite of a long waiting list that included some of New York's better-known citizens. "Things are going to be different from now on," Rebecca said. "This isn't Gramercy Park, you know."

If he didn't know, Sam thought, the monthly bill could be counted on to remind him.

"If you say I need a telephone answering service, then I'll sign up at once," he said. "Now that the Admissions Committee of this swank cliff-dweller's paradise has accepted me, I don't want to slight any of the club's traditions."

"I wish you wouldn't agree so readily to everything I suggest," said Rebecca, who claimed—and, Sam was convinced, really believed—she had asked her husband for a divorce three years ago because their marriage had lacked what she called an abrasive quality. During her decade of matrimony, Rebecca had told Sam shortly after they met, her slightest wish had been law. It had never occurred to kind, decent, simple-minded, and eminently solvent Anton, who adored her, that to make a woman truly happy it was essential on occasion to cross her. "I'm just trying to help you furnish and settle into a new apartment, Sam," she added. "I'm not trying to run your life."

"Well, it's a good way to begin," Sam said, and because she looked hurt, he shifted the conversation hastily to the level on which Rebecca was always happiest, and at which she was extremely proficient: imparting factual information. He said, "What makes you say the telephone answering service was practically invented for men like me?"

Rebecca's faintly troubled scowl changed at once to the small warm glow that Sam supposed must have appeared on the face of Annie Sullivan when she first beheld the young Helen Keller.

"To begin with," Rebecca said, "you live alone."

"Correction," Sam said. "I live with an almost thirteen-year-old and, according to this morning's bathroom scales, already one-hundred-and-twenty-pound son who might resent that remark."

Rebecca brushed aside the irrelevance with a gesture that set to tinkling like a miniature carillon the four-thousand-dollar diamond-studded charm bracelet that Anton, a civilized type, had given her as a gesture of continued friendship when she came home from Reno.

"You know what I mean," Rebecca said impatiently. Sam did. So long as he was not officially married—in the eyes of Rebecca Meissen he would be "living alone." Rebecca, who would have been outraged if Sam had revealed that for him one of her greatest charms was that she radiated propriety the way some women exude lubricity, said to him, "In addition to living alone, you don't go to an office. You work right here in your apartment. So that when you're out, and somebody tries to get you on the phone because it's an important business matter—"

"They'll keep calling again and again until they do get me," Sam said. "Anyway, that's what my mother says."

"Your mother is an eighty-year-old Rumanian peasant who, even though she's been living in this country for almost six decades, still thinks the I.R.T. subway is a personal plot against her."

It was a joke. Rebecca Meissen, who did not have a mean bone in her beautifully put-together body, would sooner—well, almost sooner—have died than say anything catty about an older person related to someone she liked. But it was no joke to Sam. His relationship to his parents troubled him more than he cared to admit, even to himself, and so he had never mentioned it to Rebecca. There were areas about which you could not talk. People who trafficked in words had a tendency to exaggerate their importance. Sam Silver, who had been writing for his living since the age of twenty, suspected in his more troubled moments that he knew something even Shakespeare, who clearly had known everything, had not had occasion to learn: there were corners of the heart out of which you could not talk or write your way. You could only escape by living the outward journey, and he had never learned how to do that.

"Mom is not eighty. She's only seventy-eight," Sam said. "And as a man who practically spent the first twenty years of his life in the I.R.T. subway, I think she's got a point."

"Your mother has many points and many virtues, I'm sure," said Rebecca, who had never met Mrs. Silver. "But her opinion about telephone answering services is not one of them. Does it make sense to buy an apartment that costs sixty thousand dollars? Calls for a monthly maintenance fee of almost five hundred? Decorate it to the tune of what will come to at least twenty thousand—possibly more, if you decide on the white iron terrace furniture, which I hope you will—and then draw the line at a silly fifteen dollars a month for a woman to answer your phone when you're not in?"

Sam had not drawn the line, but there were times when he wished Mrs. Harrison would.

"She's the best, and I ought to know," Rebecca had said some months later. "I tried three other serivces before I found Mrs. Harrison. I can't understand why you dislike her."

"I don't dislike her."

"Yes, you do. I can tell by the way the moment her name is mentioned your face freezes in a look of excessive politeness and your voice begins to practically curdle with the milk of well-bred human kindness. I've come to know you pretty well, Sam Silver," Rebecca said, poking her slender forefinger lightly at the solid-gold knot that held his tie neatly to the front of one of the half-dozen twenty-dollar shirts she had given him for Christmas. Rebecca did not know, of course, that Jennie had given him the gold square knot on their wedding day, or that he had worn it all these years as a good-luck piece. How could she know? How could anybody know? Rebecca was constantly saying she wanted to hear all about Jennie and what had happened to her, but on the three or four occasions when Sam—his guard dropped by a moment of unexpected tenderness that eased the tension of living alone with a puzzle that still stained his days—had tried to tell her, Rebecca had changed the subject. She now said, "One of the things I've learned about you, Sam, is that people you like, you call 'Hey!' People you dislike, you call Missiz Harrison in great big round pear-shaped tones as though you were conferring a knighthood on them."

Giving her a quick look of surprised appreciation, Sam could feel the part of his mind that functioned independently, like a perpetually turned-on vacuum cleaner, suck up Rebecca's observation and tuck it away for future use. Everything, Claude Sargent had said sixteen years ago when he took Sam on as a client, is grist to the writer's mill, and the trick is to keep the mill grinding away, all the time, twenty-four hours a day, without thought or pause or shame or hesitation or anything, regardless of what you're doing, even while you're making love.

"Knighthoods are not conferred on members of the female sex," Sam said. "Women are made Dames of the British Empire. And while I deny that I dislike Mrs. Harrison, I admit that if I had the power to make anybody a D.B.E., hers would hardly be the first name that crossed my mind."

"I wish I knew why," Rebecca went on. "She not only gives you good value for your money. She gives more. Mrs. Harrison is constantly calling me back, a half hour after she's read off my messages, to remind me of the important ones and make sure I haven't forgotten to return the calls."

"I know," said Sam. "That's precisely why I'd never make her a Dame of the British Empire."

"You dislike Mrs. Harrison for *that?*" Rebecca said with a touch of incredulity. "For doing her job conscientiously?"

"For doing it too damned conscientiously," Sam said. "Service above and beyond the call of duty is fine in a soldier going over the top. In a woman you dial for your telephone messages, it's a pain in the neck." The puzzled frown, which did such pretty things to Rebecca's cheekbones, by remaining intact did something not very pretty to Sam's temper. "Don't you see?" he said irritably. "There are some telephone messages a man doesn't *want* to return."

Rebecca looked hurt. In spite of her chic, highly polished, expensive exterior, she was all marshmallow inside. She could no more face the raised voice than the raised hand. Sam, who liked her and wished he could love her, at once felt like a dog.

"I'm sorry," he said. "I didn't mean to shout."

"Tell me quietly," Rebecca said quietly. "Like for instance what kind of messages you don't like to return."

"Oh—" Sam made a short gesture in the air, as though he were erasing an unpleasant word from an invisible blackboard, and the vacuum cleaner that stoked the mill of his craft sucked that up, too. For future reference, of course. Writers, he had learned, never really lived in the present. What counted was the past, where the bits and pieces and lumps sucked up lay aging patiently, like wine, against the day when they would be needed. What mattered was the future, where the refashioned bits and pieces would appear in the form of printed words the public would either clasp to its bosom or on which it would turn its back. "There aren't any special messages," Sam said vaguely. "It's just that some people who call you—" He stopped again, horrified as much by what he suddenly grasped from her face was going through Rebecca's mind as by his realization that she might be right. "For God's sake!" he said sharply. "Not *your* calls!"

The cheekbones promptly grew pink again with relieved delight. Like so many people who lived their lives chin up, avoiding no man's glance, making the daily round with fearless strides under the boldly unfurled pennant of Truth, Rebecca Meissen had only to sight a fragment of it—and she would turn and run.

"I know *that*, silly," she said with the smile that always warmed but never really melted him, the way Jennie's smiles used to melt him. Probably because Jennie's smiles, unlike Rebecca's, had not come easily. In the game of love the cheaply won victory moved many things, but never the heart. "If I thought for one minute that you hated returning my calls," Rebecca said, "I'd—I'd—I don't know *what* I'd do."

"Good," Sam said. "Because you don't have to do it. I like your calls. They brighten my day. Please keep making them. What I don't like is being hounded, and that's what I feel Mrs. Harrison does to me when she calls back a half hour after giving me my messages and says now don't forget that call from your mother, Mr. Silver, she seemed terribly anxious to hear from you."

"You mean it's your mother's calls you hate to return?" Rebecca said with a quick lift in her voice.

The vacuum cleaner, gobbling with relentless, unemotional, business-like greediness, nudged him into another moment of awareness to which he knew, as a human being rather than as a writer, he was not entitled. All at once he was staring at Rebecca the way at unexpected moments he used to stare at Jennie—with a sense of pleased discovery: she loved him enough to be constantly on the alert, probing for the weakness that, if and when she found it, would give her total possession.

"No, it's not my mother's calls I hate to return," Sam said, and he touched her cheek gently, as though she were a puppy that had earned a reward for laying a bone or a stick at his feet. "I'm not my son Billy. I'm a great big grown-up boy now. What I hate is being picked up after."

Rebecca laughed. "Anton used to say the same thing," she said. "And he was constantly dropping things behind him and forgetting them, including our marriage."

"Well," Sam said, "I'm not Anton."

"No, you're not," Rebecca said, and the touch of wistfulness in her voice made him laugh. The laugh caused her to blush. "Not that I want you to be," she said firmly. "I've had my fill of men who are open books. I'd rather have you, even though deep down I don't *really* have you, with all those footnotes in Latin or Yiddish or whatever the language is, that I don't understand but which make the book interesting because they give me something to work on, and some day, by God, I *will* understand."

"When you do," Sam said, "let me know. Meantime, see what you can do to get Mrs. Harrison off my neck."

"No," Rebecca said. "You're a great big grown-up boy. Do it yourself." "How?"

"Call her up," Rebecca said. "Tell her to stop hounding you. She understands English."

Sam wondered if she did. He *had* called her up. With the result that now, several months later, Mrs. Harrison was still dragging him out of the kitchen, just as the water for the coffee was starting to boil, to tell him something she had told him a half hour before, when he had called in for his messages after shaving.

"Yes, thank you," Sam said into the white phone on the eighteenth-century writing table that Rebecca had insisted, when she found it on Third Avenue, would "make" his study and was a "steal" at seven hundred dollars. "You gave me the message about Mr. Sargent. Half an hour ago."

"Yes, I know," said Mrs. Harrison in the throaty, well-bred voice that Sam, who had never seen her, always found vaguely troubling. "Hold it a moment, please," Mrs. Harrison said. "My board is buzzing."

"Listen," Sam said sharply, but she was gone, and as he held the dead phone, he became aware of the sounds in the kitchen behind him. The study had been intended, by the architects who drew the plans for Sutton Crescent, to serve as a dining room. But Rebecca had insisted it would be a crime to waste the magnificent river view on guests. They would spend at most an occasional hour or two in the apartment, Rebecca pointed out, whereas Sam was in it all day long, working. Besides, he didn't really need a dining room. With the proper furniture, which she would find for him, a corner of the huge living room could be converted into a dining alcove that would be more than adequate for his infrequent dinner parties and the meals he and Billy ate at home. Rebecca's point had seemed sound. She had found the right furniture for the dining alcove, and the swinging door from the former dining room into the kitchen had been blocked off by ceiling-to-floor bookcases painted to match the lime-green wall-to-wall carpeting. The result, from the cosmetic standpoint, was a huge success. Everybody, or almost everybody, who visited Sutton Crescent's apartment 16E, remarked on the beauty of Sam's study. Sophie Sargent, who was Claude's wife as well as the second half of Sargent & Sargent, Literary Agents, had remarked on seeing it for the first time that it was the sort of room in which she could imagine Henry James—staring out not at the East River but the Thames, and not from Sutton Crescent but Cheyne Walk—putting the finishing touches to *The Golden Bowl*. As the phone came alive against his ear, he said testily, "Mrs. Harrison, I wish you wouldn't do this to me."

"Do what, Mr. Silver?"

"Call me up, start to tell me something, then say hold on, and disappear."

"Surely, Mr. Silver, you don't for a moment believe I do that deliberately?"

"What?" Sam said, startled by the unexpected temperature drop in her voice.

"I said surely, Mr. Silver, you don't for a moment believe—?"

"I heard that," Sam said, and all at once he knew what it was that the throaty, well-bred voice reminded him of: Mrs. Harrison sounded like a visiting British author lecturing to an American audience and bearing down on his accent in an effort to make it plain that while reverses in his fortunes had made it necessary for him to do this sort of thing for a living, he didn't want the people for whom he was doing it to make the mistake of thinking the highly temporary and purely commercial relationship raised them in any way to his social level. Sam, who had been born in a tenement at the corner of Tenth Street and Avenue C, duly noted that the icy elegance in his voice was even more spurious than Mrs. Harrison's British accent as he said, "I'm not accusing you of deliberately annoying me, Mrs. Harrison, but that's what it amounts to when you call me up and—"

The accents of an ersatz Brasenose, pouring forth with relentless reasonableness, cut him off as effectively as a cataract. Billy, appearing in the study doorway stark naked and carrying a slender volume bound in the purple and white colors of the Porte School, drew Sam's ear away from the numbing stream of icy self-justification.

"I'm interrupting, huh?" Billy said.

"Nothing very important," Sam said. "It's that pain in the neck Mrs. Harrison."

"Oh, yeah," his son said. "She called last night while you were out."

Sam said, "Mrs. Harrison called *you?*"

"Well, not exactly," Billy said. "Or maybe she did. Depends on how you figure it. The point is she had this important message for you—"

"What message?" said Sam.

"Say," Billy said, "what's eating you this morning?"

Sam stared at the slender figure with the handsome, neatly made, crew-cut head, and his heart lurched, as it did every morning, with the curious pain that was not unlike the secret toothache he used to carry around in Grover Cleveland High when he was in love with the movie actress. The boy was all that remained of the years with Jennie. When those years ended, Billy had been only two. Even through the shock of bereavement, which had been almost unbearable, Sam had been made abruptly aware that Jennie had left him with a total stranger. Not until she was gone had he realized that from the moment she had come into his life, there had been no room in it for anybody else. Not even for their child. Made aware in spite of his grief that even to a stranger he had a responsibility, Sam had cast about for some clue to its nature. He knew nothing about children. Now that she was gone, he saw that neither had Jennie, and he also saw why: she had no interest in them. And his own interests, of course, had been limited to Jennie's. Unable to find the clue for this new interest that had been thrust upon him in the real and now empty life to which he was condemned, Sam found it in the life he preferred: his work.

He had just cracked, as Claude Sargent put it, the *Saturday Evening Post*—or, as Claude Sargent wrote it, the *Satevepost*—with a story about a Middlewestern minister's son who comes to New York's Lower East Side at the age of twenty-one to work as a social worker in a settlement house and is assigned to lead a boy scout troop composed of slum-area kids with standards of values, honesty, and sportsmanship utterly different from his own.

"The boys in Philly," Claude—whose nickname was, of course, Top—Sargent had written to Sam, "are particularly keen on the relationship between the Midwestern scoutmaster and the slum boy scouts. It's fresh. They never like to commit themselves to a series, but I have a hunch from the way they talked about this story that they'd like to see more of that scoutmaster and those kids. I'd take a chance if I were you. It might pay off."

It had paid off in a way that Top Sargent couldn't possibly have foreseen when he made the suggestion. Out of the fictional relationship between the scoutmaster and the boys in his troop, which Sam kept going for almost twenty stories before the vein ran thin, he had invented a relationship between himself and his son Billy which they had both kept going for ten years. For almost eight of those years—from the time Sam discovered to his surprise that what he felt for the total stranger who had been left in his care was at least as strong and possibly stronger than what he had felt for Jennie—Sam had been wondering if the vein had not started thin. Every morning, when he first saw his son, Sam Silver wanted to take the boy in his arms. Instead, every morning he was forced to dip up, out of his mind's accumulations, samples of the snappy, unsentimental, men-of-the-world dialogue to which, because of the way he made his living, he had committed them both.

"Nothing's eating me," Sam said.

"Well, you sure sound off your feed," Billy said, scratching his bare behind with a corner of the purple and white book.

"It's that Mrs. Harrison. She gets paid to take my messages, not to interrupt you when you're studying. The whole point of my having a telephone answering service is when I'm out, and you're in, you shouldn't be disturbed."

"Mrs. Harrison knows that, Pop. Don't get your blood pressure up. This was an exception, she said. The message was important."

"What message?" Sam said.

"Mr. Sargent called, Mrs. Harrison said, and he wanted you to call back first chance you got, and she got the impression it was too important to wait till this morning, so she asked me to tell you about it when you came home, but I guess I was asleep."

"You sure were," Sam said. "Snoring like a ripsaw. Listen, do me a favor. In the kitchen. The coffee water. It's boiling. Pour it in the Chemex, will you?"

"Sure," Billy said. "But I want you to run me through this scene once more. The show goes on right after chapel, ten-thirty, and I still don't know what the hell Calpurnia means when she says—"

"I'll run you through it at breakfast," Sam said. "And let's watch the language, shall we?"

"For saying hell? Hell, Pop, you ought to hear some of the stuff Ronnie says."

"Ronnie Meissen's language is his mother's responsibility," Sam said. "Yours is mine. Now stop standing around with your rear end out in the open or you'll catch a cold and won't be able to go to school and this great performance for which you've been preparing by driving me crazy for three weeks will be wasted. Get some clothes on and pour that water into the Chemex."

"Which first?"

"The water first," Sam said. "Before it all boils away."

"If I catch a cold it'll be your fault, then. Come on, Pop, no kidding, I have to know what this damn—excuse it, please!—this darn Calpurnia, I have to know what she means with this *Caesar, I never stood on ceremonies, yet now they fright me.* If I don't, Mr. Bronson, that creep, he'll make a monkey out of me in front of the whole auditorium."

The protective instinct, to which the *Satevepost* scoutmaster's creator would never have allowed his creation to succumb, leaped like a raw nerve.

"Mr. Bronson giving you a bad time?" Sam demanded.

"Relax, Pop, will you? Mr. Bronson is a teacher. All teachers are creeps. Creeps give everybody a pain. Some do it one way, some another. This particular creep likes to make a monkey out of you in front of the whole class when you're not prepared perfectly, and when he's got a chance like today to do it in front of the whole school, wow! I know this scene pretty good. It's just this part about Calpurnia."

"We'll run through the scene at breakfast," Sam said. "For which there won't be any coffee if you let that damn water boil away before—"

"See?"

"See what?"

"You said damn water. The way I figure it, there's this famous old proverb, it goes what's sauce for the goose is sauce for—"

The remainder of the famous old proverb vanished along with the handsome little face as Sam's slipper, thumping against the jamb of the study door, sent Billy scurrying toward the kitchen and returned his father's attention to Mrs. Harrison's nonstop description of the rare virtues and unique talents she brought to the service of her clients with the full knowledge, quixotic fool that she was, that by so doing she was merely casting pearls before swine.

"I'm sorry if I hurt your feelings," Sam said, stepping out firmly into the phone's stream of words. "I didn't mean to be rude, Mrs. Harrison."

"I'm certain you didn't, Mr. Silver. Nor do I mean to be rude to you, sir. I merely tried to explain—"

"You have," Sam said. "Would you explain to me now what makes Mr. Sargent's message important? Did Mr. Sargent use the word urgent?"

"He did, Mr. Silver."

"And that's why, instead of waiting until I called in this morning for my messages, you rang me here last night until my son answered and you gave him the—?"

"Precisely," Mrs. Harrison said. "And may I say, Mr. Silver, that a very polite and gentlemanly young man he is, too. I would like to compliment you on having raised such a thoroughly nice boy."

"Why, thank you, Mrs. Harrison," said Sam, who wished he could think of something more original to say. It was not that he was ungrateful for the compliment. It was simply that he didn't feel he deserved it. Not, at any rate, in the secret ledger of his own heart where the record was kept with scrupulous accuracy. On that page, which neither Mrs. Harrison nor any other human being had ever seen, Sam had the uneasy feeling he was failing Billy just as surely as he had once felt, uneasily, that he had failed Jennie. The fact that he didn't know how he had failed, or how he was failing now, did not ease the problem.

Replacing the phone, Sam allowed his eye to linger on the bright, sunlit river at his feet. A freighter, angling toward Welfare Island to make better time against the outgoing tide, was beating its way north. Sam had stopped calling it "uptown" soon after they moved into the apartment, when Billy, fascinated by the river traffic, had pointed out that they might as well start using the proper nautical terms.

"Not only on account of I mean you don't say a ship is moving uptown, Pop, I mean you just don't, but what the heck, you might want to write a story about the sea some day, like say maybe this Joseph Conrad that creep Mr. Bronson is always beating his gums about."

"I'm no Conrad," Sam had said, regretting the words as soon as they were uttered. Fortunately, the remark seemed to have no significance for Billy, or perhaps the boy had not heard it, and his father had covered the uneasy moment by adding casually, "It's getting so I recognize some of the ships."

He recognized this one now. She was the *Owl's Head,* dun-colored and tired-looking, with enormous scabs of ugly rust spotting her sagging sides and oil-stained well-deck. The *Owl's Head* passed the terraces of Sutton Crescent several times every day, working her lumbering way north and south on God knew what ignoble missions for the city's Department of Public Works, which Billy had finally identified as her "registry" from the DPW painted on her forward stack. There was something reassuring about the sight of the *Owl's Head*. It was like a glimpse, in the midst of a strange nightmare, of a familiar, undemanding, commonplace figure: the old newsdealer with the red nose at the Fifty-seventh Street corner; Jason, the ancient Negro who lived somewhere in the complicated bowels of Sutton Crescent and delivered to the apartment doors packages that were too large to fit into the lobby mailboxes. Watching the *Owl's Head's* familiar struggle with the waters of the tidal estuary Billy had taught him not to call a river, Sam could feel an easing away of the twinges of pain set in motion by Mrs. Harrison's unconscious tap at the inner bruise around which he lived. Turning from the eighteenth-century desk to face the day, Sam saw that Billy, now only half naked, had reappeared in the study doorway.

"Pop, can you do something about this darn tie?"

"Let's have a look," Sam said.

The slender figure came to the desk and Sam's fingers began to undo the lumped knot of black knitted silk that formed, along with the button-down blue Brooks Brothers shirt, part of the Porte School's lower-classman's uniform.

"You know, aside from the fact that these ties cost almost six dollars," Sam said, "a sum which is not to be sneezed at but about which I won't comment at the moment, you might get to knotting them properly if you stopped treating them like hawsers and tried looking in the mirror while doing it."

"How can I look in the mirror when I'm pouring the coffee water in the Chemex?"

"You don't pour the coffee water into the Chemex every morning. You just happened to do it this morning because I was tied up on the phone and I didn't want the water to boil away. There." Sam gave the neat knot a final pat and pulled Billy's chin down. "Next time you might also try knotting your tie after you've put on your underwear and pants."

"I'll let you in on a little secret, Pop: the way a guy knots his tie has nothing to do with whether he's wearing his underwear and pants while doing it." The brown eyes, not quite as dark as Jennie's, crinkled in a wink and the merry little face vanished. As Sam lifted the receiver, and started to dial Top's home number, the grin reappeared in the study door. "You done me tie," Billy said. "I'll do the oh jay."

"I've already squeezed the orange juice," Sam called toward the now empty doorway. "If you feel the compulsion to make yourself useful, get out the Rice Krispies and slice us a banana!"

"Ugh!" said a voice in Sam's ear. "What a revolting way to start the day!"

"Oh, hi, Sophie," Sam said into the phone. "I hope I didn't wake you up. It's Claude I want."

"Well, you can't have him, darling. He's off to the neck tugger, and as for waking me up, I've been up and about since dawn reading the new Titterton, God save us all, and railing at staff."

The speaker's client grinned into his ivory-white phone as the *Owl's Head*, making headway against the outgoing tide, slid from his range of vision. The Sargent staff consisted of a superb cook, a magnificent maid, and a marvelous butler-chauffeur, and few things pleased Sam more about Sophie Sargent, who had been born Melisande Kelly in an already far-too-crowded three-room flat over a grocery store in Wilkes-Barre, than the fact that she referred to her servants as "stahf," always minus the possessive pronoun or the definite article.

The reasons were crystal-clear to Sam Silver. They were the reasons why he liked Sophie and why, even though they had never discussed those reasons, he knew Sophie liked him: she and he were like a couple of adventurers of different nationalities—Columbus, perhaps, and John Cabot, or stout Cortez and skinny Amerigo Vespucci—who had set out, from different corners of the world and totally unaware of each other, to find the wealth of the Indies and, on reaching it or its equivalent, and discovering with delight that there was more than enough to go around for both, had been able in the flush of triumph to find room for an admiring salute to the enterprise and intrepidity of another.

The forty-block voyage uptown from East Tenth Street to Sutton Crescent had taken all of Sam's almost forty years. The much longer journey from Wilkes-Barre to the seventeen-room duplex facing Central Park at Sixty-first and Fifth had taken half that time. But Sophie Sargent would have been the first to admit what neither she nor Sam had ever put into words: the climb was easier for a woman, especially if she was beautiful. And Sophie, who at fifty-eight was still nearly that, had been at sixteen, when she shook the cracker crumbs of the elder Kelly's Wilkes-Barre grocery from her feet, a stunner.

"Top's sacroiliac again?" Sam said into the phone.

"Darling, you know Claude," said Sophie, who liked the fact that in the trade—as the world of letters was identified in the offices of Sargent & Sargent—her husband was known by an endearing, and therefore commercially useful, nickname but who would sooner have been seen lunching at a Nedick's hot-dog stand on Easter Sunday than herself call him any-thing but Claude. She said, "His back is always bad when there's a crisis."

"Oh," said Sam, hating the knot of apprehension that suddenly began to grow in his stomach. "So there's a crisis, is there?"

"How could there not be?" said Sophie. "I warned Titterton about this a year ago, when he started on the damned book, but you know these bloody English authors. They never seem to grasp the point that it's per-fectly all right to be greedy about money—after all, nobody adores the sound of gold doubloons chunking against each other more than I do, as you well know—but the surest way not to earn it is to show your greediness to the world."

The wonderfully entertaining voice was momentarily cheering. It al-ways reminded Sam of the sound tracks of early talking pictures: exciting in a way that had nothing to do with the often preposterous words they were sending out into the theatre, because the noises carried to the listener an awareness of being present not only at an entertainment but at a mo-ment of history; a new way had been invented for the voice of one human to reach the ears of another. The voice did not, however, fool Sam. He had been a Sargent & Sargent client for sixteen years. He had learned how to read the dun-colored depressing words between the brightly hued tinkling lines.

"What's happened?" Sam said, playing the game Sophie's way, because he knew it was only after she had been given a chance to perform for an inning or two that she would get down to the business of delivering the pitch that counted. "Metro drop the option?"

"Darling, what else could they do?" said Sophie. "These damned English novelists spend the first four decades of their lives writing and rewriting the same tedious account of their homosexual experiences at Eton or Har-row or some other thinly disguised public school, which sell four thousand copies if you give away a wrist watch with each copy and never earn back a fraction of their reprint advances, and then in their middle fifties, pre-sumably as a reward for their longevity, the addlepated Foreign Office sends them off as cultural attachés at a thousand quid a year to some out-post of empire in the Sudan, where they stumble into the first new material that has come their way since puberty, and they repay their gov-ernment's soft-headed generosity by writing a steaming novel about misce-genation in the upper echelons of Government House."

"That's pretty harsh an estimate of *Venery in the Sun*, don't you think?" said Sam, who didn't mind the harshness at all. He had learned long ago how to live with the most difficult problem his trade posed for its practi-tioners: jealousy of the success of his contemporaries. "I thought the sections about the Governor's Ball during the feast of Ramadan showed an extraordinary grasp of the difference between Coptic and Christian cultures."

"That, my dear loyal darling," said Sophie Sargent crisply, "is because you don't know any more about the difference between Coptic and Christian cultures than I do, and you think anything Claude and I sell must be good. It isn't, as you well know, if only because in the past two decades we've sold quite a bit of your own product that was not up to snuff. What made *Venery in the Sun* sell, as you also well know, was all those harem scenes in which Titterton, who has never been closer to a naked woman than I've been to William Jennings Bryan, described all the girls, with what I'm sure the silly ass still thinks is strict accuracy, as possessing four breasts."

"Has he given them fewer in this new book?" Sam asked, wondering how to phrase the question he really wanted to ask.

"If he had, we wouldn't be in this mess with Metro now," said Sophie. "The trouble is that not only are all his females equipped precisely as his epicene imagination equipped them in *Venery,* but he's placed them in the same harem on the same island with the same Balliol-trained undersecretary, who on the surface seems so worldly but in actual fact has never really known what it was all about until the pasha's favorite sneaks into his bedroom one night during the big diplomatic dinner and opens his, if you will pardon the euphemism, eyes."

From the other end of the wire came the sharp little expulsion of breath that couldn't really be described as a snort of disgust. Sophie Sargent had copied it from Pamela Poitier, the American rights to whose novels about Mayfair—drawn with brilliant and recognizable accuracy from her several decades as wife of Lord Kirriemuir, Physician in Ordinary to four reigning British monarchs—Sargent & Sargent had handled for years with enormous financial success. Lady Kirriemuir, whom Sam had met twice at Sargent dinner parties, was a formidably tiny woman of about eighty pounds and approximately the same number of summers, with a face of incredible distinction who did not snort. The effect, however, when she expelled her breath, was the same. And Sophie—who added to her arsenal of mannerisms only those that had been tested and proved effective in those areas where she felt the person into which, since leaving Wilkes-Barre, she had fashioned herself belonged—had learned how to achieve the effect as easily, and with as much conviction, as though she had spent her life, not in peddling manuscripts to the American "trade," but in gracing an ancestral estate and a London town house.

"What Titterton has done is make the mistake all you writers make,"

Sophie said. "Instead of fleeing from a success, he's embraced it and tried to repeat it."

"Is it really a mistake?" said Sam, wishing he did not sound so defensive. In between the brightly uttered lines of contempt for Henley Titterton, which only someone who did not know Sophie Sargent might have considered irrelevant, he had begun to glimpse the dreaded words that spelled trouble for Sam Silver. He said, "It's easy enough to toss off an aphorism about fleeing from a success, but what about Tom Sacheverell and Harry Carver and Quincy Holmes, just to take three examples at random who happen to be Sargent & Sargent clients and whose books sell like flypaper in August, even though those boys have been writing the same book year in and year out since Dewey sailed into Manila Bay, and you know it, Sophie."

"No, they haven't, Sam," said Sophie, and he could tell from the slight change in her voice that the performance for the bleachers was coming to an end and she was getting ready to deliver the pitch that counted. "There's a world of difference between dreary repetition, which is what Henley Titterton has done in this new book, and planting your flag in an area of either experience or geography, announcing to the world that from here on in it's your province, and then exploiting it to the full. Tom Sacheverell did that when he discovered the Pacific after the war. Tom does not write the same novel every year. He really doesn't, Sam. He merely writes a novel about the same *place* every year. Tom's wrapped up the subject of the Pacific. He's made the area, or books about the area, his own. So that poachers, and all you have to do is look in the *Times Book Review* any Sunday, to see how many there are, these poachers simply don't have a chance. The same with Harry Carver. Clinical descriptions of sexual congress, if you will pardon another euphemism, in American Eastern Seaboard moneyed society. Harry Carver has wrapped *that* subject up. Other men try it every year. Claude and I even sell some of their manuscripts. But the public doesn't buy many copies of the printed books. To the American book-buying public, when you want a book on screwing in Scarsdale, darling, you don't go to the amateurs. You go to the master, Harry Carver. Ditto for Quincy Holmes. Yes, sure, certainly, I'll grant you the novels are all about Boston's Beacon Hill and the adjacent worlds of New York and banking and all the rest that are tied to Boston by money and family and tradition, and it's always that same yearning mood for *this-is-the-house-our-fathers-dwelt-in*, but it's the yearning not of a novice, not of a newcomer who has just discovered a vein that might be profitable. It's the yearning of a professional, of the man who owns the subject, and that's what makes readers buy Quincy's books. They know they're getting the real thing. Or when Harry Carver takes you to that Westchester country club dance at which terrible things are going to happen because the nubile heroine is menstruating, or Quincy Holmes takes you into the Athenaeum where a great-great-grandson of Henry Wadsworth Longfellow has invited to lunch a young Bronx paratrooper who has returned from Tarawa to ask, while completing his studies on the G.I. Bill of Rights for a B.A. in Office Management at the Harvard School of Business Administration, for the hand of the Brahmin's daughter in marriage—"

"You know you're in good hands," said Sam.

"Precisely," said Sophie.

"Am I?" said Sam.

"What?" said Sophie.

"I've got to run Billy through a scene from *Julius Caesar* before he goes off to school," said Sam. "But I don't want to hang up before I learn what the trouble is."

"Trouble?" said Sophie.

"My answering service tells me Claude called last night while I was out," Sam said. "He left word for me to call him as soon as I could, saying it was urgent. The only thing at the moment that can possibly be urgent is *They Told Me You Were Dead,* which went over to *American Bride* ten days ago—no, twelve—almost two weeks, Sophie, and Bud Bienstock has never taken this long to reach a decision before, so I assume—"

"That *Bride* doesn't like the story and is rejecting?" Sophie said.

"Well, no, not necessarily," said Sam uncomfortably. The free-lance magazine writer felt about the verb "to reject" the way a general might feel about the verb "to surrender": even when it applied to the situation, it was better to employ a euphemism. "Not necessarily rejection," Sam said firmly. "After all, I did discuss the story with Bud before I started work on the damn thing, and I've always found him fair and reasonable and not a double-crosser. We agreed on all the characters, certainly the main ones, and where the story should break so the magazine could run it in four parts without confusing the reader. I mean, damn it, Sophie, it seems to me when an editor says that's fine, that's what I want, and he gives you a go-ahead to write it—"

Pamela Poitier's elegant snort, delivered through the nostrils of Sophie Sargent, cut him short.

"Sam darling," she said. "You're too old a hand at this game not to know the world of difference that exists between an editor's cheerful acquiescence over his third luncheon martini, and the icy eye with which he scans the writer's finished manuscript. It doesn't matter what Bud agreed to or seemed to be agreeing to when you outlined *They Told Me You*

Were Dead to him three months ago. What matters is your completed manuscript of a serial intended to run in *American Bride* that's on his desk right now."

"What does he say about the manuscript that's on his desk right now?"

Sophie Sargent laughed. "Sam, *save the flowery comments for my biographer, and just send me the checks,*" she said. "Remember?"

Sam, who certainly did remember, could feel his face grow hot. Sixteen years ago, when Claude Sargent took him on as a client, Sam had been nineteen. Two weeks after he had turned over his file of manuscripts, Sam received a note from Top:

Dear Silver:

I had a notion that, of all the stories you gave me, *Two Shall Withstand Him* had the best chance with Biff Burgoyne over at *Collier's*, and while the notion hasn't proved to be 100% accurate, it seems to me from the attached letter by Biff that we came awfully close. I thought you might like to read what he said about the story, so I am sending his letter along herewith.

Yours,
C. Sargent

Biff Burgoyne's letter had been something new in Sam's at that time understandably limited experience. This particular experience proved to be not unlike opening a piece of second-class mail—a circular urging, say, the purchase of a new kind of electric can opener—and finding instead the citation for a Congressional Medal of Honor.

Dear Top—*the letter began*—This new Silver kid smells like a big one. Hold onto him. Don't let him stop writing. I picked up *Two Shall Withstand Him* the other night after a long, hard, wearying day. You know the kind of crap that crosses an editor's desk and reduces him by five o'clock to the state of an apathetic flounder. I expected nothing from the story, and instead I got myself an experience I'll probably never forget. Thus it must have been with the now forgotten editor at Chapman & Hall when he picked up the ms. of a totally unknown youngster and started to read the first line of that first sketch by Boz.

This Silver kid's story starts with a fine Byronic sweep and gusto. It continues with the magnificent, relentless, hypnotizing control over the material that fixes the reader's eyes to the page and keeps them there come hell or high water, a control that few writers are born with, and even fewer achieve after a lifetime of practice. And the story ends with a moment of shattering terror and loveliness precisely at the point where only a great artist with a shelf full of masterpieces behind him would have known it must end. That a boy of nineteen should have known it, and done it, seems to me unbelievable.

And yet it is totally believable—and totally wonderful—for this is how greatness manifests itself and heralds its own arrival: without warning, at the end of a dreary day, in a handful of typed pages plucked at random from an "In" tray.

I am not in the crystal-ball business, as you know, but I have been around the literary game long enough to know rhinestones from diamonds. This Silver boy is pure diamond. He doesn't write with his fingers. He pounds with his fists. He is going right to the top. He is the biggest new talent to hit the American scene since Kenyon Poole knocked us all on our you-know-whats with *The Small Meal*. Some day, when you and I have run our courses, Top, the only reason we may be remembered is because you found young Sam Silver and took him on as a client, and because I was the first editor to read *Two Shall Withstand Him*. It will be glory enough for me.

Congratulations, Top. You've done again what you did when you found Kenyon Poole—added a new star to our American literary firmament. Thanks from the bottom of my heart for letting me read— no, for letting me add to my life!—the experience of *Two Shall Withstand Him*.

I return the ms. to you herewith. Unfortunately, we cannot use the story since, as you know, *Collier's* never publishes material dealing with intermarriage.

Always yours,
Biff Burgoyne, *Fiction Editor*

Sixteen years later, in the elegant lime-green study overlooking the East River, Sam could feel again the moment of shock by which he had been engulfed in the sleazy East Tenth Street kitchen when his racing blood, beating the pulse of ecstasy through his veins with such mounting violence that his head ached, came slamming into the betrayal of that final paragraph. It was like moving up the aisle of a crowded auditorium, listening to the reading of the citation with a joyous wonder that eradicated disbelief and discovering only on reaching the platform that it was all a cruel hoax: the Medal of Honor was not for him after all.

In spite of the numbing shock, during which a score of emotions darted wildly through Sam like shooting stars, the nineteen-year-old boy was able to pick out and fasten his thumping heart to the one that hurt most: he had been made to look a fool.

As he thought of the way his pulse had raced while he read the first paragraphs of Burgoyne's letter, Sam's face burned with humiliation. It was true, of course, that nobody had witnessed the humiliation. He had been alone in his kitchen when he read the letter. But already at nineteen Sam Silver knew what succeeding decades of more crowded living would confirm: pride was the ultimate fortress.

Everything else could be vanquished or repulsed or at least handled. Poverty could be lived with. Despair could be cheated. Love could be fooled. Failure could be laughed at. Hope could be renewed. Everything could be twisted or disguised to look like something else, preferably its opposite. Only pride refused to be camouflaged. Only pride, when wounded, insisted on bleeding. Because only pride, of all the emotions, was the true hermaphrodite: sexless, lonely, doomed to depend on nothing but itself for sustenance and survival.

Out of his instinctive knowledge that survival was all that mattered, the boy was able, after the wave of shock began to ebb, to write to the man:

Dear Mr. Sargent:

Thanks for sending along Mr. Burgoyne's letter about *Two Shall Withstand Him.* I'm glad he liked the story. I'm sorry he didn't buy it. I can understand your wanting me to know why. I am writing this note because I want you to understand me: Sam Silver, your new and grateful client. Unless you do understand me, our relationship, which has just begun, and from which I hope and believe we will both profit, will die a-borning. I don't know how your other clients— eminent men like Kenyon Poole, for example—feel about letters like Mr. Burgoyne's. I can tell you how Sam Silver feels about them: they drive me nuts. To me, Mr. Sargent, it doesn't really make any difference if Mr. Burgoyne returns a story with the statement that it's the greatest thing since *Hamlet* but unfortunately *Collier's* does not publish stories about Danes, or if Mr. Burgoyne returns it with the statement that it's the worst piece of junk he has ever read. The effect on me is exactly the same in both instances. Any way you slice it, Mr. Sargent, it's a rejection. And rejections depress me. And when I'm depressed, I don't write very well. Since I prefer to write well rather than poorly, I think it would be best from here on in if you did not keep me posted on what is happening to a story until it is sold, if ever. Spare me the rejection slips, however enthusiastic they may be. In short, sir, save the flowery comments for my biographer, and just send me the checks.

Sincerely,
Sam Silver

Sincerely was, of course, the wrong word. Defiantly would have been more accurate. Or arrogantly. Perhaps—because at nineteen Sam Silver had already begun to learn how to handle his emotional problems and conceal them from the world—perhaps therapeutically would have been the most accurate word of all. Sincerely, however, proved surprisingly effective. It, and the letter to which Sam appended it, accomplished something that took him by surprise and then began to provide him with a great deal of pleasure: the letter converted Top Sargent from an agent to a friend.

"You should have seen Claude's face as he walked into my office with your letter," Sophie had said to Sam when, a short time later, he came to dinner at the Sargent apartment for the first time. "You know how he loves writers. Or perhaps you don't know because you've only just met him. That's why Claude went into the literary agency business in the first place, and that's why he's been so good at it. He has this feeling about writers that teen-agers have about movie stars. Claude thinks they're all touched by God. He also thinks that they're dreadful people, but don't quote me on that, and if you do I'll deny it. Perhaps dreadful isn't quite accurate. What I mean is that while Claude is absolutely starry-eyed about writers, his vision is twenty-twenty when it comes to their characters, of which he feels that by and large, as a group, writers have very little. He excuses this lack on the ground that you can't have everything, and talent is more important than character. When you get him on the subject, Claude will tell you that Wagner was one of the worst bastards who ever drew breath, but it doesn't matter because he composed some of the best music ever written. Just the same, Claude feels it would have been wonderful if Wagner, in addition to being a genius, could have been a decent human being. Which is why, when Claude discovers a trait of character he admires in a man who also happens to be a good writer, Claude acts as though his sweepstakes ticket has come in, and the trait he admires most is dignity. A human being's sense of his own worth. Not his press agent's sense of his own worth. Or his publisher's sense of his own worth, or anybody else's. The man's true worth is what Claude means, and the man's awareness that above all and no matter what, he must do nothing to stain it.

"By and large, Claude feels that writers will do anything to achieve success. No matter how undignified or even downright disgusting, from kissing the right rear ends to get themselves elected to the National Institute or changing a story to suit an editor who otherwise would not buy it, to appearing in an advertisement endorsing canned beer or fountain pens or what have you. Now, mind you, Claude doesn't condemn them for it. In fact, if it helps sell the man's books, Claude approves of it. But he just can't help wishing they didn't have to do it, or didn't want to do it, because it's undignified. That's what knocked him galley west about your letter. This kid is only nineteen, he said to me with that touch of wonder and excitement in his voice that I know so well. Why, the little punk has sold only one story, and to a silly thing like *Landscape* at that, a kid, a mere kid, still wet behind the ears, and look what he writes me: *save the flowery comments for my biographer, and just send me the checks.* Claude repeated it two or three times, and then he laughed and he said let's invite him to dinner."

Sophie had smiled as she led Sam across the largest living room he had ever been in, toward the first private bar he had ever seen outside the movies, and she said, "That's why you're here tonight, Mr. Silver, whom I am now going to call Sam whether you like it or not, and may I add that while I'm the member of Sargent & Sargent who doesn't give a damn about our clients' characters, so long as they can write and sell, I happen to admire it when I run into it, so may I welcome you not only to our stable of authors but to our much smaller family of friends."

It was an astonishing dividend to reap from a letter written in cold fury to wipe out an intolerable moment of private embarrassment. A stab of conscience had caused Sam to think for a moment of correcting the interpretation Claude and Sophie Sargent had placed on his letter. The moment vanished, however, along with the stab of conscience, and for sixteen years, whenever some anxiety about the fate of a piece of work caused Sam to forget he was supposed to be above anxiety, and he called either Claude or Sophie to ask about an editor's verdict, they laughed as though he had attempted to amuse them with a private joke, and then with amiable chuckles quoted back at him: *save the flowery comments for my biographer, and just send me the checks!* Hearing the quotation from Sophie on this morning, when his anxiety suddenly seemed out of proportion to the fact that his telephone answering service had reported an urgent message from Claude Sargent, did not reassure Sam.

"Look, Sophie," he said. "I've got sixty thousand dollars riding on *They Told Me You Were Dead.* It's taken you and Claude sixteen years to get my price for a serial up to that figure. It went to Bud twelve days ago, and we haven't had a peep out of him, and last night I get a call from

Claude saying I should call him back because it's urgent, and when I do call back, all I get out of you is a cheery laugh and a reminder of a silly remark I made in a letter to Claude years ago when I was as green as a shutter and practically in knee pants."

The pause at the other end of the phone was suddenly for Sam as distressing as Claude Sargent's still unexplained message.

"And a very handsome young man you were in your knee pants," Sophie finally said, hurling the words forward into the phone with all her accustomed vigor, but the unaccustomed pause had done its damaging work. At least in Sam Silver's mind. Something was up. Which meant, in a writer's life, something unpleasant. Even a writer who lived in Sutton Crescent and was paid sixty thousand dollars for a magazine serial. When it sold, that is. Sophie said, "There's absolutely nothing wrong about Bud Bienstock and *They Told Me You Were Dead*. He loves the story. I'm absolutely certain he's going to buy it, Sam, so relax. He may want a few changes, of course, but isn't that normal?"

"I don't know," Sam said. "What makes you so certain he's going to buy it, and what kind of changes?"

"Darling, don't bite my head off," Sophie said. "Without it I wouldn't be much use to you as an agent, would I?"

"Sophie, put your head back on," Sam said. "And stop beating around the bush."

"It's all in a note I dictated to you yesterday," she said. "You'll have it in the mail as soon as Hilda gets it off the dictaphone tape."

The knot of uneasiness rolled over in Sam's stomach like a restless sleeper. In the writer's life, he had learned, good news came by phone. Only bad news arrived via the mails.

"Hilda gets things off the dictaphone tape at approximately the same rate of speed that Hannibal got across the Alps," Sam said. "Tell me now."

"Well, I ran into Bud at the National Book Awards do the other day, which by the way was grand fun, and you were a fool not to come with us. We had a ball, really we did. You would have enjoyed it."

"I doubt that," Sam said. "I don't have a ball watching other writers win awards."

"But, Sam darling," Sophie said. "You can't win the National Book Award unless you write a book, and you haven't written one for almost twenty years."

Again there was a pause at the other end of the line. This time, however, Sam did not have to guess at the reason, or probe for the area of his discomfort. He knew what had brought Sophie up short. The knowledge did not, of course, diminish the pain, but there was a small, sardonic satisfaction in the awareness that Sophie Sargent, who believed and not infrequently told people she had the tact of Talleyrand, had walked head on into a moment of gaucherie that would have raised both of Lady Kirriemuir's false eyebrows.

"What I mean, Sam," said Sophie hurriedly, "I mean you're not a novelist. I mean you're not known that way primarily, to the *public* I mean. The public doesn't think of you as a novelist. I mean they don't think of you as a *book* writer. You're a magazine writer is what I mean, and a damn fine one, too, one of the best in the country, if not *the* best, and what's wrong with that?"

"Nothing," said Sam, who knew that Sophie knew what he knew: everything was wrong with it. "At the moment, however, I'm not interested in what the public thinks of me. I want to know what Bud Bienstock thinks of *They Told Me You Were Dead.*"

"Sam darling," said Sophie. "You're not broke, for God's sake?"

The note of distaste in her voice caused Sam, in spite of his uneasiness, to grin. Sophie Sargent felt about people who were broke the way Helena Rubinstein might think about people with acne.

"People who earn a hundred thousand a year and better are always broke, and you know it," Sam said. "The quarterly installment on my estimated tax for this year comes due next week; the annual payment on the four annuity policies that will enable me at sixty-five to look down my nose on Howard Hughes, or so Claude's investment man said when he sold me the damn things, come up the week after; and my parents are bound to need one of their periodic plumbing jobs at Mount Sinai before the summer, which as usual is icumen in, finally makes it. No, of course I'm not broke. But I don't like to sell off stocks and bonds to make my peace with Uncle Sam or underwrite my mother's expensive taste in surgeons. I've been counting on this sixty thousand from *They Told Me You Were Dead* to tide me over the financial bump of the next six weeks and help me preserve the illusion that I'm as rich as my gold-plated neighbors here in Sutton Cresent, so tell me what's eating Bud."

"Nothing much, really," Sophie said. "Nothing that can't be fixed, I mean. He loves the story. He's crazy about the mood. Just the sort of thing readers of *American Bride* look for, he said. And it breaks beautifully as a four-parter."

"Then where's the check?"

"Oh, God!" Sophie said. "When will you writers learn about money? You sound exactly like Henley Titterton when he embarked on this damned tit-and-sander!"

"Watch your language, Sophie. I'm interested in what's standing be-

tween me and the sixty thousand dollars Bud Bienstock is supposed to pay
for *They Told Me You Were Dead*."

"Two things, as I said in the note I dictated to you," Sophie said. "First,
the relationship between the hero and heroine, and second, the ending."

"What's wrong with the relationship between the hero and heroine?"
Sam said. "I explained it to Bud in detail."

"He says you didn't tell him about the apartments."

"About what?"

"Sam, if you're going to shout, why don't you hang up the phone and
just open your window?"

"I'm sorry, Sophie. Tell me what's eating Bud about the apartments."

"Your hero is a handsome young widower who lives with his twelve-
year-old son in a swank apartment house on Sutton Circle. Right?"

"Right, and so I told Bud at our editorial conference."

"Good," Sophie said. "Your heroine is a beautiful young divorcée who
lives with *her* twelve-year-old son in the same elegant and highly expensive
apartment house. Right again?"

"Of course right again, and again so I told Bud at our editorial conference."

"I know, darling, but it turns out what you didn't tell Bud, and what
bothers him very much, is that the apartments are one above the other,
the hero living in 16E and the heroine in 15E."

"What in God's name is wrong with that?"

"For *American Bride* readers, according to Bud, a great deal," Sophie
said. "The implication is clear, and I'm only quoting Bud, darling; he says
the implication is clear that the minute the kids go off to school, the parents
go trotting up or down the stairs and hop into the sack."

"That's a God-damned lie!"

"Oh, my God!" Sophie said.

"*Now* what's the matter?" Sam said.

"You and that Rebecca Meissen, that's what's the matter. I didn't realize
that was still a thing."

"Sophie, I don't know what the hell you're talking about."

"No, of course not," Sophie Sargent said. "It just so happens that you
live in 16E at Sutton Crescent while your hero in *They Told Me You
Were Dead* lives in 16E at a place beautifully disguised as Sutton Circle, and Rebecca Meissen, as I recall that little Taj Mahal on the East
River her family built and you both inhabit, Rebecca lives just below you
in 15E while your heroine in this story lives, by sheer coincidence, I'm
sure, in 15E at Sutton Circle."

"Well, it *is* sheer coincidence," Sam said irritably. "And it's not my fault if Bud Bienstock, that great big white knight in shining armor who is paid God knows how much to choose the fiction for *American Bride's* blushing readers, happens to have a dirty mind."

"Sam darling, Bud Bienstock happens to have precisely the same kind of mind I have," Sophie said. "If you're not sleeping with young Mrs. Meissen you ought to have your head examined, and why you keep on hesitating and shilly-shallying about marrying a girl as lovely and rich as that is not only beyond me but obviously comes under the heading of None of My Business."

"It does," Sam said.

"So I'll stick to what *is* my business," Sophie Sargent said. "And that's selling *They Told Me You Were Dead* to Bud Bienstock for that sixty thousand dollars you're all of a sudden in such a tizzy about."

"I'm not in a tizzy," Sam said. "I'm just annoyed by an editor who asks you to tell him a story before you write it and then, when you do, he—"

"That's not what you're annoyed about, Sam."

The quietly spoken words, purring in across the wire with the mixture of friendly warmth that always moved him and steel-edged truth on which he depended, brought him up momentarily out of the shapeless uneasiness that he did not understand.

"Sophie," he said, matching his voice to hers, "what am I annoyed about?"

"Life," she said. "All the things that you damn writers make up your stories about. When will you learn not to use real things and real people to create fiction?"

"Never, I guess," Sam said. "You're right, Sophie, and so is Bud. I should have had more sense than to tie the facts in *They Told Me You Were Dead* as closely as all that to the real facts. But writers don't have much sense. God knows you ought to know that by now."

"Why *can't* they have sense?" Sophie said. "Does it take an Einstein to point out that changing Sutton Crescent to Sutton Circle is not going to fool anybody? Why, to stick to this particular and preposterous instance, couldn't you have called the building East River Manor or Tannenbaum's Towers or just plain Elmer?"

The exasperation in her voice was amusing, and an amusing reply—or even a stab at humor—would have released him from the circle of embarrassment by which he was trapped, but Sam suddenly felt the compulsion to return truth with truth.

"Because if I call the building something unreal, the building itself becomes unreal for me," Sam said. "And if the building is unreal for me,

I can't write real people into it, and unless I can write real people, or start with real people, I can't write at all."

"I don't understand you," Sophie said irritably. "Other writers make it all up out of whole cloth."

"Writers like Henley Titterton?" Sam said. "Who produce carbon copies of *Venery in the Sun?*"

"Henley is an extreme case," Sophie said. "He's not really a novelist at all. He's a British university-educated bum with no career who years ago fell into journalism, as so many careerless bums do, and then later made the discovery so many journalists make, namely, that if they report what they see and change the names, they can call it a novel and earn more than they do at space rates. But you're a genuine novelist. You have what these journalists don't have and what only a true novelist does have, namely, imagination. You have what Claude calls the X quality that produces fiction. It can't be taught or learned. It's a knack or a gift one's born with. You were born with it. Many years of successful work have proved that. Why, then, do you have to nail yourself down to real facts? Other people don't. Why, at my own dinner table you've heard over the years dozens of writers say they never start with real people or real things."

"The most charitable thing I can say about those writers is that they're either lying or mistaken," Sam said. "All right, I'm sorry about putting the heroine in an apartment immediately below the hero. You can tell Bud Bienstock it was a mistake. I had no intention of sneaking over something lubricious on his seven million antiseptic, odorless, cellophane-wrapped readers. I'll move the heroine of *They Told Me You Were Dead* to some other part of the building, a nice safe distance away from the hero. Now tell me what's agitating him about the ending?"

Again there was that troubling pause from a woman who was not a pauser.

"Bud says the ending doesn't flow from the plot," Sophie said. "I'm afraid I have to agree with him, Sam. It's a *come-to-realizer.*"

Sam winced. It was a phrase he hated, the way a professional golfer might hate the word slice, but it contained a truth from which there was no escape.

"What happens to people in a story," Top Sargent had told him years ago, "has to be much more logical than what happens to them in real life. Most readers don't know it, but what draws them to fiction, the reason they prefer even a cheesy magazine story about love in the advertising agency set to the article called *You Too Can Wear a Truss* that appears on the facing page, is that they turn to fiction, unconsciously of course, the way they go to church: for a feeling of organization and order in a universe that all their senses tell them daily is totally disorganized and disordered. The minister and the priest and the rabbi, those boys have the answers. Ditto for the fictioneer. To the reader he's God. Why shouldn't the reader think that? These people he's reading about were created by a man who signs his name to the story. If he created them, how can there possibly be anything about them he doesn't know? How can there be any problems he can't solve for them? So when the reader comes to the climax, when he reaches the point in the story where the people in it resolve their difficulties or problems or whatever, the reader expects the resolution to be laid out for him the way God lays it out, or the way the preacher or priest or rabbi says God lays it out: clearly, without equivocation, step by step, in a way he can follow, with none of the troubling shaded areas that bother him in real life, where very little is clear, and what happens to us is often so difficult to follow and so utterly pointless that it seems insane. Therefore, when you as the writer are stuck for a resolution of the story characters you created, when you try to duck out on your job as God by saying the hero suddenly *came to realize* he loved the heroine he's been kicking in the shins for twenty-two or three hundred and twenty-two pages, and you send them off into the sunset with their arms around each other, the reader feels cheated. He's come to church and God has let him down. He doesn't want to be told the hero *came to realize* something. He wants to be told the girl didn't steal the bushel of uncut garnets, or the boy isn't really a gangster at all but an F.B.I. man masquerading as a hood to break the counterfeit ring that has framed the girl's father, or whatever. A reader who feels cheated, like a parishioner who finds the sermons unsatisfactory, joins another church, so to speak. I mean he turns to another writer for his fiction. We don't want that to happen, do we? So let's just watch that *come-to-realize* gimmick. When you're stuck, and you feel a *come-to-realizer* creeping up on you, better come in and have a chat about the story."

Over the years, Sam had come in for scores of these chats. Most of them had proved fruitful. The stories, at any rate, had sold. There were some stories, however, about which Sam had been unable to come to Top for help. There was something about the characters that made it impossible for him to talk about them. He could only write about them. Sometimes he managed to write his way around the *come-to-realize* hurdle. Sometimes he didn't. In *They Told Me You Were Dead* he obviously hadn't.

"I'm sorry Bud feels that way about it," Sam said into the phone. "I thought the ending worked out very well."

"Sam darling, if you think that, your thinking is not of a very high order this morning," Sophie said. "What is this story about? A handsome young

widower is drawn to a beautiful young divorcée who is similarly drawn
to him. Yet something prevents them from falling in love and marrying.
What is it? With your usual skill, at the proper moment, you let the
reader discover that what stands between them is the memory of the hero's
dead wife, who was a woman of great . . . Oh, my God!"

"What?" Sam said, startled.

"I just came to realize something of my own," Sophie said. *They Told
Me You Were Dead* is the story of you and that Meissen girl and your
first wife Jennie, isn't it?"

"Suppose it is?" Sam said sharply. "What difference does that make,
so long as it's a good story?"

"Sam, it isn't," Sophie Sargent said. "Not with the present ending, which
is what Bud Bienstock is beefing about. You give absolutely no reason why
the hero, who has been prevented all during the first three parts from falling in love with the heroine because of the memory of his dead wife—you
give absolutely no reason why in the fourth part he suddenly does fall in
love with her. All you do is make him *come to realize* he really loves her,
and you blithely assume the reader is going to swallow that and be satisfied, whereas you know darn well, as Claude has said over and over again,
a reader comes to fiction the way a parishioner goes to church, because he
expects to get—"

"I know what Claude says about fiction," Sam said. "Every word of it
is engraved on my heart. Did Bud have any ideas about how to fix the
ending?"

"None that added up to anything sensible," Sophie said. "You know
these National Book Award things. Very wet affairs they are. By the time
I ran into him, Bud was already carrying a rather large load of Scotch
whiskey, to which he kept adding liberal doses all during the rest of the
evening, but he did say if you would fix those two things, the apartments
one on top of the other, which is easy of course, and the ending, which is
admittedly more difficult but Bud has confidence in you, and so do I,
darling, the story is in. So why don't you just get out your carbon, and
make the fixes, and we'll all be in clover? Can I call Bud and tell him
you'll have the corrections for him—when?"

"I don't know," Sam said.

"Now, look here, darling, I'm not going to have you go all tempera-
mental on me," Sophie Sargent said crisply. "You're not an arty fraud like
Henley Titterton. You're a hard-headed pro, the best Claude and I have
ever dealt with, as I need hardly remind you, and there's sixty thousand
American dollars riding on this number. What Bud wants is nothing more
than he and a dozen other editors have asked you to do over and over again

in the past. You've done it a hundred times if you've done it once, without a whimper of complaint, and there's absolutely no reason why you can't do it with this story."

"Yes, there is," Sam said.

"What reason?" Sophie demanded.

I don't know the ending to this story, Sam wanted to say. Not only because the statement was the simple truth, but also because he was aware of the wistful hope that saying it out loud, to a tough old friend like Sophie, might somehow break the spell of puzzling uneasiness to which his relationship with Rebecca Meissen, as well as the rest of his life, had in recent weeks been reduced. But of course Sam knew he couldn't tell the truth to Sophie. This was one of those stories about which, no matter how badly he was stuck, he had been unable over the years to come in and talk with Top in the hope of finding a solution. Once again, Sam saw, he had fallen into the writer's trap of confusing the real world with the world of his characters in the hope that the latter, since he controlled their existence, would ease his path in the former, over which Sam realized, more and more as he grew older, he, like most people, exercised no real control at all.

"The reason I can't make the corrections today," he said, deliberately misinterpreting Sophie's question to steer himself out of the circle of embarrassment he had himself created, "I've got to go to this damn thing at the Porte School. They're doing *Julius Caesar*, don't ask me why, and Billy plays Calpurnia, and I've got to—"

"Sam Silver, for the love of God, nobody said you have to make the corrections today," Sophie said irritably. "What's the matter with you this morning?"

"I don't know," Sam said, and the simple statement, which suddenly seemed to be winking on and off in the lime-green study like a warning signal, gave him a moment of terror that took him by surprise. "I mean I haven't had any coffee yet."

"Well, have some, and then go watch Billy play Calpurnia, and I'll call Bud Bienstock and tell him you'll get the *They Told Me You Were Dead* corrections to him some time this week or next. Okay?"

"Sure, fine," Sam said. "That's peachy."

"Good, darling," Sophie said. "Think of me kindly. You're going off to watch Shakespeare but I have to go back to Henley Titterton and all those oddly constructed females he thinks make love in mosques."

"Sophie, wait."

"Yes, darling?"

"Top's call?" Sam said. "The one he made last night and told my answering service was urgent? It wasn't about Bud Bienstock and *They Told Me You Were Dead,* was it?"

"No, it wasn't," Sophie said, and then, apparently annoyed with herself for having said more than she intended, she continued with a casualness that, since it did not fool Sam, underscored his uneasiness. "I mean I don't think Claude would have called you about Bud and the fourparter, since Claude knew I was writing to you about that."

"For God's sake, Sophie, what's all the mystery about?" Sam said, speaking with more anger than he intended. "If Claude didn't call me about Bud and the serial, what the hell did he call about?"

"Claude wants to tell you that himself."

"Sophie, what are you—?"

"Darling, I've got to go," Sophie said. "It isn't only Henley Titterton. It's staff, as I told you earlier. They're getting slack and I've got to pin their ears back before I go down to the office. But just before he went off to the neck puller, Claude said when you returned his call to tell you he'll be expecting you in the office for lunch. Take care, darling, and why don't you come to your senses and marry that heavenly girl with all those even more heavenly millions?"

But she was gone before he could invent a joke to cover the fact that he did not know the answer to Sophie's question. It was not enough to say because he didn't love Rebecca. That merely raised a more troubling question: why couldn't he? God knew he had tried hard enough. It was only after he had put down the phone that Sam realized, with a renewed stab of worry, that for the first time in his experience Sophie Sargent had played her customary two or three verbal innings for the bleachers without delivering the pitch that, after her performance was over, he had learned to expect was intended for him alone. She had not called him. He had got her on the phone only because he had returned Claude's call and Sophie happened to answer. So everything she had said to him about *They Told Me You Were Dead* had been made up on the spot—or repeated from the already dictated memorandum on Hilda's tape—to cover the fact that she did not want to speak for Claude about something more important. Sam was wondering what Claude Sargent could have to say that Sophie didn't feel it was right for her to tell him herself, when Billy, fully clothed, appeared in the study door.

"Oh jay, Rice Krispies in bowls, bananas sliced over same, coffee poured," the boy said. "Come and get it, Pop."

Following his son out of the study to the dining alcove, Sam was suddenly aware that Billy's head, across which his father had as late as yesterday—or so it seemed—been able to look with ease, now loomed up inches higher.

"What do they feed you for lunch at that school?" Sam said as he sat down. "You're growing like a locust."

"Aah, now, Pop, don't kid a defenseless minor," Billy said, pushing the book bound in purple and white across the table as he picked up his spoon. "You don't know anything about locusts."

"A thorny-branched, white-flowered American fabaceous tree," Sam intoned. "Pass the sugar, please."

"Holy cow!" Billy said, shoving across the table the blue and white Spode bowl that was part of the housewarming present Rebecca Meissen had brought up from 15E when she finished decorating 16E. "How'd you know that, Pop?"

"You'd be astonished by the things writers know," Sam said smugly, sprinkling sugar over the hill of Rice Krispies and sliced bananas. "Locust is also the word for any of the grasshoppers with short antennae which constitute the family *Locustidae,* including the notorious migratory species, such as *Locusta migratoria* of the Old World, and the Rocky Mountain locust, *Melanoplus spretus,* which swarm in immense numbers and strip the vegetation from large areas. Had enough?"

"Holy cow, yes, plenty," Billy said around a mouthful of cereal. "But no kid, Pop, how do you know that kind of jazz?"

"I had to look it up once for a story I was doing," Sam said. "Or rather, I was looking up something else, and you know what happens when you're looking something up in the dictionary. You find yourself reading all the definitions near the word you're looking up, and if you've got a vacuum-cleaner mind like your old man's, you pick up and remember a lot of stuff it wouldn't hurt you one bit to forget. Where do you want to begin?"

"Top of the page, there," Billy said, pointing with his spoon. "Where Caesar's just got up out of bed. He couldn't sleep and he's pacing around."

"Nor heaven nor earth have been at peace tonight"? Sam asked.

"Yeah, that's the place, except skip the part about the servant coming in," Billy said. "I mean begin after the servant says *I will, my lord* and then he blows."

"You're Calpurnia," Sam said.

"Right," Billy said.

"Okay, then," Sam said. "Shoot."

"What mean you, Caesar?" Billy recited, and the intense seriousness that suddenly masked the merry features, plus the ludicrous throatiness that invaded the childish voice, caused Sam's heart to roll over with a thump. *"Think you to walk forth? You shall not stir out of your house today."*

"*Caesar shall forth*," Sam read, and he took a hasty sip of coffee to still the thumping in his chest. "*The things that threaten'd me ne'er look'd but on my back; when they shall see the face of Caesar, they are vanished.*"

"*Caesar, I never stood on ceremonies, yet now they fright me.*" The look of intense seriousness changed to petulance. "That's the part I don't dig," Billy said. "What's with this ceremonies jazz? It's a bedroom, isn't it?"

"The word ceremonies as Shakespeare uses it here does not mean ceremonies as you and I understand the word," Sam said. "The Romans were great believers in omens. They were always cutting up pigeons and chickens to examine their insides for auguries. Tips on how things were going to come out. Sort of like reading tea leaves to see if you should invest in the stock market today, let's say. Or wait until next week to get married. That sort of thing. Well, Calpurnia never believed in all that jazz, as you put it. But now, all of a sudden, she does believe in it. In omens, I mean. So when Calpurnia says to Caesar here that she never stood on ceremonies, she simply means that while she never gave serious thought before to omens, now she *is* giving serious thought to omens because now she's scared because now she suspects the plotters plan to kill her husband. Get it?"

Billy, loaded spoon poised in air, did not answer for a moment. He was staring at his father in astonishment.

"Holy cow," he said finally, and the spoon completed its journey to his mouth. "Don't tell me you learned all that, Pop, from looking something up in the dictionary for a story."

"Nope," Sam said, refilling his cup from the Queen Anne coffeepot that Rebecca had admitted was outrageously expensive but in the long run worth every penny it cost him because it was the sort of thing that showed visitors to the apartment at a glance "who you are." Sam, who more and more found himself wishing he knew, now said to his son, "You might learn that sort of thing by looking up something else in the dictionary, but I didn't."

"Where'd you learn it, Pop?"

"From your mother," Sam said. "She loved Shakespeare."

"She did?" Billy said, and the funny little look on his face caused Sam's heart to hurl itself again at the wall of his chest. The boy said slowly, "You never told me that about her."

"I'm sorry," Sam said, and he didn't realize until he had lifted the silver pot that he was attempting to fill an already full cup. "I'm sorry I never told you," he said, replacing the coffeepot with great care. "But she admired Shakespeare enormously. Your mother felt he was the greatest writer who ever lived. I know that doesn't sound like a very original observation, since I'm sure Mr. Bronson and your other English teachers at the Porte School have made the same point to you any number of times. I know when I was a kid my teachers kept saying it, over and over again, until it meant nothing to me. Or rather until I stopped listening, the way most kids in school do when something is hammered at them. But it makes quite a difference to hear a thing like that in school, and hearing it in a Greenwich Village bedroom, from the girl you've just married. I mean that Shakespeare, his greatness, was very real to Jennie. His plays were a part of her daily life, like brushing her teeth and going to work in the morning. I mean this thing here, what Calpurnia says to Caesar, it was as real to your mother as, well, here, this, these bananas you just sliced or these Rice Krispies we're eating."

Sam's voice stopped. The funny little look had etched itself deeper into the small, neatly made face at the other side of the table.

"Pop," the boy said, "why didn't you ever tell me?"

Sam gave himself a couple of moments, during which with his spoon he carefully scraped three vagrant Rice Krispies from their tenuous hold on the inside of his bowl down into the shallow pool of milk at the bottom. By the time he had them afloat, Sam's voice was all right again.

"I don't know," he said. "I guess it's just you never can tell anybody everything about a person they never knew. I mean, even if you tried, you'd never be able to cover everything. There are always hundreds of things, maybe thousands, that would never come to your mind except by association. Like here now, this scene, we happen to be running through it, and so I happen to remember that your mother admired Shakespeare. I mean we've never discussed Shakespeare before, so I've never had occasion to tell you how Jennie felt about him, if you see what I mean?"

Billy nodded thoughtfully, and added another spoonful to the several previously inserted and as yet unswallowed spoonfuls he was chewing.

"Sure," he said, and then, after a gulping swallow that cleared his mouth, the boy cleared his throat. "Pop," Billy said, "what was she like?"

Thus, Sam supposed, came the impact of tidal waves and earthquakes, without warning, while peaceful citizens, who thought themselves safe and had every reason to believe they were, sat munching their breakfasts, thinking of crops and jobs and dentists' bills.

"Well," Sam said slowly, "as I said, she liked Shakespeare, and she hated being poor, and she loved—"

"Was she poor?" Billy said in surprise.

"Not starving poor, no," Sam said. "She always had enough to eat, or just about enough, but she was gone long before you and I made it up here to Sutton Crescent, if that's what you mean."

Billy's scowl, as he ran the tip of his tongue along the tops of his teeth, probing for stray bits of food, made it abundantly clear that he didn't mean that at all.

"No, I mean what she looked like," the boy said finally. "It's funny, I've never seen a picture of her."

"What's funny about it?" Sam said.

"Well, like take in *David Copperfield*, which this crumb Mr. Bronson says is one of the ten greatest novels in the world, so we had to read the whole damn—"

"Darn."

"—thing, all twelve hundred pages, when his wife dies, this drip Dora —boy, was I glad to get *her* out of the story—but David, when Dora dies, every room in the house, every wall, every table—I suppose he'd've had them in the bathrooms, too, if they *had* bathrooms in those days—every flat surface, vertical or horizontal, it was full of them."

"Full of what?" Sam said.

"Pictures of David's dead wife," Billy said. "This pill Dora. But you, Pop, I've never seen a picture of her in my whole life."

Sam gave himself another moment, during which he started scraping the inside of his bowl with the spoon, realized there was nothing to scrape, and put down the delicate piece of silver as though it had suddenly become unbearably heavy.

"Your mother didn't leave any pictures," Sam said.

"Not a one?" Billy's voice rose with incredulity.

"Not a one," Sam said.

"Not even a class graduation picture?" Billy said. "Or a passport, like last summer, when you and I went to Europe, we had to have our pictures taken?"

"Your mother never graduated from any place," Sam said. "And her passport was lost long ago."

The buzzer of the lobby switchboard, exploding on the kitchen wall behind them, drove from Billy's face the puzzled look in which there was more than puzzlement; and it reminded Sam of Top Sargent's observation that the cliché, while it must be eschewed, should not be derided, "because when you examine a cliché with care, and not merely with contempt, you find it has earned its place in the language honorably."

The cliché Sam examined now, as he moved from the dining alcove to the kitchen, needed a bit of adjustment, but Top's observation remained unchallenged: Sam wished he could honestly deny that he had just been saved if not by a bell then certainly by a buzzer.

"Hello?" he said into the wall phone in the kitchen.

"Mr. Silver?"

Sam recognized the voice of the doorman who came on duty at seven in the morning.

"The car is here, sir."

Sam, who had been hearing this simple announcement every school-day morning at seven forty-five since he and Billy had moved into Sutton Crescent, was certain that even a total stranger, hearing the words for the first time, would have known from the way Charlie uttered them that the doorman was referring to a chauffeur-driven vehicle.

Sam sometimes wondered if a total stranger would have suspected what Charlie surely knew, namely, that the sleek maroon and black Bentley with the liveried Frenchman behind the wheel, which every morning carried Billy Silver across town to the Porte School, was not the property of the highly successful magazine writer who lived in 16E. The beautiful car, like the four-thousand-dollar charm bracelet that tinkled on Rebecca Meissen's wrist, was another gesture of her ex-husband's continued friendship.

Anton, who did not want to lose contact with his son merely because his wife had divorced him, felt that sending his car for Ronnie every morning provided a bond between himself and the boy. Rebecca had seen no reason why Billy Silver, who was in Ronnie Meissen's class at the Porte School and lived in Sutton Crescent immediately above his classmate, should not benefit from Anton's civilized gesture. She had suggested to Sam that the two boys ride to school together every morning.

Sam would have resented the accusation that, like Sophie Sargent, he dearly loved a lord. He was honest enough, however, at least with himself, to admit that he did not dislike the trappings of lordship. Especially when they were thrust upon him for free, and more especially when one could read into them significant meanings: he felt there was something symbolic in the fact that Sammy Silver of East Tenth Street, who used to stuff cardboard in his shoes to soak up the water that came in through the holes during the walk to P.S. 64 on rainy days, should now send his son off every morning to a school that charged two thousand a year as basic tuition in a car that cost more than Sam had earned during all the first twenty years of his life. It was a yardstick he was ashamed to find himself using, and every morning, after savoring the symbol, Sam wiped his conscience clear by reminding himself that he would have drawn the line at purchasing the symbol with his own money. This morning the reminder did not perform its customary laundering job.

"Thank you, Charlie," Sam said into the mouthpiece of the kitchen wall. "I'll tell Billy."

"Okay, Pop," Billy said as he erupted out of the hall closet, dragging his briefcase in one hand and punching at an empty sleeve with his other like a fighter working his opponent across the ring with a series of left jabs as he probes for an opening for his cocked right. "See you at school. Ten sharp. Don't be late."

"I won't be," Sam said. "And remember what I said about Calpurnia and the—"

But he was talking to the closed front door in which the chimes hummed distressingly. Sam stood there for several moments, in the center of the living room, as conscious of his own heartbeats as of the glaring brightness that flooded in off the river through the huge terrace windows, trying to decide what to do with the day's first few moments of total privacy.

This was seldom a problem. Years of disciplined routine usually sent Sam, as soon as Billy went off to school, back into the study where, for half an hour before he started thinking about what to wear that day, he emptied into his neatly indexed notebooks the accumulation of scraps that the vacuum cleaner of his craft had industriously sucked up for him while he had been living through the preceding twenty-four hours. On this morning, however, the proddings of routine failed to provide the emotional climate for which they were built: the sense of security, the feeling that he was honorably enmeshed in the pattern of the world's sensible affairs, had suddenly vanished.

Claude Sargent's puzzling message, which Sophie Sargent's refusal to clarify had rendered even more puzzling, had something to do with it, of course. How Billy's questions about Jennie could have intensified the uneasiness of a still unexplained telephone call from his agent, Sam did not know. But he did know that the two were in some way connected, and that together they were responsible for the way he now felt. Perhaps because what he felt was not unlike the chill of nakedness, Sam turned abruptly away from the study and strode into the dressing room.

It was twelve feet square, larger than the living room of the East Tenth Street apartment in which he had spent the first twenty years of his life, and probably his greatest single source of secret pleasure.

His wry and only half-serious objections to the free hand with which Rebecca Meissen had spent his money when she decorated the apartment had not extended to the expensive mirrored cupboards she had insisted on building into Sam's dressing room. He knew Rebecca had been puzzled by his failure to complain about this extravagance. Sam had thought it best not to enlighten her. Rebecca had no way of knowing what Jennie would have understood at once: Jennie, like Sam, had been raised with "toilets in the hall."

It was a phrase for which Sam looked in vain in the novels he read about the rise of poverty-stricken youngsters from the mean streets of New York or London slums to the penthouses of Park Avenue and Mayfair.

Like most professional writers, Sam had long ago lost the capacity to read a book purely for the entertainment it might provide. One part of his mind was constantly at work, as his eyes skimmed the pages, picking apart what, no matter how eminent or unknown the author might be, had to be considered the work of a competitor. These works all fell into a recognizable pattern.

A prominent feature of the pattern was the obligatory scene in which the tattered urchin, who has just been splashed with mud by the passing carriage of a leading banker or sprayed with hauteur by the passing daughter of a misleading duke, clenches his fists and, addressing the always attentive heavens, states fiercely and bitterly the nature of his ambitions.

What always surprised Sam, who had lived through his own version of this scene, was that the authors never touched on the one desire that was Sam's most vivid recollection of poverty: the lust for cleanliness.

The sanitary facilities of the three-room walk-up on the sixth floor of the tenement at 390 East Tenth Street in which Sam was born had consisted of a kitchen sink with two taps. Both ran cold water that looked like diluted tomato juice. Out in the hall there was a single-seat toilet for which the five families that lived on the sixth floor of 390 East Tenth were in constant and bickering competition. There were no bathtubs. And soap, which had to compete with all the other items on the Silver family's budget, was watched as carefully as bread and butter. Sam was eleven years old before he had the heady experience of washing his entire body at the same time: boys in the sixth-grade gym class at P.S. 64 were ordered—in some cases physical force on the part of the teacher was necessary to make sure the order was obeyed—to take a shower after calisthenics. Also, Sam's mother taught him early to hang up at night his shirt, socks, and underwear: each of these items of apparel had to be worn for three days before it could be placed in the Hecker's flour sack that served the Silver family as a laundry hamper, and Mrs. Silver believed that night air, if allowed to circulate freely around soiled linen, eliminated the odors of dried perspiration. She was wrong.

Because Mrs. Silver was wrong, one of the strongest ambitions of her son's life took shape early. Almost as far back as Sam could remember he had yearned for the time when he could begin each day not only with a shower of hot water and foaming soap, but with freshly laundered clothes from, as his small boy's mind had phrased it, the skin out.

The ambition had, of course, been realized long ago. Anybody whose youth had been spent on the Silver family's East Tenth Street budget would not have had to earn very much in later life to enjoy the illusion that he had achieved riches. To the adult Sam Silver, soap and freshly laundered linen and dry-cleaned clothes had been a commonplace for years. There was nothing commonplace, however, about the pleasure Sam drew from them, and nowhere since he had been earning his own living had this pleasure been so intense as here in this expensively-put-together dressing room at Sutton Crescent. He would have been ashamed to tell anybody, even Rebecca and especially Billy, how much he enjoyed the morning routine of choosing shirt, socks, underwear, shoes, tie, and suit from the cunningly contrived shelves, the cupboards with mirrored sliding doors, the chromium racks that purred in and out soothingly on oiled bearings like the doors of a vault. They were so soothing that the telephone, tinkling delicately out in the bedroom, jolted Sam like the old fire-drill bell in P.S. 64. He walked out of the dressing room, carrying a shirt, and picked up the phone.

"Hello?"

"Oh, so you're alive, thank God."

Automatically, without thought, Sam dropped onto the bed. As the years went by he found it increasingly difficult to talk with his parents while standing up.

"Hello, Ma," he said, and Sam was aware of the small almost physical movement inside his head, like the shifting of a car's gears at the approach to a hill, as he moved his mind from the kind of English he talked with Billy and Mrs. Harrison and Sophie Sargent, to the locutions and word patterns he used with his parents. Sam said, "Why shouldn't I be alive?"

"Who knows?" Mrs. Silver said. The brisk, forthright voice came in across the wire from Queens with all the clarity and vigor of a football coach letting the members of his disappointing team know between halves in the locker room what he thinks of their performance thus far. There was no hint in the clean, sharply defined, aggressive syllables that they were being uttered by a fragile old lady of seventy-eight who stood four feet eleven in her bedroom slippers, weighed just under a hundred pounds, and whose hands shook so badly that she had to use both to hold the phone up to her mouth. Mrs. Silver said, "A person has a son, she sees him every time they elect a President, like maybe once in four years, so how should she know if he's alive?"

"Knock it off, Ma," Sam said. "I was out there week before last."

"So I'll send right away a telegram to Congress they should give you a medal."

"And I called you yesterday."

"Once in two weeks he was here, and he called me yesterday," Mrs. Silver said, as though she were dictating to a secretary at her side, and then, into the phone, "So I'll change the telegram. I'll tell them to send you two medals."

"How do you feel, Ma?"

"How should I feel?"

"I mean I hope you're okay."

"Naturally this is what you hope, because if I'm not okay you'll God forbid have to come out to Queens to see me."

There was not even the hint of bitterness in Mrs. Silver's replies, just as there was not even the hint of genuine interest in her son's questions. They were both engaged in a ritual as inflexible as the law of gravity. It had come into being, Sam was aware, by mutual even though unspoken agreement, to bridge the gap that the passing years had slowly and brutally and to their considerable astonishment opened between them. Once there had been so much to talk about that they had been forced to invent a sort of conversational shorthand—gestures that completed sentences; facial expressions that told paragraphs; shrugs that condensed pages—in order to get it all said to one another. Although she had been forty-two when Sam was born—the unexpected and fiercely desired child—she had seemed young to him while he was growing up. Now that she was old and he was no longer young and they had nothing to say to one another, now that their relationship had been reduced to an almost automatic obeisance to the tradition of filial love, they both found safety from the contemplation of their tragedy in the strict observance of their private litany.

Sam's questions always came first: about her health; about his father's health; about the health of Abe Ostreich, a distant cousin of Mr. Silver who was the superintendent of the apartment house in which Sam's parents lived; about the health of Abe's wife Hannah; and, of course, about the weather in Queens. Then came Sam's mother's questions: about his health; about Billy's health; about Billy's schoolwork; about what she called Sam's "business"; and, naturally, about the weather in Manhattan, which was two miles, as any witless crow determined to make the pointless flight from Queens to Sutton Crescent would have discovered, from Mrs. Silver's telephone.

All this took time, of course. One day, when his mother rang up just as he was about to leave the apartment to keep a lunch date with Bud Bienstock of *American Bride*, Sam, who hated to be late, especially for appointments with men in whose hands his livelihood rested, had tried to save time by condensing his part of the telephone litany into a single question about the health of "everybody out in Queens," and an all-encompassing utility assurance that his health and business, Billy's health and schoolwork, and the weather in Manhattan were all in remarkably fine shape. Sam never tried to save time in that way again.

Even now, almost two years later, he could feel the pain behind the voice—suddenly gone as weak and shaky as the liver-spotted hands that held the telephone—in which his mother told him she was sorry she had bothered him "at a time when he was busy with other people, those that they live outside in the world."

It was as much the sound of her voice as the words she used that tore away the shroud in which the nature of their relationship had for so long lain uneasily concealed. She had not said that as he grew older and started the long, slow, but steady move uptown from East Tenth Street to Sutton Crescent, he had also grown ashamed of his immigrant parents. She had not said that as her son began to make his way in the world he had thrust his mother out of it. She had not said that while he dwelt in the sunlight of movers and shakers she had been banished to the shadows in which the useless wait for death. Her words had said none of this, but her voice had said all of it, and more: that she did not blame him; that, having helped to fashion him, she also understood him, and if their positions were reversed she would have done with him as he had done with her; that it was his success and happiness she wanted, even if to achieve both it was necessary to consign her to failure and misery; that above all, because it could only distract him, he was to disregard her pain.

It was because of his anxiety to disregard his own pain as well that, to avoid a recurrence of the unexpected moment of shocking revelation, Sam from then on always sat down when his mother called and allowed their liturgical substitute for love to run its ceremonial course unhurried.

"How's Abe?" he said patiently.

"How should Abe be?" Mrs. Silver said. "A man he's a superintendent for an apartment house?"

"And Hannah?" Sam said. "How does she feel?"

"How should Hannah feel? A superintendent's wife?"

"How's the weather out there in Queens, Ma?"

"How should the weather be in Queens in April?"

Like a runner ticking off the passing landmark that tells him how much of a familiar route he has already run, Sam's mind, which was primarily concerned with computing how much time he had left before he was due at the Porte School for Billy's performance as Calpurnia, ticked off the fact that the familiar telephone ceremony had rounded the halfway pylon, and again without thought, almost unconsciously, he made the mental adjustment from interrogator to answerer.

"So how do you feel?" Mrs. Silver asked.

"I feel fine, Ma," Sam said.

"And Billy, how does he feel?"

"Fine, Ma. Billy's fine."

"And in school?" Mrs. Silver said. "His schoolwork, how is it?"

"It's fine, Ma."

"What's by you fine, tell me?"

"Well, I just received his report for the second quarter, and Billy is fourth in his class."

"Fourth isn't first," Mrs. Silver said.

"No, but it's closer to first than fifth."

"Third is still closer."

"I know, but I don't like to crowd him, Ma."

"Why not? It hurt you, maybe, when you were Billy's age in P.S. 64 your mother told you if you can't bring home a report card with on it all A's then don't bring me home nothing?"

"That was different, Ma."

"What people have inside their heads it's never different," Mrs. Silver said. "You're telling me maybe in brains the styles change every season like in clothes?"

"No, of course not," Sam said, craning to identify the flag of a foreign-looking tanker that was sliding past his bedroom window on its way downstream toward the open sea. "I merely mean that when I was a kid we were poor, so it was only natural for me to want to get ahead by piling up high marks in school and things like that."

"So now you're rich it's natural for Billy to want low marks?"

"Fourth in a class of sixteen isn't exactly low, Ma."

"You were first in a class of sixty."

"Okay, Ma, I'll tell Billy to step on the gas."

"But not he should step so hard he'll get sick, please. A boy that age, he needs plenty rest."

"Billy gets plenty of rest."

"If you tell him to work harder, he'll need more."

"I'll see he gets more, Ma."

"Good," Mrs. Silver said. "So now how is business?"

"Fine, Ma, wonderful," Sam said, and into his mind, replacing the idle preoccupation with the unidentified tanker's flag, slid an image of the manuscript of *They Told Me You Were Dead.* One half of the image showed the neatly typed top copy resting on Bud Bienstock's desk in the *American Bride* offices. The other half of the image showed Sam's carbon copy of the story resting in one of the concealed filing cabinets in his study. Between the two halves lay a road of unidentified length marked "Corrections." How long it would take to travel that road, and whether he would be able to make the journey at all, were questions Sam could not answer. To his mother in Queens, in a loud, clear voice that rang with confidence, Sam now said, "Business has never been better, Ma."

"Good," Mrs. Silver said. "This I like to hear. And how is the weather over there by you uptown?"

"Fine," Sam said, staring out at the river as he found himself suddenly wondering if anything was to be gained by calling Bud Bienstock and having a chat with the editor about the ending of *They Told Me You Were Dead.* "It's nice and sunny, Ma."

"It's good weather to get married in."

"Sure, Ma," Sam said as he decided it would be unwise to call Bud Bienstock. Like most editors, even good ones, Bud had fallen into the kind of work he now did after he had failed at the work he really wanted to do, namely, writing. As a result, while his ideas for improving an already written story might be excellent, his ideas for composing an as yet unwritten story were almost invariably bad. The creative act, which like life itself remained at its core a mystery, was beyond him, as it was beyond most editors. Bud Bienstock couldn't possibly know how to invent an ending that would leave any reader, whether of *American Bride* or *Barron's Weekly,* emotionally satisfied. If he had possessed this knowledge, Bud Bienstock would not have failed as a writer or, paradoxically, succeeded as an editor.

Furthermore, Bud Bienstock was a success worshipper. He liked to buy his fiction from people who were on top and looked as though they were going to remain there for a while. Sam, who had been on top of the magazine market for a long time, knew that much of his own success was due to the fact that, unlike many and perhaps even most writers, he was inclined to taciturnity.

Talk, he had discovered early, was the enemy of writing. It was easier to pour a story into an available ear than put it down on paper. Available ears, he had also discovered, did not respond with checks that paid the rent. To keep it paid, Sam learned, it was infinitely preferable to deny yourself the pleasure of an immediate and visible audience for the far greater satisfaction of seeing your words and name in print some time later before an unseen but huge audience. He had held onto that audience not only with his ability and skill but also with the portrait of himself he had self-consciously painted for the men like Bud Bienstock who decided, with their magazines' checkbooks, what this audience should read.

Sam's public portrait showed a man of thirty-six; tall; still slender; dark-haired; good-looking in an unobtrusive, rough-hewn way; who tended to keep, in addition to his own counsel, his trap shut, and could be counted upon never to miss a deadline.

To call Bud Bienstock on the phone now for a chat about the ending of *They Told Me You Were Dead* might very well, to a man with Bud's highly developed instinct for spotting the first faint signs of failure, seem an indication that the portrait of the close-mouthed man of action to whom he paid sixty thousand dollars for a serial was getting out of focus.

Sam Silver, who like all successful writers lived with the constant terror that at any moment he might start to slip, saw the stupidity of providing Bud Bienstock with a suggestion of impending catastrophe, and thus his mind was set free to hear the words his mother had just uttered at the other end of the phone. Startled, Sam said, "What did you say, Ma?"

Mrs. Silver's voice came in across the wire from Queens as though each word was a separate brass plate and she was nailing them one by one on a wall.

"I—said—it's—good—weather—to—get—married—in."

"Ma, for God's sake," Sam said, "what are you talking about?"

"The same thing this Walter Winchell he's talking about."

"Walter *Winchell?*"

"What's the matter? Over there by you uptown, where it's so fancy even those that they stand in front of the houses to open the door they have to wear a uniform, you never heard over there about this Walter Winchell?"

"Cut it out, Ma, and please stick to—"

"Abe Ostreich he already cut it out for me," Mrs. Silver said. "Maybe it's better you should cut it out, too, then you'll be able to read it yourself and you won't have to ask me what I'm talking about."

Out of his lifetime of experience with the circuitous but relentlessly logical workings of the sharpest mind he had ever encountered, Sam was able to pluck the key to what a stranger would undoubtedly have considered incomprehensible.

"Hold it a second, Ma," he said. "Be right back."

Sam dropped the phone on the bed, hurried out to the living room, and shuffled through the as yet unread morning papers on the breakfast table in the dining alcove. He found the *Mirror,* turned to page 10 and, like

most people accustomed to seeing their names in print, he didn't have to
hunt for his: it leaped up at him from the middle of Walter Winchell's
column, where Sam read:

Add Imminent Mergers: long-time ace mag fictioneer Samuel Silver and real-estate heiress Rebecca Meissen, who rests up from bond-
coupon-clipping sessions by wielding a wicked brush and palette.
Intimates expect the knot to be tied sometime during La Meissen's
new one-man show which opens tonight before a hand-picked Lifted
Pinky Set audience at the swank Ibram Moulage Gallery on Madison
and 62nd.

"Oh, Jesus," Sam muttered as he walked back into the bedroom with
the newspaper, sat down on the bed, and picked up the phone.

"Ma, you there?"

"No," Mrs. Silver said. "I'm by a cocktail party with my friend the
Duchess from Windsor."

"Very funny," Sam said. "How come you saw this thing in Winchell?"

"It hurts you to listen to your mother a few words once in eight years
you call her on the phone?"

"No, but I've got to get to school and—"

"What school?"

"Billy's school. He's—"

"Something is wrong with Billy?"

"No, of course not. He—"

"You just said he's fine. You said—"

"He *is* fine, Ma. I'm not going to school because anything is wrong
with Billy."

"Then for what are you going for what?"

"Billy is in a play, and I want to see him—"

"A play? Like on Broadway?"

"Well, not exactly. I mean they're just kids, but—"

"This is how they teach now in these fancy schools? With plays?"

"No, no, Ma. It happens to be their spring festival, and they're—"

"We have calendars here in Queens, too, Sam. Spring I know it is. What
I don't know is why Billy, he's in a school it's so fancy, they're supposed to
be teaching him something when he gets older he'll be able to make a
living, so in spring he's in plays like an actress?"

"Not an actress," Sam said, and then he had one of those moments of
astonishment at his mother's perception that dotted his life like chicken
pox: how could she possibly have known that Billy was playing Calpurnia?
Sam said, "All the boys are taking parts in the play, and Billy has one of

the parts, and I want to be there to see him play it, so will you please stop trying to reorganize the American educational system, Ma, and tell me about Walter Winchell?"

"What's there to tell?" Mrs. Silver said. "Abe says I hear Sam is getting married again. You hear? This is nice, no? My own son is getting married, so I have to hear it from Abe Ostreich."

"Abe Ostreich is talking through his hat," Sam said.

"And this Walter Winchell?" Mrs. Silver said. "Through what is he talking? Abe pulls out from his pocket a piece of paper he tore it out this morning from Walter Winchell and I'm holding it here in my own hand this minute I'm talking to you."

"I'm not saying it's not in the paper," Sam said. "I've got the paper in front of me. What I'm saying is it's not true."

"So this Walter Winchell, if you're not getting married, why should he say in the paper you are?"

"I don't know, Ma."

"What don't you know?"

"I don't know how these things get in the papers."

"You know a girl her name is Rebecca Meissen?"

"Yes, of course."

"You know her good? You know her not so good? A long time? A short time?"

"Ma, I know a lot of people. I don't keep track of how long I know them. Sure, I've known Rebecca, oh, I don't know, a year or two, but that doesn't mean I'm going to marry her."

"Why not?"

"Ma, for God's sake, I can't go around marrying everybody I've known for a year or two."

"Everybody, no. This I don't expect. But it's already over ten years, Sam, since Jennie—"

"Please let's not get involved with Jennie. That's all past tense, and I'm in a hurry."

"Who's talking about Jennie?" Mrs. Silver said. "I'm talking about this Rebecca Meissen. It's over ten years already you're not married, Sam. It's not good, Sam. Especially you have a boy like Billy. A man, he's got a son, he should have a wife, Sam."

"Some people don't agree with you, Ma."

"Those people, I'm sure they're so smart there where you live uptown, they think they know everything. Well, let me tell you something, Sam. In Queens there's a little smartness, too, Sam. A man like you, he's young—"

"Thirty-six, Ma."

THE *Sound* OF *Bow Bells*   / 57

"I should only be thirty-six," Mrs. Silver said. "A man like you, you're young, you have a fine boy, you're an important person there uptown—"

"Magazine writers are not all that important, Ma."

"So which other kind writers are more important, which?"

"Well," Sam said, and the deeply imbedded, familiar pain rolled over. He drew a deep breath and said, "All right, Ma, sure, I'm important."

"Everything you wanted, everything I prayed for you, down there on Tenth Street, when all we had was Papa's ten fingers and our heads full of dreams, when you were yet a baby, when you used to come home at night from the job and from night school and we used to sit in the kitchen and talk and talk and talk until—"

The voice at the other end of the wire seemed to disintegrate. Sam knew why. Into the conversation that dealt with this present they had both accepted, an intruder from the past they had shared had thrust its way; a memory of the time when everything that happened to either of them happened to both; a time when Uptown—that golden land only a mile or two from their tenement kitchen yet then as distant and beckoning and unattainable as far-off Cathay—was the goal toward which they aspired, a goal it had never occurred to either of them they would not reach hand in hand.

"Sam," his mother said, her voice coming alive slowly, haltingly, as though she had to gather all the scattered fragments before the whole could be made to work. "What's the matter, Sam?"

"With what, Ma?"

"Your life, Sam."

He pulled the phone from his ear and stared at the mouthpiece. It was as though a chair or a table in a heavily fortified citadel had in some mysterious way been transformed into a living creature and, while the complacent sentinels dozed, the creature had slipped the bolts and allowed the enemy to come storming in. Slowly, as though with the power of his will he could force the enemy out and the bolts back into place, Sam put the receiver back to his ear.

"I don't know where you dig up these large-size questions so early in the morning, Ma," he said. "But there's absolutely nothing wrong with my life."

"No?" Mrs. Silver said. "So why, ten o'clock at night, when Papa and I we're already in bed, why your agent this Mr. Sargent he comes looking for you out here in Queens, why?"

This time the shock drove the phone in the opposite direction. Wincing away from the pressure against his ear, Sam said, "Mr. *Sargent* was out there in *Queens* looking for *me?*"

"On his own two feet, no," Mrs. Silver said. "An uptownick to come here to Queens, God forbid, he could catch yet maybe a double kvetch in the kishkes. No, on his feet, himself, your Mr. Sargent didn't come. But on the telephone, last night, he called up, your Mr. Sargent."

"Why?"

"This you're asking me? And with your life you say there's nothing wrong?"

"Will you for God's sake let my life alone and stick to the point?"

"This you arranged already a long time ago, Sam."

"Ma, let's not go into that now. All I'm asking is what did Mr. Sargent want?"

"He wanted me, maybe? Or Papa, Sam? You, Sam, you're the big uptown writer. Not us. You're by Mr. Sargent a client, Sam. Not me and Papa. A couple of schnorrers from Queens, Sam, what would Mr. Sargent want with them, what? You he wanted, Sam."

"But didn't he say why?"

"He tried to call you, he said, but he got only that thing, the service, that woman she answers the telephone for you when you're not in the house."

"When you told him I wasn't there, what did he say?"

"What should he say? Mrs. Silver, I'll send you by air mail a box knishes? He said good night, that's what he said."

"He didn't leave any message?"

"In Queens? To leave messages? For someone he lives uptown? This makes by you sense, Sam?"

"Well, I just wondered," Sam said, trying to pretend he was not nearly so troubled as he now knew he was. The mental picture of soft-spoken, self-possessed, unhurried, almost phlegmatic Claude Sargent driven to the effort of trying to trace anybody by phone at that hour of the night, without the help of his office staff, exuded an aura of anxiety so uncharacteristic that Sam could no longer escape the conviction that what was involved was infinitely more serious than the possible rejection of *They Told Me You Were Dead* by Bud Bienstock. As calmly as he could Sam said, "Well, I'll give Mr. Sargent a ring later on and find out what he wants. I'm sure it's nothing important."

"If you don't know what he wants," Mrs. Silver said, "how can you be so sure it's not important?"

"The only thing my agent would consider important is business, and I know nothing important about business is cooking at the moment, so I know my agent's call can't be important."

"Good," Mrs. Silver said. "Then you can come out today, then, and look at the papers."

The phone, already half started on its return journey to the hook on the table beside Sam's bed, snapped back to his ear.

"What papers?" Sam said.

The firm voice at the other end of the wire took on a cutting edge.

"Papa and I, how should we know what papers? We're here in Queens like prisoners. They stick things under the door, we pick them up. We don't ask questions. We just sit and wait what they send us. Today they send us these papers in the mail, a fat envelope, with in the corner it's printed high, you can touch the words with your hand, like from a lawyer."

Sam could suddenly feel the knot of uneasiness about Claude Sargent's call begin to spread, putting out fingers that crept slowly into areas the morning had touched but with which Sam's agent normally had nothing to do: the conversation with Mrs. Harrison, Billy's unexpected questions about Jennie, even the imminent performance of *Julius Caesar* at the Porte School.

"Ma," Sam said with great care but no confidence: his mother's position on the subject he was about to broach had been established decades ago, before he was born, when she first set foot on American soil. "Would you mind telling me who the papers are from?"

"Mind? Why should I mind? If I knew, Sam, you can be sure you I'd be the first to tell."

"You might read me the name that's printed in that engraved lettering up in the corner of the envelope."

"Sure I might," Mrs. Silver said. "If it was printed in a language a person could read."

The languages she could read were Yiddish and Rumanian. Almost sixty years earlier, when she arrived in America and discovered that to the bulk of the inhabitants of this new land neither of these two languages was the common form of communication, she had retreated into an attitude of contempt for the backwardness of the natives from which she had never made the slightest effort to emerge.

"You don't have to read the name to me," Sam said. "You could just spell out the letters for me, Ma."

"You come here to Queens, Sam, and spell them out yourself."

"I can't, Ma."

"Why not? A policeman is standing over you with a gun? He says don't go see your mother and father or I'll shoot? Come for supper and bring Billy. I'll make knishes."

"I can't, Ma."

"With cheese and with potatoes."

"Ma, I can't. I've got—"

"I know what you've got. But two kinds knishes, with cheese and with potatoes, even uptown you haven't got. So come and I'll make."

"I can't, Ma. I've got a dinner date."

"With this Rebecca Meissen she's in Walter Winchell?"

"As a matter of fact, yes. You see, Ma, she's got this new show—"

"An actress?"

Mrs. Silver sounded as though she had just learned Rebecca Meissen was executive assistant to Jack the Ripper.

"No, an art show," Sam said. "She paints."

"Houses?"

"No, not houses. Pictures. On canvas. With brushes. Rebecca is an artist."

"It says in Walter Winchell she's rich."

"She is, but—"

"So a girl she's rich what does she have to be an artist for, for what?"

"A lot of people paint just for the fun of it," he said. "The way a lot of people write."

"*Rich* people?"

Sam, who knew the meaning of every shift in her tone the way Chingachgook knew the meaning of every rustling twig in a Fenimore Cooper forest, understood at once that a new thought had entered his mother's head.

"Sure," Sam said. "Lots of rich people write just for the fun of it."

"Books, like? In magazines?"

"Books, plays, magazines, newspapers, all over," Sam said. "Wherever they can get themselves published."

"And they get paid for this writing?"

"Certainly they get paid for it. Why shouldn't they?"

Into the firm voice at the other end of the wire came the tone of Canute addressing the sea.

"Because it's taking bread from the mouth of people who need it, that's why they shouldn't," Mrs. Silver said. "Where would you be today if seventeen years ago, when you were a boy, when you first started, if rich people were writing stories and books like you were trying to write? You'd still be on Tenth Street, that's where you'd be."

"Not necessarily," Sam said. "Just because a man is rich doesn't mean he's a good writer any more than it means he's a bad one. If an editor has two stories on his desk, one by a poor boy from Tenth Street and the other from a rich boy on Park Avenue—"

"He'll buy the one by the rich boy."

"I don't think that's fair," Sam said.

"Who is talking about fair?" Mrs. Silver said. "I'm talking about how the world is. The rich they always get the best, and you know it."

"I'm not so sure."

"No?" Mrs. Silver said. "Your own mother wants you should come eat supper with her tonight, but who gets you, who? This Rebecca Meissen, the rich painter with brushes, she's an artist, she's the one who gets you, that's who."

"Not because she's rich," Sam said. "Because it's a date we made long ago. Her show is opening, and I asked her to have dinner with me before we go over to the gallery."

"Galleries I can't give you, but knishes I still know how to make, so you can't come to supper, so come for lunch."

"I can't do that, either, Ma. I've got a lunch date with my agent."

"This date you made also a long time ago?"

"No, but it's important, and I've got to—"

"Since when it became important?"

"Since we made the date. Mr. Sargent said—"

"What *you* just said, a minute ago, you said Mr. Sargent, what he called you here last night for, it couldn't be important because in business there's by you now nothing important."

"His wife talked to me a little while ago," Sam said. "She's his partner, as you know. Sargent & Sargent. She told me he expects me in his office for lunch, and I've got to be there."

"So be there," Mrs. Silver said. "I'm stopping you maybe?"

"Ma, I wish you'd try to understand—"

"I have something better to do? All day long I'm trying. All day, when other people they're with their children, and all night, when other people they're sleeping, me, me and Papa, we're both trying, trying to understand how it could happen, how a person can dream and dream and dream, and then, when the dream comes true—"

"Tell you what I'll do, Ma," Sam said, wading out into his mother's stream of recrimination the way he had waded out into Mrs. Harrison's stream of self-justification, but what he could accomplish with his telephone answering service he was unable to do with his mother: her words, unlike Mrs. Harrison's, left echoes. "I'll come out sometime this afternoon and have a look at those papers," Sam said, disregarding the echoes. Until he found out what Claude Sargent wanted, he would have to forgo the luxury of contemplating his sense of guilt. "That be all right?"

"And if I say no, it's all wrong?" Mrs. Silver said. "A beggar takes what they throw him in his hat. What time you'll be here?"

"I don't know exactly," Sam said. "As soon as I can get there after my lunch with Mr. Sargent. Say around two-thirty, maybe? Three?"

"Papa and I," Mrs. Silver said, "we'll be waiting."

Waiting for what, Sam wondered with a touch of helplessness, as he put down the phone and slid his shirt out of the expensive-looking blue-tinted cellophane envelope that was undoubtedly the main reason why Madame Berenice's Fifty-fourth Street Blanchisserie was able with impunity to charge forty cents for laundering a button-down Oxford. How long would he have to bear the guilt of his and his parents' utterly incompatible ways of life? They were illiterate peasants who had never made the slightest effort to adjust to a civilization for which at least one of them, his mother, had never even bothered to conceal her contempt. He was a writer much of whose success depended on a total immersion in that civilization. Was he the first son in history who had grown away from his parents? The answer, which was of course no, did not drown out the silent but piercing wail of pain in the reply his mother did not have to make: he was the son who had grown away from her. So she waited, because she was helpless to do anything else, for the tide of life to do for her what it had never yet done for anybody else: reverse itself. And so Sam, whenever he was about to visit his parents in Queens, was reduced to speculation, because he, too, was helpless to do anything else.

Would his mother and father be waiting as always, Sam wondered uncomfortably as he slipped into the shirt, for some active sign of the love they had once shared and now pretended still existed? Would they be waiting, Sam asked himself irritably as he slipped the tie under his collar, for him to rescind the order of their banishment on which they had themselves insisted, or seemed to be insisting, when ten years ago they had agreed firmly with his decision, now that Jennie was gone, to live alone with, and raise, his then two-year-old son?

His mind was beginning to fight off the shocking but inevitable wish in which his speculation on this subject always ended, namely, that death would do its merciful work before too long, when he became aware of the chimes in the front door, which sounded, Sam thought as he forgot his anger and hurried out to the living room, like a Christmas TV show gone slightly crazy.

"Oh, it's you," he said to the handsome Negro girl out in the hall. "I thought it was the cops."

"I'm sorry," Charlene said. "Mrs. Meissen's been trying to get you on the phone, but it was busy, so she sent me up with—"

"I was talking to my mother," Sam said.

Charlene smiled and said, "Oh, well." As a part-time maid who spent her mornings working for Rebecca in 15E and her afternoons tidying up for Sam in 16E, Charlene answered the phone quite often when Mrs. Silver called. As a pre-med student in Columbia's evening session who was majoring in geriatrics, Charlene was constantly dispensing nuggets of helpful information intended to ease Sam's burden, the way a lion tamer flings out scraps of meat to keep the animals under control during a performance. Charlene said, "Mrs. Meissen figured it was probably your mother, verbosity being a common geriatric phenomenon, so she asked me to run up and give you this."

She held out several sheets of Rebecca's engraved notepaper.

"What is it?" Sam said.

"The copy for the catalogue."

"Now?" Sam said in surprise as he took the sheets of paper. "The show opens tonight. I thought the catalogue was printed weeks ago."

"So did Mrs. Meissen," Charlene said. "As a matter of fact, it *is* printed. The main catalogue, that is. These are some program notes for a two-page folder, a sort of program, you might say, for the specially invited guests tonight. Mrs. Meissen was talking to Mr. Moulage at the gallery a little while ago—"

"This *morning?*"

"Oh, Mrs. Meissen's been up for hours." Charlene smiled again. "You know how she is, Mr. Silver."

"I guess she's pretty excited," Sam said. "Come on in, Charlene."

"I don't think she slept a wink all last night," Charlene said, coming in. "Then this thing, I mean remembering all of a sudden on the phone a little while ago talking to Mr. Moulage there was no program for tonight, she really almost blew a gasket. When I arrived to make breakfast, Ronnie said she'd been scribbling away for over an hour."

"My God," Sam said, leafing through the sheets. "You mean she wrote all this in one hour?"

"An hour and a half maybe," Charlene said. "Why?"

"She ought to give up painting and take to fiction," Sam said. "I'm lucky if I can squeeze out a coherent twenty-five words in that time."

"Well, it may not be very coherent," Charlene said, and her smile changed slightly to indicate that while an outsider might consider her remark presumptuous, Mr. Silver could be trusted to know exactly what she did mean. "That's why she's been trying to get you on the phone. She wants you to read it over and see if it's okay. Mr. Moulage is sending a messenger at ten o'clock to pick it up and rush it to the printer so the program will be ready for tonight."

"Okay," Sam said. "Pour yourself a cup of coffee and relax while I make like an editor."

"Thanks, Mr. Silver, but I can't," Charlene said. "I've got to go over to that darned Madame Berenice's Blanchisserie to pick up the dress Mrs. Meissen's wearing tonight. When you finish, Mr. Silver, why don't you ring the elevator, and ask Howard or Vincent, whichever one is on, I think Howard probably by now, ask him to take the papers down to Mrs. Meissen?"

"All right, fine," Sam said. "I'll do that."

"See you later," Charlene said, opening the door.

"I may not be here," Sam said. "I've got a lunch date, and then I have to go out to Queens to see my mother, which means God knows when I'll get back, but I'll turn on Mrs. Harrison before I go."

"I'll see Billy, then," Charlene said. "Please give Mrs. Silver my regards."

Carrying Rebecca's scented notepaper into the study, Sam wondered how his mother would react to Charlene's greetings if he were thoughtless enough to convey them. One of the things that confused Mrs. Silver about the land in which she had lived for more than five decades was her discovery, soon after as a young girl she had been driven out of Rumania by anti-Semitism, that in America there were minority groups more minor than her own. She had been forced to trade the solid satisfaction of being an underdog for the uneasy gratification of becoming a middleman. Sam sat down at his desk, spread out the sheets of paper, and began to pick his way through Rebecca's decorative, ladylike, and almost totally illegible handwriting:

The centripetal eye or inverted vision, these are the words I have chosen to explain the matrix of physical and psychological phenomena that, at least to this artist, dominate the creative act.

Depending for a vision of the external world only on the optic nerve is, in the artistic sense, committing oneself to a form of blindness. To properly see the world around us, we must employ all our senses. Only when the strands of all our senses are intertwined in a single rope of sensitivity, so to speak, can we hope to achieve true contact, a sort of oneness, with the mind and intent of the artist whose work is spread before us.

The pictures you have been invited here to see tonight are the product of two years of groping, a quest toward some meaning in the life by which, unexpectedly but totally, the artist found herself two years ago suddenly engulfed . . .

Sam looked up. Rebecca, wearing the pale blue peignoir he had given her for Christmas, was standing in the study door.

"Oh, dear," she said, "is it as bad as all that?"

"What?" Sam said.

Rebecca came into the room and touched the key with which she had let herself into the apartment to the sheets of notepaper on the desk.

"You were scowling as though you hated it," she said.

"Don't leap at conclusions," Sam said. "Facial expressions have nothing to do with the creative act or its appreciation. I once read somewhere a report by Goethe's cook that when he was in the middle of knocking out what later proved to be some of his most celebrated poetry he looked as though he'd bitten into a bad oyster."

"I've noticed an interesting thing about you," Rebecca said. "Whenever you're in a tight spot you think you can get out of it with an appropriate quotation."

"Now what sort of tight spot am I trying to get out of now?"

"You were scowling at what I've written and you know it."

"No," Sam said. "That's not what I was scowling at."

"Then what?"

"This," he said, touching the key in her hand. "We've got to cut out all this running up and down stairs."

"Why, Sam Silver, what an unchivalrous thing to say! I can remember the day when you could hardly wait for us to swap keys and start running up and down those stairs."

"So can I, but your Ronnie and my Billy were two years younger then." The expression on her face caused Sam to add quickly, "It isn't only that I don't want the kids to get any ideas, so get that look off your face."

"If it's not only the kids, what else is it, then?"

"My agent disapproves of it."

"All right," she said in a low voice, looking very grave and very small and suddenly very desirable. "I'm not going to ask you what that remark means and give you an opportunity to duck out with another quotation."

"Rebecca, now, look. I didn't mean—"

"I know you didn't, but oh God how I wish you would. I mean just this once, please, I wish just this once you would."

"Would what?"

"Say what you mean in a way that I can understand."

He said slowly, "But haven't I always—?"

She shook her head, fast, almost desperately. "No, never. Not once. Not once in all the two years—"

Rebecca paused, as though mentioning the length of time they had known each other had a significance she did not dare discuss. She drew a deep breath and started again.

"Sam," she said, "I know I've failed you in some way. I don't know how, even though I've tried to find out. I've tried until it's almost killed me, but I haven't found out. So all I know is I've failed you. I also know you won't tell me how. Maybe you don't know yourself. That happens. I never knew what was wrong between me and Anton. For years I didn't know, until one day—" Rebecca paused again. She seemed to be waiting, as though she had for the moment forgotten some crucial lines she had carefully memorized, but she didn't doubt they would come back to her. "For a long time after we met," she said finally, "I thought I was willing to wait years for you, too. But today, this morning, this show tonight, Sam, I *can't* wait. I don't expect you to understand what this show means to me—" Her voice stopped and then, with a funny little look in her eyes, she said, "What's the matter?"

She was obviously referring to the expression on his face, so it was too late to change it.

"What's the matter is how you can be so wrong," he said. It was never too late to lie. "What I was scowling at was that I'd never before realized, not until I started reading this—" He tapped the pages of perfumed stationery. "I never before realized how good a writer you are."

It was as though his words had thrown an electric switch. The high, finely made cheekbones glowed as they always did when he pleased her.

"Sam," she said, "you're joking."

It was the reply with which even the greatest and most conceited of prose stylists had been known to greet the first news from the Swedish Academy.

"No, I mean it," Sam said. "When you know somebody for two years you think you know all about them, and then one day, by sheer accident, you discover something like this."

He tapped the perfumed sheets again and Rebecca, with a small gurgle of ecstasy, dipped down and kissed him.

"Sam," she said. "Darling." She kissed him harder and picked up the papers. "You've made my day, that's what you've done," she said. "You've even made the whole puzzling two years worthwhile. I never realized—I mean I never thought—I never dared dream—"

Neither, Sam thought dryly, had Chaucer and Milton.

"That's a damn good piece of prose," he said.

"Sam," Rebecca said. "Then I can have Moulage send this to the printer?"

"You certainly can."

She turned and strode to the door, her delicately voluptuous figure trim and purposeful in the pale blue peignoir, and then she stopped and turned, as though she had suddenly been assailed by a moment of doubt.

"Sam," she said worriedly. "You're not kidding me?"

"Cross my heart," he said.

"There isn't anything in this you think I ought to fix?" Rebecca said. "Nothing you feel I ought to change?"

"Well, there's a split infinitive in paragraph two," Sam said. "You say: *to properly see the world around us.* A purist might feel you should say: *properly to see the world around us.*"

Rebecca scowled at the second paragraph as though he had suggested that the news from Sweden was a mistake after all, and the great prize was actually going to somebody else. Then her face cleared.

"But I'm not a purist," Rebecca said with a small smile. "I'm just an artist trying to make myself understood. Under those conditions I feel a writer is entitled to a little what do you call it, yes, poetic license, don't you think?"

She was entitled to more than that. What had suddenly brought his confused and troubling morning to this moment of crystal-clear hopelessness was the knowledge that he could give her none of it.

"You're entitled to anything that will make you happy," Sam said. "Anyway, that's what I want you to have."

"Sam, do you?" She came back to the desk. "Do you really, Sam?"

He looked at her for several silent moments, with a sense of disbelief, as though the two years of intimacy had never taken place and he was staring at a total stranger, while the words she had written strode through his head like accusing paragraphs from an indictment: *The pictures you have been invited here to see tonight are the product of two years of groping, a quest toward some meaning in the life by which, unexpectedly but totally, the artist found herself two years ago suddenly engulfed . . .*

The vacuum cleaner of his craft had recorded everything: her special beauty; her odd moods; her likes and dislikes; her passion for imparting factual information; the way she radiated a sense of delicious propriety; her moments of astonishing perception; her lust for the Truth which she could not face; the marshmallow behind her expensively polished exterior; her unfailing and therefore sometimes infuriating goodness—everything had gone down into his mental notebooks, everything except the only thing that to a writer really mattered, the one thing without which even the finest craftsman could never rise to the stature of an artist: the capacity to feel.

"Sam," she said, putting her arms around his neck. "Please tell me."

"Not now," he said, feeling through the warmth of her embrace as a woman the chill of her superiority as an artist. "There isn't any time," Sam said, standing up, knowing at last why he was unable to love her as she loved him. "You've got to get that copy to the printer," he said, hoping he was managing to keep out of his voice the jealousy that churned in his heart. "And I've got to get myself to the Porte School."

The Porte School, which had been founded in 1777 by a French nobleman who served on General Washington's staff, entered the twentieth century high on the list of America's scholastically respectable prep schools. By the time the century had passed the halfway mark, and Sam Silver enrolled his son Billy in the eighth grade, the Porte School's scholastic reputation was even more elevated, but its chief distinction, at least in the conversations of parents whose sons wore the purple and white, was the school's location.

Sam naturally had no firsthand knowledge of what Seventy-fourth Street, between Broadway and West End Avenue, had looked like in the days when Charles Louis Vieullière, the twelfth Marquis de la Nantes, decided to settle permanently in the country he had just helped liberate from the yoke of George III. Today it looked like hell.

The West Side brownstones, built to the Victorian standards of elegance once considered suitable for a moneyed middle class, had been cut up long ago into rooming houses and cramped flats to accommodate the needs of an expanding lower class.

Perhaps because a prep school, at least geographically, is not as responsive to sociological pressures as, for example, a corset manufacturer or an orthodontist, the Porte School had held its ground as well as its enviable scholastic standing. As a result, many of the parents of Billy Silver's class-mates were somewhat annoyed by the fact that to prepare for the graces of an Ivy League education it was necessary for their sons to spend nine hours every day in the heart of what was known to many of its inhabitants, because of their predilections in fur garments and table delicacies, as the Fox and Lox Belt. To Sam Silver, who with the proceeds of his first *Sateve-post* sale had hurried to buy his mother a silver-fox jacket, there was nothing annoying about the Porte School's location. Or rather, being a writer, he could with ease convince himself that his annoyance was ac-tually the reaction of a trained observer who found it secretly amusing that for an institution to which his son and Ronnie Meissen were delivered daily in Anton's maroon and silver Bentley, the equivalent of a campus should be a forty-foot stretch of cracked sidewalk cluttered with overflow-ing garbage cans, and the nearest thing to the traditional prep school Sweet Shoppe in which the students lounged away their free time was either Pedro's Chile Parlor on the southwest corner of Seventy-fourth and Broadway or, facing it on the northwest corner, Drubinsky's Kosher Delly.

Sam could see, as his taxi nosed to a halt at the corner and he climbed out to pay the driver, that at least one prep-school tradition, namely, the dietary habits of boys in their early teens, was being vigorously observed: in the window of Drubinsky's Kosher Delly at least a dozen crew-cut youngsters, who looked like the drawings in the Rogers Peet back-to-school ads, were bellied up to the counter, wolfing down, at ten twenty-five in the morning, hot pastrami sandwiches, slabs of pickle, and nickel-a-shtickel lumps of knubblewurst dipped in mustard.

Turning the corner into West Seventy-fourth Street, Sam saw some-thing else: the campaign against the city's Sanitation Department, which had been launched early in the year with a speech in chapel full of Shakespearean allusion by Mr. Bronson—who in addition to teaching seventh- and eighth-grade English was Head of the Lower School—was not going well. Picking his way among the orange rinds and eggshells that spilled down the sides of the hopelessly overloaded rooming-house garbage cans like streaks of paint in one of Rebecca Meissen's abstracts of a cornucopia, Sam had a recurrence of the impression that had struck him on his first visit to the Porte School: a small beleaguered citadel hold-ing out, with a gallantry that contained more than a touch of foolishness, against a tide of lava that kept inching relentlessly closer and closer to the inevitable moment of extinction.

The feeling that the enemy was gaining ground at an accelerated rate was clear to Sam as soon as he descended the three worn stone steps that led from the street into the Porte School's cramped lobby: Mrs. Lothrop, whose switchboard occupied almost a full third of the lobby, was blinking irritably through her thick glasses as she jabbed her plugs at the tiny holes under the winking lights with all the concentrated ferocity of a matador going in over the horns.

"Porte School, good morning. I don't think so, but I'll ring his office and see. Hello, Mr. Silver. Wait one moment, Mr. Silver, please, won't you? No, I'm sorry. His office does not answer. I can't give you his secretary. She's in chapel with Mr. Bronson and I can't get her on the phone because she's about to start prompting *Julius Caesar*. I have a message for you, Mr. Silver. Mr. Bronson said when you arrived would I tell you to be good enough to please sit in the last row."

"The last row?" Sam said, puzzled.

"Yes, at *Julius Caesar*," Mrs. Lothrop said. "Excuse me. Porte School, good morning. Yes, he is. One moment, please. On the aisle, if you can, Mr. Silver, Mr. Bronson said."

"But why?" Sam said.

"He didn't say," Mrs. Lothrop said. "Just would you please sit in the last row at the back, preferably on the aisle. Porte School, good morning. I think he's in the gym, but let me try."

Turning away from the switchboard, Sam's glance fell on the painting of the round, dewlapped face of the Porte School's founder, and he had a moment of shock: Sam had never before noticed the resemblance between Charles Louis Vieullière, who looked like a pumpkin, and Claude Sargent, who resembled a basset hound.

Noticing the resemblance now, as he climbed the worn white marble steps to the first floor, Sam was reminded of Claude Sargent's still unexplained telephone message of the night before, which had been the source of so much uneasiness all morning. Walking down the corridor lined with gray steel student lockers, Sam found that he was even more uneasy about the message than he had been when he left home. It was almost as though the oil-painted face of the Marquis de la Nantes had deliberately changed shape to remind Sam that whatever was waiting for him in Claude Sargent's office during the lunch hour could in no way be avoided by spending the preceding hour playing the role of what the Family Guidance Section of *American Bride* called "the interested parent." Sam was wondering how many of the parents who had come to watch this morning's performance of *Julius Caesar* were actually interested, when he stumbled on one of the steps that appeared unexpectedly at odd intervals on almost all of the Porte School's level surfaces, and he fell into the chapel, where

Mr. Bronson, who was moving toward the door, caught him in his arms.

"Oops," the English instructor said. "Oh, it's you, Mr. Silver. Good. I'd begun to think you were not coming. Mrs. Lothrop gave you my message, did she?"

"Yes," Sam said. "Sorry to come flopping in like this. I never seem to remember those steps."

"Neither does most of our faculty and a large part of the student body," Mr. Bronson said. He was a tall, stoop-shouldered, tweedy man with fiery eyes and an enormous, knife-thin nose that twitched constantly, so that Sam always felt he was bringing into Mr. Bronson's presence a slightly unpleasant odor about which, if their positions had been reversed, the English instructor would have spoken to him sharply. "It's because we're not really a single building but an accumulation of structures out of which the walls have been knocked. You'd think they'd build these brownstones all on one level, wouldn't you? Do take a seat in the last row, please. There's one on the aisle at the left."

"I was wondering why you—?"

"Ssshhh!" Mr. Bronson said. "It's the Twenty-third Psalm."

It was always the Twenty-third Psalm, Sam thought, as Mr. Bronson hurried out of the chapel and Sam tiptoed toward the empty seat in the last row on the left. Even down in P.S. 64, where the schoolday had always begun with the Pledge of Allegiance and a reading from the Bible by the principal, Assembly had always been associated in Sam's mind with being led beside the still waters, a phrase that had never failed to move him, even though he had not then understood what it meant.

Sam was wondering if three of the words—*The Still Waters*—might not make a better title for *They Told Me You Were Dead*, when he reached the last row and stopped short. In the second seat in from the empty one on the aisle sat Anton Meissen, his patrician head slightly bowed and tipped ever so slightly to one side as he listened with a concentrated attention that may have been genuine but, Sam suspected, was actually no more than another manifestation of Anton's impeccable manners which would clearly dictate that, during a reading from the Bible in a school chapel, the proper posture for a civilized visitor would be to approximate as closely as possible the one chosen by Rodin for his celebrated statue of The Thinker.

Still on tiptoe, Sam backed hastily toward the empty seat in the last row at the other side of the aisle, making a mental note for tomorrow morning's session with his notebook about a man who, for all his supposed worldliness, was unable to shake the guilty conviction, whenever he ran into his mistress' ex-husband, that in spite of her perfectly legal divorce, he was nonetheless her partner in adultery.

"May I?" Sam whispered to the man in the second seat from the vacant one on the other side of the aisle. The man nodded without looking up, and as Sam dropped into the empty seat, he was swept by a feeling that translated itself at once into a title—*Out of the Frying Pan*—he knew would never find its way into his notebook, not because it was so obvious that Sam was certain it had been used many times before, but because it made embarrassingly clear the fact that what he was being swept by was simple, uncomplicated, garden-variety jealousy. The man in the seat beside him was Tom Sacheverell, whose latest novel, *The Barrier Reef,* had been glowingly reviewed only a week ago and was already high on the best-seller lists.

"Oh," Sacheverell said, and into his watery, unworldly, martyred eyes, which had flicked toward Sam with unmistakable terror of the human contact, there came a look of reluctant recognition that Sam knew was not quite total.

They were both Sargent & Sargent clients, and both their sons attended the Porte School, and any number of times during the past dozen years they had shared the pheasant and wild rice that were a staple of Sophie Sargent's tax-deductible dinner parties, but Sam knew that Tom Sacheverell did not really know who he was. It should have helped, Sam told himself irritably, knowing full well it didn't, to be aware that there was nothing personal in Sacheverell's vagueness. Sam had reason to believe, from everything he had seen and heard of the other man, that Sophie Sargent was telling the truth when she said Tom Sacheverell lived so deeply and totally in the private world of his obsessed imagination that she doubted if he recognized his own wife except when they met in bed. And—according to Madge Sacheverell, who drank more than was good for her, or anybody who happened to be around when she was doing it— these meetings took place only on ceremonial occasions: when the Book-of-the-Month Club chose a new Sacheverell novel for its subscribers, the Pulitzer Prize Committee sent him another of its coveted telegrams, or a Hollywood studio turned over in exchange for the use of one of his works one more fragment of Fort Knox. These occasions may not have been frequent enough to keep Madge Sacheverell sexually satisfied, but they were far too frequent to make it possible for Sam Silver to be in her husband's presence without being thoroughly ashamed of the way he felt.

"Hi," Sam whispered, hoping he sounded neither curt nor eager.

"Oh," Sacheverell said again and then, as his tortured face twisted in what was clearly intended to be a polite smile, he added, "Nice to see you."

"Sorry to be late," Sam said, but Sacheverell had already turned, jerking his saintly head as though in flight from temptation, toward the platform at the front of the chapel. Turning with him, Sam saw that the Twenty-third Psalm had given way to ruddy-cheeked Mr. Sundstrom, the Porte School's drama coach, who was explaining with academic jocularity that for a variety of reasons, including limited production facilities as well as time, the version of *Julius Caesar* they were about to see would be somewhat shorter than the one Mr. W. Shakespeare had written, but Sam found it difficult to concentrate on Mr. Sundstrom's humorous remarks.

The vacuum cleaner of his craft, which Claude Sargent had taught him to keep turned on at all times, was gulping in large lumps of his jealousy for Tom Sacheverell, and the mental habits that years of practicing his craft had made almost automatic, insisted on picking apart the nature of that jealousy.

Sam knew he could dismiss Tom Sacheverell the novelist as a second-rater who happened in the Pacific area to have stumbled on a hitherto unexplored literary vein so lush that he could fool not only the public, but the critics as well, into believing he was a first-rater. Sam knew he could dismiss Tom Sacheverell the man as a pretentious neurotic who always looked as though he was on his way to the Last Supper and was trying to decide whether or not to take the head of the table. What Sam knew he could not dismiss, and what he suspected was the source of Sacheverell's appeal to the public and the basis of his fascination for the critics, was his extraordinary skill as a technician in an area where men of even moderate ability deserved applause: the flashback.

The prose of *The Barrier Reef*, as well as Sacheverell's half-dozen other novels ranging the Pacific from early Tasmania to late Pago-Pago, was without any doubt, at least in Sam Silver's mind, assembled as skillfully as a chuck-wagon hash. The level of the thinking behind the loftily impenetrable mysticism that spouted like water from a burst water main from the mouths of the preposterously sketched characters was inferior, Sam felt, to that which had informed the passionate discussions he and Jennie used to have over their soggy bologna sandwiches in the Grover Cleveland High lunchroom with other members of Miss Mercator's Stratford Club. But when Tom Sacheverell, with effortless ease, lifted his reader from the mind of his U.S. paratrooper hero on a Melbourne street in 1943 and deposited him on the deck of a British man o' war in 1787 entering Sydney harbor with the first contingent of resettlement convicts from London, what happened between the words on the printed page and the reader absorbing them was pure magic. Sam knew. He had been trying to do it for years, without much success.

Sam was almost, although not quite, ashamed—nothing he did in the interests of improving the tools with which he worked caused him shame— of the hours he had spent poring over those inept pages, trying to figure out how Sacheverell did it. The pages of Dickens and Thackeray, Balzac and Tolstoy, had yielded up at least some of their secrets to the relentlessly probing young man in the East Tenth Street bedroom and the still curious older man in the Sutton Crescent study. Only the pages of J. Thomas Sacheverell had resisted and kept their extraordinary secret.

Here and there, under the scrutiny of an eye that Sam prided himself was as sharp as most and perhaps sharper than some, a hint or two had escaped.

Sometimes, Sam saw, Sacheverell did it by referring to an odor, evoking through the reader's eye a reaction in his nose that carried him backward in time. Sometimes it was done by leading the reader from a present-day scene into a past-tense scene of exactly the same kind, so that the parallel, working on the reader's mind without the reader's knowledge, performed the trick for the writer. Occasionally it seemed to Sam that Sacheverell worked his magic with no more than a shrewdly chosen word, a few simple syllables that flowed like an unrolled carpet from the present back into the past.

The hints, however, remained no more than that. They were not enough to provide Sam with the additional tool for his work kit that he so very much wanted. For lack of it, because he could not handle flashbacks in a manner he would have considered worthy of the rest of his skills, he had been forced to abandon stories he had wanted desperately to write. Now, sitting beside the master of the skill to which Sam had never been able to come closer than apprenticeship, he found himself poring somewhat irritably over the hints he had managed to glean from his study of Sacheverell's work, wondering why they refused to add up for him to the sum they provided for the other man.

The odor of the Porte School chapel today was certainly not unlike the odor of the Grover Cleveland High auditorium almost eighteen years ago. The uniquely acrid combination of cheap disinfectant, chalk dust, and dried sweat was probably characteristic of school assembly halls the world over. The student performance of *Julius Caesar* that was now jerking and lumbering into some sort of life on the stage up front was undeniably close enough to the Stratford Club's performance of *The Merchant of Venice* with which Miss Mercator had decided to enliven the Grover Cleveland High graduation exercises. And since so many of Shakespeare's lines, at least when uttered by schoolchildren, sounded alike, what was reaching Sam's ears now from the Porte School chapel stage was not unlike what had reached his ears on the night when his formal education had officially ended.

With all these similarities to work with, why was he unable to do what Tom Sacheverell could have done without strain or even thought? Why couldn't Sam Silver carry himself, much less a reader, back into the past? Was it because the parallel situations were not really parallel? Because he had come here today from a lime-green study in Sutton Crescent, whereas he had come to his Grover Cleveland High graduation exercises from a tenement kitchen on East Tenth Street? Yet how could it have been otherwise? Studies had been unknown on East Tenth Street. Certainly they had not existed in three-room walk-ups "with toilets in the hall." The Silvers, like most of their neighbors, used two of these rooms as sleeping quarters. The third, which was called the kitchen, also served as living room, laundry, dining room, and library. It was the center of all the family's activities during waking hours. Where else would a boy of eighteen, getting dressed for his high school graduation exercises, go to find his mother with the button that had just popped from his cuff?

"Take off the shirt," Mrs. Silver had said, putting down the long wooden spoon with which she had been stirring the tzimiss in the pot on the gas range. She stepped across the small room and took down from the shelf over the sink the round Quaker Oats box in which she kept her needles and thread. "I told you not to give it to the Chink."

Sam did not understand why she had been so set against his taking his one good white shirt to the Chinese laundryman around the corner on Avenue C.

"It's not on account of the Chink," Sam said. "It's just the button fell off." He held out his arm. "Sew it on, Ma, will you?"

For years Sam had secretly admired the older men of the neighborhood who, unlike himself, did not have their laundry done by mothers or wives, and could afford to have their collars and cuffs starched stiff by the Chink. It seemed to Sam well worth the twenty-five cents, or half his weekly allowance, it had cost him to achieve for this one night the look of distinction he hoped sometime to be able to afford every day.

"If you didn't take it to the Chink, the cuffs wouldn't be hard like rocks with starch, you could push the button in the buttonhole without a shoehorn, and it wouldn't tear off." Mrs. Silver squinted up toward the small window that opened on the backyard crisscrossed with clotheslines as she sucked the end of the thread to a point and then aimed it at the needle's eye. "Take off the shirt."

"I can't take off the shirt," Sam said. "I'll be late. Sew it on like this."

"Why can't you take off the shirt?" Mrs. Silver said. "A policeman is standing over you with a gun?" She caught the wet end of the thread at the other side of the needle's eye, whipped it out with a long upward sweep of her arm, bit the length of thread from the spool, and dropped the spool back into the Quaker Oats box. With another, shorter sweep of her arm, she brought the needle to the center of the severed length of thread, and with a series of short, swift, brushing movements of thumb and fore-finger, as though she were powdering a bit of cinnamon stick into the tzimiss pot, she worked the two ends of the thread into a knot. "You sew something on a person when they're wearing it, you also sew up their brains," Mrs. Silver said. "Take off the shirt."

"Aah, for Pete's sake, Ma, you don't really believe that," Sam said. "That's just another one of your old superstitions."

"By you maybe it's better to believe in new superstitions?" his mother said. "My cousin Itzik, in the old country, when he was a boy he had brains almost like you, smart from here to here, till one day his mother, my Aunt Bella, the dope, she should rest in peace, she sewed him on a button without taking off the shirt, and from that day my cousin Itzik the smart one became Itzik the potato head, a dope as big as his mother, across the street they couldn't even trust him to go alone. Take off the shirt."

"But, Ma, I'll be late!"

"For what? Standing in the street waiting in front of the locked doors? Seven o'clock it starts, no? And now it's not even yet five. Stop with the arguments, or when Papa comes home from work, instead of tzimiss for supper he'll have burned coals in the pot. Take off the shirt."

Mrs. Silver watched with pursed lips as her son took off the shirt. It was not a simple process. The band down the front, like the collar and cuffs, was starched stiff as a ruler. Working the buttons in had been a fingernail-cracking business. Working them out was not only a repetition of the process but also involved the infliction of another series of defacing cracks in the smooth façade that had cost him half a week's allowance.

"Take it easy, Ma, will you?" Sam protested as her needle flashed up and down swiftly. "You're bending the cuff!"

"You know maybe how to sew on a button without bending the cuff?" She bit off the thread and held out the shirt. "Here, lock yourself up in it again." He took the shirt, slipped into it gingerly, and turned toward the bedroom. His mother's voice said quietly, "Sam."

He turned back. "What?"

"You're worried about the speech?"

"Nah," Sam said and then, because his mouth felt dry and his heart was thumping oddly, he paused to consider his mother's question. Worried wasn't exactly the word. He had rehearsed the valedictory with Miss Mercator for three solid weeks. He could rattle it off without thinking. He didn't doubt he would get through it without trouble at the graduation exercises tonight. And yet there was that dry taste in his mouth and that funny way his heart kept going. "I guess maybe I am, a little," he said finally. "Not scared, I mean, but just—*you* know."

"Sit down and eat a plate tzimiss," Mrs. Silver said. She moved back to the gas range and picked up the wooden spoon. "It'll settle the stomach."

"I can't, Ma," Sam said. "I'm not hungry."

"Tzimiss you don't eat because you're hungry." Mrs. Silver lifted a lump of the golden carroty mess from the pot to a plate. "Tzimiss you eat to hold down the stomach."

"There's nothing wrong with my stomach," Sam said, but he sat down at the kitchen table. He took a forkful of tzimiss, chewed thoughtfully for a while, and then he knew what was wrong. He always did, when it involved something that separated him from his mother. All he had to do was concentrate. All he had to do was think. Thinking hard, Sam said, "Ma."

"What?"

"You won't get sore?"

"Me?"

"Come on, Ma. No kidding. I want to ask you something."

"So ask."

"Why didn't you want me to take the shirt to the Chink?"

"Eighteen years the way I wash your shirts it's fine," Mrs. Silver said. "All of a sudden the night you're graduating from high school, me, I'm not fine any more, only the Chink."

"That's not the reason," Sam said.

"So maybe you can tell me better what's the reason, what?"

"I'm asking you," Sam said. "Why didn't you want me to take the shirt to the Chink?"

"Money to throw out we've got since when?" Mrs. Silver said. "For the same quarter I could buy two dozen rolls."

"That's not the reason, either," Sam said.

"You don't like my reasons," his mother said, "go make your own."

"I want to know why you're so sore I had my shirt done by the Chink," Sam said. "If I don't know, I'll be thinking about it all night, and I'll forget not only my God-damn lines in the play but also my God-damn valedictory."

"The God-damns you won't forget," Mrs. Silver said. "This I can see."

"What I can't see is why the hell—all right, all right, I'm sorry—what I can't see is why it's so important the way I get a shirt laundered. I'm not complaining about the way you wash my shirts. Did I ever? I never said a word. It's just tonight, this one night, I wanted—"

"You wanted to look the way on this one night you shouldn't look," Mrs. Silver snapped. "You're a poor boy. From down here on the East Side, not from uptown. In the bank, how much? Nothing! On the table, what? Bread, tzimiss, sometimes maybe a piece butter, if Papa is working. But in the head? The best brains in Grover Cleveland High School. For this, because of what you have in the head, the rest doesn't matter. For this, because you have a brain, you make the speech at the end of the graduation. For this, because of the brain, the man from uptown is coming to watch the graduation."

"He'll watch it just the same whether I'm wearing a shirt washed by you or by the Chink," Sam said.

"He'll watch the same, but he won't see the same," Mrs. Silver said. "He's a knyocker from uptown. He sees the boy with the shirt washed by me, the boy who plays in the show, the boy who at the end he makes the speech, so he says good, this is a poor boy, but a boy with brains, him we'll give the uptown money he should go to college. But he sees a boy with a shirt it's washed by the Chink, the collar it's stiff like by a gangster in the movies, this man from uptown he'll say this is a poor boy? A boy he can afford his shirts to have washed for a quarter, this is a boy who needs money to go to college, he'll say?"

"Because I'm wearing a starched collar I won't get the scholarship?" Sam said in astonishment. "Is that what you're trying to tell me?"

"So if you're maybe the one that's giving out scholarships?" his mother said. "Who you'll give it to? A boy his mother has to wash his shirt? Or a boy his family can afford for twenty-five cents the Chink should wash his shirt?"

"Ma, for crying out loud, the scholarship is all set," Sam said. "I won it. It's mine. What I wear tonight doesn't make any difference."

"Then why is he coming to look, why, this man from uptown?" Mrs. Silver said.

"I don't know," Sam said. "Just to check, I guess."

"To check what?" his mother demanded. "You're so quick with the guessing, so give me a guess about that, go ahead, let's hear."

"I'm not guessing," Sam said. "It's automatic. The scholarship was established years ago by this famous man who used to go to Grover Cleveland when he was a boy. It goes to the valedictorian, just as the valedictory goes to the student with the highest average in the graduating class.

That's me. I've got the highest average in the graduating class. That's why I'm the valedictorian. And that's why I've won the scholarship. It's all settled."

"Then why is the man coming to look at you tonight, why?"

"I don't know," Sam said. "Yes, I do. What Miss Mercator said. She said every year, before the scholarship is made official, the man from the trust fund, the people who run the money that pays out the scholarship, he comes down to the graduation exercises just to make sure they're, well, they're giving it to the right person. I mean it's just a formality, Ma."

"With these uptown knyockers what they call formalities, there's no such word like just," Mrs. Silver said. "If he's coming to look, unless he's blind he'll see, and a blind man they won't send. So it's better he should see a boy in a collar washed by his mother, not by a Chink."

Twenty minutes later, walking up Avenue A toward Fourteenth Street in his second-best white shirt, Sam had to admit, at least to himself, that it was much better. So far as his neck was concerned, anyway. Relieved of the starched collar that had scraped his skin like sandpaper and kept his mind on the pain, he was free to contemplate the arrangements for the evening and their consequences. It was odd, since all the arrangements had been settled weeks ago, that his mouth should still have that dry, sour taste and his heart should still be thumping along in that funny way.

"Where's your mother?"

Sam stopped and turned. Jennie Broom had come out of the doorway between Glanzer's chicken store and Mr. Salvemini's shoe-repair shop near the Thirteenth Street corner. She was wearing the blue pleated skirt and white middy blouse that Mr. Mueller, the principal, had decreed, when he came to Grover Cleveland High two years ago, was from then on to be the official dress for all girls attending the school.

"She's waiting for Pa to get home from work," Sam said. "They'll come along after he eats. Where's your mother?"

"She's doing the same," Jennie said. "Except what she's waiting for is Pa should say if he's found any work, which you can bet he hasn't. I got sick and tired of hanging around waiting."

She fell in beside him and, as they crossed Thirteenth Street, Sam gave her a short glance out of the corner of his eye. It was never easy to figure Jennie's mood. Her sharp, nasal voice always made her sound slightly angry, but Sam had learned that she sounded exactly the same even when she was cheerful and wanted to be friendly. It occurred to him, from the way she had stepped out of the hall just as he was passing her house, that Jennie, up in the Broom family's sixth-floor rooms, might have been watching for him out of their single Avenue A window.

"You look all clean and nice," Sam said cautiously. Jennie was just as likely to let you have it for a compliment as for an insult.

"Most people in uniforms do," she said. "That's the whole idea of making them wear uniforms."

"Aah, why don't you quit it," Sam said, not so cautiously. Sometimes, the way Jennie twisted and shaped everything to fit her own ideas, it gave him a good swift pain. "It's just a skirt and a middy blouse," he said. "The way girls wear all over."

"Sure, and those black shirts that Mussolini and his men wear, they're just shirts, the way men wear all over," Jennie said. "Except these men, they were marching on Rome, that's all they were doing."

"I don't know why, we're going to graduation, you have to bring in Mussolini."

"Because there's a lot more going on in the world than high school graduations on Irving Place," Jennie said. "The people of Italy, they're starving and being murdered by those fascists in those nice clean black shirts, and now it's starting in Germany, the exact same thing."

"How do you know?"

"I read the papers, that's how I know," Jennie said. "And you'd know it, too, maybe, if you had a little time to think of important things instead of are you going to make valedictorian and are you going to get the Hammond Haynes Scholarship and how many rear ends you have to kiss to get both."

Sam could feel his face flush, but he kept his voice steady as he said, "Thanks for saying rear ends."

"Oh, I wouldn't want to upset the delicate feelings of a perfect little gentleman," Jennie said. "You might get so rattled you'd God forbid forget that crappy poetry Miss Mercator gave you to memorize." Jennie stopped right there, in the middle of the sidewalk, and spread her arms wide and, in a simpering falsetto, began to recite the lines from Richard Hovey with which Sam's valedictory speech ended: *"You to the left, and I to the right, for the ways of men must sever; and it well may be for a day and a night, and it well may be forever."* The simpering falsetto ended in a growl of disgust as Jennie moved on up Avenue A toward Fourteenth Street. "God," she said. "It makes me sick."

"Not the words," Sam said. "That's not what's making you sick."

He had suddenly had a hint about what was giving him that sour taste in his mouth and making his heart thump in that funny way.

"Well, now, that's interesting," Jennie said to a surprised man and woman who happened to be passing. "Now he knows better than I do what's making me sick."

"You bet I do," Sam said as the man and woman, putting their perplexed heads together, were left behind. "You're sore because I made valedictorian and you didn't," Sam said. "You've been sore for three weeks, ever since the grades were posted, me number one and you number two." Jennie didn't speak. She kept her eyes front as, side by side, they turned into Fourteenth Street and headed up toward First Avenue. "I don't blame you for being sore," Sam said, making no attempt to sound reasonable or conciliatory, not because he was angry or even because he had learned when Jennie Broom was in the grip of one of her ideas it did about as much good to be reasonable as to punch her in the nose, but because he was stating what he knew to be the simple truth, and he knew Jennie knew it, too. "If it had come out the other way, you number one and me number two, so you made valedictorian and I got the salutatory, I'd be sore, too," Sam said. "But one thing I'll tell you I wouldn't do, and that's I wouldn't hide my soreness behind a lot of bull about uniforms and fascists and guys marching on Rome that have nothing to do with what you're sore about."

"That shows how smart you are," Jennie said.

"I'm smart enough to make valedictorian in a graduating class of nearly eleven hundred," Sam said.

"But not smart enough to see that the principal of the school you're graduating from is nothing but a plain lousy ordinary stinking fascist."

"Oh, for God's sake," Sam said. "Can't you lay off for just this one night?"

"The people of Italy laid off, and look where they are," Jennie said. "Now the same thing is happening in Germany, the people are laying off, and you wait and see pretty soon where *they'll* be."

"Okay, I'll wait," Sam said. "Now why don't you just do a little waiting, too? At least until these graduation exercises are over?"

"Why don't you just shut up?" Jennie said.

Sam did, and they moved in silence up to First Avenue, where, when they paused to wait for a break in the traffic, Sam gave her another glance out of the corner of his eye.

"Uniform or not," he said, "I still say it makes you look nice and neat."

"Meaning, I suppose, until that fascist Mueller came to Grover Cleveland and said we all have to wear these damn things, I looked like a slob."

"I didn't say that," Sam said, but he was saying it to the back of Jennie's middy blouse. He jumped from the curb and, darting in and out among the honking cars, he caught up with her on the other side. "What I said was only that one thing, and it doesn't mean anything but what I said: you look nice and neat."

"I wish I could say the same for you," Jennie said, but her thin, dark face—which always reminded Sam of those cold, handsome, sinister women wearing heavily brocaded gowns in the backgrounds of paintings that illustrated the chapters on Lorenzo de' Medici in the Renaissance section of his European History textbook—looked a shade or two darker, from which Sam concluded that Jennie must have liked what he said. When she didn't like something Jennie Broom did not blush. She said, "What happened to your shirt?"

"What shirt?" Sam said.

"The one you took to the Chink," Jennie said. "You told me you were going to wear a stiff white collar."

"I did take it to the Chink," Sam said. "But it came back so stiff, the edge of the collar was like a saw cutting into my neck, I had to take it off."

"Too bad," Jennie said. "Now you look like all the rest of the dopes." She paused and then added, "Which is what I suppose your mother wanted you to look like."

A moment after he turned to look at her, Sam was sorry. Jennie stopped dead, right in the middle of Fourteenth Street, threw back her head, and released a bellow of laughter.

"Oh, my God!" she said, and that was all she seemed to be able to say for a while. When the fit of laughter ended, and she resumed walking up toward Second Avenue, Jennie said as he fell in beside her, "One profession you want to stay out of, Sam Silver, don't ever become a spy."

"Why the hell not?"

"You've got one of those faces, it's like that clock Mr. Mueller has on the bookcase in his office, all the sides made of glass, so anything that's going on inside your head, all anybody has to do is look at your face and they can see right away what you're thinking."

"All right," Sam said. "What am I thinking now?"

"You're thinking you wished you hadn't given out with that speech about how I'm sore because you made valedictorian," Jennie said. "Because even if it's true, now all of a sudden you're thinking you shouldn't't've said it because it's not the sort of thing a gentleman says to a lady."

"I'm no gentleman," Sam said. "I'm just a guy wants to go to college and can't afford it, so I'm glad I made valedictorian because that gives me the Hammond Haynes Scholarship which makes me able to afford college."

"I'm sorry you're not a gentleman," Jennie said. "Because I happen to be a lady, and people they're not gentlemen a lady doesn't associate with."

She gave him a quick, hard shove and started to run. It didn't take him more than a couple of moments to recover his balance, but they were enough for him to lose her in the crowd near the Second Avenue corner.

When he caught up with Jennie in front of the electric company near Irving Place, she was walking along with Miss Mercator.

"Oh, Sam, how nice," the leader of the Stratford Club said. "I came early, hoping for a last-minute word with both of you, and before I even reach the school, I run first into Jennie and then into you. I consider that a good omen, don't you?"

"Yes, ma'am," said Sam.

Miss Mercator, a timid little dried-up prune of a woman with white hair cut in a boyish Colleen Moore bob, had a passion for omens that Jennie once remarked made the average Roman emperor's College of Augurs look like an Avenue B gypsy palm reader.

"Why do you want a minute with us?" Jennie said. "Anything wrong?"

The faintly troubled look on the wrinkled face, which was Miss Mercator's normal expression, rearranged itself as though, in the mass of cherished worries she carried lovingly through life like so many neatly packed trunks and suitcases, she was hunting for the most suitable piece of luggage for this particular journey.

"Well, no, not wrong," the little old lady said. "It's merely that this is a happy occasion for both of you, as it is for me, and I wouldn't want anything to spoil it, do you know?"

"Yes, ma'am," said Sam, because that was pretty much what he always said to teachers. He had learned they never really wanted you to do more than indicate your approval of what *they* were saying. Jennie, however, who rarely approved of anything said or done by anybody in authority, now said bluntly, "No, I don't know."

"Oh, dear," said Miss Mercator. "Now I've made you angry."

"Just because I said I didn't understand?" Jennie said.

"Not because of what you said but the way you said it."

"I don't understand that, either," Jennie said. "What way did I say it?"

The cap of bobbed white hair swung up toward Sam, and then, as though aware that she couldn't really expect to get any help from an outside source, Miss Mercator sighed and said, "As though you were rolling up your sleeves for a fight, Jennie. I was so hoping there wouldn't be any fights tonight."

"Fights?" Jennie said. "What's there to fight about?"

Miss Mercator sighed again. "Well, at least we're talking about it openly," she said. "I consider that a good omen."

"Talking about what?" Jennie said. "I'm really confused, Miss Mercator. But totally."

The worried face was washed by a small smile so fleeting that only someone like Sam would have noticed it. He knew that the roots of the old English teacher's affections were as primitive as her belief in omens: she loved anybody who loved Shakespeare. Therefore, no matter how much trouble Jennie caused, nothing would ever really affect Miss Mercator's feelings for her.

"No, you're not, Jennie," the old lady said wistfully. "You're the most unconfused person I've ever known, and I admire you for it. I really do, because I'm always confused, I really am. But this is one time when I'm not, because this is one time when I know what I want. Having you and Sam in the Stratford Club this last year was a delight for me, it really was, and while I know I have absolutely no right even to think this, I do believe, in my secret heart, I mean, I believe that being in the Stratford Club had something to do with your emerging as the two highest-ranking students in the graduating class."

"How do you figure that?" Jennie said.

"Oh, I don't," Miss Mercator said hastily. "If I were to subject my feeling to figuring, it would fall apart, so I'm not going to do that. I'm simply going to be grateful for the fact that my two best Stratfordians are going to deliver the salutatory and the valedictory tonight, as well as appear in our production of *The Merchant of Venice*, which I've been trying for years to put on as our graduation play but never succeeded, because they always seem to want something light, like *The Taming of the Shrew* or *A Midsummer Night's Dream*, and I know it was only because Jennie fought so hard for *The Merchant* that it got on, and I'm very grateful to you for that, Jennie, I really am, because it means the fulfillment of an ambition for me, so running into you on the street like this is going to be my good omen that there will be no fights tonight between you and Mr. Mueller."

"Me and Mr. Mueller?" Jennie said. "You sound as though you think I'm the one who's responsible, when the fact of the matter is, Miss Mercator, that if our dearly beloved principal were not such an obvious and shameless—"

"Aah, Jennie, for Pete's sake, pipe down, will you?" Sam said, and as soon as he said it he felt uneasy. "What I mean," Sam said hastily, adding a disarming smile to his appeasing tone in the hope that both would dissolve the cold, hard, angry look that had clamped down like a mask on Jennie's face, "I mean we know you and Mr. Mueller don't get along—"

"Would you expect," Jennie said icily, "Hamlet to get along with Claudius?"

"Not on stage, no," Sam said, wishing he had kept his trap shut. "But Mr. Mueller didn't exactly murder your father."

"In Italy men like Mr. Mueller have been murdering fathers, not to mention mothers and children, for eight years, and now in Germany—"

"Oh, dear," Miss Mercator said, and then, very fast, "Well, here we are!"

Sam looked up. They had reached the front of the school building.

"Yes, exactly, here we are," Jennie said. "The richest country in the world, with a tradition of democratic freedom that goes back to Plymouth Rock and earlier, but just because it isn't happening on our own doorsteps, just because these murders are taking place across the sea, in places called Italy and Germany, nobody in this country so much as raises an eyebrow, much less a voice, to stop these brutal, savage, barbaric—"

"Hey, Jennie!"

She stopped and turned. So did Sam and Miss Mercator. On the top step, looking neater and cleaner than usual, stood Buggo Salvemini, whose father owned the shoe-repair shop on the ground floor of Jennie Broom's tenement.

"Oh," Jennie said, and all the passionate anger fled from her face as rapidly as it had disappeared from her voice. She looked quickly at Sam, even more quickly at Miss Mercator, and then, with a hurried and surprisingly mild "Excuse me," Jennie ran up the stone steps toward Buggo, calling, "Wait a minute!"

"Oh, dear," Miss Mercator said again, but this time the distress in her voice was mixed with a pleasure that Sam understood clearly. There was something about Jennie Broom, who was not even pretty, that attracted him, but the attraction was most intense when he had just left her. She was not a comfortable girl to be with, but he never remembered that when he was not with her. What he remembered was not unlike the moments of relief that came with taking off a tight but stylish shoe. Those moments held an odd pleasure. Similarly, the moments after Jennie's departure were for Sam worth whatever discomfort Jennie's explosive temper may have caused him while he had been with her. Miss Mercator, looking worriedly up toward the huge doors through which Jennie and Buggo Salvemini had disappeared, said, "She's the most unusual girl I've ever had in any of my classes. The most unusual and the most disturbing. I wish I understood her."

Sam, who frequently wished the same thing, said, "I don't know that there's so much to understand." He paused, surprised by the fact that, all at once, he understood a great deal. Then he said slowly, "I think Jennie likes to be in the middle of things, the center of attraction, I mean, and since she's not beautiful enough to get in the middle on her looks, she does it by causing trouble."

"Oh, dear," Miss Mercator said, "I do hope she doesn't cause any tonight."

"Don't worry," Sam said. "I'll see she doesn't."

It was a silly thing to say, and he knew it. Mr. Mueller, with all the weight of his powerful office as school principal to support him, had been unable to keep Jennie from causing trouble for two years. But Miss Mercator's worried expression and general air of helplessness always made Sam say reassuring things, even when they both knew the reassurances were empty. Besides, Sam was aware that Miss Mercator had helped him make valedictorian, and thus win the Hammond Haynes Scholarship, by giving him the 98 grade in English VIII that had carried his average for all subjects two points higher than that of his only real competitor, Jennie Broom. The least he could do in return was promise the old lady something Sam wanted himself: a peaceful evening.

The chances of achieving this, he saw with surprised relief as soon as he came into the locker room, were better than he had dared hope.

The locker room, on the Irving Place side of the school gym in which the graduation exercises were to be held, had been a confused mess during the Stratford Club's two *Merchant of Venice* dress rehearsals. Tonight, in addition to serving as dressing room for the entire cast of the play, the large, low-ceilinged chamber, full of steel lockers and an odor of unwashed bodies so strong that Sam felt it could be seized in handfuls like snow, had to serve as the anteroom in which the other participants in the graduation exercises waited their turn to go out and face the audience of parents and visitors: Mr. Mueller, for example, nervously fingering the knot in his tie as he studied his notes for the welcoming address; Mr. Schnieberman, the tough old biology teacher who ran the Monitors' Squad known to students as the Schnibbies, calmly going over his list of Honors announcements; skinny Miss Tietjens, the music teacher whose figure had long ago earned her, at least among male students, the sobriquet Titless Tillie, giving last-minute instructions in one corner to the members of the school orchestra.

At the far end of the aisle, where Miss Stein, the head of the Art Department, had laid out her make-up equipment, Sam saw Jennie, whose make-up as Portia took longer to put on than that of any other member of the cast, in whispered consultation with Buggo Salvemini, whose make-up consisted of a bedsheet with a hole in the middle to go over his head, since the only part for which, because of his histrionic gifts as well as his native intelligence, he had been found suitable was one of the "other Attendants."

"Silver!"

"Yes, Miss Stein?" Sam called back.

"I'd like to do you next, please! Let's not have a repetition of the trouble with that beard tonight!"

"Yes, ma'am."

Sam slipped out of his jacket, took off his tie, and hung them in the locker. He could have taken off his shirt and pants as well, since his costume for the part of Shylock consisted of a long robe that fitted snugly around the neck and fell to the ground. But even though, like Miss Stein, he did not want a repetition of the dress-rehearsal trouble with the beard, Sam was aware that the repetition might occur. And since the trouble had taken the form of a disintegration of the adhesive, which had mixed with the false hair to form a gummy pack that required almost an hour of soaking before it was all completely removed, a repetition tonight might mean keeping the entire audience waiting until his face was clean enough for him to come out and deliver the valedictory. If that should happen, which Sam of course hoped it wouldn't, he did not want to add to the audience's wait the time it would take him to get back into his shirt and pants. Sam pulled Shylock's robe over his head, fastened the stud at the back of his neck, grabbed the corded belt, closed his locker, and hurried down the aisle toward Miss Stein. At once Buggo Salvemini straightened up and Jennie, on whose toenails Miss Stein was painting bright red dots, gave Sam one of her rare smiles.

"One advantage of being salutatorian instead of valedictorian," she said, "I get my bottom half done so I can cover it up while I'm out there delivering the salutatory, then I dash back in and get my top done in peace and quiet while Schnibby is making the Honors announcements and the rest of you are sweating to go on in the play."

"If you call that an advantage," Sam said, wondering why Buggo's grin, one of the less entrancing sights of Sam's high school career, looked more irritating than usual. "Personally, I prefer to get made up all at once."

"Okay, Barrymore," Jennie said. She stood up and said to Miss Stein, "Give Shylock a beard that can come off without the help of the police force."

"Just you see you don't put your shoes and stockings on until that nail polish is dry," Miss Stein said tartly. "And leave the make-up to me, if you please."

"That's where we left it at dress rehearsal," Jennie said sweetly. "As a result, we're lucky our Shylock's got a face with which to go on for us tonight."

Buggo laughed, a rumble of sound that started somewhere down in his stomach and was for Sam as irritating as Buggo's grin. He was still laughing when he disappeared with Jennie around the aisle of lockers.

"Some day somebody is going to slap that girl's big trap shut," Miss Stein muttered. "Sit down, Sam, and let's see what we can do to make you look like a sixteenth-century Venetian."

What she did took so long that Sam missed most of Mr. Mueller's welcoming address. He came to the locker room door, which was shielded by a folding screen from the stage out in the gym, in time to hear the principal, without much enthusiasm, introduce the salutatorian.

"Drop dead, you jerk, drop dead, oh, drop dead, drop day-id," Jennie sang under her breath to the tune of "We Sail the Ocean Blue" as she marched out on stage, and Sam's suddenly tense stomach told him the trouble Miss Mercator had feared was about to start. Happily, however, as well as puzzlingly, the message from his stomach proved wrong. Jennie, giving a highly uncharacteristic demonstration of caution, stopped singing the insulting refrain before she came within earshot of Mr. Mueller. She even smiled graciously at the principal as she bowed and thanked him for the introduction. Mr. Mueller was clearly even more surprised than Sam by this unexpected display of affability from his implacable enemy. The principal gave Jennie a suspicious glance, then bobbed his head awkwardly and backed away toward his chair. It seemed to Sam that Jennie had never looked so bright and happy as she did when she turned to the audience and cheerily said, "Parents, teachers, fellow students, and other guests."

It was as though the dark, sinister, forbidding Renaissance woman had stepped out into the foreground and stood revealed as a blond, open-countenanced, creamy-skinned young girl who, at any moment, might break into light-hearted song as she trotted off gaily to roll her hoop down the street. Sam was so surprised by the change in Jennie's appearance that he forgot to listen to her words. This did not matter, since he had been hearing Jennie rehearse the speech under Miss Mercator's direction for three weeks. Apparently it mattered to Jennie, however, because as she came off stage, with the applause trailing behind her like a long, invisible veil, she asked Sam eagerly, "How'd I do?"

"You were great," he said.

"Go on, you big liar, you weren't even listening," Jennie said, but she did not sound angry. She did not even sound angry as she disappeared around the aisle of lockers, roaring, "Miss Stein, come finish my hair! I want to watch the first scene!"

She didn't, perhaps because Miss Stein, who as a rule worked swiftly, was so annoyed with her that she tackled Jennie's hair with the cautious deliberation of a sculptor about to take his first crucial whacks at a virgin block of marble. The result, it seemed to Sam, justified the expenditure of time. Jennie looked stunning, he thought, as she hurried out, muttering curses at Miss Stein, for Scene 2 with Ida Leopolstadt, who played Nerissa.

"You were great," Sam whispered when Jennie came off and he started out on stage for his scene with Lenny (Hot Cakes) Hirsch, who in Sam's opinion was a pretty terrible Bassanio, but apparently Jennie's mood had changed.

"Don't you know any other words?" she snapped. "How can anybody be great playing a scene with a slob like Ida Leopolstadt?"

Sam, who shared Jennie's opinion of Ida Leopolstadt's talents as an actress, didn't bother to answer. He had troubles of his own. In a sudden panic he could not remember if his opening line was *"Three thousand ducats; well?"* or *"Well? Three thousand ducats?"* Luckily, Titless Tillie Tietjens' musicians scrambled their cue, and the first three lines of the scene were lost in a long, inexplicable, wailing scream from the saxophone. The rest of Act I and all of Act II were recited—even Miss Mercator's most cherished omens had never convinced Sam that what the Stratford Club did to *A Merchant of Venice* could really be called acting—with reasonable smoothness, and, in the brief intermission before Act III, Sam decided he'd better pay a quick visit to the can.

This involved a long, crouching walk down the narrow passage back of the scenery to the other side of the gym, since the toilets off the locker room were for girls only, but Sam didn't mind the trip. On the way, through a crack in the painted canvas, he paused for a long look at the audience and managed to pick out not only his parents but, down in front, a thin, gray-haired, uptown-looking man who, Sam felt absolutely certain, was the observer sent by the Trustees of the Hammond Haynes Scholarship Fund. His awareness that the intermission between Acts II and III was short would have kept him from remaining there too long, eyes glued to the crack, staring at his benefactor. And the sight of Buggo Salvemini advancing in a low crouch toward him along the narrow passage was enough to hurry Sam on his way. Buggo had never been one of Sam's favorite characters. On this night the son of the Avenue A cobbler had become, for reasons Sam neither understood nor cared to examine, a great big pain in the neck.

A few minutes later, when he tried to leave the can, Sam suddenly realized that any time he might have devoted to such an examination would have been well spent: the door was locked.

"Okay, Buggo," he called. "Stop being funny and open the door."

The only reply was another rumble of the laughter that started somewhere down in Buggo's stomach.

"Listen, stupid," Sam called in a louder voice. "I'm due on stage in less than a minute, and I've got to get all the way back to the other side, so think up some other joke, will you?"

No answer from the other side of the door. Sam, beginning to feel worried, grabbed the knob and shook it.

"Buggo!" he shouted. "Buggo, you dopey son of a bitch, open up or I'll—!"

Sam's words stopped in his throat. He listened with horror. Titless Tillie's musicians were playing the cue for the opening of Act III. Sam refused to believe his ears. Salanio and Salerio had an exchange of exactly seven speeches before Shylock entered. Hadn't anybody noticed that Shylock was not standing in the wings, ready to go on? Sam grabbed the knob with both hands and started to kick savagely at the metal door.

"Help!" he yelled. "Somebody open up! Help! I'm locked in! Open up! Help!"

This time what stopped him was the sudden silence from the other side of the door. The fact that the music had ceased could mean only one thing: the scene was going on without him. Yet how could it? Without Shylock there was no scene. Another kick at the locked door, producing a booming echo from the empty toilet behind him, caused Sam, who was beginning to feel desperate as well as helpless, to turn. His eye fell on the sink.

Quickly, balancing himself by holding onto the metal rod that ran up the side of the door to the transom, he jumped to the ledge of the basin. After a swift glance to make sure his awkward, pigeon-toed footing between the taps was reasonably solid, Sam leaned forward slowly, clutching the metal rod with one hand, and with his other clinging to the edge of the narrow wooden frame around the mirror over the sink. Thus, spread-eagled like a gigantic spider's web across the upper corner of the toilet, Sam managed to bring his face up to the transom.

It was made of gray opaque glass veined for reinforcement with a network of spidery wires. Low, indistinguishable sounds came through, but he could see nothing. Panting with the effort of supporting himself in the preposterous position, Sam inched the hand on the iron rod up and up and up, in short jerks, until his fingers reached the catch. Then, with a quick, hard, downward pull, he managed to release the transom fastening. The thick slab of gray glass fell back, and Sam almost fell with it, but his grip on the mirror frame saved him.

A moment later he did fall, but the moment had been long enough for his startled eyes to absorb through the open transom an extraordinary sight: Scene 1 of Act III—"*Venice. A Street.*"—was proceeding without him. Or rather, Sam realized as he scrambled back up onto the sink, the scene was proceeding with someone who had taken his place.

This was even more astonishing to Sam than his incredible present circumstances, since the parts of Bassanio, Portia, and Shylock—due to certain obvious deficiencies in the Stratford Club membership which even the ever optimistic Miss Mercator had been forced to recognize—had been rehearsed without understudies.

By the time the now almost frantic Sam had succeeded in once again spread-eagling himself across the upper corner of the toilet, and his perspiring face was pressed to the open transom, part of the puzzle solved itself: the costume and full-bearded make-up were almost made to order for concealment, but nothing could ever conceal, when it was tuned to its highest pitch of denunciatory rage, Jennie Broom's voice.

"He hath disgraced me," she was roaring straight out at the audience while Salerio and Salanio stood back and stared, as astonished on stage as Sam was at the toilet transom above them, *"And hindered me half a million, laughed at my losses, mocked at my gains, scorned my nation, thwarted my bargains, cooled my friends, heated mine enemies. And what's his reason?"*

As Jennie stepped forward to give the reason as Shakespeare had written it, Sam saw with horror Jennie's own reason for plotting with Buggo Salvemini to seize the part of Shylock in this particular scene: directly in front of the place to which she had advanced, in the middle of the first row, sat Mr. Mueller.

"I am a Jew," Jennie cried at the principal. *"Hath not a Jew eyes? Hath not a Jew hands, organs, dimensions, senses, affections, passions . . . ?"*

Sam could see Mr. Mueller grasp that something had gone wrong. In the reflection from the ineptly shielded footlights, Sam could see the principal's face twitch as he cast a quick look to right and left, as though seeking swiftly for some method of escape. There was none. Not at that moment, and not from Jennie's voice as, leaning down over the footlights, it poured into Mr. Mueller's flushed face: *". . . fed with the same food, hurt with the same weapons, subject to the same diseases, healed by the same means, warmed and cooled by the same winter and summer, as a Christian is?"*

For anybody in the audience who might not have grasped that what the enraged Shylock on stage was saying was intended for the now white-faced, squirming man in the front row, Jennie now dropped to one knee and pointed at Mr. Mueller as she demanded: *"If you prick us, do we not bleed? If you tickle us, do we not laugh? If you poison us, do we not die? And if you wrong us, shall we not revenge?"*

Jennie rose, and so did her voice as she screamed at the quivering principal of Grover Cleveland High, "You bet we will, you dirty fascist anti-Semitic bastard!"

Mr. Mueller leaped to his feet, but Sam lost his grip again. By the time he picked himself up from the toilet floor, he could tell from the confused shouts and the thump of running feet outside that there was no point in climbing back up on the sink. Instead, Sam began to do some shouting himself. By the time somebody heard him and unlocked the door, it was all over.

So, Sam realized with a start as he felt a tug at his sleeve, was the performance of *Julius Caesar* in which he had come all the way across town to the Porte School to see his son Billy play Calpurnia.

For several confused moments—as he worked his way back to a total awareness that almost eighteen years had gone by; that he was not a boy trapped in the toilet of a high school on Irving Place but a man seated in the last row of the chapel in an institution founded by a French nobleman who had served on George Washington's staff—Sam did not realize who was tugging his sleeve. Then he saw looming over him the tall, stoop-shouldered, tweedy man with the fiery eyes and the enormous, knife-thin nose that twitched constantly, and Sam sat up straighter to face his son's English instructor.

"Sorry," he said. "I'm afraid my mind wandered a bit."

"One can hardly blame you," said Mr. Bronson. "Happily for our students, the Porte School's reputation is based on our scholastic rather than our histrionic capacities. Although," he added with a smoothness that did not quite conceal the soothing intent of the addition, "I thought Billy acquitted himself very creditably indeed, didn't you?"

"Yes, I did," said Sam, whose embarrassment for the realization that he had not even seen Billy come out on stage was suddenly crossed by a stab of puzzlement: why should Mr. Bronson be trying to soothe him? Sam said, "But I'm prejudiced, of course."

"As indeed all parents should be," said Mr. Bronson. "I hope you didn't mind my leaving that message for you with Mrs. Lothrop at the switchboard?"

"No, of course not," Sam said, and he realized that the English instructor, who had not released his grip on Sam's sleeve, was gently but insistently tugging him to his feet. "Actually, I like to sit here in the last row," Sam said, sliding up and out into the aisle, which was beginning to fill up at the bottom with parents coming out of their seats down in front, and wishing that, when he was with Mr. Bronson, he could stop himself from talking like the English instructor. "The acoustics are a bit better, I think, and one certainly gets a clearer view of the performance as a whole."

"One certainly does," Mr. Bronson said. "Although that was not the reason why I asked Mrs. Lothrop to ask you to sit back here. I wanted to avoid our being caught in a flood of parents dripping questions about their offspring. So we would be free to pop into my office, here, for a bit of a talk."

Sam saw that they had left behind them not only the chapel but also the adjacent corridor, and were standing in front of Mr. Bronson's office door.

"Talk about what?" Sam said. He was quickly trying to bring to mind Billy's last school report in an effort to remember if there had been anything under "Comments" that he had overlooked. Had there been one of those euphemistically phrased suggestions that Billy needed tutoring in English? Or math? Or help with his Attitude Toward Extra-Curricular Activities? Sam said casually, "I thought Billy's last report was very satisfactory, considering the fact that he—"

The words stopped as Sam felt the impact of a stab of surprise. Through the open door, which Mr. Bronson was holding wide so his visitor could precede him, Sam saw Tom Sacheverell, seated on the scuffed black leather couch set at right angles to Mr. Bronson's desk. The novelist was stuffing tobacco from a pin-seal pouch into the bowl of a pipe.

"Oh," Sam said, wondering as he came into the office how Sacheverell, who in the chapel had been seated farther in from the aisle than Sam, could have reached Mr. Bronson's office ahead of them. "Hello."

"You two know each other," Mr. Bronson said approvingly as he shut the door. "Good."

Sam said casually but firmly, "Well, Mr. Sacheverell and I have the same agents."

"We do indeed," said Sacheverell, and his watery, unworldly, martyred eyes crinkled in such an obvious, even though grotesquely unsuccessful, effort at ingratiation, that Sam felt all his senses, which had come sharply awake a few moments earlier, now begin to strain almost visibly in their effort to seize the ingredients for an answer to the startled question: *What the hell goes on here?* Sacheverell said, "Sargent & Sargent clients are all more or less fellow members of an exclusive club."

Sam, who over the years had felt many things about Tom Sacheverell but never that they were fellow members of anything, decided against taking the other end of the couch, toward which Mr. Bronson was gesturing. Sam chose instead a hard, straight chair facing both the desk and the couch. Mr. Bronson, not exactly annoyed but clearly a trifle thrown off whatever line he was pursuing, dropped into the chair behind the desk.

His knife-thin nose twitched visibly as he opened a silver box, took out a cigarette, and hung it between his lips. Then the English instructor seemed to remember that whatever his line might be, the job of following it required his continuing to play the role of gracious host.

"Sorry," he said, pushing the open box across the desk toward Sam. "Cigarette, Mr. Silver?"

Sam started to smile, shake his head, and make a small politely negative gesture, when he saw that Sacheverell had struck a match and was sucking a light into his pipe. This gave Sam an idea.

"No, thank you," he said, larding the words with just enough smugness to make them impossible to overlook. "That's one habit I'm glad to say I've managed to break."

Sacheverell looked startled. Mr. Bronson, who was bringing the flame of a silver lighter to his cigarette, looked as though on an easy, open-field run, with nobody between him and the goal line, he had managed somehow to fumble and drop the ball. Whatever the hell went on here, Sam reflected with satisfaction, it was not going precisely as planned by his host.

"Lucky chap," Mr. Bronson said with unconvincing heartiness. "I wish I could give up smoking."

Sacheverell hesitated, then said, "So do I. The best I've been able to do, I'm ashamed to say, is shift from cigarettes to a pipe."

"Wish I could do even that much," said Mr. Bronson, inhaling deeply, and then, obviously with no interest whatsoever in a reply, asked Sam, "Was it very difficult?"

Samuel Silver, a lowly magazine writer, did not get many opportunities to feel superior to Pulitzer Prize-winning novelists whose books adorned the tops of the best-seller lists for infuriatingly long periods of time. He made the most of this one.

"Difficult is hardly the word," Sam said coolly.

"Tough, was it?" said Sacheverell with a sympathetic bob of the head.

"Not at all," said Sam with a Prussian nod.

Sacheverell and Bronson exchanged a glance.

"What is the secret?" Mr. Bronson said.

"Character," Sam said.

"Character?" Mr. Bronson repeated, and the fact that Tom Sacheverell did not, left no doubt in Sam's mind as to who was the superior of the two. He could not help wishing, since Sacheverell was the one of whom he was jealous, it was the other way around.

"Character," Sam said again. "All the years I was trying to give up smoking, and failing, I lacked the character to do it. Then, one day, I found the character to do it, so I did it." Noting that Mr. Bronson's fiery eyes looked a trifle quenched and Sacheverell's watery eyes a bit dry, Sam decided to wrap up for later enjoyment a moment of superiority he would probably never again enjoy in the presence of either of these two men. With an ostentatious glance at his wrist watch, he said crisply, "But I'm sure you didn't call me in here for a discussion of smoking, and since I've got a lunch date and will have to leave in ten or fifteen minutes, I wonder if it wouldn't be sensible for us to get down to business, whatever the business is."

Mr. Bronson and Sacheverell exchanged another glance, this time clearly asking each other which one was to carry the ball, and in the moment of indecision all of Sam's pleasure vanished abruptly: mentioning his lunch date had brought to mind Claude Sargent's puzzling telephone message of the night before, and as the two men in the room hesitated, Sam suddenly wondered uncomfortably if by some wild chance what they wanted to talk with him about was the same thing Claude Sargent wanted to lunch with him about. At first glance, wild was indeed the word, since Sam was almost certain Mr. Bronson had never met and perhaps never even heard of Claude Sargent. A second glance, however, underscored the still startling fact that Tom Sacheverell, who for years had been so almost rudely aloof that he had never even bothered to learn Sam's name, only a few moments ago had observed that he felt they were members of the same exclusive club.

"Odd that you should have used the word business," said Bronson, who had obviously been handed the honor of punting the ball.

"Before we go into that," Sacheverell said, apparently to his own as well as Bronson's surprise, "may I first offer my congratulations?"

"To me?" Sam said.

"Indeed yes," said Sacheverell.

"On what?" said Sam.

"Your impending marriage."

"My what?"

The somewhat drier but still watery eyes crinkled in another appalling effort at a smile of ingratiation.

"Merger is the word I think Walter Winchell used," Sacheverell said, and Sam, who had given up chewing gum years before he gave up smoking cigarettes, was now glad he had. If he hadn't he would have, as the kids on East Tenth Street used to say, just gulped his wad. It had never occurred to Sam Silver that the saintly author of *The Barrier Reef* had even heard of Winchell, much less read him. Sacheverell said, "*Add imminent mergers*, I believe, is the phrasing Mr. Winchell used."

"Oh, well," said Sam, wondering with sudden discomfort if Sacheverell was as big a boob as Sam had for years found it soothing to believe. "You know these columnists. A man stops to say hello to a woman in a restaurant, and they report a new red-hot version of *Troilus and Cressida.* How about our business talk?"

"At the moment it's hardly that," Mr. Bronson said. "No more than an idea, actually. But an idea to which I have given a great deal of thought and, I'm happy to say, so distinguished a practitioner of the art of fiction as Mr. Sacheverell has given his endorsement." The English instructor touched a bony forefinger to his bony, twitching nose as though he were silencing the hum of a tuning fork and, with a slight bow across the silver cigarette box, said to Sam, "I trust you will do the same, Mr. Silver."

"I can't endorse what I haven't seen," Sam said. "What's your idea?"

Mr. Bronson said, "The writing of English prose is, I think you will agree, Mr. Silver, one of the nobler forms of human endeavor?"

"Why—" Sam began, and he could feel his face flush with embarrassment. The fact that the man who had made the statement was either a charlatan or a fool, and possibly both, did not change the fact that Mr. Bronson had just uttered the credo by which Sam Silver, who would sooner have died than utter it himself, happened to live. He said, "I don't see how anybody can quarrel with the statement that writing good English is a good thing."

"And if more people wrote good English," Mr. Bronson said promptly, "it would be a better thing, would it not, Mr. Silver?"

"Yes, I suppose so," Sam said, wondering all at once if it would indeed be a better thing. If more people looked like Rebecca Meissen, would his pulse quicken at the sight of them as it now did at the thought of her? What a sap he had been to send her downstairs that morning in her blue peignoir! Would Billy have known or cared if his father had arrived in the Porte School chapel a half hour later? Crossing his legs to still the slow stirring in his loins, Sam said more sharply than he intended, "Just what are you driving at, Mr. Bronson?"

"The wider dissemination of this good thing," Mr. Bronson said. "Teaching more and more people how to write good English. Not by coming to a school. After all, few people, once they go out into the world to earn their bread and salt, have time for that. But by having the school, as it were, come to them. With a simple but clear textbook as a starting point, and a series of lessons or exercises that can be mailed to the school for correction by competent instructors, there is no reason, granted as a base for the operation an experienced and dedicated faculty, why the ability to write good English prose should not be within the grasp and pocketbook of every reasonably intelligent and literate American. Don't you agree, Mr. Silver?"

Making no effort at all to control the incredulity in his voice, Sam said, "You mean you are about to start a correspondence course in writing?"

"Why not?" said Mr. Bronson. Sam, who could have told him, didn't get a chance to open his mouth. "With the cachet of the Porte School as a platform," the English instructor said, "and on our letterhead the names of writers as distinguished as Mr. Sacheverell—" Mr. Bronson paused, touched his quivering nose as though for reassurance, and then said, "Is anything wrong, Mr. Silver?"

"Wrong?" Sam said. "No, no. I was just thinking—" He allowed the sentence to die as he turned back to the unworldly, watery-eyed, martyred face. "Are you involved in this?" Sam said to Tom Sacheverell. "I mean are you going to lend your name to—?"

Sam allowed that sentence to die, too. The unspoken words were more effective than any he could have uttered. The novelist squirmed as though he were trying to work his buttocks through the black leather.

"Mr. Silver, you sound censorious," Mr. Bronson said in a voice as sharp as Sam's. "Would you mind explaining?"

"I don't know that I can," Sam said, and he knew he was speaking the truth. He gave himself a couple of moments to sort out his reactions. Perhaps the most surprising one was his feeling of disappointment. The circumstances surrounding Claude Sargent's message, especially the intensification of the mystery by Sophie Sargent's refusal to clarify it on the phone that morning, had led Sam to expect that what was waiting for him at the lunch with Claude was a matter not only of urgency but of a threatening nature. He should have been relieved to learn that it was something so foolish and trifling as a proposed correspondence course. And yet Sam did not feel relieved at all. If anything, his uneasiness had increased. He said, "I did not mean to sound censorious. It's just that I'm surprised."

"Yes, but why?" Mr. Bronson rapped out, and from the intensity of the English instructor's manner, Sam concluded that he had indeed misjudged Billy's English teacher. This was no fool. This was a man of considerable strength. It occurred to Sam that Sacheverell had been swept into the plan against his will by the stronger man. Why not? Most writers, no matter how successful, lived with the constant fear that some day their creative or bread-winning juices would dry up. This fear undoubtedly contributed to the conviction, erroneously but nonetheless firmly held by so many writers, that if they turned some of their attention to what seemed to them easier ways of making money, they could amass the fortunes that were daily

earned by lesser men who devoted themselves to the childish but infinitely
more lucrative affairs of business. The fact that, when writers poured their
talents into business ventures, the results were almost always financially
lamentable, did not change the intensity of the desire to outwit fate. It had
never before occurred to Sam that Sacheverell, whose success had for so
long been so enormous, was a prey to this same desire. For a moment, as
he looked at the squirming figure facing him on the black-leather couch,
Sam was able to forget his jealousy of Tom Sacheverell. For the first time
in his life, Sam regarded the world-famous novelist almost with pleasure.
Was it possible that, after all these years, the public had finally caught on
and turned away from what Sam had for so long felt was shoddy? Could
it be that *The Barrier Reef's* position on the best-seller lists did not represent actual sales but merely the publisher's overconfidence in placing
enormous advance stocks of the novel in the hands of the book-sellers who,
in the hope of moving them, were reporting as a best-seller a book that
was not selling at all? Mr. Bronson said, "Are you surprised that Mr.
Sacheverell has joined me in this venture?"

"No," Sam said, and did not add: *not any more!* Then, because he was
ashamed of his pleasure in a competitor's bad fortune, Sam added, "I am
certain adding Mr. Sacheverell's name to the venture will increase the
cachet of which you just spoke."

"Then what does surprise you?" Mr. Bronson said. "Don't you believe
that a project of this nature would be extremely useful?"

Useful to whom? Sam wondered. To Mr. Bronson and Tom Sacheverell?
Or to the people who would pay out their good money to take the correspondence course?

"I don't really know," Sam said. "I've often wondered if writing can be
taught."

Mr. Bronson, indicating by a relaxation of the muscles in his face that
the discussion had moved into an area he did not consider dangerous,
leaned back in his chair.

"If by 'writing' you mean 'genius,' " he said, "I can answer in a word:
no. But surely you, Mr. Silver, as one of our most successful practitioners,
will readily agree that certain practical aspects of writing can be taught."

"Yes, I suppose so," said Sam, who believed firmly that the practical
aspects of writing that could be taught were concentrated in the admoni-
tion that double-spaced manuscripts were more likely to be viewed with
favor by editors than pages that were single-spaced. To treat this sort of
advice as teaching, and to charge money for imparting it, struck him as
not unlike insisting on being paid a fee for telling an innocent newcomer
to New York that his chances of getting through a subway turnstile would

be increased if he exchanged his two nickels for a dime. However, he did not want to jeopardize his son Billy's chances at a passing grade in English VIII, so Sam said, "To be perfectly honest with you, Mr. Bronson, what surprises me is that you should want me to join you in this enterprise."

Mr. Bronson's look of relief was so sudden and total that Sam, shifting his glance quickly, was not surprised to see it reflected in Tom Sacheverell's tortured eyes.

"Your modesty does you credit," the English instructor said and, with a smile that reminded Sam of the way Mr. Bronson had hastened to soothe him out in the chapel about Billy's performance as Calpurnia, he added, "Nor is it surprising in the father of a boy so generally well liked by the Porte School's student body as your son Billy."

"Hear, hear," said Tom Sacheverell, and Sam, with some difficulty, managed to suppress the crisp monosyllable with which Jennie Broom used to greet most of Mr. Mueller's public remarks at Grover Cleveland High.

"We happen to have three very good reasons for wanting your name on our letterhead," Mr. Bronson said. "First, there is the matter of your formal education, Mr. Silver."

Sam laughed and said, "I'm afraid you've been misinformed. Aside from managing to stumble through high school, I never had any formal education."

"Precisely," said Mr. Bronson.

"How do you mean 'precisely'?"

"I've done a bit of research," the English instructor said. "Most writing courses, I find, fairly reek of the halls of learning. They are all in the hands of scholars with names that trail degrees behind them that look as though they were assembled from alphabet soup. I am not one to sneer at the halls of academe." The twitching of Mr. Bronson's nose shifted slightly as he permitted himself a modest smirk. "I am forced to confess my own Oxford youth," he said. "And Mr. Sacheverell, as you undoubtedly know, is one of the brighter stars in the diadem of Yale's alumni. We feel it would give our project a touch of the down-to-earth, the, the, the, how shall I put it, yes, an up-from-the-pavements note, so to speak, if our faculty included a man like yourself, Mr. Silver, a man who has achieved success as a writer in spite of having turned his back at eighteen on a college education."

It was an odd way, Sam thought, to describe his loss of the Hammond Haynes Scholarship because he had been unable to convince either the trustees or Mr. Mueller that he had not been one of Jennie's accomplices in the graduation-night humiliation of the Grover Cleveland High School principal.

"You said there were three reasons," Sam said.

"There are," Mr. Bronson said. "Number two is obvious. We would want our course to cover as many aspects of the writing field as possible. The cinema, the novel, television, the theatre, newspaper writing, magazine writing, and so on. We have our lines out to eminent representatives in all these fields, and while I have every reason to believe we will be able to bring them into the fold, it seemed sensible to begin with what I consider the two most important fields because they are the fields to which, according to my researches, most would-be writers aspire." The English instructor's tweedy arm, gesturing toward the couch, might have been the arm of Elizabeth moving the sword of knighthood toward the shoulder of Walter Raleigh. "I am sure you will agree with me that in the field of the novel, America can display with the pride of both artistic and financial achievement no name more illustrious than that of the father of your son Billy's classmate, J. Thomas Sacheverell." The agony of squirming to which this reduced the tortured figure on the couch was underscored by the pause which Mr. Bronson clearly felt had been earned by his artful combination of accolade, apple polishing and, in another of Jennie's favorite phrases, sheer balls. "To describe your own position, Mr. Silver, in the field of magazine writing as one whit smaller would, I insist, be a shameful distortion of the truth."

In the second pause—which the squirming figure on the couch dutifully filled with a hearty "Hear! Hear!"—Sam could feel again the pain that had assailed him when Billy had once mentioned him in the same breath with Joseph Conrad and, this morning on the phone from Queens, his mother had challenged his statement that "magazine writers are not all that important."

"Your third reason?" Sam said.

"One that I trust you won't take amiss," Mr. Bronson said.

He paused again. It occurred to Sam, from the way the English instructor was lighting a fresh cigarette, that Mr. Bronson seemed to be girding himself for an ordeal.

"Do you want me to promise?" Sam said.

Startled, Mr. Bronson said, "Eh?"

"That I won't take it amiss?" Sam said.

"Good Lord!" Mr. Bronson said, and then, apparently struck by the fact that he had sounded too startled, he laughed cheerily. "No, no, of course not," he said. "Just a figure of speech, Mr. Silver. What I mean is that, as you undoubtedly know, Charles Louis Vieullière, the twelfth Marquis de la Nantes who founded our distinguished school, was a famous member of a famous Catholic family. In many areas the belief still persists, erroneous, of course, as I'm sure you are equally aware, that the Porte School is a Catholic institution. We are, in actual fact, completely nondenominational. For the benefit of any people who might think a correspondence course launched to the world under the umbrella, as it were, of the Porte School, has sectarian overtones, we feel a faculty drawn from as many creeds as possible would be reassuring. I am not a religious man, at least in the sense of being an observer of the rituals to which I was introduced in my youth, but at least in the technical sense, being Church of England, I am a Protestant. Mr. Sacheverell is a Methodist, I believe."

"Baptist," Sacheverell said.

"Sorry," said Mr. Bronson. "And you, Mr. Silver, are—"

"A Jew," Sam said.

"Precisely," said Mr. Bronson, and then, apparently catching up with something extra Sam had put into the two short words, the English instructor shot a short, sharp glance at Sacheverell, turned back, leaned far forward across the silver cigarette box and, with the excessive clarity of a master correcting a pupil, he said, "A *genius* and a Jew, Mr. Silver."

Sam gave himself a moment. He had no right to be unfair to Mr. Bronson. But the moment was wasted.

"These people who would enroll and pay out good money to take your correspondence course," Sam said. "Would I be expected to teach them how to become Jews?"

"Good Lord!" Mr. Bronson said. "Certainly not!"

"Then so far as anything I could teach them is concerned," Sam said, "it would be taking money under false pretenses."

The fiery eyes blazed with a new light: anger. "How do you figure that, Mr. Silver?"

"You called me a genius and a Jew," Sam said. "And a few moments ago you stated yourself that genius cannot be taught."

Mr. Bronson, apparently afraid to trust the quieting process to a single digit, placed both bony forefingers against the sides of his twitching nose. "Mr. Silver," he said coldly, "may I say—"

"Uh, just a moment, please?"

The English instructor whipped around toward the couch. "Yes?" he snapped.

Sacheverell shrank against the black leather, but his watery eyes seemed less uncertain than his hunched frame as he fixed them on Sam.

"I won't embarrass or insult either of us by saying some of my best friends are Jews," the novelist said. "In point of fact, none of my best friends are Jews. This is not a matter of inclination, Mr. Silver. It is simply a matter of fact. I have, however, known many Jews, and like most reasonably literate persons, I know something of their history. That knowledge makes it easy for anyone to understand what is frequently, and I might add erroneously, described as their excessive sensitivity. Since I do understand it, however, I would like to say something that may help at this point."

Sam, who preferred to be patronized by people of whom he was not jealous, said sharply, "There is no occasion—"

"If you will forgive me," Sacheverell said gently, "I think there *is* an occasion, and this is it." He stared worriedly into the bowl of his pipe, looked up, tried to put into motion the hideously unconvincing smile of ingratiation, then abandoned it for a troubled scowl. "You have just told us, Mr. Silver, that you were able to give up smoking when, after many failures, you finally found the character to do so," Sacheverell said. "Nobody knows better than I, who have never been able to find it, how great an achievement that is. I believe a man who could do that can also find the character to believe a handful of simple words, especially when they are uttered by one man who makes his living by using words to another man who does the same. May I?"

It occurred to Sam, who wanted to say no but couldn't, that the success of Sacheverell's books might be due to something more than his extraordinary technical skill with the flashback.

"Of course," Sam said, hating Mr. Bronson for having brought him into this room.

"You have my assurance," Tom Sacheverell said, "that the reasons for our wanting you to join us in this enterprise were stated by Mr. Bronson with absolute precision. His words meant only what we both intended them to mean. No more, and no less." The novelist paused, examined the bowl of his pipe again, then said, "If you honestly feel you could teach absolutely nothing to somebody who enrolled in this course, I think you should refuse to join us."

Sam gave himself another moment, but it was equally wasted. Jealousy of a man was no reason to be unfair to him.

"There might be something I could teach," Sam said. "I wouldn't let a student get away with the statement that none of his best friends are Jews. I'd make him say, or rather write, none of his best friends *is* a Jew."

Both Mr. Bronson and Sacheverell looked startled. Then they saw Sam's smile, of which they had no way of knowing he was infuriatingly ashamed.

"Am I to assume, then," the English instructor said quickly, "that you will join us?"

Sam, who was even more ashamed of the fact that now his one desire was to get the hell out of this room, said, "I'd like to talk it over with my agent first." He stood up and glanced at his wrist watch. "Sargent & Sargent clients learn soon enough not only that they are members of an exclusive club but, more important, never to make a move without first consulting the club president or his wife." Sam turned to Sacheverell and said, "I assume Claude has told you it's okay to go ahead?"

"Frankly," the novelist said, "I've been afraid to mention it to Claude."

Sam said, "Then that's not what I'm lunching with him about?"

Puzzled, Sacheverell said, "Are you lunching with Claude?"

"Yes," Sam said. "He called last night and left a message saying he wanted to see me today about something urgent, and I've been assuming, ever since I came in here and we started to talk, that what Claude wanted to see me about was this correspondence course you and Mr. Bronson—"

His voice trailed away as he suddenly felt himself swept anew by the apprehension with which he had been living since he had received Claude Sargent's message early in the morning.

"Well, whatever it is he wants to see you about, it's not about this project," Sacheverell said, and the uneasiness came flooding back into his watery eyes. "I wish you wouldn't mention it," he said. "You know how Claude feels about writers dissipating their energies. Not that I agree with him," the novelist added hastily. "It's just that, well, I mean, *you* know."

"I'll keep my trap shut," said Sam, aware that his reversion to calm politeness, which Mr. Bronson and Tom Sacheverell clearly found so reassuring, was doing nothing to diminish the weight of worry which he carried with him as he turned to leave the room.

* 3

It occurred to Sam, in the taxi that carried him downtown to Claude Sargent's office, that he always brought a certain amount of apprehension with him when he went to see his agents, even on those occasions when the visit involved good news about which Sam knew in advance. The reason for Sam's apprehension was the location of the Sargent & Sargent offices.

Lower Park Avenue, just south of Grand Central, had been for Sam as a boy and for his mother what the White House is to the fledgling politician: a symbol of the ultimate achievement. Even more than the imperial apartment houses of upper Park and Fifth and Central Park West, the area immediately surrounding the Murray Hill Hotel had for a penniless but ambitious youngster the look and the feel, indeed the smell, of big money.

This, to the boy from East Tenth Street, was where the people who belonged to the world of Uptown made the deals and cooked up the schemes that yielded the wherewithal which gave them their right to a place in the gilded circle. Intensely aware that he did not belong to that circle, the boy from East Tenth Street could not help feeling, whenever he happened to walk those streets, that the people who did belong stared at him with the contempt of the insider who instantly recognizes the interloper.

Sixteen years later, when his right to a place in that inner circle had been earned long ago, Sam Silver still felt, whenever he approached the area from which the Murray Hill Hotel had vanished, the same uneasiness he had carried with him on that memorable day when he had entered the area for the first time with the exciting knowledge in which there should have been no room for uneasiness: he was crossing a threshold.

It was a rainy day in January, almost exactly eighteen months after the night of the Grover Cleveland High graduation exercises, and the day had presented a number of problems. The most important was, of course, Mr. Brunschweig. He made his living by renting tuxedos, and he paid Sam, who delivered the tuxedos to Mr. Brunschweig's customers and picked them up after they had been worn, twelve dollars a week for six working days, each one of which began at nine in the morning and ended as soon after six in the evening as Sam could complete his final delivery. He had no official lunch hour. Like Mr. Brunschweig himself, who went out on deliveries when business was too brisk to be handled by one person, Sam took his midday meal on the run: a hot dog or a knish and an egg cream at one of the stand-up, open-to-the-street, nickel-and-dime eateries on Sixth Avenue. And Mr. Sargent's letter, which Sam's mother had waiting for him when he came home from work the night before, said with a firmness that it did not occur to either of them could be questioned: "Please drop in any day, Monday to Friday, sometime between eleven in the morning and four in the afternoon." How could he do any dropping in on anybody during hours that were not only committed to Mr. Brunschweig but were under the tuxedo renter's direct surveillance?

"You could maybe say to Mr. Brunschweig you got maybe like to go see the doctor?" Mrs. Silver had said tentatively, but even before she completed the five-foot journey with the bottle of milk from the icebox to the kitchen table at which Sam was dipping hunks of rye bread into a plate of sour cream, his mother clearly realized that this subterfuge would not work. She shook her head and said, "No, not with a man like Mr. Brunschweig. He'll say, to the doctor you have to go, so go on your own time. Don't eat so fast. You'll get sick. Take a bite tzimiss."

Sam took a forkful of tzimiss and pondered the problem. It did not occur to him until years later, when he became a father and either as a result or coincidentally he began to be plagued by memories of his youth, that the simplest solution would have been to go to Mr. Brunschweig, explain that it was important for him to visit somebody during working hours, ask Mr. Brunschweig's permission to do so, and suggest that Mr. Brunschweig dock his salary for the time thus spent away from the job.

On East Tenth Street, in 1935, the suggestion of such a solution would have been treated as a sign of either misplaced levity or mental deficiency. In that place, at that time, in the minds of the inhabitants, to all of whom each succeeding meal was not an accepted event but an obstacle to be surmounted, the relationship between an employer and an employee was like that of a knife to a throat.

"I could stay home tomorrow or the day after?" Sam said. "I mean stay away from work? And you could go down to the drug store and call Mr. Brunschweig and say I'm sick? I'll be in the day after?"

Mrs. Silver shook her head as she put the plate of applesauce on the table.

"So you come in the day after, so Mr. Brunschweig he'll have a new delivery boy," she said. "With bosses today, you give them a finger, they'll grab the whole hand. Eat the applesauce. I made it fresh. Papa had for supper with the goulash. You want maybe a little goulash?"

"On top of cream?" Sam said.

Mrs. Silver struck her forehead with an open palm. "A head I used to have before from Solomon & Solomon this letter came," she said. "By my own table, my own son, I'm talking milk with meat!"

"Sargent & Sargent," Sam said, dipping up a huge spoonful of applesauce. "Not Solomon & Solomon."

"So what's the difference?" Mrs. Silver said. "So long as they're big millionaires there uptown, and they want my Sam."

"So far, all we know is they want me to drop in," Sam said.

"If they didn't want you," Mrs. Silver said, "would they ask you to drop in?"

"I guess not," Sam said, and for several moments they were both silent, lost in the dream of glory with which they had both lived for so long. Behind him, in the bedroom shared by his parents, Sam could hear his father's delicate little rippling snores. Mr. Silver was a member of the family, not a part of the dream. From beyond his mother's solid body at the other side of the kitchen table, through the window that looked out on the backyard crisscrossed with clotheslines, Sam could hear Mr. and Mrs. Heerscheim on the top floor, bickering late into the night as usual. Above all, as he wolfed the remnants of the day's meals that his mother accumulated and waited up to serve him every night when he came home at eleven-thirty from his secretarial school evening classes, Sam could hear the erratic roll of his own heart as, from the letter signed "Claude Sargent" lying open on the table between himself and his mother, the magic words and their limitless promise seared themselves into his brain: *Please*

drop in any day, Monday to Friday, sometime between eleven in the
morning and four in the afternoon.

Mrs. Silver's body moved in a great, yearning sigh. "It's the beginning, Sam," she said quietly.

Sam swallowed the mouthful of rye bread, sour cream, applesauce,
tzimiss, and cold farina, and wiped his mouth with the back of his hand.
"Let's not give it a kinnehorrah," he said.

"You're right," Mrs. Silver said, rapping her knuckles sharply on the
wooden table. "But it's the beginning, Sam. I feel it. I know it."

"Hope you're right," Sam said. "I still got to figure out, though, how to
do this dropping in."

What he finally figured out was directly related to the second problem:
what to wear for the crucial visit.

Sam's wardrobe at the time consisted of two pairs of faded denim pants,
half a dozen shirts, a pair of sneakers, a pair of brown shoes, a heavy coat-
sweater, and a raincoat, from which each morning, depending on the
weather, he assembled the costume in which he went to work. For more
formal occasions Sam had the suit he had worn to the Grover Cleveland
High graduation exercises. It had been purchased on Stanton Street, three
years before, and even though it was pretty badly worn at the collar and
cuffs and a little tight in the shoulders, it was still adequate for wearing to
synagogue on Yom Kippur and Rosh Hashana, which were the last times
Sam had worn it. The suit was not, however, his notion of how he should
be attired when he paid his first visit to an office on lower Park Avenue.

The next day, while Sam was boxing an order and wondering if his
synagogue suit would look less tight and less shabby if he wore with it on
his visit to Sargent & Sargent a shirt laundered by the Chink on Avenue A,
he became aware that Mr. Brunschweig was calling to him from the back
of the store.

Sam walked down to the desk at which his boss opened his mail and
answered the phone. Mr. Brunschweig was on the phone now.

"One second, please," he said into the mouthpiece, which he then covered with his shoulder, and said to Sam, "You remember maybe a few
months ago, he says in April, you made a delivery, a house on Thirty-
sixth Street, a private house, near Second Avenue, with a stoop?"

"Gee whiz," Sam said, "I don't know, Mr. Brunschweig. I make so many
deliveries—"

"A Mr. Traver?" his boss said helpfully. "He's a painter? An artist? The
house is like a studio? Big glass windows over the stoop? He works at
home? Mr. Traver?"

A sliver of recollection pierced the fog of Sam's private dilemma. Mr.

Brunschweig, whose store was located on Forty-eighth Street just off Sixth Avenue, catered in the main to actors and musicians who needed a dinner coat for a specific occasion. Most of them lived in, or at any rate inhabited at the time their paths crossed Sam's, the second-rate hotels and apartment houses of the theatrical district. Sam made very few deliveries east of Fifth Avenue, and only once had he made a delivery to a man who answered the door wearing a paint-smeared smock and holding a dripping palette. He remembered Mr. Traver clearly.

"Yeah, sure," Sam said. "I remember him. Why?"

"He must be some kind of a nut," Mr. Brunschweig said. "He don't know his size. Ever hear such a thing? A grown-up man, been wearing clothes thirty-forty years, he don't know his own size! But what he does know, he knows the kid delivered his tux last time, he says the kid looked exactly the same size as him, so I should send him an outfit same size as the delivery boy. Some business this is, no?" Mr. Brunschweig shook his head and, to the ceiling of the cramped store, he said, "Boy, I'm telling you!" He then lifted the telephone mouthpiece from his shoulder and said, "Yeah, Mr. Traver, he remembers. Okay, I'll fix you up an outfit his size and get it right over." Mr. Brunschweig hung up and, again to the ceiling, said, "For a dinner eight o'clock at night he needs it, but just to make sure it's the right size, so he can check, get it to him by lunchtime, he wants. Boy," Mr. Brunschweig said as he rose to assemble the pieces of Mr. Traver's outfit, "I'm telling you!"

It was not until twenty minutes later, when he was trudging across town with his raincoat collar turned up against the slight drizzle, that Sam suddenly came awake with a start to the fact that fate—which on the night of his graduation from Grover Cleveland High had dealt him a blow from which he had for over a year believed bitterly he would never recover—had just sent up a trial balloon designed to re-establish friendly relations.

Sam stopped dead in his tracks and looked around. He was on the south side of Forty-second Street, halfway down the block from Madison, going toward Park. He looked across the street at the clock over Grand Central. It showed eleven-thirty. Sam caught his breath, reached into his pocket, touched the magic letter from Sargent & Sargent, and the decision practically made itself.

His heart pounded with excitement as he hurried across the street, counting in his head the coins he knew he had in his pocket, and thanking God not only for the fact that he had enough money but also for the terrible weather. If it had not looked so crummy in the morning, he would not have taken his raincoat when he left home, and without the raincoat the solution to the problem, with which he had been wrestling since the Sargent & Sargent letter arrived on East Tenth Street, would not have been possible.

Sam came into Grand Central through the doors at the corner of Forty-second and Vanderbilt Avenue. He went down the ramp, up the steps into the shoeshine room, and down the marble stairway to the men's washroom. Here, for a dime, he rented a toilet stall in which, working with surprising speed in spite of the cramped quarters, he took off all his clothes, put on the tuxedo he was supposed to be delivering to Mr. Traver on Thirty-sixth Street, and packed his own clothes into Mr. Brunschweig's heavy cardboard delivery box. Then Sam slipped into his raincoat, turned up the collar and, carrying the box, left the stall.

He stopped at the line of washstands for a quick check of his appearance. Sam was pleasantly surprised to discover that even though, because the toilet stall had had no mirror, he had been forced to work by touch alone, he had got all the studs into the boiled shirt correctly, and he had placed the pre-knotted, elastic-backed black bow tie in perfect position under the "V" of the stiff wing collar.

The Negro attendant who rented towels at the basins for a nickel gave Sam a second, sharper look when he became aware that the wardrobe, to which at a quarter before twelve in the morning the young man in front of the mirror was putting the finishing touches, consisted of a tuxedo under a raincoat. Sam buttoned the raincoat quickly, hurried up to the street level and, for thirty-five cents, disposed of the delivery box in the checkroom.

Dressed in a manner he now felt was appropriate to a man dropping into the Park Avenue offices of one of America's most distinguished literary agents, Sam tried to disregard the thunderous hammerings of his heart as he left Grand Central and walked the two blocks down Park to the Oatley-Wicke Building on the corner facing the Murray Hill Hotel.

Sam had never been inside the Oatley-Wicke Building, but in the desperate job-hunting weeks between his graduation from Grover Cleveland High and the day Mr. Brunschweig took him on, Sam had been in and out of enough office buildings in various parts of the city to know immediately that the one he had just entered housed only organizations of overwhelming solvency: the lobby was done in two shades of brown marble, on the newsstand in one corner he saw the *Wall Street Journal* stacked as high as the *Telegram,* and on the wall between the banks of elevators there was a bronze panel dotted with winking lights that told the uniformed starter at a glance exactly where in the upper reaches of the building every one of the cars under his command was at any moment

located. At the directory, where he paused to find the Sargent & Sargent
suite number, Sam had his first moment of surprise. The small white
metal letters stuck into the black felt background read:

SARGENT & SARGENT 2101
CLAUDE SARGENT 2101
SOPHIE SARGENT 2101

It had not occurred to Sam that the two Sargents on the letterhead he
had in his pocket could be anything but brothers or father and son. The
notion of a woman literary agent was new to him. New and, Sam didn't
at the moment understand why, a trifle unsettling.

"Twenty-one, please," he said to the elevator operator, and all the way
up, Sam wondered why the simple fact should affect him so oddly. There
were women in all sorts of businesses. Why not in a literary agency?

"Twenty-one," the operator said, and as the door slid open and Sam
stepped out of the car, he forgot all about that particular problem in a sudden flood of panic. The whole thing all at once seemed a horrible mistake.
It couldn't be Sam Silver of East Tenth Street, Mr. Brunschweig's twelve-
dollar-a-week delivery boy, who had been summoned to this gilded fragment of the uptown world. Mr. Sargent must have had somebody else in
mind, and his secretary, through some insane error, had addressed the
letter to a total stranger who happened to be named Samuel Silver. Sam
shoved his hand into his pocket, pulled out the letter, and the panic re-
ceded. The sight of his neatly typed name and address, followed by the
salutation "Dear Mr. Silver," was reassuring. Holding the letter tightly,
Sam crossed to the door with the frosted glass panel on which was lettered
in black:

2101
SARGENT & SARGENT

He pushed the door open, and stopped short.

"I guess what I was expecting," he told Sophie Sargent years later,
"was one of those high-powered reception rooms you see in movies about
big business: lots of glass and chromium, and a line of modernistic desks
manned, if you'll pardon the expression, by a row of 38-22-34 starlets
wearing low-cut blouses and toothpaste smiles. Instead, there I was in
this dingy little room without windows, just about the size of our East
Tenth Street kitchen, with those three frayed cane-bottom chairs which
my mother wouldn't have considered good enough for our kitchen, that
damned still life of three lopsided lemons on the wall, and in one corner,

behind what still looks to me like an up-ended egg crate, good old Miss Tischler."

Sam did not know at the time, of course, that Miss Tischler was good, but there was no doubt about the fact that she was old. Her round, slant-eyed face, which reminded Sam of a child's drawing of a mandarin, seemed to be made of crepe paper. It was puckered around every orifice: mouth, eyes, nostrils, even ears, so that she seemed frozen in a permanent squint and about to start whistling. She looked up at Sam across a pair of thick, sickle-shaped lenses with a faint scowl of irritation, as though he had interrupted her in some one-handed game the working out of which depended on total concentration. In actual fact, as Sam discovered later, it was a game played with unopened letters, to which Miss Tischler devoted her life and by which, Sam was convinced, her life was sustained. It was Miss Tischler's job, during the lulls in her duties as the Sargent & Sargent receptionist, to redirect the mail that arrived in the office for clients who were addressed in care of their agents. Since the Sargent & Sargent list was large and international in range, and since writers, as Sam was to learn soon enough, were neither a sedentary lot nor inclined to be very careful about leaving forwarding addresses or very precise about the addresses they did leave, Miss Tischler's job, if it was to be discharged at all, required not only skill, patience, and intuition, but above all a certain amount of devotion. Miss Tischler, who had been at it since 1911, when Claude Sargent went into the literary agency business, did her job superbly.

"Could I see Mr. Sargent?" Sam said.

"Of course you can," said the puckered old lady. "You mean *may* you see him."

"What?" Sam said, and then, when his mind caught up with what she had said, he laughed nervously. "That's right," he said. "I mean may I see Mr. Sargent?"

"Who are you?"

"Well, I received this letter?"

Sam held it out. Miss Tischler glanced at the piece of paper, then took it, and came out from behind what Sam now saw was not an up-ended egg crate but one of those old-fashioned desks with a slant top at which bookkeepers in the steel engravings that illustrated Dickens novels stood up while they worked on fat ledgers with quill pens.

"Wait one moment, please," the old lady said, and she disappeared behind a dirty green rep curtain that shielded a narrow archway at the end of the reception room. Sam stared at the still life on the wall and felt the dream of glory oozing out of him like the sand in the egg timer he had bought in Woolworth's as a Chanukah present for his mother. The totally unexpected letter from Claude Sargent had exploded in his mind an image of the world he was about to enter in which none of the individual pieces had very clear shape but all were dazzlingly bright. He had lived with the image for two days, while he struggled with the problem of how to get to Mr. Sargent's office. Now that he had solved the problem, now that he was here, the bright image lay shattered around him. This was no fragment of the great world of Uptown about which he and his mother had for so long dreamed. This was a dump, not much better-looking and not nearly so well furnished as Buggo Salvemini's father's shoe-repair shop on Avenue A.

"Mr. Sargent says come in, please."

Sam turned from the lemons. The old lady with the crepe-paper face was beckoning him toward the green curtain, which she held wide with one hand. Passing through it, Sam was assailed by a strong, sharp odor of peppermint. It apparently came from Miss Tischler, who took a paper sack from the pocket of her long brown dress and popped a small white disc into her mouth as she led Sam down a narrow corridor lighted by a single, small overhead bulb. At regular intervals the bare brown walls of the corridor, which at once brought to Sam's mind the room in the prison where Charles Darnay received Sydney Carton in *A Tale of Two Cities,* were broken on both sides by narrow archways exactly like the one through which Miss Tischler had led Sam out of the reception room, and all the arches were covered by the same kind of dirty green rep she had held aside for Sam. Near the end of the corridor the odor of Miss Tischler's peppermint was crossed by the improbable smell of canned tuna fish, which Sam attributed to the fact that his mind, struggling with the disappointment that had inundated him in the reception room, was playing tantalizing tricks on him: he had suddenly realized he was hungry, and tuna on rye, which he could afford to have for lunch only once a week, was one of his favorite dishes. Miss Tischler pulled aside the curtain at the end of the corridor, said, "Here's Mr. Silver," waited for Sam to pass through, then dropped the curtain.

"Hello, there," said the man behind the desk at the far end of the room, and while Sam's spirits did not exactly soar, he was suddenly aware that they were making an effort to get up off the ground: it was an extremely friendly voice, and while the room was still not what Sam had expected, it was a distinct improvement over the reception room.

For one thing, this room had windows; four, on two sides of the room, one of which faced the Murray Hill Hotel across the street; the other looked down Park Avenue toward Union Square. For another, while the room was small and cluttered, the things that caused the clutter had an immediate and pleasing effect on Sam: a huge wing chair upholstered in red leather and brass nail studs; several jammed bookcases; scores, possibly hundreds, of black framed photographs of men and women in formal and informal poses that covered almost every inch of the walls except for a large space facing the archway through which Sam had just entered. This space was filled with a murkily painted but startlingly specific life-size oil, in an ornate curlicued gold frame, of the nakedest girl with the largest, most exquisitely shaped breasts Sam, who at nineteen had not seen many, had ever clapped eyes on.

He gulped, wished to God he was not blushing, and said to the man behind the desk, "Hello, Mr. Sargent." This managed to drag at least part of Sam's attention from the oil painting, and as a result he noticed something puzzling: the man and the desk seemed to be one.

A moment later, taking a couple of steps forward, Sam saw why. The man, who was not exactly unusually fat, was certainly well fleshed in a curious, shapeless, and attractive way: it was as though the lumps of flesh had been added to his frame with no particular design other than to underscore by its very haphazardness the impression of amiable, uncalculated friendliness conveyed at once by the large, seamed, jowly pink face, with bright laughing eyes as smokily blue as Passover grapes, over which, from an almost totally bald head, a few wisps of gray hair hung down like dank seaweed; and the desk, which was clearly of the same vintage as the contraption at which Miss Tischler played her interminable game out in the reception room, was of a kind Sam had never seen before, even in the engravings in Dickens novels: it was of some sort of richly polished dark wood, outlined at every possible angle with strips of brass, many of which were missing, and, at the sitting side, a large half moon was cut away to the depth of perhaps twelve inches so that when the man behind it leaned forward on his elbows, as Mr. Sargent was leaning now, he seemed to be wearing the desk like a wooden skirt.

"Glad you dropped in," he said. "Here, sit here."

"Here" proved to be a squat lump beside Mr. Sargent's desk. From the rear this lump looked like a three-feet-high section cut out of one of the fluted Greek columns that, according to newspaper and magazine photographs Sam had seen, supported the portico of the White House in Washington. Coming around in front of this object, Sam saw that it was indeed a section of a column, hollowed out and upholstered in green leather to form a chair. Easing himself gingerly into it, and swiftly surveying in his mind the odd bits of furniture to which he had been introduced during the past few minutes, Sam was not only assailed again but practically overwhelmed by the odor of tuna on rye.

"Had your lunch?" Mr. Sargent said.

"Uh, no," Sam said. "But that's all right. I'm not hungry. I just dropped in. I mean you said in your letter, sir, you said to just drop in, and so I did."

"Here, have one of these."

Mr. Sargent pushed across the desk a paper plate on which one and a half tuna fish sandwiches sat in a nest of mayonnaise-smeared wax paper. The missing half-sandwich was clutched in one of Mr. Sargent's pudgy hands. With the other he was pouring coffee from a percolator into a thick green mug on the side of which was a small gold and red bas-relief in the form of a crest that resembled the United States seal on the dollar bill.

"How do you take your coffee?" Mr. Sargent said. "Black, or with?"

"Thanks, no," Sam said. "No coffee."

"Well, if you want any, just holler," Mr. Sargent said. He set the percolator on a chromium trivet that seemed to be imbedded in the window sill beside his desk, took a sip from the green mug, a huge bite from the tuna sandwich, and chewed slowly for several silent moments while his blue eyes rested on his visitor's face in the frankest examination to which Sam had ever been subjected. Not quite sure that, in spite of Mr. Sargent's invitation, he was doing the right thing, Sam took half a sandwich from the paper plate and attempted what he hoped looked like a gentlemanly nibble at one corner. His teeth had not yet met when he felt the thickly smeared lumps of tuna fish begin to escape at one side. In a swift, convulsive rescue operation, Sam dipped his head to one side and chomped off a mouthful as big as an orange. Mr. Sargent's eyes crinkled in a quick smile.

"Nice get," he said around his own mouthful of sandwich, and then, "Don't try to answer for a while. Just chew, or you'll choke to death. These drug-store sandwiches have killed more writers than Scotch whiskey."

Sam chewed desperately and managed, while Mr. Sargent continued to regard him with unconcealed interest, to reduce the mass of sandwich to several swallowable lumps. After this some but not all of his embarrassment slid away, and Sam tried to cross his legs to indicate that he was completely at his ease. The tightly buttoned raincoat prevented him.

"Why don't you take off your coat?" Mr. Sargent said, reaching for the green coffee mug. "Be more comfortable, I think."

"Yes, sir, thanks," Sam said. "I think so."

He put down the sandwich, stood up, unbuttoned his raincoat, and knew at once, from the way Mr. Sargent's eyes leaped in a startled upward flick and the coffee mug stopped on its way to the stout man's mouth, that he had chosen the correct costume for this visit. Mr. Sargent's glance traveled, in a series of separate jerky movements of his bald head, from the boiled shirt, to the black snap-on bow tie, to the satin facings on the lapels of the dinner coat, and finally to the patent-leather pumps intended for Mr. Traver on Thirty-sixth Street. Feeling much more sure of himself, now that he knew he had made a good impression, Sam slipped himself back into the lump of white column upholstered in green leather, crossed his legs, retrieved his tuna on rye, and took another bite. Mr. Sargent finished taking his sip of coffee and cleared his throat.

"I liked your story," he said.

"Yes, sir," Sam said to what seemed a pointless remark. Mr. Sargent had already indicated, in the letter inviting Sam to drop in, that he had issued the invitation because he had liked Sam's story.

"I don't usually find much to like in magazines like *Landscape*," Mr. Sargent said. "It's not that I have anything against these arty publications. It's only that I've been reading them for years, and I still do, because I like to keep in touch with what the young people are doing, but the young people, God bless and keep them, seem to be bent on— By the way, Mr. Silver, how old are you?"

Sam did not exactly hesitate. It was simply that because his mouth was full of tuna fish sandwich, he had to work it into a corner before he could speak clearly, and he took advantage of the few moments this operation consumed to wonder if he should tell the truth. He wanted desperately to make a good impression. He sensed that the sight of the tuxedo had started him off on the right foot. Would he lose that initial advantage by admitting his age? Mr. Sargent apparently placed a different interpretation on Sam's hesitation, because he said kindly, "Don't answer if you think I'm prying."

"No, sir," Sam said and decided that, while the proposition: honesty is always the best policy was still subject to proof, it was certainly a good rule to lean on when in doubt. "I'm nineteen."

Mr. Sargent smiled and said, "I wish I could say the same." He took another sip of coffee, shook his head in a way that managed to convey a sense of amused wonder, and said, "The trouble with most magazines like *Landscape* is that instead of doing the job they profess to be doing, which is to provide new talents with an outlet that is denied them by the commercial publications, they merely provide an outlet for stuff that doesn't really deserve an outlet at all. I mean most of the stories are not only noncommercial. They are also non-stories. Just the same, as I said, I read them all, because in my business you've got to find new people all the time or pretty soon you're *out* of business. The big name writers, the people you make your money on, are unfortunately human. They get older and die, or they get rich and lazy, or they run out of material and dry up. Right, Ken?"

Astonished, Sam saw, on following Mr. Sargent's glance toward the wing chair, that it was occupied, or rather part of its commodious sitting space was occupied, by a small, thin, neat-looking man. His shiny black hair was slicked back and parted in the middle. His large black guardsman's mustache curled fiercely upward at the ends, like a tiny pair of bull's horns. And his brown eyes slanted downward at the corners in a slightly sinister way. The image that all these details at once brought to Sam's mind was so sharp and total that he could never get it out of his mind or modify it, even when he came to understand how inaccurate it was: the small, beautifully tailored figure lounging in the wing chair looked like an expensive doll fashioned to represent a post-Civil War Mississippi riverboat gambler masquerading as a New York stockbroker.

"Right as rain," the small, neat, and extraordinarily attractive man said in a drawl that Sam recognized at once, from movies he had seen, as authentic Texas Panhandle. "Which means, Top, old boy, rain being right about as often as weather forecasters, that you're saying something entertaining rather than strictly accurate. Not all writers get rich and lazy, and not all writers run out of material and dry up, but all of them sure as hell get older and die."

Mr. Sargent laughed. "Have another tuna fish sandwich and stop being characteristically sardonic," he said. "You're not being interviewed. You're passing the time of day with your agent and friend. By the way, Mr. Silver, this is Kenyon Poole."

Sam, who had still not recovered from the shock of discovering that a third person had been in the room ever since he entered it, now received an even greater shock. Mr. Poole rose from the wing chair, put out his hand, and in a manner so exquisitely courtly that it made Sam blush, bowed as he said, "Pleased to make your acquaintance, sir." As Sam took the small hand, which felt as knotty and hard as a lump of tangled wire, it dawned on him who the owner was, and for a long, long agonizing moment, during which Sam was absolutely convinced he would never again catch his breath, he felt certain he was going to drop in a dead faint at the feet of the world-famous Western writer.

"I—I—" Sam's breath came whistling back into his chest, and he managed to say, "I'm very glad to meet you, sir."

It sounded so utterly inadequate, like discovering that the man standing next to you at a Sixth Avenue hot-dog stand is Henry VIII and acknowledging the startling fact by casually passing him the mustard pot, that Sam felt his face grow hot.

"Ken is right, of course," Mr. Sargent said. "Not all writers get lazy or dry up, but so many of them do, that when you add these to those who are constantly dying, you're faced, if you're a literary agent, with a steadily diminishing list of clients, and if you don't do something to replenish the list, pretty soon you find yourself beginning to think you'd better get into some other business. I've never found any business I like as much as mine, so I'm determined to stay in it, and one way I've found of doing that —or, to be strictly honest, my wife found this particular way—"

"Sophie gets all the good ideas around here," Kenyon Poole drawled, and Sam's heart walloped up against the wall of his chest. It didn't seem possible that he was actually in the same room with the great man who had written the series of novels about the American cowboy which, beginning with *The Small Meal,* had caused such an uproar in the literary world that the echoes had been strong enough to reach and shake the members of Miss Mercator's Stratford Club in Grover Cleveland High down on Irving Place.

"Let's say Sophie gets a good number of the good ideas around here," Mr. Sargent said. "I'm no slouch, but this one was certainly Sophie's. She started subscribing to these literary magazines and university reviews years ago. We've found a few clients in that way, youngish people mostly, who have done fairly well, so I can't exactly say the time I've spent has all been wasted, but I can say that most of the stuff bores the living bejesus out of me. Your story, Mr. Silver, was the first one I've read in any of those magazines in years, and absolutely the first one I've ever read in *Landscape,* that I've genuinely liked."

"Thank you, sir," Sam said.

"Me, too," Kenyon Poole said. "It's a beautiful job."

Sam's heart again made an ass of itself, and he kept his mouth shut. Mr. Sargent apparently interpreted Sam's silence as disbelief, because he said promptly, "It's true. I gave Ken my copy."

"Oh," Sam said hastily. "I didn't mean that I doubted—"

"I should think not," Mr. Sargent said through his wonderful smile. "Praise from Kenyon Poole is praise from Sir Hubert."

"Thank you," said Sam, wondering who Sir Hubert was.

"I've never read anything else by you, I'm sorry to say," Mr. Sargent said. "Have you published much?"

"No, sir," Sam said. "This story in *Landscape* is my first."

"First published, or first written?"

"Both," Sam said.

Mr. Sargent sent a sharp glance toward the wing chair, then leaned forward, as though gathering the wooden skirt of the desk around him, and said, "This is the first story you ever wrote?"

Not quite knowing why that funny sound had come into Mr. Sargent's voice, Sam gave himself a moment to think, and in the moment saw that Mr. Sargent had picked up from his desk the bright yellow copy of *Landscape* in which "The Ways of Men Must Sever" appeared.

"Yes, sir," Sam said.

"Now, if you tell me that *Landscape* is the first magazine you sent it to . . . ?"

"Yes, sir," Sam said.

"You mean it *is* the first?"

"Yes, sir."

Mr. Sargent turned toward the wing chair. "Ken," he said. "First story he ever wrote. First magazine he ever sent it to. What would you say the odds are that a writer doing that would get an acceptance?"

"Statistics are not my long suit," said Kenyon Poole. "But I think it's rare enough to fall into that not very accurate but certainly dramatic category: the thousand-to-one shot."

"Probably closer to ten-thousand-to-one," Claude Sargent said. "By the way, how did you happen to choose *Landscape?* I mean most youngsters, their first story, they usually choose some well-known magazine like the *Saturday Evening Post* or *Collier's.* Is *Landscape* popular with the people in your class who are interested in literature?"

"My class?" Sam said.

"In college," Mr. Sargent said.

"In college?" Sam said, and then he understood. "I don't go to college, sir."

"Oh," Mr. Sargent said, and then, "Got a job?"

"Yes, sir," Sam said, dreading the next question, because he did not want to lie about what he did for a living, and yet how could he reveal that he earned it by delivering tuxedos without revealing that the suit he was wearing had been borrowed for this visit?

"Then how did you happen to choose *Landscape* to send your story to?" Mr. Sargent said, and Sam relaxed. "I don't think the damn thing is sold on newsstands. Certainly not on many. College bookshops carry it, I know, but you don't go to college, you say, so unless you have a subscription . . . ?"

"No, sir, I don't, but my boss does," Sam said, and realized at once that he had made a mistake. Mr. Sargent's next question, almost inevitably, would be about the kind of boss who subscribes to obscure literary magazines published on islands in the Mediterranean. To avoid the question, Sam placed what was left of the treacherous tuna fish sandwich on the paper plate and said, "He's sort of a bug on reading. Or maybe subscribing is more accurate. He doesn't seem to read any of the things he gets. He never even takes the wrappers off most of the magazines that come in. But every time he gets one of those circular letters asking him to renew a subscription or sign up for a new magazine, he fills it right in and mails it back with a check, and the things keep coming in, a couple almost every day, and he lets them pile up on his desk like, well, you know, just pile up like lumber. Every now and then, when I have nothing else to do, I look through them and, well, that's how I happened to come across this *Landscape*."

"What made you think it was the appropriate spot for your story?" Mr. Sargent said. "Instead of, let's say, sending it to one of those I mentioned? The *Post? Cosmo? American Bride?* One of those?"

Sam thought for a moment and then, with genuine surprise, said, "I don't really know." He paused, surprised by the fact that he should be surprised, thought for another moment, then said, "I think maybe it was my feeling that the other magazines like the *Post* and so on were not appropriate. Or, no, the other way around. That my *story* was not appropriate to *them*."

Mr. Sargent, who was replenishing the green mug from the percolator, nodded and said, "That's it, of course. Coffee now?"

"Thanks, no," Sam said.

He was having enough trouble following what was going on in this room without complicating matters by juggling food and a drink.

"You agree, Ken?" Mr. Sargent said.

"Absolutely," Kenyon Poole said.

Sam hesitated, then said worriedly, "I don't think I understand what you mean."

Mr. Sargent set down the percolator, picked up the yellow copy of *Landscape,* and allowed the stiff, thick pages to slide off his thumb. When the delicate rustling sound stopped, Sam could tell, from the thickness of the batch of pages lying flat, that Mr. Sargent was staring at page 36. Sam had stared at it hundreds of times since he had received his copy. It was the page on which, under the title "The Ways of Men Must Sever," his name appeared in print, not only for the first time in his life, but for all the world—or the fragment of it that read *Landscape*—to see.

"Maybe I can make you understand more easily with a simple economic fact," Mr. Sargent said. "If you don't mind another one of my prying questions, that is?"

"Of course not, sir," Sam said.

"How much did *Landscape* pay you for this story?" Mr. Sargent said.

"Ten dollars," Sam said, and no amount of rigidly exercised self-control could completely conceal the pride in his voice. For someone who was paid by Mr. Brunschweig twelve dollars for fifty-four hours of drudgery, it still seemed unbelievable to have been rewarded with ten for three hours of pleasure.

"If you had sent this story to *American Bride,* let us say," Mr. Sargent said. "And let us say further they had accepted it. Do you know what they would have paid you? Even though it is a first story by a totally unknown writer, and it came in over the transom?"

"Over the what?"

"Without the protective shepherding of a literary agent," Mr. Sargent said. "Sent in by the author himself. Unsolicited. Do you know what *American Bride* would have paid you?"

"No, sir," Sam said.

"Five hundred dollars," Mr. Sargent said, and then, apparently in answer to the look on Sam's face, he added, "That's a fact. Five hundred dollars. Possibly even more. Bud Bienstock, the *American Bride* editor, is very generous to new talent. It's also good advertising. Or so he thinks. He likes to be known as a sort of Fourth Avenue Maecenas. It makes him feel like a big shot, I suppose, and I like to let him continue feeling that way. But even if it wasn't Bud, if you'd sent 'The Ways of Men Must Sever' to any of the big circulation magazines, and they took it, that's what they would have paid: five hundred dollars. You know the difference between that hypothetical five hundred and the actual ten *Landscape* paid you?"

"You don't mean just the four hundred and ninety?" Sam said. "The arithmetic?"

Kenyon Poole laughed. And Mr. Sargent, laughing with the Western writer, said, "I see where you and Mr. Poole would get along fine together, Mr. Silver. You seem to have the same kinds of minds. No, I don't mean the arithmetic. I mean what makes your story, which is a damn good one, worth five hundred dollars to, say, *American Bride,* if they bought it, and only ten dollars to *Landscape?*"

"I guess ten is all *Landscape* can afford," Sam said.

Kenyon Poole laughed again and Mr. Sargent said, "Don't get to be *too* much like Mr. Poole, Mr. Silver. He drinks like a fish."

"Every great writer who ever lived drank like a fish," Mr. Poole said. "It's the only way to get through a daily round that includes meetings with literary agents who can't think of a fresher simile than that. Fish, by the way, don't drink at all, Top. The water just flushes through their gills."

"If it does to their gills what whiskey does to your kidneys, I'm glad I don't live under water. How about some more coffee?"

"No, thanks," the neat little man said from the depths of the red wing chair. "Just go ahead with what you're showing Mr. Silver."

"The difference, Mr. Silver, between the five hundred dollars any large circulation magazine would have paid you for 'The Ways of Men Must Sever,' assuming they were willing to buy it," Mr. Sargent said, "and the ten dollars you actually received from *Landscape,* is in the subject matter of your story."

Trying not to sound as stupid as he felt, Sam said, "The subject matter of the story?"

The creases in Mr. Sargent's jowly face, which Sam suddenly decided looked very much like that of an endearing but sorrowful dog, rearranged themselves in a look of surprise.

"Why, yes," the literary agent said. "What's your story about? The graduation exercises at a high school on New York's Lower East Side? A boy of eighteen who has won a four-year college scholarship as well as the right to deliver the valedictory address at the graduation exercises, and his relationship with a girl who is his rival and has come in second in the graduating class and thus has lost out on the college scholarship? And how this girl, who is supposed to be your hero's friend, makes him lose the college scholarship by having an accomplice lock the hero in the school can during the graduation performance of *The Merchant of Venice,* in which she then substitutes for him as Shylock and creates a scandal by humiliating the high school principal in public? Do you think, Mr. Silver, that 'The Ways of Men Must Sever' is about that?"

Merely by posing the question, if not from the tone of the literary agent's voice, it was clear that Mr. Sargent expected an answer in the negative. All of Sam's simple-minded inclinations, however, urged a reply in the affirmative. He tried, therefore, to straddle the issue with a puzzled look, then realized this could only damage the favorable impression he was trying to make on Mr. Sargent, so Sam said a trifle helplessly, "Isn't it?"

Mr. Sargent again made that humping-himself-forward movement, as though the cut-out desk was a skirt he was adjusting around his body, and he said with a touch of irritation, "Mr. Silver, why did you write 'The Ways of Men Must Sever'?"

It was an unfortunate question, at least from the standpoint of a man trying to make a good impression, because the words brought with them into Mr. Sargent's office all the horror of the year between the night of Sam's graduation from Grover Cleveland High and the day he sat down to write the story at Mr. Brunschweig's cluttered desk. During the months since Sam had written "The Ways of Men Must Sever" he had managed to force the horror so far back into the deeper recesses of his mind that he had been able to regard the events—certainly since the wonderful morning when he had learned from the editors of *Landscape* that they had accepted his story for publication—as things that had happened to somebody else.

Now, after months of freedom, Sam found himself hurled backward in time, away from his seat beside Mr. Sargent's desk in the Oatley-Wicke Building, into the prison of despair that had seemed as much a physical reality as the East Tenth Street kitchen in which he waited, on the morning after the graduation exercises, for his mother to come home from her visit to Mr. Mueller's office. Sam could tell, from the sound of her footsteps on the stairs, that the trip to Irving Place had been a waste of time.

"What happened?" he said when the door opened and his mother came into the kitchen.

"What should you expect to happen?" Mrs. Silver said grimly as she pulled the hatpin from the narrow-brimmed pancake of black straw. "From an anti-Semitt you expect favors?"

Through the despair that had settled on him like a sodden overcoat the night before, Sam felt a flicker of surprise. "Mr. Mueller?" he said.

"How many anti-Semitts they got for principals in one high school?" his mother demanded. "He should drop dead."

All at once more uneasy than despairing, Sam said slowly, "But I always thought Jennie was crazy."

"This you can keep on thinking," Mrs. Silver said, stabbing the hatpin back into the hat as though the inanimate object were the living enemy that had dealt her plans this unforeseen blow. "Only a crazy girl would do what she did last night by the graduation, but about that Mr. Mueller, his head should grow in the ground like an onion, she was right. Jews he hates like poison, he should drop dead."

"He said something, Ma?"

"Something like *you* mean, a dirty name, this these anti-Semitts they're too smart to say." Mrs. Silver slipped the straw hat into the paper bag that kept it free of dust between journeys uptown, and she crimped the open end shut with fierce little thrusts of her fingers. "But to know an anti-Semitt, you don't have to hear dirty names. You can tell by how he says what he says."

"What did he say, Ma?"

"He said I should sit down, please, so already I know there's trouble. To sit down in his own office he has to say to me please? Why? He wants a favor from me, he's so quick with the please? So I sat down and he said what can he do for me. I said Mr. Mueller you can talk to the man from uptown he came last night to the graduation to see my son Sam is the right person for the scholarship. You can talk to him, Mr. Mueller, I said, and tell him my Sam this morning he's still the same Sam he was when he got the highest marks in the school and he won the scholarship. He's the same Sam, I said, he was before that crazy Jennie Broom she got that crazy Buggo Salvemini he should lock my Sam in the school toilet by the graduation."

Mrs. Silver paused to scowl down at the paper bag in her hands, as though she had forgotten what was in it, and Sam, who knew the outcome of the interview from the way his mother had dragged her feet coming up the stairs, could not resist hoping he was wrong. He asked eagerly, "What did he say, Ma?"

"What should he say, an anti-Semitt like that?" Mrs. Silver said. "He said he was sorry, he didn't agree my Sam was the same Sam like I said. He said he was sorry, but my Sam knew the whole thing from the start. He said he was sorry but my Sam was a partner in the whole thing with Jennie Broom and with Buggo Salvemini."

"That's a lie!" Sam said.

"Me you're telling?" his mother said angrily. "Go tell Mr. Mueller, the anti-Semitt, he should drop dead with his please and he's sorry. I said my son swears it was on him a put-up job, he didn't know till it happened what was happening, go ask Jennie Broom or even Buggo Salvemini, crazy they are, but liars no, not liars to make a boy lose a college scholarship, that they're not, not even crazy Jennie. So Mr. Mueller, he should drop dead, he squeezes together those little anti-Semitt eyes, and those anti-Semitt lips they squeeze together, too, and he's again sorry, but no, if I don't mind, he's not asking any more questions, not from any Jennie Brooms or any Buggos or from nobody else, if I don't mind, because more than he already knows he doesn't need to know, and for Jennie and for Buggo, he already told them for their diplomas they could go whistle, and your son Sam, he says to me, the scholarship he's not getting, and not the diploma, either, just like this Jennie and this Buggo they're not getting diplomas, and you should please not mind, Mrs. Silver, I should please excuse him, Mrs. Silver, if from listening to my son's swearing how innocent he is I should excuse him, because what boys like your Sam swear, he says through those anti-Semitt lips, he should drop dead, it's never the truth because boys like your Sam they don't know what it means to swear the truth, and now if you'll excuse me, Mrs. Silver, his work he's got to finish, a good day to you, Mrs. Silver." She slapped the paper bag up on the shelf beside the gas meter and said grimly, "A good day he should have when they carry him to his grave, it should only happen tomorrow, the dirty anti-Semitt. You had to eat?"

"I'm not hungry," Sam said.

"I asked you if you're hungry?" Mrs. Silver snapped as she took down the apron from the nail in the wall beside the sink. "I asked if you had to eat!" Sam shook his head miserably and his mother said, "On top of you lose the chance to go to college you want also to lose the health? Sit by the table!"

Sam took the chair in which, for the evening meal after he came home from work, his father always sat. His mother began to bring from the icebox the cracked plates and jelly jars in which she accumulated the leftovers of the family's two official meals, breakfast and supper, and from which she prepared all other meals. She set down the plates and jars on the table as though she intended each to leave its outline on the blue-and-white-checked oilcloth, and even though the sight and smell of food almost nauseated him, Sam forced himself to eat. His mother's furies had to be outwaited. So long as she remained voiceless, so long as she was able to keep them bottled up, her rages could be lived with. The trick was to do nothing that would divert her from the inner struggle for self-control that absorbed all her energies. After a while she stopped slamming things around and came to the table and sat down facing Sam.

"So all right," she said quietly. She drew a deep breath and placed both hands palms down on the oilcloth in front of her and said it again: "So all right."

"What, Ma?" Sam said.

"We'll do like this," his mother said, speaking with great care, in a low voice, like a general outlining a battle plan he does not like because of the foreseeable casualties it entails, but which in his view the circumstances dictate as inevitable. "The college is lost," Mrs. Silver said. "Crazy ones like Jennie Broom and that Buggo, anti-Semitts like that Mr. Mueller, on them to call names we won't waste time. Let them drop dead, each one separate and each one four times. We'll do what we want without the college. We'll get a job. We'll go at night to study bookkeeping and typewriting and like Mrs. Heerscheim's Yettie upstairs shorthand."

"Shorthand?" Sam said.

Mrs. Silver nodded. "Everybody thinks the typewriting and the shorthand it's only for girls. So if a boy can do it, especially a boy he's also a good bookkeeper, there's jobs he could get that other boys they can't get, and a boy with upstairs here a good head, once he gets such a job, that's all he needs. He'll move up, up, up till who knows? You understand, Sam?"

He returned his mother's nod. "Bookkeeping and secretarial school at night," Sam said. "You mean C.C.N.Y.?"

"Why not?"

"Mr. Mueller said I'm not getting my diploma, Ma. I don't think they let anybody in C.C.N.Y. without a high school diploma."

"Then we'll find a night school where we'll pay."

"With what, Ma?"

"With what they pay you on the job, Sam."

"I don't have a job, Ma."

"Nobody has a job till they get one," Mrs. Silver said. "You'll get one, Sam."

"Doing what, Ma?"

"Go down and buy a paper," Mrs. Silver said. "We'll see what a boy with brains can get these days."

What Sam got, after three weeks of trying, did not require much brains, but it was enough to pay his tuition in the evening session at the Lafayette Business Institute, and for a student the job had at least one advantage: when Sam was not out delivering tuxedos, Mr. Brunschweig allowed him to do his homework on the desk in the back of the store. After French and chemistry in Grover Cleveland High, Sam found bookkeeping, typing, and shorthand almost ridiculously simple. If he hadn't, he probably would never have mastered the basic Pitman outlines or the typewriter keyboard. His mind, which had always dealt easily with school problems, seemed since the events of graduation night incapable of dealing adequately with anything.

Even though he lived with his father and mother, worked for a fairly talkative man, and spent three hours every evening in a class with forty-eight gregarious and in some cases garrulous young men and women, Sam was weighed down by a sense of loneliness that puzzled him as much as it depressed him. It was as though the loss of the Hammond Haynes Scholarship, which had cut him off from the chance to go to college, had cut him off from the rest of the world as well. He felt isolated and suspended, like a prisoner sentenced to solitary confinement without being told why, or how long he would be incarcerated. At odd moments during the day—while lugging up Broadway a cardboard box containing one of Mr. Brunschweig's tuxedos; listening in class to a lecture on amortization or the trial balance; even sitting in the East Tenth Street kitchen late at night munching the leftovers his mother had set out for him—Sam would suddenly realize his forehead was wet with sweat and, for the past few minutes, he had not really been walking or listening or even eating, but reliving the horror of those minutes in the locked gymnasium toilet when, spread-eagled across the transom over the door, he had watched Jennie Broom, wearing his Shylock costume, scream her denunciation into Mr. Mueller's startled face.

Sam did not understand why his mind kept returning to the terrible scene. Why couldn't he turn his back on the damn thing, the way his mother had? Mrs. Silver never mentioned the event that had cost her son his college education, or the people connected with it. He sensed vaguely that she believed to look backward was a weakness. Sam even shared that belief. And yet he found himself looking backward constantly, as though by re-examining the event he could find some clue to his mysterious imprisonment and thus change the course of the events that had followed.

Years later, when he looked back on this period of his life, Sam marveled at the fact that nobody—his boss, his instructors at the Lafayette Institute, not even his mother—noticed anything wrong. From the vantage point of the years Sam could see what he had then been able only to feel: the slow, relentless downward movement from a state of uneasiness and resentment toward hopelessness and indifference out of which, before long, it probably would have been impossible to climb back to anything resembling normalcy.

Sam could only conclude, from that vantage point in the future, that some instinct of self-preservation in the stricken boy had, without his knowledge, thrown up around his inner turmoil a polished carapace that reflected to the outside world the reassuring image it wanted to see: the bright, industrious, penniless youngster working hard at his job and his studies toward the success that, for the brainy and the virtuous, was inevitable.

More than a year had gone by since the night of the Grover Cleveland High graduation exercises. One hot day in August Sam came back from a delivery to the store on Forty-eighth Street to pick up his schoolbooks before going down to his classes on Fourth Avenue. He didn't have much time. His first class started at seven, and it was almost six-thirty when Sam put his key in the lock. If he hurried he could just manage to pick up his books, grab a bite somewhere on Sixth Avenue, and get to school on time. The desire to hurry, however, had suddenly vanished.

Perhaps it was due to the fact that Mr. Brunschweig, who usually waited until Sam came back from his last delivery before closing the store, had tonight decided to go home early, and so, when Sam came in, the emptiness of the store had helped send through the outer shell of pretense inside which he lived a message that told him he could, at least temporarily, stop pretending because there was nobody to pretend for. Perhaps the heat of the day, which had been worse than usual, had worn him down further than Sam himself realized. Or perhaps it was merely that the slowly growing burden of uneasiness, resentment, and despair he had been carrying in secret since graduation night had, without any warning, reached a point in size and weight where it was all at once unbearable.

Whatever the reason, as the street door slammed behind him, and Sam started down the darkened shop toward the desk in the rear in which Mr. Brunschweig allowed him to keep his schoolbooks, he felt himself stagger. His legs, he realized, were suddenly too weak for his body. With a feeling of surprise, as though he were watching something preposterous happening to somebody else, Sam tottered down the length of the store, just managed to fall into the chair at Mr. Brunschweig's desk, dropped his head on his arms, and burst into tears.

Even in those first moments of breakup, when everything inside him seemed to be falling away, so that it was impossible to grasp through the tangle of whirling emotions what was happening to him, Sam was clearly aware of two things: a feeling of surprise for the savagery of his sobs—he had never before, not even as a baby, cried like this!—and a sense of gratitude for the fact that nobody was there to see his shameful disintegration.

For a while he allowed the sobs to shake him, to bounce his wet face up and down on his arms. Then, slowly, as he became aware that he was going to die and that he was looking forward to the moment of oblivion, he became interested in the ingredients of his agony, and at once Sam saw that they centered on the image with which he had lived for over a year: the events of graduation night.

Before he knew completely what he was doing, Sam had lifted his head, wiped his face with the back of a hand, and begun the hunt for paper. Annoyed by the fact that Mr. Brunschweig's desk contained nothing suitable, Sam was about to use the back of his boss's order pad, when he remembered the steno notebook in which every evening at Lafayette Institute he took practice dictation from his Pitman teacher. He pulled the notebook out of his stack of schoolbooks and, with the pencil Mr. Brunschweig had attached with a piece of string to the telephone so that he would never be at a loss when somebody called with an order, Sam began to write.

The start was slow, mainly because he tried for a while to open with what Miss Mercator used to call a "topic sentence," but soon after he abandoned this irritating formality, and simply started, the words were coming so fast that Sam had to abandon ordinary script and resort to short-

hand. He didn't like this very much, because the Pitman squiggles were
somehow not as satisfying to the eye as spelled-out words, but it enabled
him to get the sentences down on paper almost as fast as they took shape
in his mind.

When he finished, Sam reread the whole thing and, by the time he
reached the end, pausing only to make two corrections in punctuation,
he had decided on his title. From the second line of the Richard Hovey
poem Miss Mercator had suggested he quote in his valedictory speech,
Sam took six words and wrote them neatly across the top of his first page:
"The Ways of Men Must Sever." He stared at them for a few moments,
wondering if they were right, since what was severed in his account of
the graduation-night fiasco was not the ways of men, but the way of a
boy and a girl, then Sam decided that the slight inaccuracy added an
ironic touch he found curiously pleasing.

This feeling of pleasure was diluted for a while by the next problem:
Mr. Brunschweig's somewhat primitive stationery cabinet—an old cardboard delivery carton on top of the battered filing cabinet beside his desk—
contained nothing but a couple of reams of letterheads and a batch of
envelopes, but what Sam needed, and felt he must have at once, was some
clean, white 8½ by 11 paper. Irritated by this momentary interruption in
what he was finding an oddly pleasurable flow of movement, Sam thought
of two alternatives. He could go out and find a stationery store and buy
some clean white typing paper, or he could do it sometime tomorrow
when he was out on a delivery. He discarded both for the same reason:
they would mean more than a momentary interruption, and some instinct
told him that until the Pitman squiggles were translated into neatly typed
rows of double-spaced words, he would not really have completed the activity to which he had turned without knowing why, and from which
he was drawing a satisfaction he had never before known.

Another few moments of thought suggested a compromise: the backs of
Mr. Brunschweig's letterheads. These were printed on much better paper
than his billheads because, as Sam's boss had once pointed out, a man who
rents tuxedos for a living has occasion to write many bills but few letters.

Using a batch of these letterheads, a piece of the carbon paper from
Mr. Brunschweig's billing book, the vintage Underwood that completed
his boss's office equipment, and the touch system he had been studying at
the Lafayette Institute, Sam proceeded to transcribe his fourteen pages of
Pitman outlines into two copies of an eight-page double-spaced typewritten
manuscript. He was pleased but not surprised to discover, after reading
and rereading the finished job, that it did not contain a single typographi-

cal error. After all, he was the best student in his Lafayette Institute typing class.

Without hesitation, as though he were involved in a process with which long experience had made him familiar, Sam turned to the next step: where to send the manuscript.

Years later, when he could look back calmly on the events of that incredible night and even be amused by them, Sam saw clearly that he was acting out of an instinct as natural to the storyteller as swimming is to the porpoise: a story without a reader is not a story. He did not yet know, on the night when he did it for the first time, that he had written a story. Sam knew clearly, however, without having to think about it, that he wanted his neatly typewritten pages to appear in print where they could be read.

The pile of magazines, to which Mr. Brunschweig subscribed but did not read and which Sam had shoved aside to make room first for his steno notebook and then for the Underwood, now caught his eye. The well-known publications, such as the *Saturday Evening Post, Collier's,* and *American Bride,* did not hold Sam's attention long. The instincts that had directed him all evening now told him firmly that these publications, which he had been reading fairly regularly for years, would not be receptive to what he had just written. Working his way through the less familiar publications, most of which were still encased in brown paper wrappers, Sam finally stopped at a magazine called *Landscape.* He had never before heard of it. He went through it now with great care, page by page, studying the masthead, the title page, even feeling the texture of the paper.

Almost every aspect of the examination fascinated him: the gaudy yellow cover with the title of the magazine slashing diagonally across in bright green letters that looked as though they had been drawn with a toothbrush by a demented child; the fact that the magazine was published not weekly or monthly but every second month; the box on the cover that contained the at first cryptic letters "Vol. 1, No. 2" which Sam soon translated into the intelligence that what he was holding in his hands was the second issue of *Landscape* that had thus far appeared in America; the editorial statement that, until these first two issues had been put together in the magazine's New York office, it had been edited for several years in mimeographed form on the island of Capri. Even the fact that he had never before heard of a single name that appeared on the title page was somehow, to Sam on that hot night in Mr. Brunschweig's tuxedo parlor, significant and exciting. What convinced him, however, that *Landscape* was the publication to which he should send "The Ways of Men Must Sever" was a simple, hard fact: almost all the stories in the yellow and green maga-zine, a careful word count revealed, were exactly the same length as the story Sam had just written.

He addressed one of Mr. Brunschweig's envelopes to the magazine's office on Fourth Avenue, helped himself to the proper postage from his boss's stamp box, picked up his schoolbooks, left the store, locked the door, walked down to Sixth Avenue, dropped the envelope into the mailbox on the corner, looked at his Ingersoll, and made two discoveries, both sur-prising: it was ten minutes short of midnight, and he was famished.

An hour later, in the East Tenth Street kitchen, after he had wolfed down every scrap of food from the cracked plates and jelly jars his mother had set out for him, Sam made another discovery: the sense of despair with which he had been living for over a year had vanished.

The next morning, after his first dreamless sleep since graduation night, he made a computation as he brushed his teeth: he had dropped the en-velope into the mailbox just before midnight, which meant it probably would not be picked up before the next, meaning this, morning; the *Land-scape* office was right here in New York, however, which meant there was a good chance the envelope would reach its destination that afternoon; to be on the safe side, however, say tomorrow morning positively; give the editors all of that day to read the manuscript and write a reply, and the answer had to be in Sam's mailbox day after tomorrow.

It was—a fact that did not seem at all surprising to Sam Silver aged nineteen.

What did surprise him—what, in fact, shocked him so deeply that he did not realize until long after that his life had turned a crucial corner—was something that accompanied the one-sentence letter from the editors: "We like your story, 'The Ways of Men Must Sever,' and are accepting it for publication in *Landscape*." Attached by wire clip to the top of the letter was a long green slip of expensive paper that ordered a world-famous New York bank to "pay to the order of Samuel Silver the sum of Ten and no/100 dollars." It was not, of course, the first check Sam had ever seen. It was merely the first he had ever seen with his name on it.

When his mother saw it, and Sam had explained how the check had come into his possession, Mrs. Silver looked thoughtful for a few moments and then said quietly, "Tomorrow, when it's a delivery or maybe when it's lunchtime, you take this in by the Dry Dock Bank and start a savings account."

Sam started the account, and neither he nor his mother said anything more about the incident. Sam saw nothing odd in this. The despair that had been part of his life for more than a year had been replaced by a very pleasant sense of anticipation in which he functioned with a sense of contentment that demanded or perhaps allowed for no examination of the feelings of others. His mother was what she had always been: his mother. But he was now something he had never been before: a perfectly happy tuxedo delivery boy by day and bookkeeping student at night.

The situation did not change when, one day in October, the copy of *Landscape* containing Sam's story arrived on East Tenth Street. His mother seemed to become more thoughtful rather than excited, and even Sam, who liked the excitement, did not bother to probe for its meaning. He was content to carry the magazine around with him and, at odd moments of the day, when he was in the can or on the subway or even carrying a delivery down the street, to turn to page 36 and reread the story he knew by heart. The only thing that later struck Sam as odd about his conduct during those first few days was the fact that he did not show the published story to Mr. Brunschweig or to any of his fellow students at Lafayette Institute. To have done so, Sam guessed when later he did think about it, would have diluted the intensity of the pleasure in his achievement that he preferred to take secretly. Writing, he would begin to understand years later, was an onanistic activity.

In those early days, however, when onanism was just another of the thousands of words in the dictionary he had not yet had occasion to look up, Sam was merely content with his pleasure. Then the letter from Sargent & Sargent arrived, and he sensed that he and his mother had entered a new phase in their relationship to each other and to the world they faced shoulder to shoulder.

Knowing absolutely nothing about the literary world, Sam was unable to enlighten her any more than he could enlighten himself. Mr. Sargent's letter asking Sam to drop into the agent's office made it perfectly plain that the invitation was being extended because Mr. Sargent had seen and liked Sam's story in *Landscape,* but that was all the letter did make plain. It did not occur to Sam that Mr. Sargent had asked him to drop in because Mr. Sargent might want to take him on as a client, since it had not yet occurred to Sam that he was or wanted to be a writer. He had not yet had time to take the events of that night in Mr. Brunschweig's store, and their consequences, and relate them to the life that lay ahead of him. It had been enough thus far to enjoy the relief the events had brought to the life he had been living. Nonetheless, Sam sensed what his mother had sensed and then expressed: the letter from Claude Sargent was "the beginning."

It was very upsetting, therefore, after solving the problem that had for three days plagued him, namely, how to get to Mr. Sargent's office, to find now that he was here, sitting beside Mr. Sargent's desk in the tuxedo he had slipped into in the Grand Central men's room, that he could not answer Mr. Sargent's question about why he had written "The Ways of Men Must Sever." Sam, struggling to think of a sensible reply, did not blame the fat man with the sad but pleasant face for looking annoyed.

"I'm not trying to probe into your subconscious or any of that nonsense," the literary agent said. "I'm merely trying to explain to you why you got ten dollars from *Landscape* for a story that the *Post* or *Collier's* or *American Bride* would have been happy to pay you five hundred for—if they could have fit it in."

There was a small, preparatory squeaking of springs from the wing chair at the other side of the desk, and Sam shifted his glance from the painting of the naked girl on the wall behind Mr. Sargent to the world-famous Western writer, or as much of the neat little man as could be seen.

Flicking the tips of his mustache with a neatly manicured forefinger, Kenyon Poole said in his Panhandle drawl, "Don't you think it would be simpler, Claude, if you explained to Mr. Silver why the *Post* and *American Bride* couldn't have fit his story in?"

"Well, sure, yes," Mr. Sargent said grudgingly. He took a sip of coffee, hiked himself forward, and said, "Magazines like *American Bride* would never use your story, Mr. Silver, because it's about Jews."

Sam, whose glance had gone back to the naked girl in the oil painting, was aware as he felt his face grow hot that he had moved sharply in the hollowed-out, green-upholstered length of fluted column in which he sat.

"You know," Kenyon Poole drawled, "any time this Cordell Hull who's running the State Department gets tired and quits, and Roosevelt is looking around for a successor with real delicacy and tact, why, Claude, I think I'll recommend you."

"Huh?" Mr. Sargent said, and then, as the fleshy face flushed as red as Sam supposed his own face looked, the literary agent said, "For God's sake, Ken, you don't think I meant anything anti-Semitic by that remark, do you?"

"My thoughts are irrelevant at the moment," said the author of *The Small Meal*. "I was thinking of what Mr. Silver might be thinking."

"No, no," Sam said hastily, angry with himself because he had allowed the conversation to take a turn that he knew could only hurt him. At nineteen he had already learned that one of the problems attached to being a Jew is the gentile who wants desperately to make it plain that he doesn't believe there is a problem. "I didn't think Mr. Sargent meant anything."

"Of course I didn't," Mr. Sargent said firmly, but the firmness in his voice did not conceal the uneasy look in his eyes as he examined Sam furtively while he continued: "I don't mean that there is anything wrong with 'The Ways of Men Must Sever' because it's about Jews. On the contrary. That's the story's great strength. It tackles its subject without a hint of equivocation. The girl thinks the principal of the school is an anti-Semite. His actions for a long time have infuriated her. She has not known how to pay him back. Now, at last, on graduation night, because the school play happens to be *The Merchant of Venice,* she sees a way to fight back against the anti-Semitic school principal. She seizes the opportunity, wins what she wants, and in the process loses the boy's college scholarship. It's brilliant. Absolutely brilliant, Mr. Silver."

"But *American Bride* would never run it," Kenyon Poole said.

"That's all I meant," Claude Sargent said, the uneasy look still fixed on Sam. "I don't know why it is, but it's been that way all the years I've been a literary agent: you can sell material by Jewish writers, but you can't sell material if the subject matter is Jews themselves."

"Not in all media," Kenyon Poole said.

"No, that's true," Mr. Sargent said. "In the field of the novel, the Jew or the so-called Jewish question works fine. By that I mean if the novel is any good, the fact that it is about the Jewish question, unquote, will not stop it from becoming a best-seller, but it sure as hell will stop it from picking up the gravy that, for example, a Western novel like *The Small Meal* or any one of your other books, Ken, always picks up. I mean magazine serialization, book club distribution, movie sale, and so on."

"The theatre, too," Kenyon Poole said. "That's still open."

"Yes, Jews are still okay on the stage," Claude Sargent said. "But you know, now, it's funny. Take movies. I've been dealing with the boys on the Coast for years. Sold them I don't know how much stuff. But I've never been able to sell them a Jewish story. Which is curious, when you stop to think about it, because half the studios are owned by Jews, if not more than half. Most of the brains and talent are Jewish. Take the Jew out of the picture industry, and you've got no industry left. Almost, anyway. Yet they never think of doing a Jewish story. The British Empire? The French Revolution? The unification of Italy? Why, those Jewish boys on the Coast are madly in love with the British Empire and all that other stuff. When you look at the pictures they turn out, and the amount of money they spend on them, you'd think they worry more about the dismemberment of His Majesty's realm than Stanley Baldwin. But a Jewish story? Poison. They turn and run. I've often wondered why."

"If you've been a victim for two thousand years," Kenyon Poole said, "I imagine you become a trifle self-conscious."

"Yes, I suppose," Claude Sargent said. He picked up the copy of *Land-*

scape and again allowed the thick pages to run off his thumb for a few moments. "On the other hand, if you've been a victim for two thousand years, and then you find yourself in a position of power, I should think you'd want to stop cringing and stand up straight. Like this girl in your story, Mr. Silver. I like her guts. I like what she did to that son of a bitch of a principal. I admire her spirit. I'm sure you do, too, Mr. Silver. That's what comes through in the story. Your admiration for that girl."

Sam had enough self-control to avoid uttering the two words that erupted in his startled mind: "*It does?*" His attitude toward the characters in his story had never even occurred to him during the hours in Mr. Brunschweig's store while he was setting down his Pitman squiggles. It didn't seem possible that he could admire Jennie for what she had done to him, but if that was what Mr. Sargent had felt in the story, there was no point in upsetting or annoying him with corrections. Not at this ticklish moment in their meeting, when they were talking about Jews and Sam still did not know why Mr. Sargent had asked him to drop in.

"Yes," Sam said, "I guess I do."

"Of course you do," Mr. Sargent said. "And it is precisely because you do, that this story is so impressive and why someone like Bud Bienstock would never buy it for *American Bride,* even though Bud is himself a Jew."

"Bud serialized *The Small Meal,*" Kenyon Poole said. "And there's a Jew in it."

"*In,* yes, but not *about,*" Claude Sargent said. "Max Cohen in *The Small Meal* owns the dry-goods store in Firestone Fork, and he's a nice, decent man who hides your hero Slim when the U.S. Cavalry boys are hunting him. Ken, if the whole novel had been *about* Max Cohen, Bud Bienstock never would have serialized it in *American Bride*. You know that."

"I suppose I do," Kenyon Poole said. "But I could never write a whole novel about Max Cohen. I can only observe him from the outside. I can't feel him as a human being from the inside. It takes a Jew to write a real Jew."

"Shakespeare wrote Shylock," Mr. Sargent said.

"No," Kenyon Poole said. "Shylock is not a Jew the way this angry girl in Mr. Silver's story is a Jew, or rather Jewess. Shylock is a literary creation. Jews in Shakespeare's day were not real to the people of the worlds they lived in. They were a bundle of images and attitudes created by other people, who saw them as sort of cardboard cutouts labeled pawnbrokers, usurers, shrewd financial manipulators wearing funny clothes and curls at their temples. Shakespeare gathered all those images and attitudes and, because he was a great poet, he got some great poetry out of the gathered stuff. But great poetry is not a human being. If it's a Jew I'm looking for, a real human being, I'll take Mr. Silver's girl in this story any day rather than Mr. Shakespeare's Shylock."

"I wish I could get people like Bud Bienstock to take her," Claude Sargent said. "Know what he did once? Bud? I've got a client who shall be nameless, a woman as a matter of fact, and one of the best slick fictioneers in the business. You know the kind of stuff: love in the advertising set and so on. Well, this gal has no illusions about her work. She does it for dough. Any mass-circulation magazine on the stands is bound to run three or four of her stories every year, and Bud Bienstock is her best customer. She happens to be a Jewish girl, a fact nobody would know from her fancy by-line, and one day I guess she got sort of fed up with what she was doing, so she wrote one of her regular smooth jobs—the plot had something to do with a golf tournament in a plush commuter town and the rivalry between two young matrons whose husbands are bucking for the same vice-presidency in the same Madison Avenue agency. The only difference between this story and the three thousand others my gal had written and sold over the years was that for once, instead of naming the two rival couples Lowell or Jones or Crawford or any of those nice antiseptic names the people in magazine fiction are always named, my gal called these two couples Mr. and Mrs. Hyman Ginzberg and Mr. and Mrs. Irving Levy.

"Well, when I read the manuscript, I called her up and asked what she was trying to pull? She laughed and said never mind, just you send the effing thing over to Bud Bienstock at *American Bride* because I told him the story at lunch two weeks ago and he said he loved it and asked me to write it for him. I asked her if she'd told Bud these two country-club commuter couples were named Ginzberg and Levy? Of course not, she said, giggling, and I said well, kid, Bud will reject the story. Let's see if he does, my gal said, so I sent the story over to Bud, and of course in a few days it came back with a note saying the story was not up to my gal's usual standard and Bud was sorry but he'd have to turn it down. I called my gal, read her Bud's note, and asked her what she wanted me to do. She giggled again and said have the story retyped at her expense, changing all the Ginzbergs to Gordons and all the Levys to Lewises, and she also changed the title from something like 'Love on the Run' to 'Run for Love' or some such damn-fool thing. I did as she said, sent the story back to Bud without any comment, and a few days after that he called and said he was glad to see our gal was back in form, this was one of the best stories she'd ever done for him, and he liked it so much he was hiking her price, which was already practically astronomical, five hundred bucks per story. What do you think of that?"

Kenyon Poole laughed and said, "I think it shows, Claude, that you are a smart literary agent to have clients who not only earn pots of money but also have a sense of humor. I don't think it proves Bud Bienstock is anti-Semitic."

"I never said he is," Claude Sargent said. "I merely wanted Mr. Silver, here, who is just embarking on a literary career, to know what he's up against."

"I don't think he's up against anything," Kenyon Poole said. "Are you, Mr. Silver?"

Sam, who had not grasped the significance of much that had been said during the past few minutes, said, "I don't know."

"Let me put it this way," Kenyon Poole said. "Claude, here, is the best literary agent in the business. Everything he's said to you is at least interesting, probably sound, and possibly even helpful. But it's all been said from the standpoint of a man who is not himself a writer." The slender, beautifully manicured hand reached across and picked up the gaudy copy of *Landscape*. "What got into this story, Mr. Silver, and what the editors as well as Mr. Sargent reacted to, got into it not because of anything the author necessarily planned or intended." Kenyon Poole paused and the small forefinger made the two flicking motions toward the points of the large mustache. "What got into this story, Mr. Silver, got into it because the writer, who may not know it himself, is a natural born writer. No offense is intended by that remark, Mr. Silver. It is being made to you by another natural born writer, and no vanity is intended by *that* remark, Mr. Silver. I merely want to make it crystal-clear that one natural born writer knows he is talking to another natural born writer. *Is* that crystal-clear?"

Sam tried to say yes, but his voice refused to function, so he nodded, keeping his eyes fixed on the sharp brown eyes that slanted downward in a slightly sinister way.

"Writers like Claude's gal who writes slicks are a dime a dozen," Kenyon Poole said. "Natural born writers are not." He paused, smiled gently, and the Texas drawl emerged almost as a whisper. "We're a rare breed, Mr. Silver. Not because with experience, with the acquisition of technical skills, with a growing knowledge of the market place, we can earn more money than bank presidents. No." The small, handsomely shaped head shook slowly from side to side. "We're a rare breed, Mr. Silver, because we can do something nobody else on God's green earth can do. Something we can do for ourselves, without any help. Something human beings have been trying to do for themselves since the human brain began to understand what we have to get through every day between waking and sleeping, from the cradle to the grave. Only natural born writers can do it, Mr. Silver. Only people like you and me can go to a door, and open it, and step through, and pull the door shut behind us. Only people like you and me can turn our backs on the whole insane mess. Only people like you and me can get away. Only people like you and me are free. No matter what happens, no matter what closes in, we can always get rid of it by writing about it, the way you wrote about this graduation-night experience."

Kenyon Poole looked down at the copy of *Landscape,* then up again at Sam. "As long as we play fair, that is," the slow, drawling voice continued. "Fair with ourselves. As long as we make honorable use of the bag of tools we were born with. Once we start using them for phony purposes, for jimmying open doors that lead to fame, let us say, or vaults that contain gold, once we blunt our tools in ways like that, we lose the gift we were born with. We stop being able to do for ourselves what only we, Mr. Silver, because we are natural born writers, once had the ability to do. We stop being able to go to that door, and open it, and step through, and pull the door shut behind us on the whole insane mess. In short, Mr. Silver, we stop being free men. That's when so many natural born writers turn to other things. Things like alcohol, for instance." The small, neat head moved again, slowly, from side to side. "It's a very poor substitute. So are all the others. Nothing ever replaces that set of tools you were born with. It's better not to blunt them." Kenyon Poole dropped the copy of *Landscape* back on the desk and said, "Don't be sore at me, Top."

"For what?" Claude Sargent said.

"Okay, make jokes," Poole said.

"Look, Ken—"

"No, don't make jokes," Kenyon Poole said quietly, and it seemed to Sam that the vibrant voice suddenly sounded tired. "I'll have the book finished before I have to go up to the farm to get dried out again. That's a promise." He stood up, and Sam, jumping up out of politeness, was sorry he had. It seemed wrong to be taller than the man with the mustache. Poole held out his hand and smiled. "I've got to get to work. It was nice meeting you. By the way, what instrument do you play?"

Sam said, "Instrument?"

The Western writer touched the satin lapel of Sam's borrowed dinner coat. "Soup and fish," Kenyon Poole said. "Only waiters and musicians wear them at midday. Somehow, you don't look like a hash slinger to me. I figure you stopped in to see Claude on your way to work, and I couldn't help wondering what instrument you play in your band?"

"Uh," Sam said, "piano."

"I hope to hear you some day," Kenyon Poole said. "Don't pay too much attention to what Claude says. Keep your job with the band, and take the ten bucks from things like *Landscape,* and tell people like Bud Bienstock what they can do with the other four hundred and ninety. So long, Top. Give my love to Sophie."

For several moments after Poole was gone Mr. Sargent busied himself with the percolator and Sam was ashamed to be stealing furtive looks at the oil painting on the wall.

"Coffee now?" Claude Sargent finally said.

"No, sir," Sam said. "Thanks."

Mr. Sargent filled his green mug and said, "You really work in a band?"

Sam hesitated, then said, "No, sir."

"Why'd you say yes to Ken?" Mr. Sargent said.

Sam, who didn't know why, thought for a while and then, very slowly, said, "I'm not sure, but I think, if I'd told him he was wrong, his feelings would have been hurt."

Mr. Sargent's sad face looked sadder than ever as he nodded. "Five years ago, hell, as little as two years ago, Ken Poole would never have made that mistake." The fat man took a sip of coffee, then sighed, and his sad face broke into the wonderful smile. "You mind telling me why you *are* wearing the tuxedo?"

Sam hesitated again, and then, before he realized he had reached a decision, he found himself telling the truth. Sixteen years later, as the taxi —in which he had come across town from his son Billy's performance as Calpurnia in *Julius Caesar* at the Porte School—pulled up in front of the Oatley-Wicke Building on Lower Park, Sam realized that was the key to his long relationship with Top Sargent: he had always been able to tell the older man the truth.

"Twenty-one, please," Sam said as he stepped into the elevator. In spite of his uneasiness about this visit, and his awareness that he always carried a certain amount of apprehension with him whenever he visited his agent's office, Sam could not help smiling at his recollection of that first time when the elevator had whisked him up from the lobby done in two shades of brown marble. God, what a green kid he had been! Troubled because he had just learned from the directory downstairs that the other Sargent of Sargent & Sargent was a woman! Sam wondered what it would be like, now that Top's health and mind had begun to slip noticeably, to continue doing business through Sargent & Sargent if that woman had not been around?

"Twenty-one," the operator said, and as Sam stepped out of the car, he stopped wondering and gave himself up to gratitude. Without Sophie it would have been impossible to continue. Top, who Sam figured must now be pushing seventy, was simply not up to the job any more. Although Sam, like most of the older Sargent & Sargent clients, would sooner have taken a financial beating than let the old man suspect he had the slightest doubt about Top's capacities. Like Sam, most of these older clients were willing to pretend that Top was still the active head of the agency so long as they knew that Sophie, alert and tough, was on the job, fielding all the balls Top missed, double-checking every move he made, making the moves he now more and more frequently forgot to make. Which made it all the more puzzling and troubling that Sophie, when Sam had talked to her on the phone from Sutton Crescent that morning, should have refused to clarify the curious message Top had left the night before with Sam's answering service.

Sam pushed in the door and entered the windowless reception room that was still furnished with the same three frayed cane-bottom chairs, the still life of three lopsided lemons on the wall, and the piece of ancient furniture that still looked like an up-ended egg crate. Miss Tischler, who was obviously sixteen years older but still looked to Sam exactly as she had looked when he first saw her, glanced up from her interminable game of readdressing the mail of Sargent & Sargent clients. After surveying him for a few moments across the thick, sickle-shaped lenses, her round, puckered face spread in a small smile.

"Oh, Mr. Silver," she said, getting up. "Mr. Sargent said to bring you along the moment you arrived."

"Any of these for me?" Sam said, nodding toward the envelopes Miss Tischler, clearly with reluctance, was leaving temporarily behind.

"No, I don't think so," she said hastily, like a child trying with an unconvincing lie to prevent an adult from interfering with a game that is not yet finished. "I'll have a look, Mr. Silver, while you're in with Mr. Sargent, and if there are any for you, I'll bring them in."

She wouldn't, of course. That would spoil the game. To play it properly the readdressed envelopes had to go out of the Sargent & Sargent offices as they had come in, through the mails. Sam followed the ageless player into the narrow, poorly lighted corridor; and just before she reached the archway at the end that led to Top's office, Miss Tischler took the paper sack from the pocket of her long brown dress and, as she had been doing for years, popped a peppermint into her mouth. Then, with the gestures and intonations that had not varied with two decades of repetition, she pulled aside the green rep curtain, said, "Here's Mr. Silver," waited for Sam to pass through, then dropped the curtain.

"Hello, Sam," Claude Sargent said from behind the cut-out desk. "Come on in."

"Hello, Top," Sam said, coming in. "How are you?"

"All right for an old man," said the man who, unlike almost everybody and everything else in the Sargent & Sargent offices, had indeed grown old. "I ordered you a tuna on rye," he said, which was what Top always said when Sam came to lunch. "Hope that's okay?"

"That's perfect," said Sam, which was what he always said, and as he always did when he slipped out of his topcoat, he stole a long glance at the magnificently proportioned girl in the murky oil painting on the wall. As always it made Sam wonder whether women had been built differently during the late years of the last century, when this picture had been painted for the saloon out of which Top had bought it, or whether the artists of the day had been inclined toward a romantic exaggeration that viewers of their work would find more pleasing, especially after a few drinks. Avoiding the torture rack fashioned from the length of fluted column, Sam dropped into the wing chair, and said, "Where's your sandwich?"

"I'm not having one," Top said. "The doctor says a tuna on rye contains six hundred calories. Miss Tischler is ordering up something more appropriate for an old gaffer on a diet. Coffee now?"

"Yes, please," Sam said, aware of a sudden feeling of sadness. A time he had for so long regarded as changeless had suddenly come to an end. For sixteen years lunch with Top Sargent had meant tuna on rye not only for Sam but also for the shrewd old man who looked like a basset hound wearing a desklike skirt. Picking up half his sandwich from the paper plate, as Top busied himself with the percolator on the window sill, Sam felt not unlike the one member of a secret society who is still allowed to practice a pleasurable ritual denied by edict to other members. Wishing he could think of something more entertaining to say, Sam said, "I got your message."

"Of course you got my message," Top said. "Or you wouldn't be here. That sandwich any good?"

"Fine," said Sam, whose affection for tuna on rye had remained as constant as Miss Tischler's passion for peppermints. "They still make the best one in New York."

"Well, they used to," Top said, setting the green mug full of black coffee at Sam's elbow. "When I first rented this office and Miss Tischler first started ordering them up for me, they were just a hole in the wall, around the corner on the Fortieth Street side of the building, treating every customer like a long-lost brother, and for fifteen cents they gave you a sandwich you could hardly lift. Now it's practically a damned night club, with fancy leather stools that squish up and down, and indirect lighting that makes everybody look the color of a baboon's ass, and the waitresses wear those foolish lace caps, and when they take your order on the phone they act like you've interrupted them in a conversation with the Pope, and not only have the sandwiches gone up to fifty-five cents, but they're now about as big as a silver dollar, and Miss Tischler says she's sure they're cutting the tuna fish by mixing it with diced white bread to make a can of the stuff go twice as far. Some world we've come to live in, eh, Sam?"

"Oh, it's not so bad," Sam said. "I imagine somebody was complaining about the size of the tuna fish sandwiches outside the tent of Henry V at Agincourt. When I was a boy, just out of high school, for a nickel you could get anywhere on Sixth Avenue a delicious piping-hot potato knish as big as that girl's left tit up there, and if you were feeling flush and could afford to splurge a whole dime on your lunch, why, man, Top, you could get—"

Sam's voice stopped as he stared at the tray with which Miss Tischler had just pushed her way into the room. On it, in separate paper plates, were two generous slices of apple pie, each surmounted by two scoops of vanilla ice cream. Between the plates stood a tall cardboard container on the side of which was scrawled "Choc. Malt." Sam grinned quickly and whistled softly and turned toward Top, and at once the grin slid away and the whistle died on his lips. The pouchy, shapeless old face was pink with embarrassment.

"You don't have to look at me that way," Top Sargent growled. "Pie is only two hundred calories a serving, and this ice cream has practically no calories at all because they make the stuff out of chemicals these days, and this thing is just a drink like any other, no more than a glass of milk really, so while it looks like a lot, counted as calories it doesn't come to as much as your God-damned tuna on rye, and besides to hell with that bloody doctor, and to hell with you."

"Okay, okay, okay, knock it off," Sam said, wishing for the first time in sixteen years that he was not here. "I didn't say anything to get your back up, so just calm down." The shrewd old man behind the desk was now merely old. Even Billy in his most unreasonable fits of petulance no longer sounded as childish as the senior member of the firm of Sargent & Sargent had just sounded. "I'm merely jealous, that's all," Sam said, and he turned to Miss Tischler. "Think you could get petty cash to pay for one of those chocolate malteds for me?"

"Of course," Miss Tischler said. "If you really want one, Mr. Silver."

"Thanks," Sam said. "I really do."

The ageless old lady nodded and went out.

"The hell you do," Top Sargent said quietly, but he picked up the paper fork and went at the pie, gulping huge lumps and making snuffling noises, as though he was afraid Sam might snatch it from him or ask to share it. In the middle of the second piece the old man slowed down, drew a deep breath, and said as he took a more leisurely bite, "Any word from Bud Bienstock on the serial?"

Playing the game all the old Sargent & Sargent clients had been playing since Top's memory had become a noticeable problem, Sam said with precisely documented casualness, "Sophie told me on the phone this morning that you'd told her Bud said he liked *They Told Me You Were Dead* and he'd buy it if I'd fix the end and separate the hero and the heroine so they won't offend Bud's *American Bride* readers by leading them to think just because I said in the story the hero and the heroine live in apartments one above the other I mean to imply they keep hopping in and out of each other's beds."

Sam paused for breath and thought back over what he had said to see if, in the nonstop sentence, he had dropped enough clues to give the old man a feeling, if Top wanted to have the feeling, that he was in touch with the situation. The old man, scraping greedily for the last fragments of pie and ice cream on the paper plate, was silent for a few moments. Then, having captured the last fragments and licked the fork clean, Top Sargent said, "Got any ideas on the ending?"

"Not yet," Sam said. "But it'll come."

"Sure," the old man said. "It always does. But if it doesn't come, if you get stuck and want to talk it out—"

"Thanks," Sam said. "I sure will."

"That's what I'm here for," Top said, and then he grinned. "That, and seeing to it guys like Bud Bienstock pay you what you're worth. Maybe after this serial I'll hit him up for a raise. Time you were getting fifty thousand out of that guy."

Since Sam had passed the fifty-thousand mark three years before, and for his last two *American Bride* serials had been paid sixty thousand, he thought it best, as an old and loyal Sargent & Sargent client, to shift the area in which the game was played.

"Brought you some greetings," he said. "Tom Sacheverell said to say hello."

Top's eyes, concentrated on the level of chocolate malted descending rapidly in the cardboard container under his nose as he sucked hard on the straw, now rose and spread wide with surprise. He released the straw, licked his lips, blew out a long, happy, satiated sigh, and said, "Tom? Where'd you see him?"

"This morning, over at the Porte School," Sam said. "The kids were giving a play, and his boy and mine were in it. I happened to get seated next to Tom, and we talked a minute."

The Passover-grape-blue eyes came alight with some of their old smoky shrewdness as the pouches of parchment-colored skin gathered tight and narrowed the lids. "Tom say anything to you about a correspondence school course in writing he's thinking of getting involved in?"

Surprised, Sam said, "No," and then, apologetically, "As a matter of fact he did, but he made me promise not to say anything about it to you. As long as you seem to know about it, though—"

Top nodded and said, "And you did hold the franchise by saying no." He hiked himself forward on his elbows in the old familiar gesture, as though the desk were a skirt and he was gathering the wooden folds around him, and said, "Sam, you're not thinking of joining Sacheverell in this damn-fool thing, are you?"

"Look," Sam said, "I've got enough work on my hands finding nice cellophane-wrapped endings for Bud Bienstock's serials."

The old man nodded and said, "You stick to that kind of work. That's your job. This correspondence course crap is just a racket. I don't mind a bunch of third-raters cooking up a scheme like this and putting it over on the poor suckers who want to be writers. Third-raters are entitled to indulge in a little petty larceny every now and then to keep their names and photographs in front of the public and give themselves the illusion that they're better than third-raters. But a first-rater like Tom Sacheverell—" Top Sargent paused and shook his head sadly.

"Is he through?" Sam asked.

The sagging pouches around the eyes drew together again to create a touch of the old sharp look. "What makes you ask that?"

Sam shrugged and said, "I remember your once saying writers never get involved in peripheral schemes like lending their names to correspondence courses until they're either washed up as writers or think they're washed up. It occurred to me that maybe this Pacific kick Sacheverell's been on since the war ended, maybe it's played out, although I must say I never suspected that from the way The Barrier Reef was reviewed and from its position on the best-seller list."

"No, that's not what's washed up," Top Sargent said. "This last book is not doing as well as the others, but that's just between us. We don't want it to get around, because the publisher's printed a hundred thousand and they're stacked up in the bookstores, and you know how people are. Just let a whisper get around that The Barrier Reef isn't moving as well as it should, and next thing you know, it won't be moving at all. Sophie and I think they'll get rid of fifty or sixty thousand, and my guess is Tom can run this Pacific thing for another two or three books, although not at the old pace, of course, so that part of it's all right. Where he's washed up, though, is in the sack."

Startled, Sam said, "Huh?"

Top nodded and said, "Poor bastard can't get it up any more."

"Oh, for Christ's sake," Sam said. "How the hell do you know?"

"Madge Sacheverell told Sophie."

"My God," Sam said. "The things women tell each other."

"Which is what makes them different from men?"

"No, but hell, Top, can you imagine one man telling another he's finished in that way?"

"Madge didn't say *she* was finished. She told Sophie that *Tom* is finished. It makes a difference."

"Does Tom Sacheverell think his sexual powers will be restored if he screws several thousand helpless victims out of money they should be devoting to studying bookkeeping or getting their kids' teeth straightened?"

Top Sargent shrugged and said, "Apparently. You know writers."

"As well as I'll ever know them," Sam said with a shrug. "What I don't know is agents."

"You don't have to know agents," the old man said. "As long as you know me."

"Well, you're getting pretty damn incomprehensible," Sam said, and then, realizing that the jocular note might be misinterpreted by a man all too conscious of his failing powers, Sam added quickly, "About your telephone messages, anyway."

"My telephone messages?" Top said, and Sam wondered if the old man realized how noticeably as he grew older his conversation had begun to take on the word patterns of a woman he had never met. Like Sam's mother, whose notion of a reply to a question was a question of her own, Claude Sargent said, "What's wrong with my telephone messages?"

"They're getting less and less informative," Sam said. "You call me last night and leave a message with my answering service I should call you back first thing in the morning because it's urgent. I call you back first thing in the morning and I get Sophie on the phone, who tells me first she doesn't know what the message is about, and then second, yes, it is important, but you want to tell me why yourself, so would I please come in for lunch, because you're out at the neck tugger getting your sacroiliac pulled back into place."

"Yes, well," Claude Sargent said. "How's that sandwich, by the way?"

"We went all through that," Sam said.

"So we did," the old man said. "More coffee?"

"Cut it out," Sam said. "What's this important thing you wanted to see me about?"

"Well, maybe it isn't all that important," Top said. "I mean I didn't mean to make it sound all that important. I just wanted to know if you owned any first editions of Kenyon Poole's books."

Sam had gone as far as "*You just wanted to know if I owned any first editions of*" before he heard his own voice, realized he was without thought parroting somebody else's words, and stopped. As soon as he did, the thinking started, and with it came so massive a jolt of the pain he had for years been certain he would never again feel, that Sam's mind, trained by his work to avoid repetition, failed him and fell back wearily on the words that had surged through his head that morning at breakfast when Billy, unexpectedly curious about his dead mother, had asked what Jennie had been like: *thus came the impact of tidal waves and earthquakes, without warning, while peaceful citizens, who thought themselves safe and had every reason to believe they were, sat munching their breakfasts, thinking of crops and jobs and dentists' bills.* Sam, who had been munching his sandwich, put it down carefully on the paper plate, and as he dabbed at his lips with the paper napkin, the pain eased slightly, or at any rate came down to a manageable level, and Sam became aware of Top Sargent's voice coming at him across the desk.

"Sorry," Sam said. "I didn't catch that."

"I said you knew him, didn't you?" Claude Sargent said. "Ken Poole?"

"I met him here in your office," Sam said carefully, guiding each word as though it were a tottering drunk. "The first day I dropped in on you, sixteen years ago."

"Yes, of course, that's right," the old man at the other side of the desk said, nodding with pleasure in his triumph of memory. "I'd read your first story in a thing called—what the hell was it called?"

"*Landscape.*"

"That's right," Top said. "Lord God save us, the names they think up for those bloody literary magazines. I liked it and I wrote you a note and the day you dropped in, Ken Poole happened to be here and—" The voice stopped and the sagging bags of flesh again gathered in tight knots around the smoke-blue eyes with a renewed effort at dredging a fragment of the past out of the tangled debris of memory. "There was something about the way you were dressed," Top Sargent said slowly. "You were wearing something funny."

"A tuxedo," Sam said.

"That's right," Top said, and the jowled face spread in a remarkably good facsimile of the old wonderful smile. "You were working as a delivery boy for that man who rented tuxedos and you thought that was the proper thing to wear when dropping in on—" The sentence petered out and the low rumblings of laughter shook the lumpy old body in its wooden skirt. "God," Claude Sargent said, "it's awful to be young, isn't it?"

"Yes," said Sam, who at the moment didn't think it was nearly so awful as being middle-aged.

"Ken liked you, I remember," the old man said. "He was in New York for a while, holed up in a hotel room, trying to get to the end of a book before he got to the end of his sanity and had to turn himself over again to that sanatorium for drunks he practically supported single-handed. I don't remember how that particular race came out, because poor Ken ran so many of them, but I do remember he liked you." Claude Sargent hiked himself further forward into the desk and, with a scowl, said, "Didn't you and Ken later become friends or something?"

"No," Sam said, keeping clear of the raw spot in the middle of the slowly ebbing pain. "I'd hardly call it that."

"Funny," Claude said in a worried voice. "I had this recollection that you and Ken became friends, or something like that." The old man paused, looked at Sam anxiously and said, "You did know him, though, didn't you? I mean there was more to it than that first meeting here in my office, wasn't there?"

"Yes," Sam said. "There was more to it."

The anxiety sank like spilled ink into the creases of the old man's face and he leaned back out of the wooden skirt like a woman shedding her girdle after a tiring day.

"Well, then, good," Claude said. "That's what made me think you might have some first editions of Poole's books. You do have, I hope?"

"I don't know," said Sam. "I got rid of an awful lot of stuff when Billy and I moved into this Sutton Crescent apartment, but I can always look."

"I wish you would," Claude Sargent said. "And if you do have any, Sam, you won't mind lending them to me, will you?"

"Of course," Sam said. He paused, to test the sensitivity at the point of impact, and was pleased to discover that it wasn't too bad. The pain had nothing to do with Claude Sargent. The old man had no way of knowing the things Sam knew. Sam could go back to talking about Kenyon Poole as though the discussion dealt with a total stranger. He said, "But what's all the mystery about, Top?"

"Who said there's any mystery?"

"Oh, knock it off," Sam said. "If there's no mystery, why couldn't you have told my answering service last night what you wanted? I could have looked at my shelves before I left the house this morning and either brought you the answer or the books themselves. This way, because you've made such a damn hocus-pocus out of the thing, I won't be able to look for the books until I get home, which won't be till late, I'm afraid, since I've got to go out to Queens to see my mother."

"Well, as a matter of fact," Claude Sargent said, "I didn't want to go leaving messages with Ken Poole's name in it."

"Why the hell not?"

"Oh, you know, Sam. When he died in that plane, there was all that stink in the papers."

"But that was over ten years ago," Sam said. "The whole temper of the country has changed in that time. What in God's name is there to be worried about now? Especially about a dead man?"

"Oh, it's not Ken himself I'm worried about," Claude Sargent said. "It's his daughter."

"His daughter? I didn't know he had a daughter."

"Neither did I," Sargent said. "Until last week I didn't even know he'd ever been married."

"Was he?"

"How do you mean?"

"Well, you say he's got a daughter."

Claude's face cleared. He laughed and said, "Oh, that. No, she's legitimate all right. This was years ago, long before Ken began to write and came to New York and I met him and took him on. This was way back, when he was still a cowboy. The girl was some sort of hash-house waitress, something like that. I can't exactly ask the daughter too many questions on that score, as you can imagine. Besides, I don't think the kid knows too much about her mother."

"The kid?"

"She's twenty-two," Top Sargent said. "The way I get the background, Ken was working on this ranch somewhere near El Paso, and this girl was working *in* El Paso, slinging hash, as I said, or maybe worse, but no matter, because Ken did make an honest woman of her. The marriage didn't last long, as damn few things ever did with Ken, but long enough for him to sire a female child, and then he took to the hills. He kept sending back money, though. Ken never quit that, and the wife and the kid seemed to have got along fine. In a financial way, I mean, because after the mother died Ken set up some sort of trust fund that took the kid through boarding school and continued doing it even after Ken was killed in that plane thing. In fact, the girl's just graduated from Sarah Lawrence, which is how I found out about all this."

"I don't see the connection," Sam said.

"The trust fund was set up before Ken got into the big money," Claude Sargent said. "He replenished it a few times after he did hit it big, but Ken seems to have wanted to keep it just the right size for feeding the girl without fattening her, so to speak. Whatever his motives, and with a man like Ken I doubt that even God Almighty could honestly say He understood all of Ken's motives, the trust seems to have done just that. The kid got the best of everything out of it at boarding school and Sarah Lawrence, and now that she's just graduated and wants to get married, the lawyers tell her the fund is finished."

"And you think my first editions of Kenyon Poole's books, if I find I have any, will replenish it?"

"You sound exactly the way you do when Sophie or I tell you an editor wants you to add something to a story to give it a touch their particular readers expect, and you let me have the icy 'I think you or Sophie would be well advised to inform Mr. Bienstock or Mr. Whoever that a story, unlike a turkey, is not improved with stuffing.'"

"It isn't."

"Very funny, Sam. Very true, probably, too. But I'm not asking you to correct a story. I'm just asking you to lend me, if you happen to own any, your Kenyon Poole first editions. Now surely that's not too much to ask, is it?"

"If I own any, of course you can have them. I'm simply puzzled by all this preposterous hugger-mugger about something that—"

"Something that you as a great big fat successful writer seem to have forgotten all about," Claude Sargent said. "Love."

Upset for reasons he did not understand, Sam said more sharply than he intended, "That's neither fair nor true. If you deny my right to simple curiosity—"

"I'm sorry, Sam," the old man said. "The trouble with getting old is you don't know most of the time what the hell your trouble is. Forgive an old man's short temper, will you? This is really quite simple. The girl's in love with some Harvard kid who's won a Rhodes scholarship to Oxford. He's a math major, or something involving math, maybe atomic stuff, I don't really know. I mean the girl's explained it to me, but I don't follow any of these things any more. The last scientific principle I understood was why the *Monitor* sank the *Merrimac,* or was it the other way around?"

"I can't remember," Sam said. "It was before my time. My war recollections start with a post card from Washington that began like an English ballad with the stark and simple word *Greetings!*"

"Don't complain about your army stint," Claude Sargent said. "You got four serials out of it."

"Yes, but I had to write them myself," Sam said. "Eisenhower hired a ghost, and look how much he got for *his* memoirs."

"The literary principle we learn from this contrast seems obvious," Top Sargent said. "Next time your country needs you, go in as a general. What Ken Poole's daughter needs is some dough. If she can get it, she and this boy could get married and go to England together."

"So you're going to play Cupid by peddling her father's first editions?"

"Of course not," Claude Sargent said. "That first-edition racket doesn't produce the kind of cash these kids would need."

"What would?" Sam said.

"A revival of interest in Ken's work," the old man said. "He's been dead for ten years not only physically but in the literary sense as well. None of his books is in print. Our Extra Rights Department hasn't taken in a nickel on any of his old stuff for almost four years. He's never mentioned in literary discussions or articles. It's as though he never existed, which you and I know is a lot of damned foolishness. Kenyon Poole was one of our great American writers, and if he hadn't been smeared by all the nonsense that broke in the papers ten years ago, he'd be as well known today as Whitman and Melville."

"How well known is that?" Sam said.

"Take a look at some reprint figures and have yourself a moment of slack-jawed astonishment," Claude Sargent said. "If you owned the copyrights on *Moby Dick* and *Leaves of Grass,* out of paperbacks alone you could afford to tell Bud Bienstock to put his ideas for changing the end of *They Told Me You Were Dead* where the monkey put the nuts."

"Where was that?" Sam said.

"If I were younger I would rise from this bloody torture rack and give you a personal demonstration, you impudent young scribbler."

"Young," Sam said. "Thirty-six this month."

"I was sixty-eight last November," Claude Sargent said. "Anything younger than sixty-eight is young, and Ken's daughter is twenty-two, so I'd like to help. With the proper kind of advance work behind the scenes, I think I can get him a posthumous membership in the National Academy."

"Holy hat," Sam said. "You mean he was never elected to that?"

"Kenyon Poole was never elected to anything."

"But look at the people they've *got* in the damned thing!"

"I've looked," Claude said. "That's why I think they'd vote Ken in, now that he's dead. He's no longer a threat to them, and there's nothing a second-rater enjoys more than giving himself an upward boost by being kind to a dead first-rater."

"How do you get people to vote a man into the Academy?"

"Same way you get a man voted into any damn-fool club," Claude said. "You spread the word around for a while among other members. I can do that easily enough because quite a few of these particular members are Sargent & Sargent clients. Then you impress them with the man's worth, which I can do even more easily by passing around to strategic members on the Admissions Committee copies of Ken's books, a few of which I have and a few more of which I hope to borrow from you. Then, when the groundwork's been laid, you come out in the open and ask a few important chaps in the club to write letters proposing your chap for membership."

"Suppose he's blackballed?" Sam said.

"Dead literary figures always get honored, never blackballed," Claude Sargent said. "Wait till you hear some of the honey-scented lies they'll be spreading about me after I'm gone."

"I'll do my best to keep the record straight," Sam said.

"Oh, yes, you will, you sentimental Jew boy."

"Them's fighting words, Top."

The old man looked startled, then frightened, and finally obsequious, all in a swift flow of facial expressions that Sam wished he had not seen and which left him feeling slightly sick.

"I'm sorry, Sam," Claude Sargent said. "You know what I mean."

Since they all assumed he knew what they meant, Sam wondered why they bothered telling him. But to the old man he loved and to whom he had always been able to tell the truth, Sam now told the same lie he always told people like Tom Sacheverell and Mr. Bronson, whom he hated.

"I know, Top. Forget it. You've just got Ken Poole elected posthumously to the National Academy."

"These elections are full-dress international affairs," Claude Sargent said. "Front-page coverage in the European as well as our own press, including excerpts from the speeches and photographs and what not. On the strength of that hoopla, I can not only write such a nice fat reprint contract on every one of Ken's old books that his daughter and her young Rhodes scholar can get married and live in England happily ever after, but I might even win for our old friend Kenyon Poole nothing less than a posthumous Nobel Prize."

"Top," Sam said. "Where do you buy your opium?"

"Fact, Sam. Absolute fact."

"The Nobel Prize for a writer of Westerns?"

"Why not?" the old man said. "They gave it to a writer of Easterns, didn't they?"

"Yes, but that Chinese stuff is special," Sam said. "Lum Fong tilling his rocky scrap of good earth heap big brother of Jeb Jones scraping a living out of his handkerchief-size patch of Carolina hillside. It's that Universal Man malarkey they gave the prize to, not to a writer. Ken Poole never trafficked in cheap symbolism. He was an honest-to-God writer of Westerns."

"He was an honest-to-God writer," Claude Sargent said. "Period."

"What's the difference?"

"Hasn't it ever struck you as peculiar, Sam, that a writer as superb as Kenyon Poole was content to limit his activity to the comparatively minor field of the Western story?"

"Many times."

"Did you ever ask him why?"

"Hell, no, I wouldn't have dared," Sam said. "Besides, I never really knew him that well. Did you ever ask him?"

"I didn't have to," Claude Sargent said. "Ah, here's your rich, delicious, nutritive, and disgustingly fattening chocolate malted."

Sam turned toward the odor of peppermint, took the paper bag from Miss Tischler, who was leaning into the room from the archway, holding aside the curtain, and he said, "Thank you."

She stepped out, the curtain fell into place, and Sam turned back to Claude Sargent.

"Why not?" Sam said.

"If I'd asked Ken why he limited himself to writing Westerns," Claude said, "I think he might have asked what's the matter, aren't you happy with the size of your commissions, or he'd have told me to mind my own business, or maybe what I would have got is a punch in the nose, any one or all of which I probably would have deserved. Especially since I didn't have to embarrass either one of us by asking a question to which I already knew the answer."

"What's the answer?"

"He was scared."

"Kenyon *Poole*?"

"Absolutely."

"Top, you're not making any sense. The man's record speaks for itself."

"Oh, I don't mean physical courage," Claude Sargent said. "Ken Poole had more of that than any man I've ever known. It wasn't danger he was scared of."

"Then what?"

"Intimacy." The old man said quietly, "Nobody can really write well if he's afraid to reveal himself to the reader. There are writers who care more about not revealing something about themselves to the world than they care about the fame or fortune they're trying to get from the world by their writing. So they set limitations on the degree of intimacy to which they're going to allow their readers to have with them. The great ones, of course, never set any limitations on that intimacy. Maybe it never occurred to them to set limitations. And maybe that's what makes them great. If you want to know the kind of man Dickens was, or Tolstoy, say, all you have to do is read their novels. They're as unashamedly unbuttoned as a pair of B.V.D.'s flapping on the clothesline. But if you'd never met Ken Poole, would you have known the kind of man he was from reading, let's say, *The Small Meal?*"

Sam thought of the novel that had shaken him and Jennie when they were members of Miss Mercator's Stratford Club in Grover Cleveland High, and then he thought of the neat little dandified figure with the patent-leather hair and the guardsman's mustache he had first seen lying back like a Mississippi-riverboat-gambler doll in this red wing chair, and he shook his head.

"No, I guess not."

"Because Ken was afraid of something," Claude Sargent said. "He didn't want the reader to get too close. He had what Dickens and Tolstoy had, a great talent, but he had something they were lucky enough to be born without, a secret fear. So Ken set limitations on his talent that prevented the reader from getting close enough to get a look at whatever it was Ken was hiding. That's why he wrote Westerns. A man who writes Westerns, like a man who writes mystery stories, says to the world of letters: don't take me too seriously; don't subject me to the critical examination you give the serious novelist; scrutinize me if you like but don't use the same penetrating yardsticks you use for the other men; after all, I'm not taking myself seriously, why should you? I'm writing Westerns, he protests, I'm just an entertainer."

"I wonder if you're right," Sam said. "It's one of those theories that sounds fine until maybe when you subject it to some of that critical examination you're talking about, it could maybe fall apart?"

"I doubt it," Claude Sargent said. "I know I'm right. I've watched writers doing it for almost half a century. All sorts of writers. Take you, for instance."

"Me?" Sam said.

"You," Claude Sargent said. "You're one of the best slick writers in the business. Probably *the* best. And yet, when you were a nineteen-year-old kid in a borrowed tuxedo, when all you'd written was that one story, 'The Ways of Men Must Sever,' I never thought I'd found me just another money-maker. Hell, no. I thought what I'd found was one of those rare things, a truly great new talent that I'd be proud to have had a hand in placing before the world which—"

The old man's words drained away, and once again his pouched face looked startled, then frightened, and finally obsequious, all in a confused rush, but this time Sam did not leap to the old man's rescue. He couldn't. For this blow he had no arsenal of ready phrases.

"Sam," Claude Sargent said in a small, tight, frightened voice, "I didn't mean—" The voice stopped, almost of its own weight, as though, like the man to whom it belonged, the voice realized what it had been about to say could only underscore not erase the damage. The old man cleared his throat, and announcing firmly his intention to pretend the disaster had not occurred, very deliberately said, "As I was saying earlier, Sam, I think it's time Bud Bienstock came through with a raise, so when you've fixed the ending of *They Told Me You Were Dead*, I'm going to tell him we feel we're entitled to sixty thousand for this one, and the same for the next two."

With equal deliberation, through the blinding pain and rage that drove him to strike back, as though he were sighting a gun, Sam said icily, "We've been getting sixty thousand for over a year, now, Top, on the last two serials."

There was a moment of silence, and then the old man's head dropped, as though the shot had finally penetrated to a vital area, and Claude Sargent said to the desk blotter in a low, harsh, bitter voice, "Why don't they get me a nurse, or just take me out and shoot me?"

Sam Silver, who this time thought surely he was going to be sick, stood up, and with an effort managed to say, "I'll look for those books at home, Top." He turned toward the curtain, saw he was holding the chocolate malted, turned back to the desk, and like a child offering a present to a teacher he has offended, Sam Silver said to the old man he loved and had at least for the moment destroyed, "Here, you drink this, and nuts to the doctors and their God-damn calorie counts."

Out in the dimly lighted corridor, pausing to pull himself together, he realized he couldn't leave the office without doing what every Sargent & Sargent client had been doing since Claude's memory had begun to fail.

"You mind asking Mrs. Sargent if I could see her for a moment?" Sam said to Miss Tischler in the reception room.

"She's got Mr. Titterton in with her, Mr. Silver, and they're going over his manuscript. Could you wait?"

"Not that long," Sam said. "I've got to run out to Queens to see my parents."

"Let me check, then," Miss Tischler said, coming out from behind the stand-up desk and reaching for the peppermint bag in her pocket as she headed for the curtain. When she came back, Sam dragged his eyes from the lemons on the wall, and Miss Tischler said, "Mrs. Sargent asked could you stop by at the apartment for a drink after you come back from Queens?"

"Yes, all right, fine," Sam said, wondering how long it would take before the self-loathing began to ease away. "I'll do that."

*4

The decision by Sam's parents to move from East Tenth Street to Queens had been made, like most decisions in the Silver family, by Sam's mother. Unlike most Silver family decisions, however, this one was made possible by circumstances that Sam's father, inadvertently, it was true, had set in motion.

From the moment when he arrived in America as a twenty-two-year-old Polish immigrant, Mr. Silver had apparently devoted all his spare time to the task of helping to bring other members of his large and complicated family to this country. The task would probably not have been a very difficult one for anybody with limitless funds and, at the very least, a working knowledge of the English language. For Sam's father, who was penniless when he arrived in America and during the succeeding more than half-century never achieved either solvency or a firm grasp of the language of his adopted country, the task must have been almost insurmountable.

Perhaps, it occurred to Sam years later, that was why Mr. Silver embraced it with so much determination. A man living with someone like Sam's mother would need, the grown-up Sam finally grasped, a private world into which he could retreat for solace when the going became too rough. Whether or not these later guesses on Sam's part were correct, there was no guesswork about the facts: Sam's earliest recollections of the sweet but shadowy man who was his father contained indelible images of Mr. Silver sitting at the kitchen table late at night, laboriously studying and filling in the blank spaces on Immigration Department documents; Mr. Silver collecting dollar by dollar from relatives already in America the steerage passage for a relative still in Poland; Mr. Silver writing the endless letters of encouragement to nephews and second cousins and aunts by marriage for whom word from America was the next best thing to being there and a tangible help in sustaining the hope that some day they would be; Mr. Silver trudging off on Saturday mornings in his good suit to the office of the Hebrew Immigrant Aid Society on Lafayette Street for more documents, more advice, more instructions to be relayed to Poland in the endless game by which, like Miss Tischler in the Sargent & Sargent offices, he lived.

The rewards of the game, about which Sam's father never spoke, must have been considerable. To the inner satisfactions of performing without charge a useful service for others who desperately wanted it, was added, as the number of Silver relatives on this side of the Atlantic increased, a circle of grateful admirers whose gratitude not infrequently came embarrassingly close to idolatry. Among these was Abe Ostreich.

With his wife Hannah, Abe was removed just in time to avoid extermination from the clutches of the Nazis by an embassy clerk in Warsaw who was totally unaware, when he stamped the liberating documents, that he had brought to a triumphant close a chain of events set in motion four years earlier by a patient, poor, semiliterate pocket maker on East Tenth Street in New York. Abe Ostreich, on the other hand, never ceased being aware that he and his wife owed their lives to Sam's father. During their first years in America, when Abe worked as a dish washer in a cafeteria on Centre Street, the Ostreichs never allowed a Sunday to pass without coming down from their Bronx flat to sit for a silent, adoring hour or two in the presence of the gentle old man they called, with unabashed reverence, "Uncle Silver." Mrs. Silver, who thought Hannah Ostreich was a boob and Abe a bore, accumulated quite a repertory of caustic comments about their cowlike adoration for the husband she considered a lovable incompetent.

This attitude toward the Ostreichs changed after Pearl Harbor. By that time Abe had "improved" himself from dish-washing on Centre Street to janitoring in Queens. As a result of the wartime housing shortage, janitors assumed an importance they had never before enjoyed. Abe Ostreich was able not only to augment his official income with unofficial gifts from grateful tenants, he was also able at last to repay Uncle Silver with something more than adoration.

Sam was certain that, during the confused weeks after the death of Jennie, his mother had hoped he would suggest that she and his father come to live with Sam in his Gramercy Park apartment to help take care of the then two-year-old Billy. Sam's decision to raise Billy without help was precipitated by a series of eviction notices served by the purchaser of the tenement on East Tenth Street in which Sam had been born and in which his parents had lived all of their married lives. The new owner planned to, and in fact later did, demolish it to make room for a low-cost housing development. Most of the evicted tenants had a certain amount of difficulty in finding new quarters. None had quite the problem faced by Sam's mother.

While her son had not yet achieved, at the time of Jennie's death, the place in the uptown world for which Mrs. Silver had dreamed and schemed since Sam's birth, he was so clearly well on his way that a person of lesser character might have thought her son ungrateful for allowing her to continue living in surroundings that, by comparison with Sam's Gramercy Park home, might have been considered squalid. Not Mrs. Silver. Way stations did not interest her, except as milestones. Sam's Gramercy Park apartment was a good many cuts above the East Tenth Street tenement. But it was still not Park Avenue. Until he reached that ultimate goal, and was able to reach down and lift her to his side at the pinnacle, his mother was content to remain and watch from the place where he had started.

The eviction notice shattered her contentment. She and her husband had to live somewhere. Sam's failure to invite them to live with him on Gramercy Park meant they would have to find a place in which to wait it out until Sam invited them, as his mother was certain some day he would, to live with him uptown. Places of any kind were difficult to find during the war. Into the breach rode Abe Ostreich, now no longer a mere janitor but the "residential manager" of three square blocks of two-story red-brick huts known as Rigo Park Manor, in which lived 306 families. A month after he became a widower, Sam's parents became the 307th.

Nothing about Rigo Park Manor satisfied Mrs. Silver. It was in Queens, a borough for which her feelings were not unlike those Becky Sharp might have had about Lambeth. It was full of families with small children, and Sam's mother, like most people approaching old age, had long ago lost her tolerance for the wailing of infants. It was the domain of Abe Ostreich, for whose intelligence she had a very low regard. It was a modern structure, so that she had to form an entirely new set of living habits, such as, for example, carrying her garbage down the hall to an incinerator instead of, as on East Tenth Street, down to the street to a sidewalk garbage can. And worst of all, getting to Rigo Park Manor from Manhattan was a complicated and time-consuming business.

For Sam, who did not have to live there, this proved to be Rigo Park Manor's chief attraction.

As, with the passing years, the gap between his parents and himself grew wider, the excuse that going to see them took too much time from his business affairs could be relied on with increasing frequency and, with practice, greater conviction. This did not, however, eliminate the basic problem, one aspect of which Sam would have been the first to consider ludicrous if it were not for the fact that it was also relentlessly annoying.

Coming down in the elevator from the Sargent & Sargent offices Sam, in spite of his conscious effort to escape the inevitable by thinking of his dilemma as amusing, could feel the annoyance begin to close in on him.

Getting to Rigo Park Manor from Manhattan via the transportation system provided by the city for the bulk of its citizens, only a small number of whom earned sixty thousand dollars by composing for magazine editors two hundred and twenty pages of double-spaced prose, was not simple. It involved making contact with the Independent Line at some point on Sixth Avenue either by walking or taking a bus; riding out to Union Turnpike on an "E" train; taking the Queens Boulevard bus to Sixty-seventh Avenue; and then walking the remaining distance. Depending on whether the initial contact with the "E" train was made on foot or by bus, the cost for this journey in money was either thirty or forty-five cents; in time, depending on connections, anywhere from seventy minutes to an hour and a half. For citizens like Sam, to whom time was money and who could afford to waste more of the latter than the former, the obvious solution was a taxi, for which the cost was twenty minutes of the former and five dollars, including tip, of the latter.

The choice between the two methods of travel should have been a simple one. Especially to a man like Sam who could not only afford the five dollars but who preferred the speed and comfort of a taxi. The complication was provided by the Department of Internal Revenue. Sam's success as a magazine writer had thrust him into a tax bracket where, in his accountant's phrase, "you gotta nibble to stay alive."

Translated into practical terms, this meant that in order to pay for a five-dollar taxi ride Sam had to earn fifty taxable dollars. If, on the other hand, he could prove to the tax collector that the five-dollar taxi ride had been incurred during the performance of an errand legitimately necessary to the conduct of Sam's business affairs, he could deduct the amount on his tax return as a business expense, the effect of which in practical terms was that the five-dollar ride actually cost him only fifty cents.

The accountant, who had no emotional problems in relation to Sam's parents, insisted that his client keep a log of all taxi rides and, next to each item, write a brief description that would satisfy the Internal Revenue Department. As a result, every time Sam embarked on a visit to his father and mother, he was faced with the same dilemma: should he go by bus, subway, bus, and on foot, and arrive in the state of mental turmoil about his parents that had become the more or less normal condition of his existence in relation to them; or should he go by taxi, and add to his already overburdened conscience the shameful knowledge that the following morning, in his log, next to the record of his visit would appear a scrap of fiction: "To Queens by taxi to confer with Abe Ostreich re: his recollections of Warsaw in early days of Nazi take-over in connection with projected four-parter for *American Bride*. Stopped in to see Mom and Pop."

If the dilemma was always the same, so was the solution. Coming out of the Oatley-Wicke Building into the thin February sunlight of lower Park Avenue, Sam signaled to the driver of the first taxi in the parked rank and, as the cab jerked into motion toward him, Sam silently told his conscience to get off its feet and relax for a while.

If he didn't use a cab both ways, he would never get back from Queens in time to drop in at the Sargent apartment for a drink before he picked up Rebecca Meissen for dinner, and after what had just happened over the tuna and rye in Top's office, Sam knew he would have no rest until he learned from Sophie the true reason why Top had invited him in for lunch. Even if the meeting had not ended in the small disaster of unexpected brutality, Sam would have known that the old man who had been his agent for sixteen years had not told him the truth. Certainly not, as the lawyers in Samuel Silver's stories always put it, the whole truth and nothing but the truth. Claude Sargent wanted something more from Sam than his first editions of Kenyon Poole's books. What could it be? More important, Sam felt, why was Top leaving it to Sophie to tell him?

"Driver," Sam said as he climbed into the cab, dropped onto the seat, and pulled the door shut with a decisive bang. "We're going out to Queens." He made the statement sound as firm as the bang of the door. Many taxi drivers, Sam had discovered, did not want to go to Queens because they could not count on a fare back. Sam had also discovered that, if you allowed yourself to be influenced by the likes and dislikes of taxi drivers, you might just as well walk. "Go across the Fifty-ninth Street bridge and out Queens Boulevard, and I'll tell you when to turn."

"What part of Queens?" the driver said.

"It's a place called Rigo Park Manor," Sam said. "I'll show you."

"Might make better time we go Triboro and then out Grand Central Parkway?"

"No, we won't," Sam said. "I've done it both ways. Fifty-ninth and Queens Boulevard is quicker."

"Most days, yeah," the driver said. "But today they got this U.N. thing."

"What U.N. thing?"

"Them Russians flew over for this meeting? Tzinawla papers? Whatever, anyway, all of midtown they got it loused up with cops and Christ knows what."

"To hell with the Russians," Sam said. "This is my town. Let's go Fifty-ninth and Queens Boulevard."

"Whatever you say, Mac," the driver said.

What Sam said would have been blue-penciled by Bud Bienstock out of any manuscript intended for *American Bride*. Uttering the words, however, even though under his breath, made Sam feel better. It occurred to him, as the taxi swung up onto the ramp that carried Park Avenue traffic across Grand Central, that he always felt better when he left the Sargent & Sargent offices. The free-lance writer's calls on his agent were not unlike visits to the dentist. Even when the apprehension with which he went in was justified by the pain of the treatment, the relief of getting out was by contrast enough to create the illusion of exhilaration. The pattern, Sam remembered, had been established during that very first visit, when in his borrowed tuxedo he had met for the first time not only Claude Sargent but also Kenyon Poole. That night, when Sam got back to the East Tenth Street kitchen, his mother knew at once that he had made the momentous visit.

"First eat, then talk," she said. "I'll wait to hear from the beginning."

Sam, however, could not wait. He had been bubbling with excitement for ten hours, ever since he had left Mr. Sargent's office. All afternoon, delivering tuxedos for Mr. Brunschweig, and all evening, sitting through his classes at the Lafayette Business Institute, he had been waiting for this moment. He started talking at once. For a while, during his description of the scene as he switched into the tuxedo in the Grand Central men's room, the only interruptions were by Sam himself: pauses to spoon up soup or strip a drumstick. Later, when he came to a description of the Oatley-Wicke Building and the Sargent & Sargent offices, Mrs. Silver began to interrupt with questions. She was clearly as puzzled as Sam still was by a good deal of what had happened that noon in the room on lower Park Avenue dominated by the huge oil painting of the naked girl.

"It's a business, no?" she said.

"Oh, yes," Sam said. "Lot of rooms and telephones and outside a switchboard, all that. It's called a literary agency."

"What do they sell?"

"Stories," Sam said. He picked up the copy of *Landscape*, without which he had not eaten a single meal since the mailman had left it in the box downstairs. "Like mine here."

"But yours in there," his mother said, "you sold it yourself. You sent the story to the magazine and they sent you back the check."

"For ten dollars," Sam said. "If I'd given the story to Mr. Sargent, and he'd taken it up to the magazine, and they'd bought it from him, they'd have paid more than ten dollars."

"Why?" Mrs. Silver asked.

Sam chewed his chicken and thought about the conversation with Mr. Sargent that had taken place after Kenyon Poole left.

"I'm not too sure," Sam said. "I mean there was so much he said, this Mr. Sargent, that I haven't got it all straight yet, but what he said, he said there's a lot of magazines, dozens of them, maybe even hundreds, I guess, all over the country, and all over the world, too, I guess, and the people who run them, the editors, they keep getting stories in the mail from people, like these editors of this magazine, *Landscape*, they got mine in the mail. Just opening them and reading them is a lot of work. Mr. Sargent said with most magazines it's so much work that they can't afford to hire enough people to do it all, so a lot of the stories never get read at all. They just mail them right back. But they never do that with a story that comes in from someone like Mr. Sargent. If the story comes in to the magazine from a literary agent, they read it because they figure it can't be absolutely terrible or the agent wouldn't have wasted his time or his stamps on it, see?"

"This much, sure, what's there to see?" Mrs. Silver said. "With bread eat. Not just plain chicken. Take a bite bread. What I don't see, why should this man, this agent, why should he waste his time or his stamps on it?"

"Because he gets paid for it," Sam said. "He takes for himself a percentage of the money he gets out of the magazine for the story."

"How much?"

"Ten per cent, Mr. Sargent said."

"So from the ten dollars you got for this story," Mrs. Silver said, reaching across the kitchen table to touch the copy of *Landscape* beside Sam's plate, "if Mr. Sargent sold it for you instead you sent it in yourself, he'd take a dollar and he'd give you nine?"

"That's right," Sam said.

"Sam," his mother said. "Nine is less than ten."

"I know, Ma, but four hundred and fifty is a lot more than ten."

"What four hundred and fifty?"

"If Mr. Sargent had sold this story, Ma, he said he could have got five hundred dollars for it, which means he'd get ten per cent, that's fifty, and I'd get the rest, four hundred and fifty."

"Sam," Mrs. Silver said. "He was all right?"

"Who?" Sam said.

"This Mr. Sargent," his mother said.

"Certainly he was all right, Ma."

"Not shicker, maybe?"

"Mr. Sargent?"

"Or a little maybe in the head vermisht?"

"I don't think so, Ma. He looked fine to me."

"Five hundred dollars, Sam, you know what that is?"

"It's a lot, Ma."

"It's almost how much Mr. Brunschweig he pays you for a whole year, Sam."

"I know, Ma."

"To get almost a whole year's pay, Sam, to get that for a little story like this, a few pages, this makes sense to you, Sam?"

"Me, I don't know, Ma, but it seemed to make sense to Mr. Sargent. He does it all the time, he says. It's his business."

"A liar he didn't look?"

"I don't think so, Ma. He was telling the truth, I think. Why would he lie to me?"

"Who knows?" Mrs. Silver said. "Uptown, there, it's a different world. They live different. They act different. They talk different. Why he should lie to you, this Mr. Sargent, this I don't know, Sam. I wasn't there. You, you were there. He's a nice man, this Mr. Sargent?"

"I liked him, Ma."

"An anti-Semitt, Sam?"

"Not from anything I could see or hear, Ma. I really liked him. I mean I really did, Ma."

"Then it's all right, I think. You're a good boy, Sam. You understand about people. Mistakes with people you don't make. Except Jennie Broom, she should from Passover to Ester Tahniss have a nose it should run like a faucet, except for her you know what people are like. If you like this Mr.

Sargent, all right he must be. So now tell me, at the end what he said?"

"He said he thought I had ability and if I didn't have any other agent representing me, which naturally I didn't, he said, Mr. Sargent, he said he'd be willing to represent me."

"For how much?" Mrs. Silver said.

"For what how much?" Sam said.

"A week," his mother said. "How much each week he'll pay you?"

"There's no pay, Ma."

The smooth, round forehead at the other side of the kitchen table tightened into a series of trolley tracks under the gray hair.

"No pay?" Mrs. Silver said. "A person doesn't work for no pay. Mr. Brunschweig pays twelve dollars. To leave him you should go to work for this Mr. Sargent, it must be something better, no? Better than twelve dollars, no?"

"I guess Mr. Sargent wasn't offering me a job," Sam said.

"You guess?" his mother said. "Sam, you were there. You sat by his desk. You ate a tuna fish sandwich he gave you. You listened to him, Sam. You heard him. Sam, why do you have to guess?"

"Well, I didn't mean guess," Sam said. "I mean I thought when I first got his letter, when Mr. Sargent said in his letter I should drop in, I thought the way you did, Ma, I thought he was offering me a job, or when I got there he'd offer me one, but it's not like that at all, Ma. I mean it's not a job, Ma."

"So what is it, what, if it's not a job?"

"It's he's offering me just he's willing to be my agent, Ma."

"Your agent for what, Sam?"

"To sell my stories, Ma."

"What stories, Sam?"

"In case I write any more, Ma."

His mother was silent for a while, staring down at her hands, which were folded in front of her on the table, studying them as though they were dispatches from a fighting front about which she had to make a tactical decision before the night was over. Sam continued to eat his chicken, not thinking too hard, allowing the pleasant excitement that had sustained him all day to keep bubbling along, knowing that all the heavy thinking, the thinking that would lead to decisions, was being done at the other side of the table, by the short, round, solid, strong woman without whom it would no more have occurred to him he could get through a day than it would have occurred to him to pay his night school tuition by looting Mr. Brunschweig's till.

"So it's like this," Mrs. Silver said at last. "What I thought first, a job

in an office, a beginning in a firm, where a boy with a good head and he
knows to typewrite and bookkeeping and yet shorthand also, a job where
such a boy could get a start and go up and up and up until, who knows,
the top, maybe, this what I thought, this your visit today to this Mr. Sargent, this it's not. So it looks at the beginning, what it looks, it looks like a
disappointment. But if you look on it another way, Sam, it's not only not a
disappointment, it's maybe yet even a better beginning. Are you listening,
Sam?"

"Sure, Ma."

"So take a bite bread with the chicken, and look on it like this. The
twelve dollars a week from Mr. Brunschweig you still have. What you can
get from the stories, it's like piece work, extra money, on top of from Mr.
Brunschweig the twelve. Like the ten you put in the bank from this." Again
Mrs. Silver reached across the table and touched the copy of *Landscape*.
"But what's to remember, Sam, is this: by this Mr. Sargent, the next story
it's sold, you'll get from the piece work what's nearly a whole year from
Mr. Brunschweig. What's to remember, Sam, is from this a person could
get rich. From this a person could lift himself up and improve himself
from here on Tenth Street all the way to uptown. You understand, Sam?"

"Yes, Ma," Sam said, beginning to feel the excitement inside him change
as it bent to the shape of the excitement he could sense inside her. The
time of aimless pleasure was over. His mother had reached a decision
about the next phase in the campaign. He would have to listen attentively.
His orders were about to be issued.

"This is a whole new thing," Mrs. Silver said. "From this way to get
rich, before I never heard. But because I never heard, it doesn't mean it's
not good. It doesn't mean it's not better. It could be, Sam, that this way to
get rich, to move uptown, to become somebody, it could mean it's even a
better way than going to college or starting by a firm at the bottom with
the bookkeeping and the shorthand. This, Sam, it's like going into business
for yourself. Without money to have to rent a store or a shop. Without
money to pay people they should work for you. With nothing, Sam, with
only a piece of paper and a pencil and what you have in your head, with
just your brains and your naked fingers, Sam, you can go into business for
yourself, you can be a boss like Mr. Brunschweig. You understand this,
Sam?"

"Yes, Ma," Sam said.

"So all right," Mrs. Silver said as she stood up. "With the eating you're
finished?"

"Yeah," Sam said. "I'm finished, Ma."

"So I'll clean off the table," his mother said, picking up the soup plate. "And you can write a new story before you go to sleep."

Sixteen years later, as he stared out of the taxi at the apartment houses and delicatessen stores and laundromats of Queens Boulevard, Sam could do something it had never occurred to him to do at the time, when he had simply begun, at that cleared kitchen table, to do as he had been told: write his second story. Now, several hundred stories later, Sam could marvel at the simple, uncomplicated directness of that illiterate woman who had controlled his life.

From the very beginning the objective had always been clear: Uptown. The only thing that had been unclear was the road by which the objective would be achieved. Her primitive but shrewd observation of the new world into which she had been transplanted had indicated first that the best road was a college education. When this road was blocked, she had found another: starting at the bottom of some uptown firm with equipment provided by the evening session of the Lafayette Business Institute. Then, unexpectedly, a road the existence of which she had never suspected had appeared at her feet: the world of letters. Without hesitation, unhampered by considerations of the creative impulse or the artistic temperament, she had ordered her troops onto the new and untested path. Without hesitation, because his faith was total, Sam had obeyed. Now, on his way to visit the retired commander, Sam wished the taxi driver would do likewise.

"I told you to make a left at Union Turnpike," he said.

"You make a left there, it carries you right into the parkway, you're heading right back to the Triboro."

"That's exactly where I want to be headed," Sam said.

"The Triboro?"

"I'm not going to the Triboro," Sam said. "But where I'm going is in that direction. Will you just please make a left first chance you get and go back? I'll tell you where to turn."

"Whatever you say, Mac," the driver said, and made a left so abruptly that Sam was flung against the side of the cab. With a that'll-show-you-who's-boss-of-this-steamboat jerk of his head, the driver said, dead pan, "Now where do I turn?"

"A couple of blocks down, maybe three, I think," Sam said. "There's a statue. Guy with a sword on his shoulder. Civic Virtue, it's called."

"Used to be called the Fat Boy of City Hall Park before they moved it out here from down there."

"That's right," Sam said. "How'd you know that?"

"This is my town, too," the driver said. "It ain't the town it used to be, but God damn it, it sure as hell once was."

"That's a fact," Sam said, and he knew he would have no more trouble with this particular driver. A moment of resentment for the passage of time had made them kin. "Here we are."

The driver turned the cab into the parkway at the big white statue that, on hot July days when Sam was a boy, used to tower over tenement kids splashing in the City Hall fountain, and said, "Now what?"

"Up ahead, first exit," Sam said, "you make another left." The driver made the left and Sam said, "Now you keep going four blocks to Sixty-seventh Avenue and make a right. Not Sixty-seventh Road. I want Sixty-seventh Avenue. I don't know why they have two streets with the same number, but that's Queens."

"It's the way they do things now," the driver said. "Anything that's got a chance to screw things in a nice juicy heap, they'll do it and call it progress. Used to be they was naming streets, after Sixty-seventh Road they'd have Sixty-eighth Road, but now after Sixty-seventh Road they hit you with Sixty-seventh Avenue, just to frig things up. This okay?"

"Yes, that second entrance on the right, the fancy one, about halfway down the block," Sam said. "Where those men are working."

The driver pulled up at the most elaborate of the Rigo Park Manor entrance arches and said, "You gonna be long?"

Sam, pulling a five-dollar bill from his wallet, said, "Why do you ask?"

"I hate to ride all the way back to God's country empty," the driver said. "Besides, most guys they come out this far to Queens by cab, they're usually dropping in to see the old folks and they got no time to waste, so if you're only gonna be a little while, I might as well wait for you and drive back to civilization with my clock down."

Sam's sense of guilt about his parents urged him to deny any similarity between himself and "most guys" by dismissing the driver, but his sense of reality told him that, if he did, he would as always have trouble finding a cab to take him back to Manhattan and, as a result, he might not have time before his dinner date with Rebecca Meissen to drop in on Sophie Sargent for a drink.

"Matter of fact," he said as he handed the driver the five-dollar bill, "I don't plan to stay long, but you never can tell, so I'm not sure that I have a right to ask you to wait."

"I know how it is," the driver said and, after a glance at the meter and another glance at Sam's gesture about the five-dollar bill, he added, "Thanks, Mac. I got folks of my own. The wife and I, we drop in on a

Sunday, say hello, have a cuppa coffee, sometimes we end up we're there for the week-end. Terrible thing, growing old."

"It's not good," Sam said. "I won't be here that long, but I might be as long as an hour?"

"That's okay," the driver said. "I'll just relax and watch these boys rushing the season."

The boys rushing the season were three men muffled in sweaters who were raking and seeding the two long scraps of hard brown earth that ran from the chipped brick and plaster of the entrance arch up to the doorway marked "E" at the top of the cracked cement walk. The men gave Sam a short glance as he moved up the walk and, as always, he made a small bet with himself. As always, halfway up the walk, Sam won the bet: out of the entrance marked "D," in which was located the apartment he lived in, rent free, as part of his salary for serving as the Rigo Park Manor resident superintendent, came the eager, energetic, bouncy little figure of Abe Ostreich.

"Sam!" he squealed, his high-pitched voice rising with delight. "I was sitting by the window, keeping an eye on the workers, and I saw the taxi stop, so I jumped up without even thinking, as much as to say: it's Sam, he's come pay a visit to Aunt and Uncle Silver!"

"I talked to Mom on the phone this morning and she said she'd received some sort of letter from a lawyer or somebody, so I thought I'd better come out and have a look," Sam said as he took Abe's outstretched hand and pumped it up and down. Abe Ostreich had become so thoroughly Americanized that it was difficult to believe this short, round figure in the gaudily checked thigh-length coat and the green pork-pie hat, who looked like an illustration in an issue of an undergraduate humor magazine devoted to satirizing *Esquire*, had been not too long ago a terrified refugee from Hitler's savagery with curls at his temples and a threadbare kaftan on his back. Abe's manners, however, had retained a charming touch of Old World formality. Responding in kind to Abe's slight bow over their clasped hands, Sam said, "How are you and Hannah feeling, Abe?"

"Wonderful, no complaints, absolutely wonderful," Abe said. "Hannah suffers something terrible from the rheumatism, but in front of Aunt and Uncle Silver she never shows it, as much as to say: if two people like that, eighty years old already, they're not complaining, so why should I? And you, Sam, how is it by you, I see in Winchell you're getting married?"

"I'm fine, Abe, just dandy, and I'm not getting married. I don't know how those things get into columns, but this one is not true. I'm glad you and Hannah are okay," Sam said, and he added, knowing it would do no good, "I'm a little rushed for time, but otherwise fine, thank you."

THE *Sound* OF *Bow Bells* / 169

It would do no good, because a conversation with Abe was like a truce negotiation between the representatives of two opposing armies that had fought an exhausting but indecisive battle.

Abe Ostreich had never said so, but his relationship with Sam indicated he was clearly aware that to Sam one of the great advantages of Rigo Park Manor as a home for Mr. and Mrs. Silver was the fact that the devoted Abe and the adoring Hannah Ostreich lived right next door. Nobody knew better than Abe and Hannah how much of the load of guilt about his parents was removed from Sam Silver's mind by the knowledge that the two old people were under the constant surveillance of the superintendent and his wife. Three years ago, when Sam's mother had fallen and broken her hip, and the year before that, when his father had collapsed with uremic poisoning due to an enlarged prostate, they had been resting comfortably in private rooms at Mt. Sinai, with all the appropriate doctors and nurses in attendance, before Sam had been called on the phone to be told that anything was wrong. When Mrs. Silver wanted stockings, or Mr. Silver needed shoes, it was Abe Ostreich who drove them in his brand-new Buick to the stores in Flushing, and Hannah who supervised the shopping expedition. Everything from the daily groceries to the weekly laundry was handled for Sam's parents by the Ostreichs. In many ways Mr. and Mrs. Silver received better care in Rigo Park Manor than Sam and Billy received in Sutton Crescent. The casual observer would never have suspected that the Ostreichs expected or received anything for this care beyond the satisfaction of repaying in small measure a debt they kept insisting could never be repaid. Sam, however, was not a casual observer. He was, in fact, the chief beneficiary of the Ostreichs' attention, and Abe knew it. He never lost an opportunity to remind Sam of the obligation, and he made of each of Sam's visits an opportunity to extract the sort of payment that only people engaged in the negotiation would have realized was a payment.

"See these men working here on the grass?" said the dapper little man in the pork-pie hat. "A lot of people say to me, Abe, they say, what's all of a sudden with working on the grass? It's only April, they say, as much as to say, Abe, you're a dope, you don't know what you're doing, but you know why I'm doing it, Sam?"

Sam, who did know, also knew the rules of the negotiation, and so he said, "Why, Abe?"

"So when the grass starts coming up here in Rigo Park Manor, the first place where it'll come up it'll be here in front the windows of Aunt and Uncle Silver. For old people, to see something green from their window,

Sam, it gives them hope, as much as to say: life it's not all over, there's still green things to look at."

"That's very nice, Abe," Sam said. "I'm sure Mom and Pop will appreciate that. By the way, anything I can do for you, Abe?"

Smoothly, so that it would not sound as though he had just been offered a *quid pro quo,* Abe said, "For me, no, but for Hannah, if you only could, Sam, what a wonderful thing it would be if next Thursday, it's her birthday, I could surprise her with tickets to a Broadway show. For Hannah, it would be as much as to say, see, how wonderful, Sam remembered your birthday! You know, Sam?"

"Of course," Sam said, trying without success to suppress the touch of dryness that Abe would not notice anyway. "Any particular show you have in mind?"

"For me and Hannah, we're simple people here in Queens, it makes no difference. Any show would be wonderful, as much as to say just so long it's on Broadway, but if you could, Sam, I know what Hannah would like. She'd like that new show, the Rodgers and Hammerstein, it opened last week, but only if you can manage, Sam?"

"Of course I can manage," Sam said, and refrained from adding: *as much as to say, why not?* Were not Abe and Hannah Ostreich, who warmed his image as a dutiful son, entitled to see a Rodgers and Hammerstein show as soon after its opening as Rebecca Meissen, who warmed his bed? "As soon as I get home," Sam said, "I'll call my ticket broker. That's two for next Thursday night."

"That's wonderful, thank you," Abe said. "Will Hannah be excited! She'll jump up and down, as much as to say I'm by an important man like Sam remembered!"

"Nonsense," Sam said. "Well, I better get going, Abe. I've got that taxi waiting. Nice to have seen you."

"Likewise," Abe said. "Only one thing, Sam."

"What?"

"If Uncle Silver seems a little you know, don't pay no attention."

Sam, who had long ago grown accustomed to Abe's helpful warnings about his father being "a little you know," knew he would never grow accustomed to the small tremor of trepidation with which Abe always forced him to ask, "What's it this time?"

"He's sending for my brother Shloymeh Leib."

Abe's brother Shloymeh Leib had died at Buchenwald, along with the few remaining members of the extensive family Sam's father had not succeeded, during half a century of ceaseless effort, in bringing to this country.

"When did this start?" Sam said.

"Last week, Saturday morning, when I came to take him to schul," Abe said. "He had the papers spread out with the bottle of ink and the pen, and he said he couldn't go dovvin today, he had to get the papers ready for bringing over Shloymeh Leib, there wasn't much time, even it meant writing on Shobbiss he had to do it, because Hitler was coming closer and closer."

Sam looked at the preposterous little man in the foolish coat, and for the first time in his life he grasped something that even four years of army service had never made more comprehensible for him than a slogan in a cigarette advertisement.

"I'm sorry, Abe," he said.

"No, it's nothing to be sorry," Abe said, and the bright face under the ridiculous pork-pie hat indicated that he spoke the truth. Abe Ostreich looked genuinely pleased. "I like that Uncle Silver still worries about saving Shloymeh Leib," he said. "It's as much as to say my brother is still alive. You know, Sam?"

Sam, who for a long time after Jennie's death had tried in secret to ease his pain by pretending otherwise, nodded and said, "As long as you don't mind."

"No, no," Abe Ostreich said. "Hannah and I, we're proud Uncle Silver still cares enough to try."

Sam put out his hand and Abe, taking it, made his abrupt little Old World bow, and Sam turned up the cement walk to the entrance marked "E." Rigo Park Manor was broken up into two-story units, each of which contained eight apartments, four on the street level and four above. Sam had never met any of the seven tenants who shared unit "E" with his mother and father, but whenever he stepped into the small foyer just inside the entrance door, Sam was assailed by the preposterous notion that his parents' neighbors were all identical in appearance and that they all looked like Buggo Salvemini. What Sam remembered most clearly about the cobbler's son who had locked him in the Grover Cleveland High School gym toilet on graduation night was the way Buggo smelled. The foyer of unit "E" in Rigo Park Manor smelled exactly the same: a not unpleasant mixture of garlic and cheap hair tonic. Lifting his hand to press the buzzer on the jamb of his parents' door, Sam hesitated, as he always did, and, as always, the calculated hesitation was long enough to make it unnecessary for him to press the buzzer at all: the door opened and his mother said, "From the window to the door I can still walk faster than you can walk from talking to Abe to ring the bell."

"You're getting to be a regular Charlie Paddock," Sam said, dipping down to touch his lips to the wrinkled cheek that looked like a soiled dishrag, wondering just when, on what day, at what moment in time, how many years ago, he had stopped kissing her on the lips. "Nice to see you, Ma."

"If it's nice, so you could come more often and take a longer look," Mrs. Silver said. "What's this Charlie Paddock?"

"When you and I were young, Ma, he was known as the world's fastest human. He also married Bebe Daniels for a while, but I doubt that that had anything to do with anything. Stop breathing down my neck. I know where to hang my coat."

"A good memory you always had," his mother said.

"You know what I'm going to get you?" Sam said. "A resin box. You can keep it right here, just inside the door, and when I come to see you, as soon as I step into the house, I can dip my toes in the resin, the way prize fighters do when they enter the ring."

"This is what you came for?" Mrs. Silver said. "With an old woman to fight?"

"How's about we both stop flexing our muscles," Sam said. "That's a new sweater, isn't it?"

"Abe drove me yesterday to the store," his mother said. "Hannah wanted I should buy red, but I said red is for Indians. For an old lady, she lives like a prisoner in Queens, a black sweater is good enough. You like it?"

"Very much," Sam said. "Looks more dark blue than black to me. Isn't that the pin Billy brought you from France two years ago?"

"That's why I bought black. On black the silver looks better than on red. Sure it's the pin Billy brought me. How many other grandchildren I have to bring me pins from France? How was it in the play he acted?"

"He was absolutely wonderful and stunning and marvelous and all the rest of that malarkey," Sam said. "But just between us, Ma, I don't think he's ever going to be an actor."

"Who needs he should be an actor? Just because he plays in a school play once, this means right away a boy has to be an actor?"

"It doesn't mean that, and I'm damn well going to see it doesn't ever mean that. End of subject. How's Pa?"

"You mean Abe out there with his big mouth he didn't tell you?"

"Well, he said Pop's gone back to filling in forms to get people out of Europe."

"So this is so terrible, maybe? An old man, eighty years, maybe even eighty-one—who knows exact—he lives here in Queens all alone, like a prisoner, nothing to do he hasn't got, what's wrong he writes papers all day he thinks he's bringing over mishpoche?"

"Nothing's wrong with it, and Abe didn't say anything is wrong with it, so stop making a tzimiss about it."

"A tzimiss I make only to eat," Mrs. Silver said. "Go say hello to Pa. I'll go get you a plate. It's fresh."

"Not now, Ma, thanks. I just had lunch."

"Some lunch," Mrs. Silver said. "A spoon tuna fish on a slice bread with a cup black coffee. A person would think it's a big agent there on Park Avenue, important people, a big business with big money, a person would think they'd be ashamed to serve a big important client a twenty-cents tuna fish sandwich."

"You're way behind the times, Ma. They cost fifty-five cents now. And it isn't a question of being ashamed or not. It's a question of atmosphere. If Claude Sargent stopped serving tuna on rye to his clients it would be like if the Prudential Life Insurance Company stopped putting that picture of the Rock of Gibraltar on their policies. Hello, Pa."

"Go in and say hello. You're not in the street hollering for a taxi," Mrs. Silver said. "I'll go get the tzimiss."

She pushed him through the arch that separated the hall from the living room, and herself moved off into the kitchen with the slow, hesitant gait that was due in part to the metal splint that had mended her broken hip, and in part was the result of old age. Moving into the living room, Sam was struck by the fact that even a highly imaginative storyteller would have found it difficult to invent two habitations more totally dissimilar than his lime-green and yellow Sutton Crescent co-operative, and his parents' smudged brown and faded tan three-roomer here in Rigo Park Manor. The two apartments, nevertheless, had one thing in common: both were considered highly desirable by other tenants, as well as by the rental agents, because of the view from the living-room windows. It didn't seem possible that what the privilege of seeing the *Owl's Head* moving downstream did to the cost of Sutton Crescent's "E" co-ops, could also be done to the rents of those Rigo Park Manor apartments from the living rooms of which it was possible to see the men who were rushing the season by scraping away at the two strips of barren brown earth that ran down to the sidewalk of Sixty-seventh Avenue. It didn't seem possible, but it was so, and because his father could look up from the table at which he was writing and see the taxi waiting to carry his son back to Manhattan, the cost to Sam Silver of supporting his parents was twenty dollars a month higher than it would have been if they lived at the other side of the building.

"Sam," his father said. "You'll excuse me I don't get up?"

"Of course," Sam said. He crossed the room and touched his father's shoulder with the awkward little gesture that had come into being at the same time that he stopped kissing his mother on the lips: part caress and part fending off a physical intimacy in which all that remained for both of them was a moment of embarrassment. "How are you, Pa?"

"All right, fine, but very busy," Mr. Silver said. "Sit down, Sam." The old man nodded to the table strewn with papers, a few weighted down with a bottle of ink, and Mr. Silver made a gesture with the hand in which he held the fat old-fashioned Waterman that was filled by unscrewing the large golden pen point and squirting the ink into the barrel with an eyedropper. "It's the papers for Abe's brother Shloymeh Leib," Mr. Silver said. "It's a hurry-up job, Sam. There's not even a minute, what am I saying, not even a half a minute, Sam, not even a half a minute that it can be wasted. Sit down and rest a little, Sam, till Mama comes with the tzimiss."

Mr. Silver bent back to his task and Sam sat down in the crescent-shaped rust-brown couch that had been purchased on Main Street in Flushing under the supervision of Hannah Ostreich to fill the corner of the small room that commanded the best view of the street, but Sam did not look out at the view that cost him twenty extra dollars every month. He looked instead around the room in which the two people who had given him life had been deposited to wait for the end of their own, and the sight reminded Sam of something he had once read, while looking up Cairo street names for a spy story he was writing for *Collier's*, about the ancient Egyptians. They spent their lives, Sam had learned, building the tombs in which they would be buried, painting the walls with pictures of their favorite foods, their pets, the members of their family, their jewels and money and clothes, everything they cherished or merely liked and enjoyed, because they believed that whatever appeared as a picture on the wall of a tomb would, after the owner of the tomb died and was buried in it, be re-created in three-dimensional reality and placed at his disposal for use through all eternity in the after-life for which his brief stay on this earth was merely a preparation.

In a world where the state of Israel was faced daily with the relentless hatred of the Arab countries, Sam was aware that his parents would have resented his comparison of what they had done to their living room with what the ancient Egyptians used to do to their tombs. Everywhere he looked, however, Sam saw not only additional evidence that the comparison was apt but, with terrifying clarity, what it was his parents wanted to spend all of their eternity doing: reliving the years during which Sam's life had been in their, meaning Mrs. Silver's, hands.

From all of the faded tan walls with smudged brown dadoes by which he was surrounded, Sam was faced by memorabilia of his past: the snapshot of a bawling seven-year-old in a stocking hat being held by the hands of the otherwise concealed photographer's assistant on a pony in Tompkins Square Park; the framed diploma from P.S. 188; the formal bar mitzvah photograph that showed a round-cheeked boy wearing a prayer cloth, holding a leather-bound siddir, and staring out solemnly at the invisible but adoring relatives who were responsible, among other gifts not visible, for the four fountain pens clipped like a row of test tubes in his breast pocket; the bronze medal, mounted in a flattering cardboard mat, he had won during his junior year at Grover Cleveland High in an oratorical contest about the United States Constitution; an enlarged copy of the photograph Sophie Sargent had helped Sam choose for the jacket of his first novel; a photostat of the first page of the Dry Dock Savings Bank book that showed the deposit of the ten-dollar check he had received from *Landscape* for his first story; the snapshot he had taken in Gramercy Park the day he and Jennie wheeled the six-week-old Billy out into the street for the first time; the framed Keeping Posted page from the issue of the *Saturday Evening Post* in which had appeared Sam's first story about the Midwestern scoutmaster and the East Side boy scouts; the photograph of himself and Billy on the deck of the *Queen Mary* the day they had sailed for Europe two years ago.

Sam could understand how these and a score of others, re-creating moments of youthful glory and fragments of innocent happiness, would provide an ancient Egyptian with the serenity to face—indeed with the eagerness to embrace—death. What Sam could not understand was why the accumulation should fill him with a sense of despair so total that he turned with relief toward his mother hobbling into the room with a plate of steaming tzimiss.

"So eat while it's hot," she said, "and tell me what Mr. Sargent wanted you had to go run quick downtown have lunch with him?"

"Nothing much," Sam said. "Ma, do I have to eat this?"

"If you don't eat I'll only have to throw it out," Mrs. Silver said. "In the morning, on the telephone, you tell me to go see Mr. Sargent it's by you important. Now, here in the afternoon, you tell me it's nothing much."

"It would take too long to explain," Sam said. "Besides, it wouldn't interest you."

"What interests me I know better than other people."

Mrs. Silver sat down in the rust-brown chair that, along with the crescent-shaped couch and a tub-shaped footstool, formed a set about the virtues of which she agreed, for once, with Hannah Ostreich: it may have been a little hard to sit on, but the material didn't show the dirt.

"We'll disturb Papa," Sam said. "This is good tzimiss, Ma."

"All the thirty-six years I'm making it for you it's been good tzimiss, and when Papa is writing the papers to bring somebody over, cannons in his ears wouldn't disturb him, so start telling me, please."

"It's about a man Mr. Sargent and I both knew many years ago," Sam said. "A writer named Kenyon Poole. He's dead now and Mr. Sargent thinks he can make a little money for his daughter, this dead writer's daughter, if he can get his old books reprinted, and· he thinks I have some copies of the books."

"For this he had to drag you all the way downtown to eat tuna fish on a desk?"

Sam paused in the act of lifting a forkful of the detestable tzimiss to give his mother a sharp glance: with no more than the sketchiest knowledge of the facts, which had been conveyed to her grudgingly, she had come in a matter of moments to precisely the same conclusion he had reached only after an entire morning of troubled thought.

"I know it sounds silly," Sam said, and then, before he had time to edit himself, added, "But Mr. Sargent is getting old, Ma."

"And me?" she said. "I'm getting young?"

"I didn't mean that," Sam said. "I mean his habits are changing. He probably could have told me all about this on the phone, but he preferred to tell it to me in person."

"Maybe you don't go to see him so much any more either," Mrs. Silver said. "Maybe other clients, they don't go to see him so much any more. Like to get you to come out here to Queens once in a while, I have to pull you by the hair."

Surprised by the comparison, Sam paused again, to wonder if his relationship with Top Sargent had suffered, without his being aware of it, the same sort of deterioration that had taken place between himself and his parents.

"Well, now that you've got me pulled out here," Sam said, "I'd better take a look at that letter."

"What letter?"

"Aah, now, Ma, cut it out. You know damn well what letter. When I talked to you on the phone this morning you said you'd received a fat envelope with papers in it. You said the printing on the envelope was high, so you could feel it with your fingers, which made you believe it was important."

Mrs. Silver shook her head and sighed, as though reprimanding herself for forgetting that before adults could settle down to their serious affairs, they had to provide the children with toys. She stood up and limped out of the room. Sam glanced at his father. The old man was bent over the table, totally absorbed by the process of setting down with painful slowness the letters of a language he did not completely understand. Sam stood up and, as he always did at some point during a visit to his parents, he walked over to the TV set to check the silver eight-day alarm clock he had brought back for them as a present from Switzerland. As always, the clock showed the wrong time. Sam picked it up and was resetting it by his wrist watch when his mother came back into the room carrying an envelope.

"Again with the clock," she said.

"Just setting it, Ma," Sam said.

"Something is the matter maybe with how it was set before?"

"It happens to be ten minutes to three," Sam said. "You show half-past nine on this thing."

"So?" Mrs. Silver said. "All of a sudden it's a law a person can't show half-past nine on a clock in her own house?"

"No, it's not against the law," Sam said, putting the clock down carefully on the TV set, aware from the slight throbbing of the vein in his temple that he was approaching the point at which his capacity to handle this interminable and pointless bickering always ran out. "It's just that clocks were designed for the purpose of telling their owners the correct time, Ma. It's ten minutes to three for everybody else in New York. It might as well be for you, too."

"It might as well, but it isn't," Mrs. Silver said. "Here, in this house, for me and Papa, no matter what it says on the clock, it's always for us here the same time."

"Ma, for crying out loud, can't we just once, just one time, for God's sake, can't we spend ten minutes together without all this—?"

"Not any more, Sam."

"I sure as hell would like to know why not."

"Because Papa and I, Sam, to you we're not people any more. For years now, Sam, to you we're what your uptown important accountant he calls us a tax deduction."

"Oh, Christ, Ma!"

"Not in this house," Mrs. Silver said. "You pay the rent, but we have to eat and sleep in it till we're ready to die, and with Christ we're not eating and sleeping, Papa and I. Papa and I, we're Jews, Sam. No matter what you've become over there in your fancy world uptown, Sam, here Papa and I we're still what we always were and what we'll always be. We're Jews."

Reaching to take the envelope from her, Sam saw that both their hands were shaking, and all his other feelings were suddenly submerged by a wave of anger: he could not hide, as she could, behind the excuse of muscular disintegration due to old age. He pulled a batch of pages from the envelope and sat down on the couch. Several moments had gone by, Sam did not know how many, before he realized he was merely staring at the pages in front of him without absorbing the contents. At the same moment, he became aware that the top sheet in his hands was dominated by a large picture of a beautiful girl in a bathing suit who looked a good deal like Rebecca Meissen but, unlike Rebecca, was directing out at the world a wickedly sexy and most unladylike wink. A trifle confused, Sam forced himself to concentrate on a block of type above which the girl was poised as though for a dive, and he read: *"Reduce Size of Your Hips, Waistline, Thighs! No Diet! No Weight-Loss! Unbend-a-Cizor Is the Pleasant Modern Way to Reduce Size Through Exercise!"* Sam picked up the envelope and, running his fingers over the type in the upper left-hand corner, ascertained that the return address of The Unbend-a-Cizor Corporation was indeed engraved.

"Ma," Sam said. "This is nothing important. It's just an advertisement. A circular. Look at the envelope. It's not even addressed to you personally. They stuff them into letter boxes. It's addressed to *Householder*. Even you ought to be able to understand, just from looking at this batch of junk, even without reading English you ought to understand that it's an advertisement, not something important."

"What I understand, and what I do, that's two entirely different things," Mrs. Silver said. "If I didn't treat it like it's important, how would I get you to come out here, how?"

The vein in Sam's temple lurched, like a plodding, exhausted runner trying to avoid an obstacle that has unexpectedly appeared in his path, and he moved his head. The movement brought his glance to the window through which, across the heads of the men on the barren strips of lawn, Sam saw the waiting taxi at the curb.

"Okay, Ma," he said, bringing his glance back into the room. "The trick worked. You got me out here. Now will you tell me why?"

"In a few days is Billy's thirteenth birthday," Mrs. Silver replied promptly and clearly, the way she had talked to him on the phone that morning, as though each word was a brass plate and she was nailing them one by one on a wall. "For a long time I've been asking you, what arrangements have you made for his bar mitzvah?"

Not quite with relief, because the conditions of his entrapment made relief impossible, but with a slight easing of the tension that was hurling the vein in his temple on its throbbing way, Sam said, "I haven't made any arrangements for Billy's bar mitzvah, Ma."

"Why not?"

Aware that it was the wrong answer but unable to think of a better one, Sam said, "Why should I?"

"Because Billy is a Jew," Mrs. Silver said. "Maybe you forgot it, Sam, but Papa and I, we don't want Billy to forget it."

Making no effort to control the irrational rage that was now his only protection, Sam said, "Papa. That's a hot one. All my life in this damn house Papa's never even dared open his mouth. But any time you want something, it's not you that wants it. Oh, no. It's you and Papa who want it. When will you stop using Papa as a front for what you and only you want to do?"

The colorless figure bent over the table raised his head. The small movement was scarcely noticeable and yet, because it was so unexpected, Sam felt as though he had been shaken by a blast of explosive.

"To your mother in my house this way you won't talk," Mr. Silver said to his startled son. "A bar mitzvah for Billy we both want." The fat old-fashioned Waterman went out in a gesture toward the documents strewn on the table. "Why do you think I'm working so fast on the papers?" Sam's father demanded in a voice his son had never before heard. "The whole family," Mr. Silver thundered, "everybody, Shloymeh Leib, too, he must be here in America in time for Billy's bar mitzvah!"

Much as he enjoyed dropping in at the Sargent apartment for a drink with Sophie, there was one aspect of these visits that Sam always found a trifle unsettling: the gap between the casual phrasing of the invitation and the overpowering formality of its execution. It was, Sam thought as the taxi that had brought him from Queens pulled up in front of the canopy facing Central Park, not unlike being urged to pop in for a chat with an employee at the Vatican, and discovering on getting there that what had been issued was an invitation to a private audience with the Pope.

Neither Sophie nor Top was responsible, of course, for the things that made Sam feel, when he stepped out of a cab in front of the building in which the Sargents lived, that he was not so much crossing a strip of New York sidewalk as traversing a medieval drawbridge. After all, it was the architect, not Sophie and Top, who had modeled the entrance arch, which was three stories high, to resemble the southern approach to the cathedral at Chartres. Nor could Top and Sophie be held accountable for the fact that the doorman, who had been at his post during all the years Sam had been coming to visit the Sargents, stood well over six feet, weighed not much less than three hundred pounds, and wore his black and gray gold-faced uniform with all the arrogant and sinister authority of a Nazi gauleiter.

On the other hand, Sam didn't see how anybody but Sophie and Top could be held responsible for the weird grandeur of their seventeen-room duplex. Every item of furniture in it, like all the curious pieces in the Sargent & Sargent offices, had been chosen by Top and Sophie from the stage sets of plays that had been written by clients of the agency's Dramatic Department.

Sam had not, of course, known this when he had visited the Sargent home for the first time. He had known only that there was some connection between his invitation to dinner and the letter he had written in a cold rage to Mr. Sargent in answer to the note the agent had sent Sam along with a copy of the wildly enthusiastic rejection slip Biff Burgoyne of *Collier's* had sent Claude Sargent when he returned Sam's second story, "Two Shall Withstand Him."

Claude Sargent had not, of course, known that it was Sam's second story. After he finished writing it at the table in the East Tenth Street kitchen late in the night of the day he met Claude Sargent for the first time, Sam had been assailed by a moment of doubt. Not about his ability. After all, had not Kenyon Poole, the great man who had written *The Small Meal*, said only a few hours ago in Mr. Sargent's office that Sam was a natural born writer? What Sam suddenly began to worry about was whether he was capable of carrying out his mother's orders.

The composition of his first story had presented no difficulties. "The Ways of Men Must Sever" had practically written itself. "Two Shall Withstand Him," even though it was the result of a more self-conscious effort, had been almost as easy to set down on paper. When his mother had cleared the dishes from the table and ordered Sam to get started on a new story, however, Mrs. Silver had clearly meant that he was to embark on a career consisting of an endless series of stories, the way his job with Mr. Brunschweig consisted not of delivering one or two tuxedos but an endless series of tuxedos. How did he know he could write an endless series of stories? Suppose he sent "Two Shall Withstand Him" to Mr. Sargent and then discovered he couldn't think of a third story?

The thought that the fat man with the sad but pleasant face on lower Park Avenue might feel disappointed in him was, to Sam, suddenly intolerable. He decided he would feel better if, before he sent "Two Shall Withstand Him" to Mr. Sargent, he found out whether or not he was capable of writing a third story.

The following night, after he finished his mother's midnight snack and his third story, Sam decided, before sending the second and third to Mr. Sargent, he would wait and see if he could write a fourth. The night after that, when he finished his fourth story, Sam decided he would probably make a much better impression on Mr. Sargent if he gave him half a dozen stories in a batch.

A week later, when he dropped into the mailbox on Sixth Avenue the fat envelope containing six neatly typed stories, Sam made a calculation similar to the one he had made after sending "The Ways of Men Must Sever" to *Landscape*. There were, of course, slight variations. After all, the six new stories were not going directly to a magazine. They were going first to Mr. Sargent and then to a magazine, or perhaps several magazines. This meant that instead of learning about the sales within two days, as Sam had learned about the sale to *Landscape*, he would probably not hear from Mr. Sargent for at least three days, and possibly four.

He was wrong: two days later Sam received a post card from Mr. Sargent's office on the back of which, following the printed words THIS IS TO ACKNOWLEDGE RECEIPT OF, appeared the typewritten message: "Your six short stories" and a list of the titles. Sam was pleased.

Obviously, he grasped as soon as he saw the printed post card, in an organization like Sargent & Sargent, where dozens, perhaps even hundreds, of writers were constantly sending in material for Mr. and Mrs. Sargent to sell, it was important to let the writers know at once, even before Claude Sargent or his wife had a chance to read the stories, that they had arrived safely. Sam, in addition to being neat in his personal habits, had a neat mind. Anything that contributed to a sense of order earned his admiration. He knew it was silly to admire Mr. Sargent for inventing so simple a thing as the printed post-card acknowledgment, but Sam was in a mood to admire everything that could be admired about the friendly fat man on Lower Park Avenue, and so he let himself go.

The next day Sam began to feel a cooling at the edges, so to speak, of this warm outward flowing pool of admiration: there was nothing in his mailbox.

As the days passed, Sam was in a state not too far removed from panic because he had not had further word from Mr. Sargent's office, and the only thing that prevented him from calling or writing to ask about the fate of his stories was the thing Sam had, only seven days before, so much admired: the printed post-card acknowledgment.

Since, because of it, he knew the stories had arrived in the Sargent & Sargent office, Sam was denied the only excuse his pride would allow him to use as a reason for calling or writing to Mr. Sargent for the news he so desperately wanted.

Almost two full weeks after the stories had disappeared into the Sixth
Avenue mailbox, came the envelope containing the copy of Biff Burgoyne's
letter about "Two Shall Withstand Him." The day after that, when Sam's
coldly furious reply to Mr. Sargent had somewhat eased the humiliation
he had felt when he was slammed into the treacherous final paragraph of
Burgoyne's letter, Sam received Sophie Sargent's invitation to dinner.

For several hours he was not at all sure that he would accept. Sam was
still sore about Burgoyne's letter, and his anger extended to everybody
connected with it, including the unknown secretary who had typed it and
the faceless mailman who had carried it, so it was not surprising that some
of this anger should have spilled over onto the man who, regardless of his
good intentions, had passed the letter on to Sam. Also, he had never before
been invited to anybody's home for dinner and, while the thought of going to the Sargent & Sargent apartment did not intimidate him as much as
he had been intimidated by the thought of going to the Sargent & Sargent
office, Sam anticipated certain problems such as how to acknowledge the
invitation and what to wear, and in his angry mood he did not feel like
tackling these problems. Most important, however, was the feeling that he
had been invited to dine, the way a child might be asked to join the grown-
ups for cocktails, as a sop to the wound in his pride that the Sargents had
obviously never dreamed would be the result of passing on Burgoyne's
letter.

By four o'clock that afternoon, however, after he had made the delivery
to the Mercury Films office in the Paramount Building, Sam was so eager
to attend the dinner party that he didn't see how he was going to live
through the five days before the party was to take place.

There was nothing about the Mercury Films delivery to make Sam
suspect anything unusual was in the wind. All during the time it took
to walk across from Mr. Brunschweig's shop, get the Mercury Films suite
number from the directory in the lobby, and ride up in the elevator, Sam
was only partially aware of what he was doing. His mind, or most of it,
was on the man he had never met but knew he would for the rest of his
life identify as That Son of a Bitch Biff Burgoyne, the Bastard. Sam was not
even completely aware of the girl at the reception desk in the Mercury
Films outer office in front of whom he set down the brown cardboard box
and to whom, as he held out his receipt book, he said, "Sign, please."
His first awareness of anything unusual came with the interruption of a
flow of movement that, since he had gone to work for Mr. Brunschweig,
had become automatic: the girl, placing one hand on the receipt book to
hold down the page for her signature, and reaching for Sam's pencil with
her other hand, stopped moving. She looked up at Sam, pulled over the

cardboard box to examine the name on the label, then looked up at Sam again.

"Oh," she said. "You mind taking this down to Mr. Umberg's office?"

"What?" Sam said, and then he said, "Sure," and a moment after that, "Why?"

"I don't know why," the girl said sweetly. "I was told a box comes for Mr. Umberg from Brunschweig Tuxedos, my instructions were tell the boy please take it down the hall to Mr. Umberg's office, please. You mind doing that, please? It's twenty-seven-oh-nine down the first corridor through that there door on your left, please?"

"Sure," Sam said again and, because he had not really been listening, he asked as he picked up the box, "Where's that again?"

"Twenty-seven-oh-nine is just about where you'd expect it to be in any office in America," the girl said as she pressed a button that caused the door on her left to jerk open with a sharp click. "Between twenty-seven-oh-eight and twenty-seven-oh-ten. If you get lost, just holler, and we'll send one of them dogs with a whiskey barrel around his neck."

"Brandy," said Sam, who was now fully awake, and the girl gave him a quick look, as though she had never seen him before, which pleased him, because now that he was really looking at her, Sam saw that she was pretty. Before he realized what he was saying, not because he wanted to, but because in all the movies he had ever seen this was what young men always said in this scene, Sam said, "What are you doing Saturday night?"

"I don't know yet," the girl said. "But maybe by the time you come back from Mr. Umberg's office, good-looking, I will."

"Don't go away," Sam said, wondering if that was how the scene went. "I'll be back."

Going through the door on the left and then down the corridor, Sam wondered uneasily what he would do if the girl said yes. His dates with girls had been limited to a few of his classmates at the Lafayette Business Institute, where, like the rest of the male students, his choices were always based not on how a girl looked, but on whether she had "a place." No matter how beautiful, girls who lived with their parents were, to the men of Lafayette, a waste of time and money, very little of which a night student in 1935 could afford to waste. On the other hand, even a homely girl, so long as she lived alone or with a roommate who could be counted on to be somewhere else or make herself scarce at the crucial moment, was worth the investment in a couple of fifty-five-cent tickets to the R.K.O. Jeff on Fourteenth and, after the show, a snack at the Automat or in Stewart's. Sam's few investments of this nature had paid off quite well, but he had never gone out with a girl about whom he knew absolutely nothing, and he was wondering if this girl out at the Mercury Films reception desk, in spite of her good looks, was worth the financial risk, when he came to 2709, opened the door, walked in, and realized the room was empty.

He stepped back out into the corridor, took another look at the door to make sure he had the right room, and walked in again. Sam was looking around at the office furnishings, which struck him as pretty cheesy for a movie executive, and trying to decide what to do, when he heard the door open behind him. Sam turned, felt his heart bang up against the wall of his chest, and he dropped the big flat brown cardboard box with a slap that made him realize this could not possibly be Mr. Umberg's room: no movie executive, however low his position on the company's table of organization, would have an office without a carpet on the floor. As Sam, his face flushing, bent down to pick up the box, Jennie Broom laughed and said, "Butterfingers."

"Well, what the hell—" Sam started to say and, hearing the apologetic note in his voice, he stopped. This was the girl who had cost him his college education. Reminding himself that he hated this bitch, Sam said, "What the hell is this?"

"It's an office in the Paramount Building," Jennie said. "Looks like the year and a half since I saw you last, you haven't got any smarter."

"Your big trap hasn't got any smaller, either," Sam said. "Now what's this all about? Who is this Mr. Umberg?"

"He's my boss," Jennie said.

"You *work* here?"

"See? Just a few seconds back with the old team, and you begin improving right away. All I have to tell you is Mr. Umberg is my boss, and right away, just like that, you catch on I work here."

"All I meant," Sam started to say, and stopped. What he had meant was that the best he had been able to do for himself was a job delivering tuxedos, whereas Jennie had managed, somehow, to land a berth in an office. Knowing Jennie, or rather remembering the girl with whom he had gone to Grover Cleveland High, the "somehow" suddenly seemed more interesting than the fact that he wasn't nearly as angry at her as for a year and a half he had believed he was. Sam said, "I'm surprised, that's all. I get an order to deliver something to a Mr. Umberg, and I meet you."

"Because I arranged it that way," Jennie said, and then, irritably, "Oh, stop looking so stupid. You know if I had written you or called you and asked you to meet me, you wouldn't have showed up."

"You arranged this whole thing"—Sam lifted the brown cardboard box a few inches—"got me to deliver this thing, just to meet me?"

"Well, you wouldn't have come to meet me any other way, would you?"

"Damn right I wouldn't."

"So it was a matter of simple common sense to arrange some sort of trick to get you to show up."

"I still don't see how you arranged it," Sam said, speaking irritably because he wanted to get his distracting curiosity fed and put away so he could concentrate on his other feelings, which were not even remotely what he had believed they would be when he met Jennie Broom again. "How did you know where I work?"

"Your questions are always so simple-minded," Jennie said. "If you'd been around when Isaac Newton discovered gravity, what you would have wanted to know is was the apple that hit him on the head a McIntosh or a Winesap. What difference does it make how I found out where you work? I sat down with a directory of literary agents and started calling. When I got down to 'S,' the switchboard operator at Sargent & Sargent said you worked for a Mr. Brunschweig on West Forty-eighth. I called, got Mr. Brunschweig, asked if he had somebody named Sam Silver working for him, and he said yes, why did I want to know? I hung up without answering that one, and an hour later I called again, ordered a tuxedo delivered to Mr. Umberg, told the girl out at our reception desk to make sure the delivery was made to room twenty-seven-oh-nine, and here you are. Satisfied?"

"Yeah," Sam said, trying to figure out what was wrong with Jennie's explanation. "What do you mean your directory of literary agents?"

"All the literary agents in town," Jennie said patiently. "In fact, in the country, although most of them are here in New York. We have to call them all the time, so we have an office directory of them."

"Why do you have to call them all the time?"

"Sammy dear," Jennie said, "this is Mercury Films you delivered that tuxedo to. We make movies. Movies get made from stories. Literary agents sell stories. We— Oh, wait. I see." Jennie laughed and said, "Mr. Umberg is the head of Mercury's story department, and I'm his assistant."

"Pretty nice," said Sam, who grasped only vaguely what Jennie was talking about but understood with diamond-hard clarity the mixture of pride and contempt in her voice: the gap between a delivery boy, whose status all the world understood without explanation, and the assistant to the head of a motion picture company's story department, even if her status was not quite understood by all the world, was wide enough for anybody to understand. "Congratulations," Sam said. "I didn't even know you had a job. I thought—" He stopped. His mind had suddenly poked its way through to what was wrong with Jennie's explanation. "What made you call literary agents to find out where I worked?"

"Actually," Jennie said, "I called *Landscape* first, as soon as I read the story, but they said they gave out no information about their contributors. All they could do, they said, if I wrote to you care of the magazine, they'd forward the letter to your home, which would have done me a fat lot of good so far as getting to see you is concerned, wouldn't it?"

"Yeah," Sam said, aware that once again, and with equal abruptness, the balance of power in the room had shifted, this time in his favor. Trying for a tone that would mask the glow of pleasure that suddenly warmed him from scalp to toenails, he said, "So you read the story."

"Yes, I did," Jennie said, and the tone of her voice caused him to look at her sharply, but Sam could see nothing in the thin, dark face to clarify the puzzling sound that had drawn his attention.

"How come you read a thing like *Landscape?*" he said. "It's not very well known."

"The story department subscribes to everything," Jennie said. "Mr. Umberg is too important, or so he thinks, to read these obscure literary publications. My personal opinion is the big shlemiel has trouble grasping what he reads in the *Saturday Evening Post,* so naturally, as his assistant, things like *Landscape* fall into my area of responsibility."

Abandoning the echoes of the puzzling sound that had invaded the room a few moments ago, Sam applied himself to Jennie's last remark, which conveyed a message as clear as the electric sign that carried news bulletins around the Times Building, and he said, "How come you're willing to work for an anti-Semite?"

She looked annoyed, and said, "You think the only people in the world I don't like are anti-Semites?"

"It certainly looked that way in Grover Cleveland High," Sam said.

"To a dope it looked that way maybe," Jennie said.

"All right, I'm a dope," Sam said.

"You sure are."

"Then you just mind signing this so I can get out of here?"

Sam held out Mr. Brunschweig's receipt book and a pencil, but Jennie did not take them.

"Sam," she said, "why'd you write that story?"

"Why'd you fix up all these fancy shenanigans about renting a tuxedo to get me to come here?" he said.

"I wanted to thank you," Jennie said.

Sam looked at her more closely and saw that Jennie, whose dark face seemed to have become a trifle darker, might just conceivably be blushing. Dismissing this as preposterous Sam said, "Thank me for what?"

"And also to apologize to you," Jennie said.

"Apologize to me for what?" Sam said.

"You're in a rut, Sammy."

"You go ahead and get me out of it," Sam said. "I don't know what the hell you're talking about."

Jennie smiled and said quietly, "You're going to make me say the words, aren't you?"

Not knowing what she meant, but understanding that she felt he had her at a disadvantage, Sam said, "I certainly am."

"I'm sorry for what I did to you a year and a half ago on graduation night," Jennie Broom said, and even someone who had never seen her before would have known from the way she spoke how much she hated to say it. "You satisfied?"

Sam, who was disappointed rather than satisfied, said, "That's the apology. What's the thank you?"

Jennie hesitated, which in itself was so uncharacteristic that Sam's puzzlement about being disappointed in her apology was jostled by a sudden nudge of warning.

"Ever since it happened," she said, "I've been sorry, and I wanted to come over to Tenth Street and tell you I'm sorry, but I was so sure you hated me, for which I couldn't blame you, that I just couldn't get up the steam to come over and say it. Then I happened to read your story in *Landscape* and, well, aside from the surprise, I mean I never knew you wanted to be a writer or were even interested in writing, so naturally it was a big surprise, and at first, to be honest, I didn't connect you with the Samuel Silver whose name was signed to the story, but once I got into the story, reading it, I mean, the subject matter of a graduation night and the description of the school and the people like Miss Mercator and that bastard Mueller, all that, well, there was no doubt about the identity of this Samuel Silver who'd written 'The Ways of Men Must Sever,' and my first reaction was Jennie Broom you are a bitch on wheels not to have got up steam this last year and a half to go over to Tenth Street, and my second reaction was to hell with pride and all the rest of that crap, I'm going to thank Sam for what he's done, so I did all that stuff I told you about calling *Landscape* and then the agents to get you here today, and now that you're here, I'm saying it: thank you."

"For what?" Sam said and knew at once, from the expression on Jennie's face, that he had said the wrong thing.

"You bastard," she said quietly. "You want your pound of flesh, too."

"You got me here," Sam said. "You better give me everything I'm entitled to."

Jennie's thin lips came out in a small, wry pout, and she nodded, as though admitting with reluctance that if their positions had been reversed, she would have made the same demand.

"I want to thank you for not hating me," she said. "The way you portrayed that girl in the story, I mean anybody else, under the circumstances, any other writer, I don't see how he could have resisted making the girl a bitch, as a sort of revenge, paying her back for what she did to him in real life. But you didn't. You, you, well, what you did, Sam, anybody reading that story could see, could feel, the reader just knows it in his bones the author of that story admires that girl for what she did to that school principal, and well, under the circumstances, as I said, for having understood that and had the courage to put it in the story, and even though it's only private, something nobody else reading the story except you and me would know, for that, Sam, I want to thank you."

For several moments Sam was reminded of the way he had felt after an intermediate algebra test at Grover Cleveland High. He had been afraid of the exam, because mathematics had always been his weakest subject, and as soon as he read the questions Sam realized his fears had been justified: he could not possibly pass this exam. He struggled with it for a while and then, to his as well as everybody else's surprise, Miss Vostermann, the proctor, left the room. At once everybody who needed help asked for it, and Sam, along with a dozen other students, got it. By the time Miss Vostermann came back, Sam had been given so many correct answers by his neighbors that, when the marks were announced several days later, he was astonished to discover he had earned the highest grade in the class. Miss Vostermann, equally astonished but totally unsuspecting, complimented Sam on his achievement.

Sam remembered now, in this room in the Paramount Building with Jennie Broom, how he had felt then: excited and pleased by the compliment, yet ashamed because he knew it had not been earned.

Sam knew he had been totally unaware, when on that hot night in Mr. Brunschweig's store he wrote "The Ways of Men Must Sever," that he had any attitude toward the story's heroine. He had not even been aware, in the strictest sense, that he had been writing a story. Sam had been acting out of an instinct to get rid of something that bothered him, an instinct as basic and unplanned as the instinct that drives an ailing dog to eat grass. Having got rid of it, he had lost all interest in the content of the story. Sam's concern from then on had been merely for its fate.

Would *Landscape* accept it? Having accepted it, would they pay for it? Having paid for it, when would they print it? If he had been surprised to learn, during his first visit to Claude Sargent's office, that what the literary agent had liked best about the story was the author's unstated but implicit admiration for the heroine, Sam could now think of no word more accurate than dumfounded for the way he felt on discovering that Jennie Broom held the same view.

"There's nothing to thank me for," he said. "I wasn't doing anything to pay somebody back. I mean, it wasn't an act of revenge, as you put it. What I was doing, I was writing a story. I wanted it to be as true as I could make it."

Jennie nodded, and since she did it very slowly, with an air of thoughtfulness, almost of solemnity, Sam forced himself to think of the words he had just uttered without thought, and at once he began to blush. Pomposity in anybody, even himself, he found embarrassing.

"Yes," Jennie said. "That's the wonder of it."

"Oh, hell," Sam said to dilute the embarrassment. "There's nothing wonderful about it."

"To you, no," Jennie said, and all at once, with the sharpness of a stab of pain, Sam understood the puzzling sound that had come into the room moments ago, when Jennie first announced she had read his story: it was admiration. Reluctant admiration. Grudging admiration. Even admiration that she resented feeling. But admiration nonetheless. Sure of that, Sam was no longer sure of anything that dealt with Jennie, least of all that he hated her. For the first time in the years since he had met her in Grover Cleveland High, Sam looked at the dark, sullen, intense girl he had never understood, the way he had looked at other classmates: as though they were his equals. Jennie said slowly, "What gets me is I never suspected you had it in you."

Sam, who had never suspected it either and was not at all sure that he grasped all of what Jennie meant by the "it" she felt he had in him, was nevertheless ready to accept what was clearly intended to be an accolade.

"Neither did I," he said generously and then, lest this be interpreted as a diminution of his achievement, he added what for the moment at any rate he was almost ready to believe, "I mean wanting to be a writer is one of those things you don't talk about. You either want to be, or you don't want to be, and you never know whether or not you *can* be until one day, for some reason or other, you decide to try it and see if you are."

"What was your reason for deciding to try it?" Jennie said.

The attitude of "The Man Who Has Arrived Having a Chat with the Adoring Neophyte" fell away from Sam abruptly. To the question he could no more answer now for Jennie Broom than he had been able to answer it for Claude Sargent, Sam said with a shrug, "Oh, hell, I'd rather not discuss it."

"I suppose you've got all sorts of writing plans," Jennie said.

"Well," said Sam, who had absolutely none, "you know."

"Of course," Jennie said. "Otherwise an outfit like Sargent & Sargent wouldn't have taken you on as a client."

"They're quite an outfit," Sam said, and only by throwing all his self-control into the effort was he able to prevent himself from adding the nervous question: *aren't they?*

"They're the best in the business," Jennie said. "They've been at it longer than almost anybody, and they're not only effective but completely honest, which is more than you can say for some agents. The Sargent & Sargent list is practically a Who's Who of American letters, and the mere fact that they've taken you on as a client, which they don't do very often with new young writers, is quite a compliment."

"Oh, well," said Sam, who suddenly thought it damned significant that his second, third, fourth, fifth, sixth, and seventh stories, which had been written since he acquired an agent, had not yet sold, whereas his first had been snapped up by *Landscape,* agent or no agent, "I figure it's a two-way street."

"I don't imagine too much of it is coming up your side of the street," Jennie said dryly. "Or you wouldn't still be delivering tuxedos for a living."

Sam came down to earth with a thud. He was talking to the old Jennie. He grinned and said, "Ever try to live on what *Landscape* pays?"

"I'm having enough trouble trying to live on what *Mercury* pays," Jennie said. "Now that I've apologized for graduation night, and thanked you for treating me the way you did in the story, would you come to dinner if I invited you to my place?"

Sam's first thought was how odd that the only two invitations to dinner he had ever in his life received should both have come to him on the same day. His second thought centered on the way Jennie had used the word "place" and he said, "You mean on Thirteenth Street?"

"I certainly do not mean on Thirteenth Street," said Jennie. "I got the hell out of that dump. You still living with your parents?"

"Well—" Sam began.

"I know," Jennie said. "You're not making enough to get a place of your own, and besides, you have to help support your parents."

"Don't you?" Sam said.

"My parents," Jennie said abruptly, "are dead. What about Saturday night?"

"I can't," Sam said. "I'm going to dinner at the Sargents' on Saturday."

"Boy, you really landed in it with both feet," Jennie said.

"Aah, hell," Sam said. "It's just dinner."

"At other places you get something else in addition to food?"

"What?" Sam said, and then he saw the look on Jennie's face, and he could feel his own face get hot.

"You got a few minutes now?" she said.

"Sure," Sam said. "Why?"

"There's something I'd like to discuss with you," Jennie said. "It won't take long and it could make you enough money so you'd be able to quit this tuxedo delivering and devote all your time to writing. You interested?"

"Sure," Sam said.

"All right," Jennie said, pointing to a chair. "Take a load off, and listen."

An hour later, flushed with excitement, on his way out of the reception room, Sam heard the pretty girl at the desk say something to him, but Sam didn't stop. A few minutes later, out on Broadway, he did. That curious thing about his relationship to Jennie Broom, the way he was never really comfortable in her presence but always found he missed her and liked her best as soon as he left her, had hit him again.

All the way back to Mr. Brunschweig's shop he couldn't stop thinking about her. By the time he got home late that night, the recollection was still with him, more exciting than it had been that afternoon when he left Jennie, and as a result of it he decided not to tell his mother about the events of the day. Sam was aware that this was the first time he had ever withheld anything from his mother, but the defection did not trouble him. This was something he did not want to share. Sam wanted to keep to himself the memory of the way Jennie had looked in that tight white sweater.

The next morning, with the memory more vivid than ever, he wrote on Mr. Brunschweig's typewriter a note to Sophie Sargent, accepting her invitation to dinner, and Sam asked his boss to lend him, as an advance against his salary, the price of a new dark blue suit. Mr. Brunschweig, whose moments of generosity were as unpredictable as his tastes in reading matter, did better than that: he called a friend, who manufactured men's clothing on lower Fifth Avenue, told him to provide Sam with "something you wouldn't be ashamed your own son should wear," and send the bill to Mr. Brunschweig. As a result, on Saturday night, promptly at seven forty-five, when Sam turned the corner into Fifth Avenue and saw the building in which Claude and Sophie Sargent lived, the sudden tremors of uncertainty by which he was assailed were not due to any worries about what he was wearing. On the contrary. They were caused by what the man at the door was wearing.

As Sam approached, feeling himself grow smaller and smaller with each step, the black and gray gold-faced uniform seemed to swell, like a lump of dried sponge immersed in water, until the doorman inside it, who from the corner had struck Sam as an approximately three-hundred-pound six-footer, looked as tall as the three-story entrance and broad enough to block both the enormous wrought-iron-and-glass doors before which he stood guard. He made no move, when Sam reached him, to open either one.

"Does Mr. Claude Sargent live in this building?" Sam said.

"Are you expected?" the monster retorted.

"Yes, sir," Sam said, and even in the midst of his agony of embarrassment for a mistake he could not possibly have stopped himself from making, he caught himself wondering if what he had just said might not be a funny bit of revealing detail to include in a story some day. If he ever *wrote* another story, that is.

"Name, please?" the doorman said, and as Sam told him, he saw to his considerable surprise that he was no longer out on the sidewalk nor in the presence of the terrifying doorman. Somehow, with a deftness that seemed to Sam appropriate to the elegance of the uptown world, he had been transferred like a relay race baton from the care of the uniformed giant out on the sidewalk to the attentions of a wisp of white-haired old man, wearing a variation of the same uniform, who was uttering weak little sounds into a switchboard sunk flush with the ormolu and marble wall of the lobby. The chirping sounds ended in a deferential gurgle and, turning from the switchboard, the old man quavered, "The elevator on your left, sir."

Sam managed to find it, even though for several confused moments he couldn't seem to remember his left from his right, and then during the journey upward all the confusion, timidity, and uncertainty fell away under the sudden jolting orders from a cold, hard, inner voice that was saying imperiously, "Now, look, stupid. Let's just knock off all this ooh-I'm-just-a-poor-boy-from-the-slums crap, and let's unbutton the old brain and pay some attention. All this is going to be useful to you some day, so pull in your teeth and start remembering what you see and hear."

What Sam saw and heard, during the next ten minutes, was recorded by his brain as completely and precisely as a meticulously prepared library catalogue but, while it was happening, he was totally unaware of the recording process. It was as though his eyes and ears were two sets of cameras capable of doing their work without human manipulation or even attention. Later, when his thoughts went back to that evening, Sam had no difficulty in recalling everything that had been said by, to, or near him and, as though he had at his disposal a series of snapshots that could be plucked from a file and examined at will, he was able to see in his mind the most minute detail of every physical object by which he had been surrounded, including the people who had on that night shared with him Claude and Sophie Sargent's hospitality, down to the colors of the men's neckties and the shape of the jewelry the women had been wearing.

At the same time, however, the evening reminded Sam of a movie crowd scene into which he had been sucked inadvertently by a surging mob. As he was walloped about helplessly, he would find himself every now and then caught up, motionless and yet in motion, quivering like a speedometer needle in a racing car, on the outskirts of some particular little eddy of action.

Sam was unaware of the sequence of these bumps, but he remembered that one of the first involved Sophie Sargent, who came hurrying across the enormous living room, which was furnished in a manner that reminded Sam at once of the odd pieces in the Sargent & Sargent offices, to rescue him from the butler and astonish him with the news that he had been invited because Claude had been so impressed and amused by the save-the-flowery-comments-for-my-biographer-and-just-send-me-the-checks letter. Before Sam had time to adjust to the mixture of guilt and pleasure he took in this piece of intelligence, she had darted off in a puff of bright chatter that seemed to emerge from her red velvet, mink-trimmed hostess gown like the gaily colored balloons that rose above the heads of Winnie Winkle and Orphan Annie in the Sunday comics.

The next bump proved to be the butler with a large silver tray loaded with glasses of different shapes containing liquids of different colors which he held out in a manner that reminded Sam of the scene that followed Nazimova's dance in the movie called *Salome* he had seen from the Loew's Avenue B second balcony when he was in P.S. 188. Gathering that he was expected to make a choice, Sam decided after a few moments of hesitation to try a short glass that resembled a stunted ice cream cone set in a base shaped like a large lump of sugar. This seemed safest because the glass was filled with an almost colorless liquid that looked like tap water tinted pale green by the reflection from an olive at the bottom of the glass.

As the butler glided away, Sam took an experimental sip, managed to restrain a startled scream, and almost spat the horrid stuff back into the glass in an effort to get rid of the stinging sensation on his tongue. Even a boy from East Tenth Street knew that spitting in Fifth Avenue drawing rooms was not the way to make a good impression on uptowners, so Sam managed to restrain himself, and with an effort he swallowed the small mouthful of bitter liquid. It reminded him of the ground horseradish his mother always prepared to go with gefüllte fish before she added the ground beets. Wondering how he could get rid of the glass unobserved, Sam suddenly found himself caught on the fringes of a small group that had apparently been listening with interest to a tiny woman seated on a couch Sam later learned had come from the first act of *Miss Lulu Bett*. The members of the group seemed to have stopped listening and were staring, or so it seemed to Sam, at him with disdain. Convinced that this was due to the fact that they had seen his difficulty with the first swallow from the dreadful glass, Sam drained it with a gesture that was intended to convey a worldly disregard for the opinion of gawkers but ended in a strangled gulp. A searing flame raced from his tonsils to his toenails and left him clinging to the back of a chair (from the closing scene of *Turn to the Right*), gasping for breath. By the time he caught it, Sam realized his cheeks were wet with tears. Wiping them away hastily, he saw that the butler had reappeared with the tray, and the disdainful group had returned its attention from him to the tiny lady on the couch. Sam started to take another stunted ice cream cone from the butler's tray, remembered the horror of the past few moments, and changed his mind. He chose instead a tall glass which contained a pleasant-looking amber fluid in which three ice cubes were afloat.

Sam took a long pull at his glass and was horrified to discover that the pleasant-looking amber liquid was almost as revolting as the pale green stuff in his first glass. Sam swallowed it hastily, and since this was his second experience, he did a little better with the inner flame that reduced his entrails to a crisp. He was thus able to bring into focus not only the face of the tiny red-haired woman on the couch but her voice as well.

Sam had seen enough movies to recognize an English accent in the dark, and he had thumbed through enough copies of the *New York Times Book Review* to recognize Pamela Poitier in profile. He was not filled at once with the same feeling of awe that had overwhelmed him when on that first visit to Claude Sargent's office he had become aware that he was in the same room with Kenyon Poole. There was, after all, only one *The Small Meal*. But Sam was not unimpressed, either. It was not every day in the week that a boy from East Tenth Street who delivered tuxedos for a living found himself within the same four walls that enclosed a woman who was not only the wife of the Physician in Ordinary to the King of England, but who also wrote novels about life in Mayfair that sold in Macy's like pretzels in Hamilton Fish Park. Furthermore, even though Lady Kirriemuir was admittedly unaware of the fact, she and Sam, now that he had sold his first story, were members of the same profession. One— if one was Sam—might almost say they were colleagues. It seemed sensible to Sam to pay close attention to what his colleague was saying. The people around Pamela Poitier were not only hanging on, they were practically lashed to her every word.

"—taxes," was the first one Sam heard. "Yew Ameddicans dewn't knew the meaning of the wudd, yew really dewn't, you knew. *Mayfair Maiden,* which hezzint even been published yet on this side—Sewfie tells me she's sewld the first serial rights to your *Ameddican Bride* magazine, and your Book Each Month Club has chewzin it for distribution to its membahz, and Mercury Films is paying I forget whut, a hundred thewsand pewnds I believe Sewfie said, all in all a tewtal of whut, hahf a million et the lewest, and according to Titty, bah the tahm the tex chaps hev finished with me, I'll regret the day I ever thought of writing *Mayfair Maiden.*"

Sam regretted it already, although he did not know whether this was because he had expected to hear some hints about how to become a successful writer, or because of the ominous churning in his stomach. To quiet the inner disturbance, he took a long pull at his glass and allowed himself to be carried by the tide of moving guests from the group listening to Lady Kirriemuir's complaints about the houndings of the tax gatherer out into the main stream of the party. Here, as he floated about, it occurred to Sam that the long pull at the amber fluid had been a mistake, and he was looking about a trifle desperately in another attempt to find a place where he could dispose of his glass, when he saw Kenyon Poole, and Sam's heart leaped. The neat little man with the patent-leather hair and the guardsman's mustache was standing near a cobbler's bench, holding with one hand a glass of amber fluid and with his words a group enthralled. Forcing his mind from the game of leapfrog taking place among his intestines, Sam used his elbows as a sort of rudder and managed to tack across the stream of guests toward the cobbler's bench, eager to drown Lady Kirriemuir's vulgar comments about money in the flood of exciting talk about life and letters of which, during that first memorable meeting in Claude Sargent's office, Sam had received such a thrilling sample. He had a moment of disappointment when, on attaching himself to the outskirts of the group, he saw Kenyon Poole turn to give him a glance and realized the author of *The Small Meal* had not recognized him. Sam decided this was probably due to his new blue suit—after all, the last time Kenyon Poole had seen him, Sam had been wearing a tuxedo—and he gave himself over to the pleasure of the great writer's words.

"There's only one way to beat it," Poole was saying. "That's to throw your money ahead. The amount of dough I've pissed away on accountants and tax lawyers and fiscal counselors, not to mention some of these bastards who call themselves things a guy who talks nothing but English can't even pronounce, Christ, you could wipe out the national debt with what it's cost me in fees, and when you boil it all down, no matter what fancy language these leeches use, that's what it always adds up to: throw your money ahead."

Casting himself loose from the group around the cobbler's bench and allowing himself to be carried away again by the stream of the party, Sam was aware with a sense of almost unbearable regret that his feeling of nausea could no longer be attributed entirely to the combination of liquids he had swallowed. In fact, as though anxious to wipe away the unpleasant taste in his mouth with a flavor even more unpleasant, he took a swig of the amber fluid and welcomed the burning sensation that made him wince and once again brought the tears to his eyes.

"For God's sake, is anything wrong?"

Sam opened his eyes and saw, with a surge of pleasure, that the stream of guests had carried him to the edge of a group around a mahogany whatnot near which Sophie Sargent was standing with her husband.

"No, just a cinder," Sam said hastily, because he had learned from his reading that people uptown did not get, as they did on East Tenth Street, dirt in their eyes. "Anyway, I thought it was a cinder, but I was wrong. Good evening, Mr. Sargent."

"Good evening, young man," said Claude Sargent.

"We've just decided that I'm going to call him Sam," Sophie Sargent said to her husband. "So you might as well do the same."

"With pleasure," said the literary agent. "That letter you wrote me about Biff Burgoyne's pile of hogwash, Sam, is one of the more memorable communications I have ever received," Claude Sargent said, and as the older man flapped his elbows to hike himself forward into an apparently more comfortable stance in his clothes, Sam saw why the literary agent looked so different: the cut-out desk that he wore in the office like a wooden skirt had been replaced by a maroon smoking jacket with black lapels. "It wasn't very bright of me to send Biff's letter along," Sargent said. "It's just in all my years in the business I've never read such a wild rave for a new writer, and I thought it would please you. It never occurred to me it would make you sore."

"It didn't make me sore," Sam said.

Claude Sargent laughed and said, "You're not as good a liar as you are a writer. The sheet of paper you wrote that letter on is still warm. When am I going to get a new story from you?"

When are you going to sell the six I've sent you during the past two weeks? was what Sam wanted to reply, but he would sooner have begged on the street for his bread than reveal to anyone how hurt he was by the failure of the stories he had written after his first one. Instead, Sam said, "After I finish a movie project I'm working on."

"Movie project?" Claude Sargent said and, turning to his wife, added, "You cook this up?"

"Not that I know of," Sophie Sargent said, and to Sam, "Is something going on behind my back?"

"Oh, no!" Sam said quickly. "The only reason I came here tonight is I wanted to tell you all about it. Wait, no. I don't mean it's the *only* reason. I mean that's the reason I accepted your invitation. So I could tell you about— No, I don't mean I wouldn't have accepted your invitation unless—"

"Sam," Sophie Sargent said, "what are you drinking?"

Sam looked down into his glass, said, "I don't know," and felt his face flush as the joke caught up with him. "I really don't," he said helplessly, and then, because it sounded rude, he added quickly, "But it's delicious, it really is, thank you very much."

"You're quite welcome," Sophie said. "Perhaps you'd better have another and tell me what this is all about." She turned and, almost as inaudibly as the rustle of her hostess gown, said in the general direction of Central Park, "Mortimer." As promptly as Aladdin's genie, the butler came out of the surging stream of guests with his silver tray. Sophie Sargent plucked from it a full glass, removed the half-empty glass from Sam's hand, made the switch as gracefully as a pianist crossing his hands for a gymnastic arpeggio, and said to her husband as she took Sam's arm, "Claude, I think you'd better get over into Ken Poole's corner. He looks as though he's beginning to take blue water across his bow. Sam, you come with me."

Sam came with her to a pale green tub chair and allowed himself to be pushed into it. Sophie then pulled over a hassock, gave the party a quick glance across her shoulder, like a playground instructor making certain all the children are occupied before she sneaks out for a cup of coffee, and sat down at Sam's feet with a crisp "Now!"

"Well," said Sam, heaving a long inward sigh of gratitude for being seated because he was feeling dizzy in a funny way, "it's all kind of peculiar."

"Most movie projects are," Sophie said. "Begin at the beginning."

"Well, there's this girl," Sam said, and then decided that beginning at the beginning would merely confuse Mrs. Sargent, so he amended the statement with: "I've known her for a long time and now she's the assistant story editor for Mercury Films."

"What's her name?"

"Jennie Broom."

The inner ends of Sophie Sargent's plucked eyebrows came together in two small ridges of muscle over the bridge of her nose.

"Here in New York?" she said. "Or the Coast office?"

"Here in New York," Sam said.

"Then she must be new," Sophie said. "I know Marshall Umberg very well. We're old friends. I knew him when he first came down from Yale and was practically no more than an office boy on *College Humor*. I know Marshall's whole staff."

"Yes, she's new," Sam said. "I mean, I don't know how long she's been working there, but it can't be too long because she—" Sam paused, decided that Mrs. Sargent did not have to know he and Jennie had graduated, or rather failed to graduate, from Grover Cleveland High less than two years ago, and said, "Anyway, being assistant to this Mr. Umberg, it seems Jennie has to read a lot of stuff he doesn't have time for, which is how she happened to read my story."

" 'The Ways of Men Must Sever'?" Sophie Sargent said. "In *Landscape*? And now Miss Groom wants—?"

"Broom," Sam said.

"And now Miss Broom wants you to enlarge the story for motion picture use?"

Astonished, Sam said, "How did you know?"

"She feels there's a great movie in it?" Mrs. Sargent continued. "You don't have to write a screenplay, of course? They can always get some Hollywood hack to do the actual script? What they want from you is merely a synopsis? An outline, really? Just a few pages in which the main characters and the story line are sketched clearly so that they can have something to show their producers on the Coast? And as soon as one of their producers gets interested, which naturally will happen at once because your story is so wonderfully tailored to pictures, why, then they'll be in a position to make you an offer? Until then, until you provide them with this outline or synopsis, they really have nothing to sell to their producers, so it's in your interest, if you want them ultimately to hit you over the head with one of their sacks of gold, it's to your interest to do this synopsis job for them for free, except that Miss Broom naturally didn't use the word free, did she, Sam?"

"No," Sam said, wishing he didn't feel so dizzy in that funny way. "But, Mrs. Sargent, how did you—?"

"Let's be fair, now," Mrs. Sargent said. "You agreed to let me call you Sam. The least you can do in exchange is call me Sophie."

"Yes, ma'am," Sam said. "But how did you know that Jennie—how did you know that's what Miss Broom said to me?"

"My dear Sam," Sophie Sargent said, "I would love to own a nice little mink pelt for every time some fast-talking smart aleck in a picture company's story department has said to one of my clients precisely the same thing that your Miss Broom said to you. It's the oldest racket in the world. In the world of pictures, anyway. The wonder is not that the picture companies try to get writers to work for nothing. After all, aside from the foolish publicity that gets into the papers about the millions of dollars they're supposed to be hurling at stars and what not, they're as cheap a group of people as you're likely to find on God's green earth. No, my dear Sam, the wonder is that so many otherwise intelligent writers fall for the cheap trick. You'd be astonished how many manage to get hooked. Even people as smart as Ken Poole, to take just one example at random. Your Miss Broom may be new in her job at Mercury Films, but she certainly has learned fast. She's even added a new wrinkle to the old racket. The other picture company vultures I've known were merely trying to hoodwink a writer. Your Miss Broom has struck out into new terrain. She's trying to hoodwink a writer who also happens to be her personal friend."

"That's not fair," Sam said. "You don't know Jennie."

"I'm not supposed to be fair," Sophie Sargent said. "I'm supposed to be your agent. And as for your dear little Jennie, I think, from what you've just told me, I know her somewhat better than you do. You take my advice and forget this little attempt at literary highway robbery on her part. The only work a writer should ever do on spec is work he does for himself. The picture companies have absolutely nothing to offer a genuine writer except money, and until they put some of it on the table, don't you ever lift a pencil or— Oh, my God, here, quick, it's through this door."

Actually, it was through the door and halfway down a corridor, but Sophie Sargent, with an efficiency that even in his agony Sam could not help but admire, managed to get him into the bathroom and pull the door shut on him in time. Later, when the dizziness was gone, and he had carefully rinsed away the last traces of his shame, and before rejoining the party was giving himself a few moments of rest, Sam found himself considering the words she had used about Jennie, and he was aware of a feeling of resentment.

Mrs. Sargent, whom he had been instructed to call Sophie, had no right to speak that way about Jennie. Even after he left the bathroom and immersed himself again in the stream of guests, Sam could not shake off the resentment. He did not doubt that what Mrs. Sargent—no, Sophie—had said was true about Mr. Umberg and other people who worked in picture company story departments. It was simply not true of Jennie. It couldn't be. Every detail of her thin face, every flicker of her brown eyes, as she had outlined the plan in Mr. Umberg's office, was as clear and vivid to him now as it had been five days ago.

There was only one way to prove to Sophie Sargent that she was wrong, and late that night, after he got home from the Sargent party, even though he still felt somewhat drained and wanted desperately to go to bed, Sam forced himself to sit down at the table in the Tenth Street kitchen and start work on the proof.

Jennie had not been specific about the length of the synopsis. A few pages, she had said, would be enough, although she had added that, if Sam felt he could make his characters and his story more clear by describing them at length, he was not to worry about length. In actual fact, Jennie had said, movie producers not being the brightest people in the world, it was probably safer to err, if err one did, on the side of verbosity rather than brevity.

Sam had no intention of erring. He was determined to prove to Sophie Sargent that she had misjudged Jennie Broom, and as he worked, with the image of Jennie in that tight white sweater before him, Sam's determination strengthened. So did his grasp of the task on which he had embarked.

It was not really writing. Not in the sense that he had found the composition of "The Ways of Men Must Sever" to be writing. The compulsion to make decisions was gone. The tension of selection was lacking.

In writing the short story, he had been aware on every line of the necessity to choose among the many words that came to mind the single one that would most precisely convey what he wanted the reader to see and feel, whether it was the color of the heroine's hair or the hour during which the crucial act of betrayal occurred. In writing the movie synopsis, Sam was aware that he was not trying to make a reader feel or see or even hear, but that he was spreading a net in which he hoped to catch a large number of dollars.

He did not say, as he had said in the story, that the heroine's hair was satiny black, like the skin of the fresh olives in Mr. Fromkin's appetizing store on Avenue C. Sam said instead that if the heroine was going to be played by a blond actress, the sense of brooding mystery she aroused in the hero could be changed to a feeling of carefree gaiety, because the climactic act of betrayal would work just as effectively that way. Sam did not say, as he had said in the short story, that the act of betrayal took place at night, where the horror was intensified for the hero by the fact that, watching it through the transom of the toilet in which he had been locked, the dirtiness of the act was underscored by the detestable smell of half a century's accumulation of dried urine. Sam said instead that if a scene in a toilet could not be shown on the screen, then the graduation exercises could just as easily take place during the day, and the hero could be forced to watch it from the window in the principal's office, which could be made to abut on the gym, or the exercises could be moved outdoors and the principal's office could have a window that looked out on the school-yard.

Since the decisions on every line were not being made by the writer to satisfy himself but in the hope of pleasing an unknown customer who would more likely be induced to purchase if presented with a wide variety of, so to speak, colors and sizes, the task lacked the peculiarly secret gratifications of literary composition, and seemed to Sam not unlike the accumulation by an industrious employee of a mail-order catalogue.

By the time he had included all the varieties he could recall or invent, Sam had used up six of his writing nights and covered almost seventy pages of his steno notebook with Pitman squiggles. Another six days of stolen half hours with Mr. Brunschweig's Underwood reduced this to forty-seven neatly typed double-spaced pages that Sam felt would cause Sophie Sargent, when Mercury Films bought them for a huge sum, to retract what she had said about Jennie Broom.

He did not bother to figure out how much of the eagerness that carried him the next morning across from the tuxedo store to the Paramount Building was due to this sudden passion for dispensing justice, and how much to the desire to bring together the image in the tight white sweater with the real girl who had left its disturbing presence in his mind. What made it more confusing was the fact that the girl at the reception desk in the Mercury Films outer office happened to be wearing a tight white sweater, and for several moments, as he absorbed the sight, Sam forgot completely why he had come here.

"Come on, snap out of it," the girl said and, as Sam did, she recognized him. "Oh, it's you," she said. "How's the tuxedo business?"

"Great," Sam said. "Could I see Miss Broom, please?"

"Who is she?" the girl said.

"Miss Jennie Broom," Sam said. "Assistant to the story editor."

"Stop with the jokes," the girl said. "Who is she?"

It seemed wrong to be irritable with anybody who looked like that in a sweater, but Sam was still too young to know what he would learn later, namely, that the inadvertent encounter is more exciting than the calculated conquest, so he said sharply, "Miss Broom is assistant to Mr. Marshall Umberg, and I'd like to see her, please."

"What did I ever do to you, good looking, to get hit in the puss with that tone of voice?" the girl said. "First time you show up here you ask me what I'm doing Saturday night, then walk out before I can answer, and this time, the second, you come in here asking for people don't even work here. This is a way to start a friendship?"

"Who doesn't work here?" Sam said. "Miss Broom?"

"Look, handsome, why don't you come clean?" the girl said. "What do you want here?"

"I want to see Miss Jennie Broom," Sam said. "She works in your story department."

"Not in mine," the girl said. "In my story department, which it should only *be* mine, boy, we got like you said Mr. Marshall Umberg, who runs it, and we got Mr. Gerald Horowitz, who is his assistant, two sterling types, God should forgive me, the lies I tell, and between them these two slobs have one secretary, Yetta Kenzler, a peach of a girl, not only because she's my friend, but because Yetta *is* a peach, and that is all we got working in our story department, except a fatzo who is in charge of the outside readers named Grimsby, which thank you again for calling it *my* story department, except these assorted readers who come in and out all the time on a piece-work basis, but this babe you're looking for, this Groom girl—"

"Broom," Sam said automatically, feeling helpless and, in the face of this girl's sardonically chanted monologue, pretty damn foolish. "Jennie Broom."

"Her, my friend, we ain't got," the girl said. "Any more questions?"

"But I saw her here two weeks ago," Sam said. "When I delivered a tuxedo to Mr. Umberg. You sent me through that door and down the first corridor on the left to twenty-seven-oh-nine. You remember everything else, how come you don't remember that?"

"Who says I don't remember it?" the girl said. "I remember it like anything. What I don't remember is this Miss Jennie Gloom—all right, all right, all right already, don't nail me to the wall with that look, for God's sake—Miss Jennie Broom. Her I don't remember because her we ain't got."

Sam could scarcely wait for the elevator to carry him down to the lobby, where he went to a phone booth, looked up the number, and then made his call.

"Mercury Films, good morning."

"Miss Broom, please," Sam said. "Miss Jennie Broom."

"Who was that, please?"

"Miss Jennie Broom," Sam said, and spelled it out. "She works in your story department."

"One moment, please." The girl at the other end took a great many more than one, but when she came back on the wire she was firm. "I'm sorry, sir, we have nobody working for us by that name."

"You sure?" Sam said.

The firmness took on a cutting edge. "Positive," the girl said.

"Well," Sam started to say, then slowly replaced the receiver. He sat there for a while, staring out into the lobby of the Paramount Building, resenting the fact that his anger was running down, because, without it, all that remained was a sense of baffled confusion. It made him feel stupid. Finally, when a woman holding a nickel peered in at him reproachfully, Sam got up, left the phone booth, walked back to Mr. Brunschweig's shop, and put the envelope containing his manuscript in the desk drawer where Mr. Brunschweig allowed him to keep his schoolbooks.

The sense of stupidity remained with him all day. Occasionally, on his way to or from one of Mr. Brunschweig's customers with a delivery, the anger would return, or try to break through the feeling of stupidity, but it did not get very far or help very much. The trouble was that Sam didn't know precisely what to be angry about. Just being sore at Jennie didn't seem to be enough. She had asked him to do something. He had done it, and when he tried to give it to her, he learned she had vanished. More accurately and more bafflingly, he had learned that, at least so far as Mercury Films was concerned, she had never existed. This was, of course, preposterous. Sam knew Jennie existed. Yet what could he do with his knowledge? To whom could he go and say, "A girl I've known for years doesn't seem to work in the office where I know she works because I saw her there two weeks ago when she asked me to do something for her firm that my agent then warned me not to do but I did it anyway and now that I've done it what the hell goes on, anyway?"

The answer was "nothing" until a few minutes before seven that night, when, as on the night when he wrote "The Ways of Men Must Sever," Sam came back to the shop after his last delivery to pick up his schoolbooks and discovered that Mr. Brunschweig had gone home. Sam unlocked the door, walked down to the back of the store, took his books from the desk drawer, and heard the front door open and close.

"Sam?"

"What the hell you doing here?"

"Oh, God," Jennie said as she came down the store toward him, "don't you know any other way to start a conversation?"

"Don't you know how to tell the truth once in a while?"

"What's eating you now?"

"You told me you work at Mercury, didn't you?"

"And I do work at Mercury," Jennie said. "What else is eating you?"

"You work there," Sam said. "But the girl at the reception desk never heard of you, and when I called up, on the phone, the switchboard operator said nobody by that name works here."

"That's why those two will never be anything but receptionists or switchboard operators," Jennie said. "Did you do it? Did you write the synopsis?"

"Certainly I did it," Sam said, allowing his words to rise with the anger that had started again and was coming through very well now. "I told you I'd do it, didn't I? I'm not a liar like some people around here. I said I'd do it and I did it. That's why I went over there today. To give it to you."

"Where is it?" Jennie said.

The eagerness in her voice took him by surprise. The anger seemed to halt like a motion picture that has suddenly been stopped, and Sam looked at her curiously.

"Look," he said. "One thing at a time. Do you work at Mercury or don't you?"

"I just told you I did."

"So now tell me are you the assistant story editor or are you not? Assistant to Mr. Marshall Umberg?"

"What the hell difference does that make?"

"You mean the answer is no?"

Jennie's thin lips came together until her mouth was a line in her tense, dark face. "All right," she said. "No."

"Then you did lie to me?" Sam said.

"Only about that."

"Why only about anything?"

"I was afraid, if you really knew what I do up there, you wouldn't write the synopsis for me."

"All right, tell me," Sam said. "What do you do up there?"

"I'm a reader," Jennie said. "Part time or piece work, whatever you want to call it. Me and about thirty others. That's why the switchboard operator and the girl at the reception desk don't know us. We're not really on the payroll. They have hundreds of novels and plays and things, everything being published. Umberg has to cover them all, and naturally he can't. Aside from being stupid, I mean, he wouldn't have time to read everything personally, so he has these outside readers. Me and these others. We get paid so much per report and the only time the people in the office see us is when we come in to pick up an assignment or deliver a report. That's what happened just now. Around six. I came in with a report for Umberg, and when I told the girl to say Miss Broom was here, the girl at the reception desk, she said hey, wait, are you Jennie Broom, and when I said yes she said a delivery boy from a tuxedo place had been in looking for me before lunch, so I figured you'd brought in the synopsis."

"When you asked me to write it, what did you think I'd do with it when it was finished?" Sam said. "Stick it in a bottle and throw it in the river and hope it would float around till it hit you?"

"Oh, don't be so smart," Jennie said irritably. "I thought when it was finished you'd mail it to me care of the Mercury story department and they'd give me the envelope the next time I came in, the way they give me other mail I get there. How the hell was I to know you're one of these eager beavers would deliver it in person?" She stood up on her toes and peered across Sam's shoulder, as though she had heard the rustle of an intruder, and said, "Where is it?"

"Will you tell me something?" Sam said.

"Certainly," Jennie said.

"What the hell is the matter with you?" Sam said.

Jennie plopped back on her heels and, in the darkened store, as she looked up at him, Sam saw the brown eyes light up, as though two little bonfires of anger had been ignited somewhere deep inside her.

"What makes you ask a stupid question like that?" she said.

"The things you do," Sam said.

"What things do I do?"

"Nutty things," Sam said. "Stupid things. Like graduation night. What did it get you? Aside from being fired out without a diploma?"

"They know what they can do with their diploma."

"Then this thing," Sam said. "You want me to write that synopsis, why don't you ask me? Why all that crap first you fix up I should deliver a tuxedo, then you lie you're assistant story editor, all that. Why? It's crazy. Sometimes I think you're as crazy as a bedbug."

"Suppose I hadn't lied?" Jennie said. "Suppose I'd said I'm a part-time reader for Mercury Films and I think 'The Ways of Men Must Sever' is a wonderful short story that could make a wonderful movie and earn you a fortune? Suppose I'd said that? Would you have sat down and written the synopsis? The hell you would. You'd've said what the hell can *you* do about it, *you*, a crummy part-time reader? Isn't that what you'd've said?"

Sam, who didn't know what he would have said, felt the conversation slipping away from him, the way it had done two weeks ago in Mr. Umberg's office, and he made an effort to recapture it by saying, "Stop the crap and stick to the point."

"I *am* sticking to the point," Jennie said angrily. "Did that great big brain Mr. Marshall Umberg approach you about there's a movie in 'The

Ways of Men Must Sever'? Or his bonehead assistant Mr. Gerald Horowitz? Or for that matter any other studio? Or anybody else?"

"Listen—"

"To what?" Jennie said. "To more of your gratitude? I'm the only one who saw the possibilities. I'm the only one who took the trouble. And believe me, it sure as hell *was* trouble, arranging that whole business about you coming into the office when Umberg was out, me not even being a regular employee, just in and out of the place all the time—"

"But why, for Christ's sake, why?" Sam said. "That's what I don't get. Why did you *take* the trouble?"

"Because, because, *because,* you stupid, pig-headed dope, I wanted to repay you for the harm I did to you on graduation night, and now for all my troubles you won't even give me the lousy manuscript so I can—"

Somehow, inexplicably, incredibly, the screaming stopped and, even more incredibly, she was sobbing in his arms and then, even more inexplicably, what they were doing made the breath burn raw at the back of his throat, and then Jennie was saying quietly, "No, wait, not like that, I'll take off my sweater, but first you better lock that front door."

Three days later, when he unlocked it and came into the store, the telephone was ringing. Wondering what sort of nut would be calling for a tuxedo at this hour, Sam ran to the desk, picked up the receiver, and was astonished to hear a voice he knew saying, "Sam, is that you?"

"Yes, Mr. Sargent," Sam said. "You in the office so early?"

"What? Oh. Now, what difference does that make? You ask the damndest questions. I happen to be calling from home, and I've been doing it for an hour in the hope of catching you before you go out on one of your deliveries."

"I'm sorry," Sam said. "Anything wrong?"

He said it as casually as he could, but his heart was suddenly thumping with excitement. He knew why Claude Sargent was calling. He had sold one of Sam's six short stories. Or possibly even more than one.

"Well, I don't want to discuss it on the phone," Mr. Sargent said. "Could you drop in at the office around noon?"

"I think so," Sam said, wishing Mr. Sargent wouldn't be so cautious and give him the good news at once. "I may not make it exactly twelve on the button, because I have to wait till I'm out on a delivery, but I'll do it as close to twelve as I can."

"That's fine, Sam," Claude Sargent said. "A few minutes one way or the other won't make any difference, just so long as I know you'll be there."

"Yes, sir," Sam said. "I'll be there, Mr. Sargent."

By the time he got there, Sam had behind him four and a half hours of feverish speculation, the result of which was an uneasy compromise between the wild optimism to which he did not dare succumb and the dreary pessimism he did not want to feel: yes, at least one of the six stories had sold, he had decided, but the purchaser wanted some changes made in the manuscript, and Mr. Sargent, not being sure that Sam could or would be willing to do the job, preferred to discuss face to face rather than on the phone what amounted to a conditional sale.

"Oh, yes, Mr. Sargent is waiting for you," Miss Tischler said as she rose reluctantly from her endless game of readdressing envelopes. She led Sam through the green curtain, down the dimly lighted corridor, and popped a peppermint into her mouth just before she pushed aside the curtain at the far end and into the air of Claude Sargent's room said, "Mr. Silver."

Sam stepped past her and stopped.

"It's all right, Sam dear," Sophie Sargent said from the red-leather wing chair, "I assure you we won't bite. Take that look off your face and sit down."

"Hello, Sam," Claude Sargent said from behind the desk, and he nodded toward a pasty-faced man slumped down in the lump of white column upholstered in green. "This is Marshall Umberg."

Mr. Umberg nodded coldly and Sophie Sargent said, "Here, Sam, try this."

She patted a red-leather footstool that apparently belonged to the wing chair. Sam sat down, and as she leaned back into the chair, Mrs. Sargent allowed her hand to brush lightly against his shoulder. It was so obviously a pat of reassurance that Sam's spirits, which from the moment he stepped into the room had been poised ominously on the brink of disaster, now took the plunge. He didn't have to be told that this meeting, whatever else it had been called to consider, had not been called to discuss changes in a short story.

"Sophie, you want to talk?" Claude Sargent said.

"Not much," his wife said. "Sam dear, you went and did what I warned you not to, didn't you?"

"How do you know?" Sam said.

"Claude is right," Sophie said. "You do ask the damndest questions. Does it matter how we know? Or did you really think you could write a forty-seven-page movie treatment and submit it to a picture company and nobody, especially your own agents, would find out?"

"I didn't submit it," Sam said. "I gave it to this friend of mine."

The slumped body in the green and white chair stirred. "See?" Mr. Umberg said bitterly. "I told you it's a God-damn conspiracy."

Sam stared at Mr. Umberg with distaste. His tiny, petulant mouth sat like a navel in the round, soft, white face that looked like a pregnant woman's naked belly.

"Marshall," Claude Sargent said, "I see no need for words like that."

"Naturally," Mr. Umberg said. "Why should you see the necessity? Is it *your* position that's been endangered by this shitty plot?"

"Marshall dear, you're no longer at Yale," Sophie Sargent said. "You don't have to use all that manly language." She moved slightly in the chair and said, "Sam dear, what was your understanding with your friend Miss Broom, if I've got the name right?"

"Yes," Sam said. "Broom."

"What was your understanding of what she planned to do?"

"To do?" Sam said.

The navel moved in the fat round belly of Mr. Umberg's face. "Look at him," he said. "Joe Innocence."

"Shut up, Marshall," Sophie Sargent said. "Sam dear, when did you give your manuscript to Miss Broom?"

"Three nights—" Sam paused, suddenly overwhelmed by the memory he had been carrying around like a fever. "Three days ago."

"She didn't waste any time," Marshall Umberg said. "The bitch."

"Sam dear," Sophie Sargent said, "what did your Miss Broom say she planned to do with your manuscript?"

Sam opened his mouth for a reply, and discovered he didn't have one.

"Go ahead," Mr. Umberg said. "Invent something real good."

Sam looked at the little navel of a mouth in the white belly of a face and considered the satisfactions of shoving his fist into it.

"As a matter of fact," Sam said to Mrs. Sargent, "Miss Broom didn't say anything."

"Ha," Mr. Umberg said.

"Now, Sam," Claude Sargent said.

"Sam dear," Sophie Sargent said.

"Miss Broom didn't say anything to me about what she planned to do with the manuscript," Sam said slowly and carefully, the way his mother spoke when she wanted to make it plain that any further questioning of her motives, statements, or intentions would earn not a verbal but a physical reply.

"When you invited me to this meeting," Mr. Umberg said to Claude Sargent, "I wish you'd told me in advance it was on account of you wanted me to meet Hans Christian Andersen."

"Sam dear," Sophie Sargent said, "don't you realize yourself how improbable your statement sounds?"

"No, I don't," Sam said. "Miss Broom is a friend of mine. We went to school together. She told me she works for the story department of Mercury Films and she felt 'The Ways of Men Must Sever' would make a fine movie if the short story were expanded in synopsis form to adjust to the cinema medium. If I trusted her enough to go ahead and do all the work of writing the synopsis on spec in spite of my own agent's warning not to do it, why shouldn't I trust her enough to assume when I gave her the manuscript she would submit it to her boss?"

"Because she didn't, Sam dear," Sophie Sargent said.

"Then what did she do with it?" Sam said.

"Oh, no," Mr. Umberg said. "This is too much."

"She sent it out to the Coast," Sophie Sargent said. "To Mr. Umberg's boss, Nate Schroeder."

"What's wrong with that?" Sam said.

"What's wrong with it, Sam dear," Sophie Sargent said, "is that Miss Broom sent along with your manuscript an accompanying letter addressed to Nate Schroeder."

"I don't want to sound stupid," Sam said, "but I still ask what's wrong with that?"

The slumped pile of blubber suddenly began to bounce and tug and push and sway, as though the seat under him had all at once become red-hot and Mr. Umberg, wedged in more tightly than he had realized, was trying desperately to free himself.

"I'll tell you what's wrong with it, you little son of a bitch," Mr. Umberg screamed. "She said in the letter the reason she was sending your God-damn manuscript to the Coast was because the New York office, the office I happen to run, you little son of a bitch, it's run so inefficiently, so badly, it's run so lousy, she said, that this manuscript, *your* manuscript, you little son of a bitch, she said you and your agent, you submitted it four times and each time it was assigned to her to read, and four times, she said, four times, the little lying bitch, four times she wrote a rave report recommending the studio buy, and four times the report got lost and the manuscript was sent back without even a covering letter, so now she was giving up on the New York office, *my* office, she was giving up on the New York office because the way I run the New York office, she said, it's hopeless, and she was sending the manuscript out to the Coast direct, attention Mr. Nate Schroeder, who only happens to be my boss, that's all, for any action he sees fit to take, *that's* what's wrong with it, you little son of a bitch, the accompanying letter your friend Miss Broom, the bitch, the letter she sent with your manuscript, that's what's wrong with it."

The sounds stopped emerging from the little mouth, but the lump of blubber kept heaving up and down. Not quite so violently, however. It was as though the effort poured into the screaming words had depleted the energies available for escaping from the blistering heat. Into the strained silence that now filled the room, Sam heard himself saying to Mrs. Sargent, "Is this, what he just said, is it true?"

Claude Sargent, holding up a sheet of paper, said, "Here's a copy of the letter, Sam."

Sam took the paper and, for a while, he stared down at the typewritten lines, as though he were reading them with care, but in actual fact Sam did not even see the words. He was stalling for time, trying to separate his attempts to understand the meaning of what Jennie had done to Mr. Umberg, from his recollection of what had happened three nights ago in Mr. Brunschweig's store when Jennie had convinced Sam to let her have the manuscript.

"Sam."

He looked up. Claude Sargent was leaning far forward across his desk.

"Yes, sir?" Sam said.

"You didn't know Miss Broom planned to use your manuscript as a support for this letter?"

"No, sir," Sam said.

"You," Mr. Umberg snarled. "You dirty rotten little lousy lying slob."

"Marshall," Sophie Sargent said icily, "if you don't shut your stupid mouth, I will slap it shut for you. Proceed, Claude."

"Nevertheless, Sam," Claude Sargent said, "I'm sure you see that indirectly you've been a party to Miss Broom's attempt to injure Mr. Umberg?"

"Yes, sir," Sam said. "I guess I have been."

"I take it, Sam, you don't know *why* Miss Broom wanted to injure Mr. Umberg?"

"No, sir," Sam said.

"Did she ever mention Mr. Umberg to you?"

"Just that he's her boss," Sam said. "And that she didn't think he's very —well—you know."

"Yes, Sam dear," Sophie Sargent said, tossing at Mr. Umberg a look of distaste as though she were whipping a dart across at a target, "we know."

"The reason we asked you to come here, Sam," Claude Sargent said, "I'm sure you can see from that letter that you're not the only one who has been used. Miss Broom wrote to Nate Schroeder that Sargent & Sargent, your agents, submitted your manuscript to Mercury Films four times. That is not true, and Sophie and I intend to comply at once with Mr. Umberg's request that we write a formal denial to Mr. Schroeder on the Coast. The reason we asked you to come here, Sam—"

"You deny it, too!" Mr. Umberg shouted. "That's what I want. If it's a lie, like you say it is, you deny it, too, you little shitass."

The words stopped pouring out of the petulant navel as Sam rose from the footstool.

"Mrs. Sargent," he said, wishing his voice was not shaking, "I think I'm going to take away from you the privilege of slapping this bastard's mouth shut."

"Now, Sam," Claude Sargent said.

"Sam dear," Sophie Sargent said.

"What did I say?" Mr. Umberg screamed. "All I said—"

"Don't repeat it," Sophie Sargent said.

"Sam," Claude Sargent said. "I apologize for Mr. Umberg's rudeness. Miss Broom told the truth about at least one thing. Mr. Umberg is not very bright. Nonetheless, he has been injured and, bright or stupid, common decency insists that those of us who have been used to injure him do what we can to correct the damage. Will you join Sophie and me in signing a letter of denial to Nate Schroeder?"

"Yes, sir," Sam said. "On one condition."

"Condition?" Mr. Umberg squealed. "What condition?"

"That you tell me where Miss Broom lives," Sam said.

Again the room was filled with a strained silence, and again the strained silence was broken by the chirping sounds of indignation from the petulant navel in the bellylike head.

"You're the one to make conditions?" Mr. Umberg shrieked. "Who the hell are you, you little jerk, to make conditions?"

Sophie Sargent rose like a battleship gun turret swiveling into firing position.

"Marshall," she said in the most magnificently final enough-is-enough tone Sam Silver had ever heard, "get on that phone, and call whichever one of your office flunkies handles the staff of outside readers, and get Miss Broom's address, and don't say another word to anybody in this room or you will never be able to say another one to anybody in any other room."

The lump of blubber managed to separate its bottom from the grip of the green and white chair, and the pudgy hands took the phone Claude Sargent shoved forward, and the nail-bitten forefinger dialed a number, and the petulant voice announced its ownership and asked the appropriate questions, and the information was scribbled on Claude Sargent's desk pad, while Sophie and Sam stood side by side, watching, and without knowing how he knew it, Sam knew that Sophie knew what had happened, or an approximation of what had happened, three nights ago in

Mr. Brunschweig's store, and he knew she knew why Sam wanted that address. As though to indicate that she approved of what Sam planned to do, Sophie reached out and took the slip from Mr. Umberg, handed it to Sam, and touched his arm lightly before she turned back to the Mercury Films story editor.

"Our letter to Nate Schroeder will be in the mails this evening," she said coldly. "Good-bye, Marshall."

It was Claude Sargent who broke the silence that followed Mr. Umberg's departure.

"Sam," he said, "I'm sorry about this." Sam sent a quick glance at Sophie. He was relieved to see that she, too, understood that what Claude Sargent meant by "this" was not what Sam meant. The older man hiked himself forward into his desk and said, "I guess you'll be wanting to get back to your job, so maybe we'd better get that letter written and let you sign it."

"Yes, sir," Sam said, and then, as Claude Sargent buzzed for Miss Tischler, he said, "Did this Mr. Schroeder send back my manuscript?"

"Yes, it's right there," Claude said, tapping an envelope on his desk. "Why do you ask?"

"I was wondering what you think of it," Sam said.

Sophie Sargent shook her head slowly and, in a voice as dry as one of the martinis for which Sam later learned she was famous, she said, "Claude tells me Ken Poole called you a natural born writer. I now see why."

More eager for an answer to his question than for an understanding of the exact nature of Mrs. Sargent's only partially understood compliment, Sam said, "I'd like to know what you think of my synopsis."

Claude Sargent looked worriedly at his wife. Sophie frowned, as though she wished her husband would not saddle her with the task of answering Sam's question, and then her shoulders moved in the almost imperceptible shrug of a soldier turning back to a distasteful duty.

"I hope Sam, dear," Sophie Sargent said, "you won't think me a dirty old woman for borrowing a fragment of Marshall Umberg's loathsome vocabulary to tell you that Claude and I both feel you should forget this." Her hand touched the envelope on Mr. Sargent's desk. "It's a hopeless lump of dreary and thoroughly unmarketable dreck, dear."

Sam did forget it, for exactly five and a half hours, during which his one thought was to get through the day he owed to Mr. Brunschweig. He finished his last delivery at twenty minutes after six, but even though he was only five blocks from the store, Sam did not go back for his schoolbooks. He was not going to the Lafayette Business Institute tonight. He went, instead, into the Seventh Avenue subway, got off at Sheridan Square, and asked a cop how to get to Commerce Street. When he stopped in front of the house with the number Mr. Umberg had scrawled on the slip of paper from Claude Sargent's desk pad, Sam had a stab of surprise: the house was even more shabby and disreputable-looking than the Avenue A tenement in which Jennie had lived all of *her* life, and yet, when she had told Sam that she had a place of her own, he had received the distinct impression from the pride in her voice that Jennie felt she had, in Mrs. Silver's phrase, improved herself.

Sam climbed to the third floor and knocked on the door marked 3-A. There was no answer. He knocked again, and while he waited, Sam became aware of an odor that was suddenly tugging his memory. He looked around, hunting the source of the not unpleasant smell that seemed to be a mixture of garlic and cheap hair tonic, and the door opened behind him. Sam turned back, and did what the figure in the doorway did: he jumped slightly.

"Hey, what is this?" Buggo Salvemini said. "Some new kind of a dance?"

"What're you doing here?" Sam said.

"Don't steal my lines," Buggo said. "Me, I live here."

"You live here?" Sam said, aware that he sounded stupid. "But I came to see Jennie?"

"Come on in and wait," Buggo said. "She's not home yet."

"You mean she *lives* here?"

"Now where the hell else would she live?" Buggo Salvemini said, pulling the door wide. "She's my wife, ain't she?"

Sixteen years later, stepping out of the cab that had brought him from his mother's house in Queens to the Sargent apartment house on Fifth Avenue, Sam Silver could still blush for his first reaction to Buggo's revelation: *Thou shalt not*—his stunned mind had reminded him as it brought alive what had happened in Mr. Brunschweig's store three nights before —*commit adultery,* but he sure as hell had.

"Mrs. Sargent," Sam said to the front of the gauleiter in the black and gray uniform at the front door and, as he passed the huge man, "I'm expected."

"Yes, sir," the doorman said.

"Mrs. Sargent," Sam repeated to the wisp of white-haired old man dozing with eyes wide open. The old man came awake with a start, and squeaked, "Yes, sir, elevator on your left, sir."

The elevator on the left, which had been installed before the electronic wonders that carried the tenants of Sutton Crescent to and from their river-view apartments had even been dreamed of, was a soothing reminder to Sam, who had just lived through quite a day, that he had lived through a great many days since he had first been carried up in this contraption, and he was still on his feet. "So just don't knock yourself out with the oh-God-if-people-only-knew-what-I-have-to-go-through bit," he told himself curtly. "You don't have to go through any more than anybody else goes through."

"I do think, Sam, after you finish those corrections for Bud Bienstock on *They Told Me You Were Dead,*" Sophie Sargent said as she pulled open the door, "you should go off somewhere on a short holiday. Or even a long one, darling, since people who mumble to themselves as they ring other people's doorbells are usually ready for a nice long rest. How are you, Sam dear?"

"You've just told me," Sam said. "What are you doing answering the door yourself? If Lady Kirriemuir hears about this, you'll be run out of the International Set."

"There's no longer an International Set," Sophie said. "Pam Poitier says the whole damn thing fell apart when word got out that Cholly Knickerbocker was not a real human being but just a newspaper by-line for any reporter who happened to be free that day. Here, let me take your hat. We're quite honest, you know. Nobody's lost a hat or a pair of rubbers in this place for years. And I'm answering the door myself because Mortimer is at the dentist."

"A fine way to run a house," Sam said as he followed Sophie into the drawing room. "I can just see Lady Kirriemuir letting the butler go get his teeth filled at a time when she's invited a dear, distinguished, devoted and whatever else I am friend to drop in for a drink."

"Lady Kirriemuir doesn't know what the servant problem is," Sophie said. "The British still haven't tipped off the lower orders to the fact that Magna Charta is part of the record. If you knew what the Poitiers pay for a maid, you'd fall over in a dead faint, and Mortimer is not having his teeth filled. What will you drink?"

"A little Scotch and a lot of water," Sam said. "What's Mortimer getting at the dentist? A permanent?"

"Remember this morning when we talked on the phone and I said staff had been getting slack and I had to pin their ears back before I went down to the office? This all right?"

"Perfect," Sam said. "Except a little more water, please, and another lump of ice. Yes, I remember."

"Well, when I got round to the ear-pinning-back business, it turned out Mortimer, poor lamb, hadn't been slack at all. He'd been in absolute agony for three days with an impacted wisdom tooth and the poor dear had been too terrified to say anything about it. You're sure that drink is all right?"

"Why are you making all this fuss about my drink?"

"Because you just had a message from that adorably rich Mrs. Meissen, who wants you to call her the moment you show up here, and from the sound of her voice I think it would be wise for you to have something truly fortifying in your hand while she pours her words into your ears. Why don't you make the call in Claude's study? He's still at the office."

She opened the door to the small room, and as Sophie pulled the door shut behind him, Sam took a long pull at his glass. It *had* been quite a day, no matter what he told himself curtly as he rang other people's doorbells, and the only favorable thing that could be said for what he had been involved in since Billy had gone off to school that morning, was that the complications of the day had kept Billy's father from thinking about the problem of his relationship to Rebecca Meissen. Now that he was being forced to think about it, Sam found that his only sensible thought was a disturbing one: it was totally unlike Rebecca, with whom self-control was a passion, to leave telephone messages, especially with another woman, that were, if Sophie's description could be trusted, on the excitable side. Sitting down at the desk, which had come from the middle, or 7:00 P.M. to 9:00 P.M., section of *Strange Interlude*, Sam set down his drink and took up the receiver of the old-fashioned phone that had not, when it was part of the set of the original company of *Yellow Jack*, been equipped with a dial. Wearily, wishing all at once that he knew what to do with his life, Sam ran his forefinger through the familiar pattern.

"Sam?"

"Yes," he said, startled. "How did you know it was me?"

"Oh, darling, don't you know you're as regular as the tides?" Rebecca's voice said in a manner that made Sam realize Sophie, in describing the way the leaver of the message had sounded, had not been bitchy. "Mrs. Sargent said you were expected at five, and she'd give you the message the moment you arrived, so when the phone rings at two minutes after five, who can it possibly be but you?"

"I wish I had as much confidence in my solid, stable qualities as you have," Sam said, wondering how best to sneak up on her obvious distress without adding to it by indicating that he was aware of it. "Are you excited about tonight?"

"I wish I had the character to say I'm not, but the truth is I'm as excited as I was the night I went to my first ball," Rebecca said. "And, Sam, I think you'll be pleased to know that your judgment about that piece of copy for the catalogue this morning—remember?"

"I certainly do," Sam said.

"Well, Ibram agreed with you," Rebecca said. "He says it's a superb piece of writing."

"Then that can't be why you called me," Sam said.

"What?" Rebecca said, and then, "No, darling, it isn't." There was a pause at the other end of the line, and Sam, who was so fond of her that the wish to love her frequently became confused in his mind with the fact that he didn't, now wished he could smooth away the troubled frown he knew he had brought to her brow by his inept attempt at easing her discomfort. "What I called about—" Rebecca said in the spuriously forth-right tone of someone making a determined fresh start, and paused again. "Sam," she said, "we *are* having dinner together before we go on to the gallery, aren't we?"

"Do you really think a man as regular as the tides is likely to forget that?"

Rebecca laughed and said, "Of course not. Sam?"

"Yes, honeybunch?"

"I love it when you call me that."

Sam, who was intensely aware that she did, could please her only with an effort: it was what he used to call Jennie.

"What's on your mind, honeybunch?"

"What makes you think anything is on my mind?" Rebecca said, and Sam could see the frown deepening as she changed course and sped away from her true purpose with: "Where were you all day? I tried reaching you on the phone at the apartment several times."

"What about?" Sam said, pleased that the opening had finally come. "I ran up to have a sandwich with my agent about some changes *American Bride* wants in that new serial I've just done for them, and then I went out to Queens to see my A.P.'s."

"A.P.'s?"

"Aged Parents. It's from Dickens. *Chuzzlewit*, I think."

"How are they?"

"I'm afraid my mother and father are suffering from an incurable disease."

"Oh, Sam, no! Is there—?"

"No, there isn't. This disease is something nobody can do anything about."

"Sam, for heaven's sake, what are they suffering from?"

"Being eighty years old," he said.

"Oh," Rebecca said, and then, in a new burst of determination to face up to the Truth she spent as much time fleeing from as pursuing, she said, "What I called you about, Sam, did you see Winchell this morning?"

Sam had a moment of relief mixed with disappointment. He had been expecting something bigger, something more troubling. The fact that what had finally arrived was neither did not compensate for the feeling that he had been cheated.

"Yes, I did," he said. "I meant to mention it this morning when you came up, but we got so involved in your copy for the catalogue that it slipped my mind. Does it upset you?"

"No, of course not," said Rebecca, who was so obviously lying that Sam at once lost—and immediately regretted the loss—his feeling that he had been cheated out of an impending disaster. "It's a little embarrassing, of course. People have been calling all day. Ibram from the gallery. My father and then my three brothers, all of them, one after the other. Anton, who must have had it pointed out to him by his secretary, since he doesn't read anything but the *Wall Street Journal* and Proust. Even Charlene, although she didn't call, of course. She just came running out of the bedroom where she should have been dusting, holding a cloth and a copy of the *Mirror,* and wanting to know what they all wanted to know, what it says here in Winchell, you're going to marry Mr. Silver, is it true, Mrs. Meissen, are you?"

"Well, honeybunch, are you?"

"Sam, is this a proposal?"

"I don't know," said Sam, who didn't. The words had emerged not because he wanted to utter them but because his sense of neatness as a storyteller had nudged him, telling him that here, at this point in the scene, if he were writing it rather than living it, the hero should say something startling, something that would shock the protagonists into pulling together the carefully laid-down strands of their relationship into a dramatic knot of resolution. Floundering, caught between the unmanageable uncertainties of his real life and the manageable certainties of his professional life, Sam said, "Do you want it to be a proposal?"

"Yes, very much," Rebecca said. "But not when it comes that way."

"What way?"

"By accident," she said. "A bunch of words you don't mean."

Torn again, this time between surprise at these recurring illustrations of her acute perceptions and annoyance with himself for providing the opening through which she had tagged him, Sam said, "Look, honeybunch—"

"No, don't say it that way, Sam, please. Not in that tone of voice. I hate it when you say it that way."

"I'm sorry," he said. "But I'm also confused. You call me here at Mrs. Sargent's apartment, you leave a message asking me to call you back and it's urgent, and when I do, you ask me if I've forgotten our dinner date and what do I think of an item in Winchell's column. I can't believe that's why you called."

"It isn't," Rebecca said. "I called because I don't want you to do anything foolish."

"That's a pretty tall order for a man of thirty-six," Sam said. "The habits of a lifetime are not easily broken."

"No, I'm serious, Sam."

"About what?"

"On the page facing Winchell, in the horoscope—"

"The what?"

"The horoscope," Rebecca said. "Don't you read it every day?"

Her tone, which was laced with incredulity, left him stunned: it was as though he had been asked with deadly seriousness if he did not, like all other members of the civilized community, fight a duel every morning before he shaved.

"Of course I don't read it," Sam said. "Don't tell me you read that nonsense."

"I certainly do read it," Rebecca said sharply. "And it's not nonsense."

He stared helplessly at the phone, remembering what he had said to Billy that morning when the boy had asked why Sam had never told him that Jennie was so fond of Shakespeare: you never could tell anybody everything about another person. No matter how hard you tried, there would always be things you left out, things you didn't know you had left out until they came up accidentally, by association. Similarly, you could never *know* everything about another person. No matter how close you were, or how long the closeness had existed, there would always be moments of discovery that took you by surprise and changed you both.

"Is that why you called me?" Sam said. "Because of something you read in the horoscope?"

"Yes, and I wish you'd drop that tone of voice, Sam. Just because you don't believe in something doesn't mean it isn't so."

"Do you believe in it?"

"I certainly do," Rebecca said. "Our destinies are written in the stars, and I can prove it."

"Oh, come on."

"I said I can prove it."

"How?"

"It was the horoscope that told me my vague feelings about Anton should be brought to a head in divorce, and when Ibram Moulage asked me to set a date it was the horoscope that told me tonight is the right night for my show. That's just two examples at random, and it's what the horoscope said about you this morning that's made me try to reach you all day."

"How can the horoscope say anything about me?" Sam said. "We haven't even met."

"You save that joke for Bud Bienstock and *American Bride*," Rebecca said. "You're Aries."

"Who says so?"

"The zodiac," Rebecca said. "Aries is anybody born between March 21 and April 19 and your birthday is April 4th, so you're Aries, and what it says about Aries in today's horoscope, which I am holding right here in my hand, is as follows, and I quote. Sam, are you listening?"

"That's hardly the word."

"It'll serve for the time being, so keep right on doing it," Rebecca said. "Aries, it says here, and I quote: *A dangerous day. Be on your guard. A series of innocent events, dealing with social, business, and family matters, will absorb your morning and afternoon, and at first merely annoy and irritate you. Unless you are alert and watchful, however, each of these events, which when considered separately seem so small and casual and matter-of-fact and no more than part of the daily routine, will contribute toward the end of the day to a general feeling of dangerous dissatisfaction that could drive you to a culminating act that would affect your whole life, a change that might be disastrous. The decision is in your hands. Keep your eyes open. Remember the old adage: whom the gods would destroy they first make mad. Perform no act, make no decision without first reviewing the events of the entire day, no matter how small or innocent any one of these events may seem.*" Rebecca's voice stopped and then, worriedly, she said, "Sam, did you hear that?"

"Every word of it," he said.

"Do you understand now why I've been trying to reach you on the phone all day?"

"Yes, and I think it's very sweet of you," Sam said. "The only thing is—"

Into his abruptly created silence leaped Rebecca's sharp, concerned "What, Sam?"

"I don't know," he said slowly. "I mean, it's all so general, the things it says could apply to anybody, not only that thing I'm supposed to be."

"Aries."

"Yes, well, for instance, what about you? You're what?"

"Gemini."

"No kidding."

"Oh, Sam, please do stop joking. This is serious. Didn't you hear what it said? Your whole life might be ruined."

"It also says whom the gods would destroy they first make mad, so isn't it safer for me to be kidding?"

"Except that you always start kidding when things are most serious," Rebecca said. "People who want to deride the horoscope always say what you've just said: it's all so general, it could fit anybody, Gemini as well as Aries, Capricorn as well as Leo—"

"Are those some of the others?"

"Yes, and if you'd read what it says today for every one of them, you'd find that it's entirely different from what it says about you, and yet if you wanted to be mean about them and dismiss them, you could say what you just said about Aries, that it's all so general that it could fit anybody."

"Rebecca?"

"Yes, I'm here."

"What does it say about you?" There was a pause, and Sam said again, "Rebecca?"

"I told you I'm here," she said.

"Now tell me what it says about Gemini."

"Sam, that's not why I called."

"I know it isn't, but that's what I want to know."

"I'll tell you when I see you."

"Why not now?"

"I'll tell you when I see you."

"All right," Sam said. "I'll pick you up at six. If I'm not there by six, say six-fifteen, I'll meet you at Tony's at six-thirty."

"Oh, Sam!"

"Aw, shucks, it's nothing. I figured your father and your brothers and Anton would want to make it a gold-plated full-dress thing at '21' or the Colony, and if that's what they want, fine, let them have it. But you and me, this is your big night," Sam said, "I thought we'd have dinner alone at Tony's," and, making the effort, he succeeded in adding, "honeybunch."

"If I weren't such a fool," Rebecca said, "I would accept your proposal of a few minutes ago whether you meant it or not. You're the nicest, handsomest, sexiest, most thoughtful, loyal and all-around decent magazine serial writer in the Western Hemisphere."

"I know," Sam said, fiercely turning his back on the bright beam of despair she had inadvertently admitted into the delicious gloom of their intimacy. *"The Second Largest Outdoor Swimming Pool in the East."*

"The what?"

"I'll tell you when I see you," Sam said. "We'll swap. You tell me what the horoscope says about you for today, and I'll tell you about *The Second Largest Swimming Pool in the East.*"

"Fair enough," Rebecca said. "See you here at six or at Tony's at six-thirty, and remember the warning I just read you from your horoscope."

"I'll remember," Sam said and, lowering the receiver, he held it in his lap for a few moments, so she would be able to hang up first. The mechanical click that ended a telephone conversation was exactly the same, he had discovered, whether what was being terminated was a screaming quarrel between deadly enemies or the whispered endearments of lovers parting reluctantly for the night.

When he heard the click in his lap, Sam replaced the receiver on the hook, stood up, and went out into the drawing room, where he was stopped in his tracks by a sight that disturbed as much as it startled him: Sophie Sargent, arms folded across her chest, was standing by the window, staring out into the dusk gathering over Central Park.

With the shadows changing her graying hair to a soft purple, and her strong, cleanly cut features outlined in sharp profile against the glass, she reminded Sam of figureheads he had seen in pictures of Cape Cod whalers.

A moment of thought, and he realized what was startling about the sight: Sophie's immobility. She was a woman of apparently limitless energy who, even when sitting at her desk, created the impression of restless movement. Another moment, and Sam knew why he was disturbed: was it possible that even Sophie, who was no more than fifty-eight, fifty-nine at the most, was also running down?

The thought was intolerable. What would he do without her? He was too old to turn to another agent. No, not too old. Thirty-six was young. At any rate, that's what he always implied about his heroes in *American Bride* stories. But Sam knew he suffered from an infirmity almost as bad as age: habit. He was set in his ways. Ever since he was a kid of nineteen, his life had been inextricably intertwined with the Sargent & Sargent office. When the first Sargent had begun to slip, it had been easy to conceal the truth of his own fears beneath the thickly smeared lotion of loyalty, telling himself he didn't mind doing everything twice. After all, he loved Claude, didn't he? And besides, there was always Sophie to carry on. Jolted inadvertently into facing the fact that always was a foolish word on which to lean, that inevitably Sophie would some day also slip, Sam's first thought was that the inevitable day must be postponed. Sharply, unaware of the passion in his voice, he said, "Sophie!"

She turned, shattering the illusion created by the interplay of twilight

and shadow, coming back to the grayness and wrinkles of her nearly six
decades, and she said, "Sam darling, why are you screaming?"

He laughed uneasily. "I didn't mean to," he said. "But you did look
so—so—" He made a gesture with the hand in which he was holding the
glass, saw it was empty, and moved toward the bar. "This seems to be
my day for collecting clichés," Sam said. "Would you drop yours into the
hopper by repaying me for the penny I offer for your thoughts?"

"They aren't worth that much," Sophie said. "I was just thinking about
Wilkes-Barre."

The Scotch decanter clinked sharply against the lip of Sam's glass.
"Good God," he said, and didn't bother to modify his astonishment: it
was the first time in all the years he had known her that Sophie Sargent
had ever mentioned in his presence the place where she had been born
and raised. "What brought that on?"

"Come here and take a look."

Sam carried his refilled glass to her side. "At what?" he said.

Sophie Sargent nodded down toward the park, where the lights were
twinkling over the tiny figures roller-skating back and forth, some alone,
some hand in hand, like beautiful little dolls brought to life in one of those
fairy tales Sam's kindergarten teacher used to read to the class in P.S. 188.

"When I was a little girl," Sophie Sargent said, "across the street from
Papa's grocery store, there was a vacant lot. In the summer it was full of
weeds, and my older brothers and other kids on the block used to play
ball there. In the winter, though, the middle used to fill up with snow or
rain or what not, I don't remember. I remember only that it would freeze
and form a crude sort of skating rink on which all the kids on the block
used to slide about. All the kids except me."

The tone of her voice caused Sam to turn and say, "Why not you?
Sick? Or some sort of injury?"

Sophie shook her head. "No," she said. "I had a better game. I used to
hide at dusk up in our front room. We lived in three rooms, over the
grocery store, and the front one, like all the others, was a bedroom at
night. It had to be. There were ten of us, counting Ma and Pa. But
during the day, when the beds were all covered, we pretended that front
room was a parlor. Nobody ever used it, of course, because Ma and Pa
were always downstairs, working in the grocery, from early morning to
late at night. But Ma liked the idea of a parlor, and she had a fat green
plush-covered chair near the window. At dusk, in the winter, I used to
hide in that chair and pretend it was a golden chariot. I used to look
out on the kids sliding around on that patch of frozen empty lot and I'd

pretend they were all pure-bred Arabian steeds hitched to my golden char-iot. And you know what they were doing?"

Sam nodded. "Yes," he said quietly. "They were drawing your chariot toward the palace where the handsome young prince was giving a ball at which he would choose the most beautiful girl to be his wife and share his kingdom."

Sophie shook her head again. "No," she said. "That was the trouble."

"How trouble?"

"What you just said, that Cinderella thing, that's normal for any little girl to dream," Sophie said. "But me, my dream, in my dream I dreamed those horses, those Arabian steeds, they were pulling me in my golden chariot to New York."

"Just New York?" Sam said.

"Just New York," Sophie said.

"But to a child, especially a child over a grocery store in Wilkes-Barre, New York isn't a place. It's just two words."

"Not to this child," Sophie said. "Like all the other kids on the block, my chief source of entertainment was my public library borrower's card. This was before the days of TV and radio. There were a few comic strips in the daily papers, but the comic book as we know it today had not yet been invented, and the movies were a once-a-week affair to which you could go only if you had a dime. You didn't need a dime to go to the public library, and we all went. I soon had a whole, absolutely real, three-di-mensional dream world built for myself out of fairy tales and other books I read, and I lived in it quite happily, like most little girls."

"And most little boys," Sam said.

Sophie gave him a short glance. "Yes," she said, "I imagine you did."

"What destroyed yours?" Sam said.

"A copy of *Leslie's Weekly*," Sophie Sargent said. "There was a maga-zine section in our library, and there used to be quite a bit of competition among the kids for *St. Nicholas* and *Boys' Life* and so on. One day, when I came too late for the *St. Nicholas* I wanted, I tried to hide how I felt by turning the pages of the first magazine I saw in front of me, but suddenly I stopped turning pages. There, in front of me, was a picture I've never forgotten. It changed my whole life."

"A picture of what?" Sam said.

"A dinner party," Sophie Sargent said. "I don't know if you remember *Leslie's*, or ever saw it. It was a sort of cross between one of today's slick picture magazines and one of those butcher's paper jobs edited up in Bos-ton that are full of think pieces about cartels and summit conferences. Anyway, this was a picture, a snapshot of a dinner party given for Richard

Harding Davis at Rector's. He had just come back from covering the
Spanish-American War, and his friends were giving him this dinner, and
this was a snapshot of the guests sitting about, walking toward tables, bowing to one another, holding glasses, smiling, that sort of thing. Nothing
spectacular or even unusual. And yet I knew. Out there in Wilkes-Barre,
at the age of eight, I knew."

"Knew what?" Sam said.

"I knew this was it," Sophie Sargent said, nodding down toward Central Park. "Don't ask me how that little girl knew, but she did. Right then
and there, in that Wilkes-Barre public library, the dream world about
the prince and the ball fell apart and was replaced by the dream of New
York. I suppose I grasped at that moment that one was an unattainable
dream, and the other an attainable reality. Something inside me said girls
who dream about princes end up in Wilkes-Barre, but girls who dream
about wearing the kind of dresses the women in that *Leslie's* picture were
wearing, and going to that kind of party with men in those kinds of
clothes, why, I knew at once that those girls get to wearing those kinds
of clothes at parties with those kinds of men."

"You were right," Sam said.

"Yes, I was," Sophie said. "About everything except one thing."

"What's that?" Sam said.

"The end of the dream," Sophie said. "I could hear the music, the sound
Dick Whittington heard, those bells that drew him to London."

"Bow bells," Sam said.

"That's right," Sophie said. "We had to learn the poem by heart in
school. Along with *Evangeline*."

"No, *Evangeline* came later," Sam said. "Dick Whittington came around
the time of *Hiawatha*, in sixth grade."

Sophie nodded and, with a wry smile, said, "I suppose uptown was to
East Tenth Street what New York was to Wilkes-Barre."

"What's wrong with it?" Sam said.

"Who said anything is wrong with it?"

"You did," Sam said. "You said the Cinderella thing is normal but this"
—he nodded down toward Central Park, then added a short gesture to
include the elaborate drawing room—"this you implied isn't."

Sophie opened her mouth, then closed it, and did a curious thing with
her fingers: she laid them delicately against her cheek, as though to ease
a pain, and Sam suddenly found himself holding his breath, as though the
answer to his question, over which Sophie was so obviously hesitating,
contained a great truth for which he had for a long time been searching.

"What's wrong with it is," she said finally, "it lives up to your expectations."

She scowled, as though checking in her mind the words she had just spoken to make sure they expressed what she had meant. Apparently they did not, because Sophie made a small gesture of impatience, and said, "Didn't you ever stop to ask yourself why fairy tales always end with the words *happily ever after?*"

"Because there isn't any more to tell," Sam said.

Again Sophie made the gesture of impatience. "No," she said. "It's because happiness is dull. It doesn't make exciting reading. People never really think about what they want. They just want it. And most of what they want seems to fit very nicely under that general heading: happiness. So the boys who write fairy tales very shrewdly devote their storytelling skills to the struggle *for* happiness. When the struggle is over, they know the story is over, so they wrap it up with that wonderful all-purpose pink ribbon: *happily ever after.*"

"You got here," Sam said slowly. "You made it all the way from Wilkes-Barre to the place from which Dick Whittington heard those bells. You say it's lived up to your expectations. And you say that's the trouble?"

"Sam, you've made it, too," Sophie Sargent said. "Don't you feel the same way?" To avoid answering he looked down into his glass, because she had put her finger on what had been wrong with his whole day—he didn't know how he felt—and Sophie said, "Sam dear, don't you see? The story ended when I made it, years ago. Ever since then I've been living the part that comes after the pink ribbon: *happily ever after.* And the trouble is the difference between a story and a life. The story ends. Life goes on. I didn't mind it for a long time. Maybe I should say I didn't notice it for a long time. But these last couple of years, since Claude's memory started to go, since old friends like you started coming out of business conferences in Claude's office to have a drink with Sophie at the apartment so the conference could really be held—"

"The same thing would be true in Wilkes-Barre," Sam said. "If you were still there today."

Sophie turned, and from the way she looked at him, a look that came to her face as a rule when she greeted him after reading a new manuscript of his that she liked, Sam knew he had said the right thing.

"It would, wouldn't it?" Sophie Sargent said, and again she did that curious thing with her fingers, only this time she placed her fingers gently against *his* cheek. "You're very sweet," she said. "And like most writers, just about as wrong as you can be. If I were still in Wilkes-Barre today, I would not yet have got as far as that *happily ever after* pink ribbon. To abandon plain English for a moment and use the sort of fancy lingo Henley Titterton adores, if I were still in Wilkes-Barre, Sam dear, I would not yet have known the disappointment of fulfillment. All this"—she repeated Sam's nod toward the park below and his gesture toward the expensive room that surrounded them—"would still be ahead of me. No matter how old I am, I'd still be that little girl curled up in the dusk on a green plush chair looking out on the world spread and waiting for her to take it."

"No," Sam said, and then found he could say no more. There was something wrong with Sophie's statement. If what she had said was true, then Sam Silver would have been happier if he were still living on East Tenth Street, and Sam Silver knew that could not be true. There were things worse than the disappointment of fulfillment. There was the bitterness of frustration. Disappointment might hurt you. Frustration could kill you. Sam knew. It had killed Jennie.

"Sam dear, Socrates and his chums couldn't even put a dent in this one," Sophie Sargent said. "You and I are not likely to lick it between now and your dinner date with that enchanting Mrs. Meissen."

"How the hell do you know I have a dinner date with her?"

"Darling, you mustn't be so simple. People will think you're an agent rather than a writer. I had a card about her show from the Moulage Gallery, and any man who wouldn't take a girl to dinner on the night of an event like that is either disinterested in her or doesn't have the inside track, and if either of those things were true, you couldn't have written the love scenes in *They Told Me You Were Dead*, which, by the way, are the best things in the story and Bud Bienstock thinks so, too, so let's get on with what it is you came to see me about and then you'll be able to get on to dinner with Mrs. Meissen. Why don't you let me dampen that just a bit?"

"No, this is fine," Sam said, swinging his glass out of her reach. "It's about Kenyon Poole."

"Then I think perhaps I'll have one, if you don't mind," Sophie said, moving past him toward the bar. "What about Kenyon Poole, darling?"

"Sophie, if you're going to fade off into the Lady Kirriemuir vagueness act, I'm never going to get to my dinner date with Rebecca Meissen."

"Sam, I don't understand how the sweet, innocent, open-faced youngster I met sixteen years ago can have become the cynical, crabbed, suspicious man glaring at me today."

"The answer is simple enough," Sam said. "Sixteen years of immersion up to my belly button in the sweet, innocent, open-faced world of letters. Now let's really cut the crap, Sophie. I want to get out of here before Claude comes home."

"Yes, you must," Sophie said. "I'm sorry, Sam. Of course I know what it's about. How much did Claude tell you?"

"He told me about Kenyon Poole's daughter, and that he thinks he can make the girl rich if I lend him my copies of whatever Kenyon Poole first editions I may happen to have, and on second thought, I think maybe I'd better have a bit more of this lubricant."

"Yes, do, Sam dear," Sophie said. "That was quite a sentence. You must be parched."

"I'm also annoyed," Sam said as he went to the bar.

"Don't take it out on the rug, dear," Sophie said. "It's from *Rain From Heaven*. Why are you annoyed?"

"Because Claude should know better than to think I'd swallow that pile of farfel."

"Sam darling, you mean you don't believe it?"

"Sophie darling, bring your eyebrows down to where they belong. No, I don't believe it, and I've got a couple of damned good reasons."

"One at a time, then, Sam dear."

"First, because it's so obviously a piece of fiction fabricated by a man who knows all there is to know about putting together a story but has never actually written one. People come to fiction, Sophie dear, the way they come to church. Remember? What Claude has done, in feeding me this little number about Kenyon Poole and his daughter, is put together an embarrassing *come-to-realizer* that stands up to the test of logic just about as successfully as Hitler's protestations that far from being the enemy of the Jews, he was actually trying by driving them out of Germany to help them achieve their Zionist goals. If I came to you or Claude for an editorial discussion before going on to lunch with Bud Bienstock to outline a few stories for *American Bride*, and I told you the plot Claude told me across the tuna and rye in his office today, you'd both scream."

"All right, Sam dear, all right. There's no need to scream now. What's your second reason?"

"What you just said a minute ago," Sam said. "You said to me: *how much did Claude tell you?*"

Sophie nodded and took a sip from her glass. "Yes," she said, "I did say that."

"I assume from it that you and Claude discussed in advance how much he was to tell me, but because his memory is not what it used to be, you don't know whether he told me too little or too much or what. I can set your mind at rest on that point. So far as I'm concerned, Sophie, he told me too little, and if you want me to do anything on this, whatever the hell it is, you'd better tell me the works."

She gave him one of the long, appraising glances that used to make him blush and still made him feel a trifle awkward.

"Sam," Sophie Sargent said, "whatever happened between you and Kenyon Poole?"

"That's none of your business."

"Are you sure?" Sophie said.

"Positive," Sam said.

"I don't want to pry—"

"Oh, yes, you do."

"Only for the purpose of—"

"Sophie, I don't give a good God-damn about the purpose."

"I wouldn't tell anybody, Sam dear. You know that."

Sam, who did know it, nevertheless said, "No."

"But why not?"

"If I told you," Sam said, "it would make two people who know."

"And that's one too many?"

Sam nodded, and Sophie, nodding with him, said slowly, "Yes, I see that." She pursed her lips, looked down into her glass, then looked up and said, "If Claude and I want those first editions out of you, we'll have to tell you the truth?"

"If that's *all* you want," Sam said.

"If you won't tell us what happened between you and Ken Poole," Sophie said, "I guess it *is* all."

"Don't guess, Sophie. Tell me what you know, and I'll tell you if I'll do what you and Claude want."

Sophie set down her glass, then seemed to regret having deprived herself of something to do with her hands, and she picked up the glass.

"The part about Ken's daughter and the nuclear physicist and their wanting to get married and their being broke, all that's true," Sophie said. "It's also true that we want the first editions so we can start the campaign of reviving Ken's reputation, about which I'm sure Claude told you?"

"He did," Sam said.

"What he didn't tell you is that the daughter has discovered a new Kenyon Poole manuscript."

"New?" Sam said. "Poole was killed in that plane disappearance ten years ago."

"New to *us*," Sophie said. "New to the world. Apparently he wrote it and then put it in the safe deposit box in the same bank that was in charge of the trust fund that educated the daughter, and when she graduated and had her session with the bankers who told her there was no more money, she discovered there was a manuscript in the box, and since she knew Claude and I had been her father's agents, she brought it to us, asking if we thought it was worth anything."

"Is it?" Sam said.

"Have I ever lied to you about money?" Sophie Sargent said. "Or even exaggerated?"

"Not that I know of."

"No, Sam, I'm serious."

"Sophie, I don't think you've ever lied to me about anything."

"That's not true," she said. "In the early days, when I was feeling my way with you and I didn't know how tough or soft you were, I used to tell you, before I got around to suggesting corrections, I'd say some of your manuscripts were better than I actually thought they were."

"I knew you were doing it," Sam said. "So you weren't really lying."

"If I were twenty years younger I'd dispose of Claude with a sashweight, which still seems to me the only stylish way to get rid of a spouse, and I'd marry you," Sophie said. "But about money, I never lied. You know that."

"Yes," Sam said. "I know that."

"So there's a good chance you'll believe me when I tell you, in answer to your question is this just-discovered Kenyon Poole manuscript worth anything, I personally would rather own all the rights to this number than own a Shakespeare first folio."

"All right, now that you've got that out of the way, say something sensible."

"No, it's true, Sam."

"How can it possibly be? Even *The Small Meal*, which was Poole's most successful book, with an earning record that even a Greek shipping magnate might envy, still it's not in a financial sense anything like—"

"This manuscript, speaking purely financially, Sam, is to *The Small Meal* or any of the big best-sellers of the last twenty years, as the Empire State Building is to an F. A. O. Schwartz doll house."

"I must say I admire your capacity for maintaining the posh note in even a highly exaggerated figure of speech."

"Sam dear, I'm not exaggerating."

"I can't believe you're doing anything else," Sam said. "Kenyon Poole was a writer of Westerns. There is a group, and I admit I belong to it, that feels he was potentially a greater writer than he allowed himself to be. But they don't pay off at the wickets on potentialities. Kenyon Poole undoubtedly wrote the greatest Westerns of our time, but they're still Westerns, a secondary art form, like the magazine serial, of which I will punch you in your lovely nose if you call me once more the greatest living American practitioner. There may be a certain amount of curiosity value,

I admit, in discovering, ten years after his death, an unpublished magazine serial by a man who once was the hot shot of the field, and similarly with discovering a Western by the man who wrote the greatest of them, but how that literary oddity can be equated financially with a first folio is something—"

"Sam, this manuscript by Kenyon Poole is not a Western."

"Oh," Sam said.

"Yes, dear, oh," Sophie Sargent said, and she waited until he could have asked the question two or three times before, a trifle irritably, she said, "Aren't you going to ask what it is?"

"Of course," said Sam, who was sick at heart because he knew what it was, and now, in the clutch, when he needed the skill he had acquired by so many years of resolute self-schooling, the capacity to handle the success of a contemporary, even a dead contemporary, had deserted him. With simulated interest, he said, "If it's not a Western, what is it?"

"The book we always thought Ken was too scared to write," Sophie said. "Well, apparently he finally decided to stop hiding behind the Western and come out into the arena as a serious novelist. He never said a word to me or Claude or anybody else. I can understand that, and I can even understand his locking the manuscript away in a safe deposit box after it was finished. He probably wanted it to season for a while, look at it later, a year or two after it was written, to see if it was what he thought it was, before he turned it over to his publisher and the world. If it hadn't been for his daughter going to the bank last week, God knows how much longer it would have been before the manuscript was discovered, if ever."

"Sophie."

"What?"

"Is it good?"

"Claude says it's better than *Moby Dick.*"

"What do you say?"

"I haven't read it yet."

Sam's mind recorded but did not flinch from the fact that his jealousy was pierced by a sudden stab of hope.

"Then how do you know it's good?" he said.

"I trust Claude's judgment," Sophie said.

"About magazine serials, yes," Sam said. "Young Loves for *American Bride,* yes. But *Moby Dick?*"

Sophie lifted her glass, but did not drink. Sighting across it, as though the glass were a telescope and she was adjusting it to get him into sharp focus, she stared at Sam for several moments in silence. The lower half of her face was hidden by the highball glass, and the expression around her eyes remained neutral, but Sam could tell about the temperature of that silence. It was cold.

"Sam," Sophie said finally, "I never thought it was necessary to set you straight on this particular point: it is Claude's memory that has failed, not his judgment."

"I'm sorry," Sam said.

"I should jolly well think you would be," Sophie said. "Now that we've got that nonsense out of the way, here's the pitch. Claude feels that we are sitting on the biggest property of our careers as agents, and I couldn't agree more. Ken Poole's potential greatness was established long ago. Now, here, ten years after his death, the potentiality becomes fact. Claude and I feel this is the most important literary event of the decade. What's going to happen when Claude and I spring this Kenyon Poole manuscript on the world will be little short of a national holiday. On the publicity side, I won't even try to describe it. On the financial side, we are a shoo-in for a huge magazine serialization, a whopping book club guarantee, a monster movie sale, a colossal paper-back advance, an unprecedented second serial fee, a history-making hard-cover sale, and everything in the way of diamond-studded extra rights that your active mind can dream up, from foreign editions to Kenyon Poole costume jewelry. In short, my dear Sam, if this manuscript does not earn for Ken's daughter at least a cool million during its first active year, I am willing to forgo my commission. Now what do you think of that, my dear Sam?"

"I think there's something fishy about this junior Fort Knox being dependent on a few first editions that an obscure magazine serial writer might or might not have on his shelves."

"You are not obscure," Sophie said sharply.

"Knock it off," Sam said.

"And Ken must be made respectable."

"He's dead," Sam said. "What's more respectable than that?"

"The men who run the movie studios, the editors of magazines that serialize novels, the judges of book clubs, they all have long memories, Sam. They're afraid of their audiences. The first thing they're going to remember when the name Kenyon Poole comes up is not that he wrote *The Small Meal* and half a dozen other great Westerns. The first thing they're going to remember is that mess he was involved in when he died."

"And if they remember that mess," Sam said, "you think the men who run the studios, and the editors who serialize novels, and the book club judges will refuse to buy for their audiences, and I quote, the most important literary event of the decade?"

"There's a good chance they won't," Sophie said.

"What's wrong with their not buying?"

"Sam *dear*."

"Shut up, Sophie. I'm punching holes in your corrections and additions to Claude's story."

"Such as?"

"Suppose all those people refuse to buy?" Sam said. "That won't stop Kenyon Poole's old hard-cover publisher, or indeed any hard-cover publisher in the business, from leaping at the chance to publish, will it?"

"No, of course not," Sophie said.

"In fact, the hard-cover publisher will undoubtedly be delighted that the cream of the book has not been skimmed off by a magazine serialization prior to publication. Isn't that right?"

"Suppose it is?" Sophie said. "What are you driving at?"

"The great big yawning hole in your story, Sophie dear. Even if nothing of a financial nature happens to this book except straight royalties from a hard-cover publication, it should still add up to what I'm sure Henley Titterton would describe as A Tidy Sum. Correct?"

"Yes, of course," Sophie said. "So what?"

"You and Claude tell me your entire motivation in this matter is to provide enough money for Kenyon Poole's daughter to marry her nuclear physicist and accompany him to England. True?"

"Yes, certainly. But what—?"

"Isn't A Tidy Sum adequate for that modest purpose?" Sam said. "Or do these two young cats expect to set up housekeeping in Buckingham Palace?"

"Our entire motivation, as you put it, Sam dear, is not merely to provide these youngsters with the price of a marriage license and the cost of a couple of plane tickets to London. Claude and I would like them to have the pink ribbon on the package as well. Sam, she's Kenyon Poole's daughter. She's entitled to the *happily ever after*."

"So she can live like you and me, Sophie dear? In gold-plated misery? Nibbling out-of-season fruit? Looking down over her cocktail at the most expensive side of Central Park? And yearning for the bygone days in Wilkes-Barre?"

"Sam Silver, why do all you writers have to be such bastards?"

"Because only a bastard is free from Freud's boring interpretation of the Oedipus complex, and can therefore devote himself full time to trying to possess the only mother worth possessing, namely, his Art."

"Jesus, Mary, and Joseph," Sophie Sargent said. "On two drinks, yet."

"On two drinks and your hot air," Sam said. "Sophie dear, after sixteen years you have finally cracked the ice on one front between us. You have finally evaded an issue with me. Sophie, what is it you want from me?"

Sophie said, "You don't know the pressures I'm under."

"That's right, I don't," Sam said. "And until I do, dear, I'm not playing ball on this thing, whatever it is."

"Where are you going?"

Sam, who had reached the mahogany whatnot from *Paris Bound,* turned with his glass.

"Home to change," he said. "As you pointed out to me a few minutes ago, I have a dinner date."

"Sam."

"I'm waiting," he said. "But not much longer."

"It's fish or cut bait, isn't it?" Sophie said.

"If that's the Wilkes-Barre equivalent of what used to be known on East Tenth Street as crap or get off the pot," Sam said, "the answer is yes."

Sophie sighed and stood up and carried her glass to the bar. "That mess Kenyon Poole was in just before Pearl Harbor," she said. "You weren't in it, too, Sam, were you?"

"Until I learn what you're driving at, Sophie, I'm taking the Fifth."

"Claude and I want you on our side," Sophie said. "You won't tell us what it was between you and Ken Poole. All right. We won't insist. But will you tell us, will you promise that, when we spring this manuscript on the world, and these people come to you for the true story, you'll tell one that won't hurt Ken's daughter?"

"Or your commission," Sam said.

"You can't separate one from the other," Sophie said quietly. "Will you promise, Sam?"

He turned with his glass, saw the tiny, lovely dolls skating back and forth under the lights in the park, and quickly turned back. This was no moment to be caught up in the emotions of a little girl in a green plush chair staring out across a mean street into an empty lot in the winter dusk of half a century ago. This was a moment of decision, and what held Sam motionless was not the knowledge that for over ten years it had never occurred to him he would ever have to make this decision. What held him motionless, holding the empty glass with both hands as though for support, was something at which, a quarter of an hour earlier, he had laughed: Rebecca's warning that because he was not merely what he had been all his life, namely, Samuel Silver, but because he was also something he had never suspected, namely, Aries, he must be on the alert and bear in mind the horoscope's prediction that whatever decision he did reach could easily prove disastrous.

"I realize, of course," Sophie said, "that I don't know the exact nature of what we are asking. Just the same, Sam dear, I do ask it."

Sam dropped one hand from the glass and said, "You can have the promise."

"Thank you, Sam."

"On one condition," he said.

"What's that?"

"I want to read the manuscript first."

Sophie took him by surprise: she laughed.

"What's funny?" Sam said.

"You," she said. "You're always making conditions. Remember that time when Jennie caused that mess with Marshall Umberg at Mercury Films, and he wanted us to write a letter to his boss on the Coast denying the whole thing?"

"What about it?" Sam said.

"You said on one condition," Sophie said. "You'd sign the letter on condition, you said, that Umberg give you Jennie's address."

"Well, he did," Sam said. "Will you do the same with Poole's manuscript?"

"I can't, Sam. It's hand-written, and it's down at Shirley Shaefer's, being typed."

"How long has she had it?"

"Since Claude finished reading the hand-written original, a week, no, eight, wait, yes, eight days ago."

"Then it's finished," Sam said. "Shirley's done novel-length serials of mine in three days. Call her it's all right for me to have it."

"Sam dear, it's almost six o'clock."

"Shirley's never out of that office before seven except the night before Yom Kippur. Call her and tell her."

"But, Sam, even if she's there, and even if it's finished, it's too late for a delivery boy."

"I'll taxi down and pick it up myself," Sam said. "Call her."

Sophie gave him one of those long looks. This time it did not make him feel awkward.

"My God," she said. "I didn't realize this meant that much to you."

"If you had," Sam said, "it wouldn't have stopped you from asking for the promise."

"No, it wouldn't," Sophie said, starting for the telephone in Claude's study. "What's involved here is a client's money. I couldn't let friendship or personal feelings interfere with that." She stopped and turned. "Sam."

"Just call Shirley, will you?"

"One promise I'm going to ask for even before you read the manuscript," Sophie said. "Please promise you won't mention this to Mrs. Meissen."

"What the hell has she got to do with it?" Sam said.

"Everything," Sophie said. "You say you're an obscure magazine writer. Maybe so. But you know people who are not."

"People like the Meissens?"

"I'm sorry, Sam, yes. What those studio heads and magazine editors and book club judges would be afraid of, is what people like the Meissens could pass on, and spread."

For a rueful moment Sam wondered what Rebecca would say to that, but only for a moment. "Okay," he said. "I won't mention it to Rebecca."

"Thank you, Sam," Sophie Sargent said and then she seemed to be struck by something. "Wait a minute," she said. "Before I call Shirley Shaefer and tell her you're coming down for the Poole manuscript, let me just get the terms of our deal straight. In exchange for my letting you read the manuscript, you promise, if asked about the mess Ken Poole was in just before Pearl Harbor, you promise to tell not the truth, whatever it may be, but a story that won't scare anybody off. Is that the deal?"

"That's the deal," Sam said, "and it's one of the poorest you ever made."

"How do you figure that?" Sophie Sargent said.

"I couldn't tell the truth if I wanted to," Sam Silver said quietly. "I've been writing *American Bride* serials too long."

* 6

One of the reasons why the Sargent & Sargent list contained such a high percentage of loyal old clients, at least in Sam Silver's opinion, was Shirley Shaefer.

He doubted that these clients were all aware of the important role Shirley had played in forging their feelings for the agency.

The fact that Sam Silver was probably more aware of that influence than most Sargent & Sargent clients, was due, he knew, to admittedly special circumstances.

For one thing, he and Shirley were almost exactly the same age. For another, they had entered the Sargent & Sargent orbit at approximately the same time. And finally, their professional relationship had begun with a *first* for both of them.

Several months before Sam Silver came out of Mr. Brunschweig's store in a borrowed tuxedo to meet the literary agent who had liked his story in *Landscape*, Shirley Shaefer came out of Washington Irving High School in a homemade guimpe—known on East Fourth Street, where Shirley lived, as a chimp—to take a job as an assistant in the Sargent & Sargent bookkeeping department. The simple fact that she got the job was, to anybody who knew anything of the Sargent & Sargent attitude toward its clients' money, as eloquent a testimonial to Shirley's character as all the letters of recommendation Julien Sorel carried with him up to Paris. The fact that Shirley did not remain very long in the bookkeeping department would have been as predictable to Sam, who came from almost exactly the same background, as it was predictable to Shirley, who actually did make the prediction to him soon after they met, that Sam would not remain long in the employ of Mr. Brunschweig.

By forces not too dissimilar they were both driven toward goals not too different.

Shirley was the oldest of six children, all girls. When she came to work in the Sargent & Sargent office, only one of her five sisters had, like Shirley, made it to Washington Irving High. Even though it looked, because Shirley's father had died while she was in her senior year, as though the four youngest girls might have to do without a high school education, Shirley did not care how it looked. Her sisters were going to have the same advantages she'd had, if it killed her.

Of all the people who watched Shirley operate, Sam was the only one who was not amazed by the fact that she managed to remain alive. If you wanted something fiercely enough, no amount of work involved in moving toward the goal could hurt. It was being denied the wherewithal to work and move forward that killed you.

Shirley was a first-rate bookkeeper, but she was also a superb typist. In the office of a literary agent the most commonplace recurring crisis is the manuscript that must be copied immediately at a time when all the professional typists known to and regularly used by the agency are too busy to do the job. Shirley watched this crisis occur four times during her first two weeks in the Sargent & Sargent office. The fifth time, as she put it herself, she stuck in her two cents and offered to type the manuscript, a six-thousand-word short story, during her lunch hour.

Sam was never quite sure in his own mind whether Shirley knew, when she made the offer, that she would be paid for her work. He certainly did not, when Shirley told him the story years later, dare ask her. Sam was certain, however, that by the time she made the offer, Shirley, who was an extremely bright girl, had reached a fairly accurate assessment of her boss's character. Even a slow-witted person would have known soon after meeting him that Claude Sargent was a fair-minded man. He insisted that the client, whose short story had been involved, pay Shirley what he would have had to pay the professional typist who normally copied his work.

Another thing Sam did not know was Shirley's weekly salary during those early days in the Sargent & Sargent bookkeeping department. He did know, however, because he had written scores of them, that a six-thousand-word short story came to eighteen double-spaced pages. At thirty-five cents a page, plus two carbons, this meant six dollars and thirty cents to the typist. Sam was not surprised, when one day Shirley described her feelings about the transaction, to discover that they were not unlike his mother's feelings about the ten-dollar check he had received from *Landscape* for the hour and a half it had taken him to write "The Ways of Men Must Sever."

"I mean, Mr. Silver, figure it out for yourself," Shirley had said. "You know what salaries were like back in 1931. Especially for kids just out of high school. No reflection on Mr. Sargent. I love him like my own father, he should rest in peace, one of the fairest-minded men who ever lived, that's what I think of Mr. Sargent. But to stay in business in 1931, it was no picnic, either, believe me, Mr. Silver. Paying the office rent and getting up those salaries for the help every week, honest, there were times I used to worry myself sick how Mr. Sargent was going to do it in those days. Well, one of the ways he did it, like everybody else in those days, eighteen-year-old kids from Washington Irving High in the bookkeeping department, them every week they didn't pay off with no satchel full of goldfish, believe me. So when I got this six dollars and thirty cents for typing that story, which actually it took me two hours, but they were so desperate to have it, you know how it is when an editor is hot and he's gotta have it that afternoon or he won't buy it, they were so glad, nobody said boo about my lunch hour that day it was two hours, not one hour, and I said to myself Shirley Shaefer, wake up. A whole week you work five and a half days, from nine to five-thirty, and what you get, while it's perfectly respectable, the national debt it won't pay off neither. And here, for one little extra job, done on your lunch hour, you get almost one third as much as a whole week's salary. Shirley, I said to myself, Shirley Shaefer, give a little think."

The results of Shirley's thinking proved to be, in the long run and in her immediate circle, spectacular.

From solving an occasional crisis during her lunch hour, she moved on to remaining after hours to do longer manuscripts, and when she had earned enough to buy a typewriter, Shirley started taking work home to do at night and during the week-ends. Within six months, she had purchased a second typewriter, and the sister who was still in Washington Irving High School, when she was not doing her lessons, was helping Shirley with the Sargent & Sargent manuscripts. By the time this sister graduated, Shirley was doing such a large after-hours typing business, that her job in the Sargent & Sargent bookkeeping department represented a financial loss for her. She suggested to Claude Sargent that it might be better for all concerned, but especially for the agency, if Shirley were to be replaced in the bookkeeping department by her younger sister, who had just come out of Washington Irving with top honors in bookkeeping, so that Shirley could devote all her time to the manuscripts of Sargent & Sargent clients.

Claude Sargent agreed, and he continued to agree each time one of Shirley's remaining four sisters graduated, always with top honors in bookkeeping, from Washington Irving High School. As a result, during all the years of Sam's association with Sargent & Sargent, there had always been a bright young Shaefer in the bookkeeping department, and a whole group of Shaefers typing away at the manuscripts of Sargent & Sargent clients.

By the time Sam Silver moved into his river-front co-operative in Sutton Crescent, Shirley Shaefer had moved into her own three-room suite nine floors below the Sargent & Sargent offices in the Oatley-Wicke Building; she had six girls on her staff, no longer including the sisters who had done their tours of duty in the Sargent & Sargent bookkeeping department upstairs; and her gross income was large enough to make it necessary for Shirley to employ the services of an accountant and lard her conversation with the latest jokes about taxes.

The reasons for Shirley's success, from which Sam drew almost as much satisfaction as Shirley herself, were several.

First of all, as Kenyon Poole had once put it, she made a damned good mousetrap: a Shirley Shaefer manuscript was attractive in an un-fussy, businesslike, clean way, and guaranteed to contain no errors not put there by the author. Secondly, Shirley dealt exclusively with Sargent & Sargent manuscripts, or at any rate they were given preference over any other work Shirley might have in what she called her shop, so that a Sargent & Sargent client always had the feeling that in turning over his brain child to Shirley, he was not releasing it into the hands of an indifferent stranger who was interested only in how much money could be earned from boarding it temporarily, so to speak, but giving it over into the loving care of a member of the family who was as anxious as the parent himself to have the child look its best when it was all dressed up to go out and face the world. The main reason for her success, however, Sam was convinced, was Shirley's personality.

She had not been a pretty girl, although the years had repaid her for that by making her a handsome woman, but she had always had a scrubbed, open, forthright look that made people in her presence feel good. Kenyon Poole, who had admired Shirley enormously, once said to Sam, "If that girl had sex appeal, she'd be sitting in the White House some day, and I don't mean as the wife of the incumbent, either. Shirley's tragedy is that she doesn't do anything for a man below the belt, but oh, God, how she makes you wish she was your sister!"

Nobody, Sam had discovered with the years, wanted a sister more than a writer. This was not, of course, what the writer told the world. For the public, which needed a satisfying image at whose feet it could place its homage and its royalties, the writer let it be known that what he wanted was an insatiable mistress, preferably several. But it was the sister for whom, in a purely platonic way of course, he lusted. Whether Shirley Shaefer had figured this out in her extremely good brain, or merely knew it instinctively in her very large heart, Sam had no way of knowing. He did know, however, that Shirley acted on it.

While, like most writers, he would have denied hotly that he gave a damn about what a typist thought of his story, Sam knew that in actual fact he would have given a good deal more than a damn to get her opinion. The typist was the first human being who saw the story after it came out of the creative kiln. The typist's reaction was the first public response to an intensely private act. A man would have had to be made of flint to be indifferent to that response, regardless of the intelligence of the source. If, as Voltaire had said, a dog that sniffed with eagerness at his unblotted page could warm his heart, why shouldn't a magazine writer be reduced to a pool of molten ecstasy by a typist who said "Wow!"?

The fact that Sam, and so far as he knew no other Sargent & Sargent client, had ever been thus reduced was due to the fact that Shirley Shaefer was not the "Wow!" type. She had grasped early that her business was not as simple as it looked.

To live with the work of a creative person for several hours or several days and return it, neatly typed, with no comment other than a bill, was the equivalent of suggesting that the creative person take his copying work to someone more sensitive. To add to the bill the assurance that the writer had just conferred on the typist the rare honor of copying the equivalent of the Twenty-third Psalm, was to invite, once the fine drunken glow of the compliment wore off, the inevitable resentment of the hangover. To walk the judicious tightrope of "I'm just a dumb typist and no judge of these things, of course, but it seems to me," was merely to leave oneself wide open for the withering "Who the hell asked for your opinion in the first place?" None of these approaches, or rather their consequences, is good for business.

The solution, which it had taken Benjamin Franklin a crowded lifetime to reach, was arrived at by Shirley Shaefer in her teens: honesty is the best policy. Without the modification of personality, however, it is rarely the best business policy. Sam Silver suspected that Benjamin Franklin would have admired the way Shirley Shaefer shaped his general precept into a working business tool.

For every manuscript, no matter what the length or the content, regardless of the eminence or the obscurity of the author, Shirley Shaefer had one of two comments, and Sam Silver, like every other Sargent & Sargent client, had learned to watch for it, while his stomach knotted with tension, the way a gladiator once watched for the sign from the emperor's box: thumbs up, or thumbs down.

If Shirley Shaefer liked something she or one of her girls had typed, her smile was like the sunrise when she handed over the manuscript to the author and said, "This one's got my label in it."

If Shirley did not like the story, her smile looked no different to the uninitiated, but the Sargent & Sargent client could detect with a sinking heart, as she handed over the manuscript, the wintry, faintly pitying edge in Shirley's voice as she said, "There's always people they'll be crazy about this sort of thing."

It was not the sort of critical phraseology one found in the back pages of the fifty-cent magazines, but Sam had learned to value it more highly. For this reason he never asked Shirley to deliver his manuscripts by office messenger. He always came for them himself.

In the taxi that carried him from the Sargent apartment to the Oatley-Wicke Building to pick up the Kenyon Poole manuscript, it occurred to Sam, as it always did when he was on his way to Shirley Shaefer's office, that the person who introduced him, indirectly, of course, to Shirley's talent as a literary critic was Jennie Broom.

From the open doorway on Commerce Street through which, on that dreadful night, Buggo Salvemini had delivered the stunning news that Jennie was his wife, Sam had turned and run. He had almost reached East Tenth Street before his boiling emotions had simmered down enough to allow him to become interested in their nature.

Was he running away because, struck by the realization that he was an adulterer, he feared the reprisals of a wronged husband? Or was he running away from the rage of jealousy that had shot through him when he was hit over the head with the fact that Buggo Salvemini, the boob of Grover Cleveland High, was his successful rival?

The realization that he was not sure, the awareness that there were alternatives, had a calming effect. Sam stopped running. Walking along and thinking about it, picking the situation apart, he began to see that what he really was sore about was the fact that Jennie Broom had used him again; just as, on graduation night, she had used him in her fight against Mr. Mueller the school principal, so now she had used him in her fight, whatever the fight was about, against Mr. Umberg, the New York story editor of Mercury Films. The second thing Sam began to see was that there might be a good story in the situation.

"What's the matter?" his mother said when he came into the East Tenth Street kitchen. "You're maybe sick?"

"Sick?" Sam said. "No, I feel fine."

"Then what are you doing home eight o'clock?"

"Oh," Sam said. He had forgotten that in his furious desire to confront Jennie with her duplicity, he had skipped his classes at the Lafayette Business Institute. "I decided not to go to school tonight," he said. "I got an idea for a new story and I wanted to start on it right away."

"Sopper you had already?" his mother said.

Sam suddenly realized he was famished. "I could eat a little something," he said.

"So sit down," his mother said. "And here, it's a letter. After you went to work it came."

Sam sat down and took the letter. It was from *Landscape*. He pried open the flap, pulled out a sheet of paper, and read:

Dear Mr. Silver:

We are pleased to announce that we have just completed arrangements with Trafalgar, Singlenight & Co., Inc., book publishers, to sponsor jointly with this magazine a first-novel contest which shall be open only to writers whose work has appeared in *Landscape*.

The manuscripts must be at least 300 double-spaced typewritten pages in length, and the prizes are $2,500 for first place, $1,500 for second place, and $1,000 for third place, these sums to be paid outright to the winners and not to be applied against normal book royalties, which will be paid in the normal way by Trafalgar, Singlenight & Co., who undertake to publish the winning manuscripts.

The judges of the contest are the combined editorial staffs of this magazine and Trafalgar, Singlenight & Co. All manuscripts should be submitted to the above address on or before April 1, 1935, when the contest closes.

We realize this is extremely short notice. Or rather, it may strike you as short notice. May we add, therefore, a clarifying note.

The purpose of this contest is not to set in motion a wave of hurried novel writing. It is our firm belief that great writing must age, like great wine. We know, from our intimate contacts with writers over many years, that every really good writer has a novel on the drawing board, so to speak. It is these novels, these long pieces of work over which writers have been anxiously meditating for years, that we want to flush out. Unless you have such a work in progress, this letter does not apply to you, since it is obviously impossible to compose an entire novel of three hundred or more pages within six weeks.

We trust that, as one of the new writers it has been our privilege to present to the American public through the pages of *Landscape*, you have a novel-in-progress which is near completion and will enter it in this contest for our consideration. When you send it along to us, please attach this letter, which will serve as your entry blank to the contest.

Sincerely,
THE EDITORS

"What do they want?" Mrs. Silver said as she came to the table with the plate of noodle soup.

"They want to make me rich," Sam said.

"So don't put anything in their way to stop them," his mother said. "Eat with bread."

"I'm going to make it easy for them," Sam said.

His mother gave him a sharp look. "What happened tonight that's so special?" she said.

"I just told you." Sam waved the letter as he gulped a spoonful of noodle soup and took a huge bite of rindle, the chewy end of the rye loaf that his mother always saved for him. "Here's a bunch of people that want to make me rich."

"No, I mean before you read the letter," his mother said. "Something happened."

"You bet it did," Sam said.

"And your own mother you're not going to tell?" Mrs. Silver said.

"Nope," Sam said.

"This is very nice," his mother said. "You come from Europe in a ship like an animal. For thirty-eight days to eat there's only black bread and herring. By Ellis Island they stick you and push you and slap you like a package. For a whole life in a crazy new land you work and work and work, like a machine, to keep a house clean for a son, to make him good things to eat he should be healthy and grow up tall and strong, to see he goes to school and learn. So it comes thank God the time he's almost twenty years old, he's tall like you wanted, he's good-looking like you prayed he should be, he's got a job like you worked he should have, he's already beginning a shreiber, so now, he's ready to be rich, what do you get from it? You get his own mother he's not going to tell!"

Sam laughed. "If I tell it," he said, "I won't get rich."

"What's telling the mother got to do with getting rich?" Mrs. Silver said.

"If I tell it," Sam said, "I won't write it."

"You mean this to get rich," his mother said, "it has something to do with writing?"

"It has everything to do with it," Sam said.

"So why are you wasting time with the soup like its chung gum?" Mrs. Silver said. "Stop with the fancy chewing and hurry up finish so I can clean the table."

After she did and disappeared into the bedroom, Sam laid out his campaign. He re-examined the synopsis, eliminating the ambiguities, making decisions wherever he had allowed two or more choices to stand, and sketching several clarifying scenes of the kind that Claude Sargent had pointed out to him were responsible for the success of the only story he had thus far managed to sell, namely, "The Ways of Men Must Sever." This proved to be fairly simple, since the synopsis was little more than an elaboration of that first short story, and by one o'clock in the morning Sam had what seemed to him a good, clean outline that came to thirty-one chapters.

Assuming that each chapter ran to approximately ten pages, which was what he had learned during the past few months he could write without strain in a single session, Sam figured he should be able to finish the novel in thirty-one nights. Allowing two weeks for the typing, or twenty-five pages a night at Mr. Brunschweig's Underwood, and he would be able to have the novel in the *Landscape* offices two full days before the April 1 deadline.

He almost made it.

Thirty-one nights after he sketched his chapter-by-chapter outline, Sam scrawled "The End" at the bottom of Chapter 31. The following night, after Mr. Brunschweig left the store, Sam started typing, and a half hour later realized he was in trouble: the shift key on Mr. Brunschweig's vintage Underwood went out of business.

"Find a typewriter repair place and get it fixed," Mr. Brunschweig said the next day. "Otherwise I won't be able to get out the bills comes the first of the month."

Sam found a typewriter repair shop on Sixth Avenue, and while the owner was sure he could get the machine in shape in time for Mr. Brunschweig to send out his bills, he could do nothing to solve Sam's problem.

"It ain't only the shift key," the repairman said to the young novelist, who had exactly sixteen days in which to type a 310-page manuscript. "That's only like a guy he falls down in the street and breaks a leg, you can't just go treating him with a plaster cast. You look into it, why he fell in the first place, you find he's got maybe a screwed-up gall bladder or something. This machine, it's got everything from ingrown toenails to galloping dandruff. It needs a new platen, the letter *s* is hanging by a thread, for the space bar and the zero I wouldn't give you a nickel, and without a complete and total overhaul, you might just as well throw it in the ash can and start over fresh. I'll have to keep it two weeks."

Sam looked around the crowded shop and said, "While you're working on it, could you lend us another machine to use till this one is fixed?"

"If everybody they brought in a machine to fix, I had another one to lend them, my family instead of bread they'd be eating stones," the repairman said. "But I got some nice rebuilt models, good as new, I could sell you one of them."

"How much?" Sam said.

"I got a beauty here, Remington, forty-five bucks. Of course, it's not the greatest machine in the world. What can you expect for forty-five bucks? But you wanna go a little higher, say sixty, or here, this Royal, for eighty-five dollars I defy anybody, I absolutely defy them, to find in the whole city of New York a better machine, new, used, rebuilt, anything, than this Royal for eighty-five dollars. Take a look."

Sam took a look. It was a beauty, all right, but he had in the Dry Dock Savings Bank the ten dollars he had received from *Landscape* for "The Ways of Men Must Sever," and he still owed Mr. Brunschweig eight dollars on the dark blue suit he had bought to wear to the Sargent dinner party.

"It's a nice-looking machine," Sam said. "I'll go ask my boss."

He went, instead, into a phone booth and called the Sargent & Sargent office.

"Miss Shaefer, please," he said to the switchboard operator. "In the bookkeeping department."

A few moments later a girl's voice said, "Hello?"

"Miss Shaefer?"

"Yes, who is this?"

"Miss Shaefer, you don't know me, and I wish you wouldn't mention my name, just in case anybody happens to be near you, but I'm a client of the office—"

"The Sargent & Sargent office?" Shirley Shaefer said. "Here?"

"Yes, I'm a client," Sam said. "A new one. I mean I haven't sold anything through the office yet, but Mr. Sargent has just taken me on, and the other night, when I was at a dinner party at Mr. Sargent's house, I heard someone tell a story. How you did a hurry-up typing job one day? And now, once in a while, you take manuscripts home to type?"

"Yes, I do," Miss Shaefer said. "Who is this, please?"

"You won't mention my name?"

"No, if you don't want me to, but why not?"

"Well, I've got this manuscript I want typed, but I don't want Mr. or Mrs. Sargent to know about it until I've had a chance to read it in typed form."

"Oh, it's in longhand?"

"Yes, but it's very legible," Sam said. "You won't have any trouble following it. I know it sounds sort of silly, my not wanting Mr. and Mrs. Sargent to know about it until it's in typed form, I mean until I've had a chance *myself* to see it in typed form."

"I don't think it's silly at all."

"You don't?" Sam said, surprised.

"I make my own dresses," Shirley Shaefer said. "The early stages, when I'm cutting and basting and all that in the rough stages, I don't like my mother and sisters to see it. When I got it looking nice and neat, all the rough seams smooth and the basting out, *then* I let them see it."

"Well, I never thought of it that way," Sam said. "But I guess it's pretty much the same."

"Of course it is, Mr.—?"

"Silver," Sam said. "Samuel Silver."

"Oh, I know you," Miss Shaefer said.

"You do?"

"Well, I mean I know your ledger card," Miss Shaefer said. "Like you said, it's new, and there's nothing on it yet, but there it is, nice and fresh and clean. I hope it gets all filled up soon with big fat sales."

"Why, thanks," Sam said, and in the pleasure of realizing that he actually had a card all to himself in the Sargent & Sargent clients' ledger was suddenly so intense that he forgot completely why he had called.

"Is this a long manuscript?" Miss Shaefer asked.

"Is what a—? Oh," Sam said, coming back to the matter in hand. "It's four hundred and sixty-five hand-written pages, and I know from my own typing that I get a page and a half of hand-written onto a single page of double-spaced typewritten, so it'll come to three hundred and ten typed pages."

"Your first novel, huh?"

"Yes," Sam said, succeeding with only a small effort in giving no more weight to the word than if she had asked if he wore shoes. "Could you type it for me, Miss Shaefer?"

"It would be a pleasure, Mr. Sil— Oops! It would be a pleasure. Period. Because it's *my* first novel, too."

"Thanks, Miss Shaefer. There's only two things."

"What are they?"

"I've absolutely got to have the job finished in two weeks," Sam said. "By March twenty-ninth, the thirtieth at the latest, but the twenty-ninth preferably. I promised to show it to somebody on that day, and he's going to, uh, to Europe the next day."

"Well, now, let me see," Miss Shaefer said. "You'll want two carbons, I suppose?"

"If that's regular, yes."

"It's regular for the Sargent & Sargent office," Shirley Shaefer said. "But you can have more if you want them. I can make six legible at one typing."

"No, whatever is regular is fine with me," Sam said.

"So if you want it in two weeks, that's fourteen nights into three-ten, comes out twenty-two pages a night, yes, I can do it."

"That's swell," Sam said.

"What's the other thing?" Miss Shaefer said.

"Well, I—" Sam paused and wondered how to say it. "It's sort of funny, Miss Shaefer. I don't mean humorous funny. I mean I know typing is labor, and it's not like buying machinery or anything like that, things a business firm gets billed for, and they post it in the ledger, and they wait to send out checks until—"

His voice trailed away into a puddle of embarrassed silence out of which Miss Shaefer's friendly voice said, "Listen, if you mean you haven't got the money to pay for it right away all in a lump, don't worry about it. By me the credit of any Sargent & Sargent client is good."

"I don't really know how to thank you, Miss Shaefer."

"So why waste time trying?" she said. "When can I get the manuscript?"

"I don't want to take it into the office," Sam began slowly, and then something about the way Miss Shaefer had sounded made him say, "Where do you live?"

"East Fourth Street," she said. "Between Avenue D and Lewis."

Sam laughed and said, "I live on Tenth, between Avenue B and A."

Miss Shaefer laughed and said, "No kidding?"

"Fact," Sam said.

"Hello, landsmann," Miss Shaefer said.

"Hello," Sam said. "How would it be if I delivered the manuscript to your house tonight? Say around seven o'clock?"

"That will be fine," Shirley Shaefer said, and she gave him the address.

The Shaefer flat on East Fourth Street was not much different from the Silver three-roomer on East Tenth Street, except that Sam suspected it was at least one room larger, unless all those sisters slept in shifts, and the

Shaefer flat, unlike the Silver home, was dominated, not by the mother of the family, but by Shirley. Sam did not realize until he called for the finished typescript and she greeted him with unmistakable enthusiasm, that he had been somewhat apprehensive about Shirley's opinion of the novel.

"You don't have to worry about showing it to Mr. and Mrs. Sargent or anybody else," she said with a smile that from then on, Sam began to cherish. "This one has my label in it, Mr. Silver."

The contest judges, to whom Sam sent the manuscript after pledging Shirley not to mention it to anybody in the Sargent & Sargent office, apparently felt the same way about it. On April 16, less than three weeks after he mailed off the package, Sam received another letter from *Landscape*. This one, unlike his previous communications from the magazine, which had all ended with the typed words: "The Editors," was signed in green ink: "Keeley Cuff, Managing Editor." The letter said:

Ham Farnsworth of Trafalgar, Singlenight and I are crazy about *Yours Is the Earth* and want very much to talk to you about it. Please meet us for lunch next Thursday at twelve-thirty in the Murray Hill Hotel.

For several moments, as he sat there at the kitchen table, staring at the piece of paper, Sam did not hear his mother's voice. Then, as she set down the plate of cold chicken in front of him with a thump, he came out of his trance.

"I'm sorry, Ma," he said. "I didn't hear you."

"I said what it says in that letter you should look like that?"

Sam did not know how he had looked, but he knew how he had felt when his mother had been staring at him, and it seemed best not to tell her about that. It seemed best not even to think about it. He had read over the years, in newspapers and magazines, a great many interviews with people who had achieved literary success. Under the influence of Miss Mercator and the Stratford Club at Grover Cleveland High, Sam had even read several biographies of eminent literary figures.

All these men and women, in describing the emotions that assailed them at the moment of learning that their first major work had been accepted for publication, touched chords that any reader, even a crude, inexperienced high school student, could tell were a measure of man's ultimate nobility. These were the moments when the lonely artist, working in obscurity, living on crusts, despised by his respectable brethren, was rewarded for his selfless devotion to the muse. These were the moments when it was given to him, the outcast, to know that in his hands was placed the sacred trust of guarding, and preserving for the generations to come, the flame of life itself.

Sam was disturbed to discover that he did not feel like that at all. What he felt seemed, in fact, rather shameful. Reduced to reasonable coherence, his feelings as he looked at the letter announcing his triumph, were: "This will show that bitch Jennie Broom. She thought she was making a monkey out of me again. Well, wait till Miss Jennie Broom, that bitch on wheels, wait till she finds out that instead of using me, I've turned the tables and used her. Wait till she learns I took that lousy synopsis and turned it into a prize-winning novel, the God-damn bitch. How do you like that, Miss Broom? Excuse me, I mean Mrs. Salvemini? And while we're at it, how do *you* like it, Buggo, you son of a bitch?"

The necessity for editing these thoughts into some sort of palatable shape for presentation to his mother was obvious. "Remember a couple of months ago?" Sam said. "I told you these people wanted to make me rich?"

"Sure I remember," Mrs. Silver said. "So what?"

"So they've done it," Sam said. He explained about the contest, the thirty-one days it had taken him to write the novel, the two weeks it had taken Shirley Shaefer to type the manuscript, and the less than three weeks it had taken the judges to reach their decision. Sam explained everything except Jennie Broom's connection with the affair, and then held up the letter from Keeley Cuff. "I won, Ma," he said. "Here's the proof."

Mrs. Silver, who did not read English, took the letter and turned it over and over in her hands, gingerly, as though she expected it to explode. "Sam," she said finally. "Where's the check?"

Sam laughed and took a huge bite of cold chicken. "This isn't like paying for a short story," he said. "This is prize money. They make a kind of ceremony out of handing it over. That's why they're asking me to come to lunch."

"After the lunch, you'll do me a favor, Sam?"

"Sure, Ma. Anything."

"After the lunch, don't go right away to the Dry Dock," Mrs. Silver said. "Bring the check home. To the bank you can take it in the morning the next day. I never saw—once in my life I want to see a piece of paper it's worth two thousand and five hundred dollars."

So did Sam, but of course he didn't say that. None of those men and women, whose interviews and biographies he had read, ever said things like that. It occurred to Sam that they probably had their reasons, and until he learned what they were, common sense indicated the wisdom of borrowing their reticence. Sam applied himself, instead, to the problems raised by Mr. Cuff's invitation. These, as always, were what to wear, and how to get there.

The first was simple. Sam now owned the dark blue suit he had worn to the Sargent party, the cost of which had been underwritten by Mr. Brunschweig. It was this fact, that the suit was still unpaid for, that affected Sam's second problem.

Unlike Claude Sargent's original invitation, which asked Sam to drop into his office any time between ten and four, this invitation from Keeley Cuff was for a specific time. To get to the Murray Hill at twelve-thirty, Sam could not depend on the accident of being sent out with a tuxedo delivery around that time. He had to be free to go, and the only way he could be free was to ask Mr. Brunschweig's permission. For two full days the fears that had prevented Sam from asking his boss's permission the first time kept him from asking this second time.

Then, on Wednesday, when he was beginning to feel desperate, Sam was struck by a sudden thought: he would not be asking a financial superior for a favor; since Mr. Brunschweig was constantly complaining that after he finished paying his expenses, his tuxedo-renting business netted him little more than forty dollars a week, which came to two thousand a year, Sam—who was going to the Murray Hill for lunch to pick up a check for twenty-five hundred dollars—would actually be doing no more than asking for a minor accommodation from a man who was—for one year, at any rate—Sam's financial inferior. The thought was so exhilarating that Sam acted on it at once.

"Mr. Brunschweig," he said to his boss, who was rearranging into more becoming patterns, on the desk in the rear of the store, the stacks of unread magazines to which he subscribed so pointlessly, "I'd like an hour off tomorrow, from a little before twelve-thirty. Is that okay?"

"It's important?" Mr. Brunschweig said.

For a wild moment Sam was tempted to tell his boss precisely how important, but some instinct warned him that the sense of superiority his success as a writer had given him over his fellows including his boss, was dependent to some extent on secrecy: the things available to you for writing about existed in direct proportion to the number of people who did not know you were capable of writing about them.

"Well, yes, pretty important," Sam said. "The dean down at Lafayette Business Institute has these interviews once a year with all the students. To check on how they're doing and all. You know. Anyway, he set me down for twelve-thirty tomorrow, on account of I suppose he figures it's my lunch hour."

"Lunch hours," Mr. Brunschweig said bitterly. "The Lafayette Business

Institute doesn't know nothing about one kind of business, the tuxedo-renting business, this you can be sure, or he wouldn't be making dates for interviews for twelve-thirty."

"If he'd asked me," Sam said, "I'd have told him, but he didn't, so can I go?"

"As long as it's not an interview for another job," Mr. Brunschweig said, "sure you can go. If I lose you, Sam, I'm going into the herring-training business."

This was Mr. Brunschweig's figure of speech for the ultimate in stupidity, and since, by implication in this context, it was the only compliment Mr. Brunschweig had ever paid him, Sam wished his boss had chosen some other time to utter it: now he felt guilty about the lie he had told. The guilt did not last long. The next day, as he walked into the Murray Hill Hotel at twelve twenty-nine, Sam had forgotten not only what he had said to Mr. Brunschweig, but Mr. Brunschweig as well. He was suddenly worried by another problem: how was he going to recognize his hosts? That he was not alone in worrying about this was demonstrated almost immediately by a thin young man with thick horn-rimmed glasses who appeared unexpectedly at Sam's side.

"Excuse me," he said in an anxious, whining voice. "Are you Samuel Silver?"

"Yes," Sam said.

"I'm Keeley Cuff," the young man said as he put out a hand that, when Sam grasped it, felt like an order of chopped chicken liver. "Glad to meet you. Ham Farnsworth's going to be a bit late. He's driving in from Connecticut. He only comes in three days a week, you know. Let's have a drink while we're waiting, shall we? I'm absolutely parched. Say, how old are you, anyway?"

He had been leading the way deeper into the hotel as he talked, flinging the words back across his almost shoulderless body in little bursts, like women Sam had seen in Tompkins Square Park throwing out sprays of crushed stale bread to the pigeons. They entered the dining room just as Cuff asked the question, so that Sam had time, because a man in a dark cutaway appeared in front of them and started mumbling to Cuff with crisp obsequiousness, to think over his answer to the question about his age. When Claude Sargent had asked it during their first meeting, Sam, who had wanted to make a good impression on the agent, had hesitated because he felt the truth would make him seem something he certainly did not feel, namely, a freak. He decided, as he watched Mr. Cuff chirping away whiningly at the headwaiter, that being a freak was something the young man with horn-rimmed glasses would find interesting.

"Twenty," Sam said.

"Yes, fine, thanks," Mr. Cuff said to the headwaiter, and as he started to follow the man in the cutaway, he flung at Sam across his shoulder, "Lordy me, this boy genius thing gets more difficult every year. I thought I had it sewed up on the editorial end. I'm twenty-seven. Maybe I still have it sewed up. In the editorial end, that is. I'm probably the only twenty-seven-year-old managing editor in the magazine game. But the writing end, Lordy me. Twenty. You mind if we have our drinks at the table? I loathe all this jockeying from the bar to food nonsense just when you're beginning to feel juiced up and the conversation gets good. Yes, this is fine, thank you," he said to the waiter and, to Sam, as he gestured to a chair, "This one? Or would you rather here? We'll save the middle one for Ham. He's got a bad ear, poor man, so we'll put him here, where he can hear you. Lordy knows it's not me he's coming to lunch to hear. You sure now?"

"Yes," Sam said, sitting down. "This is fine."

"Good-oh, then," Keeley Cuff said. "What will you drink?"

"I'll have a—" Sam said, and stopped. He had remembered the Sargent dinner party. "I'll have a glass of water," he said, and then, grasping at once from the look on Mr. Cuff's face that he had not said enough, Sam added, "I'm working this afternoon."

The addition seemed to do the trick, because Mr. Cuff's bony face cleared. He said, "Good-oh," to Sam, flung "Martini, very dry, no olive" at the waiter, who bowed and vanished, then swung back to Sam and, with an arch little smile that was clearly intended to be winning, said, "New novel?"

Not grasping what Mr. Cuff meant, Sam concentrated on what it was about the young man's coat that bothered him, and in a moment he had it: the bristling tweedy brown folds, wrapped around the skinny stick of a body at the top of which perched the bony head with the large horn-rimmed glasses, made Mr. Cuff look like a caterpillar sitting up. Having got that straight in his mind, Sam caught up with Mr. Cuff's question and realized what the managing editor of *Landscape* had assumed as a result of Sam's statement that he was working that afternoon.

"No," he said, and because he didn't think Mr. Cuff ought to know that his work that afternoon would consist of delivering tuxedos for Mr. Brunschweig, Sam said, "Just a short story."

"Just a short story," Mr. Cuff said admiringly. "Lordy me, ah, youth, youth." From the tray of the waiter, who had appeared at his elbow, the energetic little caterpillar swept up a long-stemmed glass and said, "Well, here's to *Yours Is the Earth*."

"Thank you," Sam said.

Mr. Cuff took half his drink in a single swallow, shuddered slightly, smacked his lips, set down the glass, and said, "I suppose I ought to wait until Ham arrives, so we can both tell you, in unison, what we think of your novel, but frankly, Mr. Silver—I say, look, do you mind if I drop the Mister? It seems a bit silly when talking to a twenty-year-old. Lordy me, Mr. Silver, it sounds like the headmaster in a British novel addressing a lower-form boy who's come back to school late from his hols, or has been guilty of some other infringement of the rules. You know?"

"Yes," said Sam, who didn't.

"Suppose I call you Silver, and then, after my second drink, I'll have a go at Sam. Agreed?"

"Sure," said Sam, who wished Mr. Farnsworth would hurry up and get here. Mr. Cuff was beginning to strike him as being a rather large horse's ass.

"The thing about *Yours Is the Earth*," Mr. Cuff said, squinting at his glass as though the words he sought were swimming about elusively in the pale green liquid, "I think what got us both, Ham Farnsworth and myself, what got us both was the book took us by surprise. I mean to say, you know *Landscape*. You've appeared in it. You know the kind of story we run. Well, that's pretty much the kind of novel we thought we'd get in this contest. In fact, frankly, we did. Limiting the contest the way we did, making it only for first novels, and only for chaps, as well as lassies, of course, who had appeared in the mag, the mag being quite new here in the States, and on top of that giving everybody only six weeks, meaning that of the already quite narrow field we'd pinpointed, we were narrowing it down even further to chaps, or as I said lassies, too, of course, who'd had a novel in the works for a longish period, we naturally expected a very small turnout, and small it was, too. We received only thirty-three manuscripts. That's a mere drop in the bucket as novel contests go, you know. But that limitation of time, a mere six weeks, that's what did the trick, of course, by automatically eliminating any whiz-bang fireballs whose chief virtue is that they write fast, so you see we didn't have to waste time wading through any garbage that might have been ground out in a hurry just to meet the deadline. Which reminds me, by the way, how long did it take you to write *Yours Is the Earth*?"

"Well," Sam said, scowling hopefully into Mr. Cuff's glass as though, having provided the youthful magazine editor with the proper words, the pale green fluid might be charitable enough to do the same for his guest. "It's hard to say," Sam said, and indeed it was. Until the twenty-five hundred dollars in prize money was handed over and safely banked, at any rate. "You know how those things are," Sam said.

"Lordy me, yes," Mr. Cuff said. "I do indeed. After all, how does one count writing time, anyway? Remember what Arnold Bennett said?" Sam nodded, but this did not stop Mr. Cuff, which was just as well, because Sam had no idea what Arnold Bennett had said. "The thing a writer's wife does not understand, Bennett said, is that when he's sitting in an easy chair, staring out the window, he's working. So it's probably damned stupid of me to ask you how long it took you to write *Yours Is the Earth* because anybody can see, with half an eye anybody can see, Lordy me, Ham and I both remarked on it at once, anybody could see this was more than a novel, this is a piece of a man's life."

Mr. Cuff paused, perhaps to drain his glass, which he did, but without any doubt, from the way he fixed his horn-rimmed stare on Sam, because he wanted corroboration. Sam, who wanted to give it to him, thought perhaps the best way, under the circumstances, was not with words. Shyly he dropped his own glance, and because a preoccupation with the state of his cuticle did not seem quite enough for someone like Mr. Cuff, Sam added a small, a very small, sigh.

"That's what I thought," Mr. Cuff said with satisfaction. "Ham Farnsworth, when he finished *Yours Is the Earth,* Ham said you can always tell a manuscript that's been aged the way you can tell a good bottle of wine or a cheese that's *a point.* Ham is a big wine and cheese man, you know. He's doing a book on cheese. Not a cook book or anything like that. Ham is probably the most important book editor in the business, as I'm sure you know. The poop in the trade is that his base pay at Trafalgar, Singlenight is twenty thou a year, plus an expense account from here to here, and he's worked out this theory about literature, based on his years of experience as an editor. Ham's got this theory that just as the old saying has it that the way to a man's heart is through his stomach, the way to greatness in literature is through the alimentary canal, and cheese being the greatest and most noble of man's foods, at least in Ham's opinion, the story of literature, from the first crude fable scratched on the wall of a cave by Paleolithic man to, Lordy me, anything that's truly great in our own day, say Kenyon Poole's *The Small Meal,* Farnsworth feels that the only way to see the story of literature truly, and see it in the round, is to see it through the lens of cheese. He's been on the book for years, and nobody really knows when he's going to finish it, but everybody knows that when he does, it will be something all right, truly something, which is why, when Ham Farnsworth said he could tell that the man who wrote *Yours Is the Earth* had spent years at the task, I knew at once that my own judgment had been substantiated, because I read the book first. That was the arrangement we made with Trafalgar, Singlenight, that up at *Landscape* we'd go through all the entries first, weed out the impossibles, and send on to Ham and his staff at Trafalgar, Singlenight only the ones we thought were promising. That's how I happened to read *Yours Is the Earth* before Ham did, and I remember distinctly my first reaction was Lordy me, and great jumping J. Pierpont Popocatapetl, what a book! The precision of the style, the care with which each paragraph, each sentence, Lordy me, each *word* is set in place, my first reaction was how right we were to plan a first-novel contest limited by that six-week clause, because in that way, and only in that way, could we flush out the great works of art that have been in the oven, so to speak, for years."

The waiter, who so far as Sam could judge had received no signal, appeared with a second martini, which Keeley Cuff whipped off the tray like a train scooping up a mailbag while thundering through a station. As he took a long pull at the glass, his eyes, fixed on Sam, started to blink rapidly behind the thick lenses, and Sam wondered uneasily if Mr. Cuff, listening to some of his own words, was suddenly thinking what Sam had been thinking for several minutes: if the author of *Yours Is the Earth,* who had just confessed to being twenty, had taken years to write the book, he would have been wearing knee pants, and conceivably even diapers, when he first took pen in hand.

"That theory about literature and cheese, Mr. Farnsworth's theory," Sam said in a changing-the-subject maneuver that he hoped was not too obvious, "I'd certainly like to hear more about that."

"You will, Oscar," Mr. Cuff said dryly, and Sam wondered if he should remind the little cockeyed caterpillar, who had promised to call him by his first name with his second drink, that his first name was Sam. "Ham is a bit of an effing bore on the subject, although I hope you won't quote me, and once he gets started, it's a bit difficult to stop or even deflect him, so perhaps I'd better say here and now, without any lily gilding or what have you, that I think *Yours Is the Earth* is a magnificent piece of work that compares favorably, and I know you'll think I'm exaggerating when I mention the name but I assure you I mean every blessed word, I really do, compares favorably, I say, with the best of Ronald Firbank."

He paused to stoke himself with another dose of the pale green liquid, and Sam realized that Keeley Cuff was waiting for a comment.

"Well," said Sam, who was wondering how this Firbank joker spelled his name, because he wanted to look him up in the library, and he added, "I really don't know what to say."

Mr. Cuff nodded, as though the reply was precisely what he had hoped for, and said, "Why should you? You've said it in your manuscript, and said it superbly. Why should you be called on to say anything more? It's

like that marvelous plaque in St. Paul's that says if you want to see the
monument to Sir Christopher Wren, look about you. Very well, I say. Or
rather, you do, Sam. You see? I said I'd call you Sam with my second
drink. Do you mind?"

"No, of course not," said Sam, who preferred it to Oscar.

"Very well, you say. I'm glad you think my novel is as good as the best
of Ronald Firbank, and if you add anything to that, my dear Sam, you
would add only the simple word: why? Because, having added it, having
asked yourself that simple question, why, I will tell you, my dear Sam, if
you care to hear?"

"Please," Sam said, realizing it was foolish to expect silent prayers to
speed Mr. Ham Farnsworth's journey from Connecticut, but he prayed
nonetheless.

"*Yours Is the Earth* compares favorably with the best of Ronald Firbank
because it has delicacy," Mr. Cuff said. "*Grace* and delicacy. Yes, that's
better. Not only delicacy. Grace *and* delicacy. I am fed up to but here
with the tough boys, with the I-Bit-Her-Tit School of Modern American
fiction. These uncouth slobs tell us that sex is the greatest motivating factor
in our lives, that we spend more time at it than any other single function,
and therefore to write with truth a writer must include sex, presumably,
to judge by the way these thinly disguised pornographers include it, by
describing this most sacred of all acts between a man and a woman the
way a manufacturer of toy electric trains describes for his customers how
to assemble his product once they buy it and get it home. If what these
boys say is true, then I counter by saying something else. How about the
other bodily functions? Do we not spend as much time peeing and defe-
cating as we spend screwing? Indeed, as any constipated individual can
testify, many members of the human race spend more time in the can than
in the sack. How do the members of the I-Bit-Her-Tit School answer that?
Just one word: sales. Which is why *Yours Is the Earth* is such a wonderful and welcome relief. What is your novel about? Life on the Lower
East Side of New York. More accurately, life in a large, crowded, slum-
area New York City high school. What a magnificent opportunity for one
of the I-Bit-Her-Tit boys! Lordy me, just think of the possibilities. Slum
kids! At the age of puberty! Boys and girls in their teens crowded together
in a poorly supervised high school! Great J. Pierpont Popocatapetl and
Lordy me! The opportunities for lubricity fairly stagger the imagination.
But has the author of this novel seized the opportunity? No! He has turned
his back on the money-grubbing pornographic potential of his material and
written, instead, something lovely, something hauntingly beautiful, something as delicate as a rose petal at dawn, something enduring. In short, be-

cause like Ronald Firbank he has written with grace, he has in *Yours Is
the Earth* achieved a work of art. Oh, hello, Ham."

Sam turned with relief, and then the relief turned to uneasiness: the
man who had just arrived at the table looked enough like Mr. Brunschweig
to be the tuxedo-renter's brother.

"Hello, Keeley," the newcomer said. "Sorry to be late. First the frigging
car wouldn't start, then the son of a bitch who came to start it forgot half
his God-damn tools, then the state cops, the bastards, just because it's the
day I'm driving in, they decide to give up pinochle for a few hours and
man the bloody speed traps. This rosy-cheeked ad for Zweiback is, I take
it, the author of *Yours Is the Earth?*"

"Yes, indeedy," Keeley Cuff said, half rising in his chair. "Samuel Silver,
Ham Farnsworth."

"How do you do?" Sam said, taking Mr. Farnsworth's hand and wondering if there was such a thing as the Publishing Palm: touching hands
with the editor of Trafalgar, Singlenight & Co., Inc., was like making
sudden contact in the dark with something that felt like an unbaked lemon
meringue pie.

"I'm absolutely lousy," Mr. Farnsworth said. "Nothing pisses me off more
than mechanics who don't know their ass from a hot rock about things
mechanical, and cops who go on a once-a-month-look-what-a-frigging-vir-
tuous-public-servant-I-am spree at my expense. Is this chair for me?"

"Yes," Mr. Cuff said. "I thought you'd rather hear what Mr. Silver has
to say than anything I might manage to utter."

"You're not kidding," Mr. Farnsworth said as he deposited his plumpish
bulk in the chair between Sam and Keeley Cuff with all the grace of a
teddy bear slipping on a banana peel. "I see you've started. Christ, the
spectacle of a human being stunning his palate with gin just before consuming food is just too grisly to contemplate."

"I work hard," Keeley Cuff said. "And I have to do it all myself. Up
at *Landscape* we don't have all those expensive flunkies you've got at your
beck and call at Trafalgar, Singlenight, secretaries and what not. By midday, I need a bracer. Waiter, *une autre* of these for little old me, *et pour
Monsieur Farnsworth,* I give you the great man himself."

The waiter bowed and Mr. Farnsworth, who had struck Sam as an
irascible but on the whole rather peaceful individual, suddenly seemed
to turn on the waiter like Dempsey coming out of his corner at the sound
of the bell. The waiter, apparently responding to the same signal, met Mr.
Farnsworth in the center of the invisible ring, and for a few minutes,
before Sam realized they were merely talking French, he could have been
watching a vaudeville re-enactment of Pickett's Charge. When he grasped

what was happening, Sam found himself regarding Mr. Farnsworth with
the respect he had counted on feeling for an editor who had awarded
him first prize in a novel contest, but which had vanished as soon as Sam
saw him.

Sam saw now that the fact that Mr. Farnsworth looked like Mr. Brunschweig, who exuded an aura of inept foolishness, could not—or rather,
should not—be held against him. The curious hairdo—straight up and very
long all around, so that Mr. Farnsworth's silly little face seemed to be surmounted by a light brown grenadier's busby—probably had to be scored
on the debit side of his ledger sheet. After all, the public had a right to
expect a grown man to take steps to avoid looking like one of the little
apple-cheeked wooden soldiers in a *Babes in Toyland* set of dolls. Nonetheless, the air of authority with which Mr. Farnsworth hurled the foreign
language at, under, over, and around the waiter, the dexterity with which
Mr. Farnsworth parried his opponent's far from inept counterattacks, the
unmistakable zest Mr. Farnsworth brought to the battle, all contributed
to the clear impression, Sam felt, of a person who, though he might not
look *the* part, was, however, a man of considerable parts.

"*Alors!*" he concluded with a gesture of finality that sent the waiter
scurrying, and Mr. Farnsworth turned back to his table companions.
"I've ordered for all of us," he said. "I hope you don't mind, and if you
do, for Christ's sake don't tell me. I've got to be in the office at two. Semi-
annual sales meeting. It saves time if one person who knows what he
wants polishes off the God-damn waiter with a single punch instead of
everybody indulging in an individual and time-consuming bout of hem-
ming and hawing."

"Oh, Lordy me," Keeley Cuff said. "And all I wanted was another one
of these and a ham on rye."

"You're muttering into my bad ear," Mr. Farnsworth said. "From which
I conclude you're saying nothing complimentary, so don't repeat it." The
editor-in-chief of Trafalgar, Singlenight turned to Sam and, with a sardonic
smile, said, "Don't pay any attention to this little putz. No business is perfect, and the publishing business is no exception. Every once in a while
one of these goyim creeps in past the best efforts of the office exterminator,
and we talented Chinese just have to put up with them. Mr. Silver, I
think you're one hell of a writer."

Sam nodded, and while he may have seemed to be doing it shyly, the
way he had done it earlier to avoid replying in kind to Keeley Cuff's silly
words, this time he was doing it uncomfortably. It had not occurred to
Sam until this moment that somebody named Ham Farnsworth was a
Jew. The fact that this could not possibly be Mr. Farnsworth's real name,

that he had obviously changed it from something recognizably Jewish to something that now seemed ludicrously non-Jewish, was to Sam, for reasons he had never before encountered and did not pause now to examine, distinctly unpleasant. Mr. Farnsworth, who had just changed in Sam's eyes from a foul-mouthed fool to a man of parts, had not only worked the trick again, but had gone back, at least in Sam's eyes, to being a fool. Worse than that, by reminding Sam that they were, so to speak, members of a secret fraternity that set them apart, Mr. Farnsworth had diminished the size of his compliment. Sam, who had come to be told by a famous editor that he had won the prize because, in Mr. Farnsworth's words, he was one hell of a writer, had been made to feel by the editor's other words that the award was being made to him because he was a Jew.

"In my business," Mr. Farnsworth said, "new writers are a dime a dozen. We find new ones every day. If we didn't, the publishing business would fold as soon as the living writers died, just as a butcher would fold if he sold off all the meat in the shop and didn't arrange to have new stuff coming in from the slaughterhouse. So we publishers, we arrange to have new stuff coming in all the time. These new writers we have coming in all the time, they're people who can supply our market, and as long as they can do that, frig it, who asks for anything more?"

"Some of us do, Ham," Mr. Cuff said. "That's why magazines like *Landscape* come into existence."

Mr. Farnsworth, keeping his eyes on Sam, jerked his head toward the skinny little man, and said, "These shmucks, they think the way to add to a conversation is to interrupt it. What I was saying, before this boob goy interrupted, I was saying as a rule, like in any other business, if we can keep the market supplied, we're reasonably content. This afternoon, for instance, at our sales conference, the Trafalgar, Singlenight salesmen, who have come in from all over the country, will be presented with our complete list, all the books we editors have found and got ready for these salesmen to sell all over the country to the American public during the next six months. What's interesting is that among all these packages, I think Trafalgar, Singlenight is publishing sixty-two new titles this fall, what's interesting is that among those sixty-two new titles there is not a single book. I startle you?"

"No, no," Sam said. "I was just looking at the waiter."

"Don't," Mr. Farnsworth said. "It makes them self-conscious and they start doing tricks to show off. Like look. Now he's twirling in the ice bucket like the bottle is a God-damn pneumatic drill, because he knows we're watching, and as a result the wine, which is a 1929 Bandol, and should be served at no lower than forty-five degrees Fahrenheit, is well on its way to being fit for the palate of an Eskimo. *Cochon!*" he rapped out at the waiter, and for a few moments the battle was resumed. It ended with two goblets of pale reddish wine on the table, one in front of Sam and the other in front of Mr. Farnsworth, who said, "This stuff is too good for goyim, so we will let Mr. Cuff continue the process of destroying his taste buds with grain alcohol while you and I, members of the chosen race, will sip slowly. How you like?"

"Very much," said Sam, who thought the wine was sour and not nearly so good as the rich, thick, sweet stuff his mother and father made every year for Passover.

"I thought you'd like it," Mr. Farnsworth said. "Good wines always like good writers and vice versa. Don't gulp it. It's not a malted. Just keep sipping. And if you want to look startled when I say the Trafalgar, Single-night list contains sixty-two packages of manure this fall but not a single book, go right ahead and look startled. You're entitled. Because this is where you come in. More?"

"Yes, thanks," Sam said, holding out his glass.

"Out of Christ alone knows what," Mr. Farnsworth said as he refilled Sam's glass, "a sense of guilt or a feeling of boredom, I've never really made up my mind, we publishers get to feeling every once in a while oh, God, wouldn't it be nice to get away from all this packaged shishkebob and stick our noses up out of the sewer and inhale a breath or two of clean air. In short, every once in a while we get to remembering what brought us into this business, and what we ought to be doing, and the lust to publish a piece of literature becomes absolutely overpowering. So what do we do? We run a novel contest."

"That's where dumb goys like me come in," Mr. Cuff said cheerfully.

"Incredible, isn't it?" Mr. Farnsworth said to Sam as, once again, he jerked his head toward the skinny little managing editor of *Landscape*. "Did you ever hear the word pronounced like that?"

"Lordy me, Ham," Mr. Cuff said, "I wish you wouldn't always be so infuriatingly Jewish and better than everybody."

"Get a load of that," Mr. Farnsworth said to Sam with another jerk of his head toward the third man at the table. "Even with a bum ear I can hear that whine of the poor son of a bitch who knows all his life he's going to run no better than second." Mr. Farnsworth took a delicate sip of his wine and turned in his chair. "Keeley," he said, "I hate to read you the hard word, but facts are facts, and at your age you ought to know what they are. In a nutshell, Keeley, you're never going to make it. Life has a way of evening things off. Us Heebs can't ever make it into Skull and Bones, and you white Protestant goyim can't ever make it into the inner circle of brains. Tough tookey, old chap, so you just keep on corroding your palate with that poison and shut up, Keeley boy. I'm talking to a landsmann." Mr. Farnsworth turned back to Sam, who wished the editor of Trafalgar, Singlenight would just hand him the check for twenty-five hundred dollars and let him go back to Mr. Brunschweig's store. Delivering tuxedos, which had never struck Sam as one of the more admirable achievements of the human animal, was suddenly beginning to look like an extremely attractive way for a man to spend his time. Across his wine glass, Mr. Farnsworth said, "You'd think we publishers were perfectly equipped to discover a hunk of literature, wouldn't you? I mean, Christ, we've all got expensive editorial staffs that are supposed to be devoted to finding great works of literary art for our employers to publish. I'm not a bragging-type Jew, but I've heard the gossip in the trade that my base pay at Trafalgar, Singlenight is twenty gees a year plus a shmaltzy expense account, and since you will undoubtedly hear it soon, too, I might as well tell you now, my dear Sammy boy, that the gossip is not too wide of the mark. Wouldn't you think that an editorial staff topped by a fat-salaried, bright young Chinaman like me would be able to handle Trafalgar, Singlenight's sudden desire to publish a good novel? Well, if you think that, you're wrong, Shmeelick, because in the full flush of our lust for a piece of literature we turned, as all publishers turn, to these little ass holes."

Mr. Farnsworth's gesture, as he pointed to Keeley Cuff, involved his wine glass, as a result of which the young managing editor of *Landscape* received a rather generous dose of 1929 Bandol full in the face.

"Aah, now, Ham," he said amiably as he swabbed his bony cheeks with a napkin, "I'm sorry you never made Skull and Bones, I really am, and if I could arrange for you to make it, I would, honestly I would, but I'm just the managing editor of an almost unbearably precious literary magazine, and I haven't got the influence of a Roxy usher, so would you quit spilling wine on me and show a little gratitude for the fact that I was directly responsible for your finding this boy genius here and his great novel called— Say, Sam, why the deuce do you call it *Yours Is the Earth?*"

Sam looked at him with a mixture of surprise and suspicion, then decided that Mr. Cuff was not kidding.

"It's from Kipling," he said. "*If you can keep your head when all about you men are losing theirs and blaming it on you, if you can trust yourself when all men doubt you, yet make allowance for their doubting too—*"

"*If you can fill each unforgiving minute with sixty seconds' worth of distance run,*" Mr. Farnsworth's chanting voice interrupted. "*Yours is the earth, and everything that's in it, and what is more—*"

"Which *is more*," Sam said.

Mr. Farnsworth's eyes narrowed as he ran through the line in his head, then he grinned and nodded and said, *"And* WHICH *is more, you'll be a man, my son."* He took a sip of wine and giggled with delight as he nodded toward Keeley Cuff and said to Sam, "Look at Joe Yale. Look at the expression on that Irish kisser. Oh, for a Leica shot of that, oh, oh, oh!"

"Well, Lordy me," Mr. Cuff said sullenly. "Hell, Ham, *Kipling* for God's sake."

Mr. Farnsworth giggled again, and then, seeing Sam's face, he must have gathered that his guest did not understand the joke, because Mr. Farnsworth leaned forward, jerked his thumb toward Cuff, and said to Sam, *"Cette goy la,* he works for this precious little dreck of a magazine, it's so delicate and rarefied, when somebody lets one go, they think it's a whiff of Chanel Number Five, and it's all so frigging *Yellow Book* and Aubrey Beardsley and Ronald Firbank, and along you come, the great big new star they've helped discover, and what do you take your title from? A smelly old armpit-and-muscles writer like dear old Rudyard!"

"But that's the point," Sam said uncomfortably. "I mean the title—it's supposed to be ironical."

"You know it, kid," Mr. Farnsworth said, "and *I* know it, son, because we have brains, but this putz melamed here, all he's got is that little gold dingus on his watch chain, and that may be a help if you want to get in for a shvitz and a massage at the Yale Club, but it is absolutely no help up here." Mr. Farnsworth tapped his temple and added, "Which is where the power is."

"I find you infinitely more witty, Ham, old boy, when you're on a subject you know something about," Mr. Cuff said. "Like publishing, for example. So why don't you continue with that?"

"Being a Jew happens to be a subject I know a good deal about, too," Mr. Farnsworth said. "I've been one all my life." He turned to Sam. "And so have you, so we don't have to waste time on a subject with which we are only too intimately acquainted, so I will continue, as our shaygitz here suggests, with publishing, about which I was saying that we discover new writers every day and why we have to, to supply our market. But there's one thing we don't discover every day, and that's why we enter into these embarrassing arrangements for novel contests with twittering aviaries like this *Landscape,* and that new thing we *don't* discover every day is new *writers.* You get the distinction?"

"No, sir," Sam said.

"Sir?" Mr. Farnsworth said. "Sir is for cowering little immigrants with peddler's packs on their back who knock on white Protestant back doors and try to earn another two bits toward their son's college tuition by selling some pigeon-brained shickseh a coffee pot or a yard of hair ribbon. You and I, Sammy boy, we are beyond that. My father has hung up his pack and now sits in Prospect Park every day bragging to his cronies about his brilliant son who earns twenty thousand bucks a year for telling a bunch of goy publishers on Fourth Avenue what books to publish. I don't know what stage your old man has reached, but I think for a boy who at twenty has written a novel as good as *Yours Is the Earth* it is fair to let some of the glory wash off on the poor old pants presser or peddler who sired him and move him up a notch or two, so that even if he still is peddling or pants-pressing, let's pretend he isn't, which means the Sir crap is out for you as well as for me, especially when us Chinese are talking to each other, and most especially when we're talking to the lower orders, like our shmendrick luncheon companion here."

"Boy, Ham, you sure ride that Jewish thing into the ground," Keeley Cuff said. "Lordy me, I don't know what your beef is about. At thirty-six you're one of the most successful men I've ever known, everybody in the business envies you, you've got a beautiful wife, an apartment on Park Avenue, a lovely home in the country, a national reputation, and the most brilliant future in publishing that anybody can imagine, and yet to hear you talk, dripping bitterness and venom all over the place like a pair of wet swimming trunks, you sound like Oliver Twist holding up that bloody porridge bowl. What's your complaint, Ham? What have you got to be sore about?"

Mr. Farnsworth turned and, from the way the wine glass suddenly hung in the air, as though it were a bell that had been struck in a village square to gather the attention of the scattered populace, Sam knew that an invisible line had been crossed.

"I'll tell you what I've got to be sore about," Hampton Farnsworth said slowly and clearly, enunciating each word the way Sam's mother did when she wanted to make it perfectly plain that the discussion phase is over and she is now reading out the law. "I'll tell you what my complaint is," Mr. Farnsworth said. "If I were not a Jew, if in addition to my ability and talent that one stupid card of race had fallen at birth for me as it fell for you, you loathsome little louse, I would not now be working for Alfred Trafalgar and Calder Singlenight, but those two pudding-headed slobs would be working for me—as shipping clerks."

There was a pause, during which Keeley Cuff tried to drain his empty glass, saw what he was doing, started an embarrassed grin, apparently felt it was the wrong thing to do, and set the glass down slowly as his bony face puckered in an expression that might have reflected no more than puzzlement but, to Sam, seemed also to indicate something not too far removed from pain.

"You Jews," the cockeyed little caterpillar said, and then that seemed all he was capable of saying.

"Yes?" Mr. Farnsworth said sardonically. "We Jews?"

Mr. Cuff shook his head, irritably, as though annoyed with himself for being unable to get the words out, and then, poking the horn-rimmed glasses up on his nose, it was as though he had poked a latch that released the gate that held back his words.

"You Jews don't know when you're well off," he said with a bitterness that made Sam feel uncomfortable. It was not as colorful as Mr. Farnsworth's, and it lacked his volume, but it seemed to cut deeper as Mr. Cuff said, "You get it all handed to you, and then instead of being grateful, you kick it in the groin."

"Get what handed to us?" Mr. Farnsworth said icily. "What is this mysterious 'it' that you feel we are not sufficiently grateful for?"

"The bur under your saddle that makes you what you are," Mr. Cuff said angrily. "You say if you were not a Jew then Alfred Trafalgar and Calder Singlenight would be working for you instead of you working for them. *Au contraire,* my dear Ham, if I may borrow the language of your adoption. If you were not a Jew, you wouldn't have built into you the drive to show the Alfred Trafalgars and the Calder Singlenights that you're as good and better than they are. If you were not a Jew, Ham old man, you know what you'd be? You'd be me, that's what you'd be. You wouldn't be the hottest editor in the biggest publishing house in the business, earning twenty thousand and better. You'd be working on some crummy little precious magazine like *Landscape* for thirty bucks a week and chiseling your drinks on a big-shot editor's expense account. That's what you'd be, Mr. Hampton Farnsworth, if you were not a Jew."

"In your opinion," Farnsworth said.

"It's the best one I know," Keeley Cuff said. "You say being a Jew is a subject you know all about because you've been a Jew all your life. Well, my dear Ham, I have a spot of information for you. Being what you call a white Protestant is a subject *I* know all about, because I've been a white Protestant all *my* life, and shall I tell you something, my dear Ham?"

"If it makes more sense than the rest of this garbage you've been letting go, yes," Mr. Farnsworth said.

"I'd swap with you like a shot," said the bony-faced little man. "You can have my little gold dingus on this watch chain, and you can have my access to the Yale Club steamroom. I'll take your Jewishness any day in the week."

"I have a spot of information for you, too, Keeley old boy," Mr. Farnsworth said sarcastically. "That particular day in the week they left out when they made up the calendar. It's easy enough to make grand statements about how you'd prefer to be a Jew, especially with three martinis inside you, or is it four? The hard fact is, however, and you God damn well know it, that there is no swapping, and there is no changing, and there is no going back. If you're born a Jew, you're stuck with it, and one of the toughest things about being stuck with it is having to listen to white Protestant boobs like you telling us being a Jew is a great big wonderful advantage, when every day of our lives it is rubbed into us over and over again that it's the biggest disadvantage since the harelip."

"Is it?" Mr. Cuff said. "Here I am, sitting at a table with two Jews. Has either of you suffered any disadvantage that amounts to a hill of beans? You're thirty-six, and I've already sketched the size of your mess of pottage. Here's Mr. Silver. At twenty he has written a magnificent novel that is about to be published. How has his being a Jew hurt Mr. Silver?"

"You know God damn well how it's hurt him, you double-dealing little vontz of a shaygitz," Mr. Farnsworth said, and he turned to Sam. "That novel of yours is one of the most magnificent things I have ever read. My opinion may not mean much. Why should it? I'm just a slob and a hack. I'm a cheap whore. No, an expensive whore, spreading my intellectual legs for gentile boneheads like Alfred Trafalgar and Calder Singlenight. But I know honest writing when I see it, especially when it deals with material I've lived through. I'm a Brooklyn boy, Sammy boy, and I went to exactly the same kind of high school you describe in *Yours Is the Earth*, and I know how great a job you've done. The temptation, in dealing with that kind of material, is to duck it, to go all delicate and literary, to hide the truth behind a lot of Ronald Firbank delicacy and grace, as those boys call it. What I like about your novel, Sammy boy, is that you didn't succumb to that temptation. You walked up to your material, the way an honest writer should, and you called a spade a spade. These frigging Ronald Firbank lace-pants cream puffs, they turn my stomach. The way they write, you couldn't say sewage to them if you had a mouthful of it. But not you, Sammy boy. You wrote it honest. You wrote it true. You won that contest hands down. There wasn't another manuscript in those thirty-three that were submitted that could come within miles of *Yours Is the Earth*." Mr. Farnsworth whipped around to Mr. Cuff. "So why didn't he win first place?"

"Well," Mr. Cuff said.

"Why didn't he win second place?"

"Well," Mr. Cuff said.

"How about third?" Mr. Farnsworth said. "Why didn't Mr. Silver win that?"

"Well," Mr. Cuff said.

"Well, my ass," Mr. Farnsworth said. "Because there were six judges in this effing contest, and only one of them is a Jew, namely, me, and Mr. Silver happens to be a Jew, too."

"I voted for *Yours Is the Earth*," Mr. Cuff said angrily.

"Hooray for you," Mr. Farnsworth said. "There's always one goy like you to make it legitimate. Like that prop Negro they always have down in the front row at all those damn meetings at Mecca Temple and Webster Hall to show it's a liberal, broad-minded gathering. You voted for him. How nice, you little Judas goat!" Mr. Farnsworth swung back to Sam. "He voted for you, Sammy boy. As a result of Mr. Cuff's broad-mindedness, you got two votes out of six, so that three goyishe stumblebums, who can't write home for money, are walking off with the twenty-five-hundred-, fifteen-hundred-, and thousand-buck prizes, while you, Sammy boy, the biggest fresh new talent to hit this country since Kenyon Poole set us all on our asses with *The Small Meal*, you have won the great big fat honor of having your novel published as a regular part of the Trafalgar, Singlenight list of dreck. What's the matter, kid?"

Sam, who could not say that he was afraid he was about to be sick, did manage to point to the tray the waiter had just brought to the table. Mr. Farnsworth followed Sam's finger with his glance, then turned back.

"They're snails," he said. "And this stuff is a special cheese sauce of my own invention that I had them make up. Wait till you taste this, Sammy boy. You've never— Hey! Hey, Sammy! Where you going?"

Sam went back to Forty-eighth Street, where, after several hours of delivering tuxedos, he calmed down sufficiently to be able to examine his position. It was not, he decided, too bad. In fact, it was quite good. True, he did not have the twenty-five hundred dollars in prize money. But nobody, he had to admit, had ever said he was going to get it. It was an assumption to which Sam had leaped when he read Mr. Cuff's letter inviting him to lunch. Even if it was a reasonable assumption, and from what both Mr. Cuff and Mr. Farnsworth had said about *Yours Is the Earth* it seemed to Sam that the assumption was at least reasonable, it was still no more than an assumption. It was not easy, after you had believed for a week you had won a first prize, to face the fact that you had not won even a second or third prize. But saying something was not easy eliminated neither the something nor the necessity for facing it. So Sam faced it and found that he still had more than he'd had before he entered the contest. Just how much more, he did not know, but he now knew how to go about finding out. He went into a phone booth and called Shirley Shaefer in the Sargent & Sargent bookkeeping department.

"Miss Shaefer?"

"Yes. Who's this?"

"Sam Silver."

"Ooh, am I glad to hear from you!"

"I'm sorry," Sam said. "I didn't have anything to call about."

"Don't I know that?" Miss Shaefer said. "But even so, three weeks, nearly a month biting my fingernails, this is a diet for a person to be on?"

"I'm sorry," Sam said again. "I thought I'd wait to call you until I had some news."

"So please, Mr. Silver, don't make me wait any longer. How'd we make out?"

"Not too bad," Sam said. "They like the novel well enough to want to publish it."

There was a pause at the other end and then, on a rising note of incredulity that was almost a scream, Shirley Shaefer said, "You mean it didn't *win?*"

"No, but they're willing to publish it in the regular way," Sam said.

"Isn't that nice of them!" Miss Shaefer rapped out. "Isn't that just too darling and oh, my, so generous of them! They're willing to publish it! How nice! How sweet! I hope you told them to drop dead?"

Sam, whose heart had disintegrated into a molten pool of gratitude and affection for this wonderful creature at the other end of the wire, did his best to sound crisp and businesslike as he said, "No, because I thought that was a decision for my agents to make."

"I suppose you're right," Miss Shaefer said. "But honestly, it makes my blood boil. A story like that, a book so wonderful, a piece of work like that—"

"And so beautifully typed," Sam said.

"No, I'm serious, Mr. Silver. That story is something nobody who reads it is ever going to—" Her voice stopped and then, sharply, she said, "Who won, Mr. Silver?"

"I don't know," Sam said.

"You mean they didn't tell you?"

"No."

"Just what I thought," Shirley Shaefer said.

"I don't think I understand," Sam said. "You thought what?"

"Mr. Silver, please, don't be so naïve," Miss Shaefer said. "Since when do gentile firms like Trafalgar, Singlenight & Company give prizes to Jewish authors?"

"Oh, now, Miss Shaefer, wait a minute."

"For what? The next pogrom or something? Listen, Mr. Silver, it's as plain as the nose on my face, and I think you're absolutely right to have nothing to do with those anti-Semites."

"I didn't say I was going to have nothing to do with them," Sam said. "I want Mr. and Mrs. Sargent to decide that for me, so would you do me a favor, Miss Shaefer?"

"Anything, Mr. Silver."

"You know the second carbon that I left with you?"

"Locked away in my bottom bureau drawer at home as safe as my father's tvillim, he should rest in peace."

"Good," Sam said. "Now here's what I'd like you to do. Tomorrow morning, when you come to work, bring the manuscript with you, and then take it in to Mr. Sargent or Mrs. Sargent, whichever one happens to be free, and say to them— No, wait. Maybe it would be better if I called them up and said— No, I don't know, I'd have to say— How about this? Suppose I write a note and mail it right now, so they'll have it tomorrow morning, so by the time you come in with the manuscript—"

"Mr. Silver."

"Yes?"

"Could I make a suggestion?"

"Certainly."

"Why don't I go in to Mr. Sargent or Mrs. Sargent and tell the truth?" Shirley Shaefer said. "Mr. Silver wrote this novel, I'll say. It's his first novel, so naturally he was a little embarrassed about showing it to you, but onna konna this contest, for which he happened to be eligible, he thought he'd test it out and see before he wasted your time with it. So me —that's Shirley Shaefer talking—I typed it, and Mr. Silver sent it in, and while it didn't win, Trafalgar, Singlenight says they're willing to publish it, so Mr. Silver feels at least now he knows it's something that he wouldn't be wasting your time if he asks you to read it, so here it is, and after you read it, would you call Mr. Silver and sort of like you might say take it from there. Hoddizat sound, Mr. Silver?"

"Like Talleyrand at the Congress of Vienna," Sam said. "Miss Shaefer, you are not only the world's greatest typist, you are clearly a born diplomat, and for both talents I thank you."

"Don't thank me," Miss Shaefer said. "Just write me another novel as good as *Yours Is the Earth*."

"I'll start tonight," Sam said.

He didn't, because that night, after he had told his mother about the lunch in the Murray Hill Hotel, Mrs. Silver did not clear the table and go to bed, as she did every night after Sam had eaten, so that he could write. That night Mrs. Silver sat and watched in silence as Sam ate.

"Sam," she said finally. "What these two men said to you, these men with the names?"

"Cuff and Farnsworth."

Mrs. Silver shook her head and said, "This is a country." She pushed a plate closer to Sam and said, "With bread, eat. So these two men, what they said about your book, they were telling the truth?"

"I guess so," Sam said.

"Guessing anybody can do," Mrs. Silver said. "What I'm asking, Sam, when they said it was so good, you're such a first-class writer, all those good things they said, what I'm asking, Sam, I'm asking did they tell the truth?"

Sam chewed in silence for a while, trying to reconstruct the scene at the luncheon table, and found that he couldn't quite do it. Or rather, he found that the scene, when reconstructed, differed slightly from the original through which he had only a few hours ago lived. It was as though the real scene, and the scene Sam was now putting together in his mind, were a double exposure, two snapshots of the same subject taken inadvertently on the same piece of negative, so that while in general outline they were similar, the details varied just enough to indicate where one image was superimposed on another. In the real scene, for example, what Sam remembered was the praise that Keeley Cuff and Hampton Farnsworth had heaped upon him. In the reconstructed scene, however, Sam saw that the nature of the praise had been shaped by each man's prejudice. If Keeley Cuff liked *Yours Is the Earth* because it reminded him of the work of Ronald Firbank, which he loved, and Hampton Farnsworth liked *Yours Is the Earth* because it was so refreshingly different from the work of Ronald Firbank, which he detested, wasn't it possible that to both of them Sam Silver was not really a human being but an instrument to be used in the advancement of their special causes? Would Mr. Farnsworth's praise, for example, have been so fulsome if Sam were not a Jew to whom the editor of Trafalgar, Singlenight could point as further proof of his conviction that the world, and particularly his world of publishing, was riddled with anti-Semitism?

"I don't know, Ma," Sam said finally. "They sounded as though they were telling the truth, but how can I tell?"

"There's one way to tell," Mrs. Silver said.

"What's that?"

"Behind the words, how much is there in money?"

"I don't know that, either," Sam said. "All I know is they said they're willing to publish. That means they're willing to take a chance on losing some money."

"In what they're willing to lose, this I'm not interested," Mrs. Silver said. "What I'm interested, I'm interested how much you're going to win."

"I'll know more about that, Ma, after I've had my talk with Mr. and Mrs. Sargent."

"So after you talk with Mr. and Mrs. Sargent," Sam's mother said, "I'll talk some more with you."

"About what, Ma?" Sam said. "What have you got on your mind?"

"A question he asks?" Mrs. Silver said. "What I got on my mind, he wants to know? How President Hoover, now he's out of a job, how he'll get money for rolls and coffee every morning, this is what I got on my mind? You, Sam, and your life, what you're going to do with it, how to use it, it shouldn't be wasted, how to get from here by the garbage pails to uptown there by the money, that's what I have on my mind, Sam."

Two nights later, when Sam got home from the Lafayette Business Institute, his mother had a message for him.

"A girl from Mr. Sargent's office," Mrs. Silver said. "A Shirley Shaefer she was here."

"Here?" Sam said, surprised. "Here in the house?"

"No, here on the roof," his mother said. "A boy, twenty years old, so all of a sudden he starts asking questions like in his head, where once it was brains, now it's a tepple buppkiss. Sam, who is this Shirley Shaefer?"

"She works in Mr. Sargent's office."

"This I just told *you*, Sam," Mrs. Silver said. "Now you tell *me* something."

"Stop making a great big tzimiss out of it, Ma, will you? She works in the bookkeeping department, and in her spare time, at night and on weekends, she types manuscripts to make a little extra money. She typed the manuscript of my novel for me."

"For money?"

"Certainly for money," Sam said. "What do you think she is? Crazy?"

"Not if she types for money," Mrs. Silver said. "When she starts with the typing for nothing, then first she'll be crazy, and you'll learn how big a tzimiss I know how to make."

"Well, before you drive me crazy," Sam said, "I'd like to know what Shirley was doing here?"

"Shirley?" Mrs. Silver said. "And what does she call you?"

"Rudyard," Sam said. "Will you for God's sake quit it, Ma? This is just a girl works in Mr. Sargent's office and types. I'm not going to marry her."

"Jennie Broom, wherever she is she should only stay there two times over, she also was just a girl you knew in school and I should for God's sake quit it, Ma, and look what happened to you from her, I should live so long till the day I want to see *her* again."

"What the hell has Jennie Broom got to do with Shirley Shaefer?"

"Both of them, when you talk about them to your own mother, it's all of a sudden with the hells from the gutter, hah?"

"Okay, I'm sorry. I won't say hell. I won't say anything. I'll just sit here quietly and go out of my mind until you get good and ready to tell me what Miss Shaefer wanted."

"All of a sudden calling her Miss, with this you could maybe fool Papa in there in the bedroom, not me. What she wanted, this Miss Shaefer, two minutes ago it was Shirley, she came with a message from Mr. Sargent."

"What does he want?"

"You should come in see him tomorrow. We have no telephone he could call here, she said, and he couldn't get you by Mr. Brunschweig in the store, so the only way he could get in touch with you, she said, Mr. Sargent could send you a letter, but he was afraid the letters they don't get here on East Tenth Street so early before you go to work, so he sent Shirley, excuse me, he sent Miss *Shaefer,* with the message because she lives on Fourth Street by Avenue D, only a few blocks from here. This you knew?"

"Yes," Sam said. "When I gave her the manuscript to type, I took it over to her house."

"That's nice," Mrs. Silver said. "To bring it in the office, to give it to her there so she could carry it home herself, too heavy for a girl, hah, Sam?"

"She's got five sisters, Ma. A guy is picking a Shaefer for a wife, he doesn't want to be hasty and just grab the first one he sees. I wanted to look them over, all six, make sure I pick the best of the bunch, and the only way to do that was go over where they live and look them over at home. You know what I mean?"

Mrs. Silver apparently did, because, after giving him a long look, she said quietly, "This meeting with Mr. Sargent tomorrow, no matter what Mr. Brunschweig he wants or doesn't want, he says yes or no, for this meeting, Sam, don't even tell Mr. Brunschweig. Just go."

Sam did, shortly before noon, after making a delivery on Forty-fifth Street, and when Miss Tischler showed him into Claude Sargent's room, the agent said across Sam's head, "Tell Mrs. Sargent, will you?" Miss Tischler nodded and disappeared through the curtains, and the fat man hiked himself forward and said, "Well, boy."

"I'm sorry," Sam said.

Claude Sargent laughed and said, "I suppose that remark makes about as much sense as mine does."

"Yes, sir," Sam said, understanding all at once that he had been looking at this meeting only from his own standpoint. Looking, or trying to look at it now, from Mr. and Mrs. Sargent's standpoint, Sam saw that he had placed them in an embarrassing position. The green curtains billowed again and Sophie Sargent came in.

"Well, boy," she said, and as her husband burst out laughing, Mrs. Sargent said irritably, "What's funny about that?"

"It's what I just said to our young genius," Claude Sargent said. "Guess what he said?"

"He's sorry," Mrs. Sargent said.

"Well, I am," Sam said.

"Naturally," she said as she sat down in the red-leather wing chair. "Geniuses are always sorry, or so they say at any rate, once they've done what they planned to do in the first place."

"I didn't plan it," Sam said.

"Of course not," Sophie Sargent said. "Right here in this room, on that dreadful day when we had the meeting with Marshall Umberg, you asked me what I thought of that appalling movie synopsis you had written, and I said out loud and clear, in front of Claude, that I thought it was worse than appalling. Then that dreadful movie synopsis shows up here in this same room in the form of a superb novel which doesn't even have to be shown by us to anybody, since Trafalgar, Singlenight have already read it and agreed to publish it, and you sit there and tell me you didn't plan it."

"You put it that way, yes," Sam said. "I planned the novel, and then I wrote it, and then I had it typed, and then I submitted it to this contest, and then I learned they wanted to publish it, so I thought you and Mr. Sargent better take over. Told that way, it sounds like a plan. But it wasn't a plan when I was here in this office that day. When you said the synopsis stank—"

"You were furious," Mrs. Sargent said. "So when you got home, and you found this announcement from *Landscape* about a novel contest, you said I'll show that bitch. I'll take this stinking synopsis, and I'll turn it into a novel, and I'll win that contest, and that'll show that bitch whether something I write stinks or not. How close am I, Sam dear?"

"Pretty close," Sam said. "Except for two points."

"What are they, darling?"

"I didn't win the contest," Sam said. "And you've got the wrong bitch, Mrs. Sargent."

There was a long silence, during which the ice-blue eyes in the angular, handsome face stabbed at him like probing hat pins, and then Sophie's husband broke the silence.

"The wrong bitch?" Claude Sargent said. "Now what the hell does that mean?"

His wife's eyes stopped stabbing at Sam, and Sophie Sargent smiled slightly, and she said, "What it means is none of our business as literary agents, Claude. The second point is. Am I right, Sam dear?"

"Yes, Mrs. Sargent."

"I thought we'd settled the Mrs. Sargent thing months ago at our house?"

"I'm sorry," Sam said and, because she was waiting, he added, "Sophie."

"That's better," she said. "Now, just to clear the air, the truth is that what you did has proved a little embarrassing to us."

"We're agents," Claude Sargent said. "We look like fools, Sam, when an editor reads something by one of our clients before we read it, or even before we know of its existence."

"Worse than that," Sophie Sargent said. "It weakens us in the one area where we must always be strong, the area of negotiation. If we bring a manuscript to Trafalgar, Singlenight, and they like it, we can tell them what we want for it, and if they won't give it to us, we can threaten to go elsewhere. However, if Trafalgar, Singlenight gets a manuscript from an author and read it, like it, and then we come running up, panting and breathless and say we're the agents on this item, and this is how much we want for it or we'll take it elsewhere, Trafalgar, Singlenight can say sorry, chums, but this manuscript is already committed to us, so don't waste your breath with empty threats about taking it elsewhere, and this is what we're offering for it, not take it or leave it, but take it *and* leave it, the 'it' being the manuscript, Sam dear."

"You mean I've screwed things up," Sam said.

"Not hopelessly, dear," Sophie said.

"But badly enough," her husband said.

"I'm sorry," Sam said.

"Of course you are," Sophie Sargent said. "But that doesn't help, you see. So before we go on to a discussion of what might help in this case, I think I'd better make something clear for all future cases. You agree, Claude?"

The fat man looked uncomfortable as he cleared his throat and said, "Yes, I think he'd better understand it right from the beginning."

"Understand what?" Sam said.

"That we are your agents," Sophie Sargent said. "This does not mean that we get ten per cent out of every dollar you earn. It means we get ten per cent out of every dollar we earn for you. If you don't allow us to earn it for you, then we don't want you as a client."

The words were uttered quietly, in a pleasant, conversational tone, through the small smile that sat like an enhancing cosmetic arrangement on the attractive face, and yet the effect was not unlike that of reading at the point of a gun a blackmail note delivered in the dead of night by a masked stranger.

"It won't happen again," Sam said.

Sophie Sargent's smile changed, not much, but just enough to indicate that she appreciated his taking the trouble to phrase his reply in such a way that they would both understand that what had just taken place was more than a polite conversational exchange: a binding pact had been made.

"Good," she said. "Now that the future has been neatly taken care of, let's see what we can do about the untidy present. Claude and I have both read the novel, Sam. We will dispense with the hot air. It is more than an extraordinary piece of work. It confirms what Claude and I both felt when we read your first story. You are not just another writer who can be taught the tricks necessary to tailor his talents or improve them to a point where he will be turning out a product out of which we will all make a great deal of money. You are a *real* writer. You are unique. What you have to say, and the way you say it, is different from the way other people have said it before. I don't know if I'm saying it right. Claude, help me."

The fat man said, "Sam, they teach you any Latin down in that high school?"

"No, sir," Sam said. "But I know a few phrases from reading and then looking them up."

"*Sui generis* happen to be one of them?"

"Yes, sir."

"That's what Sophie means."

There was another pause, during which Sam thought about what Sophie meant, and he didn't like it. Underneath the compliment there was a nagging suggestion of something unpleasant. She seemed to grasp what was bothering him.

"Sam dear," she said. "You don't like being *sui generis?*"

"It isn't that," he said slowly.

"Then what is it?"

"I'm not sure," Sam said. "It's you said we'll dispense with the hot air."

"And *sui generis* sounds like hot air?"

"Not because I think you're lying," Sam said.

"But because there's a footnote to it?" Sophie said.

"Yes, something like that," Sam said. "Like you're telling me the good part, so I'll be feeling all right when you hit me with the bad part and it'll go down better."

"Well," Sophie said. "That's close enough."

"What's the bad part?" Sam said.

"You can't be both," Sophie said. "You can't be *sui generis* today, and write those crappy synopses for Mercury Films the next day."

"Why not?" Sam said.

"Both things suffer," Sophie Sargent said. "That synopsis was really awful, Sam, it really was."

"But the novel you just said is good," Sam said. "So the *sui generis* part didn't suffer by my writing the synopsis."

"Not yet," Sophie Sargent said. "But if you continue this literary double life, so to speak, the next novel won't be good."

"How can you be so sure?"

"It's been tried, Sam dear. There's a long track record on this subject. We've lived through it with dozens of poor bastards who helped create that record. Every one of them, at the beginning, thought he could do both. Every one of them ended up in trouble, or in a Spanish-type mansion in Hollywood, which for a *sui generis* writer is just another way of saying trouble."

"Sam." He turned toward the fat man behind the desk. Claude Sargent said, "Remember a few months ago? That first time you came to see me? Ken Poole was here? You remember that?"

"Yes, of course."

"You remember what he said? About what a writer's got? A real writer? A door he can open and walk through and close it behind him, something nobody else in the world has got? And you've got it only as long as you play fair with your talent? With the tools of your trade? As long as you don't blunt those tools?"

"Yes, of course I remember all that," Sam said, trying not to sound annoyed. He had done something that everybody told him was extraordinary. Keeley Cuff, Hampton Farnsworth, Claude Sargent, Sophie Sargent, all had used variations of the word. He had come here expecting to be praised. Instead he was being made to feel like a once promising schoolboy who had been summoned to a conference in the principal's office because his grades had unaccountably begun to slip. "What I don't understand is why you should be lecturing me about this now."

"We knew you were a good writer when we read your first story in *Landscape*," Claude Sargent said. "But we didn't realize then that you were a novelist."

"What's the difference?" Sam said. "A writer is a writer."

"No, there's a difference," Sophie Sargent said. "*Sui generis* writers who also have the wind for the long pull are extremely rare. But they don't always make much money." Sophie Sargent paused, and she looked at Claude Sargent, who nodded, and Sophie said, more slowly, "Sam dear, they don't always make much money."

Sam, who understood at last why they were lecturing him in this way, said, "You've talked to Mr. Farnsworth."

"We did," Claude Sargent said. "Or rather, Sophie did. She's much better with those book people than I am. The magazine boys are my cup of tea."

"Nobody's very good with any kind of people when their hands are tied, but I'm not afraid of Ham Farnsworth," Sophie Sargent said. "I knew him when his name was Irving Feuerknecht and he was teaching freshman English at C.C.N.Y. and picking up pocket money translating LaFontaine for the Trafalgar, Singlenight juvenile list. He's slightly crazy, all that nonsense about wines and cheese, but in the literary and publishing sense he's completely sound and, more important, basically honest."

"Here it comes," Sam said.

"Yes, Sam, I'm sorry," Sophie Sargent said. "Ham told me pretty much what he told you. He likes the book, and he wants to publish it. Or rather, he wants to publish you. He thinks you've got a fine future as a novelist, and he'd like to have you on the Trafalgar, Singlenight list. He's sorry you didn't win the prize, or any of the prizes, because that was your only chance to make some decent money out of the book. He thinks it's the kind of book that will attract a certain amount of attention because it's a first novel and because of the slightly controversial fuss that might be aroused because of the frank treatment of the subject matter. Ham feels it will get excellent reviews, which will also help, and as a result he feels they can sell somewhere between a thousand and twelve hundred and fifty copies. At a two-dollar retail price, and a straight ten per cent royalty, or twenty cents a copy, that comes to two hundred and fifty dollars, which is what Ham Farnsworth offered as an advance. What are you laughing at?"

"My mental arithmetic," Sam said. "I owe Shirley Shaefer one hundred and eight dollars and fifty cents for typing the manuscript, which means my end of it comes to a hundred and forty-one dollars and fifty cents."

"No, Sam dear," Sophie Sargent said gently. "Your end of it comes to one hundred and sixteen dollars and fifty cents. You're forgetting our twenty-five-dollar commission."

"It doesn't seem like much for all your work," Sam said. "Why don't you ask Mr. Farnsworth to come up a little in the size of the advance? Now what did *I* say that's funny?"

"Writers are alike in many ways, but in no way are they more alike than in their reaction to a disappointing price," Sophie said. "They always suggest that the agent go back and ask for more, as though this were as brilliantly fresh and original a notion as the invention of the wheel."

"Sophie's right," Claude Sargent said. "When we tell you this is what somebody has offered for something, you can be absolutely sure, Sam, that's final and rock bottom, that we've made every conceivable suggestion, presented every argument, and made every threat, and we've been fought to a standstill represented by the price we bring you."

"If the book is as good as Mr. Farnsworth and you think it is," Sam said, "maybe some other publisher might feel the same way about it and offer a little more?"

"Yes, they might," Sophie said. "In fact, I'm damn sure they would. Not much more, perhaps, because they're all as good as Ham Farnsworth at the simple arithmetic involved in the dismal sales of first novels, but I know half a dozen editors in the trade who are jealous enough of Ham to risk losing a couple of hundred dollars of their employers' money for the pleasure of sneaking a new writer, especially one Ham has himself discovered, out from under his nose."

"Should we provide one of those editors with that pleasure?" Sam said.

Claude Sargent and his wife exchanged a short glance.

"We are pleased to note, Sam dear," she said dryly, "that, like most good writers, you are not hampered by any old-fashioned scruples about fair play."

Feeling his face grow hot, Sam said, "I didn't mean—"

"Of course not," Sophie said even more dryly. "Neither, I'm sure, did you mean to sign away your right to act freely."

"My right to do what?" Sam said.

Claude Sargent leaned forward across his desk and said, "That letter you got from *Landscape* announcing the contest?"

"What about it?" Sam said.

"They asked you to return it with the manuscript, if you entered the contest, and the letter would serve as your entry blank?"

"That's right," Sam said. "And I did return it."

"After filling in the blank spaces at the bottom?"

"Yes," Sam said. "They wanted some biographical material, things like that. There were about a dozen or so blanks to fill in."

"And one for your signature?" Sophie said.

"Huh," Sam said.

"Your signature, Sam dear," Sophie said. "You signed your name to this document, didn't you?"

"I think so," said Sam, who knew damn well he had signed it but knew also, from the tone of Sophie's inquisition, that he had made a mistake. "I guess I shouldn't have, huh?"

"Well, it would have been better if you hadn't," Sophie said. "But on the other hand, under the circumstances, I don't see what else you could have done, except perhaps let your agents submit the novel to the contest for you, but that puts us under those circumstances again, Sam, doesn't it?" She smiled and said, "Don't look like that. All the other contestants probably were hooked in the same way."

"What way is that?" Sam said.

"There was some small print immediately above the place where you put your signature," Sophie said. "It's still there, Sam dear. Ham Farnsworth showed it to me when I was in his office yesterday. It says that whether you win any of the three prizes in the contest or not, you grant to Trafalgar, Singlenight the right to publish your manuscript under terms currently considered equitable in the publishing business."

"Boy, I not only tied your hands," Sam said, "I practically cut them off."

"Not quite," Sophie said. "There's that phrase *currently considered equitable*."

"But you just said a two-hundred-fifty-dollar advance was pretty much what any of those half-dozen other editors would consider fair for a first novel like this one," Sam said.

"So I did, and so they would," Sophie said. "But if I wanted to put on the gloves with Mr. Farnsworth, I could without too much trouble dig up half a dozen other editors whose testimony, in the arithmetical sense, would be more to my liking."

"Oh," said Sam, who was beginning to sense something he could not quite explain, a feeling that he was being led slowly, step by step, to a conclusion Mr. and Mrs. Sargent wanted him to reach, but they could no more admit they were leading him to it than they could, without jeopardizing his chance of getting there, omit any of the steps. "In other words," he said, "I've pretty much committed *Yours Is the Earth* to Trafalgar, Singlenight on the terms you just outlined. But if I want to break the commitment, you'd be willing to fight it out with them and break it for me?"

Mr. and Mrs. Sargent exchanged another glance, as though checking with one another to see if the process of leading Sam to the conclusion they wanted him to reach was going according to plan. Apparently it was, because Sophie nodded to her husband, and like a climber pausing to tighten his belt before tackling the last lap of his upward journey, Claude Sargent hiked himself forward into the desk and said, "*If* you want to break the commitment, Sam."

"Oh," Sam said again because, while he *felt* closer to the conclusion, he still didn't know what it was. "Do I *want* to break the commitment?"

"Sam dear," Sophie said. "All that stuff Claude and I were telling you at the beginning of this talk, about being *sui generis* and so on, we pointed out that the serious novelist, the man who is true to his talent, doesn't always make a lot of money. We should have added that he doesn't always make a lot *at the beginning*. Even Kenyon Poole made almost nothing out of his first three books. As a matter of fact, the advance on his first novel was exactly what Ham Farnsworth has offered you. Two hundred and fifty dollars. Then along came *The Small Meal*, and he not only made a fortune out of that, but the value of those first three books was suddenly enhanced. They all sold to the movies, for example, for nice fat prices, whereas at the time they were published, the studios were not interested. What it amounts to, Sam dear, is setting your course, so to speak, with your first novel. If the course is set right, you're bound to sail into the money harbor eventually. But if you wobble at the beginning, if you deflect yourself with junk to earn an immediate buck, you'll be putting yourself off course, and you'll miss the money harbor in the future. Do you follow me, Sam?"

"I don't know," Sam said, which was certainly true. "I think you're trying to tell me that I should take Mr. Farnsworth's offer."

Once more Claude Sargent and his wife exchanged a glance.

"Sam we *think* you should, yes," Mr. Sargent said. "But we don't want to *tell* you to do it."

"Why not?" Sam said. "You're my agents. Why shouldn't you tell me?"

"We can only point out the facts," Sophie Sargent said. "You must make the decision yourself."

Sam could see that they had gone as far as they intended to go. There was something missing, something they would not, or perhaps could not, tell him. Sam sensed that he was supposed to have grasped it from what they *had* told him, and because he hadn't, both the Sargents were uncomfortable. So was Sam. Not only because he felt stupid to have missed what they clearly thought he should have seen, but because by missing it he had so obviously let them down.

"Do I have to make the decision now?" he said and, from the look of relief the fat man behind the desk exchanged with his wife, Sam knew that he had made the right move.

"No, of course not, Sam dear," Sophie Sargent said enthusiastically, as though, instead of breaking into an almost lumberingly obvious stall for time, he had done something brilliant. "Ham Farnsworth is in no hurry. Take your time. Take a few days to think it over."

Sam knew he wouldn't have to take that long. All he had to do was get back to the East Tenth Street kitchen. When he did, late that night, he explained the problem to his mother.

"Tell me from the beginning," Mrs. Silver said. "And with bread eat."

Sam ate with bread, and told her everything. When he finished, his mother sat quietly for a while, scowling down at the oilcloth cover and, apparently unaware that she was doing it, running her forefinger slowly around and around the perimeter of a small block of the blue and white checks in the design.

"This man you had two days ago the lunch with," she said finally. "The one he's with the wine and the cheese and he's by this big publisher the main knyocker?"

"Mr. Farnsworth?" Sam said.

Mrs. Silver nodded. "Him," she said. "Mrs. Sargent she said she knew him once his name it was Ira Feuerknecht?"

"*Irving* Feuerknecht," Sam said. "Yes."

"And you he said the reason the twenty-five hundred dollars you didn't win it's because you're a Jew?"

"That's what he said, Ma, but I don't believe—"

"What you don't believe we can talk some other time," his mother said. "But to you he said it?"

"He certainly did."

"Mr. and Mrs. Sargent, what they said to this?"

"They didn't say anything about it."

Mrs. Silver looked puzzled. "Nothing?" she said. "Not a word?"

Sam shook his head. "Not a word. How could they? I didn't tell them about it."

Mrs. Silver's face cleared. "You didn't tell them, to Mr. and Mrs. Sargent you didn't say this Mr. Farnsworth he said you didn't win because you're a Jew?"

"No," Sam said. "It seemed completely beside the point."

"Never mind the point and what it's beside," Mrs. Silver said. "One more thing, Sam. The book, what you wrote, it's about Jews?"

"Not about Jews as subject matter, Ma. It's about a group of people on the Lower East Side and especially about the kids in the group at this high school they go to, people and kids who just happen to be Jews."

"Sam, nobody just happens to be a Jew," his mother said. "When you're a Jew, you're a Jew one hundred per cent, no matter how fancy you become with cheese and with wine, and no matter what you change your name to."

"What are you driving at, Ma?"

"What Mr. and Mrs. Sargent wanted you should understand there in the office today but with their own mouths they couldn't tell you."

"You mean you know, Ma?"

"What's there to know?" Mrs. Silver said. "Anybody with a head that's a head and not a potato can figure it out. What they want, Mr. and Mrs. Sargent, they want you should let this Mr. Farnsworth, his firm, they want you should let them publish the book."

"Why couldn't they tell me that?" Sam said. "It seems simple enough."

"When it's with goyim, and they got something to say it's about Jews, it's never simple," Mrs. Silver said. "Mr. and Mrs. Sargent figure like this, they figure: this Mr. Farnsworth, it's not about wines and cheese that he's crazy. It's about being a Jew that he's crazy. This is a kind of craziness that it can't be stopped, no matter what, even it means losing your friends, your good name, even your job. Because he has in him this craziness, this Mr. Farnsworth he'll do anything against the people that he thinks are against *him*. He thinks you didn't win because you're a Jew. The book, it's about Jews. So if he publishes it, he'll break his back and his neck and his life even, *everything*, to make you and this book you should be a bigger success than the books that they gave to them the prizes, the prizes they didn't give to you because you're a Jew. This is what Mr. and Mrs. Sargent wanted you should understand. This is what they were ashamed to say to you in words."

"That I'll do better on the Trafalgar, Singlenight list because I *am* a Jew?" Sam said.

Mrs. Silver nodded. "And because Mr. *Farnsworth* he's a Jew," she said. "He'll make from you and your book something he can use to slap in the face those goyim they're his bosses."

Sam shook his head. "That sure is the latest wrinkle in anti-Semitism," he said.

"With anti-Semitts there's never no latest," his mother said. "With anti-Semitts there's always, every day, it's something new."

"You think I ought to do this, Ma?"

"Why not?" Mrs. Silver said.

"It feels sort of cheesy," Sam said. "I'd be letting myself be used as a sort of, I don't know, a gun or a rock or something in Mr. Farnsworth's war against his enemies."

"And your enemies they're not?"

"Ma, for Pete's sake, I never even met Mr. Trafalgar and Mr. Singlenight."

"Why you have to meet them?" Mrs. Silver said. "They're goyim, no?"

Sam shook his head again. "It doesn't seem right, Ma."

"For a Jew in this world it's not a question of right," his mother said. "For a Jew the only question is to live."

"I can live if my book is published by somebody else than Trafalgar, Singlenight."

"By them, so long this Mr. Farnsworth is working there," his mother said, "you'll live better."

This certainly proved to be true, in a way that neither Mrs. Silver nor her son could have contemplated, at least during the months that elapsed between the time Sam signed the contract and the time *Yours Is the Earth* was published.

That first lunch at the Murray Hill, from which Sam fled when the snails arrived, was followed by a dozen or more other lunches in various small restaurants in the midtown area that Mr. Farnsworth apparently chose, or so it seemed to Sam, because the waiters were able to give as well as they got in the inevitable battle about the cheese and the wine, always conducted in French, that ran in and out of each meal, disappearing for a few minutes, or even for an entire course, only to erupt again into shrill violence with the next course, like the bar sinister in a genealogical table.

The lunches presented certain problems for Sam. Each one, merely from the standpoint of getting to it, involved a complicated manipulation in his relationship with Mr. Brunschweig, who was becoming, if not suspicious, then certainly curious about Sam's activities outside the tuxedo-renting business. Once he did get to the lunch, Sam was faced with a couple of other problems. When he bought his own lunch, the only problem was how to get up the dime to pay for his potato knish and hot dog. When Mr. Farnsworth was buying Sam's lunch, Sam rarely knew what he was eating until the process started, and by then it was often too late. One mouthful of tripe, if the mere thought of tripe makes you sick, is as bad as an entire plateful, and the fact that the sauce, which Mr. Farnsworth had himself invented, cost as much as Sam's blue suit, did not change the reactions of Sam's gastric nerve centers. It did not, on the other hand, cause them any permanent damage and, on the plus side, there was the educational factor.

Before he met Hampton Farnsworth, Sam's gastronomical horizons had been limited by his mother's idea of a great delicacy, which was tzimiss, and his own, which was tuna on rye. By the time *Yours Is the Earth* was published, these horizons had not only been extended considerably as a result of the generous expense account Trafalgar, Singlenight placed at the disposal of its editor-in-chief, but Sam had learned a basic truth about the career into which he had stumbled and on which Mr. Farnsworth was apparently determined to launch him properly: the publishing business, like Napoleon's armies, traveled on its stomach.

Sam's biggest problem with these lunches, however, was that for a long time he could not figure out why Mr. Farnsworth invited him to them.

Common sense told Sam that even if lunching with authors is a regular part of an editor's job, on a list that Mr. Farnsworth had said contained sixty-two items for the half year and therefore presumably a hundred and twenty-four for the entire year, Sam was clearly getting more than one one-hundred-and-twenty-fourth of the Trafalgar, Singlenight editor-in-chief's available lunch time. Why?

Because Mr. Farnsworth liked him? If so, the plump little man with the toy soldier's face crowned by the busby of light brown hair had an odd way of showing his affection. When he was not screaming at the waiters in French, Mr. Farnsworth was sneering in monosyllabic Anglo-Saxon at all people who wanted to be writers, had become writers, thought they had become writers, or would some day think they were writers.

Did Mr. Farnsworth invite Sam to these lunches because he wanted to get to know this particular writer better? If so, he had an even more odd way of accomplishing *that*. He never asked Sam a question or gave him a chance to say more than yes, he did like the kidneys in that wine sauce. Mr. Farnsworth did all the talking, and after the second or third dose of it, Sam wondered why the editor bothered. It was always a repetition of the basic theme Mr. Farnsworth had sounded during that first lunch with Keeley Cuff: he, Mr. Farnsworth, may have looked like a great big roaring success to the uninformed, but in actual fact he was just a shit and a hack because his natural talents, which were enormous and should have carried him to the heights, were completely nullified by one overwhelming fact that would forever keep him harnessed to the shafts of lesser, meaning gentile, men's chariots: he was a Jew.

There were times when Sam found himself wishing even harder than Mr. Farnsworth that the editor was not. He was the first man who ever planted in Sam's mind the heretical thought that being a Jew could also mean being a bore.

One night, when Sam came home from his classes, his mother said, as she started bringing the cracked plates and jars from the refrigerator to the table, "Sam, I think it's time already we got a telephone."

"Here in the house, Ma?"

"Where else? Outside in the street? Telephones to put in, it's to talk here in the house, no? To the meat, take a little chrein."

"It's five dollars a month, Ma."

"No, four dollars twenty-five cents. I talked with Mr. Tinniff in the grocery today. A bite bread, Sam, take. He says it's four dollars and a quarter with sixty-six calls you can make. Only if you make more than sixty-six calls, only then it's more than four dollars twenty-five cents. To come in, the calls people they call you, this it's no limit. All day and all night people could call you, and you it doesn't cost a penny. What's the matter, Sam, all of a sudden by you the bread is poison?"

"Ma, we can't afford it."

"Sometimes it's better not to think what you can afford, but to do. You're now a shreiber, Sam. With soon a book it'll be in the stores, people all over they'll be buying. You're becoming an important person, Sam. It isn't right, other important people they want to talk to you, they have to send somebody, like in Europe, when a cow was sick, the little shaygitz they sent in the middle of the night for the doctor."

"I'm an important man, Ma, sure, so important that up to now this important man, he's sold one short story for ten dollars and he's earned a hundred and sixteen dollars and fifty cents out of a big fat novel. If I didn't spend six days a week delivering tuxedos for Mr. Brunschweig, what I'm eating now, we'd have to save it for tomorrow's supper. We've got along up to now without a telephone, we can get along without one a little longer. Let's wait until the book is published, and if it sells better than the twelve hundred copies everybody says it's going to sell, okay, then we can discuss luxuries like telephones. Hey, what's happening around here tonight? Where's the bread?"

"Wait, I'll get more. A person would think he never saw a piece rindle before. Here, eat slow. Sam, it's not right people should come running when they want you."

"Who came running?"

"Who said running? She came to tell, so it's enough without the running."

"To tell what, Ma? Who?"

"First it's hurry up, where's the bread? Then, you bring it, he lets it stand like a soldier by Franz Joseph. That Shirley Shaefer, that's who came running, from Fourth Street, she's by Sargent & Sargent a bookkeeper, but for you all of a sudden she knows how to make extra money with the typewriter."

"Shirley was here tonight?"

"No more Miss Shaefer? All of a sudden again with the Shirley?"

"What did she want, Ma?"

"What she wants, this she'll tell a mother?"

"Ma, she must have had some reason for coming over."

"Reasons? Sure, they always have reasons. This Mr. Farnsworth from the publisher, he wanted to talk to you, she said, but who can talk to my Sam? To call him by Mr. Brunschweig, no, he's never there, and to call him here by his house, again no, because if he had a telephone, the Shirleys they couldn't come running. So this Mr. Farnsworth, if she's telling the truth, this Shirley, he called you by the office by Sargent & Sargent, they should give you a message, and by Sargent & Sargent, they know already this Shirley she lives only six blocks from here, on Fourth Street, so they told her when she goes home, she should come here and give you the message. This is what *she* says, this Shirley from Fourth Street."

"What's the message, Ma?"

"Look," Mrs. Silver said. "Just one word he has to hear, this Shirley, so right away he's jumping out of his skin. The message, she said, tomorrow this Mr. Farnsworth he wants you should call him up, it's important."

It didn't seem important when, the next day, Sam got Mr. Farnsworth on the phone.

"Who?" he said. "Oh, Sam Silver. Hello, Sam. What's on your mind, son?"

"Nothing much," Sam said. "When I got home last night, my mother gave me a message saying you wanted me to call you?"

"Did I?" Mr. Farnsworth said. "Let me think. Wait a minute. Maybe my secretary knows what the hell I had in mind. Cynthia! Hey, Cynthia! Miss Sheridan, where the hell is Cynthia? Well, then, ask Margaret, will you? Christ, they saddle you with a bigger staff than Marlborough had at Oudenarde, and all day long they're tripping you up under foot like wet bathmats, but the moment you want one of them, they're all gone."

"Maybe it was about the publication date?" Sam said helpfully.

"The publication date of what, son?"

One thing Sam had learned during his puzzling lunches with Mr. Farnsworth: the editor always seemed to know what he wanted in the way of cheese or wine, but apparently he could never make up his mind whether the person for whom he was ordering them was a friend or an enemy. In the midst of a glowing compliment about Sam's prose style Mr. Farnsworth would stop to say something cruel about the cheap cut of Sam's still unpaid-for suit.

"My book," said Sam, who had learned that while Mr. Farnsworth was struggling with the problem of whether at that particular moment he loved you or hated you, it was sensible to bear in mind that the problem was not yours but his. *"Yours Is the Earth,"* Sam said. "My book."

"Oh, *that,*" Mr. Farnsworth said. "No, I couldn't have called you about that because we haven't set a pub date yet on any of the books that came out of the *Landscape* contest. Oh, here she is. Hey, Cynthia, my love, what the hell did I call Sam Silver about yesterday? I did? Well, I'll be damned. Okay, thanks, sweetie. Sam?"

"Yes?"

"What I called about," Mr. Farnsworth said, "I wondered could you come out for the week-end?"

"Out where?" Sam said.

There was a pause at the other end that, it occurred to Sam, was long enough to enable Marlborough to move his staff from Oudenarde to Malplaquet.

"Out to my home in Westport," Mr. Farnsworth's voice said finally. "Where did you think I meant?"

Sam couldn't tell him that he hadn't really been thinking at all. Not about what Mr. Farnsworth meant, at any rate. Sam, who had never been away for a week-end, knew all about them from novels he had read. They involved week-end bags, which he did not own, tips to servants, which he could not afford, and racket and golf clubs, or sticks if it was an English novel, he did not know how to use. Furthermore, Sam did not mind, or he did not mind very much, being alternately praised and insulted by Mr. Farnsworth for an hour or two every couple of weeks in a French restaurant. After all, like David Copperfield, Sam had his way to make in the world, and even that estimable young man had grasped soon enough that a bit of trimming now and then was essential. But the prospect of serving as Mr. Farnsworth's emotional punching bag for a whole week-end did not cause Sam's heart to leap up.

"What I meant," he said into the phone, "I meant I'm afraid I can't come out for the week-end."

"Why the hell not?"

"I work all day Saturday," Sam said.

"Oh," Mr. Farnsworth said, and there was another pause, during which the editor may have been consulting Cynthia, because at the other end of the phone there was a great deal of twittering that sounded like several people raking leaves across a pavement. Mr. Farnsworth came back on the phone with: "How about coming out Saturday night after work? There's a good train at six-ten and a not so good but it's the last one at seven-twenty, and I could meet—"

"I work until eight-thirty on Saturdays," said Sam, who had never been kept later by Mr. Brunschweig than seven.

"For Christ's sake," Mr. Farnsworth said. "Can't you ask your boss to give you an hour off once in a while?"

"Saturday is our busiest night," Sam said.

"Well, then, come on out on Sunday, and I'll drive you in to work Monday morning."

"I have to be on the job at eight-thirty on Monday morning," Sam said and, before Mr. Farnsworth could go to work on that, he added, "But if there's a train back to New York Sunday night—?"

"There are dozens of them," Mr. Farnsworth said. "Here, I'll put Cynthia on. She'll square you away, then tell me what you've fixed up, and I'll meet you at the train."

He did, in a Buick convertible with the top down, and Sam saw, through the window as the slowing train slid past the line of cars parked at the edge of the platform, a girl in a peasant blouse seated beside Mr. Farnsworth on the front seat. The editor, wearing sandals, a dirty sweatshirt, and red swimming trunks, was coming up the platform toward him when Sam stepped down from the train.

"Hi, son, glad to see you," Mr. Farnsworth said, and Sam, who had been forced to become something of an expert on the editor's moods, saw that his host was telling the truth: Mr. Farnsworth did look glad to see him. "I'm whipping up a little surprise for lunch, and I want to stop in at the grocery for a few things, but my secretary came along in the car, so you can talk to her while I'm shopping. She's no beauty, but she's as bright as a button, and you better keep your legs crossed, unless you don't mind getting banged in a convertible with the top down at high noon on an August Sunday with half the town of Westport for an audience. This chick and the male zipper are as iron filings to a magnet."

"Cynthia?" Sam said as he fell in beside Mr. Farnsworth.

"Hell, no," the editor said. "Cynthia's mother wouldn't let her go away for a week-end at the home of a guy with my rep."

"Miss Sheridan?"

"Miss Sheridan is *Mrs.* Sheridan, and when she goes away for a week-end, Mr. Sheridan goes with her."

"Then it's Margaret," Sam said.

"Margaret was here last week-end and is now home with a bad case of what we both hope actually *is* poison ivy," Mr. Farnsworth said. "How do you know all my secretaries?"

"They keep getting into the conversation every time I call you on the phone," Sam said.

"Well, this one gets into more than conversations, and she's not one of my Trafalgar, Singlenight staff," Mr. Farnsworth said. "I've hired this one to help me with my cheese book. I'm putting on a final push on that, and hope to have it finished by the end of the summer. Sam, I'd like you to meet Miss Broom. Jennie, this is Sam Silver. What's the matter?"

"I think Mr. Silver and I have met," Jennie said from the front seat of the convertible.

"Well, Christ," Mr. Farnsworth said. "It couldn't have been that bad, could it?"

"Oh, no, not at all," Jennie said, and she laughed. "It's just that I feel such a fool. I can't remember where it was. Can you, Mr. Silver?"

"No," said Sam, who wondered if he would have been able to say anything if she hadn't laughed. "But I'm sure it'll come back to me."

"Well, why don't you two work on it while I do my shopping," Mr. Farnsworth said. "I won't be long."

He walked across the street toward a line of shops facing the station, and Jennie opened the front door and slid along the seat until she was behind the wheel. After a moment of hesitation, Sam got in and pulled the door shut. Jennie took a cigarette from a pack in the crevice between the two leather cushions, punched in the dashboard lighter, and looked at Sam coolly until the lighter popped out. Then she put the glowing filaments to the end of her cigarette, inhaled deeply, replaced the lighter, and said through the thick outpouring of smoke, "I don't know what the hell *you've* got to be sore about. I turned you into a novelist, didn't I?"

"Oh, I see," Sam said. "I owe it all to you."

"I don't know how much *all* is," Jennie said. "Ham brought out an advance copy on the train with him yesterday, and I read it last night. I agree with him that it'll probably sell about twelve hundred copies, which won't put you into fur-lined underwear, Sammy boy, but a novel is a novel, and you can't deny that this one is nothing more than an expanded version of the movie treatment I got you to do on your short story for Mercury Films, although I haven't told that to Ham."

"I see it's Ham," Sam said.

"Why not?" Jennie said. "I call all my bosses by their first names."

"Including Marshall Umberg?"

"He's different," Jennie said. "He was my enemy."

"What was I?" Sam said. "The bullet in the gun you were using to ambush him?"

"Ham thinks you've got quite a future as a novelist," Jennie said. "Figures of speech like that one, Sammy, might make him change his mind. You want to know the truth?"

"How would *you* know it?" Sam said.

"If I've got the birthdays figured correctly, you're twenty years old now," Jennie said. "Maybe by the time you're allowed to vote you will have learned something that most people pick up at their mother's knee: to be a good liar you've got to be an expert on the truth."

"What was it this time?" Sam said. "Was Mr. Umberg an anti-Semite like our old principal Mr. Mueller, and your great big liberal anti-fascist heart couldn't rest as long as he was the head of the Mercury Films story department?"

"That's only part of it," Jennie said.

"What's the other part?" Sam said.

"I thought if I could get him drop-kicked out on his big broad ay for being incompetent, which he was, I could maneuver myself into the job," Jennie said. "I think I could have done it, too," she added. "Except for a certain letter that was sent to Umberg's boss on the Coast, a letter signed by Claude Sargent and Sophie Sargent, who are no friends of mine, and a third party who I thought was."

"When did you get that idea?" Sam said.

The look in Jennie's brown eyes changed slightly as she took a long puff and then, slowly, blew the smoke in his face. "The night I came to that Mr. Brunschweig's tuxedo store," she said. "To pick up the manuscript of your screen treatment."

"You might have told your friend that night," Sam said, "that since you and he had seen each other last, his visitor had become Mrs. Buggo Salvemini."

"Suppose I had told him that?" Jennie said. "Would he have kept his fly buttoned?"

Mr. Farnsworth, appearing at the other side of the car with a paper sack, said, "Jennie, for the love of God, what have you been telling our Sam to get his face as red as that?"

"We both just remembered where it was we'd met," Jennie said, sliding back across the front seat, toward Sam, as Mr. Farnsworth opened the far door and slipped in behind the wheel.

"Where was that?" the editor said.

"Oh, some dull party," Jennie said as the car started. "When we were both still in high school."

"When I was in high school, no party was dull," Mr. Farnsworth said. "But then, as we all know, the cultural level of Brooklyn has always been several cuts above most of our other fashionable Eastern watering places. Jennie, my love, don't sit on that bag. It contains a pound of Gruyère imported especially for your host, who intends to build not only our lunch around it, but also chapter eight of his *chef d'oeuvre*. Train trip out okay, Sam?"

"Uh, yes, fine," said Sam. He had been worried all the way out by the fact that his round-trip ticket had used up all except $2.84 of the half of his salary, which Mr. Brunschweig had paid him the night before, that belonged to Sam, and who was now wishing desperately that he could concentrate on something as reassuringly simple as a financial problem. Jennie's bare arm, since she had moved across to make room for her boss, was resting on Sam's thigh.

"Do you know Westport?" Mr. Farnsworth said.

"Huh?" Sam said.

"Jennie," the editor said. "Will you pinch him awake?"

"How can you tell when he is?" Jennie said.

"Oh, boy," Mr. Farnsworth said. "That must have been some party where you two met."

"I meant no," Sam said. "I've never been here before."

He moved slightly to the right. Jennie's arm moved with him.

"It's the last oasis of sanity within commuting distance of New York," Mr. Farnsworth said, swinging the car from the road running along a river, that had carried them away from the station, onto a paved highway. "That's the Saugatuck River down there, and this thing we're on now is the Boston Post Road. We won't be on it long, just until we get through town, and then we fork off."

"Isn't it pretty early in the day for an orgy?" Jennie said.

"Did she make jokes like that at this party where you met, Sam?" Mr. Farnsworth said.

Sam tried not to say "Huh?" again, but Jennie's hand, lying on his thigh, was no longer motionless, and there was no room in Sam's head for the effort involved in inventing small talk that would look large, so he abandoned the effort and settled for another "Huh?"

"Our young novelists, as you may have noticed, Miss Broom, get wittier and wittier," Mr. Farnsworth said. "This is the town, Sam."

Sam forced his eyes into focus, became aware of a sleepy, sun-hazed street running at right angles to the Post Road, saw an A. & P. sign and a red-brick structure that could have been a bank, felt the bright shock of a flower garden behind the bank or perhaps it was behind the white clapboard house next to the bank, and then the car was purring along a narrow, poorly paved, tree-shaded road.

"Pretty, what?" Mr. Farnsworth said.

"Yeah," Sam said as Jennie's fingers, gently kneading the cloth of his pants, sent the deliciously squirming rays of warmth up and down his thigh.

"It's what keeps me alive," Mr. Farnsworth said. "If I didn't have my place here, and a clause in my Trafalgar, Singlenight contract saying I don't have to come into the New York office more than three days a week, I'd have been locked away in the booby hatch a long time ago. I'm just over the top of the next hill. Right on the river. I hate the shore places. The sea bores me. The ocean is like a whore. Zip, and there it is, the whole works. After you've looked at an ocean for thirty seconds, you've seen all it has to offer. A river, though, a river is like a dame, no matter how often you've been there, there's always something draws you back, something you haven't had yet. A river view, I mean a narrow woodsy river like the Aspetuck, surrounded by a good stand of timber, there's always something for the eye to be caught by. See what I mean?"

Sam, who had opened his mouth as the car started up the hill in the hope that this would keep his breathing inaudible, made another effort to absorb his surroundings. This time he saw that the Buick had emerged into a small parking area behind a low house on which, it seemed fairly obvious, a good deal of money had been spent to create the impression that it had been put together from timber felled in the immediate vicinity by a man who, eschewing the advantages of civilization available in any local hardware store, had preferred to work with nothing more than his bare hands and the ax that a direct ancestor had carried across the plains and the bad lands in a covered wagon.

"It's beautiful," said Jennie as she gave Sam's thigh a final squeeze, and he managed, in a croak that hurt his dry throat, to say, "Yeah."

"Come around the front," Ham Farnsworth said. "That's where you'll see what I mean about the view."

He took the paper grocery bag, held the door of the convertible until Jennie and Sam had stepped out on the gravel, then banged the door shut and herded his guests up some rough flagstones to a porch that ran all the way around the house. Sam, who was absorbed by the rise and fall of Jennie's peasant blouse, did not at once see that Mr. Farnsworth's enthusiasm for the beauties of his country retreat was not unjustified.

"Get a load of that," the editor was saying, and Sam, once again making an effort, saw that Mr. Farnsworth was standing at the rail of the porch, which dropped away abruptly to the rocky riverbed far below. "You wouldn't think you're an hour out of New York by train, would you?" he said. "You could be in the heart of the Maine woods, or the center of Tibet, assuming they have maple and sumac in Tibet. Some view, hey?"

"It's beautiful," Jennie said again, and Sam managed another croaking "Yeah."

"I chose this spot because of the way the river bends," Mr. Farnsworth said. "There's a house up beyond that bend, and another one below this one, but because of the zigzag, this spot right here, between the zig and the zag, you get the feeling of complete isolation. Anybody want a swim before lunch?"

"I don't think so," Jennie said. "Sam?"

Sam remembered that the croaking was painful, so he swallowed before he said, "No, thanks."

"Well, it's free, and if you change your minds, there are plenty of trunks and a couple of my wife's bathing suits in the bathhouse down below," Mr. Farnsworth said. "Just be careful climbing down. It's almost a hundred feet and those rocks are not exactly featherbeds. I'm making a fondue for lunch, which is a simple peasant dish, but I don't like to melt the cheese too rapidly, and the kirsch should be properly heated before it's poured in, and unlike some Swiss peasants who will dip it up with anything from Shredded Wheat to cigarette butts, I insist on absolutely nothing but toast made from day-old bread because day-old bread is neutral and does not impinge its own flavor on the cheese and kirsch. All this will take a little time, and if you two want to fill my absence with a drink, the ingredients are over there, in that birchwood chest, as Jennie knows. If you have anything else in mind, don't be bashful. My wife is visiting her mother in Chicago, and I always whistle the opening bars of the 'Marseillaise' before I enter a room or come out on a porch."

Several moments, or so it seemed to Sam, after Mr. Farnsworth disappeared into the house, Jennie whispered, "No, not here," and Sam, who realized he had no idea how long they had been alone on the porch, became aware of a sharp, familiar odor. The son of a bitch, he thought, turning in a panic of embarrassment toward Mr. Farnsworth, and then Sam saw that he had made a mistake. The familiar odor, which his confused senses had assumed came from a reappearance of the cheese in the paper grocery sack, was older than that. Jennie, to whom it was obviously just as familiar, turned with him, toward the curiously not unpleasant mixed smells of garlic and cheap hair tonic and, in what was to Sam a totally unfamiliar voice, she said, *"Buggo!"*

The unfamiliarity, the realization that Jennie, whom he had never known to lose control, was suddenly frightened, did a curious thing to Sam. The panic of embarrassment vanished, and the control passed from her to him. Holding Jennie close, astonished as he had been on the night in Mr. Brunschweig's store by how thin she was, nervously aware that he would have to do something and do it fast, he nevertheless remained at dead center completely calm. It was as though a part of him, in spite of the realization that he and Jennie were in grave danger, had decided it was more important to record rather than participate in what was about to take place. Like a war correspondent standing up in the face of a cavalry charge to make sure he was observing it properly, that central core, which seemed totally independent of the nervous, confused, and frightened Sam, recorded the following:

Buggo Salvemini, who had apparently climbed up the rocky path from the river below, was standing at the porch rail, breathing hard. His white shirt and duck pants were damp, either with sweat or river water, so that he reminded Sam of the graduation-night production of *The Merchant of Venice,* in which Buggo, too slow-witted for an important part, had played one of the white-robed "Other Attendants." His dark, not unhandsome, slightly stupid face looked out of focus, as though a lifetime of slack-jawed amiability was making it impossible for him to adjust to the unexpected savage rage that consumed him. Crouched forward, like a tennis player waiting for the serve, he held in one hand, as though it actually was a racket, a kitchen knife as long as a fly swatter.

"Didn't expect me, huh?" he said, hurling the few syllables out in jerky sobs.

"Buggo," Jennie repeated, somewhat pointlessly, Sam thought.

"Son of a bitch," Buggo said, and Sam, seeing the tears streaming down his distorted face, realized Jennie's husband was addressing him. "It's you," Buggo sobbed. "I thought it was that bastard she works for. It's him I come out here to get, but it turns out it's you. I see something now, you son of a bitch. All the other guys I thought it was before this Farnsworth, it wasn't any of them. All the time, from the beginning, it was always you, you son of a bitch, wasn't it?"

"You're crazy," Sam said, and paused, trying to think of something more effective, anything that would drive the awful look of crazed misery from that broken face, and then he heard the piercingly whistled opening bars of the "Marseillaise." Buggo also heard them. A touch of surprise raced through the wild grief on his face and he turned toward the door. A moment later he obviously realized this was a mistake, and Buggo started to turn back, but the moment was enough.

With a shove that sent Jennie staggering back and himself forward, Sam jumped. He knew where he wanted to hit, at the elbow or above, so that the knife would be temporarily immobilized, but Sam also knew as his feet left the ground that he was too late. Buggo had started to turn back.

"Jennie old girl," Ham Farnsworth was saying as he came through the door, holding a long loaf of French bread. "Somebody's gone and hooked my best kitchen knife, and since you're the only one who's been on these premises since—" His voice stopped as Sam hit the half-turned Buggo, and then, in a piercing falsetto, the editor shrieked, *"Jesus Christ!"* and turned to run back into the house. Jennie, however, had recaptured her balance.

Sam, his arms locked around the squirming Buggo, saw her send a quick glance at the struggle on the porch floor, another at the disappearing host, and then she moved.

"Give me that!" Jennie screamed as she ran forward. She caught Farnsworth at the door, snatched the French bread from him, and turned back.

"*His hand!*" Sam grunted as Buggo, heaving above him, kept banging Sam's head on the porch floor. "I can't hold him! He's—"

The breath went out of him as Buggo came down again, hard, but Jennie got the idea. Using the French bread as a club, she began to hammer at the hand in which her husband held the knife. Sam, flat on his back as he rolled about under Buggo, could see her face. It was calm, as though she were performing a stupid chore, beating dust from a carpet, perhaps, while her mind was on something else, but the lips were drawn back slightly from her teeth, and there were tiny pinpricks of light in Jennie's eyes, and Sam's mind, aware that his life was in danger, could not help recording the fierceness with which at this moment he wanted her.

"*Let go!*" she said in a low, hard, mechanical voice, repeating the words with each blow of the bread. "*Let go! Let go! Let go!*"

When Buggo did, a few seconds later, Jennie straightened up, and swinging the side of her foot as though it were a broom, she gave the knife a sweeping kick. Sam heard it skitter across the porch floor and, because the sliding sound stopped without a thump, he knew the knife had gone over the edge of the porch. He found himself waiting, as he struggled with the thrashing Buggo, for the sound the knife had to make when it landed. It seemed a long time coming, and then the echoing clatter from the rocks below seemed to touch off in Buggo a final spasm of fury.

"You son of a bitch!" he screamed. "You dirty bastard!"

On the last syllable he heaved himself up and out. Sam's slipping fingers dug into Buggo's wet shirt, but the shirt tore free along with the wearer, and the impact of Buggo's last blow sent Sam sliding backward. As he hit the birch chest with the back of his head, the central recording device etched a final tableau: Ham Farnsworth, standing in the open door with his lower jaw quivering stupidly as he stared at the porch rail; Jennie, still holding the broken French bread, looking backward, in the same direction, as she started toward Sam; and Buggo hanging against the rail, apparently suspended in the air, like a leaf blown by the wind against the side of a house.

Two things puzzled Sam's dazed mind about the tableau: the rail looked crooked, and the air was full of a thin, reedy, tearing noise. A moment later the puzzlement fell away. So did Buggo and the porch railing. It took them about the same amount of time as it had taken the knife to reach the river, Sam thought stupidly as his mind seemed to draw away from him, but the sound they made when they hit the rocks was different.

When the recording device started functioning again, it was as though two different strips of film had been spliced together. The sun, which had lighted the porch when Sam's head hit the birch chest, had vanished. So had the porch. Sam was lying on a couch in what looked like a living room although, from the rough-hewn timbers that formed the wall surfaces, he supposed it could also be a barn or a stable. Ham Farnsworth, who had been a slack-jawed image of terror in the final tableau of the first film strip, had become once again the pink-cheeked wooden toy soldier surmounted by a brown busby, except that now he was holding a tall glass from which he took short, nervous sips as he walked back and forth, following and talking to Jennie, who was moving between the open drawers of a birchwood chest at one side of the room and an open suitcase on a trestle table at the other side.

The recording device was clearly out of order so far as its sound mechanism was concerned, because while Sam could see Ham Farnsworth's and Jennie's lips moving, he could not hear what they were saying. He thought it odd, but not particularly interesting, that he did not care. It was very pleasant, lying on the couch and watching Jennie. Sam had never before realized how graceful she was. He wondered why, and in order to learn the reason, which suddenly seemed terribly important, he pretended to himself that he wanted to describe the scene in a story, and in a few moments the recording device provided him with the answer. There was no waste motion in Jennie's movements. Most women, including Sam's mother, surrounded each major move in the act of packing with a series of fussy little adjusting pats. Not Jennie. Each shirt and tie, every pair of socks and pajamas, as she brought it from the drawers of the birchwood chest, was placed in the open suitcase on the trestle table the way a good chess player, after careful thought, finally moves his piece, without a series of shilly-shallying back-and-forth movements, but with a single, clean, decisive thrust. Even when the suitcase was full, and Jennie was closing it, there was that same crisp, graceful finality in the way she snapped the catches, pulled the straps tight, and turned to give the room a final glance.

By comparison, Ham Farnsworth's movements were a mass of fluttery, indecisive gestures as he set down his glass, pulled a wallet from somewhere under his dirty sweatshirt, counted out some money, gave the bills to Jennie, and continued talking to her as he retrieved his drink and Jennie put the money into her purse. The contrast was even sharper between the way she snapped the purse shut and slung the long strap over her shoulder, and the way Farnsworth dragged the suitcase lumberingly off the trestle table. The recording device was admiring her quick, clean strides and deriding Farnsworth's awkward hopping steps as he and Jennie moved side by side across the room and out the door, when the mechanism seemed to jump slightly, as though it wanted to point out to Sam that while he was so busy noting everything down, he was also being left alone.

He started to sit up on the couch, found this was impossible, and was trying to remember if it was the Lilliputians or the Brobdingnagians who had nailed Gulliver to the ground while he slept, when Jennie and Mr. Farnsworth, minus her shoulder purse and his suitcase, came back into the room, and helped Sam to do what he had been unable to do for himself. He thanked them kindly as they walked him out of the room, through a kitchen, and down some stone steps to the parking area back of the house, but they did not seem to be interested in what he was saying.

They had their hands full, Sam could see, helping him onto the front seat of the Buick convertible. The suitcase, he also saw, as he helped them make him comfortable, was on the back seat. Jennie and Mr. Farnsworth were still talking, or at any rate their lips were moving, as she came around, slipped in behind the wheel, and the editor slammed the door shut. The recording device noted that Jennie's movements, as she set the car in motion, were just as graceful and decisive as when she had been packing the suitcase, and that Mr. Farnsworth, standing on the gravel, raised his glass in a salute as the car rolled away, and then Sam snuggled down more comfortably on the front seat, and the recording device went out of business again.

It went back to work in a peculiar way, recording the image of its own restoration to life, as though it were a stopped watch that noted not only the moment when it resumed its normal function of telling time, but also the preceding moment when the resumption was accomplished by its owner's sharp tap.

Even before he was awake, Sam knew that what had awakened him was the delicate jolt as the soothing forward motion of the car came to a halt. He opened his eyes and saw a number of things simultaneously: sometime after the departure from Mr. Farnsworth's house in Westport, somebody had tucked a blanket around his shoulders; the Buick had stopped against the curb of a street lined with stores that were shut up for the night; at the far end of the deserted street, a neon sign over a dimly lighted marquee carried the words Hotel Nathan Hale; and Jennie, on the seat beside Sam, was lighting a cigarette.

"This isn't Westport," Sam said, remembering the tree-shaded street with the white clapboard houses and the small red-brick bank through which Ham Farnsworth had driven them shortly before noon.

"No, and it's not New York, either," Jennie said.

Sam started to say, "Where are we?" but the recording device, which suddenly identified itself as part of a remark Mr. Sargent had made about the vacuum cleaner of a writer's craft, took another one of those small leaps, as though to warn its owner that this particular combination of words, in this sort of scene, had been worn threadbare by the countless repetitions of other writers. Involved all at once against his will in the irrelevant search for a new and fresh way of asking "Where are we?" Sam suddenly remembered the events on the porch, and he said, "What happened to Buggo?"

"He's dead," Jennie said.

This seemed reasonable. Sam remembered the sounds, first made by the knife, then by Jennie's husband and the torn-away porch railing as they landed on the river rocks below. What did not seem reasonable was the way Jennie sat there, a cardigan across the shoulders left bare by the peasant blouse, smoking slowly and steadily as she stared down the silent street toward the "Nathan Hale Hotel" sign.

"I guess a lot of things have to be done," said Sam.

Jennie shook her head. "No," she said. "Ham's done all of them." She gave Sam a short glance, then turned back to look down the street, and Sam, turning toward her, saw that Jennie was not as calm as she looked or sounded. Her right forefinger was tapping rapidly up and down on the cigarette, which she held low, resting the heel of her hand on the leather seat between them, and it was only because he saw the movement that Sam was able to hear the delicate sound, like an endless string of minuscule firecrackers going off somewhere far away in the night. Jennie said, "Ham's got some drag with the local authorities. In addition to cheese and wine, he seems to be nuts about small-town politics. Nuts enough to have worked on committees and things like that in Westport, anyway, and while you were out cold, he did some telephoning. How's your head?"

"I don't know," Sam said, touching it gingerly. "All right, I guess."

"Well, you don't have to guess," Jennie said. "Among the people Ham called was a local doctor who happens to be Ham's friend, and he said there was no concussion. Just you'd be out for a while, which you were, and then you'd be a little woozy, which if you're not, you ought to be."

Sam again touched the back of his head, and this time, since it had been pointed out to him, he noticed that it did throb.

"It doesn't feel too bad," he said. "Who else did Farnsworth call, and what are they doing?"

Jennie hesitated, took a long drag on the cigarette, replaced it on the seat between them, where her forefinger resumed its tapping, and said, "Helping him pretend you and I don't exist."

A lot of other things came back to Sam. He turned on the seat, put one arm on her shoulder, the other in her lap, and said, "But we do."

Jennie pushed his hand away and said, "That's the trouble. No, stop, not now. Don't you see the mess?"

Sam made a suggestion about how to dispose of the mess, and Jennie said grimly, "Yes, that's the male cement-from-ear-to-ear approach. Unfortunately, when somebody dies by falling from a porch that shows clear signs of a terrible struggle because the railing is torn away, the police start asking embarrassing questions."

"Oh," Sam said, and he sat back abruptly.

"That's right," Jennie said. "That's why Ham made this arrangement."

"What arrangement?"

"You're supposed to have a sore head, so keep that tone out of your voice. It's your neck as well as everybody else's that's involved."

"Yes," Sam said. "That's right. It's my neck that's involved. So you'd better tell me just how you and Mr. Farnsworth have involved it."

"Oh, for Christ's sake," Jennie said, and she flung the cigarette over the side of the car. "Will you stop being a God-damn writer and listen to a piece of the real world?"

"Go ahead," Sam said. "Make it real."

"Ham Farnsworth is a perfectly respectable member of a perfectly respectable community," Jennie said. "His wife goes to Chicago for a week to visit her sick mother, and that week-end the husband of Mr. Farnsworth's secretary is found dead at the foot of Mr. Farnsworth's house. The husband is twenty-one, Sammy dear, the secretary is twenty, Sammy dear, Mr. Farnsworth is thirty-six, Sammy dear, and what she's a secretary about to Mr. Farnsworth, Sammy dear, the reason this twenty-year-old girl is spending the week-end with Mr. Farnsworth, she's helping him with a book on cheese, for Christ's sake."

"It's true, isn't it?" Sam said.

Jennie gave him another short look, then said, "Is that sarcasm?"

"It might turn out to be that," Sam said. "At the moment it's just a question."

"The answer is yes, it's true," Jennie said. "I know Ham Farnsworth has told you nasty things about me. Why shouldn't he? He's a nasty man who tells nasty things about everybody, including you."

Astonished, Sam said, "Me?"

"Yes, you," Jennie said.

"What sort of things?"

"They're not the point now," Jennie said. "The point is that Ham Farnsworth talks that way about everybody, especially girls. But it's all just talk. He makes it up and throws it around so people will think he's part of it and a great ladies' man. The truth is he's scared to death of women. I've been working for him for over a month, in his New York apartment, while his wife's been out in Westport, and two week-ends in Westport, while his wife's been out in Chicago, and I've been safer than I ever was in the gym locker room down at Grover Cleveland High."

"Some people didn't find that place so safe," Sam said.

"You may have lost your college education there, but you never got raped there," Jennie said. She paused, as though her own words had struck an unpleasant chord of memory, and she fished for another cigarette as she said, "Neither did anybody ever get raped working for Ham Farnsworth. He takes it all out in dirty words, cheese sauces, and vintage wines. The book about cheese is absolutely true. I don't know if it will ever be finished, but there's a stack of stuff this high, and I've been getting twenty-five dollars a week to help him make it look like some day it might be a book."

"*Twenty-five dollars a week?*"

"Twice what I was making as a free-lance reader at Mercury Films," Jennie said, and then, with an odd little twist of her lips, as though she knew it was the wrong moment to say it, but knowing also that resisting the remark was beyond her powers of self-control, she added, "Twice, I'll bet, what you get from Mr. Brunschweig."

"Jesus," Sam said.

"Jesus what?" Jennie said.

"I just remembered. I've got to be on the job tomorrow morning," Sam said. "What time is it?"

"We're talking about necks," Jennie said. "He wants to know what time it is."

"But I've got to be back in New York in time to—"

"No, you don't," Jennie said. He turned on the seat and she turned to face him. "This is what we're in," she said. "The way it would look, if the cops came and found Buggo dead, a jealous husband had got into a fight with the respectable member of the community, and the jealous husband was killed in the fight."

Jennie paused, lighted the cigarette she had brought up from the pack on the seat between them and blew out the match with a long, slow, gentle expulsion of breath, as though she were cooling a spoonful of hot soup.

Slowly, understanding that she wanted him to pick up the next point himself, Sam said, "That's the way it would have been, if I hadn't showed up."

"Not necessarily," Jennie said. "If you hadn't been there, if Buggo had found only Ham Farnsworth, as he expected, Buggo might have won the fight."

"I see," Sam said.

"What do you see?" Jennie said.

"In that case only you would have had a problem," Sam said. "Assuming Buggo won the fight."

"He would have won it," Jennie said. "Ham Farnsworth is as yellow as the Sahara Desert on the Grover Cleveland High School wall map."

"So he would have been out of it," Sam said.

"That's right," Jennie said. "Dead men have no problems."

"In addition to you, then, Buggo would have had a problem, because Buggo would still be alive."

"He's better off dead," Jennie said.

Sam, who agreed with her but preferred not to think about his reasons, suddenly found himself thinking about Jennie's.

"Why did you marry him?"

Jennie shrugged. "Don't ever put this in a story," she said. "No editor would ever buy it," Jennie said. "I had to marry Buggo."

"An editor would snap at that," Sam said. "If he knew the story was about you."

"About some things everybody is the same," Jennie said. "Even me."

"Like what?" Sam said.

"Like money, for example. Trouble, if you want more examples. And most important—" She stopped, and shrugged again, and said, "Oh, the hell with it."

"No," Sam said. "Nothing doing," he said, aware that he might never have another chance. Everything that had happened, from the moment this girl he tried to hate had placed her hand on him in the car at the Westport station, all of it had been beyond his control. If, after all that had happened before that moment, he could not hate her, he saw with a shattering clarity even more hateful that wherever Jennie was concerned, everything, all of it and forever, no matter what "it" was or how long forever lasted, would be beyond his control. He had to make a stand now. He had to try. Unless he dug in his heels, if he didn't make the effort while there was still a chance, he would go over the edge of sanity just as surely as Buggo had gone over the edge of the porch. Because he wanted her so badly, because it took every scrap of his strength to keep his hands off her, Sam knew his life was at stake. Speaking slowly, trying to sound

convincing, knowing that no matter what he said or how he said it, he
didn't really have a chance at all, Sam said, "You want me to do something. You always want something. Now it's you and Farnsworth that
want it. I'm not doing anything any more, never, not till I know why."

Jennie looked at him for several moments, then turned away, toward
the neon sign over the hotel, and she said, "Okay." But apparently it wasn't.
Not yet, anyway. Because she continued to sit quietly, motionless except
for the nervous tapping of her forefinger on the cigarette. After a while,
with a quick little sigh, Jennie said, "You think you can stand anything,
and as long as you think that, you're all right, because thinking it is as
good as being it, but then one day something happens, and you find out
what it is you can't stand, and then you're finished. I can't stand being
alone. I don't mean alone in a room. That kind of alone is easy to handle,
because you know it's got to end. Somebody is bound to come along sooner
or later and open the door. The kid with the groceries. The landlord asking for the rent. Somebody who came to the wrong door and wants to
know can you tell him where Mr. Jones lives. It's when you know nobody
is ever going to open the door, because nobody knows you're there, not
even the grocery store, and the landlord doesn't even want your rent, because it isn't really a room, it's nothing, absolutely nothing, and you're in
it, and there's nobody in the whole city or state or country or world who's
ever going to snap his fingers and say hey, Jennie Broom, she owes me
money, I better go try and collect, or I owe *her* money, I'll go see if I can
find her and pay it back, or she used to make me laugh, or I like her, or
even, for Christ's sake, I hate her guts and I hear she's in trouble and I'm
going to have myself some fun by looking her up and doing a little gloating
over her."

Jennie's voice stopped, and with a sense of helplessness, aware from
what the sight was doing to his heart how hopeless the process of digging
in his heels had been, Sam watched the tears bobbing crazily down the
side of her face.

"I always seem to want something, and then when I get it, it's not
what I wanted," Jennie said to the neon sign over the Nathan Hale Hotel
at the end of the silent street. "I wanted revenge on Mr. Mueller, and then
when I got it, it didn't seem like anything. What good was it? I'd humili-
ated a stupid high school principal, and he deserved it, I could tell myself
that. But there I was, still living on Avenue A with my drunken father
and mother, without a job, flat broke, and nobody around." Jennie paused
and then said, "Nobody except Buggo."

The curious emphasis she gave to the name caused Sam, in a spasm of jealousy that was in no way eased by the knowledge that Buggo was dead, to say, "The son of a bitch."

"Oh, hell, no, not really," Jennie said with a tired little shake of her head. "Except that he did prove to be that, too. But that was later. In the beginning it was just that he was around, downstairs there, in his father's shoe-repair shop. So we went job hunting together, without any luck, and then he got a job in the mimeograph room at Mercury Films. When he found out the story department used outside readers, Buggo introduced me to the woman in charge and she tried me on a couple of things. She liked my synopses, so at least I had something to do and some money coming in, and Buggo was right there, and I was grateful to him for getting me the job and then, well, when I thought I was pregnant, I got scared, and I suppose Buggo did, too, so we got married." Her head made the same tired little movement. "It wasn't bad at first," Jennie said. "There was the fun of being away from that Avenue A sewer. There was the fun of fixing up your own place. And there was, well, there was Buggo. It wasn't his stupidity. It wasn't that he was no better than what he was doing, running a mimeograph machine. After all, what was *I* doing? Writing synopses for the story department? No, I wouldn't have hated him for that. For that, I'd have contempt for him, because he would always be on the mimeograph level, whereas I, what I wanted—"

Jennie paused again, and catching up with the sound of her last words, Sam was reminded of the way his mother sounded late at night in the East Tenth Street kitchen when she talked about Uptown. The parallel made Sam a little uneasy. But he grasped at it just the same, because this was something Sam could understand, and he knew with the desperation of a drowning man that anything he grasped at, even fragments of understanding that would in the long run do no good, were for the moment better than grasping at nothing.

"No," Jennie said. "I didn't hate Buggo for being stupid. What I hated him for was you were right. He was a son of a bitch as well as stupid. When I found out after we were married it had been a false alarm, and I wasn't pregnant, I started remembering how it happened, and I guess no woman ever forgets, if that's the way it happened to her the first time, no woman ever forgets she was raped, or ever forgives the man who did it to her. No, I don't care how it sounds, but it's true and I'm saying it," Jennie said. "I'm glad Buggo Salvemini is dead."

"If he wasn't," Sam said, "I'd kill him all over again."

Jennie gave him a glance out of the corner of her eye and said, "That's the writer in you talking. It ties up the scene. Those things I used to do synopses on for Mercury, there was always a scene like that. But I'm glad you feel that way about it. It makes it easier for both of us to be sensible about what Ham Farnsworth has arranged."

"You better tell me about that," Sam said.

"He wants us to stay out of the way for a few days," Jennie said. "His doctor friend, the one who looked at you, is apparently better than just a friend. He doesn't know he saw you. After he left, Ham called some local bigwig who is also a friend of his, and told him he was in trouble. When this man came out, I stayed out of sight, in the house with you, and Ham told him he'd hired a secretary a month ago to work on his cheese book, and the girl had been doing the work in his New York apartment, and Ham said he hadn't known when he hired her that she was married or having trouble with her husband, and this week-end, when Ham was out here working, the secretary had apparently had some sort of fight with her husband in New York and walked out on him. The husband apparently thought she had come out to Ham's place in Westport, so he had followed her, or come out thinking he was following her, and demanded to see her. When Ham couldn't produce her, because in this version he was telling she was not there, the husband had pulled a knife, Ham had been forced to fight for his life, and in the struggle the husband went over the edge— knife, porch railing, and all. The bigwig was very sympathetic, told Ham to calm down, and he would go get the state cops. While he was off doing that, Ham and I got you into the car with a bagful of Ham's clothes, and he gave me some money and, well, here we are."

Sam didn't answer. He couldn't. He was thinking of the opportunity that had suddenly opened up, he was thinking of the next few minutes, and the next few hours, and the next few days, and it was as though he welcomed the fact that his dug-in heels were slipping, but Jennie apparently didn't know that. Jennie apparently thought he was probing for holes in her story. He could tell by the way she promptly went about plugging them. Sam could tell, and he didn't care.

"It isn't that Ham is being generous to you and me by keeping us out of it and taking the blame all on himself," Jennie said. "He's just as selfish as anybody else, probably more than most, and he knows this way is best for him. Any man can be the innocent victim of a jealous husband who makes a mistake. But if the man has a secretary staying with him while his wife is away, he doesn't look so innocent, and the jealous husband doesn't look as though he's so obviously made a mistake. Ham's got a rich wife. He's got a big job. He might lose both if the true story got out."

"Would the true story be true?" Sam said.

Jennie turned on the seat, and her mouth twisted in a funny way, and she said, "If a worm like Ham Farnsworth ever put a hand on me, I'd shove him off that porch faster than Buggo went." She took another cigarette from the pack on the seat but made no move to light it. "That goes for whatever nasty little inventions Ham may have poured into your ears when he was telling you about me this morning, and the crazy things Buggo said when he was coming at you with the knife. I can't help what's said by a dirty-minded slob like Ham Farnsworth or a crazy moron like Buggo Salvemini, and I can't make you or anybody else believe the truth when you hear it, but I can tell it to you, and this is it: I've never slept with any man except my husband."

"Except in Mr. Brunschweig's store," Sam said.

"By that time Buggo Salvemini was my husband only in the legal sense," Jennie said. "We'd been finished for months, and I was looking for a way out."

"And today you found it," Sam said.

"That's right," Jennie said. "But I can't take it without you."

He didn't answer. He didn't want to hear any more words spoken. He didn't want to ask any more questions. Above all, he didn't want to think.

Twenty minutes later, after the car was parked and they had checked into the hotel, and he was sitting on the bed, shivering with anticipation as he waited for her to come out of the bathroom into the dark chamber that looked out on what he later discovered was a sliver of the Yale campus, Sam suddenly did have a thought. As the bathroom door opened, and he stood up, and he slipped out of Ham Farnsworth's pajama top, and he came forward to meet her, and he took Jennie in his arms, Sam Silver remembered that he had told his mother he would be home by nine o'clock that night, nine-thirty at the latest.

The next morning, before he and Jennie left the Nathan Hale Hotel and headed north, Sam called Shirley Shaefer in the Sargent & Sargent office.

"Mr. Silver?" she said, clearly surprised.

"Yes, it's me," Sam said.

"You sound so funny."

"Maybe because it's long distance."

"Where are you?" Shirley said.

"In Connecticut," Sam said. "I wonder if you'd do me a favor?"

"A question? If I can, of *course*."

"Thanks," Sam said. "Tonight, on your way home, I wonder if you'd stop in at my house and tell my mother I missed my train last night, so I stayed over?"

"You missed your train," Shirley Shaefer said. "So you stayed over."

"That's right," Sam said. "And I'm going to be out here for a few more days, maybe a week, so she shouldn't worry."

"You're going to be out there a few more days, maybe a week," Shirley said, "and she shouldn't worry."

"That's right," Sam said. "We have no phone, as you know, so I can't call myself."

"And a note to write her, what's the use?" Shirley said. "Probably, like my mother, she can't read it."

"That's right," Sam said. "Thanks, Shirley."

"For what?" Shirley said. "Anything else, maybe?"

"Well," Sam said and, after a few moments of thought, he decided that it was better to take a chance on his boss's gullibility after it was over, than to widen the area of advance explanations by asking Shirley to call him. "You might tell my mother that Mr. Brunschweig knows I'm going to be away, and it's all right."

"Mr. Who?" Shirley said. Sam spelled it, and Shirley said, "Mr. B, r, u, n, s, h—"

"S, *see*, h," Sam said.

"Mr. S, *see*, h, w, e, i, g knows you're going to be away, and it's all right."

"Yes," Sam said. "Well, thanks again, Shirley."

"You're welcome," she said. "Mr. Silver?"

"Yes?"

"You say you're in Connecticut?"

"That's right. Why?"

"You're not anywhere around with that Mr. Farnsworth?" Shirley said. "That big cheese up at Trafalgar, Singlenight? Your publishers?"

"No," Sam said, which was true enough, and, as casually as he could, he asked, "Why?"

"You mean you didn't see the papers?"

"Not yet," Sam said, and he kept his mouth open, to ease his breathing and the sudden jumpiness in his chest. "What's in them?"

"Oh, boy," Shirley Shaefer said. "Yesterday, out there, he's working on his porch, it says, a book on cheese he's writing, a young man, he's the husband of some girl, Mr. Farnsworth's secretary, he hired her part time, it says, to help him with this cheese book, she was supposed to be working on it in New York, but she wasn't. Anyway, her husband said she wasn't, and he thought she was out there with Mr. Farnsworth, so he goes out there, this young husband, you hear?"

"Yes," Sam said. "What happened?"

"Wait till you hear," Shirley said. "People, honestly, they're the limit. You know what this young husband did?"

"What?" Sam said.

"He comes busting in on Mr. Farnsworth with a knife," Shirley said. "A knife, you hear? Like one of these things something in the movies, a knife he stole from Mr. Farnsworth's own kitchen yet, while he was working on the porch, Mr. Farnsworth, and Mr. Farnsworth, it says, he had to fight for his life, and in the fight, they're rolling around on the floor of the porch, with that knife yet, can you imagine?"

"What happened?" Sam said.

"The wood, there, whatever you call it on a porch—"

"The railing?" Sam said.

"That's right," Shirley said. "It broke, this railing, and this young man, the secretary's husband, he fell off the porch with the knife and everything, almost a hundred feet, it says, down to a river with great big rocks, and guess what?"

"What?" Sam said.

"He was killed," Shirley said. "The husband. Can you imagine?"

"Holy smoke," Sam said.

"You can say that again," Shirley said. "That poor Mr. Farnsworth, all he was doing was writing a book on cheese, and look what happens. These literary people, I'm telling you, honest."

"What are they going to do?" Sam said. "I mean the police and all?"

"What can they do?" Shirley said. "The young husband they can't make alive again. Mr. Farnsworth they can't give the electric chair because he stopped a crazy man from sticking a knife in him. So you know how the police are. They're looking for the secretary, the husband's wife, the one she wasn't even there when it happened. Some place, that Connecticut, no?"

"Not all of it," Sam said. "It's pretty dull where I am."

"Better dull than dead," Shirley said. "Have a good time, Mr. Silver, and I'll tell your mother like you said."

During the next three days, on which years later Sam looked back as the happiest of his life, one small, nagging worry ran like a flawed thread through the fabric of bliss: there was something wrong with Shirley Shaefer's account, which had been confirmed by the paper Sam bought as soon as he hung up on her, but he could not figure out what it was.

He did not try very hard. There was too much to see and enjoy. Jennie's presence was, of course, the most important element in his happiness. There were others, however, that contributed to a heightened, almost painful sense of being alive such as Sam had never before known.

Up to this time, for example, all the hours of his life had been committed to others by forces over which he had no control: to his mother, to his schoolteachers, to Mr. Brunschweig. For himself, for time in which to be Sam Silver, he had been dependent on moments stolen from the hours indentured to others, and each of these moments had possessed, like the midnight curfew imposed on Cinderella, a terminal point: this chapter of the book he was reading had to be finished before his mother came up from the grocery store and demanded why he was not doing his homework; this daydream had to end by the time he got to the store on Forty-eighth Street and Mr. Brunschweig ordered him out on a new delivery. The concept of time, not as a bolt of cloth to be measured by numbers marked on the face of a clock, but as an element, like water, to float around in, had never before entered Sam's consciousness. This was his first holiday.

Neither had he ever known before the sense of freedom that was part of moving forward, with no particular destination, in an open car. Or the enlarging effect on the human spirit of a full pocket. Sam had no idea how much Mr. Farnsworth had given Jennie, who spent it without hesitation or even counting as their needs demanded, but it was clearly so much more than Sam had ever possessed, that as he steeped himself in the sensations it purchased, he had his first understanding of the force that drove people to the acquisition of wealth. And, of course, seasoning the whole bowl of new sensations, was the spice of excitement: they were, or at any rate Jennie was, being hunted.

She was not being hunted very hard. After the report on Monday that police were looking for the wife of the young man who had fallen from Ham Farnsworth's porch, the papers, which Sam and Jennie bought in every town through which they passed, had apparently become bored with the story. By Tuesday it had moved from the front pages, and by Thursday it had disappeared from the papers entirely. The sense of excitement, however, remained.

It added to the things with which they filled their days. Jennie, for example, taught Sam how to drive the car. When he asked who had taught her, she disregarded the question and, along with the stab of jealousy, Sam learned what he had always grudgingly suspected, even in Grover Cleveland High: in some areas, she was smarter than he was. One day, when they stopped for lunch at a small clam bar on a sandy stretch of Massachusetts coast and he asked for a tuna on rye, Jennie objected and suggested that he have some sea food. Sam told her about his first lunch with Ham Farnsworth and Keeley Cuff at the Murray Hill Hotel. Jennie at once started to teach him how to eat oysters, clams, lobster and, the next day, in a better restaurant in Boston, she introduced him to snails. He did not ask who had introduced her.

It was the questions Jennie asked, however, that seemed to bring them closest together. The questions gave Sam the sense of superiority without which, because of her own strength, the relationship, after the first days of physical frenzy, would have diminished rather than grown. And they provided him with something he did not understand but felt very strongly: she needed some sort of nourishment, the exact nature of which she did not seem to understand, either, but like those children with calcium deficiencies who, Sam had read somewhere, instinctively turn to claw at and stuff into their mouths the plaster of their nursery walls, Jennie seemed instinctively to turn to Sam. Her questions dealt with his writing.

Essentially, they were all the same question: how he did it? Since Sam could not seem to provide her with a satisfactory answer, Jennie continued to probe. It was as though the child, finding that the plaster of the walls did not still his craving, turned to the ceiling, to the walls of other rooms, to the masonry that held together the bricks of the house itself.

When had he first felt the desire to write? Sam's description of the night in Mr. Brunschweig's store when he wrote "The Ways of Men Must Sever," to which Jennie listened attentively, merely caused her to ask, "But how did the idea for the story come out of the way you felt?"

"I don't know," Sam said. "It was just there."

Jennie shook her head impatiently as she guided the Buick around a milk truck.

"How about the novel?" she said. "That wasn't *just there*. You had to plan that, didn't you?"

"Yes," Sam said, and described the night at the kitchen table on East Tenth Street when he plotted the thirty-one chapters of *Yours Is the Earth*. "Of course, by then, I'd gone through the material twice before, once as the short story that appeared in *Landscape*, and then as the movie synopsis you got me to do for Mercury, so that the chapter-by-chapter outline for the novel was fairly simple."

"Was it simple to write?" Jennie said.

"I don't know," Sam said.

"You keep saying that, but it doesn't make sense," Jennie said impatiently. "How can you *not* know?"

"I don't know," Sam said. "I just wrote it."

"How?"

"What do you mean, how?"

"You say you just wrote it, the way Hank Greenberg might say I just hit it."

"Well," Sam said, "I guess that's all he could say."

Jennie shook her head, and the black hair, streaming in the wind, whipped about in a tangled halo that moved Sam's heart.

"That's not true," she said. "He could say I chose my bat. I swung a few until I found the one that felt right, then I walked out to the plate, and I knocked the dirt out of my shoe cleats. I pulled the cap straight on my head. I put the bat across my shoulder. I squinted down at the pitcher. I watched his windup. Just before the delivery, I shifted the grip on my bat. At the right moment, I swung and my bat hit the ball."

Sam laughed and said, "You can't describe writing in that way."

"I wish you wouldn't laugh," Jennie said. "I'm serious."

"So am I," Sam said. "Sure, I can give you a lot of physical detail, the way you just did about Greenberg hitting a ball. I could tell you I use the red and black Parker my father gave me for my bar mitzvah. I write on those steno notebook sheets we use in class at the Lafayette Business Institute. I sit at the kitchen table after Mom's cleared away the dishes. I use blue-black ink in the Parker. I write on one side of the page, and so on. But no matter how much of that I give you, no matter how detailed, there's no avoiding the moment you got to."

"What moment?"

"About Hank Greenberg hitting the ball," Sam said. "After all that stuff about picking his bat and squinting at the pitcher and shifting his grip, you come to what you said: *At the right moment, I swung and my bat hit the ball.* You're asking me to pick apart the right moment, to put down in ay, bee, see form each step in the selection of the right moment and each step in the movement of the bat from his shoulder to the ball."

Jennie nodded. "That's right," she said. "Why can't you tell me?"

"Nobody can," Sam said. "Greenberg couldn't tell you."

"Why the hell not?" Jennie said.

"Because he doesn't know," Sam said. "The thing in the middle, the thing you said for Greenberg is the right moment he selects for swinging at the ball, the moment that's so right that it results in his connecting, the same thing in writing. The thing in the middle, the place where it actually happens, I mean after you've filled the pen and got out the kind of paper you like, and so on, all that stuff, the moment when it *really* happens, that moment, it's—it's—"

"It's what?" Jennie said.

Sam hesitated. He knew it was not the answer she wanted, but it was all he had to give her, and because he loved her, he could not hold back anything he had, even if it was inadequate.

"It's a mystery," he said. "It just happens."

Jennie risked both their lives by taking her eyes from the road to give him the long look with which, during the ten days of their flight, he had become so familiar: the look of a child who, having carefully stalked a kitten or a puppy that has stupidly allowed itself to be trapped, finds, when she makes the final triumphant lunge, that she has caught nothing: her prey, clearly not so stupid as she had thought, has escaped.

As always, after one of these question-and-answer sessions that were so obviously unsatisfactory to Jennie and yet left Sam with the puzzling sense of superiority he found so embarrassingly satisfying, she seemed to leave him, to disappear into a brooding silence where he could not follow her, an inner place where she either licked her wounds or regrouped her forces or perhaps only rearranged her thoughts for the next session. There always was a next session. Sam never knew when it would begin. He suspected that Jennie didn't, either, because once the questioning started late at night, while they were in bed, locked in each other's arms, and he had the feeling that what she said at that moment was as surprising to her as it was to him. It was not really surprising, therefore, that Jennie should have been asking, as they sat sipping Cokes at the soda fountain in the Portland drug store, how Sam chose the correct simile for a description, when the two men came up behind them and said, "Which one of you is Samuel Silver?"

Sam, who almost fell off his stool, never forgot that Jennie didn't. She didn't even turn. She took a final sip of her Coke, looked up into the mirror behind the soda fountain, and, as though she were asking Sam for the time, Jennie Broom said, "Only a cop would consider that a good joke."

"You'll get plenty of opportunities to make better ones," the man said. He pulled something from his pocket and held it out, palm upward, the way a father might hold out a handful of small change for a child to choose the dime he wants for his soda, but it was not a handful of small change. It was a silver badge pinned to a piece of worn black leather. After thrusting it first under Sam's nose, and then under Jennie's, the man said, "Pay for your Cokes and let's get going."

"Where?" Jennie said.

"You'll find out when you get there, Mrs. Salvemini," the man said. "You're both under arrest, and it's my duty to inform you that anything you say may be held against you. Let's go."

The second man put his hand on Sam's elbow and Jennie said, in a low but clear voice, "Unless you tell us what this is all about, you are in for some trouble, gentlemen. I am one hell of a screamer."

Her manner, her words, and the tone in which they were delivered were clearly something new in the experience of the two plainclothesmen.

They exchanged a quick, uneasy glance. Then one nodded to the other, who pulled a folded newspaper from his pocket, and held it out to Sam and Jennie. It was a New York paper dated that day, which explained why Sam and Jennie had not yet seen it. The largest headline on the front page dominated a boxed story:

Young Novelist Sought in Death of Secretary's Husband

Samuel Silver, twenty-year-old author of *Yours Is the Earth,* was today revealed to have been a guest at the home of his editor, Hampton Farnsworth of the book publishing firm of Trafalgar, Singlenight & Co., Inc., on the fatal Sunday, ten days ago, when the husband of Mr. Farnsworth's secretary, a twenty-year-old mimeograph clerk in the New York offices of Mercury Films, fell to his death from the porch of Mr. Farnsworth's home in Westport, Conn., leaving behind clear signs of a violent struggle.

Police, who suspected at the time that the motive for the struggle was jealousy and have been hunting Mrs. Salvemini ever since, were informed last night that she had fled the scene of the accident in Mr. Farnsworth's car with Samuel Silver, the young author of *Yours Is the Earth,* whose name had hitherto not appeared in the case. The unidentified source from which this information was obtained also revealed that the youthful novelist and Mr. and Mrs. Salvemini had been fellow students at Grover Cleveland High School here in New York City, and apparently advised the police of the whereabouts of the fugitives, because a police spokesman said they did not believe the problem of apprehension would prove difficult.

"We know not only the license number and description of Mr. Farnsworth's car," he said, "but also exactly how much money the novelist and Mrs. Salvemini had when they vanished ten days ago, so that—"

Sam dropped his corner of the paper. Jennie, holding the other corner, looked up. Their eyes met. He started to speak, changed his mind, and shook his head. This was not the place to tell her that he finally understood what it was that had bothered him, from the moment he had first heard it on the phone from Shirley Shaefer, about the story Ham Farnsworth had given to the police ten days ago: it differed in one respect from the story Jennie had said Ham Farnsworth planned to tell.

"You want any more explanations?" one of the plainclothesmen said. Jennie shook her head. The man said, "Let's go."

They went, somewhat to Sam's surprise, in Ham Farnsworth's car, which Jennie had parked in front of the drug store. All during the long drive, when his confused and troubled thoughts became too much for him, Sam was able to retreat into the soothing distraction of pointless speculation: had the two policemen come to Portland by train, or by car? If by car, one of them would have to come back to Portland to pick it up. Or perhaps three of them had come to Portland, and the third man was driving their car back. Back where?

It was easier, Sam found, to set his mind in circular motion, in this fashion, than to send it out on a straight line. Whenever he did, his mind always came up against that difference: Jennie had said that Farnsworth wanted her as well as Sam out of the way because then Farnsworth would be able to tell the police that he had been alone, and in total ignorance of any trouble between his secretary and her husband, when Buggo attacked him. And yet the next morning, when Shirley Shaefer gave Sam an account on the phone of what the newspapers reported Ham Farnsworth had told the police, the account ended with the statement that the police were seeking Buggo's wife.

Who had brought the name of Buggo's wife into the story? And why? Was it the same "unidentified source" that had brought in the name of Sam Silver? Who else but Ham Farnsworth could this unidentified source be? And how could it help Ham Farnsworth, who according to Jennie did not want to lose either his rich wife or his good job, to admit that when he was attacked by her jealous husband, his secretary was spending the week-end in his house? Most confusing of all, why should Sam Silver, who had been so stealthily removed from the picture ten days ago, be kicked into it now with a front-page splash?

More troubling than these questions were the inevitable memories they evoked: the way he had been used on graduation night in Jennie's fight against Mr. Mueller; the way he had been used later in Jennie's struggle to get Mr. Umberg's job at Mercury Films. During the past days Sam had managed, if not to eradicate those memories, then at least to accept Jennie's explanations of them. Now, when all he wanted was to hold onto the memory of these days, it was being dragged from his grasp by these earlier memories that brought with them the most troubling question of all: was he being used again?

It was indeed simpler, especially since the policemen had separated Sam and Jennie by putting her on the back seat with one man and Sam on the front seat with the driver, to go back to the squirrel cage of circular thinking: had the two policemen come to Portland by train or car? If by car, one of them would have to come back to Portland to pick it up. Or perhaps three of them had come to Portland, and the third man was driving their car back. Back where?

The sudden awareness of a tree-shaded street, lined with white clapboard houses and a small red-brick structure that could be a bank, provided the answer. Sitting up straight on the front seat, Sam saw in the windshield mirror that Jennie had done the same on the back seat. The policeman at the wheel pulled Ham Farnsworth's Buick to a stop in front of the red-brick structure, and Sam saw that it was not a bank. The next thing Sam saw, striding firmly down the steps of the police station toward the car, was Sophie Sargent.

"Hello, Sam," she said. "Are you all right?"

"Yes, sure," Sam said. "I mean yes, I'm fine, but what are you doing here?"

"I'm your agent, aren't I?"

"Look, lady," one of the policemen said. "Would you mind stepping aside, please?"

"Of course I'd mind," Sophie said. "Didn't you just hear me say I'm Mr. Silver's agent?"

"Mr. Silver happens to be under arrest," the policeman said. "Step aside, please."

"When I was a girl and first started week-ending in Connecticut, the Nutmeg State certainly bred a more refined type of law-enforcement officer," Sophie said coldly from her commanding position on the second of the police station's four stone steps. Then she moved her head, toward Sam, and said, "Don't say a word to any of these ill-bred country bumpkins. Everything is under control. Ken is on his way over right now." Sophie moved her head again, toward Jennie, and said, "Those instructions apply to you, too."

"Oh," Sam said, and then, "This is Miss Broom."

"So I gathered," Sophie Sargent said.

"I mean she—" Sam paused and tried again. "Miss Broom is my friend."

"How nice," Sophie said. "I still don't want her saying a word to these specimens of the brute man. Ken said to keep you both quiet until he gets here."

"Ken who?" Sam said.

"Sam dear, how many Kens do I know well enough to call Ken? That sanatorium at which he gets himself dried out is just down the road a piece, this side of Darien, and when I got him on the phone and explained— Here's the sanatorium car."

She made a small flicking motion with her silver-lacquered forefinger. It affected the policeman holding Sam's arm as though Sophie had lashed him with a whip. As the man stepped back, she stepped down and across the sidewalk to the black sedan that had drawn up at the curb. From the back seat, moving with gingerly grace, came Kenyon Poole.

He straightened up, squinted at the group gathered in front of the police station, and with three nervous, darting movements of his beautifully manicured fingers, touched swiftly one waxed end of his mustache, the part in the middle of his patent-leather hair, and the red silk scarf knotted into the open collar of the white shirt he wore under a hound's-tooth sports coat.

"Why are we gathering crowds on street corners?" he said. "Is our young friend running for office?"

"No," Sophie said. "They just arrived. A moment before you did."

Poole stuck out his hand and Sam, startled, saw that it was pointed at him. He took the small lump of bone and muscle that reminded him of a ball of twisted wire, and Kenyon Poole said, "Why don't you stick to writing?" Before Sam, whose face grew hot, could reply, Poole's squinting glance was again swinging back and forth, and he said, "Who's in charge here? I mean aside from you, Sophie?"

The policeman holding Jennie's arm swallowed so hard that Sam, four or five feet away, heard the gulp, and then the man said angrily, "Who are you, buddy?"

Kenyon Poole turned directly toward him, and said with contempt, "Clearly not you," and then, with a friendly smile, took the man's arm and, in an even more friendly voice, said, "Let's go in and find your boss."

As they turned, so that the policeman and Poole were at right angles to Sam, he saw the friendly smile stop on Poole's face, as though the neat little man had received some sort of unexpected message that had made him forget the necessity for maintaining the appearance of friendly relations with the enemy. Kenyon Poole looked startled. Turning quickly, to see what he was looking at, Sam saw Jennie. She was staring at the Western writer in a way that reminded Sam of his own reaction when, during his first visit to Claude Sargent's office, he had suddenly understood that he was in the same room with the man who had written *The Small Meal*. Sophie Sargent, who had started up the stone steps with Poole, stopped, turned, saw what had happened, and pulled her mouth to one side in a dimple of distaste.

"Ken," she said, "this is Jennie Broom."

"Oh, yes," Poole said. "The young lady who writes letters to the Coast." He turned back to the now completely confused policeman, gave the man's arm a friendly pat, and, through a smile that would have made superfluous a chandelier in a ballroom, said, "Come, my friend, let's go dispose of a murder charge."

It was the first time the word had been spoken aloud. It was just as well, Sam realized later, that he heard it at a moment when he was still absorbing the realization, from Poole's reply to Sophie's introduction of Jennie, that she had told the Western writer about Jennie's attempt to use Sam in her efforts to get Marshall Umberg's job. Sophie could not have told the story to Poole without including the fact that Sam had taken his story from *Landscape,* which Poole had admired, and turned it into a movie treatment. That this was an act of debasement, Sam had grasped long ago. If he had been too stupid to grasp it, what Claude and Sophie Sargent had said would have made the nature of his act clear. In fact, it was because Sam, who was far from stupid, had grasped all too clearly the nature of the debasement, that he had tried, in his shame and rage, to wipe out what he had done by turning the screen treatment into a novel.

For months, ever since Shirley Shaefer had finished typing *Yours Is the Earth,* Sam had been convinced he had erased the stain. Why should he have felt otherwise? Shirley's naïve enthusiasm had been substantiated by the more sophisticated opinions of Keeley Cuff, Hampton Farnsworth, Sam's own agents, and the hard, although admittedly minuscule, cash of Trafalgar, Singlenight's contractual advance. He had done something good. Why should it matter that, on the way to doing it, he had paused to do something bad? Since nobody would ever ask such a question without the reassuring certainty of the answer built into it, Sam had for months lived with the serenity of the reply: it didn't matter. The way Buggo Salvemini, who once explained to Sam and Jennie in the Grover Cleveland High lunchroom the advantages of his faith, said your sins did not matter so long as you admitted them in the confessional.

Now, however, in the presence of this neat little tortured man who had just stepped out of a car from a drunkards' sanatorium, Sam had been jolted into a frightening awareness: for the artist there was no confessional. You could hide your sins, but you could not wipe them out. Because the sins blunted what Kenyon Poole had called the tools of your craft. You could, of course, carry on with blunted tools. You might even, by picking up the skills Poole had said were the inevitable accretion of experience, turn out with the blunted tools a product that to the public would look as good as your best and possibly even better. But it would not look that way to you. Because you could see what the public could not see: the artificial color that had been laid on to cover the nicks and scars left by the damaged tools. And you, Kenyon Poole had made it plain, were the only judge who mattered.

It was terrifying to grasp, at twenty, that because of a couple of dozen pages he had written not for himself but for a girl with whom he wanted to sleep, he would never again be precisely as good a writer as he had been at nineteen. It was so terrifying that, by comparison, being charged with murder seemed unimportant. Jennie seemed to feel otherwise.

"Listen," she said, tugging Sam's sleeve as they all climbed the steps into the police station.

"Don't you dare," Sophie snapped across her shoulder. "You were both told to shut up. Do all your listening to Ken, please."

This proved to be difficult, since when they came into the large, high-ceilinged room that formed the center of the police station building, Kenyon Poole went to the desk, over which a fat man in a blue shirt was leaning, and for several minutes all Sam could hear was the rasping murmur of a voice so much stronger than Poole's that the Western writer might have been completely silent. He was not, however, motionless. His arms moved in a series of swift gestures that indicated the intensity with which he was arguing. Finally, he seemed to win some sort of point, because he turned sharply to Sophie, talked to her for a few moments, and then she came across toward Sam and Jennie, followed by one of the policemen.

"I told you things would begin to look up as soon as Ken arrived," Sophie said. "We've scored our first victory."

"What sort of victory?" Sam said.

"You're to be allowed to wait sitting down," Sophie said, and to the policeman, "Where?"

"In here," he said.

The policeman opened a door and held it, while Sophie, Jennie, and Sam filed past him, then closed the door behind them. They were in a small office decorated with framed photographs of beefy-looking men with walrus mustaches and heavy gold watch chains strung across old-fashioned waistcoats sitting at banquet tables and staring sheepishly at the camera.

"Sophie," Sam said, "what are we waiting for?"

"Ham Farnsworth," Sophie said, and then the fact that Sam should have asked the question seemed to surprise her. Irritably, with a touch of disbelief, Sophie said, "He sent you off on this jaunt ten days ago, didn't he?"

"Yes, but at that time I thought it was because—" Sam paused. Sophie did not have to know what he was really worried about. "I mean," Sam said, "I don't understand the whole thing."

Sophie gave him a long look, eyes slightly pinched at the corners, and then she turned the look on Jennie.

"You've seen the papers?" Sophie said. "Haven't you?"

Jennie pulled the folded copy of the *New York Times* out of Sam's pocket and said, "The cops gave us this up in Portland."

"I don't mean that front-page stuff," Sam said impatiently.

"Neither do I," Sophie said. She took the paper from Jennie, opened the folds, and held it out to Sam. "Take a look at the back page."

As Sam took the paper, the door opened and Kenyon Poole looked in. "Sophie," he said. "Come out here a minute."

Sophie went out. The door closed. Jennie snatched the paper from Sam. Across her shoulder he saw that the entire back page consisted of an advertisement for a new book which had just been published. There was a frenetic quality about the advertisement which, since Jennie was not holding the paper very steadily and Sam was able to absorb the contents only in snatches, it took him a few moments to realize was due to the publisher's distribution problem. The demand for the book, the advertisement told the public, was so great and so sudden, that the initial modest printing had been exhausted within the first few hours of publication date, which happened to be today. New printings were being rushed to the bookstores. The public was advised to do likewise. Sam had absorbed snatches of almost a dozen highly colored reasons why the publisher felt this advice was sound before he saw, with a stab of shock, the name of the book the advertisement was screaming about: *Yours Is the Earth.*

"Holy Benny!" Jennie said softly. "You know what an ad like this costs?"

"What?" said Sam, who had no interest at the moment in what anything cost, but Jennie apparently interpreted his question as an answer to hers.

"Not counting agency fees and commissions," she said with unmistakable awe, "just the space alone, this little number set Trafalgar, Singlenight back fifteen hundred bucks."

Sam, to whom this was as impressive a figure as it was to Jennie, was aware that it had significance for her in this case that he had not grasped.

"I don't understand," he said. "I mean I know that's a lot of money and all that, but what I mean, I don't see what the hell it's got to do with this murder rap it looks like your friend Mr. Hampton Farnsworth has hung around our necks."

There was something so odd about the way Jennie looked at him that for several moments Sam found himself beguiled into grappling with the nature of the oddity: this, he realized, was the way Sophie Sargent had just looked at him, and realizing that, Sam realized something else: this was the way most women with brains—women like Sophie and Jennie and his mother—looked at one time or another at even the brainiest of men: as though they were constantly being reminded of a fact that there really was no reason for them ever to forget, namely, that men, in the long run as well as in the mass, were not very bright.

"Sammy boy," Jennie said. "Have you any idea how much money is spent on advertising first novels?"

"How should I?" Sam said. "I don't know anything about publishing."

"You've seen ads for other first novels," Jennie said. "Most of them look like postage stamps. This is the back page of the *New York Times,* Sammy. Does it look like a postage stamp?" Sam examined the advertisement with new interest. Jennie, clearly sensing that she had brought her horse to water at last, proceeded to make him drink. She said, "Remember Ham Farnsworth's prediction about the sales of your novel?"

"Twelve hundred copies," Sam said.

Jennie nodded. "A prediction shared by your own hard-headed agents. Right?"

Sam nodded.

"Does it seem likely to you," Jennie said, "that a publisher in his right mind would spend fifteen hundred dollars for space alone on the first advertisement for a book that is going to sell twelve hundred copies?"

Sam thought for a moment, figured out that this meant $1.25 per copy, then said, "I guess maybe they're not in their right minds."

Jennie shook her head. "Try again," she said.

Sam shook *his* head. "Come on," he said. "If you know what it means, tell me."

"It means, Sammy boy," Jennie Broom said, "Mr. Hampton Farnsworth is seeing to it that your book is going to sell many, many, many more than twelve hundred copies."

Keeley Cuff said it somewhat differently when, the next day, Sam was able, by pleading the necessity for a visit to the bathroom, to get away from the people in Sophie Sargent's office, sneak into the bookkeeping department, and call the young managing editor of *Landscape* from Shirley Shaefer's phone.

"Silver?" Cuff's nasal voice said at the other end. "*Samuel* Silver? What are you doing out of jail?"

"Keeping a promise," Sam said. "When we had lunch a couple of weeks ago, you asked me to let you know as soon as I found out that a publication date had been set on my book."

"Yes," Keeley Cuff said. "Over the spaghetti and meat balls at Tony's."

"Well," Sam said, "I didn't find out until yesterday, when I saw that ad in the *Times,* but this is the first chance I've had to get to a phone. Not that I suppose the information, whatever you wanted it for, can do you any good now."

"No, but this call can," Keeley Cuff said. "And is."

"Is what?" Sam said.

"The papers said this morning you and that girl and Farnsworth were all cleared late last night?"

"Yes," Sam said. "We all had to make depositions or whatever they're called, and at first they wanted a formal inquest, but Mr. Farnsworth is so well known in the town, he serves on the Selectmen's Finance Committee, or something like that, and Mr. Poole was so tough about everything—"

"Kenyon Poole?"

"Yes."

"What was he doing there?"

"My agent brought him up," Sam said. "Sophie Sargent. Mr. Poole is a client of the Sargent & Sargent office. It seems he knows a lot about criminal law, and he certainly knows a good criminal lawyer. He kept things going on his own for a while, managing or stalling, I don't know which, until his friend Morris McKewen arrived. You know him?"

"Only from the papers," Keeley Cuff said.

"Well, he's as good as it says in the papers," Sam said. "Between Kenyon Poole and Morris McKewen, the whole thing was finally straightened out, but by then it was almost three in the morning, which didn't seem the right time to call you, so I had to wait until this morning."

"Where are you now?" Keeley Cuff said.

"In the Sargent & Sargent office."

"Alone?"

"Well, at the moment, yes," Sam said. "I sneaked in here to make this call."

"Sneaked in from where?"

"Mrs. Sargent's office," Sam said. "It's like being in a malted machine. Reporters and radio people and photographers, all asking a lot of damn-fool questions and, oh, you know."

"I don't, really," Keeley Cuff said. "It's never happened to me. But I've watched it happening to other people, which is why I said the information you called to give me, it's too late for that to do me any good, but Lordy me, the mere fact that you made the call is doing me a lot of good."

"Well," Sam said, "I'm glad."

There was a laugh at the other end of the phone, and Keeley Cuff said, "You don't know what I'm talking about, do you?"

Sam hesitated. He had begun to grasp that it was not always a good thing, when you didn't know what somebody was talking about, to admit it.

"I don't know why you wanted to know when the publication date on my book was set," he said.

Keeley Cuff laughed again and said, "All right, we'll clear that up first. You know what I want out of this contest. No, wanted."

"A lot of publicity for *Landscape,* you said."

"Correct," Keeley Cuff said. "Am I getting it?"

"Well, the books that won the contest haven't been published yet," Sam said.

"No, but the book that lost," Keeley Cuff said, "has."

"Oh," Sam said.

"Uh-huh," Keeley Cuff said. "Did you see the *Times* again this morning?"

"Yes, I did."

"You any idea what an ad that size costs?"

"It was explained to me yesterday," Sam said.

"You take what that ad cost yesterday, and you add it to what today's ad cost, and then you just sit back and consider that these are merely the two opening guns in a campaign, and you'll get some inkling of how far Ham Farnsworth's special passions are going to carry a new young novelist named Samuel Silver."

"Even assuming all that is true," Sam said, "I still don't see why what you wanted when you cooked up this novel contest, a lot of publicity for *Landscape,* why that should be affected. When the winning novels are published—"

"There will be no money in the Trafalgar, Singlenight till," Keeley Cuff said. "And publicity costs money."

"Why should Trafalgar, Singlenight have less money when your winning novels are published than they have today?"

"Oh, Lordy me, they won't have less," Keeley Cuff said. "Matter of fact, after what they're going to rake in on your little number, they'll have more. The difference is that they won't be under any obligation to spend it."

He paused, and Sam, without seeing the bony little head held together by the black bands of the thick glasses, knew that Keeley Cuff's face was twisted in a sardonic smile. The pause at the other end of the wire was so obviously the stage wait of the skilled performer who knows when he has reached his best line and wants to make sure it achieves its maximum effect.

"You see," Keeley Cuff said, "I've made a few inquiries since I saw that first ad yesterday, and I've learned something I didn't know before. Trafalgar, Singlenight have a space contract with the *New York Times*."

"What's that?" Sam said.

"A way of buying advertising space more cheaply," Keeley Cuff said. "Trafalgar, Singlenight have such a large list, they buy so much advertising space regularly for so many books, that it's to their advantage to buy in bulk, because they can buy cheaper. The *Times* says to Trafalgar, Singlenight at the beginning of the year, look, last year you bought X number of advertising lines from us at so much per line. If you will guarantee to buy the same number of lines from us next year, or the same number plus, if by contract we can be certain of selling that many lines to you next year, for that certainty we are willing to pay out good money in the form of giving the space to you at a lower rate. Last year Trafalgar, Singlenight published one hundred and eight titles. They signed their contract with the *Times* on the assumption that they would publish at least the same number of titles this year. Their calculations went out of whack, however. As of today, Trafalgar, Singlenight have thus far this year published exactly fifty-nine titles, and their contract with the *Times* runs out by August thirty-first. In other words—"

"In other words," Sam said slowly, "between now and August thirty-first, which is—"

"Three and a half weeks from today," Keeley Cuff said.

"They have left and must use up advertising space that they assumed when they signed the contract would be used up on—let's see." Sam paused to make calculation. "One hundred and eight titles last year," he said. "Minus fifty-nine titles published this year—"

"I've done the arithmetic, Silver old boy," Keeley Cuff said. "During the next three and a half weeks Trafalgar, Singlenight must use up, since it's paid for anyway, advertising space in the *New York Times* that would ordinarily be spread out over forty-nine titles. My inquiries indicate that between now and August thirty-first, Trafalgar, Singlenight will not have any other new titles ready for publication, not even, I might say with a certain amount of bitterness *especially* not even, the winners of my little contest."

"Why not?" Sam said.

"You might ask their editor-in-chief," Keeley Cuff said. "Mr. Hampton Farnsworth. If you and he are not talking, I'll answer for him. No other books on the Trafalgar, Singlenight list are ready for publication because Mr. Farnsworth didn't want them to be ready. But he wanted yours to be ready, and it was. When the right moment came, when he could put your name on every front page in the country, he was also ready to put your book on every book counter in the country, and during the next three and a half weeks, what will be sweeping those books from the nation's book counters to the nation's book buyers will be an advertising campaign so large that under normal conditions, it would have been used to service not one book but forty-nine books."

In the pause that followed, Sam glanced across the Sargent & Sargent bookkeeping department, toward the desk to which Shirley Shaefer had discreetly withdrawn with a batch of ledger sheets. She was bent over them, making marks with a pencil, and the sun, coming in off Park Avenue, turned the back of her neck to a golden fuzz that made Sam think of Jennie, early in the morning, sitting on the edge of the bed, smoking the first cigarette of the day, and his heart moved with the pain of possession.

"There's only one thing wrong with your calculations," Sam said into the phone.

"What's that?" Keeley Cuff asked.

"They're all based on a pretty wild assumption," Sam said. "That Mr. Farnsworth knew in advance Miss Broom's husband, that Salvemini guy, was going to jump up at me with a kitchen knife from the Aspetuck River."

"How do you know he didn't?" Keeley Cuff said.

"What?" Sam said.

"How do you know Ham Farnsworth didn't know it was going to happen?" Keeley Cuff said. "It, or something like it?"

"Aah, now, wait a minute," Sam said.

"For what?" Keeley Cuff said. "Divine inspiration? Silver, old boy, somebody tipped off that poor Salvemini cluck that his wife was going to be out at Farnsworth's house for the week-end. Who?"

"I don't know," Sam said. "And neither do you."

"No," Keeley Cuff said. "But we know who invited Samuel Silver, the brilliant young author of the about-to-be-published sensational new novel *Yours Is the Earth*, so he'd be on the scene at the same time."

Again Sam looked across at the golden fuzz on Shirley Shaefer's neck, and he wished Jennie was here with him. Jennie would have known how to handle this.

"Silver?"

"Yes," Sam said into the phone.

"There's nothing to be upset about," Keeley Cuff said. "You've got a best-seller."

"You're saying I got it because Mr. Farnsworth risked his life," Sam said.

"What?" Keeley Cuff said.

"If your analysis is correct," Sam said. "If it's true that Mr. Farnsworth tipped off Salvemini about his wife being there, it might have been Mr. Farnsworth he went for with that knife."

"But it wasn't," Keeley Cuff said. "Besides, the Martin Luther type doesn't mind risks."

"What's Martin Luther got to do with Mr. Farnsworth?"

"Both are religious fanatics," Keeley Cuff said. "Or rather, one was and the other is. Luther hated the hypocrisy of Rome. Ham Farnsworth hates the hypocrisy of his life. He believes you lost that contest because you're a Jew. He'll go to any lengths to prove to the gentile members of the committee of judges how wrong they were. If I were you, Silver my boy, I would say screw the lengths and enjoy the proof. It's going to come to a lot of money. Congratulations."

"Thanks," Sam said.

"Let's have lunch some day."

"When?" Sam said.

Keeley Cuff laughed. "Lordy me," he said. "I should have known it wouldn't work with a man who'd worry about keeping a promise like the one you made to call me."

"What wouldn't work?" Sam said.

"The let's-have-lunch-some-day gag."

"You mean you didn't mean it?" Sam said.

"Lordy me," Keeley Cuff said, "of course I meant it."

"Okay," Sam said. "When?"

"Next week sometime?"

"What's the matter with today?" Sam said. "You busy?"

Keeley Cuff laughed again and said, "No, but I imagine you are. There must be a lot of loose ends to tie up."

Actually, there was only one. That night, after he left Jennie and sat down at the kitchen table on East Tenth Street to face his mother across the jars and cracked plates of leftovers, Sam decided the best way to approach it was through the problem of Mr. Brunschweig.

"Who says it's a problem?" Mrs. Silver said. "There's something with the lotkes the matter they don't taste good?"

"No, they're fine," Sam said. "It's just I had a big dinner, and I'm not hungry."

"A big dinner before school?"

"I didn't go to school tonight, Ma."

"Why not?" Mrs. Silver said. "Ten days you were riding around all over America in an automobile, with no school, it wasn't enough for you? More vacation you need yet?"

"That's not it, Ma," Sam said. "And I've explained all about those ten days and how they happened. They were no vacation, so let's drop it and stick to the problem. The Lafayette Business Institute and me, we're part of the same problem as Mr. Brunschweig and me."

"So tell a person," his mother said. "Who says it's a problem?"

The answer was: Jennie did. But Sam did not think it politic to say so.

"I do," Sam said, "but I don't know how to explain it."

"So if you don't know," Mrs. Silver said, "I'll do the explaining. Try a lotke. A bite out of you it won't take." Sam bit into one of the cold potato pancakes, and his mother said, "The person that you were ten days ago, Sam, that person is finished. Today, Sam, you're a different person, and a different person, Sam, he has different problems. What's the matter?"

"Nothing," Sam said. He couldn't tell her that Jennie, across the dinner they had eaten in Tony's three hours ago, had made precisely the same point. "I'm listening, Ma."

"Ten days ago you were a boy with a job tuxedos to deliver and at night you were studying bookkeeping. That you wanted more, that you expected more, that you had plans, this was inside. I'm talking what you were to the world outside, what the world saw, and what the world saw was like I said, a delivery boy by day, night school by night. Today, Sam, it's different. Today, Sam, your picture it's in the papers. Today, Sam, you have a book people they're buying it over the whole country. Today there's big advertisements they have your name printed. Today, Sam, you're not a boy. Today, Sam, you're like Lindenbergh, you're like this one with the fur coat down there by the South Pole he's all the time running around, this you know."

"Admiral Byrd," Sam said.

His mother nodded. "Like him, Sam," she said. "You're today a famous man, Sam."

"Let's not overdo it," Sam said, wondering how to steer the discussion around toward the loose end he had come to tie up. "But I know what you mean."

"If you know," his mother said, "then this you also know: a famous man, a man with his picture in the paper and a book a best-seller, such a man doesn't shlep tuxedos for a Mr. Brunschweig for twelve dollars a week, and such a man he doesn't go at night to sit with a bunch other shleppers in a night school there on Fourth Avenue studying how to be a bookkeeper."

The best opening was, after all, the front door. Sam decided to walk right in.

"That's what Jennie says, too," he said.

Mrs. Silver's lips tightened slightly, and she said, "What Jennie says, here in this house I'm not interested to hear."

"I know how you feel about her," Sam said. "I don't blame you. For a long time I felt the same way, but now that all this has happened, it's all due to Jennie, really, if you just look at it the right way."

"You mean Jennie's way," Mrs. Silver said.

"I mean the fair way," Sam said. "If she hadn't done that thing on graduation night, I never would have written that short story, and if I hadn't written that short story—"

"You would have written another one," his mother said. "Jennie didn't make you a writer, Sam. God did that. What Jennie did, she gave you something your first story you should write about. She didn't give it to you for a present. It was an accident, something you got out of a bad thing she did to you, something that if God didn't thank God make you a writer, you never would have got, and the bad thing that Jennie did to you on graduation night would still be what it was then and what it is now, Sam, a bad thing. That's the fair way to look at it, Sam, and you could eat great big dinners with Jennie in fancy restaurants from today till Tishibuff becomes Christmas, God forbid, and she could talk to you with the fancy lies twice as fast, it won't change what's true, Sam. Eat another lotke."

He ate two, forcing them down, because as always she had outmaneuvered him, and he had to think of some other approach. It was better to do this while eating because so long as his mouth was full of food he was reasonably safe from uttering words she could twist to suit her own purpose.

"So now we got Jennie out of this kitchen," Mrs. Silver said, "we have room for plain talk. You're now a different man, Sam, so you'll do like a different man. No more Mr. Brunschweig, and no more night school. From now on, only one thing: the writing. You hear?"

"Yes, Ma, but—"

"Tomorrow you'll go see Mr. Sargent and you'll ask him he should find out from the publisher how much the book is selling. A hundred per cent, to the last penny, no. This nobody can expect. But an estimate, something a person can figure, this they can give you. From this estimate we'll figure how much money it'll be coming to you by the end of the year, and then we'll figure how long it'll take you to write the next book. How long it takes, that's how we'll spread out the money, every week, like you were getting it from Mr. Brunschweig a salary, except this much even without talking to the publisher, this much I know: more than twelve dollars a week, Sam, this I guarantee it'll be." She stood up and said, "You're finished?"

Sam stood up, too, and said, "Yes, Ma, but wait a minute. I want you to listen."

"Not tonight," Mrs. Silver said. "Tomorrow, maybe, when a big dinner with Jennie somewhere you didn't eat, when your head is back where it belongs, on your own neck, and you're using it like the Sam I know all my life, not like a potato sack full of words somebody else spilled in, tomorrow we'll talk some more. Bring me the dishes to the sink."

He hesitated, gathering his strength, knowing he would never have enough to vanquish her, but hoping he could manage an orderly retreat, and he said, "All right, Ma, I'll see you tomorrow."

The three steps to the kitchen door, which led out of the flat, accomplished more than any words he had ever used in her presence: she looked apprehensive rather than astonished, as though, having always been able to read his mind, she had once again read it now. That was the way her voice sounded, too, as she said, "Sam, where are you going?"

"To my wife," he said, wishing he did not have to see her face as he said it. "Jennie and I were married three days ago."

Almost sixteen years later, stepping out of the taxi that had brought him downtown from his drink with Sophie Sargent, Sam suddenly stopped short. It seemed odd that in the murky dusk, on the Park Avenue sidewalk in front of the Oatley-Wicke Building, on his way up to Shirley Shaefer's office to get the copy of Kenyon Poole's manuscript that Sophie Sargent had promised to let him read, he should finally have understood something that had puzzled him for almost two decades: the look on his mother's face that night.

There had been pain in it, of course. Pain, disappointment, and anger. These he had seen at once, because these were what anybody could be expected to feel under the circumstances. But to him Mrs. Silver was not "anybody," and it was her son's business to record not what was expected but what was actually there. What was there, what eluded Sam for years, was something extra, something beyond the pain, the disappointment, and the anger, something that had made the pain and the disappointment and the anger memorable, and the moment worth recording. Walking into the Oatley-Wicke Building, Sam saw it so clearly that, for a stunned moment, he felt as though he had walked back into that East Tenth Street kitchen. What he had seen on his mother's face was the look of the fiercely proud master of a vessel he has himself constructed who has just learned that he has been removed from his command.

"Eleven, please," Sam said to the elevator operator.

When Shirley Shaefer's business had grown so large that she could no longer handle it in one of those tiny rooms behind a green-curtained archway off the Sargent & Sargent central corridor, and she had applied to the rental agents of the Oatley-Wicke Building for space of her own, Claude and Sophie Sargent had urged her to ask for something on the twenty-first floor. After all, she did most of her work for the Sargent & Sargent list. It would save a lot of leg work and be more convenient all around to have her next door rather than in some other part of the building. Shirley had disagreed.

"Convenient, yes," she had said to Sam when she explained why she had rented an office ten floors below, on eleven. "But better, no. All these years I been typing manuscripts, I've learned a little something about writers. They gotta have like a Switzerland."

"A what?" Sam had said.

"A place to talk," Shirley had said. "You ever notice? All those wars they're all the time having over there in Europe? This one invades that one. That one grabs this. But no matter how much they invade or how big the grabber, even that Napoleon, and you know what a pig he was, they never grab Switzerland. With that shrimp Switzerland, nobody ever fights. You know why? Because the fighters and the grabbers, they know when the time comes to stop fighting, they know they gotta have a place it doesn't belong to either side, a place where they can talk and arrange how to get out of the mess they're in with all their fighting and grabbing. The same with me and with writers. I'm like a wife right there in the office. Most of them, the minute they leave Mr. Sargent's room, they step in to see me. On the face of it, what they step in to see me about, it's just to say hello, how are things going, Shirley, and then, before you know it, it's oh, by the way, on that last story, I'm afraid you're going to have to retype it in a few days, Shirley, what a bore, isn't it, that Ellery Yiffniff who seems to think he's an editor, he wants a few changes, and I must say, while I don't mind making them, they're so childishly simple they won't take more than a few minutes, just the same you'd think a man like Claude Sargent, with his experience and his literary taste, you'd think he'd know better than to knuckle under to a stupid so-and-so like that Ellery Yiffniff, and if you think they say so-and-so you are mistaken. After a while, when they got it out of their system, they feel better, and they go home, and they make the corrections, and I retype the story, and everybody is happy. But the place to get it out of their system, what I call the Switzerland, this they gotta have. It's part of Shirley Shaefer's service."

Sam, who had made use of it more often than he cared to remember, was pleased to note, as he opened the door marked "S. Shaefer, Complete

Manuscript Service," that at the moment nobody else was making use of this aspect of Shirley's service. His talk with Sophie Sargent had left him uneasy. The problems of the day, which his common sense told him had been no more difficult than the problems of most of his days, had left a residue that a couple of drinks late in the afternoon usually dissolved. The Scotch Sophie had given him had not done its usual healing work. On the contrary. The alcohol had made more acute a feeling that had nothing to do with common sense: a feeling that Kenyon Poole's manuscript had some personal meaning for Sam Silver. He wanted to get at it without further delay. His chances of accomplishing this were increased by the fact that Shirley, whose office usually hummed until almost eight o'clock with the clacking of typewriters over which the seven girls on her staff hunched like racing-car drivers over their steering wheels, was alone.

"Hi," Sam said.

Shirley rose from the desk in the far corner, which she referred to as her Executive Suite, and said, "How are you, Mr. Silver?"

"I'm fine," Sam said. "And let's not have any cracks about age. We're both in the same bracket, remember."

Shirley laughed and said, "Who can forget?"

The laugh simmered down into a small smile, the way it always did when either of them alluded to the fact that their careers had started at the same time and in the same place, and her eyes seemed to go out of focus and mist over slightly, as though the past was for her so much brighter than the present that she could not, like staring into the sun, contemplate it without protection. In the moment of unspoken reminiscence, Sam noticed that, since he had seen her last, Shirley had again changed her hairdo. This time it was one of those Italian basket affairs, or perhaps it was French, that Sam had noticed recently on the mannequins in the windows of Bonwit's and Bergdorf's. He had heard some of the Sargent & Sargent clients make jokes about the amount of money Shirley spent at the hairdresser in an effort to improve on nature's indifferent handiwork, and while some of the jokes were good, since a number of Sargent & Sargent clients were professional humorists, they did not make Sam laugh. He understood that relentless, tireless effort at self-improvement. It was what had driven him to study bookkeeping in the evening session of the Lafayette Business Institute. It was part of growing up where he and Shirley had grown up, with "toilets in the hall." And, as he examined the trim, self-possessed woman in the expensive, severely tailored tweed suit and the slightly preposterous hairdo, and he thought of the girl who years ago had typed his first novel, Sam felt that at least that part of what he and Shirley had grown up with was a good thing. Hunger was not necessarily the evil that the champions of a regimented society branded it. True, the effort to fill an empty stomach produced cutthroats and thieves. It was equally true, however, that it produced a Shirley Shaefer.

"I'm glad Mrs. Sargent called and said you were coming to pick up that manuscript," she said. "It saved me the trouble writing you a note."

"A note?" Sam said. "About what?"

"What it said in Winchell this morning," Shirley said. "That you're getting married."

It had never before occurred to Sam that Winchell might have almost as many readers as Matthew and Luke.

"What were you going to say in the note?"

"A question!" Shirley said. "What does a person say in a note to another person that's getting married? Congratulations."

"Well, you save your congratulations until they're called for," Sam said. "Mr. Winchell got a bum steer from somebody this time. I'm not getting married."

The look of disappointment that raced across Shirley's face was so intense and so genuine that Sam felt as though he had done her a personal injury.

"Oh," she said. "Oh, what a shame."

"You're such a great big champion of the married state," Sam said. "I've often wondered why you never took the plunge yourself."

She gave him a funny little look, and Sam realized that his remark, intended as a joke, had touched something unfunny.

"Who needs it?" Shirley said. "When I was a kid, the time most girls they don't think about anything else, I didn't have time to think about it. I was too busy figuring out how to feed Mama and my five sisters, not counting myself, and get the whole bunch through high school. Then, when the business started going, and the problem how to feed them was pretty much under control, and I might have had a little time to think what other girls think, I mean about marrying, my sisters it turned out *they* were thinking about it, and since they were all younger, somebody had to keep an eye on them, and Mama, she should rest in peace, a wonderful woman she was, but in that department she was but absolutely and one hundred per cent helpless, so I had to do it, and frankly, even if I say it myself, I did a good job. Comes Sunday, no kidding, I got my day off, I need a personal traffic cop he should tell me which way to turn, and I'm not joking. I mean it's should I go up to the Bronx to see my sister Elsie and her family, or to Queens where Yetta lives with her husband and the kids, or down to Peter Cooper Village where it's Hannah, or over to Brooklyn where Lena's husband he's in the liquor store line, or out yet to New Jersey, Rachel's husband, he's a Ph.D., he's a research physicist there by Johns Manville, they have their own home near New Brunswick, a ranch type with two and a half acres, nearly three. I mean it isn't as though I'm complaining. I got more to be proud of than lots of people I know. I got my own business, it throws off a nice substantial profit, I got a nice little something put away, when her working days are over nobody is gonna have to take care of Shirley Shaefer, believe me, I got five sisters, every one of them married to a nice clean-cut Jewish boy, and I've got eleven nieces and nephews, by next week, if Elsie is as dependable as she was with the first two, it'll be twelve, and every one of those kids, not to mention my sisters and their husbands, every one of them they love their Tante Shirley. The only thing is—"

She paused, and the funny little look came back into her face, except that this time it didn't seem to be directed at anybody. Or rather, it seemed to be turned inward, and Shirley's eyes misted slightly, as they did when she or Sam happened to mention their similar origins, but he could see that this time the funny little look had nothing to do with him. This time Shirley was not looking at a moment in the past that was for her brighter than the present. This time she was caught by something that might have been but hadn't. This time Shirley Shaefer was looking at something that had never happened. It was not Sam, who was too fond of Shirley to hurt her, but the habits of his craft, over which he had no control, that said, "The only thing is what, Shirley?"

She gave a tired little poke at the preposterous basket that, for a sum she would have once considered an excellent week's salary, somebody with an odd accent and, in all probability, an odder sex life, had made of her mouse-colored, unglamorous, honorable hair, and Shirley Shaefer said, "The only thing is you're young and you're young and you're young, and you think you'll always be young, and then one day, you're combing your hair, and you take a good look in the mirror, and you realize you're—"

Her voice stopped. She couldn't say the word. Neither, however, could she let an old friend think that she was not what she had spent her whole life demonstrating to the world she was, and Shirley Shaefer, with a laugh that was almost convincing, said, "You think you're a bright young businesswoman, piling it up so you won't have to grab just for a meal ticket the first man who comes along and says how about it, kid, and then all of a sudden you realize you're not a bright young businesswoman any more, you're Tante Shirley to eleven, almost twelve, like grandchildren."

She paused again, and the misty look vanished as her bright, merry eyes came back into the sharp focus that Sam had grown to accept as her normal look, and Shirley Shaefer laughed, really laughed, the way she had laughed all the years Sam had known her, as she said, "Besides, I'll be honest, this marriage business, after all the stories I've typed, who needs it?"

"That's right," Sam said. "Blame it on somebody else. You shouldn't let the stories fool you. They're not real."

"They're real enough for Shirley Shaefer," Shirley Shaefer said. "At least when I finish typing a story, and I've lived through sixteen double-spaced pages of this here incompatibility, I don't have to go out and buy myself a plane ticket for Reno. By the way, how did Mr. Bienstock over at *American Bride* like your last one, that there *They Told Me You Were Dead?*"

It was the question of an interested friend, a friend who wished him well and wanted, Sam was certain, to hear a reply that they would both consider good news. Yet Shirley was human, and Sam could not help wondering if she also wanted to hear a substantiation of her own judgment. Twelve days ago, when Sam had stopped in to pick up the typescript of his latest serial, Shirley's observation, as she handed it over, had not been the thumbs-up "This one has my label on it." Shirley's comment about *They Told Me You Were Dead* had been the thumbs-down "There's people they'll be crazy about this."

Sam said, "He liked it all right, but you know Mr. Bienstock."

"He wanted some changes?" Shirley said.

"What else?" Sam said.

"The hero and the heroine?" Shirley said. "That they live in those apartments one on top of the other? That he wanted changed?"

Surprised, Sam said, "Yes, how did you know?"

Shirley's editorial comments had never, so far as he could remember, gone beyond her thumbs-up or thumbs-down observation.

"I can't exactly say," she said and then, apparently aware that by saying what she had already said, she had broken a precedent, Shirley seemed to feel the compulsion to mend it. "I didn't have so much a reaction as I had like you could say it made me uncomfortable. You know?" She paused again, and Sam nodded again, urging her on beyond what suddenly began to look like the brink of an important discovery. "What I mean," Shirley said, "I mean it's good. When I was reading it, I had the feeling it was real, and when something is real I get all tied up in it and I forget where I am, and then every now and then, once in a while, something would hit me wrong, and I'd come out of it, you might say, and I'd realize it wasn't real, it was just a story, and one of the things that bumped me out of it like that, one of those things was the two apartments, one on top of the other."

She paused, and looked a little frightened, as though aware that she had done something she might later regret.

"You're absolutely right," Sam said, craftily choosing his tone and manner. He didn't give a damn about the apartments being one above the other. What he wanted was a clue to the end of the story. "Mrs. Sargent felt the same thing," he said. "Mr. Sargent, too."

"Oh, well," Shirley said with obvious relief. "Then I'm in good company. I mean they *know,* and me, well, it's not my job."

"You do it very well," Sam said and, as casually as he could: "Mr. Bienstock also wants the ending changed. He says it's a come-to-realizer, there's no real reason why the hero, who couldn't seem to fall in love with the heroine all through the story, should suddenly decide at the end he does love her."

He paused, and Shirley, who clearly did not want to say anything, said, "Oh, really?"

If he were not so deeply concerned, Sam would have laughed. Shirley Shaefer was not the "Oh, really?" type.

"Yes," Sam said, and because he was now convinced she had the answer, he attacked head on: "Did you feel that, too?"

Looking absolutely neutral, Shirley said, "I can't really say."

"Why not?" Sam demanded.

Shirley looked startled. "Oh, I don't mean that I *know* but I won't *tell* you," she said hastily. "I mean I can't because I don't *know.*"

In the pause that followed, Sam was aware of a sense of regret. Not for the fact that he had failed to bludgeon from her the solution to the end of his story, but because he sensed that by trying to involve her to a greater degree than her own inflexible code had ever before allowed her to venture, their relationship had changed.

"Well, no point keeping you here all night," he said. "If you'll give me that manuscript Mrs. Sargent called you about, I'll carry these weary old bones back to the stable."

Shirley stepped over to her Executive Suite, picked up a fat envelope, and handed it over.

"It's not proofread," she said. "Mrs. Sargent said it was a rush, so I didn't have time."

"Oh," Sam said. "You typed this yourself?"

"Mrs. Sargent asked me to," Shirley said. "She didn't want the other girls to know about it."

Sam, who had opened the clasp of the envelope to peer inside, said, "Where's the title page?"

"There isn't any," Shirley said. "Mrs. Sargent said the author's name was to be kept a secret for a while."

"That's right," Sam said, "I forgot she did say that," and he paused, but nothing happened, so he said, "Well, good night, Shirley."

"Good night, Mr. Silver," she said.

It wasn't until he was out in the hall, pressing the elevator button, that Sam realized the full significance of the fact that during the pause he had provided for Shirley, nothing had happened: Kenyon Poole's manuscript was the first one Shirley Shaefer had ever handed to Sam without uttering either her thumbs-up or thumbs-down verdict.

"Hi, Pop. Watcha got?"

    "Oh, just a manuscript Mrs. Sargent wants me to read and give her an opinion on," Sam said. He pulled his key out of the lock, nudged the front door shut with his elbow, slid the hall closet door open, and as he disposed of his hat and coat, he nodded toward the table in the dining alcove at which Billy was eating his dinner. "That any good?"

    Coming out of the kitchen with the silver platter, Charlene said, "It must be. This is his third helping. Good evening, Mr. Silver."

    "Hi, Charlene. You're spoiling him good, all right."

    "I'm a growing boy," Billy said, lifting a slab of barbecued spare ribs from Charlene's platter to his plate. "Besides, everybody knows overeating is a symptom of preternal neglect. If my busy father could find time to eat with his lonely little son once in a while, instead of taking chorus girls to night clubs all the time, I'd have only two helpings."

    "In the pig's ear," Sam said, reaching across Billy's shoulder and stealing an olive from the condiment dish, without the complicated contents of which his son considered any meal except breakfast incomplete. "And I think you mean parental, not preternal."

"Lay off my olives," Billy said. "I mean I'm not only a growing boy, which I've been for some time, but I'm now an actor, too, and I need every ounce of food I can get to keep my talent at like what they call my peak. What did you think of my Calpurnia?"

"If Sarah Bernhardt wasn't cremated, she's spinning in her grave." Sam touched the top of Billy's head and said, "Don't you ever ask Charlene to make you anything else for dinner?"

"Listen, Pop, you lead your life and I'll lead mine," Billy said. "I happen to be but crazy about ribs and Charlene happens to make them but better than anybody in the whole wide world."

"Listen to that blarney," Charlene said as she started back to the kitchen. "And not quite thirteen yet, either."

"Speaking of that," Billy said, "what's a bar mitzvah, Pops?"

The old vacuum cleaner relentlessly noted that Sam's first reaction was a swift glance at the kitchen door, which was chunking back and forth, and the mind that would have explored the reaction in a story, except that Sam Silver had long ago given up writing that kind of story, was equally relentless in noting the reason for the reaction: he had wanted to see if Charlene, who was on her way out of the room when Billy started asking the question, had heard it.

"What makes you ask that?" Sam said.

"You know, Pops, you're getting more and more like Grandma," Billy said. "You once told me her idea of answering a question is to ask one of her own. I ask you what's a bar mitzvah and you answer me with a what makes you ask that?"

"I don't have time to answer a lot of questions now," Sam said. "I've got to shower and change my clothes and pick up Rebecca downstairs in exactly fifteen minutes."

"You're all out of gear today, Pops." Billy looked at his wrist watch and said, "You've got like a full hour or better before you pick up Rebecca, and you're not even doing that. She called a few minutes ago. There's some foul-up at the printer about her catalogue for this show thing of hers, so she had to do something about it, and she said she'll meet you at Tony's at seven-thirty. It is now twenty-one, hold it, bong, twenty-*two* minutes after six, which gives you an hour and eight minutes, and if you can't work in an answer to what's a bar mitzvah in that time, then, man, you have slowed down but I mean *down*."

"It's a ceremony," Sam said. "Jewish boys go through it at the age of thirteen. It means a sort of crossing of the line from childhood into manhood. Let me just get rid of this, will you?"

He crossed into the study, put the fat envelope Shirley Shaefer had

given him on his desk, started back into the living room, stopped, returned
to the desk, picked up the envelope, ran his glance slowly around the lime-
green room, decided on one of the concealed filing cabinets, placed the
manuscript in the top drawer, closed it carefully, and then, with a troubled
start, wondered why he had done it.

"Pops?"

"Hey, quit that," Sam said. "You're dripping grease all over the rug. In
the civilization to which you and I belong, we do our eating at a table."

Billy, backing out of the study as Sam followed, continued gnawing the
barbecued spare rib and watching his father. The bright brown eyes, not
quite as dark as Jennie's but close enough to make Sam's heart ache, were
narrowed in the sort of open, unabashed, speculative examination that was
exactly like Jennie's.

"Only Jewish boys?" Billy said as he reached the table in the dining
alcove.

"What only Jewish boys?" Sam said. "That's better. Now for the fun of
it, how about trying a knife and fork?"

Scooping a slice of pickle from the condiment dish as he settled himself back in the chair, Billy said, "Eating ribs with a knife and fork is like
doing algebra with your gloves on. Here, have an olive on me, Pops, and
lay off for a few minutes this trying to turn me into a little gentleman, and
in the time thus left free, you can tell me if this bar mitzvah thing, this
ceremony, only Jewish boys go through it?"

"Other religions have other forms of it," Sam said. "I don't know too
much about it, but I think with Catholics it's called confirmation. To answer your question specifically—no, I like the green ones better, thank you
—yes, only Jewish boys go through the bar mitzvah ceremony."

"Will I go through it?" Billy said.

"No, of course not."

"What's all this firm and positive no, of course not? I'm going to be
thirteen years old on Sunday. Why shouldn't I go through it?"

"Because it requires a lot of preparation," Sam said. "You have to learn
certain prayers, you have to memorize a speech, you have to, oh, I forget
the whole works, but it takes a couple of months to prepare for it, and
Sunday is exactly four days off, so that's how come all this firm and positive
of course not. No, thanks, two olives a day is my limit, and now you mind
telling me what's all this sudden interest in bar mitzvahs?"

"Tommy Sacheverell asked me about it at lunch today," Billy said.

"The novelist's son?"

"Pops, pull your eyebrows down where they belong and let's but knock
off this high screaming tone of surprise. Tommy Sacheverell may be known

as the novelist's son in your circles, but, Pops, in the Porte School he is known as B.B. or Boy Bonehead, the champion stupid of the Lower Eighth."

"That's hardly the way to refer to the offspring of a man who has won two Pulitzer Prizes," said Sam with a severity he did not feel.

"Pops, I am going to let you in on a little secret," Billy said, cramming a gherkin into a mouth already so loaded with meat that Sam was surprised to discover his son was able to utter sounds that emerged as comprehensible words. "The number of Pulitzer Prizes your father has won is absolutely no help with your algebra, and this Tommy Sacheverell but needs help, I'm telling you. He told me about this bar mitzvah stuff at lunch."

"That's interesting, considering that his father was telling *me* just before lunch that he's a Methodist," Sam said. "Did B.B. have any other items of interest to impart?"

"Boy, you're really burned, Pops, aren't you?" Billy said, chewing happily. "Impart yet! Boy! As a matter of fact, this slob was full of information today. He told me why we Jews have different dorks."

Sam jerked his glance toward the kitchen door more rapidly than he would have preferred, and said, "Billy, for Pete's sake."

"Pops, for Pete's sake," Billy said, imitating his father's tone of voice. "Charlene ain't no cotton-picking mammy from the Deep Sooth. That chick's got three legs up on her Ph.D., Pops, and she knows a hell—no! no! I didn't say it!—she knows a *heck*—see? ah's a good boy, ah am!—she knows a heck of a lot more than how to make barbecued spare ribs."

"That's still no reason for using words like that in front of her."

"Words like what? Dork? Pops, it's what we call in English Eight a euphemism. What's wrong with the word dork? You rather I said—?"

"No!"

"Chee-*zuzz!*" Billy said. He took a bite of pickle, stripped the meat from a barbecued spare rib, tamped them down with a wad of garlic bread, worked the accumulation into a manageable mess and, around it, with astonishing clarity, said, "Pops, you don't for one minute think in front of a clean writer like you, the star of *American Bride,* I'd use a word that Mr. Bronson, that jerk, he'd throw me out of class for? Pops, that's why euphemisms were invented. What's wrong with dork? It's just an innocent little sound that everybody who hears it they know what it means, and I figure that's pretty good. I mean a word that conveys what it means and yet it doesn't make everybody start peeing in their jockey shorts, I mean, Pops, it's—"

"I know what you mean," Sam said. "Finish your dinner. Charlene has a class at eight."

"Pops, my stomach and Charlene have got this worked out fine," Billy said. "She's never missed a class yet on account of my eating habits, and she's not going to miss it tonight on account of what Bonehead Boy Sacheverell said about us Jews having different kinds of dorks."

"What did he say?"

"He says ours are different because when we're born we hire a guy with a beard to come around and bite off the end."

"And you believe that?"

Billy stopped chewing. "Pops," he said. "You kidding? That's why I hit him."

"You hit Tommy Sacheverell?"

"Aah, it's nothing, Pops. Everybody hits him all the time. I mean he's so dumb you can't help it."

"I don't mean that," Sam said. "I mean I don't understand the connection. You mean he said this stupid thing about circumcision—"

Billy slapped the table with his palm. "*That's* the word!"

Charlene came in from the kitchen and said, "What's the fight about?"

"No fight," Billy said. "I just remembered a word I been trying to think of since I hit Tommy Sacheverell."

"That's fine," Charlene said. "Then you ought to be ready for dessert."

"Is it—?" Billy said.

"It is," Charlene said.

"Then I'm ready," he said.

Charlene took his plate and went back into the kitchen.

"Straighten me out," Sam said. "Tommy Sacheverell said this stupid thing about circumcision, and you hit him?"

"Sure," Billy said. "Because it wasn't a guy saying something, like if anybody else in my class said it because it was something they just learned, a new fact like. It was a crack. This Sacheverell dope is always making cracks like that. Against Jews, I mean."

"Oh," Sam said. "I didn't know that sort of thing goes on at the Porte School."

"Get with it, Pops," Billy said. "That sort of thing goes on all over the whole wide world."

Sam was accustomed to being astonished by the things he was constantly discovering Billy knew, but even so he was pleased by the diversion Charlene's reappearance created. Some discoveries were just too astonishing.

"What's that?" he said.

"A Silver Special," Charlene said as she set the plate in front of Billy.

"We worked it out together, Charlene and I," the boy said. "My three favorite desserts are lemon meringue pie, chocolate pudding, and watermelon, and so we asked ourselves why not put them all together and make one favorite dessert, and the answer is right here."

"It'll make you sick," Sam said.

"Oh, no, Pops. This is a tested recipe. I've had it every night for a week."

Thus reminded of the time that had elapsed since he had last eaten dinner with his son, Sam covered the small nudge of guilt with a mock serious tone.

"Charlene, if you don't start resisting this kid's blarney, you'll end up in Sing Sing."

She laughed and said, "It looks a little lurid, I admit, but the nutritive value is actually remarkably well balanced and, in view of the bulk, the caloric content is surprisingly low. How was your mother, Mr. Silver?"

"Fine," Sam said, and remembering that Charlene had asked him to convey her greetings to his mother, he said with more warmth than the small lie demanded, "She asked me to give you her best."

"Thank you," Charlene said. "Statistics indicate that nine point four out of every ten persons in the seventy-to-eighty age bracket prefer to have a greeting conveyed in person over receiving it by phone or mail. More milk, Billy?"

"No, thanks." He looked at his wrist watch and said, "You better hit the trail for Morningside Heights."

"Don't you worry about me," she said. "I'll get there."

She went out, and Billy said, "I didn't know you were going out to Grandma's today."

"I didn't know it either until you went off to school," Sam said. "She called up, and I went out after lunch."

"What did she want?"

Sam hesitated and then, because his mind recorded the hesitation, he forced himself into the area he was ashamed to realize he wanted to avoid.

"Oddly enough, pretty much what you want," Sam said. "She wanted to know if you were going to have a bar mitzvah."

"What did you tell her?" Billy said.

"Same thing I told you," Sam said, forcing himself, as a penance for his shame, to refrain from changing the subject. "I told her no."

Billy's frank, appraising glance remained on his father for a few moments. Then, with great care, the boy cut a wedge of watermelon with the side of his fork, placed on it a piece of lemon meringue pie, crowned the structure with a dab of chocolate pudding, and laid down his fork.

"Pops," he said, "when you were thirteen, did you have a bar mitzvah ceremony?"

"Yes," Sam said.

"Then how come I'm not getting one?"

"The situations are different," Sam said. "I had no choice in the matter. My parents were European immigrants, very religious people, I mean religious in the sense that they worked at it. They went to synagogue regularly, and my father said his prayers every morning, and my mother kept a kosher kitchen. Pretty much all the families in our house and even on the block were the same. In that kind of atmosphere, the bar mitzvah ceremony was a perfectly normal thing. When a boy got to be twelve and a half or around that, he was taken to a man, a melamed, a teacher, a rabbi who was paid to teach the boy the correct prayers and his speech and in general get him ready for the bar mitzvah ceremony. That's what they did with me. But you're different."

"How?" Billy said.

"You've been raised in an entirely different kind of atmosphere," Sam said. "Your parents were not religious. You've never been to a synagogue. To put you through the months of preparation for a bar mitzvah ceremony would be a highly artificial business. The thirteen-year-old boy that I was twenty-three years ago on East Tenth Street, and the thirteen-year-old boy that you are today in Sutton Crescent, Billy, they're two entirely different people."

Billy eased the fork under the structure he had built on his plate, conveyed the mess to his mouth, and chewed for a while.

"Bonehead Boy doesn't think so," he said finally.

"What?" Sam said.

"That boob Tommy Sacheverell," Billy said. "With his cracks about Jews. To guys like that, there's no difference to them between you and me, Pops. I mean all that jazz about you were raised in a religious atmosphere and me, I wasn't, so it was all right for you to have a bar mitzvah, but it's all wrong for me to have one, guys like Tommy Sacheverell don't care about that. To those guys, with their cracks, you and I, Pops, they don't see no difference. East Tenth Street or Sutton Crescent, it's the same two slices. We're just a couple of Jews, Pops."

For several moments Sam refused to believe Billy had uttered those last few words. Almost sixteen years ago, a week after he and Jennie had been married in Portland, she had said exactly the same thing to Sam across a marble-topped table in the old Lafayette Hotel on University Place.

During the first few days after the police had picked them up in Portland, and Kenyon Poole and his lawyer friend cleared up the mess in

Westport, and Sam and Jennie came back to New York to break the news of their marriage to Mrs. Silver and become caught up in the excitement of a mushrooming best-seller, they had lived in Jennie's apartment on Commerce Street. On the fourth day after the return to New York, coming back to the apartment from a lunch with Ham Farnsworth at which the editor had reported gleefully that the morning mail had brought into the Trafalgar, Singlenight offices reorders for twenty-two hundred copies of *Yours Is the Earth,* Sam suddenly realized that it was not Jennie's apartment.

"Let's get out of here," he said.

"You mean move?" she said.

"Yes," Sam said.

"Where to?" Jennie said.

"Any place," Sam said. "Just so it's out of this place."

Jennie looked around the room, as though seeing it for the first time.

"I've been thinking the same thing," she said. "This dump is hardly the proper setting for the man Lewis Gannett has called the most exciting new talent to appear on the American literary scene since Kenyon Poole."

Sam, who had been following Jennie's glance around the room, turned to look at her in surprise. That was not the reason why he wanted to move. Sam wanted to get out because he couldn't stand sleeping in the same bed Buggo and Jennie had slept in.

"I think maybe Mr. Gannett was being kind to the new boy in the class."

"False modesty will get you nowhere," Jennie said. "Besides, John Chamberlain said pretty much the same thing in the *Times.* Any idea where you think we ought to live?"

Sam had a very good idea, but he didn't dare say it aloud. He had less than three dollars in his pocket, and he was too embarrassed to ask Jennie how much she had left of the sum Ham Farnsworth had given her on the day Buggo was killed.

"I don't particularly care," Sam said. "So long as it's—" He stopped. He couldn't say so long as it's uptown. Not yet. So he said, "So long as it's with you."

The reward for this recovery from a near moment of ineptness was overwhelming: Jennie gave him one of those rare smiles that always moved his heart, and for a while everything was the way he wanted it to be forever, and it did not matter that Buggo Salvemini had once slept in this bed, too.

"Oh, wherever you move it'll be with me all right," Jennie said later. "I'm not letting you slip through my fingers, sonny boy. How about Gramercy Park?"

Sam didn't quite know what to say. All of his life, when he thought of uptown, he had meant something beyond Forty-second Street. On the other hand, Gramercy Park was certainly uptown in relation to East Tenth Street, and perhaps Jennie—whose mind darted down short cuts that were unknown to him, so that when he did arrive at her conclusions it was always to find her already there, waiting impatiently—had arrived at a conclusion now that suggested it would be more fitting to make the journey uptown in stages rather than in a single leap.

"Gramercy Park sounds pretty expensive," Sam said. "What'll we use for money?"

"It's not too expensive for a man who is earning four hundred and forty dollars a day," Jennie said.

"Who's doing that?" Sam said.

"You are," Jennie said. "Didn't Ham Farnsworth tell you at lunch today they had twenty-two hundred reorders in the morning mail? According to your contract you get a straight ten per cent royalty on retail price, and *Yours Is the Earth* sells for two dollars, which means twenty cents a copy multiplied by twenty-two hundred copies, or four hundred and forty bucks into the Silver family till today. Gramercy Park, here we come."

Again Sam looked at her in surprise. She was like a book he had read so often as a child that he thought he knew it by heart and then, on rereading it when he grew up, discovered to his astonishment that he didn't know it nearly so well as he had thought: there was something new on almost every page. He had never known, for example, that Jennie was so quick at figures. In fact, he hadn't known that she was aware of the details of his Trafalgar, Singlenight contract.

"Okay, if you put it that way," Sam said. "Gramercy Park, here we come."

But Gramercy Park didn't seem to be listening very attentively. It turned out that Jennie had made the suggestion because her ex-boss at Mercury Films, the woman who was in charge of the outside readers and shared Jennie's low opinion of Mr. Marshall Umberg, lived in an apartment house on Gramercy Park. Now that Jennie was the wife of the best-selling author of *Yours Is the Earth,* this woman was even more friendly and, after talking to her on the phone, Jennie reported that Mrs. Grimsby would ask if there were any vacancies in her building and let Jennie have all the details. Two days later Mrs. Grimsby reported four vacancies. Two proved to be much too large for Jennie and Sam, who had decided they needed no more than three rooms—a bedroom, a kitchen, and a living room in which, during the day, Sam could work—and a date was set for them to look at the two smaller apartments. They called on Mrs. Grimsby, who gave them a cup of tea, told Sam how much she admired his book, and then took them downstairs to meet Mr. Schnittmann, the superintendent. Mr. Schnittmann, who looked somewhat like pictures Sam had seen of Marshal von Hindenburg, was formal and thorough. He showed Jennie and Sam through the apartments, both of which were attractive, and agreed with them that probably the one on the twelfth floor was preferable since, while the rents were the same, this one had a better view of the park. Mr. Schnittmann said he would ask the rental agent to send Sam the lease for his signature, said good-bye to them, and they went up to thank Mrs. Grimsby, their new neighbor, for her trouble.

"Not at all," she said. "This building is so full of old fuddy-duddies, it will be a pleasure to have an attractive young couple in it. I feel like celebrating."

"So do we," Jennie said. "We were going over to the Lafayette for a drink. Why don't you join us?"

"Oh, I'd love that," Mrs. Grimsby said, and her phone rang. "Excuse me, please."

She went out to answer the phone, and Sam said, "What's the Lafayette?"

"Honestly," Jennie said, "I sometimes wonder where you've been all these years. It's a hotel on University Place. It's a famous literary hangout."

"Oh, that place," said Sam, who had thought the hotel's fame rested on the fact that its owner, Raymond Orteig, had put up the $25,000 prize for the first New York-to-Paris flight that had been won by the man Mrs. Silver called Lindenbergh.

Mrs. Grimsby came back into the room and said, "I wonder if you'd mind going on to the Lafayette and I'll join you there in a little while? Something's just come up that I've got to polish off first?"

"We'll wait for you," Jennie said.

"No, please," Mrs. Grimsby said. "I'd rather you go on ahead."

Sam did not realize, until they were in the street and Jennie flagged one, that they were going on in a taxi.

"It's not far," he said. "We could walk it in a few minutes."

"We could also carry each other piggyback," Jennie said as she climbed into the cab. "Successful novelists and their wives do neither. Take us to the Lafayette, driver, please."

"Jennie," Sam said as he dropped onto the seat beside her. "I'm worried about money."

"I know you are," Jennie said. "That's why I called up Ham Farnsworth this morning. Don't look like that. I'm your wife. It's my job to take off your

shoulders all the business and other details that interfere with your performance of the creative act."

"Oh, come *on*," Sam said.

Jennie laughed and said, "The last synopsis Mrs. Grimsby gave me to
do at Mercury before dear little Marshall Umberg gave me the ax was a
Kathleen Norris serial for *Collier's*. It was about a dreamy architect with
visions of building the perfect city who marries a beautiful but calculating
bitch whose secret attitude is screw this perfect-city stuff, what I want is
pearls as big as walnuts to wear when I'm invited to dinner by Mrs. Cor-
nelius Dressylhuys the Fourth, and at the end of the first installment, she
says that thing to him, the line I just quoted, word for word: 'I'm your
wife. It's my job to take off your shoulders all the business and other details that interfere with your performance of the creative act.'"

"Does she say it to him in a taxi?" Sam said.

Jennie gave him a sharp look, apparently saw from his face that Sam
was joking, and rewarded him with one of those smiles.

"Idiot," she said, pushing him away. "We're in a taxi."

"Who cares?"

"I do," Jennie said. "It's too short a ride. Besides, I want to tell you what
Ham Farnsworth said."

"Do you have to?"

"Yes, because it's about that thing you worry about," Jennie said.
"Money."

"How'd you ever get him off cheese and wine?"

"Look, I thought we'd come to an agreement about Ham Farnsworth
and the nasty things he said to you about me?"

"Your telling me I should forget it doesn't add up to my idea of an agreement," Sam said. "A guy can't forget what a bastard like that says about
his wife."

"I was not your wife when he said it," Jennie said. "And he may be a
bastard, but he's also your booster and rooter at Trafalgar, Singlenight,
and in that firm the boosters and rooters don't come any bigger. What is
happening to *Yours Is the Earth*, in the purely financial sense, is largely
due to the fact that Ham Farnsworth, who is practically psychotic on the
subject of being a Jew, used you as a club to beat his gentile bosses over
the head. At those prices, I say let him continue beating them, and I'm
not going to let you stop the lucrative process by tying yourself up in a
bunch of chivalrous knots over a few stupid remarks he made about me.
All men, when they're alone together, talk that kind of locker-room talk
about women, and you know it."

Surprised, Sam said, "Yes, but how do you know it?"

Jennie gave him one of those looks that reminded him of the new things he kept discovering on every page of a book he had known, or thought he had known, since childhood, and she said, "There are more things in heaven and earth, Sammy dear."

"If you'll agree to lay off Shakespeare," Sam said, "I'll agree to lay off Ham Farnsworth."

"You don't know what you're missing," Jennie said. "But I'm told all you geniuses are like that, so I'll make the deal."

"It isn't that I don't like Shakespeare," Sam said. "Or don't agree with you that he's great. It's just he doesn't talk my language."

"Thank God for that," Jennie said.

"If I did," Sam said, "we wouldn't be able to afford an apartment on Gramercy Park."

"I'm not so sure about that," Jennie said. "There are more productions of *Hamlet* and *Macbeth* being done right now in all parts of the world than copies of *Yours Is the Earth* are being sold."

"Maybe so, but they wouldn't pay your hero's rent," Sam said. "Mr. Shakespeare is in the public domain, and is earning no royalties."

"But you are," Jennie said. "Which is why you can stop worrying about money. Ham Farnsworth told me on the phone today you earned back your two-hundred-and-fifty-dollar advance and more on the day of publication, and everything that's happening now is on the gravy side of the ledger. Ham asked me how long you think it will take to finish the new book, and I said about six months. Is that right?"

"Just about," said Sam, who had not yet even thought of an idea for a new book but was ashamed to reveal this upsetting fact even to Jennie.

"Well, Ham said not to rush, because at the rate *YITE* is going—"

"Yite?"

"*Yours Is the Earth,*" Jennie said. "Wye, eye, tee, ee—yite."

"I like my title better," Sam said.

"It slows down conversation," Jennie said. "Ham said at the rate *YITE* is going, you'll be on the best-seller list for at least six months, possibly more, and it would be a mistake to put another Silver into the bookstores for at least a year after the excitement of the first one has died down, so he says you should figure you've got a full year for the actual writing. He didn't want to make any predictions about the number of copies *YITE* would finally sell, and while it's holding up beautifully and even building, which is the important thing, we must remember that twenty-two-hundred-copies days are a rarity, the sign of a book's initial excitement rather than its long-range capacities. The thing to do, he said, is to provide you with a comfortable income, so you don't worry about money while working on the second book, and yet at the same time not use up your accumulated royalties, so that when you finish the second book, there will still be a nice balance due you on the first to keep you from worrying about money between the time you finish that second book and the time it gets published, a period during which you can be working out leisurely the plan for your third book. What's the matter? Doesn't this make sense to you?"

"Yes," Sam said. "Oh, yes. A great deal of sense."

What he didn't say, what had obviously brought to his face the look of guilt Jennie had noticed, was the realization that his mother, who knew nothing about publishing and had never read a book in her life but knew thoroughly the man who had written *Yours Is the Earth*, had worked all this out for him on the night when, by telling her of his marriage to Jennie, he had relieved her of her command.

"Ham asked me a few personal questions about our expenses and our way of life," Jennie said. "I told him we didn't have any yet, but we were going to look at this apartment on Gramercy Park today, and after I told him the rent and we discussed the other elements of running a household, we decided that if Trafalgar, Singlenight paid you one hundred dollars a week for the next year, we could live very comfortably, you would use up only a portion of your accumulated royalties, and thus, after you finished the second book, there would still be a nice fat balance in the royalty account to keep us going until the second book was published and you were well into your third."

"Okay," Sam said, wishing he could stop thinking of his mother. She had made it sound so much more personal. "That's fine."

"Yes, I guess it is," Jennie said. "Except for one thing."

"What's that?"

"Your mother."

Annoyed, and ashamed of his annoyance, Sam said, "Can't we keep her out of this?"

"I don't see how," Jennie said. "She's part of our financial picture."

"If your parents were alive, so would they be."

"Yes, Sammy dear, but they're not, so there's no point in hitting me with that tone of voice."

"I'm not hitting you with anything," Sam said. "I just think it's kind of mean to imply that my mother is going to be a drain on us."

"Isn't she?" Jennie said.

"Of course not."

"You mean you're not going to help her financially any more?"

"I didn't say that."

"Then you mean you *are* going to continue helping her financially?"

"Do you have any objections?"

"Not until I know the figures," Jennie said.

"I haven't thought about the figures," Sam said. "In fact, I haven't thought about this whole damn conversation."

"Then it's lucky one of us did," Jennie said. "How much financial help have you been giving her up to now?"

"What's all this crap about financial help?" Sam said. "You make it sound like a board of directors meeting. She's my mother. She raised me and fed me and clothed me on whatever my father earned, which was never much, and as soon as I started earning, why the hell shouldn't I kick in, too? I was living there, wasn't I? I was eating her food, wasn't I?"

"You're not living there any more," Jennie said. "You're eating your own food now."

"So I should be a son of a bitch like some other people I could mention and turn my back on her?"

"Most men don't call their wives a son of a bitch until the honeymoon is over," Jennie said. "But I suppose ours is a special case. We had our honeymoon before we got married."

"Would you mind telling me what the hell we're fighting about?"

"As nearly as I can make out, we're fighting about the fact that I neglected my parents, who were two worthless drunks now happily dead, whereas yours never touched a drop and are very much alive."

"And as long as they're alive," Sam said, "I'm going to share whatever I have with them."

"Good," Jennie said. "And now, if you'll just tell me the extent to which you plan to share with them, we can wrap this one up and put it in the memory book under Our First Quarrel."

"I've just told you I don't know the extent."

"Maybe I can help," Jennie said. "How much were you giving your mother each week until you became the most exciting new American talent to hit the American literary scene since Kenyon Poole?"

"Oh, for Christ's sake, what a comparison," Sam said. "I was a delivery boy shlepping tuxedos around town for twelve bucks a week and I gave Mom half."

"Having set so generous a precedent," Jennie said, "I can see where turning your back on it would not only be bad publicity but would at once be attributed to the machinations of the bitch you married. How would it be if from now on, instead of the six dollars a week which you were giving her out of your salary from Mr. Brunschweig, you were to give your mother ten dollars a week out of the hundred-dollar check you will be getting from Trafalgar, Singlenight?"

"How many ropes of those pearls big as walnuts do you think she'll be able to buy on that?" Sam said.

"Exactly the same number your wife will be able to buy on what's left," Jennie said. "Now that that's settled, and we seem to have arrived, let's stop giving this cab driver an earful and go get a drink."

They got it in a room that Sam liked at once because the stained marble-topped tables and the wire-backed chairs reminded him of Mr. Zwilling's ice cream parlor on Avenue A, where, on several occasions when they were coming home from meetings of Miss Mercator's Stratford Club in Grover Cleveland High, Sam had bought Jennie an egg cream. He stopped liking the room very soon after they sat down because, out of a noisy group at a table near the window, Sam saw Keeley Cuff rise and approach him and Jennie. In the few confused moments before the skinny little managing editor of *Landscape* reached them, Sam wondered why, since he had thought up to now he liked the man in the horn-rimmed glasses and the brown tweed coat, he should find his approach unsettling, and then he remembered. So, apparently, did Keeley Cuff.

"How about lunch sometime?" he said with unmistakable sarcasm.

"I'm sorry," Sam said. "I've been busy as hell."

"I can imagine," Keeley Cuff said. "When the pressure lets up, how about introducing me to your companion?"

"Oh, I'm sorry," Sam said. "This is my wife. Jennie, Keeley Cuff, the managing editor of *Landscape*."

"How do you do?" Mr. Cuff said, bowing over Jennie's hand. "What's he sorry about? A guy with a book that's selling like Florida real estate and a wife like you should be sorry?"

"Why don't you sit down?" Jennie said. "Jokes, like making love, work better when the participants are not standing up."

Mr. Cuff looked startled, then pleased, and sat down.

"I'm beginning to understand why half the population of Connecticut was battling over you, Miss Broom," he said, and to the waiter, who had appeared with Jennie's rye and Sam's Scotch, the managing editor of *Landscape* said, "Martini, please. Double."

"Look," Sam said, "I really am sorry about lunch."

"Lordy me, don't make a big thing about it," Keeley Cuff said. "Lots of people tell lots of people let's have lunch sometime. It's the oil that keeps the wheels of this town from squeaking."

"Maybe, but I meant it," said Sam, who now hated the idea of lunching with Keeley Cuff. "Let's have lunch sometime."

The skinny man did that funny thing with his shoulders, as though he were hooking them to some fastenings concealed inside his furry tweed jacket, and the smile on his bony face changed.

"My doctor informs me that I must keep my diet on a more regular basis than that," Mr. Cuff said as though he were dictating a note to a slightly deaf secretary. Then, as the smile changed once more, he said to Jennie, "I'm sorry about that story."

"Now you're doing it, too," Jennie said. "But you're in good company. When Gide was a reader for a Paris publishing house, he turned down the first volume of *Remembrance of Things Past*, you know."

Mr. Cuff's eyes behind his thick lenses came together in a puzzled squint, as though he had suddenly realized that the girl to whom he had been talking was not really the girl to whom he had been talking.

Acidly, he said, "I hardly think the size of my error, if indeed it was an error, Miss Broom, will rank with the enormity of Mr. Gide's."

"How would a stupid little snotnose like you know the difference?" Jennie said.

"Hey, now, wait a minute," Sam said. "What the hell is this all about?"

Mr. Cuff's face, which was not built for withering glances, managed to come up with an astonishingly good facsimile of one. "You poor bastard," he said gently to Sam. "You poor, sad, obtuse son of a bitch."

"Go back to your table, Mr. Cuff," Jennie said. "We'll send your drink after you."

"I'll take it with me," Keeley Cuff said, skimming his martini from the tray of the waiter, who had just arrived. "I've learned never to trust the promises of bad writers."

"I asked what this is all about?" Sam said.

"Your wife seems to be under the impression," Keeley Cuff said as he started to walk away from the table, "that the way to become a writer is to sleep with a great many of them."

He was halfway across the room when Sam heard Jennie saying, "Why didn't you hit him?"

"Oh," said Sam and then, as he remembered the scene from books he had read and movies he had seen, he realized Jennie's indignation was justified. What kind of a slob was he, anyway? Dutifully, slipping into the role of the husband whose wife has been insulted, Sam growled, as he started to get up, "The little son of a bitch!"

He didn't get up very far, because Jennie, with a hard poke at the golden square knot tie clasp she had given him as a present on their wedding day in Portland, sent Sam tumbling back into his chair.

"Oh, sit down and stop making an ass of yourself," she said irritably.

Puzzled, Sam said, "But I thought you wanted me to hit him?"

"We'll try it again some day when you're a little faster on your feet," Jennie said, picking up her glass. "Drink your drink, Sir Walter."

Sam drank half of it before he managed to put the pieces of the odd conversation together. "Did he mean you wrote a short story and sent it to *Landscape* and they turned it down?"

"Couldn't we just forget the whole thing?" Jennie said. "It was after I got fired from Mercury and before Ham Farnsworth gave me the job helping him with his cheese book. I didn't have anything to do with myself all day, so I thought I'd take a crack at writing."

The phrase created a tiny island of clearly outlined annoyance in Sam's vaguely shaped confusion. It seemed to equate what he had accomplished in *Yours Is the Earth* with any number of other activities at which Jennie could have taken a crack to prevent herself from becoming bored, such as saving stamps or weaving raffia baskets.

"Have you got a copy?" Sam said. "I'd like to read it."

"No, you wouldn't," Jennie said. "That little vontz was right. It stinks."

"Then why did you act that way with him?" Sam said. "I mean when he said he was sorry he was just being polite, and if you'd let it go, I mean if you'd been polite back and said that's all right or something like that—?"

"Because it wasn't all right," Jennie said.

"But you said yourself the story stinks," Sam said.

"Will you please for God's sake shut up about the God-damn thing?" Jennie snapped, and, even more waspishly, to the waiter who had reappeared, "What do you want?"

"Are you Mrs. Silver?"

"Yes, why?"

"Telephone for you, madam."

Jennie stood up, drained her glass, said to Sam, "Order me another of these," and followed the waiter out to the lobby. While she was gone Sam, after ordering another drink for Jennie, tried to pick apart the threads of his tangled feelings, setting himself to the task as though he were straightening out the feelings of a character in a story he planned to write. He was thoroughly ashamed to discover, by the time Jennie came back, that all he really felt with complete honesty was a sense of relief: his pride, which had been severely jolted by Keeley Cuff's acidulous demonstration of the insincerity of Sam's sincerely issued invitation to lunch, had been set back on its feet. Now, because of the things Cuff had said to Jennie, Sam did not have to lunch with the little bastard.

"Who was it on the phone?" he said when Jennie came back to the table.

"Mrs. Grimsby."

"She can't come?"

"I think she can," Jennie said, picking up her fresh drink. "But she's not going to."

"Why not?"

"She's had a bad shock," Jennie said. She took a sip. "Remember when we were up in her apartment? After we'd looked at ours? We asked her to come out with us for a drink and the phone rang?"

"Yes, what about it?"

"The call was from Mr. Schnittmann."

"Marshal von Hindenburg?" Sam said. "The super who showed us the apartment?"

"That's the boy," Jennie said. "It seems after he showed us the apartment and he told you he'd have the rental agent send along the lease for signature, he'd had some second thoughts."

"What about?" Sam said.

"Your name," Jennie said. "And probably our appearance."

Sam got it, of course. And he got it at once. But facing it took a little more time.

"What about my name?" he said. "And what the hell is wrong with our appearance?"

"If you'd reacted as fast to that little drip Mr. Cuff, you might have hit him before he got all the way over there to the coast of Labrador," Jennie said. "The building is restricted, Sammy dear. Mrs. Grimsby is terribly upset because it seems the silly dope, who has been living in it for eleven years, didn't know it was restricted. If she'd known she never would have subjected us to the embarrassment of telling us there were apartments available and of being scrutinized by that Nazi superintendent, and more of the same, but I'll skip it, because none of it changes the basic fact, which is that we're apparently not going to live on Gramercy Park, dear."

"You mean to say the stupid bastards who own that building don't think a best-selling novelist is good enough to live in their God-damned building?"

"Who happens to be, according to Lewis Gannett and John Chamberlain, the most promising new talent to appear on the American literary scene since Kenyon Poole?"

Sam did not realize, until much later, that he had been blushing as he said angrily, "Yes, okay, why not? They said it, didn't they?"

"Lewis Gannett and John Chamberlain do not run apartment houses," Jennie said. "At least not to my knowledge. You may be a great new American talent to them, and you are undoubtedly a best-selling novelist to the people who make up the lists, but to the people who own Mrs.

Grimsby's restricted apartment house, you're no different from your wife, Sammy dear, to them we're just a couple of Jews."

She polished off the rest of her drink in a single gulp and then, with a calm smile that, even though it infuriated him, Sam could not help admiring, Jennie said, "The motto for today, Sammy dear, is *nil desperandum* or frig it. I'll find another place."

What she found, with the help of Mrs. Grimsby, who was so mortified by what had happened in her own apartment house that she insisted on making the Silvers' problem her own, was the top two floors of a brownstone on Eleventh Street just west of Fifth Avenue. At sixty-five a month Sam had to admit that the four rooms and two baths—which Mrs. Grimsby, with a touch of elegance that made Sam uncomfortable, called a duplex— were a bargain, but he felt his mother had a point when he called on her to explain their new financial arrangement and he gave her his new address.

"For this a person has to go get his picture in the papers and become eppis a shreiber with best-sellers?" Mrs. Silver said. "To move from East Tenth Street to West Eleventh Street?"

"It's not as bad as it sounds," Sam said. "What I mean, Ma, it's not like here on East Tenth Street, tenements and all. It's a nice quiet street, with trees, and Fifth Avenue right there at the bottom gives it a sort of, well"— he had enough sense not to say what Mrs. Grimsby said, namely, that it had a literary atmosphere—"it's got a lot of dignity and charm, Ma."

"Dignity today, charm tomorrow," Mrs. Silver said. "On the way uptown it's still only one block."

"I'm sure you'll change your mind, Ma, when you see it."

"About how far uptown it is, this even Mayor La Guardia he couldn't change his mind, but to go see it, this I can do."

"Jennie wants to get it fixed up first," Sam said. "When she and Mrs. Grimsby have the place in shape, you and Pa come on over and have a look."

"Pa, I don't know. He's busy with the papers. Shloymeh Leib he's trying to bring over from Poland, the third son from his second cousin Berel. The first son, Abe Ostreich with his wife Hannah, them Papa already finished with the papers, so with God giving a little push, maybe they'll be here soon. But me, I'll come. Who is this Mrs. Grimsby?"

"She's a friend of ours who happens to be an interior decorator," Sam said.

"What's an interior decorator?" his mother said.

The truthful answer, the answer Sam would have made if he were putting it into a story where he would have been forced to rely exclusively on his own observation, was, he felt, a trifle peculiar. An interior decorator, that observation indicated, was a plumpish divorcée of about fifty in the middle of whose fleshy face one could see remnants of the girlish, dimpled, simpering charm that had made Mary Miles Minter one of the popular movie stars of Sam's youth, had undoubtedly been responsible for hooking the now vanished Mr. Grimsby and, inevitably, just as responsible for driving him to the hills. An interior decorator did not, Sam was aware, necessarily have to live on Gramercy Park, although that was where this one lived, any more than she had to earn her base pay, so to speak, by working as head of the outside readers for the New York story department of Mercury Films, although that was how Mrs. Grimsby happened to pay for her groceries. But one thing an interior decorator definitely had to have, as Sam knew because Mrs. Grimsby had told him so, and that was what the wearer of the cloth had to have: an inner call.

"I could earn a great deal more money by giving up my job at Mercury and devoting all my time to decorating," she had said when she explained to Sam and Jennie, in the empty apartment on West Eleventh Street, why she was taking on the assignment of seeing to it that the young novelist and his wife would be living in surroundings appropriate to their position in the New York literary world. "But that would be like Nathaniel Hawthorne giving up his job as collector of customs at New Bedford or Anthony Trollope giving up his job with Her Majesty's Postal Service to devote themselves exclusively to their writing. I mean, don't you see, it would convert them from practitioners of an art form, which the artist does when the spirit moves him in his spare time, to crass shopkeepers hawking their wares in the market place, don't you see?"

Sam, who had just given up his job with Mr. Brunschweig so he could devote his entire time to writing, nodded uncomfortably. It had not occurred to him until this moment that he had done something on which Nathaniel Hawthorne and Anthony Trollope would have frowned.

"This way, with my job at Mercury taking care of the crude necessities of life," Mrs. Grimsby had said, "I am free to give my art as the man of God gives his heart, only when he has a true vocation, don't you see, for what I do to a room to make it suitable for its occupant is as much a creative act as what Hawthorne or Trollope or"—the dimples dug deeper into their fleshy surroundings—"or what you do, Mr. Silver, don't you see?"

"Is it expensive?" Sam said.

"Oh, for God's sake," Jennie said.

Mrs. Grimsby managed to look amused as well as pained as she said, "No, no, my dear. Men are the practical sex. They can't help asking these questions. It's their nature, don't you see. Mr. Silver—"

"Call him Sam," Jennie said.

"Oh," Mrs. Grimsby said, "I wouldn't dare."

"Try," Jennie said. "It might stop him from asking silly questions."

"What's silly about asking if something you're going to have to pay for is going to be expensive?" Sam said.

"Would you have asked Da Vinci if the Mona Lisa was going to be expensive?" Jennie said.

"Damn right I would," Sam said. "If I was the guy who was commissioning it and was going to have to pay for it."

Mrs. Grimsby chuckled. "Now, that's very sweet," she said. "Comparing what I'm going to do to the bare walls and floors of this duplex with what Da Vinci did to that once equally bare piece of canvas. Mr. Silver, you have given me the courage not only to begin mixing my colors but also to call you Sam."

"Fine," Sam said. "And if my wife doesn't mind, I'd like to ask again: is it going to be expensive?"

"Mr. Silver," Mrs. Grimsby said.

"You mean Sam," Sam said.

"No, I mean Mr. Silver," Mrs. Grimsby said. "Because I'm talking to the man who asked the question, don't you see, not to the friend I have just made."

"Tell us both," Sam said. "Your friend is just as interested as that crude type who asked the question. Is this Da Vinci job going to be expensive?"

"Mr. Silver and Sam, it won't cost you a penny," Mrs. Grimsby said.

Even Jennie looked surprised, but it was Sam who said, "Come again?"

Mrs. Grimsby laughed. Sam had the feeling that it was lucky for Mary Miles Minter that her career had flourished before sound was added to the American cinema art form.

"My services," Mrs. Grimsby said. "They won't cost you a penny."

"Oh, now, wait," Sam said. "Just because you and Jennie are friends, just because we're *all* friends, I mean, that doesn't mean we want you working for nothing."

"Sam's right," Jennie said.

"You're very sweet, both of you," Mrs. Grimsby said. "You needn't worry. I won't be working for nothing. I will be amply repaid by the satisfaction it will give me to watch you writing your second novel in the proper surroundings."

Sam, suddenly terrified by a vision of Mrs. Grimsby sitting in a corner of the room while he wrestled with his Parker and yellow pad, said, "We feel you should be reimbursed in a more concrete way."

"Oh, I'll get that, too," Mrs. Grimsby said. "It's kind of you to worry, but you needn't, you really needn't. My concrete form of reimbursement, as you put it, Sam, comes not from you but from the dealers who supply my paints, as one might say, if you understand me?"

"No, I don't," Sam said.

Mrs. Grimsby sighed, as though driven into an unpleasant corner from which, in spite of repeated efforts, it was her sad destiny never to escape.

"Suppose you and Jennie were to go to Wanamaker's and buy a chair to put, let us say, there," she said. "And let us say the price of that chair in Wanamaker's is fifty dollars, do you see?"

Sam, who shuddered inwardly at the thought of paying fifty dollars for a chair, could do no more than nod. Jennie, curiously less timid about money matters, said, "Yes?"

"If you bought that chair from Wanamaker's you would pay Wanamaker's the fifty dollars, don't you see?" Mrs. Grimsby said. "But when your apartment is being put together by an artist, you don't buy anything. The artist or decorator does it all. If I decide that a chair should go in that corner, I will not go to Wanamaker's to buy it, don't you see? I will go to the dealer or manufacturer who sells the chair to Wanamaker's and buy it from him for the same price he charges Wanamaker's. Then, when I send you my bill, that chair will appear on it for the same fifty dollars you would have paid Wanamaker's. My compensation of a concrete nature, as you put it, my fee for making of your home a work of art, is the difference between what I pay for the chair at the dealer's and what you pay me, don't you see? In other words, the fee is paid in dribs and drabs by all the dealers on whom I call for the colors I intend to use on my palette, but not by you, and that's why I say my services won't cost you a penny, don't you see?"

"But that chair," Sam said. "I still have to pay for it, don't I?"

Mrs. Grimsby's dimples, digging deep, helped give to the smile she turned on Jennie a look of understanding pity worthy of Edith Cavell facing the firing squad as she said, "Yes, you still have to pay for that chair."

"Well," Sam said, "I guess maybe I better set you straight about our financial picture right at the start, Mrs. Grimsby. We can't afford any fifty-dollar chairs."

"Sam, for heaven's sake, Mrs. Grimsby was just using a figure at random as an example," Jennie said. "Isn't that right, Mrs. Grimsby?"

"Of course," the plump woman said.

It seemed to Sam that her voice lacked conviction, so he said, "Could you give us some idea what this whole thing is going to cost?"

Mrs. Grimsby's hands, which had small dimples on the knuckles that

looked as though they had been placed there to match the dimples in her
cheeks, went out and up in a pretty little gesture of helplessness.

"Who can say?" she said. "At this stage?"

"There's something I can say," Sam said. "At this stage."

"No, you can't," Jennie said. "Mrs. Grimsby and I have discussed this
in detail. She knows our financial picture and she won't do anything to
throw it out of kilter. Now you just go ahead and worry about your new
book, and let me and Mrs. Grimsby worry about decorating the apartment."

Sam, who made an honest effort to keep the worries separated in this
fashion, found that it didn't work out. For one thing, he couldn't think of a
new book to write about, and he was so thoroughly ashamed of this that
he couldn't bring himself to tell either his wife or his editor, so that he
assumed both Jennie and Hampton Farnsworth assumed all the hours
Sam spent in a corner of the unfurnished living room, curled up with a
yellow foolscap pad and his Parker, the new book was growing. For another thing, the decorating process took place right in front of Sam, so that
it was impossible not to worry, as truckmen kept bringing in chairs and
couches and mirrors and draperies, how much each item cost. For a long
time, there didn't seem to be any way of finding out. Mrs. Grimsby, who
appeared at the apartment only early in the morning, before she was due
at her job in the Mercury Films office, during her lunch hour, or late in
the afternoon, when the Mercury offices had closed for the day, was always too rushed to discuss prices; Jennie didn't seem to be interested; and
the bills attached to all the items, which Sam examined furtively, were
not really bills: they looked like bills, and they had on them everything
that all the bills Sam had ever before seen had on them, except one thing:
price. It was as though everybody, including the girls who typed the bills
for what Sam Silver was buying, had entered into a conspiracy to prevent
him from learning how much he would ultimately have to pay for his
purchases. As is the case with most conspiracies, however, there came a
day when one of the conspirators slipped.

It happened shortly before noon, when Jennie had gone off to meet Mrs.
Grimsby at a shop on Third Avenue, where, during the artist's lunch hour
from her bread-and-butter job at Mercury Films, they were going to look
at bedspread fabrics.

Sam had killed the usual half hour rereading his *Yours Is the Earth*
reviews, which he could do only when Jennie was out of the house, and he
had leafed through the novel for another half hour, reading snatches here
and there and wondering wistfully how he had managed to write them
only a little more than a year ago, and he was thinking longingly of how

simple his life had been delivering tuxedos around town for Mr. Brunschweig, when he heard the clump of thick shoes on the stairs, a sound that Sam had come to recognize as the first stage of a heavy delivery: the reconnoitering ascent of a truckman who wants to make sure he has the right place, and somebody is in it to receive his delivery, before he starts carrying things upstairs. Sam put down the Parker and the foolscap pad, on the otherwise top blank page of which, around the words "Chapter One," he had in three hours managed to draw a complicated reproduction of Windsor Castle, and he was at the door, pulling it open, when the knock sounded.

"Silver?"

"Yes," Sam said to the man outside.

"You got a couch coming?"

"I don't know," Sam said. "My wife is out at the moment."

"Don't you know if you got a couch coming?"

"We divide up the work in this family," Sam said. "Couch ordering is in my wife's department."

The truckman gave him a funny look. "How about couch receiving, mister?"

"If it's for us," Sam said, "I'll receive it."

The truckman held out a piece of paper and said, "This you?"

Sam looked at the paper and saw that it was almost exactly the same as dozens of others he had seen during the months since Mrs. Grimsby had entered his life.

"Yes, that's us," Sam said, and then he saw that this piece of paper differed in one important respect from its far too numerous predecessors: this one, somewhat incredibly, had a price typed in the column at the far right, and it did not strike Sam as at all odd that as the figure sank into his consciousness, he should have in the center of his belly exactly the same feeling that had exploded there when the policeman had put his hand on Sam's arm at the soda fountain up in Portland and told him he was under arrest. By the time Sam succeeded in forcing some control over the area of panic, the truckman had disappeared, unloaded the couch, and, judging by the dual nature of the grunts on the stairs, was bringing it up with the help of an assistant. When they came around the bend of the stairway Sam, watching from the open door, forgot the feeling in his belly. What the two men were carrying, what they brought into the apartment and set down in the living room as Sam backed away, was an unupholstered frame that looked like a section of a children's playground jungle gym made not of steel bars but of wooden slats.

"It's not finished," Sam said.

The first truckman gave him another of those funny looks.

"That's right," he said, holding out the piece of paper. "Sign here, please."

"Where's the rest of it?" Sam said.

"We just make the frames," the man said. "H. E. Russo & Sons. Sign here, please."

"Who makes the rest of it?" Sam said.

"You got a decorator, no?"

"Yes," Sam said.

"She'll tell you," the truckman said. "Sign here, bud, will you?"

Sam signed, and the truckman left, and after a half hour, during which Sam had absolutely no success with his efforts to straighten out his thoughts, the door opened and Jennie came in with Mrs. Grimsby.

"Oh, look!" the decorator squealed. "It's arrived!"

Sam watched and listened while she and Jennie fluttered around the to him offensive-looking object like a couple of maiden aunts around the bassinet of a newly minted niece in an animated cartoon.

"Where's the rest of it?" he said finally.

The two women turned to look at him as though in the chattering intimacy of a female Turkish bath, they had suddenly heard the accents of a male prowler.

"What did you say?" Jennie said.

"This thing," Sam said. "I said where's the rest of it?"

"Oh, Sam," Mrs. Grimsby said through her Mary Miles Minter simper. "It has to be upholstered, don't you see?"

"Sure I see," Sam said. "Any sap can see that the damn thing has to be upholstered. What this particular sap wants to know is where's the upholstery?"

Clearly sensing from his tone of voice that the simper was the wrong weapon, Mrs. Grimsby reached for one with which she was equally skilled: wide-eyed innocence.

"Why, Sam, it's at the upholsterer's," she said.

"Then you've picked it out?" he said.

"But, Sam, of course we've picked it out." She made a gesture toward Jennie, like the star at curtain time beckoning the supporting players to come share in the applause being hurled at her, and said, "You don't think Jennie and I would choose a couch, I mean settle on it definitely, without being just as definite about the material with which it's going to be covered?"

"How much is this material going to cost?" Sam said.

"Sam," Jennie said.

"You stay out of this," Sam said.

"No, I won't," Jennie said. "We settled all this months ago."

"Shut up," Sam said. "I'm talking to Mrs. Grimsby."

"You're talking to me," Jennie said. "And you're not going to do it in that tone of voice."

"Watch me and see," Sam said. "You might learn a few things you obviously haven't found out yet about my tone of voice. Meantime, just shut up." He turned back to Mrs. Grimsby. "All right," Sam said. "How much is this material you've already picked out for this couch going to cost?"

"I don't really know," Mrs. Grimsby said. "It goes by the yard."

"Cut the bull," Sam said. "You know roughly how many yards it takes to cover a couch, and you know probably better than roughly how much this stuff you've picked out costs per yard. Do a little simple multiplication. I'm not going to hold you to it. All I want is a rough figure."

"Well," Mrs. Grimsby said.

"That's not a figure," Sam said.

"I'd say the upholstering job," Mrs. Grimsby said, "material and labor, I'd say it will come to about the same amount as the cost of the frame."

"That's not a figure, either, but it's good enough," Sam said. "According to this bill I signed a little while ago for this frame, it's setting me back one hundred dollars. If the upholstery comes to the same, that means the couch will cost me two hundred dollars. Correct?"

"Yes, and I know exactly what you're going to say," Mrs. Grimsby said. "You're going to say that's a lot of money."

"Close, but no cigar," Sam said. "What I'm going to say is that two hundred dollars is my entire income for two weeks. If I spend that on a couch, I won't have anything with which to buy food or pay my rent. Even an artist like you, Mrs. Grimsby, can see the simple logic of the situation. I can't afford this couch. I don't want it. I won't pay for it. You'd better call these Russo people and tell them to take it back, and call the other people and cancel the order for the upholstery."

Gently, as though she were leading a child out of a tantrum, Mrs. Grimsby said, "Man does not live by bread alone, Mr. Silver."

"Maybe not," Sam said. "But just plain bread and two-hundred-dollar couches are not this man's idea of the right combination. There must be something less expensive a man in my income bracket can sit on."

Mrs. Grimsby's dimples helped arrange her other features in a picture of sweet reason. "Yes," she said, "but would you sit as happily?"

"I've been sitting in various places and on various things for twenty-one years," Sam said. "The part of me that does it hasn't complained yet."

"There's no need to be vulgar," Jennie said.

"I told you to shut up," Sam said.

"Mr. Silver, look at it this way," Mrs. Grimsby said. "Two hundred dollars for a couch is a lot of money, I admit. But once you've paid for it, it's *behind* you."

"What?" Sam said.

"It's *behind* you," Mrs. Grimsby said. "That particular expense will never again face you in the future. Because you've bought something so good that you will never have to replace it. Whereas if you buy a cheap couch, it isn't behind you at all, because sooner or later, and in all probability much sooner than later, you will have to face that expense again. This way, by putting the couch behind you—"

"Get out," Sam said.

"What?" Mrs. Grimsby said.

"Get out," Sam said again, and to make sure she would not misunderstand a second time, he took Mrs. Grimsby's arm, marched her to the door, opened it, shoved the plump woman out into the hall, and pulled the door shut. When he turned back, Jennie was standing near the window, smoking a cigarette and looking down into the street. Even in profile he recognized the look on her face. It was the look he had come to know during the ten days of their flight, the look that would appear on her face after one of those question-and-answer sessions about how he wrote, the sessions that were so obviously unsatisfactory to Jennie and yet left Sam with the puzzling sense of superiority he found so embarrassingly satisfying: she had left him; she had disappeared into the brooding silence where he could not follow her, an inner place where she either licked her wounds or regrouped her forces. This time the sense of superiority made Sam feel guilty, because this time he knew what it was he had deprived her of.

"I'm sorry," he said.

"Oh, balls," Jennie said.

"Not for throwing her out," Sam said. "I'm sorry I had to tell you to shut up in front of her."

"Same old Sammy," she said. "Mama's little gentleman."

"I was on top of it, and I wanted to stay on top of it, and I was afraid if I got deflected into an argument with you, I'd lose control of it, and she'd talk me into more of this junk, so I had to get you out of it fast."

"You said shut up. People say it all the time. You don't have to make a megilla out of it like Burke's speech in defense of the colonies."

"All I'm saying is I'm sorry."

"All right, you're sorry," Jennie said with an impatient gesture that knocked the ash from her cigarette. It hit the floor like a small splash of spilled cream. "What the hell has that got to do with the price of Indian nuts?"

"It isn't that I don't want you to have a two-hundred-dollar couch," Sam said. "If I had the money, you could have a dozen of them. But I don't have the money. We're living on a weekly allowance from my publisher. Even without buying *any* kind of furniture, after I give my mother ten, and we deduct Sargent & Sargent's ten for commission, and we take off one quarter of the sixty-five monthly rent bill or sixteen and a quarter rent for each week, we've got exactly sixty-three dollars and seventy-five cents to live on each week. Two grown-up people. Sixty-three seventy-five for two grown-up people to buy their clothes and pay for their meals and their drinks at places like the Lafayette. It's impossible. You know that. We've never made it yet. Comes Saturday and Sunday we're always so broke we race each other down to the mailbox Monday morning to make sure the Sargent & Sargent envelope is there with the Trafalgar, Single-night check. On top of that, to have a dimpled, satchel-assed crook like that Mrs. Grimsby running up for us a decorator's bill the size of which, just guessing at it, it gives me the willies, it's insane, that's what it is, just plain crazy."

Jennie drew deeply on her cigarette as she watched him in silence for a while.

"You mind telling me something?" she said finally.

"Of course not," Sam said.

"Why the hell do you want to be a writer?"

Sam, having his usual difficulty following her mind along the twists and turns of its labyrinth of private short cuts, said, "I don't understand your question."

"Anybody with your intelligence, your industry, your appearance, the whole damn kit of clean-cut American boy virtues that get the hero the girl and the job in the bank in those shitty *American Bride* stories," Jennie said. "With all those things, which you have up to here, if you applied yourself to some business, if you started in a brokerage office or at the bottom in a firm that manufactures widgets, or even if you went into the grocery business and sold salami, for God's sake, *anything* like that, you'd make a fortune in no time. Why, since you never seem to worry about anything except money, why do you choose of all the ways to earn your living the one line of work where earning a living is probably its most precarious feature? Tell me, I want to know, why the hell do you want to be a writer?"

"I don't want to be," Sam said.

The answer, which after he had made it took him as much by surprise as it obviously took Jennie, caused her to say slowly, "You don't want to be a writer?"

Skimming away the surprise, examining the reply without embellishments or distortions, Sam saw that it was absolutely true. "No," he said.

"Then why are you?" Jennie said.

Trying for an honest answer, Sam in his mind ran swiftly through the pleasant aspects of the profession into which he had stumbled: the odd thrill of opening that copy of *Landscape* and for the first time seeing his name in print; the surprise of that first ten-dollar check; his picture in the papers alongside the reviews of *Yours Is the Earth;* the words Lewis Gannett and John Chamberlain had used about him; even the unexpected envy of people like Keeley Cuff. It was quite a roster, and yet it was as nothing by comparison with the secret anguish of the past months during which he had been unable to write a word.

"I don't know," Sam said.

Slowly, Jennie said, "You don't know why you want to be a writer?"

"That's right," Sam said, but of course he did know. Into his mind came a picture of that hot summer night two years ago when, unaware of what he was doing, he had worked his way out of the sobbing despair into which he had collapsed in the dark of Mr. Brunschweig's store, by setting down on paper the account of the graduation-night disaster that *Landscape* later published as "The Ways of Men Must Sever."

"But that's ridiculous," Jennie said irritably, reminding Sam of the way she used to sound at the end of one of their discussions during their flight in Hampton Farnsworth's car when he could not tell her what she wanted to know about the writing process. "People know why they want to be what they are," she said. "You *must* know why, out of all the things you could have been, you chose to be a writer."

"I didn't choose it," Sam said. "It just happened."

"Like getting hit by a truck?"

There was no mistaking the sarcasm in Jennie's voice. Neither, however, was there any overlooking the basic truth imbedded in her contemptuous remark.

"Exactly," Sam said. "I had nothing to do with it," he said. "It just happened. I couldn't help myself." He paused, measured his words, decided they were absolutely true, and said, "I still can't."

"You mean if you could help yourself," Jennie said slowly, "you *would* do something else? Like manufacture widgets? Or sell salami?"

Sam thought about that for several moments, translating the manufacture of widgets and the sale of salami into this morning's and the last couple of hundred preceding mornings' wistful yearning for the uncomplicated days of tuxedo-shlepping for Mr. Brunschweig, and he saw something he had never grasped before: his own wishes no longer counted; it was a one-way street; there was no turning back; he was, in an awful word, doomed.

"I might if I could," he said. "But I *can't* help myself."

With an angry gesture, as though it was responsible for leading her to these stupidly unrevealing answers he was giving her, Jennie flung the cigarette out into West Eleventh Street and said, "Why did you marry me?"

Wearily, but with relief, because her darting mind had led him back to an area he understood, Sam said, "Because I can't keep my hands off you, and I want to be with you all the time, and when I'm not with you, that's all I think about, being with you." The answer did not seem to satisfy her any more than his other answers had, so he said, "Why did *you* marry *me?*"

Sullenly, looking out into the street as she spoke, Jennie said, "Because I thought—because I want—" But she couldn't seem to say what she thought or what she wanted.

"Go on," Sam said. "Tell me."

She lit another cigarette, making a small, deliberate ceremony out of it, as though she wanted as much time as she could get to gather her strength.

"Because you have talent," Jennie said. "And I wanted to be a part of it. I wanted to make the frame that would show off your talent to the rest of the world. That's why I've let Mrs. Grimsby go ahead and that's why I haven't worried about how we're going to pay for it. With what you've got, in the proper setting, this apartment fixed up the right way, so I can have the right people coming into it, the money would take care of itself. You're bound to make pots of it. And at the same time, I'd be part of it. Everybody would know it's me that made the setting for you. In that way I thought what I wanted would—"

Her voice, muffled against his chest, became a sobbing, incomprehensible mumble, because he was holding her close and they were staggering across the uncarpeted floor to the bedroom, and for a while it was as it had always been, and as he wanted it to be forever, except that this time Sam was aware of a sense of impatience. He wanted to be finished with the business of lovemaking so he could get to work. After all these shameful months of inactivity, he had at last got the idea for his new novel.

Blocking it out took longer than it had taken him to plan *Yours Is the Earth.* This time he did not have as a guide a short story that had contained the original idea for that first book, or the movie treatment he had prepared for Jennie that contained a series of expanded multiple-choice

scenes from which he could select what he wanted for the novel. But
Sam did not care. He had the whole thing in his head and, besides, he
found it so exciting to be working again that he didn't mind the time.

In fact, he didn't mind anything, not even the reappearance of Mrs.
Grimsby, dropping swatches and rug samples and dimpled apologies for
disturbing him. When he got to the actual writing, and he found that
what she and Jennie were doing to the apartment *was* beginning to disturb
him, Sam carried his yellow foolscap pad and his Parker across to East
Tenth Street and worked at his mother's kitchen table. He worked so well
that he was only vaguely aware of what was going on around him, and it
came as a surprise when, on returning to West Eleventh Street late one
afternoon after an all-day session in his mother's kitchen with the pad and
the Parker, Jennie announced that she was ready for her first party.

"Who's giving it?" Sam said.

"We are," Jennie said.

"We're giving a party?"

"A week from Tuesday," Jennie said. "Cocktails and buffet."

"Why?"

"Look around you."

Sam did and saw, to his considerable astonishment, that there was more
to Mrs. Grimsby than the dimpled remnants of a Mary Miles Minter
charm: she had converted the bare, high-ceilinged room into something so
attractive that Sam found it difficult for a while to grasp that this was
his own home.

"Nice, no?" Jennie said.

"My God, yes. How—?"

"Don't you dare," Jennie said. "One word out of you about how much
it cost, and I'll punch you right in the nose."

"Well, all right, but it's going to have to be paid for."

"When this party is behind us, and I have a little more time, remind
me to teach you a little trick about crossing bridges only once, when you
get to them. Right now I'm making up my list. Anybody special you want
to have?"

"I don't know," Sam said. "My mother and father, I guess."

"Not at this party," Jennie said.

"Why not?"

"Sam, for God's sake, can't you just see the picture of them in the same
room with Ham Farnsworth and Sophie Sargent?"

Sam, who could suddenly see the picture all too clearly, said, "I guess
maybe then you better do it your way."

Jennie's way, he found a week from Tuesday, was almost exactly the same as Sophie Sargent's way. The brownstone on West Eleventh was different, of course, from the duplex at Sixty-first and Fifth; and there was no similarity between Mrs. Grimsby's muted blending of monk's cloth with French provincial, and the wild splendor of Sophie's crossing the armoire from *Desire Under the Elms* with the mahogany whatnot from *Paris Bound*. But the people standing around with drinks in his home seemed to Sam to be the same people he had seen standing around with drinks in Claude and Sophie Sargent's home, and the sounds they were making were identical.

Sam was wondering, for example, where Jennie had found the skinny Englishwoman with the choker of amber beads who was clearly not Lady Kirriemuir and yet just as clearly was saying, "Yew Ameddicans dewn't knew the meaning of the wudd texes, you really dewn't, you knew." Or the man in the green corduroy jacket who was obviously not Kenyon Poole but, with alcoholic precision, was saying, "There's only one way to beat the tax rap, and that's throw your money ahead, and even then, what the hell good does it do you if the money you threw ahead in 1935, now comes 1936 and you have yourself a good year, that frigging money you threw ahead, it comes along and hits you in the ass now in 1936?"

It was exactly the same and yet it was different, because between the large areas of similarity, there were small islands of surprise, which Sam supposed was why people continued going to parties, like the homely girl with the shy smile and the buck teeth who looked like the frightened woman at the "out" desk in the Hamilton Fish Park Branch of the public library, until Sam, who had to strain to catch her gentle, hesitant voice, realized she was saying to him, "I've screwed short-story writers and biographers, and I've screwed radio writers and poets, blank verse as well as the ones that rhyme, and I've screwed playwrights and novelists with long strings of books to their credit, but I've never screwed a first novelist, Mr. Silver." Or the tall, thin, saintly-looking man, with a gaunt face that could have been borrowed from an El Greco and a large Star of David stickpin in his tie that matched his bottle-cap-size Star of David cuff links, who talked to Sam for twenty minutes about Zionism before he said, "I liked your novel very much, Mr. Silver."

"Thank you."

"I understand from your wife that you're working on a new one?"

"Yes, sir."

"Mind saying what it's about?"

"Well—" Sam said.

"Good," the man said. "That means you'll finish it. Writers who enjoy talking about their work rarely do. How far along are you?"

"I'm on the last quarter."

"When it's finished, you mind if I have a look? I like to serialize the new young people while they're still full of piss and vinegar, before they lose their anger and decide the only place to get a decent sunburn is Cap d'Antibes."

"I'm awfully sorry," Sam said. "I don't think I caught your name?"

"Wilson Bienstock," the man said. "But my friends call me Bud."

"Glad to meet you, Mr. Bienstock."

"My pleasure," the editor said. "I'd like to see you in the pages of *American Bride.* I've had them all when they were at the top of their form, from Kenyon Poole up, and I think anybody who could write something as good as *Yours Is the Earth* belongs there, too."

"Thank you, sir."

"Bud's the name."

"Yes, sir," Sam said. "I mean Bud."

One of the Star of David cuff links came zooming toward Sam as the gaunt man thrust out his hand.

"Giving a little U.J.A. cocktail party at my house next week," he said as Sam took his hand. "Be nice if you and Mrs. Silver could make it."

"I'll ask her."

"This isn't a collection thing," Bud Bienstock said. "The bite won't be put on anybody. It's just Jekuthiel Newman is back from Palestine, and before he goes out on his regular Zionist lecture tour, I'd like my friends to hear some of the rabbi's firsthand observations."

"We'll be there," Sam said.

"I'll have my secretary call Mrs. Silver in the morning to give her the address and the time. Bright girl you've got yourself there, young man. Don't forget next week."

"Oh, no," Sam said. "I won't."

But he did forget. The next morning, from the Silver mailbox, Sam pulled an envelope with Mrs. Grimsby's name printed in the upper left-hand corner. He thought this odd, since the decorator had been a guest at the party the night before, and whatever she had to communicate to her hostess, it seemed to Sam she could have done verbally. Then he saw that the envelope was addressed not to Mrs. Grimsby's hostess but to her host, and Sam, tearing it open, smelled trouble.

Dearest Sam—*he read*— Only twenty minutes have passed since I left your lovely party and, while the warm glow of your hospitality still suffuses me, I feel I must set down these words of gratitude, set them down and carry them at once to the mailbox, so that you will know, first thing in the morning, how one of your guests feels about the special magic you and your enchanting Jennie created for her tonight. But will you know? Will my awkward words convey even a fragment of the loveliness I have carried away with me from your home? How I wish I had a smidgen of your glorious talent, a mere pinch of the genius from your overflowing cornucopia, so that I might do justice to the emotions by which I am overwhelmed and for which you and your lovely bride are responsible. She is indeed a *mignon*, as are you, my dearest Sam, and together you form the most cherished couple it has ever been the privilege of these weary eyes to behold. I cannot thank you enough for the pleasure not only of this night but for the rare privilege it has been to know you during the past year, but I can, like most of us poor hewers of wood and drawers of water, who are untouched by the glory that is part of the daily lives of the movers and shakers like you and Jennie, I can be greedy, and I know you will be charitable to a poor fellow artist whose greed takes the form of hugging to herself the knowledge that, by helping you create the frame of your lovely home, she has contributed her tiny mite toward the glorious picture that is you and Jennie and that went on view tonight for all the world to see.

Yours always,
Alison Grimsby

P.S. The dealers are becoming a bit importunate, and so I enclose herewith a bill covering the materials and labor employed in the creation of your home. An immediate check to cover will be appreciated by A.G.

Sam stared at the bill for a long time in a manner probably not unlike the way Balboa had stared at the Pacific for the first time: he had never before seen such a thing. Unlike Balboa, however, in whom the astounding sight is reported to have aroused a sense of humble gratitude to God for having granted him the privilege of making so extraordinary a discovery in the name of his sovereign, the sight of Mrs. Grimsby's bill aroused in Sam, aside from vague adumbrations of terror, like the stealthy tramp of enemy soldiers heard in the distance from the side of a lonely campfire late at night, the conviction that the decorator had made a mistake: the figure on the bill after the word *Total* was $2,840.35.

"No," Jennie said after she had read the letter, examined the bill, and listened to Sam's hopeful observation. "That's about right. She may have padded it a little here and there, most decorators do, but I've been keeping track in my mind of the larger items as we've been choosing them, and I figured it would come to around two or three thousand."

"You mean you *knew?*" Sam said. "All these months she's been dancing around here and dropping that talk all over the place, you *knew* she was running us up a three-thousand-dollar bill?"

"What did *you* think she was doing?" Jennie said. "Giving you a present because she admires your talent? Things cost money. If you buy them, you have to pay for them."

"But you buy what you can afford," Sam said. "Not what you want."

"Look around you," Jennie said. "If we'd bought what we can afford, would this place look the way it looks now?"

Sam looked around. The room that only a week ago had seemed so lovely, and in which only the night before he had taken such pride, he now found embarrassing. He felt like a thief. It was as though he had been found out after stealing a manuscript by someone like, say, Kenyon Poole, and publishing it under his own name.

"But I don't want it to look the way it looks now if I haven't got the money to make it look the way it looks now," Sam said. "What's wrong with living in a place that looks the way the amount of money you do have can make it look?"

"People who live in places that look like they can afford them never get to live in places that look the way they some day want to live," Jennie said. "What's wrong with living in a place that looks like what you and I can afford at the moment is that you don't get people like Bud Bienstock to come visit you if your house looks like a B.M.T. washroom."

"You mean you did all this, you ran us into debt for three thousand bucks, so you'd have a proper setting in which to invite Bud Bienstock?"

"Among others," Jennie said.

"Screw the others," Sam said. "Let's stick to Bud Bienstock. He's the editor of a crappy women's magazine full of popover recipes and articles about Menstruation Can Be Fun, in which an honest writer of fiction that has any resemblance to real life wouldn't be found dead."

"But Bienstock serialized *The Small Meal* in *American Bride*," Jennie said. "For I understand forty thousand American dollars."

"Because it has absolutely nothing to do with Jews," Sam said. "My work, which I assume you've read, does."

"There hasn't been so much of it that reading through it is exactly an onerous chore," Jennie said.

"Let's not get nasty," Sam said. "It's too early in the morning for that crap."

"It's too early for stupidity, too," Jennie said. "You're accusing of anti-

Semitism a man who happens to be one of the leading Zionists in this country."

"Only in his spare time and on his haberdashery," Sam said. "Mr. Wilson My Friends Call Me Bud Bienstock wears the Star of David in his necktie, but in his magazine it's about as welcome as Chaim Weizmann would be on Hitler's staff of personal advisers. And you don't know a God-damn thing about my work," Sam said. "If you did, you wouldn't spend three thousand dollars that we haven't got in exchange for an invitation to drink two-bit cocktails and hear Rabbi Jekuthiel Newman's observations about his latest trip to Palestine, which is the sum total of your great achievement in building this junior Taj Mahal as the proper setting in which to let Bud Bienstock show off his matching stickpin and cuff links."

"You were as dumb as dreck in Grover Cleveland High," Jennie said. "You are as dumb as dreck now and clearly getting dumber, and what I can't get through my head is how, in the middle of such a mountain of turd, there could be hidden that wonderful fragile marvelous thing called talent."

"This isn't exactly the morning for your Sainte-Beuve act," Sam said. "What I'd like you to get through your head now is some idea of how we are going to pay this God-damn bill."

"If you'll just stop screaming and thinking, at both of which you're not very good," Jennie said, "I'll tell you."

"Is there any more coffee?"

"In the kitchen," Jennie said. "Get me a cup, too."

When Sam came back into the living room, Jennie was hanging up the phone.

"Who'd you call?" he said.

"That girl in the Sargent & Sargent bookkeeping department," Jennie said. "The one who typed your manuscript at night."

"Shirley Shaefer?"

"That's the one."

"What did you call her for?"

"You forgot the cream."

When he came back with the cream, Jennie was scowling at the tip of her unlighted cigarette, and Sam said, "I asked what did you call Shirley for?"

"I wanted her to look at your ledger card and tell me how much money Trafalgar, Singlenight has paid you up to now on *Yours Is the Earth*. In addition to your original two-hundred-and-fifty-dollar advance, they have shelled out forty-eight weekly checks of one hundred dollars each,

or a total of forty-eight hundred plus two-fifty, say five thousand dollars
even."

"My God," Sam said. "That's a lot of money."

"Not really," Jennie said. "I mean not in view of the sale *Yours Is the
Earth* must be running up."

"It can't be running very hard any more," Sam said. "In last Sunday's
Times we were in fourteenth place, and we've been there a long time."

Jennie said, "How far along are you in the new book?"

"I'm on the last section."

"What does that mean in terms of time?"

"It's in four sections, of which the two middle ones were very long, but
the first and last, they're sort of the book ends for the story, they're quite
short, so I figure, oh, a few more days, say a week."

"Good," Jennie said.

"Why?" Sam said.

"We can stop this weekly one-hundred-dollar pension plan from Trafalgar, Singlenight," Jennie said. "In another week your new novel will be
finished. That means we're in a position to ask Trafalgar, Singlenight for
an advance on it, and since you're no longer an unknown beginner, but
a best-selling novelist with a damn good track record, that two-hundred-
and-fifty-dollar chicken feed is out. What we want, and what we'll get, is a
nice big fat sum based on the *Yours Is the Earth* sales. In addition, we'll
ask Trafalgar, Singlenight for a final accounting on *Yours Is the Earth.*
Taking off the five thousand they've already paid you, there should be a
nice juicy little lump there, too. Putting those two lumps together, we'll
have enough to pay not only this bill from Mrs. Grimsby, or a good enough
chunk of it to keep her out of our hair, but there will be enough left over
to keep us going comfortably until the new book is published and starts
selling. How does that sound?"

"Pretty good," Sam said.

"It'll sound better after you've showered and shaved. No, cut it out. Not
now, Sam."

"Why the hell not? We're paying two hundred bucks for this couch.
Let's do something more interesting on it than just support Bud Bienstock's
ass."

"The fabric is very fragile and scuffs easily," Jennie said. "Besides,
there's no time."

"The hell there isn't. That's one of the advantages of being a writer.
You make your own hours. And your own wife, ha, ha."

"Stop panting," Jennie said. "You're due in Claude Sargent's office in
half an hour."

"I am?"

"That's what I told Miss Shaefer on the phone and she said she would tell Miss Tischler, so get going."

"What am I going to tell Mr. Sargent?"

Jennie, lighting her cigarette, paused to stare at him across the flame and then, as she shook it out, she said softly, "Oh, no. No. No, no." Then she sighed, struck another match, lit the cigarette and, around the first huge exhalation of smoke, said sweetly, "Oo is dawna tell dwate big agent Claude Sargent what oo just heard from itsy bitsy wife."

"Oh," Sam said, "that."

"Yes, Einstein, that," Jennie said, but she put her hand where he liked to have it as she added, "I told the Shaefer girl to have Mr. Sargent call Ham Farnsworth at Trafalgar, Singlenight and get all the figures on *Yours Is the Earth* before you get there. How's that?"

"More."

"When you come back with the dope," Jennie said. "Right now Claude Sargent is waiting."

He was doing it, Sam noticed uneasily as soon as Miss Tischler showed him through the green curtain, with a completely uncharacteristic scowl.

"Now what sort of damn-fool trouble have you gone and got yourself into?" he said after Sam was settled in the red-leather chair. "Sugar and cream?"

"No, thanks," Sam said. "Just black."

"Getting to act more and more like a writer every day," the fat man grumbled as he shoved the cup toward Sam. "Two years ago, you first walked in here, you never even heard of coffee. Now it's just black, please, and telephone calls at ten o'clock in the morning to find out how much money you can chisel out of your publisher."

"I don't want to chisel anything from anybody," Sam said. "Jennie just thought we ought to find out how we stand with Trafalgar, Singlenight."

"Why?" Claude Sargent said.

"No special reason," Sam said.

"That's what Henry VIII told Anne Boleyn when she asked him why he wanted to give her that close haircut."

"I tell you there's no special reason."

"I hope you're telling the truth."

"Now, why wouldn't I be?"

"Please withdraw the question," Claude Sargent said. "If I were to try to answer it, if I started telling you all the reasons why writers lie to their agents, we'd be here for a week."

"Okay," Sam said. "I withdraw the question."

"You do that just about as fast as you withdraw money from your publisher," Claude Sargent said. He picked up a piece of paper, slipped his glasses on his nose, studied the paper for a few moments, then said, "I called Ham Farnsworth, as instructed, and he said he was glad I'd called because he'd been meaning to call me. Always a bad way to begin a telephone conversation."

"He'd been meaning to call you about me?"

Claude Sargent looked across the rims of his glasses and said, "Sit back, Sam, you're spilling your coffee on the only commission this office ever got out of a show called *Up Pops the Devil.*"

Sam leaned back, wiped the splash of coffee from the red leather between his legs, and said, "Sorry."

"Ham said when they made this arrangement to pay you a hundred dollars a week while you worked on your new novel, they said they'd do it for a year," Claude Sargent said. "Ham said their accounting department put a note on his desk the other day indicating they'd sent you forty-eight of these checks, and the year would be up with four more, in case he wanted to do anything about it."

"Do anything about it?" Sam said. "Like what?"

"Like ask you where's the new book you're supposed to have been working on these past forty-eight weeks," Claude Sargent said.

"What's that got to do with a final accounting on *Yours Is the Earth?*" Sam said.

Claude Sargent took off his glasses, said, "Quite a bit, Sam," then replaced the glasses and stared at the slip of paper as he continued. "The final sales figures on *Yours Is the Earth* show a total sale of a little over fifteen thousand copies. There are a couple thousand more out in the stores, but there have been no reorders for about a month, which is a sure sign that a book has run its course, as I imagine you must know yourself, if only from the way it's dropped on the best-seller list. Sophie showed me the *Times* last Sunday. Fifteenth place."

"Fourteenth," Sam said.

"In those positions, fourteenth is the same as fifteenth," Claude Sargent said. "So is thirteenth."

"I'm just trying to be accurate," Sam said.

"So am I," the fat man said, and he returned to his study of the slip of paper. "The couple of thousand copies out in the stores will probably be returned during the next few months, Ham Farnsworth said, but in a wild outburst of foolish optimism, as he put it, let's assume only half are returned, which means the book will have had a total sale of sixteen thousand copies. At your twenty cents a copy royalty, that means you will have earned thirty-two hundred dollars out of *Yours Is the Earth*. Since they paid you a two-fifty advance, plus forty-eight hundred in weekly hundred-dollar payments, or a total of in round figures five thousand, there is a debit balance in your account at Trafalgar, Singlenight to the tune of five thousand paid less thirty-two hundred earned or eighteen hundred bucks."

Claude Sargent took off his glasses, put down the slip of paper, and leaned back. Sam, who felt his agent expected him to say something, tried to keep his feelings out of his voice as he said, "You mean I owe *them* money?"

"Strictly speaking, yes," Claude Sargent said. "But the last writer who felt himself bound by that kind of strict speaking was, I believe, Thucydides."

"Who?"

"That was a joke, Sam. I take it from the fact that you didn't fall out of my commission from *Up Pops the Devil* with whoops of laughter, that you're not in a joking mood. Let me abandon my own and try for a more serious note. The point, Sam, is, that while the relationship between an author and a publisher is in one sense a business relationship, it is a sense that makes absolutely no sense in terms of any other business. If you were a baker, let us say, not a writer, and you made bread not books, which you turned over to Trafalgar, Singlenight to sell for you on a royalty basis, so much per loaf, and they overpaid you in the form of advances because you were strapped for cash and had to buy flour and yeast with which to make the bread they were going to sell for you, if it turned out they had overpaid you, as I said, because they were unable to sell as many loaves of your bread as you both thought they could sell, why, Sam, since it would be a simple business relationship, the sort that Western man has evolved over the centuries and is recognized in all civilizations beginning with that of the bead-swapping Maori tribesman, yes, you as the baker would owe the overpayment to Trafalgar, Singlenight, and they as your creditors would recover the money without any difficulty by bringing suit in a court of law, and if you did not have the money, the courts would help them throw you into bankruptcy so that they could seize your assets, such as your oven and other baker's tools, sell them, and recover from the proceeds of that sale at least part of the money you owe them. More coffee?"

"No, thanks," Sam said.

"I think you'd better," Claude Sargent said. "You're looking pale."

"No, no," Sam said. "It's just the light."

"Good," Claude Sargent said. "I'm glad it's no more than that. I've had writers faint more than once, right there in that chair, before I've got even this far in what Sophie calls my facts-of-life lecture. Sip your coffee slowly, and if a slight dizziness begins to steal over you, try placing your head between your knees. I had a client once who ghosted first-aid handbooks for insurance companies. He said it was more effective than smelling salts. It must have been. He sat right through this entire talk, including the second part, which is more reassuring. Because you see, Sam, while publishing is a business, and as I said in one sense the relationship between the publisher and the writer is a business relationship, you wouldn't think so from the way either party acts. Take you, for instance."

"Me?" Sam said. "I haven't acted in any way."

"No, but you will," Claude Sargent said. "I've known I don't know how many writers who have taken I don't know how much money from publishers to write I don't know how many books that were never written, but I have never known a writer to return the advance or a publisher to sue a writer for the return of the money. Don't ask me why. The closest I've ever come to a sensible explanation is the writer's insistence that as long as he's alive and can hold a pen or a whiskey glass, there is still a chance that he'll deliver the manuscript, and I suppose the reason no publisher, at least in my experience, has ever filed a claim for the return of an advance against a dead writer's estate, by which time the writer is clearly incapable of holding either a pen or a whiskey glass, is that writers seldom leave estates, and I would be a liar, Sam, if I did not say here and now that it distresses me to find you, who have always struck me as a sensible, solid citizen, following so soon and so quickly in that honorable, or do I mean dishonorable, tradition."

The fat man turned to the percolator on the window sill, refilled his cup, reached across, saw that his guest was not interested in coffee, replaced the percolator, and said quietly, "How much do you owe, Sam?"

Sam didn't answer. He couldn't. Even more quietly, the fat man behind the desk said, "Will a personal loan help, Sam?"

Sam shook his head. Claude Sargent took a noisy sip of coffee, set the cup down, and said, "Then here's something that might. If you've got any of the new book ready, that is. Have you?"

"It's almost finished," Sam said. "I've got only a few more days' work."

The shapeless face rearranged itself swiftly in the extraordinary smile that had shaped Sam's first reaction to Claude Sargent.

"You blithering idiot," the agent said. "Why the hell didn't you say so?"

"What difference does it make?" Sam said. "I still owe them eighteen hundred dollars."

"Not if you've got a good manuscript practically finished," Claude Sargent said and then, after only the faintest hint of hesitation, "Is it good?"

Sam, who had never thought about this before, did so now. "It's better than *Yours Is the Earth*," he said finally.

"Sam, is that true?"

Sam did some more thinking, started to phrase a modest qualification, then remembered the conclusion he had reached at the end of his first meeting with Claude Sargent: he could tell this man the truth.

Sam nodded and, with as little inflection as it was possible for him to release and still utter comprehensible sounds, he repeated: "It's better than *Yours Is the Earth*."

"Then you've got nothing to worry about," Claude Sargent said. "Ham Farnsworth told me if you deliver the new book as promised within the year, meaning within the next four weeks, they'll not only carry over the *Yours Is the Earth* debit balance as an advance on the new book, but they'll add something decent to sweeten the pot and keep your pecker up for the assault on your third book."

An hour later, when Sam told this to Jennie, her reaction puzzled him.

"On this one," she said, "I'll do the typing."

"Why?" Sam said.

"We're strapped for cash. The last one you paid that Shirley Shaefer over a hundred dollars. This one you say is a little longer. Until Ham Farnsworth has another attack of wanting to finish that cheese book of his, which may be never, I probably won't earn a penny for this team. The least I can do is save us the typing expense on your new book."

"I didn't know you could type."

"Lot of things about me you don't know, sonny boy."

Sam wished she hadn't said that, because it was a truth of which he did not like to be reminded, but Jennie was busy keeping the promise she had made before he went off to see Claude Sargent, and in a matter of moments his wishes were completely irrelevant. Later, he got out his manuscript, and after it was established that she could follow his handwriting without any difficulty, he left Jennie at the typewriter in the bedroom and went over to East Tenth Street with his pad and his Parker to finish the last section of the book.

It took him six days. During that time Jennie had a conversation with Mrs. Grimsby that apparently satisfied both of them, and she typed two hundred and forty pages of Sam's manuscript in a manner that compared favorably with Shirley Shaefer's performance.

"You're good enough to run a typing agency of your own," Sam said.

"I'm better than that," Jennie said.

"That was intended as a compliment," Sam said.

"My ambitions run in other directions," Jennie said. "Is this the works?"

"That's the whole thing," Sam said. "In what directions?"

"Some day maybe I'll tell you," Jennie said. "Right now one genius in the family is enough." She riffled through the handwritten pages he had brought home from East Tenth Street. "I've been getting one typed page out of approximately one and a half of these handwritten," she said. "So this last section should come to eighty typed, and I've got almost exactly one hundred more to go on section three, means two-forty plus a hundred is three-forty plus eighty is four-twenty. Just about the same length as *Yours Is the Earth*, which is fine, and at the rate I'm going, about forty pages a day, I can have this finished by Sunday, say Monday at the latest, in case you have any last-minute corrections, so okay, you call Claude Sargent right now and tell him you'll have the thing in his office Tuesday morning."

When Sam set it down on Claude Sargent's desk—in the manuscript paper box on which Jennie had pasted a neatly typed label:

I'll Make My Heaven
A Novel
By
Samuel Silver
(Author of Yours Is the Earth)

—he was suddenly aware of a feeling that puzzled him. For six months he had lived through the agony of sterility. Then, for another six, he had lived with the excitement of creation. The drive to get it out of his head, where he saw it so clearly and it looked so flawless, and onto paper, where only he could see the gap between his accomplishment and his vision, had been as strong and as satisfying as his most intimate moments with Jennie. He had thought, as he walked uptown with the manuscript box under his arm, that he had better make some joke when he put it on Claude Sargent's desk, something to conceal the moment of pride that the older man, whose regard Sam valued, might interpret as conceit. And yet now that the moment had come, Sam could think of nothing to say, least of all a joke, and all he knew about the peculiar way he felt was that it had nothing to do with pride.

"Hurts a little, doesn't it?" Claude Sargent said quietly, and Sam could feel his face grow hot. He had not realized the fat man behind the desk was watching him so closely. He nodded awkwardly, and Claude Sargent said, "You might as well understand something that's going to happen to you again if you keep on writing. It always starts with the second book. The first is easy. You write that not because you're a writer but because you've got to get something out of your system or bust. That's why so many first novels are their authors' best. It's the only book they really had to write because they were possessed. After that they're no longer possessed. After that they're just writers. If they go on to become writers, I mean. Many people don't. They've got just that one thing they had to say. They're possessed just once. Like Emily Brontë, for example. Only once, that first time, you're touched by God. After that, the second time, and no matter how good you are, you're a pro. It's nothing to be ashamed of. His second time out, Shakespeare was a pro, too. But it's something to understand. That Hungarian guy, Molnár, he once made a crack. It got a big laugh, I remember. Still does. But there's a lot of truth in it. He said becoming a writer is like becoming a whore. First you do it for your own pleasure, then you do it for the pleasure of a few friends, and finally you do it for money."

In the sudden silence that filled the room Sam became aware of the bubbling sounds from the percolator. Claude Sargent turned in his chair and snapped off the switch. The bubbling sounds began to subside.

"You mean what I'm feeling now," Sam said, "I feel like a whore?"

"Don't run it down with that tone of voice," Claude Sargent said. "It's called the world's oldest profession."

"I've never heard it called the most honorable."

"Look, Sam," the older man said. "Most writing careers that go off the rails, the guys who start out like Man O' War breaking from the barrier, and they go great guns for a while and then they fade out, it's been my experience, because I've had quite a few like that on my list, the basic trouble, I've found, is a lack of understanding about themselves. They see the rest of the world bright and clear, twenty-twenty vision all the way, which is what makes them writers, but when it comes to seeing themselves, they're as lost as though they were wandering around inside a cow's belly. Writers have more cockeyed notions about themselves than Cinderella's stepsisters had about their physical charms. Very few of them can face the realities about their own personalities. Yet it's probably the most important requirement for a successful literary career. Know thyself, the Good Book says, and that's the only way good books get written." The fat man's hand went out and touched the manuscript box Sam had just placed on his desk. "You didn't write this to be locked away somewhere in an attic with your first pair of baby shoes and the lock of hair your mother saved from your first trip to the barber. You wrote this to be sold. For as much money as I, your hired salesman, can get for you. There's nothing dishonorable about that hard fact. But it is a fact, and it is hard. Hard as anthracite. You'd better learn to look it right square in the face now, because from now on, every book you write, even though they get better and better, as I know they will, I also know none of them will ever have that special amateur quality of the first. You were a virgin when we first met, Sam. Now you're in business."

"I guess you're right," Sam said. "It's just I never thought of it like that."

"It isn't such a dreadful thought as it may seem on meeting up with it for the first time," Claude Sargent said. "Life, like the Constitution, is a system of checks and balances. If you can't have what you want, you'd better want what you have."

He paused, turned the box around, studied the label, and after a pause that was clearly intended to allow time for the dust of his lecture to settle, the fat man said, "What does the title mean?"

"It's from *Richard III*," Sam said. "That part where he tells about his schemes. *I'll deck myself in fine ornaments, I'll make my heaven in a lady's lap*, and so on."

"Oh," Claude Sargent said. "I didn't know you were a Shakespeare buff."

"I'm not, but my wife is," Sam said. "I hear an awful lot of it around my house."

"What does Jennie think of this?"

"She said she'd rather not give me an opinion until she's had a chance to read it again," Sam said. "She did the typing, you see."

"Oh," said Claude Sargent, who clearly did not see at all.

"I mean she got it in bits and pieces," Sam said, aware that the explanation, which had sounded unconvincing when Jennie made it to him, sounded even less convincing when it was repeated. "She's going to let a few days go by, maybe a week, then read it again."

"I won't wait that long," Claude Sargent said. "I'll read it tonight and call you in the morning."

In the morning, however, it was Sophie Sargent who called.

"Claude's sacroiliac is acting up again and he's had to go off to the neck tugger," she said. "But he wanted me to call and tell you he'd finished reading the book, and I'm reading it right now. Sam?"

"Yes," he said. "I'm on."

"I thought we'd been cut off."

"No," Sam said.

"Well, as I said," Sophie Sargent said, "Claude read it but he had to go off to that doctor who pulls his head back into place, so I'm reading it now."

"Fine," said Sam.

"Did you hear what I said, Sam?"

"Yes, I did," said Sam. He could not say he had expected her to say more.

"I'll call you as soon as I finish."

"Fine," said Sam.

"It might not be today," Sophie Sargent said. "I'm having a bit of trouble with stahf, and it looks as though ear-pinning-back time has come round again, but the moment I finish, I'll call you."

Two days later, when Sophie still had not called, Jennie threw her cigarette out into Eleventh Street all the way from her seat on the two-hundred-dollar couch.

"God damn it," she said. "If you won't call, I will."

"No, you won't," Sam said. "More coffee?"

"I don't want any more coffee," Jennie said. "I want to know why the hell neither of those two monkeys has called."

"I don't know why they haven't called," Sam said. "So you'd better have more coffee."

"They must know how anxious you are to hear what they think."

"I'm sure they know."

"Then what right do they have to keep you up in the air this way?"

"They're not doing it to be cruel."

"The hell they're not," Jennie said. "Not him, maybe. He's a great big fat nothing who remembers to blow his nose when she tells him, but her, boy, that's a bitch from Dixie."

"Wilkes-Barre," Sam said. "And you're dead wrong. She may be a bitch about the kind of things women are bitches about, but not about this. She's not calling just to make me squirm."

"You sure are the widest-eyed innocent in town," Jennie said. "How can you possibly say such a thing?"

"Because I know it's true."

"You mean she's got a sneaker for you and she wouldn't hurt the new boy friend?"

"Where do you get these ideas?" Sam said. "Sophie Sargent is twenty years older than I am."

"Ever hear of Elizabeth and Essex? Or Daddy Browning and Peaches Heenan?"

"I've heard as much of this kind of junk as I intend to listen to," Sam said. "Whatever the reason neither Mr. nor Mrs. Sargent has yet called me, I know the delay is for my own good."

"Then why can't you get on the phone and ask them what they're doing for your own good?"

Sam looked at Jennie in puzzlement. There were so many areas in which she was so far ahead of him that it didn't seem possible in this one area, the area of pride, she could be so far behind.

"I just can't," he said.

The phone rang. Jennie snatched it up and said, "Hello? Yes, this is Mrs. Silver. I'll be glad to." She listened for a few moments, then said, "Mr. Farnsworth's office at eleven, right. Thank you."

She hung up, and Sam said, "He want you back on that cheese book?"

"No, he wants you," Jennie said. "That was Miss Tischler. The Sargent & Sargent Miss Tischler. That dear sweet woman from Wilkes-Barre and that darling fat slob to whom she's married, both of whom adore you so much that they'd never do anything to hurt you, apparently they can't find the time to get on the phone and talk to you personally, so they had their switchboard operator do it for them. They've made an appointment for you to see Ham Farnsworth in his office this morning at eleven."

"What about?" Sam said.

"Miss Tischler's confidences did not extend that far," Jennie said. "But in view of your relationship with Trafalgar, Singlenight these past two years, I hardly think he wants to sound you out about going over to Germany as a special correspondent to cover the forthcoming Olympic Games at Garmisch-Partenkirchen. It's obviously about the new book, Einstein, and remember: we're not taking a penny less than five thousand dollars as an advance. Keep your mind fastened to that crucial figure, and I'll get you a clean shirt and socks while you're showering."

What Sam found his mind fastened to, while he was showering, was that uneasy area in which he and Jennie apparently functioned differently: pride. Even if they hated the book, and it seemed to him perfectly obvious from their silence that they did not like it, he felt Claude and Sophie Sargent should have called to tell him so before they sent him to face Ham Farnsworth. Forty minutes later, on his way through the Trafalgar, Singlenight offices on Fourth Avenue to face his editor, Sam was struck by an irrelevant thought that had a salutary effect on his state of mind: the gap between the splendor in which publishing-house employees lived their expense-account lives outside the office, and the squalor of the quarters in which they functioned inside the office.

Ham Farnsworth earned twenty thousand a year, lived in an apartment on Park Avenue, spent his week-ends in a twenty-thousand-dollar log cabin on the Aspetuck, and ordered snails and vintage wines at the Murray Hill with all the careless grace of a man who knows the waiters are aware the bill as well as the lavish tip will be paid by a highly solvent corporation. The room in the Trafalgar, Singlenight offices where Farnsworth performed his duties as the firm's editor-in-chief, however, made Mrs. Silver's East Tenth Street kitchen look like the Petite Trianon. The room was so small that it also made Ham Farnsworth, with his toy-soldier's face and brown busby haircut, look as though the child to whom he belonged had shut him up for the night in the wrong box: what was a toy soldier doing in a room decorated with a huge picture of Brillat-Savarin and a framed copy of the menu distributed to the guests at the dinner served after the wedding of Victoria and Albert?

The answer, Sam saw as he closed the door behind him, was dipping up gobs of sour cream from a cardboard container with lumps of rye bread that Farnsworth tore from a loaf in the middle of his desk blotter with ferocious little twisting gestures, as though he were stripping the meat from the bones of a chicken and he wanted to finish the job before he was interrupted and told he might have to share with somebody.

"Hello, kid," he said. "Sit down and take a load off. Want some of this?"

"Thanks, no," Sam said, sitting down. "I've had breakfast."

"So have I, but every once in a while I get so tired of being a goy named Hampton Farnsworth, I have to do something to remind me I'm still Itchie Feuerknecht from Bushwick Avenue, so I send one of these shickseh secretaries down to the delly around the corner and I go hog-wild in private. Fancy editors in goy publishing houses will tell you it's a thing called atavism, but us Jewish boys know better, hey, Sammy? Here, have a hunk."

"Do I have to?" Sam said, not reaching for the lump of rye bread soaked in sour cream that Farnsworth was holding out like a handful of snow.

"No, I guess not," the editor said, cramming the mess into his own mouth. "Not at your age. Not yet. You haven't learned yet what we all learn sooner or later. It's a goy's world, kid, and the sooner you adjust to it, the sooner you'll stop writing brilliant novels like this."

With his elbow, as he tore a fresh piece of bread from the loaf and plunged it into the cardboard container, Hampton Farnsworth nudged a manuscript box on his desk. Leaning forward, Sam saw and read upside down the label Jennie had typed so neatly.

"Oh," he said. "You've read it?"

"How the hell could I say it's brilliant if I hadn't read it?" Farnsworth said.

"That's not what I meant," Sam said. "I meant I didn't know Mr. and Mrs. Sargent had sent it over to you."

Farnsworth stopped munching bread and cream to give him a sharp look. "They didn't tell you, did they?"

Sam hesitated. Claude and Sophie Sargent had hurt his pride. He would not hurt it again by admitting as much. So he concealed the small wound under a neat little poultice of loyalty: he would not betray their dereliction of duty. Hampton Farnsworth apparently did not need Sam's betrayal to tell him what he clearly knew.

"Goyim," he said, shaking his head. "Even when you run into one that likes you, they don't know how to handle you."

"There isn't anything to handle," Sam said, not because he knew what he meant, but because he didn't like being a party to what sounded like a slur on Mr. and Mrs. Sargent: the fact that they had hurt his pride didn't change the fact that they were his friends.

"The hell there isn't," Hampton Farnsworth said. "You're a Jew, and they seem to like you. For all I know they may even love you, but because you're that thing, not a human being, but a Jew, they fall all over themselves asking themselves are they doing the right thing, are they maybe unintentionally hurting your feelings, when all they have to do is treat you like anybody else, the way they'd treat one of their goy clients, and say it in plain English."

"Say what?" Sam said.

"That you've done an absolutely extraordinary thing," Hampton Farnsworth said. He wiped his mouth with the back of his hand and slapped it down on the manuscript box. "You've written a second novel that is even better than your wonderful first one."

Sam, who had known this all along, did not waste time enjoying the warm glow that spread through him, but said, "You mean they couldn't call me up and tell me that?"

Farnsworth ripped off a piece of rye bread, plunged it savagely into the cardboard container, and said, "No more than Leander, when he got to the other side of the Hellespont, could tell Hero she was cross-eyed."

"But he could tell her she was beautiful, since she was," Sam said. "So why couldn't Mr. and Mrs. Sargent tell me they liked the book, if they did?"

"Because they're agents, and their job is to make money for you, and this book, which is brilliant, ain't going to make money for nobody."

Sam had learned from seeing others do it that incoherent splutterings of astonishment did not increase the stature of the splutterers in the eyes of their auditors. Therefore, when something he saw or heard aroused in him feelings that he knew would emerge, if he gave expression to them, as incoherent splutterings, he had trained himself to keep his mouth shut. Ham Farnsworth seemed to resent this.

"Why don't you knock off that strong, silent, self-control stuff?" he said. "It's a goy trait. You're a Jew. You don't fool anybody with that self-control any more than I fool anybody with a Pullman-car name like Hampton Farnsworth. Us Jews, we're screamers. I've just said something that wants to make you scream. Why the hell don't you?"

"Because I don't like to be treated like Pavlov's dog," Sam said. "Giving out with the expected reaction when somebody rings a bell."

"Jesus," Hampton Farnsworth said. "With a nose job, and a name change, you might be one of the few who could really pass."

"I'm not interested in passing."

"You will be, Sammy boy, you will be."

"When I am, I can tell you the name you'll have a right to call me, Mr. Farnsworth. Right now I'd like to know why, if this book is as brilliant as you say it is, it won't make any money?"

"Two reasons," Ham Farnsworth said, licking sour cream from his forefinger. "First, in choosing the story for your second novel you have made a perfectly understandable mistake, but a mistake nonetheless. You have chosen to continue the story of the boy and girl who are the hero and heroine of *Yours Is the Earth*, and while you have told the continuation brilliantly, with far greater skill and depth than you told the first part of their story, the part when they were kids in high school, the fact remains that what you have written in *I'll Make My Heaven* is a sequel, and sequels are poison in the bookstores. In short, Sammy boy, you have made the cardinal error of embracing a success rather than fleeing from it."

"What's the other reason?" Sam said.

"The same reason you didn't win that *Landscape* contest with *Yours Is the Earth*," Ham Farnsworth said. "This new book, like your first one, is about Jews."

"*Yours Is the Earth* was on the *New York Times* best-seller list for almost a full year," Sam said.

"Due to circumstances, Sammy boy, that had absolutely nothing to do with the book's intrinsic merits."

"What circumstances?"

Ham Farnsworth, about to ram a lump of bread and cream into his mouth, held it poised in the air. "Are you kidding?" he said.

"What circumstances?" Sam said.

The editor put the piece of bread into his mouth, chewed rapidly for several moments, then said quietly, "The only reason *Yours Is the Earth* sold, Sammy, is because I took advantage of an accident, a front-page murder story with national coverage in which I was able to inject your name at the right moment. It happened to be the moment when this bunch of dumb goyim I work for were up the creek with a newspaper advertising contract that called for them to use up close to thirty-two thousand dollars' worth of already-paid-for space in exactly three weeks, and they had no new books to use it up on, except one. They used it up, and you got to be a best-selling novelist, and I'm personally just as delighted as you are, because your success gave me a chance to sink the harpoon into these anti-Semitic scum bags, but chances like that don't come twice in a row. I can't arrange a front-page murder story every time you publish a novel, Sammy boy, and these goyim I work for are dumb, but nobody is that dumb twice, and they're not signing any more space contracts like the one they got nailed with last year, so all the help *I'll Make My Heaven* can expect from advertising is the amount we give to any second novel with a dubious subject matter, which will be just enough, I assure you, to let your more sharp-eyed newspaper reading friends realize you've published another book."

Farnsworth paused, smiled kindly at Sam, and waited for a reply. Sam, who had first thought that Hampton Farnsworth was a fool, then discovered he was a man of parts among which his foolishness was only one of many, now learned something else: the editor with the rosy-cheeked toy-soldier's face was a sadistic son of a bitch.

"Since the cat seems to have got your tongue," Farnsworth said through the kindly smile, "I will translate my remarks into dollar-and-cents terms. *Yours Is the Earth* sold sixteen thousand copies, which means you earned thirty-two hundred dollars. We paid you, however, five thousand, and so you are now in our debt to the tune of eighteen hundred. However, being an honorable man as well as a brilliant writer, a very rare combination, by the way, you have delivered to us, your creditors, the manuscript of a second novel. If *I'll Make My Heaven* were a first novel, I would expect it to sell what under normal circumstances *Yours Is the Earth* would have sold, namely, twelve hundred copies, and it would thus be worth an advance of two hundred and fifty dollars. Since you are now a best-selling novelist, however, your second book can be counted on, in spite of its unpalatable subject matter, to have a certain carryover curiosity value, which means it will probably sell twice as many as it ordinarily would, or twenty-four hundred copies. Also because you are now not a beginner but a best-selling novelist, we will be forced to raise your royalty rate from ten per cent to twelve and a half, which means you will be earning not twenty cents a copy but twenty-five, and twenty-four hundred copies at twenty-five cents a copy means six hundred dollars, which is the amount we are prepared to offer as an advance on this brilliant second novel." His hand came down with a thump on Jennie's neatly typed label and Hampton Farnsworth said, "This means instead of owing us eighteen hundred dollars, you owe us only twelve hundred, and that twelve hundred we are willing to carry forward as an advance on your third novel, on which we hope you will get to work at once and which I, for your sake, Sammy boy, hope will have nothing to do with the God-damn race of which it is our misfortune to be members." Farnsworth ripped off a piece of rye bread, dipped it into the cardboard container, and, as to the kindly surface of his smile there rose a touch of sweetness, he said, "Any comments, Sammy boy?"

"Only one," Sam said.

"What's that?" Farnsworth said.

"It's a phrase the kids on my block used to have for guys like you," Sam said.

"Let's hear it," the editor said.

"You're a prick in your heart, your feet stink, and you ride a bicycle on the roof."

Farnsworth blinked, and a mean glint suddenly burnished his sweet, boyish smile as he said, "Sounds pretty obscure."

"Not really," Sam said. "A prick in his heart is somebody who's rotten all the way down, from the inside out, so nothing can ever change him, and if your feet stink it means in addition you're physically revolting, and only somebody who is mentally defective would ride a bicycle on the roof." Sam stood up. "Any comments, Mr. Farnsworth?"

"Only one," the editor said. "You know what you've just done, don't you?"

"I sure as hell do," Sam said as he reached over and picked up the manuscript box. "I'd rather burn this than have it published by a Jew-hating animal like you."

Later, when he reported all this to Jennie on Eleventh Street, she said, "Well, that cuts off two sources of income for the Silver family."

"Two?" Sam said. "How do you figure that?"

"You don't think, do you, that after this little session you've just had with Mr. Hampton Farnsworth, he's ever going to hire me again to help him with his cheese book?"

"Do you care?"

"Not particularly," Jennie said. "But, like writers, I too enjoy eating regularly."

"Mr. Sargent said he'd be willing to make me a loan," Sam said.

Jennie shook her head pityingly. "And you believe him?" she said.

"I don't think Claude Sargent would lie about a thing like that."

"Not him. You," Jennie said. "Don't you know yourself well enough to know that you'd sooner starve, and I mean starve in the literal sense, until you're dead, than borrow a penny from anybody?"

Sam, who did know it, wondered how Jennie had found out, and wished she hadn't. To love a person completely, he was beginning to learn, it was important not to know him or her completely. There always had to be areas you were still eager to explore and possess. He had all those pages

of the once familiar book he had thought he knew intimately, the pages
on which he was discovering something new almost daily. But he did not
know what Jennie had in the way of undiscovered things about him. All
he knew was that every time she learned something new about him, the
number of strings by which she was tied to him was reduced by one.

"We won't starve," he said. "Farnsworth said it's a good book."

"But he's not going to publish it," Jennie said.

"Mr. and Mrs. Sargent think it's good, too."

"But they're so embarrassed by its dismal financial chances that they
didn't have the common decency, the simple politeness, or the just plain
guts to pick up a phone and tell you it's good."

"You don't even have to go so far as to pick up a phone," Sam said. "And
you haven't told me, either."

"Don't we have enough problems on our hands without complicating
them with a dose of artistic temperament?"

"A guy writes a book? And his wife types it? And she never says a word
one way or the other? It stinks or it's good? And he happens to wonder
about it? You call that artistic temperament?"

"It doesn't stink, and it is good," Jennie said. "But I don't understand
it."

"Hampton Farnsworth and Mr. and Mrs. Sargent understood it," Sam
said.

"They're not in it," Jennie said. "I am."

"Who says you're in it?"

"I do," Jennie said. "And since it's me you're talking to, and not those
newspaper people who interviewed you last year when *Yours Is the Earth*
came out, let's cut that crap about how odd it is that people should identify themselves with the fictional characters in novels, since they never
seem to identify themselves with the nice characters but only with the rotten ones, from which the poor put-upon novelist is forced to conclude that
it is by our faults and not by our virtues that we recognize ourselves."

"Well, it happens to be true," Sam said.

"In the pig's zudick, Sammy boy," Jennie said. "*Yours Is the Earth* is
about you and me in Grover Cleveland High and you know it, and I like
it, the way I liked the original short story you based it on when I read it
in *Landscape*, because you understood that girl, you liked her, you were
fair to her, you painted her with the warts she was born with, but you
didn't add a pair of fangs she didn't have. She came out an understandable
human being because you the writer were neither at her feet nor at her
throat."

"Say, that's pretty good," Sam said.

"You can have it for your next book," Jennie said. "And that kind of childish sarcasm does nothing but prove that my shots are going home and you're embarrassed."

"So far you haven't said anything to embarrass anybody about," Sam said. "You've uttered a highly complimentary critical judgment."

"If you shut up and listen you might hear another," Jennie said. "This new book, *I'll Make My Heaven,* is about you and me after we left Grover Cleveland High, and while it's exactly what Ham Farnsworth called it, a brilliant piece of work, in every way superior to the first book, better story, more skillfully told, deeper character exploration, cleaner writing, an all-around more professional job, it lacks the one thing I happened to like best in the first book, and that's that sense of fairness to the girl, the feeling in the book that's almost naïve, almost amateur, an open-eyed boyish desire to tell the truth, no matter what, without taking sides. The first book reads as though it happened. The second books reads as though it was written."

"Mr. Sargent says every book a man writes after his first book has that in it," Sam said. "He says it's inevitable."

"Death is inevitable, too," Jennie said. "That doesn't mean I have to like it."

"Then you were just trying to let me down easy when you said you liked this new book," Sam said.

Jennie stubbed out her cigarette as though she were trying to drive it through the ash tray into the coffee table.

"No, Einstein, dear," she said irritably. "I'm not trying to let you down easy. I'm trying to tell you the book is good and I like it, but it's not great, and if it were I'd like it better. Just as it's the doctor's job to hold off the inevitability of death as long as possible, it's the artist's job to keep out of his work those inevitable signs of the artist at work."

Sam looked at her curiously. "How the hell do you know all this?" he said.

Jennie shrugged. "I don't know how I know anything," she said. "I just feel it."

"Well," Sam said, "I never said I was an artist."

It was Jennie's turn to look curiously at him. She did it for such a long time that he began to feel uneasy.

"No, that's true," she said finally. "You never said that." Then, unexpectedly, her face broke into one of those rare, extraordinary smiles that Sam supposed it was not an exaggeration to say were what he lived for. "That's what makes living with you bearable," Jennie said.

"I wish I knew what that remark means," Sam said.

"If I felt there was the remotest chance you might," Jennie said, "I never would have made it."

"Hey, now, look."

"No, let it go," Jennie said. "I'll just have to work with the raw materials that are available. This," she said, touching the manuscript box he had carried home from Hampton Farnsworth's office, "and you."

"What do you want me to do?" Sam said.

"The only thing you seem to be good at," Jennie said. "Write."

"Write what?" Sam said.

"Your third book."

"But I don't have any third book," Sam said.

"All those months you were sitting over there in the corner with your pad and your Parker while Mrs. Grimsby and I were decorating this place, you thought the same thing about your second book," Jennie said, and he was scarcely aware of the surprise in discovering that she had known all along something he had been certain he had managed to conceal from her. He was accustomed to that kind of surprise. What he was not accustomed to, what filled him with fear every time he heard it, was the sound for which he wished he had not learned to listen: another of the strings by which she was bound to him had snapped. Jennie said, "But after a few months, you found your second book. You go on over to your mother's kitchen and try to find your third. I want to do some thinking about this one."

"Don't you think I ought to call the Sargents and tell them what happened at my session with Farnsworth?"

"Eff the Sargents," Jennie said. "They owe you a call."

Three days later it came through.

"Sam?"

"Yes. Oh, hello, Sophie. How are you?"

"Completely flabbergasted but wildly happy, which I suppose is a good combination."

"What are you flabbergasted and happy about?" Sam said.

"You, dear," Sophie Sargent said.

"I wish I could say the same," Sam said. "I don't know what to be flabbergasted about, but I'm good and unhappy about a session I had with Ham Farnsworth three days ago, which I've been meaning to call you about."

"You didn't have to," Sophie said. "He called me."

"I'm sorry about the way it went."

"I'm not," Sophie said. "We made eighteen hundred dollars as a result of your using to Mr. Farnsworth what that foul-mouthed fool had the crust to describe to me as unpardonable language."

"It was pretty rough," Sam said. "How did it earn us eighteen hundred dollars?"

"We have a debit balance at Trafalgar, Singlenight on your first book," Sophie said. "If we'd stayed there with this new one, whatever it earned, that eighteen-hundred-dollar debit balance would have had to be deducted by their accounting department before we saw a red cent on the second. This way, Sammy dear, we start from scratch with a new publisher."

"Can't Trafalgar, Singlenight go to the new publisher, whoever he is, and ask to be paid back the eighteen hundred out of whatever royalties I earn on the new book?"

From the other end of the phone came the curious little snorting sound that was not really a snort and that Sam had first heard issuing from the patrician nostrils of Lady Kirriemuir in Sophie Sargent's living room.

"They certainly can," she said. "But let them just try it!"

"It doesn't sound very honest," Sam said. "But in my present financial state I'm willing to pretend it is."

"Your present financial state, Sam dear, is what I'm completely flabbergasted and wildly happy about. Are you sitting down?"

"There hasn't been enough solid food in this house these past two weeks to provide enough strength for anybody in it to stand up."

"Well, after I hang up, you trot round the corner to the Lafayette and order yourself a coal scuttle full of plover's eggs smothered in ortolan's tongues. Bud Bienstock of *American Bride* just called. He is crazy about *I'll Make My Heaven* and wants to pay twelve thousand dollars for serializing it in four parts in his magazine." Sam looked across the room, where Jennie was lying on the couch, smoking a cigarette and watching him. Sophie Sargent's voice said, "Sam, did you hear me?"

"Yes, sure," he said. "I mean— Wait." He covered the mouthpiece, said, "Jennie," stopped, uncovered the mouthpiece, and, into it, said, "Sophie, you're not kidding?"

"Of course I'm not kidding."

"Then say it all again."

Sophie said it all again, and added, "Bud said he's aware that twelve thousand is not a huge price, not nearly what he'd pay for a Kenyon Poole serial, for example, but it's your first time out in his magazine, he said, and it does come to three thousand for each installment, which, if you think of each installment as a short story, is a damned good price, and anyway Bud says he's crazy to have you do more work for him, so if you let him have this first one for twelve thousand, he said he'd give you a nice juicy raise on the next one, and, Sam dear, I did a terrible thing."

"What?" Sam said, fear cutting through the delight in which he was bathed.

"I accepted," Sophie Sargent said.

"You—? I mean, what's terrible about that?"

"An agent is not supposed to close a deal until the terms are conveyed to the client and the client has given the agent the authorization to accept."

"Oh, Christ. Who cares about that?"

"Well, Claude and I do," Sophie said. "I promise it won't happen again, but in this case, knowing you, well, knowing your situation, I just couldn't think as an agent, and when Bud told me all this, I reacted as a friend with a wild whooping yes, and I'm so pleased you— What, Sam?"

"I said hold it a second, please," Sam said. He covered the mouthpiece and said, "What?"

From the couch Jennie said, "How much?"

"Twelve thousand," Sam said and, taking his hand from the mouthpiece, "Gee, Sophie, I wish I knew how to tell you how this makes me—" Sam's voice stopped and, immediately, on a rising note, he said, "Sophie, how did Bienstock get the manuscript?"

"Sam dear, that's what I'm calling to ask you."

"I gave you one copy," Sam said slowly, as though he were working out a complicated arithmetic problem. "You gave that copy to Ham Farnsworth, and I brought that copy home with me after the fight. So the only copies in existence were all in my possession. Then how the hell—?"

"That's what I asked Bud," Sophie Sargent said. "I mean I didn't want to, since an agent looks foolish when an editor buys something the agent never sent him, but he refused to tell me how he got the manuscript. He just laughed and said I should be content with the good news of the sale, which of course I was, but just the same it was pretty embarrassing as a situation for an agent to find herself in."

"I seem to specialize in getting you into them," Sam said.

"What?" Sophie said.

"The *Yours Is the Earth* manuscript went to the *Landscape* contest and was legally committed to Trafalgar, Singlenight before Sargent & Sargent even knew of its existence."

"Oh, dear, yes," Sophie said. "I'd forgotten that. And you promised it would never happen again."

"I didn't break my promise, Sophie."

"You mean it wasn't you who sent the manuscript up to Bud Bienstock?"

"Why would I do a thing like that?" Sam said. "Even if I were dumb enough to want to by-pass my agent, this book is about Jews, and my own agents have told me *American Bride* never runs material about Jews."

"Well, the magazine is making an exception in your case, Sam dear."

"For which I'm damned grateful," Sam said. "But I do want you to know, Sophie, that I did not give the manuscript to Bud Bienstock."

"Well, when you find out who did, let me know," Sophie Sargent said. "Whoever it was did us both a favor. Go and have your celebration. Now that Trafalgar, Singlenight is out of the picture, I want to discuss with Claude what we should do about the book publication angle."

She hung up, and as Sam did the same, he looked across the room at the couch. Jennie smiled as she took a long drag on her cigarette.

"It was quite simple," she said. "I just went to that cocktail party for Rabbi Jekuthiel Newman. While he was letting everybody in on his latest observations about Palestine, I was letting our host in on my observations about *I'll Make My Heaven,* a copy of which I just happened to have left in the bedroom, where all the ladies had left their coats, since I happened to have come to the cocktail party direct from the typist, where I'd just happened to be to pick up my husband's new novel." Jennie sat up and said, "This great agent of yours, who is going to collect twelve hundred dollars for my afternoon's work, what were her parting thoughts?"

"Now that I'm no longer with Trafalgar, Singlenight, she's going to discuss with Mr. Sargent the problem of finding me a new book publisher."

"Let them discuss it," Jennie said. "I've found one for you."

"Who?"

"Gerosa & Jellaby."

"But they're a textbook house, aren't they?" Sam said. "I don't remember them ever doing much in fiction."

"They haven't up to now, but they want to start," Jennie said. "And they mean really start, in a big way, which these textbook houses can do because they're all as rich as God, and Gee & Jay are the richest. They've hired themselves a bright, tough young editor and given him a pair of guns with instructions to use them as he sees fit, which he clearly enjoys doing, since he's pulled some of the neatest talent raids in the last few weeks the publishing business has seen in years, and because I happen to know Ham Farnsworth is number one man on his dreck list, I know the chance to take you away from Trafalgar, Singlenight would make all his piratical instincts glow with great big fat dollar signs."

"He wouldn't be taking me away from Trafalgar, Singlenight," Sam said. "I *am* away."

"He doesn't know that," Jennie said. "And if we move fast, as I plan to do, now that we've got the good news about the serialization that I've been waiting for, he doesn't have to know until the deal is set, if ever."

"He doesn't sound all that bright if you can pull something like that on him," Sam said. "Who is this genius?"

"Keeley Cuff," Jennie said. "And he's bright enough for my purposes."

"Keeley Cuff?" Sam said. "Are you crazy?"

"I just earned us twelve thousand dollars from a place that your own big-shot experienced-up-to-here agents said was for you absolutely barren ground," Jennie said. "Do I sound crazy?"

"You certainly do if you plan to deal with that little bastard," Sam said. "I wouldn't have anything to do with him if he was—"

"Sammy dear, half the conversations of writers begin with that I-wouldn't-have-anything-to-do-with-that-bastard-if-he-was-the-last-man-on-earth malarkey, and the other half are edited versions that go I-wouldn't-have-anything-to-do-with-that-bastard-until-I-need-him."

"Well, I don't need Mr. Keeley Cuff."

"You do, and you're going to have him, so start getting used to the idea."

"For God's sake, only a few months ago he insulted you in public, right there in the Lafayette, and you were sore as hell because I didn't punch him in the nose."

"That was a few months ago, and if the compulsion to correct the omission is really overwhelming, you can do it after I've got his name on a Gerosa & Jellaby contract."

"God damn it," Sam said, "I don't understand you."

"That's been obvious since the Our Gang Comedy days on Avenue A," Jennie said. "Now let me make a few things obvious to you. The ball has just started to roll. You thought it started to roll with the publication of *Yours Is the Earth*, but you were wrong. You were confusing all that publicity about Buggo and your picture in the papers and the glowing reviews by Lewis Gannett and John Chamberlain and the thirty-eight weeks, or whatever it finally came to, on the best-seller list—you were confusing all that hoopla with dollars and cents. I wasn't. I could hear the noise, but the sound of money wasn't in it, and when the noise died away, all that hoopla added up to was thirty-two hundred dollars, period. By the time it was over, we were flat broke and we owed your publisher eighteen hundred dollars and our decorator three thousand. When you woke up to the realities, all you could do about them was run around changing your underwear, but I had seen the realities from the beginning, and I knew not only that that first book was a false pregnancy, but I also knew you had it in you to get really knocked up and turn out to be the mother of a literary Dionne quintuplets.

"In other words, I knew you were worth gambling on; that's why I didn't worry about running up that three-thousand-dollar bill with Mrs. Grimsby, because I knew it wouldn't be long before the ball would begin to roll. Well, it just began, Sammy boy, with that phone call from Sophie the Four-Thumbed Agent, and I'm not going to let it slow down until it has rolled us up a nice big bundle, because this twelve-thousand serialization money is not my idea of a bundle. What I want is to get nice and cozily deep into the soft. Keeley Cuff is a piece of dreck, and when I've got what I want out of him, I won't wait for you to punch him in all four of his eyes, I'll do it myself, but right now he wants to do with you to Ham Farnsworth what Ham Farnsworth did with you to his goy employers: sink the harpoon and twist. Ham Farnsworth using you against his goy employers didn't put us into the soft, but Keeley Cuff doing it against Farnsworth is going to cost him, or rather Gerosa & Jellaby, a satchel full of money."

"If the method is a great big secret," Sam said, "I don't feel I have the right to pry."

"You know something, Sammy boy?" Jennie said. "You're the only man I know for whose conversation a dash of sarcasm does absolutely nothing. The method is simple enough. Gerosa & Jellaby know exactly the same amount about publishing fiction as Keeley Cuff knows, and that, in round figures, is zero. But Gerosa & Jellaby thinks he knows a lot because he started that dopey *Landscape* novel contest with Trafalgar, Singlenight. The winners were published three months ago. Can you remember their names? Neither can I. But the fact that they got published got Keeley Cuff this job with Gerosa & Jellaby, and before Messrs. Gee & Jay as well as Cuff find out the little shmuck doesn't know his ass from a hot rock about publishing, we will have their advance on *I'll Make My Heaven* in the bank." Jennie stood up and, as she went to the phone, said, "Run me a tub and make a fresh pot of coffee."

"Who you calling?" Sam said.

"My pigeon, Mr. Keeley Cuff," Jennie said. "We had lunch the day after you had your fight with Farnsworth. I told him I thought I could get you away from Trafalgar, Singlenight and over to Gerosa & Jellaby, but it would cost him money, because your new book was so sensational that the magazines were already bidding for the serial rights and the only way Farnsworth would let you go is if you bought back your contract, so Cuff would have to include that in his advance, and all the panting little dope could think to say was how much money would it cost."

Sam, aware of the parallel, but unable to think of anything else to say, said what Keeley Cuff had said, "How much money?"

"Will you get going on my tub and that coffee?" Jennie said. "All you've got to do is think of your third book, but I've got a busy morning ahead of me."

"Come on, cut that out," Sam said. "How much money?"

Lifting the phone to her ear, Jennie smiled one of those extraordinary smiles that Sam lived for, but this one was not directed at him. This one was directed at something in the distance, as though she were saluting a vision.

"Mr. Keeley Cuff is about to learn what it costs to insult certain people," Jennie said. "I told him on your new book I wanted a seventy-five-hundred-dollar advance."

She got ten.

"I don't believe it," Sophie Sargent said.

"Here's the contract," Jennie said, pulling it from her purse and placing it on Claude Sargent's desk. "And here's the check for ten thousand dollars," she said, putting the pale green slip on top of the contract. "I made Mr. Cuff get it certified, just in case he had any second thoughts."

Sophie Sargent looked at her husband, then at Sam, and finally reached out of the red-leather chair to pick up the documents Jennie had just set down. Sam was embarrassed by the look on Sophie Sargent's face as she leafed through the contract, so he stared up at the oil painting of the naked girl and did again the little sum in his head that he had done several times since Jennie had called him at the apartment with the news and told him to meet her in the Sargent & Sargent offices: twelve thousand from *American Bride* plus ten thousand from Gerosa & Jellaby came to twenty-two thousand; deduct twenty-two hundred for Sargent & Sargent commissions, leaves nineteen thousand, eight hundred; take away the three thousand they owed Mrs. Grimsby for decorating the apartment, and Sam and Jennie Silver were the owners of sixteen thousand and eight hundred dollars in hard cash, or, in terms that somehow seemed more real to Sam, the equivalent of over twenty-five years' salary from Mr. Brunschweig.

"I'm afraid Mr. Cuff is going to have a whole basketful of second thoughts," Sophie Sargent said finally. "I see that in addition to the ten thousand advance, you got a straight fifteen per cent royalty out of him."

Jennie smiled sweetly and said, "I'm not an agent, of course, so I had to try and put myself in your shoes, Mrs. Sargent, and think the way you would have thought, and it seemed to me you would have thought it wrong for a best-selling novelist like Sam to get only ten per cent on this book, the way he got on his first, so I asked for fifteen, and I hope I'm right?"

Sophie Sargent did that thing Sam had often noticed women do when they are about to let somebody have it: she tipped her head to one side and touched the tips of her lacquered fingers to the back of her neatly marceled hair as she said, "No, as a matter of fact, Mrs. Silver, you're quite wrong. I would have had the gall to ask for only twelve and a half per cent."

"Then it's lucky for all of us that I was there talking to Mr. Cuff instead of you, isn't it?" Jennie said. "And aren't you ever going to call me Jennie?"

"Probably not," Sophie Sargent said. "It would be like calling Lady Macbeth Daisy May."

Claude Sargent cleared his throat and said, "All right, girls. Sophie, what's all this about second thoughts you say this Cuff boy is going to have?"

"This new book of Sam's is a little longer than his first one," Sophie said, "and production costs are rising, I hear all over the trade, so this book will probably have to retail at two-fifty instead of two dollars. At a fifteen per cent royalty, that's thirty-seven and a half cents a copy, which means with a ten-thousand-dollar advance, Gerosa & Jellaby will have to sell roughly twenty-five thousand copies before the advance is earned back, and with all due respect to Sam's talent, and much as I love the book, anybody in publishing will tell you *I'll Make My Heaven* does not have twenty-five thousand copies' worth of bookstore mileage in it."

"That's Mr. Keeley Cuff's tough luck," Jennie said. "That check, as I told you, Mrs. Sargent, is certified."

Sophie looked at it again, caught her lower lip in her teeth, nibbled gently for a while, then said, "My husband and I, while we're delighted for you and Sam, Mrs. Silver, are a trifle embarrassed by all this."

"Embarrassed?" Jennie said. "Why?"

Claude Sargent leaned forward and said, "We don't feel that we've earned our commissions."

"You haven't," Jennie said. "But you will." She made them wait while she lit a cigarette, then said, "Mercury Films is interested in the movie rights."

"How do you know?" Sophie Sargent said sharply.

"Mrs. Grimsby up there is my former boss and a dear friend who wishes us well," Jennie said. "So I gave her a copy of the manuscript the same day I gave one to Bud Bienstock. She put their best girl on it at once, and they had a synopsis in Marshall Umberg's hands forty-eight hours later. He's dumb, but he's not all that dumb, and when I gave Mrs. Grimsby the news about the *American Bride* serialization and this Gerosa & Jellaby contract and she passed it on to him, Umberg called his boss on the Coast at once. Just before I came up here, I called Mrs. Grimsby from the phone booth in the lobby, as I promised, and she said Umberg told her to tell us they were willing to pay twenty-five thousand for the movie rights, but she told me in confidence she thinks they'll go to fifty, and I think so, too, which is where you come in, Mr. Sargent." Jennie turned and sprayed Sophie Sargent with a dose of the sweet smile. "You, too, Mrs. Sargent. Here's your chance to earn your commission. Get the fifty thousand out of Mercury and we can all forget about being embarrassed."

Whatever it was Sophie Sargent was about to say, she clearly would have regretted. Fortunately, she didn't get a chance to say it. Claude Sargent moved into the breach. With a great deal of throat-clearing and chair-scraping and hearty chuckling, he said, "What are you two kids going to do with all that money?"

"For a starter, go to Europe," Jennie said, taking Sam, not for the first time, completely by surprise. "I'm told travel is broadening, and I think my genius, here, could use a little of that, don't you?"

"It never hurt anybody except the boys of the A.E.F. who didn't come back," Claude Sargent said. "But the circumstances of your trip will be somewhat different. When are you going?"

"As soon as we can buy a couple of suitcases," Jennie said, "and get the passports."

This took much longer than Sam would have thought.

Doctors on the Lower East Side, he and Jennie discovered, were not especially diligent about reporting births to the Board of Health, and when they did, were not particularly accurate. It took six weeks to locate the birth certificates that the Department of State insisted on having before it would issue passports to Mr. and Mrs. Samuel Silver, and the only reason they finally were issued was the Passport Division's surprising willingness to accept as relevant to the applicants what ultimately did turn up: one birth certificate for a "Semmel Siliver" and another for a "Jean E. Brumm."

The time devoted to the hunt was not wasted, however, at least not by Jennie, whose interpretation of buying a couple of suitcases was another of those surprises Sam kept discovering on the pages of the book he had thought he knew by heart.

Aside from the time in Grover Cleveland High when she was in a rage about Mr. Mueller's insistence that all girl students wear bloomers and middy blouses, and her fury kept dragging Sam's attention back to the subject over and over again, he had never been aware of Jennie's clothes. It was a subject to which nobody paid much attention on East Tenth Street or on Avenue A, where preoccupations with how to pay for food and shelter were always of more immediate concern. When the problem of clothing had to be dealt with, the rule that governed the dealings was simple: the maximum durability for the minimum cost. It was rare, therefore, for anybody to wear anything that would attract attention for its beauty, and these rarities were limited, it seemed to Sam when he thought about it years later, at least among women, to those who possessed more than the average amount of money or more than the average amount of beauty. Since Jennie possessed neither, she had always worn the sort of clothes that all the other girls of the neighborhood had worn. Sam supposed this had changed somewhat after Jennie left Avenue A and went to work for Mercury Films, and he knew of course that during the almost two years of their marriage, she had bought dresses and sweaters and other items of apparel, but none of this had in any way impinged on his basic image of the dark brown eyes in the dark, lean face mounted on the slender, supple body surrounded by some sort of perfectly adequate, and probably even appropriately handsome, but thoroughly unobtrusive stuff.

This image changed abruptly after the checks from *American Bride*, Gerosa & Jellaby, and Mercury Films, minus the Sargent & Sargent commissions, were deposited to the credit of the "Samuel and/or Jennie Silver" account in the Washington Square Branch of the National City Bank.

The idea of going to Europe had always existed in Sam's mind on the same level with the idea of being elected President: it had happened to many people in the past, was happening to others right now, and would continue to happen to still others in the future, so in theory there was no reason, especially since there was no specific injunction in the Constitution against it, why it shouldn't happen to Sam Silver. In practice, however, he knew that Jewish boys from East Tenth Street did not get elected President, and for a while, after Jennie announced it in the Sargent & Sargent office, the idea that at least one Jewish boy from East Tenth Street *was* going to Europe proved so overpowering that Sam, trying to adjust inwardly to his happiness and good fortune, was not completely aware of what was going on around him. It was his mother's attitude toward the trip that brought him back to reality.

"Europe?" she said when Sam stopped in at East Tenth Street to break the news. "Who needs it, for what? Papa and me, we worked like animals to save a little money to run away from it, so now you, our son, we made you an American, you're running back to it?"

"It's not the same," Sam said. "You and Papa were running away from bad economic conditions and from anti-Semitism."

"Who says it's not the same?" Mrs. Silver gestured toward the kitchen table, at which Sam's father, with the same old Waterman and the same bottle of ink for a paperweight, was bent over the same endless documents, and said, "Look. Look at Papa. To get out the uncles and the aunts and the cousins, they're crying please save us, he's still working. What do they want Papa to save them from? The same thing, Sam, Papa and I we saved ourselves when we came here. The same thing, Sam, we saved you when you were born here, an American. To this you're running back? To pogroms and to Hitler and a war he's making over there?"

"All that war talk is just talk," Sam said. "And I'm not going to Europe to live or even to the Europe you and Papa knew. You lived on a small farm in Rumania, Ma. We're going to visit London and Paris and Rome."

"Why?" Mrs. Silver said. "What's in London and Paris and Rome that you haven't got here?"

"They're a part of the world," Sam said. "You can't stay in one place and pretend the rest of the world doesn't exist. I'm a writer. I've got to find things to write about."

"If to London and Paris you have to go, for a few days or even a few weeks, a quick look here, a quick look on that, from this to find things to write about, Sam, if this you have to do, then it's better to go back to the Lafayette Institute with the lessons and come out a bookkeeper, because a writer you're not going to be for long. What's in London and in Paris, Sam, it's been there a long time, and there's writers that they live there, they're the ones that write about it. Like you write about here in New York, where it's you that live here a long time. From a smell and a look, a taste and a touch, Sam, a writer doesn't find things to write about."

"I'm not actually going to Europe to find things to write about," Sam said with more emphasis than he intended. Secretly, even though he knew what his mother had said was absolutely true, he was hoping that his case would be an exception. He had been unable to think of a subject for a third book. "I'm going to Europe the way I might have gone to college," he said. "As part of my education. I couldn't afford to go to college, but I've had some luck and I now can afford to go to Europe, so I'm going. You don't have to worry, especially about money. I'm going to open an account for you in the Standard Bank on Avenue B, and I'm going to put two thousand dollars into it, and every week I want you to draw out twenty-five dollars."

"Twenty-five dollars a week?" Mrs. Silver said. "What Papa and I we'll do with twenty-five dollars a week?"

"I don't know," Sam said. "Buy some clothes, eat goldfish, anything. Everybody gets a raise when business is good. No reason why you and Pa shouldn't."

"Jennie knows you're giving me and Papa a raise?"

"Certainly she knows," said Sam, who found it easier to tell these lies than go through the labor of setting himself straight with his conscience by telling Jennie about something in which she was not really interested. "What is it? Something to be ashamed of?"

"No, but it's fifteen dollars a week more," Mrs. Silver said. "And Jennie is a wife."

"She wants you to have it," Sam said.

"Better from her a visit I'd like to have once in a while," his mother said.

"She'll be over before we go to say good-bye," Sam said. "She's pretty busy right now."

"With what?" Mrs. Silver said. "Spending money?"

Sam did not attribute any importance to the remark until later in the day when, on coming into the apartment, he saw that the top box on the stack that United Parcels Service had delivered during the day was from Bergdorf Goodman. It was one of those moments of revelation when, through the lens of objects or events totally insignificant in themselves, matters of enormous significance are unexpectedly revealed. Sam had been aware for some time that while he was tracking down their birth certificates, Jennie had been busy shopping for their trip. It had not occurred to him until this moment that she would even have dreamed of doing any of that shopping in Bergdorf Goodman. Shopping in Bergdorf Goodman was something done by people who lived uptown, people who were part of the world about which Sam and his mother had dreamed ever since he was a small boy, people with large bank accounts whose names and pictures appeared in the papers and who did not have to count pennies. Looking at the lavender and purple box, Sam finally grasped as a reality something that had been for some time merely a concept: now he, too, had a large bank account, and his name and picture appeared in the papers, and, at least for the time being, he did not have to count pennies. Having grasped it, he wondered why the reality, instead of cheering him, made him uneasy.

"It's the difference between hoping and waiting," Jennie said after she came home and started unpacking the boxes and Sam told her about his reaction. "That, plus the phrase *at least for the time being*. All your life as a kid on East Tenth Street, you were hoping some day to get out of that sewer and live uptown. All my life as a kid on Avenue A, I was just waiting to get out. You didn't really believe you'd make it. You just hoped you would. I knew damn well I was going to make it. All I didn't know was when. Now that we've made it, you can't quite believe it. That's why, when you just said all those things you now have what only people uptown have, the part about they don't have to count pennies, you said now you didn't have to count pennies, either, but you added *at least for the time being.* As far as I'm concerned, Sammy boy, it's not for the time being. It's forever. I'm out of that sewer, as I knew I some day would be, and I believe it right down to my toenails. I'm never going back, Sammy boy, and if you stick with me, neither are you. Isn't this gorgeous?"

"Yes, very pretty," Sam said. "What is it?"

"A raincoat," Jennie said. "You can't go traveling around Europe without a raincoat."

"A raincoat?" Sam took a handful of the soft red material that looked like velvet. It felt like velvet. "I always thought raincoats—"

"Look like those things detectives wear in British movies?" Jennie laughed and tossed the coat to him. "Not at Bergdorf's. Hang that up for me while I see what little goodies Bonwit sent over today."

Hanging up the raincoat as Jennie opened another box, Sam saw the price tag on the red sleeve, and he said, "My God!"

"No, not uptown," Jennie said. "Downtown, yes, that's a My God price for a raincoat, but not here. We've made it, Sammy boy, remember?"

"We're going to have to keep on making it, if this stuff is going to get paid for."

"You will," Jennie said. "I have confidence in both of us."

"I suppose that thing is a sweatshirt?"

"No, this is a dinner dress," Jennie said. "Which reminds me that in a few days, when I've got most of my big shopping behind me, we'd better start on you."

"Me?" Sam said. "What's the matter with me?"

"What's the matter with you is you look exactly what you are," Jennie said. "A Tenth Street hick who's hit the jackpot and hasn't had time yet to get out of his Howard's twenty-two-fifty double-breasted. On ships like the *Washington,* when you travel first class, you dress for dinner, and that means not only sweatshirts like these for your lady fair, but black tie for you, Sammy boy. We'll go over to Brooks' on Tuesday, no, better make it Wednesday, I've got a fitting at Jaeckel's on Tuesday, and we'll get them started on changing you from looking like what you are to looking like what you've become."

"What do they sell at Jaeckel's?" Sam said.

"Mink, dear," Jennie said.

"Oy," Sam said.

"It's chilly in Europe," Jennie said. "And you've married a very cold-blooded woman. What does that expression mean?"

"I'm trying to think like you," Sam said. "I'm trying to eliminate that *for the time being* feeling."

"You'll find it easier in our new quarters."

"What new quarters?"

"This place was appropriate for a best-selling first novelist who sold sixteen thousand copies," Jennie said. "It's a little cramped for a man whose new book is going to be serialized by *American Bride,* made into a movie by Mercury Films, and will have to sell twenty-five thousand copies before Gerosa & Jellaby come out even on their advance. Mrs. Grimsby told me the other day an apartment opened up in the building next to hers, and I went over to look at it."

"Didn't you once tell me that to those bastards on Gramercy Park you and I are just a couple of Jews?"

"Only to the bastards who own Mrs. Grimsby's building," Jennie said. "The building next door is owned by Jews, and they think we're just fine. So is the apartment. Three bedrooms and four baths, not counting a maid's room and stall shower, with a forty-foot living room that's a dream. Mrs. Grimsby thinks she'll be able to use pretty nearly everything we've put into this apartment, especially the big pieces like this couch and that commode, and she promises to have the whole place completely done, down to linen and silver, so we can move right in and start screwing and eating the day we come back from Europe. Better hurry up and shave, Sammy boy. The Bienstocks are giving a farewell dinner party for us tonight, and we don't want to be late."

Sam wondered, during the weeks that followed, why, if they didn't want to be late, they always were. They were late for the farewell dinner party the Bienstocks gave for them, and they were late for the farewell luncheon George Jellaby of Gerosa & Jellaby gave for them, and they were late for the farewell cocktail party Mercury Films gave for them, and they were so late for the *bon voyage* party Sophie Sargent gave for them in the *Washington*'s first-class dining room that Keeley Cuff, his bony face aglow with anxiety as well as its customary martini flush, was on his way down the gangplank to see if he could find them when he met Sam and Jennie coming up.

"Lordy me," he said. "We all got scared you'd miss the boat."

"That's one of the few things you can count on me never to do," Jennie said. "What's that?"

"Galleys on *I'll Make My Heaven,*" Keeley Cuff said. "They came from the printer this afternoon, and I was going to mail them on ahead to your hotel in London, but George Jellaby said you might like to read them on the way over."

"I'd love it," said Sam, reaching for the fat manila envelope, but Jennie beat him to it.

"I'll take charge of that," she said. "Much too valuable to be left in the hands of a mere writer. What other surprises are in store for us?"

"Come on up to your party and see," said Keeley Cuff.

What Sam saw first was Bud Bienstock, his saintly El Greco face hung like an accusation above the diamond-studded Star of David in his necktie, bearing down on him with a magazine.

"Here's a proof copy of next month's issue of *American Bride*," he said. "It contains the first installment of *I'll Make My Heaven*. I was going to mail it on ahead to your hotel in London, but my wife said you might like to look at it on the way over."

"I'd love it," Sam said, but again Jennie beat him to it.

"I'll take charge of that," she said. "All he did was write it, but I saw that it got to the right people, didn't I, Mr. Bienstock?"

"You sure did," Bud Bienstock said. "And call me Bud."

"I'm sorry," Jennie said. "Bud."

"Clever little girl you've got there, Sam," the editor of *American Bride* said. "Clever little girl. And here." He clicked open a blue velvet jeweler's box to reveal a pair of Star of David cuff links only slightly smaller than his own. "I always give a set of these to my Jewish writer friends when they go abroad for the first time," Bud Bienstock said. "Just so they won't forget who they are."

"Not our Sam," Sophie Sargent said, coming up with two glasses. "He knows who he is. Here, kids, drink up. Mrs. Silver, what a pretty coat."

"I'm glad you like it," Jennie said. "Sam told the man at Jaeckel how to cut it."

"Why, Sam," Sophie Sargent said, "I didn't know you had a talent for designing women's clothes."

Sam, who didn't know it, either, gave Jennie the lay-off-will-you look, and said, "Oh, well."

He said a good deal more, because a good deal more was said to him, but later, after the gongs had sounded and the last farewells had been shrieked and the smeared lipstick from the final kisses had been wiped clean and he was standing out on deck with Jennie and several hundred other people watching the city in which he had lived all his life pull away from the ship, the only thing he remembered was something Claude Sargent had said.

"Don't let it fool you, Sam," the fat man with the shapeless, wonderful face had said. "It's just another place."

"What did you say?" Jennie said.

"I was repeating something Mr. Sargent said to me," Sam said, and he repeated it again. "I was wondering what he meant."

"Nothing you need waste time or ink jotting down in your memory book," Jennie said. "These provincial hicks make me sick, and nothing is more provincial than a hick from New York. He took me aside when you and that lion tamer from Schenectady he's married to—"

"Wilkes-Barre," Sam said.

"—were nuzzling little farewell kisses at each other, and he said he wished you weren't going abroad for the first time at this particular moment, because while he approved of the European experience, if only as a yardstick to show you how good you had it over here where you came from, all this war talk tended to obscure the experience and blur the yardstick, and he hoped, as your dear little devoted wife, who like him had the best interests of your career at heart, he hoped I wouldn't let you get involved in any of this Rome-Berlin axis hysteria, because your superb talent was basically with people, and politics were not your dish of tea."

Jennie paused to light a fresh cigarette from the butt of the old one, which she flung over the rail, and said, "I said is that so, Mr. Sargent? Has it ever occurred to you that a couple of dishes of that kind of tea might make the difference between a superb talent and a great one? A human being who has no interest in politics is as much a human being as a fish is a fish who has no interest in water."

"Oh, Christ," Sam said. "Here we are back in Grover Cleveland High."

"You're still back there," Jennie said. "Not me. I've grown."

"I'm glad," Sam said. "You'd look awfully funny at your age if you hadn't. But that's no reason to get into a fight with a nice, sweet guy like Claude Sargent."

"Nice, sweet guys like Claude Sargent make me sick," Jennie said. "Especially when they're also apolitical slobs. Besides, there wasn't any fight. I just told the fat boob what he's old enough to have known for a long time, that man is a political animal, the life he lives is conditioned every minute of the day by politics, and a writer who doesn't grasp that, and doesn't interest himself in the mechanism that creates the conditions in which human beings live, is not going to be much of a writer."

"Is that why you're taking me to Europe?" Sam said.

"It's one of the reasons," Jennie said.

"What kind of a writer do you want me to be?" Sam said.

"Better than you are," Jennie said.

"The kind of writer I am paid for that twenty-five-hundred-dollar mink coat," Sam said.

"That's right," Jennie said. "Try to duck out on the argument with that artist-in-the-garret crap. You think you'd be a better writer if I was wearing a six-ninety-five from Klein's?"

"I might not get to be a worse one," Sam said.

"You'd better translate that crack," Jennie said.

"I find it interesting that you should be so terribly concerned about improving my talent when you're the only one who ever got me to do something that debased it," Sam said. "That fat apolitical slob and his bitch of a wife, who happen to be a couple of money-grubbing agents, pleaded with me not to do anything as cheap as write that movie synopsis for Mercury Films because it would hurt me, but you didn't feel that way, did you?"

"Not at the time," Jennie said. "No."

"What the hell has time got to do with it?"

"I didn't know then how good you are."

"When did you find out?" Sam said. "When Bud Bienstock decided to pay twelve thousand dollars to serialize *I'll Make My Heaven?*"

"That helped," Jennie said. "Now we'll just let this trip to Europe help some more."

"By getting me involved in this Rome-Berlin axis hysteria?"

"By getting you involved in anything, absolutely *anything* that's different from what you've been involved with all your life."

"I can only write about what I've known all my life."

"You'll have to learn something else," Jennie said. "There's no future in all this writing about Jews all the time."

"Oh," Sam said, "I see."

If she had any regrets about what she had said, if, as for a moment Sam suspected, the remark had slipped out unintentionally, Jennie gave no sign of either as she said firmly, "No, you don't. You're not going to avoid the issue by putting me in the same class with anti-Semites like our darling high school principal Mr. Mueller, or those bastards who own that first apartment house we tried to get into on Gramercy Park, or psychotics like Hampton Farnsworth, because I'm not in that class. I'm in the same class in relation to you as a fight manager is in relation to his fighter. I've got to say certain things to you. They may sound terrible. If they were said by other people, like that bastard Mueller or Farnsworth, you'd have a perfect right to call them names because you know what their motives are. My motives are different. I want you to get the best you can out of your talent. To do that you've got to reach an audience. You're never going to reach an audience if you keep on writing about Jews."

Sam reached out, pulled the proof copy of *American Bride* from under Jennie's arm, and read aloud the line printed over the painting of the girl with yellow hair smiling down at the man's hand slipping a diamond ring on her third finger: "Net paid circulation 4,075,870 copies."

Jennie shook her head. "No," she said.

"What do you mean, no?" Sam said. *"I'll Make My Heaven* is about Jews. The first installment is right here, and this thing is read by more than four million people. You don't consider that an audience?"

Jennie took from under her arm the fat envelope of galleys Keeley Cuff had brought to the ship and she handed it to Sam. "Here, you go on into the lounge and read for a bit," Jennie said quietly. "When you want me I'll be in our cabin."

The lounge looked like segments Sam remembered from comic-strip portraits of early-morning disorder following nights of revelry. The mess was so exaggerated that it seemed almost to have been staged. Ash trays not only literally overflowed, but seemed to have been hurled about like hockey pucks; drinks had not only been spilled, but many had obviously been smashed on the floor. The celebrants, however, were gone. The air was stale, but the room was quiet. Sam wedged himself into a heavy chair in the corner farthest from the door, put the envelope and the magazine on his lap, considered both for a few moments, and decided in favor of the magazine: he had seen a set of his own galleys before.

He turned to the index and saw, after the list of short stories and under the caption "A New Serial," the words:

I'll Make My Heaven, PART I .... by Samuel Silver, page 48.

He had a twinge of annoyance. Page 48 seemed pretty deep in the book to bury a story about which Bud Bienstock had made such a fuss. Sam turned to page 48 and the annoyance vanished. Page 48 was the first page of editorial matter on which no advertising appeared. Pleased by the discovery that his story had been given front position in the issue, Sam at once felt his pleasure marred.

At first he thought this was due to the shock of the four-color illustration, which spread across both pages 48 and 49, directly under the title and the author's name. The only other piece of work by Sam that had appeared in a magazine had been his first short story, and *Landscape* carried no illustrations. Sam had known, of course, that most fiction in the women's magazines was illustrated. It simply had not occurred to him until this moment that Bud Bienstock, who commissioned artists to prepare drawings to accompany all the fiction in *American Bride,* would naturally do the same for *I'll Make My Heaven.* What was bothering him, Sam felt, was the result.

The illustration, which he could tell from the nationally known name of the artist scrawled in one corner was the best that money could buy, showed a blond girl, who looked exactly like the blond girl on the magazine's cover, bent over a diary, on the open pages of which she was dropping a symmetrical stream of lavender-tinted tears, while in a cloud over her head, the same girl, but obviously much younger because in the cloud she wore braids and a middy blouse, was blowing a kiss to a curly-haired soldier who, in the uniform of a First World War doughboy, was leaning far out the window of a departing train and waving his hat.

Sam stared at the illustration with a troubled frown: not only was there no such scene in the novel; his heroine, he remembered distinctly, had black hair.

A few moments later, as his eyes skimmed the opening paragraphs of the story, Sam was jolted into the realization that it was not the illustration alone that had bothered him. He sat forward, turned swiftly to the back of the magazine where, after its expansive opening on pages 48 and 49, his story was continued in congested columns that ran like narrow pebbled paths between wide hedges calling attention to the virtues of cream deodorants, liquid depilatories, and sanitary napkins.

Sam skimmed several of these columns, started to get up, was struck by a horrible thought, and thumped back into the chair. Nervously, with fingers that suddenly seemed infuriatingly swollen, he scratched at the fastenings of Keeley Cuff's envelope and managed, after putting a small, painful gash into the side of his thumb, to tear it open. He pulled out the galleys, thumbed past the title page and the dedication to Jennie, read the opening paragraphs of the first galley, started to fumble for a glance at some of the later galleys, as he had glanced at the columns in the back of the magazine, then figured the hell with that. He had read enough.

He rammed the galleys back into the envelope, tucked it and the copy of *American Bride* under his arm, hurried out on deck, saw a familiar sight in the distance, and realized it was the Statue of Liberty, as he had seen it in illustrations all his life but never in actual fact, facing out to sea. He also realized he did not know the location of his and Jennie's cabin.

By the time he located the purser's office and found out, much of the shock had eased away. The anger, however, remained. By making an effort that was almost physically painful he succeeded in controlling the former sufficiently so that when he opened the cabin door and Jennie turned to face him, he was certain that while she could obviously see he was furious, she could not see his shame.

"Before you hit me," she said, "I'd like to point out that I got the idea from you."

"Don't you ever tell the truth?"

"Every once in a while," Jennie said. "When nothing else will do as well. This is one of those times."

"I had nothing to do with this," Sam said as he slammed down the galleys and the magazine on the upended open trunk in front of which she had been kneeling. "And you know it."

"Only indirectly," Jennie said. "You didn't know you were giving me the idea, but you did. Don't you remember telling me about the first time you went to see Claude Sargent? In that tuxedo you borrowed from Mr. Brunschweig? And Kenyon Poole happened to be there?"

"What the hell has all that got to do with *this* God-damn thing?"

"You told me something Sargent said one of his clients had done. A woman writer who sold a lot of slick stories to Bud Bienstock at *American Bride?* At one of her editorial conferences with him she outlined one of her usual stories about love in the country club set and he said great, go ahead and write it? Which she did, except that this time, instead of calling the characters Mr. and Mrs. Wheeler and Mr. and Mrs. Martinson, she called them Mr. and Mrs. Weingarten and Mr. and Mrs. Ginzberg? And Bienstock sent it back with a note saying he was sorry but he would have to turn the story down because it was not up to the writer's usual standard? And Sargent called his client and told her? And she laughed and said okay, just have the story retyped, please, and tell Shirley Shaefer to change all the Mr. and Mrs. Weingartens to Mr. and Mrs. Wheelers, and all the Mr. and Mrs. Ginzbergs to Mr. and Mrs. Martinsons? Which Shirley did, and Sargent sent the story back to Bienstock, who called to say he was glad to see the woman was back on the track again, and not only was he buying the story, but it was so good that he was raising her rate? Don't you remember that?"

"What I remember is the day you all of a sudden became daddy's little helpmeet," Sam said. "On this one, I'll do the typing, she says sweetly. I'm not earning a penny for this team, so instead of you paying out good money to that Shirley Shaefer, she says, batting her eyelashes, the least I can do is save us the typing expense of your new book, dear."

"I never called anybody dear in that tone of voice, and I never batted my eyelashes at you or anybody else," Jennie said. "And I did a hell of a lot more than save you the typing expense, dear. I got you into a Brooks Brothers dinner jacket, dear."

No, Sam thought, fighting to keep the astonishment from diluting his anger, no, I don't believe it.

"Is that all you've got to say about this?"

"What do you want me to say?" Jennie said. "I didn't do it? You know I did. You want me to say I'm sorry? I'm not. We were broke and worse. We didn't have a dime in the bank and we owed your publisher eighteen hundred and Mrs. Grimsby three thousand, and all we had to look forward to was a possible twenty-four-hundred-copies sale of your newest little epic about Tessie Birnbaum and Harry Lipschitz. I took the manuscript, and when you were communing with your muse in your mother's kitchen I typed up three copies for you, and then I typed three copies for myself, changing all the Tessie Birnbaums to Terry Bakers and the Harry Lipschitzes to Harry Lewises, and as a result we not only got out of debt, but here we are, sailing to Europe with a fat bank account under us, and here you are"—she picked up the magazine—"with an audience of four million readers, and may I ask what the hell is wrong with that?"

"You," Sam said as he grabbed the magazine from her. "If you can't see the difference between the novel I wrote and this piece of shit you've turned it into, I'm obviously talking to the wrong person."

He let it go, but either she ducked, or he hadn't really meant to hit her, because the magazine sailed past Jennie's head and landed with a rustling smack against the mirror between the beds. He saw the tumbled pages start sliding down the glass and then he could hear them scattering the bottles and boxes of Jennie's make-up kit as he slammed the door behind him.

Sometime later he found himself in the bar, facing a glass at a small table, and Sam realized from the fact that he was shivering that he must have been pacing the deck. He picked up the glass, thinking the whiskey would warm him, but the odor was so offensive that he gulped air noisily and set down the glass with a thump as he almost vomited. Easing the glass back from the edge of the table, he glanced around, to see if anybody had seen what had almost just happened, and it was obvious that several people had. Two men and two women were watching him with interest from a table so close to his left elbow, Sam could have tipped it over without moving his arm more than six inches. He moved his head, to see if there were any other members in his audience, and saw instead, through the glass door on his right, that the sky, which was moving up and down in a thoroughly preposterous way, was splashed with stars. Remembering that the ship had sailed at five o'clock, Sam was suddenly wondering, in a jumble where none of the questions seemed particularly important, yet each one fought for the privilege of being answered first, how long he had walked the decks, what time it was, and whether he was drunk. He started to get up and found that he was sitting in the lap of one of the men at the table on his left.

"Easy, boy," the man said, as his three companions giggled. "We're rolling a little."

"Sorry," Sam said. He tried to get up, couldn't, and said again, "Sorry. It's my legs. They—"

"Dempsey has the same trouble," the man said. "He can still punch good as ever, but his legs gave out. Here, Lou, how's about you take his other arm."

The other man took Sam's other arm, and while the two women spread their eyes wide and made little round circles of their mouths in front of which they held their hands as though they didn't want to release any more distracting giggles until the delicate operation was over, the two men heaved Sam to his feet.

"Attaboy," the first man said, and Sam realized with resentment that the soothing, patronizing tone was being directed at him. "Where do you live, Mac?"

"West Eleventh, just off Fifth, but I'm decorating a new apartment on Gramercy Park," Sam said. "What's it to you? And my name ain't Mac."

"I mean your cabin," the man said. "You ought to lie down, kid."

"I don't need any advice on should I stand up or lie down," Sam said. "Where the hellza purser's office, and don't call me kid."

With a violent twist, he shook himself free from both men. This proved to be a mistake, because his freedom lasted just long enough to land him prone on the table of his benefactors, with his face squashed up against the bosom of one of the two pop-eyed women, for whose self-restraint the situation proved too much. She burst into a cascade of giggling squeals while the man called Lou, his companion, and the second woman, panting, tugging, shoving, and grunting, managed to put Sam back on his feet.

"What do you want with the purser?" Lou said. "You oughta be in bed, Buster."

"I go to bed when I'm good and ready," Sam said. "I wanna send a cable, and don't call me Buster."

"Cables you send from the radio room," the first man said. "Think you can make it?"

"I've been making it for years," Sam said. "Long before I met you guys, and din I tell you don't call me Mac?"

"My error, chum," Lou said and, to his companion, "Come on, Fred, or we'll be here all night. It's just down the deck."

"Oooh, kwee come, too?" one of the women said.

"Better not," Lou said. "This one looks like it's gonna be a mess before it gets funnier."

"Why don't you two stay here and sell tickets?" Sam said to the women as the two men walked him out the glass doors and down the deck.

"Think you can write?" Lou said in the radio room after he and his companion had eased Sam into a chair at one of the small tables and he had pulled a pad of blanks into position in front of him.

"Damn right I can," Sam said. "I do it for a living."

"Poor bastard must be starving," Lou muttered to his companion.

"I heard that," Sam said. "And it just shows how much you know. I hapna be rich, see? You don't believe me, just go downa my cabin and looka my luggage. That coat my wife's wearing ain't no six-ninety-five from Klein's, Buster. That's mink. From Jaeckel's, Mac. And this apartment I'm decorating, it's a ten-thousand-dollar job, kid. Good as anything you live in, you uptown wise guy. Probably better. Ever fill anybody's teeth for twelve thousand bucks? Or maybe you're not a dentist. Maybe you're one of these Seventh Avenue boys, chum. Ever get a ten-thousand-dollar advance on one number? No? You don't manufacture dresses? Ooh! A doctor! From Park Avenue, yet, I'll bet. Well, next time you get fifty thousand bucks for conning some poor slob out of his appendix, the way I got it out of Mercury Films for one story, that's the day you can come along and give me the hairy eyeball. Can I write, this guy asks. What a laugh. Where the hell is that pencil?"

The man named Lou placed it in Sam's hand, and at once all was clarity and order. It was as though he were sitting at his mother's kitchen table facing the pad of yellow foolscap with his Parker. Without the slightest difficulty, as though he were copying the words from a blackboard inside his head, he lettered the message and signed it.

"You must get paid by the word," said the man named Lou. "Longest cable I ever saw."

"Stick around, kid, and you'll see a lot more," Sam said. He got to his feet, staggered to the radio officer's desk, and said, "Right away, please."

"Yes, sir," the radio officer said. "Anything else, sir?"

"Yes," Sam said slowly. "But I can't remember what it is."

"I can," said the man named Lou. "Officer, what's that thing signed? Simon?"

"No, sir," the radio officer said. "Silver, sir. Samuel Silver."

"You mind calling the purser's office and finding out the number of Mr. Silver's cabin?" Lou said. "We're getting a little tired of his company and would like to tuck him in."

Somewhat surprisingly, they did. Sam remembered wondering, as they pulled the blankets up to his chin, where the hell Jennie was, but that was the last thing he did remember. For a long time after he woke up he had no idea where he was, partly because he didn't really wake up. He seemed to ooze, like a slowly squeezed blob of toothpaste, from one darkish, shapeless, agonizing nightmare into another one, slightly lighter in color, and at once tried to crawl back, but he couldn't. He couldn't even throw up properly, a discovery that surprised him as well as somebody else in the cabin.

"Oh, Christ," a voice said, and it occurred to Sam that it must belong to Jennie, but that was as far as his mind would take him. He knew he was going to die, a process he had never before realized was this painful and exhausting, so that he could scarcely drag together the energy to wish that it would hurry up and finish him off. It didn't, however. It seemed to enjoy toying with him. Back and forth he went, from the darker nightmare to the lighter one, with short pauses during which it seemed to him Jennie or somebody like Jennie would appear and try to tidy him up or force warm liquids down his throat. Several times she succeeded, but it all came right back, and a great many times she or somebody else helped him back and forth to the bathroom, but these trips were the worst parts of the horror, and he made no attempt to identify the owner of the hands that pushed and pulled and swabbed him. At last, without warning, it stopped abruptly. Sam found himself sitting up in bed, staring at a ruddy-cheeked, smiling young man in a white coat who was whirling a stubby implement around in a mug.

"Morning, sir," he said. "Feeling better?"

"I don't know," Sam said.

"Well, you are, sir," the young man said. "I can tell you that."

"What happened?"

"We had a very rough crossing, sir. The doctor thinks in addition to the old *mal de mer* you had a touch of flu." He saw Sam looking around the cabin and said, "Mrs. Silver's up having breakfast. She asked me to give you a shave and a bit of a wash. You'll be going ashore in the barge soon. Plymouth, sir. Now, if you'll just hold your head back a bit. That's right, sir. That's fine. I shouldn't try to talk for a while, if I were you, sir."

Sam didn't. He didn't even try to think until they were ashore and Jennie had seen them through customs and they were in the boat train on their way to London, and then his thoughts were so confused that he welcomed the chance to say to the waiter, who had started to slap down plates in front of everybody in the car, "No, thanks. Nothing for me."

"You better get something down into your stomach," Jennie said. "You haven't had anything solid for five days." She turned to the waiter and said, "He'll eat."

The waiter looked dubious, but he set two places, and when he moved on to the next table, Sam said, "I must have been pretty bad."

"You were worse than that," Jennie said. "Don't try to explain it. The doctor couldn't. Just look out the window. This is England. It cost us a great deal of money to get here. Try not to miss it the way you missed the Atlantic Ocean."

Sam missed a great deal of it nonetheless, even though he did as he had been told and stared fixedly out the window. The trouble was with his thoughts. He could make them work up to the *bon voyage* party, and the discovery he had made in the lounge, and the fight with Jennie, but then his thoughts began to leap about, like a team of perfectly trained horses that stepped along smartly in their harness, responding promptly and dutifully to each tug of the reins, until they reached a certain place in the road, a graveyard perhaps, that held some mysterious terror for them, and at once they forgot all their training and bolted like a couple of wild mustangs. Something had happened that Sam's mind refused to accept, and while he knew he should be grateful for its efforts to spare him a recollection he was not going to enjoy, he knew also that he wasn't going to see much scenery, or anything else he stared at, until the missing piece was found.

Several minutes after they checked into their hotel at Marble Arch it looked as though he had found it. A couple of cables were waiting for him, and while Jennie tore one open and read it, Sam read the other. His was from Bud Bienstock.

Dear Sam we are getting the most wonderful reactions to your story from all readers advance copies our next issue and at editorial conference this morning was suggested you take same two characters Terry Baker and Harold Lewis with their Lower East Side New York background on a tour of Europe work out any plot you want perhaps Harold gets job with Wall Street brokerage firm and is sent to Europe to scout big cities for opening branch offices or maybe he goes over as salesman for some American product and he takes Terry along whatever plot device you use okay with us so long you keep these two brash New York kids moving London Paris Berlin Rome Brussels Vienna Edinburgh the works with Terry making her snappy wisecracks about European clothes culture men women love sex art customs et al and Harold getting into scrapes as a result her remarks and both them have to work their way out of trouble by turning tables in typical American fashion on all these frogs limeys krauts wops et al if you agree do this and earnestly hope you do will pay twenty thousand for four parts and throw in ten thousand for your expenses so you'll really be getting this trip free and will come home with a bundle please cable acceptance collect will at once deposit ten thousand expense money with your agents Sargent & Sargent all best to that bright little girl you married to and mazel tov

BUD BIENSTOCK

Sam crumpled the cable with a series of angry smacks of his open palms, dropped the wad of paper on the floor, stamped on it, then kicked the flattened lump into a corner of the room that looked out on Hyde Park.

"I see you're feeling better," Jennie said.

"Much," Sam said.

"What was that?"

"A long insult, probably the longest ever sent since they laid the Atlantic cable, from that great Zionist leader and your admirer, Mr. Bud Bienstock, the son of a bitch. What's yours?"

"It's from Keeley Cuff," Jennie said. "Apparently in answer to a cable you sent him from the ship."

"That's right," Sam said, reaching out. "Let me have that."

The missing piece that his mind seemed to want to keep from him was apparently about to fall into place.

"In a minute," Jennie said, pulling the cable out of his reach. "What did you tell Cuff in your cable?"

Speaking slowly and clearly, so there would be no room in her mind for thinking there was any difference between his feelings on making the discovery the day they sailed and his present intentions, Sam said, "I told him I'd just discovered that *I'll Make My Heaven* had been offered to him without my knowledge in a bowdlerized version and therefore the contracts had been signed and I had taken the advance under false pretenses. My characters were not named Terry Baker and Harold Lewis, as they appear in the galleys and obviously must have appeared in the unauthorized manuscript that had been offered to him. My characters, I said in the cable, were named Tessie Birnbaum and Harry Lipschitz. If Gerosa & Jellaby were prepared to make this correction in the galleys, I was prepared to bear the expense, and they could go ahead with our agreement to publish the novel simultaneously with the appearance of the fourth installment in *American Bride*. If they were not prepared to make this change, I said in my cable to Cuff, I hereby released him from the contract to publish the book and he could use my cable as an authorization to my agents Sargent & Sargent to return to Gerosa & Jellaby the ten-thousand-dollar advance they paid me. That's what I cabled Mr. Keeley Cuff," Sam said.

Jennie shook her head slowly. "You shouldn't have done it, Sam," she said.

"You didn't ask my opinion when you did that thing behind my back," Sam said. "I'm not asking your opinion now that I'm undoing it in front of your face."

Jennie's head continued to move slowly, from side to side, like a metronome.

"You shouldn't have done it, Sam," she repeated. "Between the *American Bride* serialization and the Gerosa & Jellaby advance and the Mercury picture sale, we took in a gross of seventy-two thousand, Sam. Sargent & Sargent took seventy-two hundred in commissions, three thousand went to Mrs. Grimsby for the Eleventh Street job, we spent thousands getting ready for this trip, and we've given Mrs. Grimsby the authority to spend between nine and ten thousand on the Gramercy Park place, every penny of which she has undoubtedly already committed. You can check my figures later, but I assure you they're right, and what they come to is this: out of our original seventy-two thousand gross, when you take off all the things I just listed, we have almost exactly twenty thousand left after taxes. I figured that was enough to carry us through this trip and the writing of your next book. I figured wrong." Jennie held out the cable. "Cuff says Gerosa & Jellaby will not make the changes you request. He says if they had known the book dealt with the kind of characters you say you wrote, they would not have offered the ten-thousand-dollar advance because they know a book with those kinds of characters cannot sell enough to earn back such an advance." Jennie thrust the cable out a little further. "Cuff says they don't want to publish *I'll Make My Heaven* under your conditions, so they consider themselves released from the contract and they are asking Sargent & Sargent to follow your instructions and return the ten thousand dollars. Here, Sam, read it."

"I don't have to," he said, making no move to take the piece of paper. "This is one time, probably the only time, I feel pretty sure you're not lying."

"With that advance paid back, Sam, we're down to a few thousand dollars. You shouldn't have done it, Sam."

"I'm a better judge of that than you are," he said.

"No, you're not," Jennie said. "Not any more."

"What the hell do you mean?"

"I mean you shouldn't have done it, Sam."

"Why the Christ not?"

"Because I'm pregnant, Sam," Jennie said.

By the time Billy arrived in Doctors Hospital on East End Avenue, the European trip, and the advance Sam had received from Bud Bienstock for *In a Sense Abroad*, were behind him.

But Sam's credit was good, Bud Bienstock was clamoring for another serial, and other editors were asking Claude Sargent if this new man Sam Silver would work for them. The fact that he was able to, it seemed to Sam, could be attributed directly to Billy. The baby, by providing Jennie with an interest that absorbed at least some of her energy and a good deal of her time, had brought Sam's relationship with her to a plateau. On it he found it possible to function, if not with the same passion that had informed every moment of their ten-day flight through New England and which Sam now saw could not possibly have been sustained indefinitely, then with a serenity that provided an ideal climate for the kind of life on which he was now embarked.

The presence of an infant in a nursery down the hall brought a sense of purpose and stability to the large apartment on Gramercy Park that had been lacking in the smaller duplex on West Eleventh Street. It was as though all the lumber and bricks and window sashes and other materials necessary for building a house, which had been lying tumbled about on a building site, had suddenly begun to be converted into a habitable structure by the appearance of the foreman in charge of the job. On West Eleventh Street, Sam saw, he had been a talented neophyte who, somewhat to his own surprise, had published a fairly successful first novel. On Gramercy Park he became a working writer.

In the light of the satisfaction this gave him, he was able to see something else: what Jennie had done, which less than a year ago had caused him to hurl a copy of *American Bride* at her head, was the most convincing illustration he had ever encountered that there was some truth in a phrase he had never believed: *his own good*.

Sam was reasonably sure she had not done it with only his interests in mind. He was equally sure she had not done it merely for the obvious reason, namely, because she wanted a mink coat and Bergdorf dresses. But since Sam's greatest certainty now about Jennie was that he would never understand completely why she did anything, and it seemed to him not unlikely that she did not know herself, he was prepared to work with what he did understand, and this much Sam Silver understood about himself: his creative faculties, such as they now were, were atrophied rather than stimulated by poverty.

If he had been unable to pay for the nurse who helped Jennie care for his son down the hall, Sam would have been unable to earn the nurse's salary with his Parker and his yellow pad. The fact that Jennie's machinations had made it possible for Sam without a tremor to hire a nurse, in turn made it possible for Sam to write the stories that earned the money that made it possible for him with equal peace of mind to hire the maid Jennie felt they needed to help the nurse. As long as he was free from money worries the money rolled in, and as long as the money rolled in he worked without difficulty.

Part of the reason for this was a sense of organization Sam had not hitherto realized he possessed. His first story had been an act over which he had almost no control. The next six, written after his first visit to Claude Sargent's office, had been self-conscious acts performed with materials which it had not occurred to him then to examine for the purpose of discovering how much control he had over them. In the Gramercy Park study, which Mrs. Grimsby at his request had furnished to look like a commonplace but efficiently laid-out office, Sam examined those six stories and discovered at once why they had not sold: the intense reality of the material crossed with the artificiality of the craftsmanship aroused in the reader a sense of confusion. By changing the names of the characters, by converting Birnbaums to Bakers, as Jennie had done with *I'll Make My*

Heaven, Sam was able to blunt the edge of the reality and bring it into closer alignment with the smooth texture of the narration.

All six of the stories sold, to Claude Sargent's but not to Sam's surprise. He was beginning to understand where his strength lay, and he organized his working life to exploit it.

Discovering that ideas for stories, scraps of dialogue, outlines for characters, titles, and all sorts of literary odds and ends came to him all day long, in all sorts of places, and that inevitably the new ideas crowded out of his head the older ones, he set up a system of notebooks in which to store and season what he saw was as much the raw material of his trade as lumber is to the carpenter. Learning that after a lifetime of being forced to rise at six, he could not learn to sleep later, he trained himself to go to the study as soon as he woke up, while the rest of the household was asleep, and get his work done before the distractions of his home and the people with whom he dealt, such as editors and agents, interfered. Experimenting for a while with various methods, in the hope of hitting on the one best suited to his temperament, he decided finally that his chances of getting a job done were increased if he knew how much of it he expected himself to accomplish within a given time, and from then on he made it a point every morning to fill at least ten pages of yellow foolscap with his own invented mixture of abbreviated longhand and Pitman squiggles. In this way, assured of a steady flow on which he could count, he had no hesitations about cutting or discarding pages that did not meet the standards he gradually began to evolve for himself.

These standards, which were nobody's business but his own, were at the core of the disciplined existence in which he had imbedded himself. Sam was aware that Claude and Sophie Sargent, though pleased by the financial aspect of his success, were troubled by it. He knew they felt, although they were too discreet to say, that he had deliberately abandoned the high road of the dubiously remunerated artist for the somewhat lower path of the handsomely paid journeyman. Even in his own home, where what he did for a living was rarely mentioned because Sam did not care to talk about it and Jennie was clearly not very interested, he sensed that she had no very great regard for his work. None of this bothered him. He knew what he was doing. He refused, when the Sargents suggested and Jennie, obviously after some behind-the-scenes prodding from Claude or Sophie, also urged him, to seek book publication for *I'll Make My Heaven.*

"It's still exactly the same manuscript you wrote," Sophie Sargent said. "The fact that it's appeared in a magazine and on the screen in a somewhat different version does not change what you have on paper. Trafalgar, Singlenight and Gerosa & Jellaby are not the only publishers in the business, you know. Half a dozen of them have asked me if you're free, and I took the liberty of telling Duke Svaboda of Pinnacle Press at lunch the other day about *I'll Make My Heaven*. I don't mean I told him the details of what happened and who did it. I merely said that while you were in Europe certain liberties had been taken with the manuscript up at *American Bride* which, when you found out about them, drove you into a rage but it was too late to do anything about it, and so you had withdrawn the book from Gerosa & Jellaby. Duke asked if he could read the original manuscript, and I hope you don't mind, Sam dear, but I let him read it, and he called this morning to say he loves it, and you can have a Pinnacle Press contract on exactly the same terms you got from Gerosa & Jellaby. Why don't you let Pinnacle do it, Sam? What have you got to lose?"

The answer, which Sam did not make, was: my self-respect. He had lost it once—in his disciplined mind he was careful not to say it had been taken from him; he knew that Jennie could not have done what she did without a laxity on his part that amounted to unconscious consent—and he had no intention of losing it again. He could not, however, lose what he did not have, and at the core of his disciplined existence was the determination to win it back.

To do this he had chosen his own arena: the heart of enemy terrain; and his own weapons: those that could do him the most damage. To have made it easy for himself would have destroyed the value of the prize he sought. He wanted to make certain that when he won it back, he would have something that even Kenyon Poole would consider worth winning.

For Sam had never forgotten what the author of *The Small Meal* had said to him on that first day in Claude Sargent's office, or the moment in Westport after Kenyon Poole had stepped out of the car from the sanatorium when it had dawned on Sam that already, at twenty, because he had debased a piece of his work by turning it into a movie treatment, he had gouged irreparable nicks in the finely honed edges of the tools of his craft.

All during the trip to Europe, while he and Jennie moved from country to country gathering the material for Bud Bienstock's four-parter, Sam had thought about the problem. It was something he couldn't, nor would have wanted to, discuss with Jennie or anybody else. It was a moral problem. The morality involved nobody but himself. He would have to find the answer for himself.

He found the answer in Paris, in a kosher restaurant in Montmartre called Chez Kirschner, to which he and Jennie had gone because, from the description in the guidebook, they both agreed that it sounded like a wonderful background for some sort of episode in which those two brash kids from New York, Terry Baker and Harold Lewis, could with typical American methods turn the tables on a bunch of frogs. Sam and Jennie were wrong. The frogs all looked like Sam's father and mother, and the waiter, a thin, round-shouldered, hollow-eyed man, who appeared to be sixty and proved to be forty, told Sam in Yiddish that he should not take his wife to Berlin on this trip because, even with an American passport, a Jew was not safe in Germany today.

Jennie had at once embarked on an animated discussion with the waiter about Hitler in which Sam had become involved mainly because, Jennie's Yiddish being almost as bad as her French, he had to act as interpreter. Sam had acted efficiently enough, since his Yiddish was excellent, but without much interest because the questions Jennie asked and the answers the waiter made were all on a large, round, impersonal level, like the editorials about Nazism in the *New Republic*, and besides, Sam was preoccupied with his private problem. Then the waiter had said something about his own escape from Germany and, all at once, Sam's senses came alive.

"I'm sorry, I missed that," he said. "Would you say it again?"

"I live every day in a cooking pot of shame," the hollow-eyed man said sadly. "Because I ran away."

"But you would have been killed if you hadn't run away," Sam said. "Besides, thousands of Jews are running away from Germany every day."

The bowed shoulders moved in a shrug of hopelessness. "Those thousands they're not me," the waiter said. "And to be dead is better than to be ashamed."

"That's ridiculous," Jennie said impatiently. "If you're dead you can't fight back. So you do feel ashamed, so what? At least you're alive, and when this war we're all heading for finally does come, you'll live to see Hitler and all his damned Nazis destroyed. Sam, tell him that. Tell him he's wrong to think to be ashamed is worse than to be dead. Tell him."

But Sam did not tell him, because all at once Sam was reliving that moment in Westport when Kenyon Poole had stepped out of the car, and Sam knew the bowed man in front of him was not wrong.

"How do you get through your days?" Sam said instead. "If you feel that way, what keeps you alive?"

"I hope," the waiter said.

"That it will all be over some day?" Sam said. "That Hitler will be destroyed?"

The gaunt head moved slowly from side to side. "No, no," he said. "That will happen anyway. Hitler is not the first one that he tried to wipe us out. On his grave, like on all the others, some day we'll all pee. What

I hope—" The bowed shoulders moved again in the shrug of hopelessness. "I hope some day before it happens, before others they do it for me, I'll find somewhere the strength to climb out of my cooking pot of shame, and go back, and do a little something myself, so when the time comes, I'll not only do it, but also I'll have the *right* to pee on his grave."

Sam never learned whether the hollow-eyed man ever found his courage. He and Jennie left Paris for Rome the next morning. But the man's words went with Sam, and by the time he and Jennie returned to New York, Sam had worked out the technique of his penance and regeneration: he would do what nobody had ever done before; what Claude and Sophie Sargent had said they had watched others try and fail to do; what Kenyon Poole had said was impossible.

He would take his beautifully honed tools into the market place. With them, on materials better suited to the sledge hammer and the ax, he would hew for himself a place on which the journeyman would look with envy and the artist with contempt. And then, when in the eyes of both it looked as though he could go no further, he would prove they had both been wrong. Far from ruining his tools in the market place, he would prove that he had honed them to a finer cutting edge than they had possessed when they were placed in his keeping at birth. In short, when he had taken enough money from the Bud Bienstocks to achieve financial independence, Sam Silver at thirty intended to write the novel he had thought he was writing at twenty.

Living with a secret goal of this kind proved to have certain advantages that had not even crossed Sam's mind when the plan first began to take shape in it.

For example, while he would drop in on Claude Sargent every now and then to "talk out" the plot of a story with which he was having difficulty, Sam never had to come in, as almost all of Sargent's other clients did when a fit of depression blocked them from working, for one of those morale hand-holding and pep-talk sessions that Top called "soul swabbing." When Sam felt depressed he didn't tell anybody about it. He merely turned up the flame of the inner fire by which he lived, so to speak, and was soon warm enough to go back to work. As a result, he found to his surprise that he was getting a reputation in magazine circles as a man of strength and dependability, and he could point to several stories that, whatever their merits ultimately proved to be, had been sold before they were written because an editor had needed a piece of fiction by a certain date to flesh out a meager issue, and he had learned that Sam Silver could be counted on to deliver.

Similarly, since most of the time he spent with other people, at the parties Jennie was constantly giving or taking him to, he was only vaguely aware of what was being said to him, Sam soon developed a protective manner, consisting of a small, bright, interested smile and a slight, almost imperceptible nodding of the head to the tempo of his companion's speech, behind which, in the small private joke he had invented for himself, he could peacefully contemplate his novel. As a result, and again to his surprise, he began to be known as a friendly, affable person with whom it was fun to be, because unlike most writers, instead of constantly talking about himself, he was interested in hearing you talk about you.

It was not unlike, Sam decided, living in a monastery from which, when the peaceful pleasures of the contemplative life became a bit dull, you could pop out for an evening at the Stork Club. Sam supposed it was because he had not popped out for some time that he was unaware how he had become involved with the C.T.D.A.B.C.U.O.O.B.Y. He popped out now, carrying the letter from his study into the living room, where Jennie, in her robe and over her breakfast tray, was going through her own mail.

"What's this damn thing?" Sam said.

Jennie looked up at him across her glasses, took the piece of delicate pink note paper with the heavy black monogram, glanced at it quickly, then looked up again.

"It's a note from Trish Teal thanking you for agreeing to be a sponsor."

"I know it's a note of thanks," Sam said. "A sponsor of what?"

"The C.T.D.A.B.C.U.O.O.B.Y."

"What the hell is that?"

Jennie took off her glasses with the right-to-left slashing gesture that always reminded Sam of a hurrying officer impatiently returning the salute of a passing private soldier.

"Sam, for heaven's sake, you were there."

"There where?"

"The Teals' for dinner, three nights ago."

Sam closed his eyes, flipped through the neatly indexed slides in his mind until he got back to three nights ago, and turned on the light switch of his memory. Bethany Teal was a poet who wrote verse that appeared in *Harper's* and the *Atlantic* at the bottom of short stories and articles that ended without quite filling the page. His wife Trish was a Shlansky from Chattanooga, the department-store not the textile Shlanskys, and she and Bethany lived in a magnificent town house on East Sixty-first Street, just around the corner from Claude and Sophie Sargent.

"Jesus, yes, the masks," Sam said, opening his eyes. Between poems Bethany Teal collected Japanese Noh masks that made the walls of his home look like pages from a gigantic Oriental stamp album. "What happened?"

"After dinner?" Jennie said. "In the upstairs drawing room? You mean you don't remember?"

Sam closed his eyes again and flipped to another slide. "Oh, yes," he said. "All those people who came in later and sat on those tiny gold chairs. I thought it was that string quartet again. Wasn't it?"

"Weren't you listening?"

"Well, sort of. What did I miss?"

"You missed the organization of the Committee to Defend America by Cleaning Up Our Own Back Yard, that's what you missed."

"It sounds noisier than that damned string quartet."

"You know, Sam, there are times when I think you live in a private world of your own. How you can make jokes at a time like this about a thing like the C.T.D.A.B.C.U.O.O.B.Y. really beats me. There's a war on over there in Europe, Sam, and there are influential people and powerful interests in this country that are trying to get us into it. Unless other people and other interests do something to stop them, this country sure as hell is going to be dragged into this war to pull England's chestnuts out of the fire again, the way we did in 1917."

"All I did was come out here and ask you what Trish Teal is writing me a note of thanks for," Sam said, "and what I get is tomorrow's editorial from the *Daily Worker*."

"Are you implying that the C.T.D.A.B.C.U.O.O.B.Y. is communist-sponsored?"

"How can I imply anything about something I know nothing about?" Sam said. "But isn't that the current C.P. line? Let's stay out of Europe's quarrels because Uncle Joe is staying out, too?"

"I see when something like the C.T.D.A.B.C.U.O.O.B.Y. is being organized, you're in such a fog you don't even know you're present," Jennie said. "But when a bunch of fascists are sitting around making cracks about a perfectly reasonable non-aggression pact, you memorize every word that's uttered."

"Not all circles consider that little deal Joe made with Adolf just before the Nazis went into Poland as perfectly reasonable," Sam said. "But I didn't come out here to argue that. I've got a lunch date with Bud Bienstock at one-thirty, and I've still got almost a thousand words to go before I can close up shop for the day. What do I do about this?" He tapped Trish Teal's note.

"Nothing," Jennie said. "You agreed to be a sponsor."

Sam looked at her sharply. "When did I do that?"

"You mean to say you're not even aware of what you did?"

"Who did it, Jennie? You or me?"

"Some writer. You or me."

"I'm not writing now. I'm asking a question. Did you commit me to this foolish plate of alphabet soup?"

"I suppose only a writer of those crappy stories Bud Bienstock uses to separate the sandwich-spread ads from the brassière ads would refer to an organization that is intended to save this country from destruction as foolish."

"Paul Revere saved this country from destruction, or so I was taught in school, and he made his living by hammering out pewter chamber pots," Sam said. "Don't obfuscate the issue with cracks about the way I make mine."

"Where did you get that one? Win it in a raffle?"

"No, I looked it up in the dictionary one day. Maybe if you learned to spend a little time with that book instead of going to all those meetings with Trish Teal you'd learn the words with which to answer a simple question. What have you got me into?"

"An organization that intends to do precisely what its name says," Jennie said. "Defend America by cleaning up our own back yard."

"What's wrong with our back yard?"

"It's littered with the kind of dangerous junk that spawned fascism in Italy and Germany," Jennie said. "Jim Crowism. Slums. Child labor. Primitive factory conditions. Shameful minimum wage laws. Anti-Semitism."

"I see in at least one circle we Jews have made it down to the bottom of the list."

"You'll see something else, my friend. You'll see full-scale fascism in this country unless we devote our energies to clearing up these shocking conditions in our own back yard," Jennie said. "There are people who don't want this mess cleared up, just as there were people in Italy and Germany who didn't want it cleared up, because they wanted fascism, which pays them enormous dividends, while decent minimum wage laws and slum clearance cut into their profits. The same kind of profiteering bastards in this country are now urging us to get into this war to save poor, bleeding, noble England. Why? Because for these bastards wars are profitable and that's what they want, profits, but the profits they make do nothing to strengthen this country, whereas if we stay out of this war and devote our energies to clearing out our slums and getting some decent medication to the disease-ridden mountaineers of Tennessee, the specter of fascism will be pushed back, away from this country, and we'll be a stronger country because our people will be healthier and happier, and nobody attacks a strong country, not even a maniac like Hitler, and that's why the Committee to Defend America by Cleaning Up Our Own Back Yard was organized, and that's what I've got you into, Sammy boy."

"How far in?" Sam said.

"Don't worry," Jennie said. "You won't have to do anything that will interfere with your steady cranking out of fictional sausage for *American Bride.*"

"Just what will I have to do?" Sam said.

"Nothing," Jennie said. "Your name will appear on our letterhead, along with a lot of well-known people in various fields, including some real writers like Tom Sacheverell, by the way, so you'll be in good company and ought to feel honored."

"I don't," Sam said. "Has the stationery been printed?"

"I don't know," Jennie said. "Why?"

"You'd better find out," Sam said. "Because if my name appears on it, they're going to have to chuck it all in the ash can."

"Now, listen, Sam—"

"No, *you* listen," he said. "Your political thinking and what you do about it, which I happen to feel makes about as much sense as my mother's thinking about the English language, are your own business. I won't interfere, mainly because I know it won't do any good, but also because I've never really been able to follow your thinking, and I've decided the energy devoted to making the attempt is wasted. But you're not carrying me with you. This thing you call the Committee to Defend America by Cleaning Up Our Own Back Yard is cut from the same nutty bolt of cloth that once made you believe you could stamp out fascism in Grover Cleverland High by dressing up as Shylock at the graduation exercises, and later made you think you could get Marshall Umberg's job at Mercury by sending a letter to his boss in California. Count me out, Jennie. You better call Trish Teal right now, or whoever is in charge of printing that stationery, and have them take my name off. If they don't, I'll call my lawyer and raise a stink that will blow the whole silly enterprise out of the water before it is even launched."

Jennie replaced the glasses on her nose, leaned back into the five-hundred-dollar sofa with which Mrs. Grimsby had replaced the two-hundred-dollar couch she had put behind Sam on West Eleventh Street, and said quietly, "Sam, what are you afraid of?"

It was a serious question, asked in a way he had learned meant she expected a serious answer, and all at once the monastic life, from which he could escape at intervals by popping out to the Stork Club, seemed inadequate, and he wanted desperately to tell her, but he couldn't.

"Sam, are you afraid you'll be called a radical or a communist or a troublemaker?" Jennie said. "Are you afraid if you get that kind of reputation people like Bud Bienstock will stop buying your stories?"

"No," Sam said, because this much of the truth, since it was peripheral, he didn't mind revealing. "They'll never stop buying my stories, no matter what I do politically or in any other way, so long as the stories are as good as they are, which at the moment is better than the work anybody else is doing in the field, and they are steadily getting better."

Jennie whipped off the glasses with that saluting gesture and said, "That's the first conceited thing I've ever heard you say."

"It's not conceit," Sam said carefully. "It's the truth, and you'll never hear it again, but I've felt for some time that maybe you ought to know, and since you presented me with the opportunity, I thought I'd take it."

Jennie looked at him carefully for several moments, and then, as though what she saw was out of focus with some other and perhaps preferable image, she replaced the glasses on her nose.

"Is that the truth?" Jennie said. "Can I accept that? You're not afraid?"

"I'm afraid of lots of things," Sam said. "But not of that."

"What kinds of things?"

"Walking under ladders. Something happening to Billy. You dying."

"You're afraid of that?"

"Terrified," Sam said.

She gave him one of those smiles that moved his heart, and the temptation to tell her the central truth was suddenly so overwhelming that he felt himself gripped by an even greater terror, the terror that he would succumb, but Jennie saved him by breaking the silence.

"But you're not afraid of economic reprisals from people like Bud Bienstock?" she said.

"Not so long as I keep turning out as good a mousetrap as the one I'm making now," Sam said.

"Then why don't you join us?" Jennie said. "Why won't you let the C.T.D.A.B.C.U.O.O.B.Y. use your name on its letterhead?"

Because to join anything was to share something, and in the fierce jealousy of his secret devotion, sharing was not possible on any level. To belong to a group, no matter what its function, regardless of how irrelevant were its activities to the inner fire by which he lived, was to diminish his exclusive right to tend the flame in his own way, without considering the wishes of companions to whom he was pledged. His penance was his private affair. Regeneration could be earned only if the effort remained inviolate. He was alone, and the sustenance he drew from moving toward his secret goal depended entirely on his remaining alone.

"Why don't we just say I'm what you once called Top Sargent?" Sam said. "An apolitical slob?"

"Because for the first time in all the years we've known each other," Jennie said, "I'm beginning to think maybe you're not."

Shying away from the dangerous area, Sam laughed and said, "Whether I am or whether I'm not, and frankly I don't really know, I'm still asking you to call Trish and keep my name off that letterhead."

"It's not on yet," Jennie said. "I mean we haven't gone to the printer yet because there are a couple of biggies we're angling for, and there's no point in paying out all that money to the printer and then, the day the letterheads come in, you find out you've landed someone like Kenyon Poole, for instance."

"Him you'll never land," Sam said.

"Sam, where have you been? Don't you read anything? Ken Poole is a mover and shaker. He's been involved in all kinds of what you call liberal activities. He'll be there all right," Jennie said. "Alison Grimsby said she could bring Poole to the buttoning-up dinner."

"The what?" Sam said.

"Trish is giving a dinner party Thursday night to finalize everything. Come to definite and final decisions on who's to be chairman, vice-chairman, secretary, treasurer, and of course the list of sponsors, and you know how she talks. She calls it her buttoning-up dinner."

"And Alison Grimsby thinks she can bring Kenyon Poole to it?" Sam said.

"So she says."

"How much do you want to bet?" Sam said. "And name your own odds."

"I'll do something better than that," Jennie said. "You come to the dinner with me. If Poole does not show up, you'll never hear another word out of me about the C.T.D.A.B.C.U.O.O.B.Y. If Poole does show up, give me one more chance to try and argue you into becoming a sponsor. And if Poole agrees to become a sponsor, you also agree. How's that?"

Sam didn't really know. Something curious was going through his mind. He could catch only glimpses of it, as though it were a message on one of those streamers that airplanes trail along over crowded beaches urging people to buy some product or patronize some establishment, and the streamer had been caught by the wind and was being whipped about.

"If Kenyon Poole shows up at the dinner," Sam repeated slowly, "I have to listen to one more sales talk from you."

"And if he agrees to become a sponsor of the C.T.D.A.B.C.U.O.O.B.Y.," Jennie said, "you do likewise."

"Fair enough," said Sam, and went back to the study. But the words came slowly. Between the gold nib of the Parker and the yellow page of the pad, that pennant kept whipping about with the urgent message he could not read clearly. Sam knew, as he added the finally finished tenth page to the pile in his desk drawer and went to the bedroom to dress for his lunch date, that most of those last thousand words would be discarded tomorrow. What he did not know, as he stepped into the elevator in the American Bride Building on Fifth Avenue, was why the message, which seemed to have something to do with the bet Sam had made with Jennie, should be so elusive.

"Oh, Mr. Silver," Bud's secretary said when Sam came into the editor's mahogany-paneled outer office. The *American Bride* editorial quarters had been designed and decorated to look like a series of Episcopal chapels. "Mr. Bienstock is at a circulation meeting and won't be coming back here. He said would you go right up to the dining room? He'll meet you there."

Sam's spirits, which were in an inexplicably depressed state, moved a trifle lower. When Bud Bienstock was in a good mood, he took his business guests to "21" and made a fuss about getting a good table. When Bud's mood was bad, usually as the result of either a report in the papers of a setback in the Zionist movement or the loss of a skirmish in his ceaseless circulation war with the *Ladies' Home Journal*, he fed his guests in the company dining room and made pointed remarks if they left anything on their plates. It was difficult, Sam had found, not to.

The *American Bride* company dining room was part of the magazine's widely advertised home economics testing laboratory, in which every product advertised in its pages was subjected to a series of secret tests before it was granted the famous, and so far as Sam had been able to discover, much coveted A.B.G. or American Bride Guarantee seal. He had often wondered what these tests consisted of in the case of, for example, brassières and sanitary napkins. Sam did not have to wonder about the tests on food products. He had been a part of too many of them.

"Yes, sir," the plump, smiling, gray-haired woman in the neat gingham housedress said to Sam as he came into the dining room. "Mr. Bienstock is waiting for you, Mr. Silver."

The company dining room was furnished to look like part of the maple and chintz New England home of an economically comfortable but definitely not rich small businessman, and all the employees in it were fiftyish; weighed a hundred and forty or better; wore gingham, perpetual smiles, and no make-up; and looked like the beaming grandmother in the canned cranberry-sauce ads at the moment when, faced by her entire eager clan gathered round the festive board, she brings in the Thanksgiving turkey.

"Hi, Sam," Bud Bienstock said from the maple breakfast nook in the sunny bow window that looked out on nothing. The sunlight was the result of a concealed arrangement of electric bulbs and mirrors. "You're two minutes early."

"Some day I'll beat you yet," Sam said.

"You're just about the only one I can think of who might," Bud said. "The rest of the people I have to deal with, they have no more notions about promptness than a Borneo head hunter has about vegetarianism. How's that bright little girl you're married to?"

"Fine," Sam said. "Sends you her best."

"Little Tommy?"

"Billy. He's fine."

"That's right," Bud Bienstock said. "It's Tom Sacheverell's son that's named Tommy. He walking yet?"

"Just about," said Sam of his son who had been walking for a year. "Mrs. B. okay?"

"Except for worrying about the war," Bud said. "Christ, women. She thinks Roosevelt is a fascist because in that destroyers-for-bases deal he gave Churchill only those fifty old four-stackers instead of throwing in all our aircraft carriers, the state of Florida, and Cordell Hull's left nut. It's carrot juice mixed with strained eggplant sauce."

"No, sir, Mr. Bienstock, if you'll be excusing me, sir, please," said the plump woman who had set down the glasses. "It's kumquat juice mixed with the strained eggplant, sir."

Bud Bienstock took a sip and said, "So it is, Mrs. Pembroke, so it is." She went bustling off to the kitchen as though he had told her the magazine planned to put her picture on the cover of its Mother's Day issue, and Bud said, "Seen Kenyon Poole lately?"

"Me?" Sam said. "Not lately. Once in a while. Is he in town?"

"He's in town all right," Bud Bienstock said. "I thought you and he were good friends or something?"

"I see him around," Sam said. "Why?"

"He must be on the sauce again," Bud Bienstock said. The Star of David in his cuff link winked in the artificial sunlight as he drained his glass. "Good stuff, no?"

"Great," Sam said, forcing down a mouthful. It was in the *American Bride* company dining room that he had finally grasped something that had puzzled him for years: what some writers meant when they said of a character that his gorge rose. "What's Poole done?"

"Done and doing," Bud Bienstock said. "Christ, writers. To hell with Kenyon Poole. That's not why I asked you to lunch. Thank you, Mrs. Pembroke."

"You're welcome, sir, Mr. Bienstock," said the plump, smiling, gray-haired woman, and as she set the plate down in front of Sam, she said, "Would the gentleman like, sir, the French or the Russian dressing, sir?"

"French, please," said Sam. In the *American Bride* company kitchen Russian dressing was made with cream cheese and chopped filberts.

"No, wait, Mrs. Pembroke," said Bud Bienstock. "Give him some of the Z-248."

"Yes, sir, Mr. Bienstock, of course, sir. For you, sir, too, Mr. Bienstock, sir?"

"No, thanks, Mrs. Pembroke, I'll just stick with the oil and vinegar."

She hurried away to the kitchen, and Sam, who had learned his dialogue for this scene long ago, said, "Something new on the drawing board?"

"Peerless Products is all steamed up about this one, and we're working with them on it, because if it pans out the way they think it will, and our tests up to now show their confidence seems justified, this stuff is going to drive mayonnaise off the map. No, don't use a knife. Cut it with your fork. The bacon is made crisp so it'll crumble, and the applesauce and diced calf's liver filling squirts if you go at it with a knife. Good, no?"

"Great," said Sam.

"Why I asked you to lunch, Sam, I've got a hole in next year's Christmas issue. I'm all set for this year with your story about the Harlem kids who cut down the pine tree in Central Park as a Christmas present for their schoolteacher, but I'm stuck for my Christmas 1941 issue."

"Isn't that pretty far ahead?" said Sam, who was beginning to find that the heat of this June, 1940, day, which on his way over to the American Bride Building had seemed seasonably pleasant, was becoming, with a mouthful of bacon, applesauce, and diced calf's liver, pretty unbearable.

"Not any more," said Bud Bienstock around a juicy lump of his charcoal-broiled, beautifully rare porterhouse. Bud was on a special diet because his doctor felt that the tensions of his job combined with his passionate involvement with the Zionist movement might at any moment result in ulcers. "The damn printers' unions, especially the bastards that work on color, the hours they've got in their contract these days, I have to close my book three months earlier than I used to, and I hear rumblings, when this contract runs out they're going to ask for a six-hour day. Christ, unions. You like that, don't you?"

"Great," said Sam.

"The trouble is this damn Pamela Poitier," Bud Bienstock said. "I've used her before, not because she's a good writer, frankly I think she's pretty terrible, but let's face it, she *is* Lady Kirriemuir, and one thing all our circulation studies always show clearly, without any qualification, is you put a piece in the book about royalty, particularly British royalty, now that that Balkan crap is all washed up, and you can count on a newsstand jump for that issue anywhere from a quarter of a million to a million copies, depending how close to the throne the member of the royal family the piece is about happens to be, and Pamela Poitier does that kind of tutti-frutti better than anybody in the business."

"No, thank you, this is fine," said Sam to the plump, smiling, gray-haired woman with the cruet.

"Take some more," said Bud Bienstock. "The Peerless Products tests, which check out with ours, show that to get the full flavor you have to put it on the salad at least twice as thick as mayonnaise. Let's be generous to our star author, Mrs. Pembroke."

"Yes, sir, Mr. Bienstock," said the woman as she buried Sam's sliver of tomato and two lettuce leaves under what looked like a pint of used crankcase oil.

"The trouble is you can't tell these damn British writers what you want the way you can tell an American writer," said Bud Bienstock. "I commissioned the story last time she was over here, back in January, and I explained to her carefully what I wanted was something that combined the spirit of Christmas with the spirit of royalty, and she said sure, or as close as anybody named Lady Kirriemuir can come to saying sure, and she goes home to England, and last week what do I get? A story about the Crucifixion with a note saying nothing combined the spirit of Christmas with the spirit of royalty better than a story about the King of Kings."

"Sounds interesting," said Sam, who had learned long ago that it was a mistake to disparage other writers in front of editors. They liked to do that themselves.

"Until you read it," said Bud Bienstock. "What's the matter? Don't you like it?"

"No, no, it's great," Sam said. "It's just this is quite a helping."

"Go ahead, finish it," said Bud Bienstock. "A clean plate leads to a clean conscience, as the hero of Tom Sacheverell's novel says. You know the one I mean, the one the natives call Father Kind Smile?"

"Yes," said Sam, picking up his fork again, "I know."

"It wouldn't be so bad if she'd done a straight historical job," Bud Bienstock said. "I mean, what the hell, I've got nothing against the Crucifixion, but what she's done, this British broad, she's used the short-story form to advance a theory. The story reconstructs the events of that night, as seen through the eyes of a little servant girl who works for the wife of Pontius Pilate, and according to Pamela Poitier, this British broad says it was not the Sanhedrin who condemned Christ and got the Romans to kill him so it wouldn't look like they had anything to do with it. Not at all. According to Lady Kirriemuir the Sanhedrin had the power to condemn anybody and execute anybody who preached heresy and threatened the foundations of the Jewish faith, so that if they really felt Jesus was doing that, there would have been no reason to hide behind the skirts of the Romans, because what they did, if they did it, would have been perfectly legal and receive the approval of the entire population. So this British broad writes this story in which she pins the entire rap on the Romans, especially Pontius Pilate, and instead of the way he's been pictured for two thousand years, a kind of Colonel Blimp who did what he was told, Pamela Poitier shows him to be a tough, ruthless, ambitious administrator, who deliberately set out to get rid of Jesus because Jesus was an agitator who was upsetting the smooth functioning of this country Pontius Pilate was administering, and if word of that got back to Rome, old Pontius would have found his ass in a sling. This way, by wiping out the source of the unrest, he got himself to look good with the boys in the top spots in Rome, and it turns out the Jews, who for two thousand years have been accused of all that You Crucified Our Lord stuff, they had absolutely nothing to do with it, except for two thousand years they've been the victims of a fake."

"Sounds like quite a story," said Sam.

"Not for my six million readers," said Bud Bienstock. "Theories about the death of Christ don't boost newsstand sales. A good Christmas story does. Got any ideas, Sam?"

Sam had several, which he outlined, and Bud Bienstock, as the plump, smiling, gray-haired woman set in front of him an individually baked deep-dish apple pie topped by a mound of vanilla ice cream as large as a baseball, chose the one about the Vassar-educated schoolteacher who gives, at her own expense, a Christmas party for her slum-area pupils, who think she is trying to punish them by forcing them to eat the traditional hard candies that mean only one thing to these underprivileged children who have never known the benefits of dentistry: agonizing toothache.

"And at the end her boy friend, who is a medical student, gets wise to what's happening and saves the day by signing up all the kids for a series of free treatments at an uptown dental clinic?" Bud Bienstock said. "Is that right?"

"Right," said Sam. "Say, that looks good. Got another one of those out in the kitchen, Mrs. Pembroke?"

"Yes, sir," said the plump woman.

"No, wait," said Bud Bienstock. "Give him some of the D-210."

"Yes, sir," she said, and went lunging off to the kitchen.

"It's a gelatine concentrate Friendly Foods is going all out for with a

national campaign this fall," Bud Bienstock said. "You'll love it. I hear it
tastes like a mixture of caramel custard and sherry. I like that story, Sam.
It's just the sort of thing we do well with here at *American Bride*. Can I
have it by Labor Day?"

"Sure," Sam said.

"How's the four-parter coming?"

"Fine," Sam said. "You'll have it on time."

"Christ, it's a pleasure to deal with a real pro," Bud Bienstock said. A
slurp of vanilla ice cream oozed out of the corner of his mouth and started
down his chin, but Bud fielded it neatly with his spoon and said, "I think
I'm going to call Top Sargent this afternoon and tell him I feel a certain
writer on his list named Samuel Silver is entitled to a hike in price."

"Why, that would be very nice," said Sam, and to the woman who had
appeared with the plate, "Thank you, Mrs. Pembroke."

"You're welcome, sir, Mr. Silver."

"Gee, that looks great," Bud Bienstock said, spooning up apple pie à la
mode.

"I have another one out in the kitchen, sir, Mr. Bienstock, if you'd like,
sir?"

"I'd love it," Bud Bienstock said. "But my doctor says no alcohol, and I
hear the sherry content in that number is but sensational."

"I think I'll get Jennie to serve this stuff at our next cocktail party instead of martinis," said Sam as he smacked his lips around a mouthful of
the pale brown horror. "I'm beginning to feel looped already," he said and
then, casually, as the streamer with its indistinct message whipped tantalizingly across his mind, Sam added, "What's Kenyon Poole done that's
made you sore?"

"Given me a royal screwing," Bud Bienstock said. "That's what. Writers,
God! Two years ago, the minute I heard he was working on this new book,
I went to Top Sargent and said I wanted it for *Bride* sight unseen and he
could name his own price, and the very next day we had lunch, all three of
us, right there in '21,' and Poole promised me up and down, cross his heart
and hope to die, the first serial rights are mine and nobody else is even
going to see it, so what happens? By accident, the other day, just because
I happen to run into Marshall Umberg at the National Book Awards do,
I find out Mercury Films has already made an offer for the book, and me,
I didn't even know it was finished. I got right on the phone to Top Sargent
and said what the hell gives, why haven't I seen the manuscript, and Top
says nobody's seen it, not even Mercury, and all that's happened is Marshall Umberg ran into Poole at the Authors Guild cocktail party and asked
him how the new book was coming, and one drink led to another, and

next thing you know, Poole promised him if Mercury can get Clark Gable for the main character they can have the book, because he had Gable in mind when he started writing it, but as for an actual manuscript, Top said, nobody has seen it, not even Top himself, and he's Poole's agent, as you know."

"Well, then, you're okay, aren't you?" Sam said. "I mean when he finishes the book you've still got Poole's promise, haven't you?"

"I can tell you where I'd like to stick it," Bud Bienstock said. "And ram it into place with the jagged edge of a broken bottle. Writers, Christ! Top says there's nothing he can do with Poole any more, now that he's in the hands of this damn broad."

"What broad?"

"Oh, a satchel-ass named Grimsby."

"*Alison* Grimsby? She's in charge of the outside readers up at Mercury's New York story department?"

"That's the tomato."

"Hell," Sam said, "I know her."

"Who doesn't?" Bud Bienstock said. "My house is full of five-hundred-dollar couches she's been putting behind me for years, the bitch."

"No, but I mean, Bud, she's a woman of fifty. More."

"So was Madame Pompadour. Some guys go for that fruity type. Besides, Poole's no bar mitzvah boy, you know. He's my age, maybe a couple of years older, and I'll never see fifty-five again. Also, although if you quote me on this I'll say you're a liar, I've always had my doubts about Kenyon Poole in the sex department."

"Aah, now, Bud, come on."

"Oh, I don't mean he's queer or anything like that," Bud Bienstock said. "But he ain't like you and me, neither. All the years he's been around, he's never had a wife, you never see him with a dame, he goes stag to all the parties, and I can tell you from what a couple of girls I know have told me he always leaves stag, too, because they tried and didn't even bunt, and when you stop and think a minute, is there any other celebrity of Kenyon Poole's stature, any other guy I mean, whose name, just his name alone, it's news, there any other guy that big you can think of who in the columns, Winchell and all those boys, you've never seen his name linked to some dame? Not once? Never?"

"I don't think that's necessarily conclusive," Sam said.

"With Oscar Wilde it wasn't conclusive either, because it never is unless you're in there in the bedroom with the boys, watching, and how often does that happen? But that's the way the judges voted."

"But you just said you didn't mean to imply Poole is queer?"

"Not queer like that," Bud Bienstock said. "But queer like different. I once had a guy here in the art department, big handsome son of a bitch, shoulders out to here, dark hair, the works, with a set of equipment, we all went swimming bare-ass up at Bear Mountain one of our staff outing days one summer, this boy was really hung, let me tell you, and as you can imagine, the dames here in the office, brother, it was something. All this guy had to do was come in a room and they'd start to cream, and you know what? He never gave one of them a tumble, so naturally pretty soon the talk started, and everybody was saying he was mint, when one day, out in Brooklyn, one of our office boys saw this guy in the movies with a girl, she had one leg in a brace. Polio. The kid said she was quite a looker, so he stuck around, and when the show was over and they were all going out, he saw the leg. Pretty soon other people started seeing him in other places with other dames, and it was always the same. Good-looking but crippled in some way. This guy just couldn't get it up with a girl that wasn't, and in my book that's queer."

"Well," Sam said, "Alison Grimsby is no cripple."

"No, but she's got something, I'll bet you, a crooked snatch, maybe, or a third tit, I don't know, *something*, and whatever it is, Kenyon Poole goes for it, because she sure as hell has him tied up. She made him promise, Top Sargent said, get this, she made him promise not to show the manuscript of his new book to anybody until she's read it and okayed it, and she's not even sure I'll ever see it, she said, because he doesn't need the dough, it all goes in taxes anyway, and he's too important a literary figure to have his work serialized in a woman's magazine. Y'ever? Kenyon Poole, the author of *The Small Meal*, which I happened to serialize, by the way, but never mind that. Kenyon Poole, what did Gide call him? The Dostoevsky of the American prairie. Kenyon Poole, the biggest thing we've had since Melville, and a satchel like that, a clerk in a movie company's story department, for Christ's sake, with a little interior-decorating racket on the side yet, too, from now on this, this, this *thing*, *she* decides whether a Kenyon Poole manuscript is ready to be given to the world!"

"It sounds pretty bad," Sam said. "On the other hand, it's like what you just said about the boys. Nobody really knows unless you're in there in the bedroom with them, watching, and I've never yet met anybody who has, and the story of her influence over Poole may be greatly exaggerated. Grimsby may even have spread it herself to look important. I'm pretty sure Poole didn't tell that to Claude Sargent himself, did he?"

"No, but he doesn't have to," Bud Bienstock said. "She's got him under her thumb, and everybody can see it. For Christ's sake, she's even got him as a sponsor on this new committee, what the hell is it called, yeah, the

Committee to Defend America by Cleaning Up Our Own Back Yard. Y'ever hear such a thing?"

"Yes," Sam said. "Jennie was telling me about it this morning. Matter of fact, she said Kenyon Poole was going to be one of the sponsors, and I bet her they'd never land him."

"Well, you're wrong, Sam. Not that I wouldn't have bet the same way. Why, until he met this Grimsby broad Kenyon Poole never even knew who the hell was President. I know for a fact he's never voted, and once, a few years ago, he was at our house for dinner and he was sitting next to a woman who was working on La Guardia's campaign, friend of my wife, and she was telling some stories about the Little Flower's platform manner, and Kenyon Poole says in a loud, clear voice everybody could hear, he says what's he running for. How about that? Yesterday he doesn't know who the hell is running for mayor, today he's a sponsor of the Committee to Defend America by Cleaning Up Our Own Back Yard."

"Is it definite?" Sam said.

"They haven't come out with their letterhead yet, but it's definite, don't worry. My wife tells me there's going to be a big dinner Thursday night at the Teals' where the whole damn thing is going to be finalized."

"No," Sam said. "Buttoned up."

The breeze had suddenly died down. At last he could see clearly the message on the streamer that had been whipping tantalizingly in his mind ever since his talk with Jennie.

"That's right," Bud Bienstock said. "One of Trish Teal's buttoning-up dinners. Christ, that dame with her cute phrases, she burns my ass. All that Shlansky dough, and our last Zionist drive I ask her for a contribution, she sends me a check for five hundred bucks. Y'imagine? That great big goy poet she's married to, him with those God-damn things they don't rhyme and they don't end, just a lot of dots, he spends more than that every week on those God-damn Japanese masks, for Christ's sake. Her family owns all of Chattanooga practically, and to found a Jewish homeland she can afford only a lousy five hundred bucks. You going to that dinner?"

"I don't know," Sam said, but he did. The message on the streamer had been a warning. "I'll have to ask Jennie."

He didn't.

Sam waited until late Thursday afternoon and then said to Jennie, "Listen, you think Artie Bergman is in his office now?"

"Of course he's not in his office now," Jennie said. "You know Artie's at the hospital every day from three to six. What's the matter? You sick?"

"I don't know," said Sam. "I feel sort of woozy, and I've got this pain in my gut."

"Well, if you're going to eat lunches in the *American Bride* laboratory, you have to expect to carry away something more than bundles of money."

"That was three days ago, and I've been perfectly okay yesterday and the day before and all of today, up to now."

"Been to the john?"

"Three times."

"I understand Flaubert once said he did his best work when he had a touch of diarrhea."

"Terribly funny."

"Go lie down," Jennie said. "I'll take your temperature."

"I just did," Sam said. "It's one of those little lines over a hundred."

"If you've just been working on a love scene, that would be about normal." Jennie's eyes suddenly crinkled. "Say, you're not trying to duck out on going to Trish Teal's dinner tonight, are you?"

"With a temperature of over a hundred I wouldn't go to the Last Supper," Sam said. "But what difference would that make? Our bet's still on."

"All right," Jennie said. "Lie down and I'll call Artie's office and ask his girl to have him call back when he checks in from the hospital."

Loosening his tie in the bedroom, Sam was aware of an odd little mixture of surprise and uneasiness. It was as though he had been trying to push open a door against the resistance of somebody on the other side and, as he was gathering his strength for a final shove, the door had suddenly sprung open. Sam supposed, as he lay down on the bed, that Jennie didn't really care whether he went to the dinner or not, so long as he agreed to let them use his name on their letterhead.

"It's Artie," she said, coming into the bedroom an hour later. "He wants to talk to you."

Sam picked up the phone from the table between the beds and said, "Hi, Artie."

"Jennie tells me you're dying."

"Well, except if you get shot or hit by a truck, it always starts slowly like this, doesn't it?" Sam said. "How are you?"

"Pretty good," Artie Bergman said. "Except I feel a little woozy, and I've got this pain in the gut, and my temperature is just one of those little lines over a hundred."

"Nobody's ever going to say my wife is not an accurate reporter," Sam said. "How's Sally?"

"Fine, thanks."

"The girls?"

"Great, except for Betty."

"What's the matter with her?"

"She's getting married."

"That little bundle of charm in pigtails I was dandling on my knee only yesterday?"

"Only yesterday, my eye," Artie Bergman said. "That little bundle of charm in pigtails is nineteen, and I'd like to have her around awhile."

"There once was a boy who felt the same way about a chick named Jocasta," Sam said. "Who's she marrying? Not a doctor, I hope?"

"Well, he's not a doctor yet, but he will be after he gets out of college, and graduates from medical school, and finishes his internship, and starts collecting his social security."

"Don't be bitter," Sam said. "You've still got that cute little Amanda."

"I know," Artie Bergman said. "Now let's figure out what you've got."

"Everything Jennie said, plus she left out a light touch of diarrhea."

"Are you uncomfortable?"

"I don't know," Sam said. "Not very, I guess. I just don't feel like getting all greased up and swimming the Channel."

"Don't do it, then," Artie Bergman said. "Want me to come up and have a look?"

"Not unless you think it's necessary," Sam said. "This time of day you must be bushed."

"I'm bushed all times of the day," Artie Bergman said. "Most doctors are. I could be there in an hour."

"I hate to make you make the trip," Sam said. "Can't you tell me over the phone what's wrong with my gut?"

"Most people I'd tell them it's the bug," Artie said. "That always works, and most of the time that's what it is. You, I'd say it's writer's cramp."

"You know, if you and my wife got together you could bring back vaudeville."

"I think Jennie and I could do better than that," Artie Bergman said. "Seriously, Sam, it doesn't sound like anything serious. Why don't you have a drink or two, get a plate of hot soup into you, if you can't sleep take a Seconal, that's one of the red ones, and call me in the morning."

"If I'm alive," Sam said, "I will. Love to Sally and ask her to let Jennie know what Betty wants for a wedding present." He hung up and said to Jennie, "Artie prescribes I shouldn't go out tonight, stay in bed, and force Scotch whiskey."

"Well, don't force it too hard," Jennie said. "We want all the sponsors of the C.T.D.A.B.C.U.O.O.B.Y. to be sober."

"I'm not a sponsor yet," Sam said. "You have to land Kenyon Poole first."

"We'll land him, and you will be," Jennie said. "Don't worry."

Sam tried not to, but long after Jennie left, and in spite of the Scotch whiskey, a small, nagging uneasiness persisted. It was as though, after careful consideration and thorough study of the maps at a crossroad, he had taken the right fork, only to find, after he had gone along for a while, that some instinct that resisted the information on maps was telling him he should have taken the left fork.

Sam got out of bed; slipped into his robe; paced around the apartment; looked in on Billy, who was asleep; nodded to the boy's nurse, Mrs. Lempke, who was washing silk stockings in the kitchen; said no, thanks to Aggie, the cook, who came out of her bedroom to ask if he was feeling better and could she get him something to eat; went into the study and tried without success to get the Christmas story for Bud Bienstock off the ground; added two pages of foolscap to the four-parter; tore them up; read a chapter of *Nostromo* before he realized he had not absorbed a single word; tried *Pendennis* with the same result; went out to the bar; started to make another drink and, for the first time in years, looked at the picture over the bar.

The essence of Kurt Schneerboehm's art, as the artist had himself told Sam at a cocktail party in Schneerboehm's honor at the Ibram Moulage Gallery to which Jennie had taken Sam two years ago, was that the artist did not force his emotions on the viewer of his paintings but, rather, provided the viewer with a key that helped him unlock his own emotion. Sam had, the following morning, jotted this down in his notebooks under the section headed: BUSHWAH, CREATIVE.

He now saw, to his amazement, that he had done Kurt Schneerboehm an injustice. The abstract over the bar, which had cost twelve hundred dollars, consisted of three dots of red paint, arranged in the form of a triangle, that looked down from the upper left-hand corner of an otherwise bare canvas to a blob of black in the lower right-hand corner that could have been either a bathtub seen through a prism or a helping of omelette made with soy-bean sauce and coal dust. Staring at the canvas now, as he had stared at it hundreds of times during visits to his living-room bar, Sam saw that the three red dots were the eyes and nose of a face, and the black blob was a mouth that was trying to say something to him. Sam put down his glass and listened.

"Stop krotzing around like a chicken without a head," the painting said in the accents and tones of Sam's mother. "You want to go take a look at this party, so shlep on your pants and go take a look."

Sam went to the bedroom, got dressed, told Mrs. Lempke he was going out for a while, and did. The walk up Fifth Avenue relaxed him, and when he climbed the steps of the Teal house and rang the bell at a couple of minutes short of eleven o'clock, it seemed to Sam that what he was doing was a good idea.

"Oh, Mr. Silver," the butler said. "Good evening, sir."

"Hello, Nathan. Where's the meeting?"

"In the drawing room, sir."

"I'll just go right up."

"Very good, sir."

Sam climbed the stairs, past the lines of horribly grinning Japanese masks, and ran into Trish Teal, carrying a handful of pencils, just outside the arch that led to the drawing room.

"Sam Silver, for heaven's sake, I thought you were sick."

"So did I, but you know that Artie Bergman. The grotto at Lourdes has nothing on him. I feel fine now, so I thought I'd come on over and join the fun. How are you, Trish?"

"Distracted but aglow with excitement. I'm glad you came. You don't happen to have a pencil sharpener on you, do you?"

"Damn," Sam said, "I just smoked my last one."

"Oh, you," Trish said. "Go on in and make yourself a drink while I see if maybe Nathan can restore these to life."

The moment he stepped into the crowded room Sam, who could have picked her face out of the packed bleachers from the other side of the Yankee Stadium, knew Jennie was not there. He nodded to several people he knew, circled several animated groups, and arrived at the bar, where Bethany Teal was splashing brandy into a glass and onto the black lapel of his red velvet dinner coat.

"Ah, Lazarus," he said. "I see they managed to roll away that stone."

It was his one joke. With it he greeted all guests at all times. Sam often wondered if he had worked it out because of his name, or whether he had chosen his name after he had worked out the joke.

"You know how it is," Sam said. "Can't keep a good man down. Seen my bride?"

"She's around somewhere," Bethany Teal said, swinging the bottle out toward the crowded room behind him in an alcoholically expansive gesture that sent a spray of twenty-dollar brandy splattering like rain across several thousand dollars' worth of hideously grinning Japanese masks on the wall near the bar. "How about a dose of this?"

"Thanks, no," Sam said. "I'll just inhale the fumes off the wall and your lapels."

He moved on, nodding and smiling when he caught the eye of someone he knew, but refusing to become engaged. He would locate his quarry first, then attach himself to a group from which he could watch Kenyon Poole furtively. What he would do after that, Sam did not know. He did not want to talk to Poole. He merely wanted a glimpse of him. He was not sure how this could be managed without becoming engaged in a conversation, but Sam was hoping that alcohol would help. From what he had seen on a number of occasions, when Kenyon Poole was on the sauce, by eleven o'clock he was usually incoherent. He was also, Sam realized after his second circuit, not in the room.

"Ouch!" Sam said, and turned.

"Just testing," said Trish Teal, holding up the pencil with which she had stabbed him. "Nathan does do a lovely point, doesn't he?"

She was one of those handsome, highly polished, completely sexless women who had convinced herself, with the help of several psychoanalysts who had a proper regard for the resources of the department-store not the textile Shlanskys of Chattanooga, that men wanted a woman's body only when they could not have her brain, and Trish Teal's notion of how to give it to them was to take the simplest phrases in the language and distort them grotesquely, so that talking to her was not unlike reading one of those instruction sheets composed in English by someone in a Tokyo factory to accompany a product manufactured for export to the United States.

"If he did them any better, I'd bleed to death," Sam said. "Where's Jennie?"

"Oh, she went off with the Liberty Plane Committee to plot itinerary and compose personnel."

"What's the Liberty Plane Committee?"

"A flinging of truth into the teeth of our detractors," Trish Teal said. "There's been such a cry and hue from people of a vicious stripe that the purpose of the C.T.D.A.B.C.U.O.O.B.Y. is solely, merely, and exclusively to avert the eyes of America from the plight of Albion the not perfidious but virtuous, that we've decided to charter a plane, fill it with nationally respected observers, fly them to England, with their own eyes and ears tour the country, and return to report to this nation which it is our determination firm and true shall not perish from this earth."

"Who's on the committee?" Sam said. "Jennie?"

Trish Teal nodded.

"And Alison Grimsby and Kenyon Poole."

"Oh, so you landed him?"

"Sinker, line, and hook," Trish said. "How about you?"

"I'm still thinking," Sam said. "Where does this committee hold its meetings?"

"Alison Grimsby's apartment," said Trish, and she rolled her eyes archly. "I understand Poole finds the atmosphere congenial. Here, take one of these and ask Bethany for a pad. We're drafting the full-page advertisement we plan to overwhelm the *New York Times* with, giving the lie to our detractors with the veracious facts about England that our Liberty Plane Committee will bring back. Why aren't you consuming of the grape and the grain?"

"Artie Bergman told me to lay off for a couple of days."

"I've heard tell you're one of those writers who fuels the creative motor with the juice of the cow," Trish said. "Well, get a pad."

Instead, Sam got his hat. Walking back to Gramercy Park, he decided that he was relieved. Wanting a glimpse of Kenyon Poole was one of those sudden passions, like the pregnant woman's midnight urge for pickled pig's feet, that are better left ungratified. The momentary satisfaction is hardly worth the inevitable bellyache. Sam remembered the first dinner party he had attended years ago at the Sargent apartment and, all at once, he could hear again the sound of Kenyon Poole's voice as he held forth on the subject of taxes. The votary of a private faith, feeling the need for a glimpse of his god, was wise if he arranged to take it when the god was not in his cups.

Turning into Twenty-first Street from Fourth Avenue, Sam was glad his attempt had failed. His problem now was what to do about the bet he had lost to Jennie. Kenyon Poole was indeed under the thumb of Mrs. Grimsby if that foolish woman could get him to let the C.T.D.A.B.C.U.O.O.B.Y. place his name on their letterhead. Sam, who saw now that he had been a fool to make the bet with Jennie, was determined not to be a bigger fool by paying off. But how could he avoid it? He had given Jennie his word. He was morally bound. As he stepped under the canopy of his apartment house, a taxi pulled up in front of the canopy of the building next door. There was something familiar about the shape of the body gathering itself to rise from the rear seat, and Sam, turning in toward the entrance of his building, paused to see why. When he did, his mind, which had been chugging along in low gear, came sharply awake. It was as though he had been drowsing in the sun on a beach and suddenly, without warning, somebody had pitched him into the icy water. He stepped across to the taxi and said, "Hi, Alison."

Mrs. Grimsby, turning with her open purse, saw Sam and dropped it.

"Oh, Jesus," the taxi driver said, getting out, and all three of them went down on their knees on the sidewalk to gather the rolling lipstick and spinning coins.

"I'm sorry," Mrs. Grimsby said, apparently to the taxi driver, because there could be no doubt who was being addressed when she said, "You took me by surprise."

"So did you," said Sam, straightening up with a crumpled handkerchief, a nicked silver compact, and a crushed pack of Chesterfields. "Trish Teal just told me you were up in your apartment plotting itinerary with the Liberty Plane Committee."

"Oh, thank you, Sam. You, too, driver. I'm awfully sorry for the mess. No, no, do keep the change. Not at all. Good night." The taxi pulled away from the curb and she turned her plump face directly toward Sam. "We decided after we left the Teals' we'd had enough of apartments, not that the Teal house is an apartment, but you know what I mean. It's a *home,* and we'd been cooped up in a home all evening, and my apartment is a home, too, not on the scale of the Teal house, of course, but as my husband used to say, he was a Dartmouth man, you know, and when people said something about somebody else's home, something that he felt was disrespectful, he always quoted Daniel Webster in the Dartmouth College Case when he said it's a small college, but there are those who love it, and I've always felt that way about my own home. Small as it is, it's still my home, and so when Jennie and Kenyon and I left the Teal house—"

Sam's alerted senses recorded every syllable of this pointless monologue, but it was the vacuum cleaner of his craft that demonstrated it was not pointless. Dispassionately sucking up the fact that the monologue was unreeling on a sidewalk at one o'clock in the morning, out of a face that Sam had never before seen reflect confusion and even fear, it was made possible for him to see that Mrs. Grimsby looked like someone who has been caught in a lie and is trying, under cover of a desperately invented verbal surface, to think of a plausible solution.

"—and we started downtown to my apartment to work out the personnel and the itinerary for the Liberty Plane, we all thought, no, not from one home into another. I mean we were so excited by the project that we didn't feel like shutting ourselves away in another home, and it was Jennie, always so quick at understanding moods, it was Jennie who suggested it."

"Suggested what?" Sam said.

The confusion and the fear vanished as the Mary Miles Minter charm carved the traditional dimples into the fat cheeks. Mrs. Grimsby had obviously worked her way to the solution for which she had been scrabbling.

"Jennie said I make a motion the Liberty Plane Committee move on to

Tony's to finish its work for the night," Mrs. Grimsby said. "And of course Kenyon and I seconded it at once, so we went to Tony's."

"Thirty-six?" Sam said. "On Eighth Street?"

"Of course," Mrs. Grimsby said. "You know Tony's, Sam dear."

He also knew something Mrs. Grimsby didn't: Tony's was closed on Thursdays.

"Of course," Sam said, and he found himself wondering about the sex life of the gods. If everybody knew—when something was known to Bud Bienstock and Trish Teal, it was safe to use the word everybody—that Alison Grimsby was sleeping with Kenyon Poole, it was safe to assume, Sam felt, that Alison Grimsby wanted everybody to know about it. Women, Sam had observed, did not want from adultery the same things men wanted. Or rather, they wanted more. Most men were satisfied with the sexual gratification of an illicit relationship. Most women, however, were not satisfied until other women also knew they were being sexually gratified, and by whom. That Kenyon Poole, famous, rich, attractive, and sought after, should have spurned the lovely creatures who were constantly hurling themselves at what was euphemistically known as his head, and chosen as the object of his desire this middle-aged, almost elderly, sagging, lumpish dumpling, was enough to turn a head as level as that of a Portia. Alison Grimsby, whose head was on the hilly side, could be excused for a bit of bragging. Having excused her, Sam wondered why he couldn't dismiss her. Why all this coy and inept lying about having spent the last couple of hours with Poole in a restaurant after all the hard work she had put in during the past months to create an atmosphere in which Sam, along with everybody else, would know she had spent them in Poole's bed?

"I guess I'll turn in," Sam said. "It's been a long day for everybody."

She gave him a sharp look, a look that so clearly said: *have I fooled him?*, that Sam had to force back his quick smile, the gentle reassuring pat he wanted to place against her fat face, and the words "Yes, you have."

"It certainly has been a long day," Mrs. Grimsby said, and then she took him by surprise again. She said, "I could certainly use a nightcap."

Had success gone to her head? Sam wondered. Was she trying to add his—the euphemisms became as preposterous as the idea—scalp to her belt? Was Alison Grimsby making a pass at him?

"I could use one, too," said Sam, testing to see if she was serious. It was just possible that the foolish woman thought by giving him a bit of what she was giving the author of *The Small Meal*, she could raise Sam to Poole's level as an artist. "But it's too late to invite you up to our place," Sam said. "We'd wake everybody up."

"And we can't go up to my place," Mrs. Grimsby said. "Not at this hour. I mean, the elevator man and all."

"Of course," said Sam, disappointed. An interesting solution to a dull puzzle had evaporated, leaving only the dull puzzle.

"That's the trouble with Gramercy Park," Mrs. Grimsby said. "There aren't really any nice places one can walk to. I mean at this hour. But perhaps on Third Avenue? We might find a bar that isn't—too, you know?"

"I think not," said Sam. The puzzle had become a bore. Mrs. Grimsby, clearly brimming over with confidences about this new and exciting phase of her life, did not feel sleepy and wanted an ear into which she could pour the details of her triumph. Sam said, "I really am tired. Good night, Alison."

"Oh." The dimples vanished beneath a flashing reappearance of the confusion and fear, and Mrs. Grimsby put out her hand, as though to restrain him physically, but the recorder had stopped working. Sam knew there was nothing more to hold him here. He continued moving toward the entrance of his building, and Mrs. Grimsby, apparently accepting the inevitable, said in a tired voice, "Good night, Sam."

Letting himself into the apartment, he found himself wishing Jennie was awake. He wanted to tell her about his curious adventure. But Jennie was not awake. In fact, Jennie was not in her bed.

Staring at the neatly turned-down, untouched sheets, feeling the first rumblings of the rock-slide of comprehension, Sam forced himself to say aloud, "No, she's in Billy's room." But she wasn't, nor was she in any other part of the apartment, and when Sam heard the key in the lock of the outer door, and he glanced at his watch, he knew he could no longer hold it back. He could feel his teeth clench, and his eyes squeeze tight as he bowed his head, and he even put his arms up to shield it, as though what was crashing down on him was indeed a physical cascade: his watch had recorded the interval, and the instrument of his craft had recorded its meaning.

Eleven minutes. Just long enough for Mrs. Grimsby to reach her apartment, relate *her* curious adventure to another woman while the other woman flung on her clothes, and for the other woman to come down in the elevator from Mrs. Grimsby's apartment and go up to her own in the elevator of the building next door.

"Oh, hello," Jennie said, pulling her key from the lock and shutting the door. "You must be feeling better."

Feeling the way he did, it took Sam a moment or two to realize she was not being sardonic, to remember that when he had seen her last, at seven o'clock, he had been in bed, pretending to be sick. She was still playing the game. How long had she been playing it? When did it start? For the only certainty in the whirling mass of doubts by which he had been suddenly surrounded was that nothing new had happened tonight. The newness was his discovery of something that had been going on a long time. Into the sickening mixture of shame and rage and jealousy came the terrible knowledge that until he found out where he had failed, he, too, had to continue playing the game.

"Yes, I'm feeling fine," he said, taking the cue for his tone of voice from hers. He did not know what to do about the rock-slide of comprehension that had thundered down on him. He knew only that the time would come when he would have to do something about it, and when that moment arrived he must not face it the way Buggo Salvemini had faced *his* moment of comprehension, his mind lost to reason, a knife in his hand. Wishing he did not have to look at her, wanting fiercely to speak from behind a mask or a door, so that he would not have to divide the terrible effort at self-control between his voice and his face, Sam said steadily, "I began to feel fine about ten, so I got dressed and went over to the Teals', thinking I'd finish out the meeting with you."

"I'm sorry," Jennie said. "They put me on this subcommittee, the Liberty Plane. We're sending a group to England to check on conditions at first-hand, and the three of us, the committee is me and Alison Grimsby and Kenyon Poole, we decided to get out of the Teal house and do our work somewhere else, so went down to Tony's and did it over a drink."

Not until she said it did he realize he had been clinging to one last hope: self-deception. Jennie knew that Tony's was closed on Thursdays, and she knew that Sam knew it. She knew, therefore, that this was the flaw in Mrs. Grimsby's account of what had happened on the sidewalk between her and Sam. If Jennie had said the committee had gone to Sardi's, or "21," or to any other place, Sam would have been able to tell himself that Alison Grimsby, a foolish woman who only rarely knew where she was, had not known tonight. The flaw in the story would have looked like nothing worse than a mistake, certainly to a man who desperately preferred a mistake to a flaw, and with that tiny platform to stand on, the desire not to accept the truth that had been hurled at him would have provided the leverage with which to lift himself up and out of the debris of disaster. But Jennie had not given him the platform. Since she knew its significance, and what he could have done with it, he knew therefore that she had not wanted him to have it. Knowing that, he knew the worst: that his finding out meant nothing to her.

"You must have done a lot of work," Sam said. "You look tired."

"I can't understand why I should," Jennie said. "It was pure pleasure."

He did not want to hit her. Not yet. The image of Buggo's crazed face coming up over the edge of Ham Farnsworth's porch was too vivid. She was not going to do that to him. He must not act until he found out exactly how much she *had* done to him. Did everybody who knew about Alison Grimsby and Kenyon Poole also know what Sam Silver now knew? That Alison Grimsby was no more than camouflage for Kenyon Poole and Jennie Broom? The instinct that told him he must not go the way Buggo had gone told him also that it was just possible that he had learned something nobody else yet knew. It was a slim possibility, but his life depended on it, and so he would hold onto it as long as he could.

"I think I'll go out for a walk," he said.

"At this hour?" Jennie said. "It's almost two in the morning."

"I don't think you'll miss me."

Jennie hesitated, as though she had not expected the showdown to come so quickly. She obviously would have preferred more time to choose the weapon with which to fight the final skirmish. But there would be no more time. So she said, "By the way, Alison Grimsby tells me she told you we've managed to land Kenyon Poole. So you've lost your bet."

"All bets are off," Sam said. "My name stays off that letterhead."

Jennie tipped her head to one side and said, "What's wrong, Sam?"

"I just looked through the drawer in the bathroom where you keep your diaphragm," he said. "It's not there. I didn't realize until tonight that you've been wearing it to committee meetings."

She tipped her head the other way and smiled. "That's almost as good as Kenyon Poole," she said.

"But not quite," Sam said.

"No, not quite," Jennie said. "And it hasn't been for a long time."

He went out, and rang for the elevator, and started walking without any idea of a destination, but he was not surprised when, some time later, he found himself on East Tenth Street. His mother asked only one question.

"Billy is all right?"

"Billy is fine."

"You're sure?"

"Positive, Ma."

"So sit down and eat a little something while I go make your bed."

He awoke, as usual, at six, meeting the pain like a blow before his feet touched the floor. He gave himself a few moments, sitting on the edge of the bed with his head in his hands, but it did not help, and he knew nothing was ever going to help, yet he knew something else: if he went down, it would be his own fault, not theirs. *They* had not meant to destroy him. They didn't really care what happened to him. The core of the pain was what he had read so clearly in Jennie's face last night: he meant nothing to her; he had merely been in the way when she made her move, just as Buggo Salvemini had once been in the way.

Sam went out to the kitchen, where his mother had insisted the telephone he had given her as a present be installed, and called the apartment. Mrs. Lempke answered.

"How's Billy?" Sam said.

"Fine," she said. "I mean he's still asleep. I mean, Mr. Silver, is something wrong?"

"No," Sam said. They were not going to destroy him. "Put Mrs. Silver on, please."

"She's not here," Mrs. Lempke said. "I mean she hasn't been here all night. I mean neither have you, Mr. Silver. I mean is something wrong, Mr. Silver?"

"No," Sam said again. They were not going to destroy him. "We've been at a committee meeting, working all night, Mrs. Lempke. If Billy wakes up and asks for us, tell him I'm on my way home right now."

He hung up, went back to the bedroom, pulled on his soiled clothes, and when he came back into the kitchen, found his mother waiting with orange juice, a glass of cold milk, and a buttered roll.

"Thanks, Ma, but I can't."

"And you're not going to tell me?"

"Not yet, Ma."

"So I'll tell you," Mrs. Silver said. "She never wanted you. Just like she never wanted that Buggo Salvemini. She wanted something from both of you. From him, when she got it, when she was finished with him, she moved to you. What she wanted from you, I don't know. For five years in my head it's going around like a clock—what? what? what? But the answer to what, no, this I never knew, and I don't know now. But if there's trouble, Sam, I know this: whatever it is, if she can't get it from you, she'll try somebody else. Remember that, Sam. It's the whole thing, Sam. She never wanted you."

It was not the whole thing. What his mother was leaving out was that he had wanted her. He still did. He supposed he always would. But that was irrelevant now. What mattered now was that they were not going to destroy him. He would destroy them first, the woman he loved and the god he worshipped, before he went under.

"Don't worry, Ma," he said. "It's all going to come out all right."

"From your mouth into God's ear," Mrs. Silver said. "For me, a favor, take at least one bite roll."

Sam took one bite, was surprised to discover it tasted good, took another bite, gulped the orange juice, drank the glass of milk, kissed his mother, and hurried back uptown munching the remainder of the roll. It was a few minutes before seven when he came into the apartment. Billy was having breakfast in the kitchen with Mrs. Lempke and Aggie. Sam wasted a few minutes with them, uttering meaningless remarks that nobody listened to, and then made a swift check of the closets and the bathroom. Three pieces of Jennie's matched luggage were gone. He did not bother trying to remember which dresses and make-up items were gone. The gaps in the closets and on the shelves were enough. He went into the study, closed the door, sat down at his desk, pulled the phone forward, and it started to ring. He picked it up.

"Sam?"

"Yes. This Sophie?"

"Thank God you're in," Sophie Sargent said.

"Where would I be at seven o'clock in the morning?" Sam said.

"If you were a butcher, a baker, or a candlestick maker, I might be able to tell you," Sophie Sargent said. "Since you're a writer, for all I know, at seven o'clock in the morning, you could be in an airplane on your way to England."

Sam's heart lurched, and he tried hard to think of something witty to say, something that would not let Sophie know how she had shaken him, but the best he could manage was, "What are you talking about?"

"Kenyon Poole," Sophie said. "He's driving me and Claude out of our minds. We've been up half the night trying to figure out what to do, and it just occurred to us that you might be able to help."

"In what way?" Sam said, trying not to sound cautious.

"You know, of course, that he's been carrying on with that Alison Grimsby, the one who works at Mercury Films and lives in the apartment house next to you and did your place?"

"Yes," Sam said, and he let his breath out slowly. Sophie Sargent, like Bud Bienstock and Trish Teal, was part of everybody. If she didn't know the truth, then everybody didn't know it. Not yet. Sam said, "I'd heard that."

"What a man like Ken Poole sees in a cow like that is beyond me, but I've long ago given up trying to understand the sexual drives and habits of writers, and all these months he's been practically living in her apartment Claude and I figured it was all to the good, because he did seem to be making progress with his new book, but last night we learned that he hasn't even been working on the book. This Grimsby creature has got him involved in something called—wait, I've got it written down, yes, here—the

Committee to Defend America by Cleaning Up Our Own Back Yard, and
don't make witty remarks, that's exactly what it is, the Committee to Defend America by Cleaning Up Our Own Back Yard, and he and this
Grimsby thing have been assigned to fly to England for some fool reason,
and unless we do something about it, the fool will do it, I know he will."

"Suppose he does?" Sam said, feeling the vein in his temple begin to
throb. "What's wrong with it?"

"Sam darling, stop being a writer and use your head," Sophie Sargent
said irritably. "There's a war on. Aside from the fact that I don't think
Ken Poole knows who is fighting whom, there is a great deal of hardware
flying about in Europe. I wouldn't lose any sleep if that Grimsby fool was
hit by some of it, but I don't want to lose a valuable client who happens
to be an ornament of American letters, certainly not until he finishes this
book and I've sewed up the serial rights with Bud Bienstock and the movie
rights with Mercury."

"Sophie," Sam said, trying to sound casual, "what can I do about it?"

"You, no," Sophie Sargent said. "But I think your wife can."

Sam's heart lurched again, and his mind recorded the interesting fact
that it was lurching for the man who was determined not to be destroyed,
not for the way he wanted the woman who could destroy him, and he
said, "Jennie?"

"That's her name, Sam, isn't it?"

"What's Jennie got to do with all this?"

"A good deal, I hope," Sophie Sargent said. "I know she doesn't like me,
and I must say I don't blame her, ambitious women not exactly being my
cup of tea, but I've heard that Alison Grimsby thinks the world of her.
Is that true?"

"I think they're pretty good friends," Sam said. "Yes."

"That's what Claude and I heard, too, and that's why I'm calling, Sam
darling," Sophie Sargent said. "Would it be too much to ask you to talk
to Jennie and ask her to talk to that detestable Grimsby creature and reason with her? Claude and I understand from Trish Teal that they've chartered a clipper, and Serge de Shertzieff says—"

"What's he got to do with it?"

"Nothing, Sam dear, except he's written all those books about flying
that we handle, and he knows more about airplanes than any man alive,
and Claude called him at once, and Serge says flying to England in a
clipper at this time of year is practically the equivalent of signing a suicide
pact. The Germans have air patrols ranging the coast of Europe from Lis-
bon up to Ireland, Serge says, and they've even managed to shoot down

Lancasters, which Serge says fly many times faster than clippers. They'll be sitting ducks, Serge says. They haven't got a chance. Sam?"

"Yes, I'm on."

"There's no point in talking to Ken. He doesn't know what the word fear means, and I can't talk to that Grimsby creature. Besides, they're not answering the phone in her apartment. But you can talk to Jennie, Sam. She's a sensible person. She's not in the throes of a menopause love affair with a great American novelist. She'll listen to reason. Won't you ask her to go up to that Grimsby woman's apartment and talk sense to her? She does live in the building next to yours, doesn't she?"

"Yes," Sam said.

"Well, that makes it very convenient for Jennie."

It certainly had.

"Sophie?"

"Yes, Sam?"

"How urgent is all this? I mean I gathered from Jennie that the committee to fly over had just been formed yesterday."

"Bethany Teal was in the office yesterday with a new quatrain and he told Claude they'd chartered the plane weeks ago and cleared away all the papers and other red tape and were just waiting to choose the members of the committee at a meeting in his house last night, so it's damned urgent, Sam. For all I know, Ken and his paramour may be in the air right now. Will you please talk to Jennie?"

"I'll do what I can," said Sam.

He hung up and sat quite still for a long time, staring at his hands spread flat on the green desk blotter. Sophie had no way of knowing, of course, that she had asked the impossible. Or what, by asking it, she had done to Sam. The card index of his memory had flipped crisply and come up with two slides. One showed the steps of the police station in Westport on the day when Kenyon Poole had stepped out of the limousine from the sanatorium and, passing Sam, the neat little head with the guardsman's mustache had suddenly whipped to the right, and Sam, turning to follow Poole's glance, had seen what he was staring at, and the way Jennie was staring back: Sam had his answer to when it had started. The second slide showed a thin, hollow-eyed, stoop-shouldered waiter in a kosher restaurant in Montmartre telling a couple of American tourists how it was impossible to live with shame: and Sam was unable to pretend that the man who had betrayed him was merely a man.

Wearily, wishing he was free to act merely as a man and not as a votary, Sam turned the pages of his desk directory, found Alison Grimsby's number, dialed it, and waited. There was no answer. Sam hung up the phone, went out to the kitchen, told Mrs. Lempke he would be back soon, and went downstairs.

"Would you ring Mrs. Grimsby's apartment?" he said to the doorman in the lobby of the building next door. "Mr. Silver."

"I'm sorry, sir," the doorman said. "Mrs. Grimsby is out."

"Is there anybody in the apartment?" Sam said.

The doorman's eyelids moved in a funny way, but Sam forced himself to disregard it. Everybody blinked all the time.

"No, sir," he said.

"Thanks," Sam said.

There was nothing to do but wait. He went back up to his apartment and did it in the study, holding the Parker his father had given him as a bar mitzvah present, staring at the blank sheet of yellow foolscap, aware of the household noises behind him, the muted street noises in front of him, and the dull, heavy, slow heartbeats inside him. Mrs. Lempke and Billy came in to say they were going out to the park, and Sam said something that must have been appropriate because they left, and later Aggie came in to ask what he would like for lunch, and he said he wouldn't have any lunch today. There were probably other interruptions, but Sam did not bother with them. The vacuum cleaner would suck them up and, if they were interesting, he could examine them later. Right now he was completely absorbed by the business of waiting. When the phone rang, he glanced at his watch. Eight minutes after six.

"Sam?"

It was the first of a series of surprises that were not really surprises since they popped up within the framework of something he knew at once was what he had been waiting for: he had not expected to get the news from Claude Sargent.

"Yes, Top?"

"Sam, my God, Sam, I just heard it on the radio. I turned on the six o'clock news, the way I always do when I come home from the office, and at first, when he was talking about this plane disappearance over the Atlantic, I didn't realize—Sam?"

"Yes, Top?"

"I mean we didn't realize, Sophie and I, we had no idea your wife, we didn't know, Sam, it never occurred to us that Jennie would be on the plane."

That was the second surprise: the Sargents obviously assumed Sophie's call that morning had somehow been responsible for Jennie's joining the flight. Sam saw the advantage of that from his point of view, and so, to the man he had always been able to tell the truth, he told his first lie.

"Neither did I," said Sam.

There was a pause, and then Sophie came on the wire.

"Sam, Sam darling, oh, Sam, I have no words to tell you—"

"Then don't," he said.

There was a pause, during which Sophie Sargent was clearly weighing his reply, and then, quietly, completely under control, she said, "Sam, if there's anything we can do—"

"Thanks," he said. "There isn't anything anybody can do."

He hung up, aware that the pain was on its way, and that handling it would take everything he had, so he forgave himself for the pleasure he took in the first, clean, hard feeling he'd had all day: he was safe; nobody knew.

Then, as though they were anxious to get to him before the pain arrived and caused them to go unnoticed, the last two surprises showed up together, stumbling over one another in their eagerness: the secret flame that had been kindled in a kosher restaurant in Montmartre, and by which Sam Silver had lived for so long, had finally gone out; and he had found the opening for the Christmas story he had promised Bud Bienstock at *American Bride*.

*9

Eleven years later, hurrying into the Ibram Moulage Gallery on Madison and Sixty-second, Sam wished he could stop remembering the opening line of that Christmas story: *The plane was late.*

So was he. And as Sam glanced at his wrist watch, the feeling of guilt he had been carrying all the way uptown from Tony's became a sense of dismay: it was almost nine o'clock.

"Ah, Sam."

Turning and recognizing Anton, Sam remembered the moment in the Porte School chapel that morning when he had made a mental note, for tomorrow morning's session with his notebooks, about a man who, for all his supposed worldliness, was unable to shake the guilty conviction, whenever he ran into his mistress' husband, that in spite of her perfectly legal divorce, he was nonetheless her partner in adultery.

"Hello, Anton. Is Rebecca here?"

"But yes, of course," said Anton, only his fluttering eyelids resisting his otherwise successful attempt not to display ill-bred surprise. "I mean it's her show, and all." He turned his handsome, bloodless head for a glance at the crowded rooms behind them, said, "Everybody's here," and then, with a slight grimace, as though wincing at the impolite familiarity his concern made it impossible for him to resist, Anton said, "Sam, is Rebecca all right?"

Sam, whose mind was on Kenyon Poole's manuscript in his Sutton Crescent study, felt it come back to the Ibram Moulage Gallery with an almost audible snap.

"Is Rebecca—?" he started to say, then realized he probably sounded as foolish as Anton looked, and he said irritably, "Of course she's all right." A moment later he realized he really had no right to this opinion and so, more reasonably, Sam said, "I mean she was all right when I saw her this morning, and she seemed fine when I talked to her at five. Why do you ask?"

"Well, I thought you and she were going to dine together. I mean I wanted to give a small party for her before the show, but she said no, she couldn't, she was dining with you, and—" Anton paused, frowning with anxiety, and Sam wondered whether Rebecca had said that to get out of a date with Anton, or, even though Sam had not yet invited her, she knew he would when he remembered. "But then she came in a little while ago, all by herself," Anton said. "And I wondered—"

His voice trailed away, like the end of one of Bethany Teal's poems, and Sam realized with a bump of embarrassment that Anton, in an agony of awkwardness, was really asking whether the relationship between his ex-wife, about whose happiness Anton worried constantly, and Sam had fallen apart.

"No, of course not," Sam said sharply, and stopped. How was he going to reassure Anton? By telling him that he and Rebecca were still sleeping together? More quietly, Sam said, "We both got fouled up. At the last minute Rebecca learned there was some trouble at the printer about her program notes for the show, and she left a message for me to meet her later, and me, like a fool, I started looking at a manuscript my agent had asked me to read and give him an opinion on, and I lost track of the time. By the time I got down to Tony's, he said Rebecca had eaten and gone, so I came belting up here in a cab. Have I missed anything?"

"No, no," said Anton. "I mean it's going very well. Some of the things are really quite remarkable. I didn't realize Rebecca had moved so deeply into this new phase. The collages particularly have an almost unendurable searching quality. I've heard some quite extraordinary comments. I think the reviews are going to be excellent. Sam, you're quite sure Rebecca is all right?"

"She ought to be more all right than I am," Sam said. "At least she's had dinner. Where is she?"

"I saw her only a moment ago in the west wing, just beyond the bar, talking to the man from *Art News*. I'm so glad she's all right, Sam. She looked so, not distraught exactly, but yes, troubled, that I couldn't help worrying. Thanks so much for relieving my mind, Sam. And by the way, I thought Billy's performance this morning as Calpurnia was remarkably good."

"Thanks," Sam said. "I better go find her. See you later."

He started directly for the west wing, saw Rebecca's massive father and her two bulging brothers standing a few feet away like an Epstein group depicting Finance, at once shifted the angle of his approach, and walked into Bud Bienstock's Star of David stickpin.

"Oops," the editor said, swinging to safety the two glasses he was carrying, and then, "You lucky stiff. Some guys marry girls that are beautiful, and some guys marry girls that are rich, but you, you land one that's not only both, but she paints yet like a Cimabue. Here." Bud Bienstock thrust one of the glasses into Sam's hand and raised the other. "Here's to you, boy."

"For what?" Sam said.

Bud Bienstock laughed and said, "You ought to read Winchell and find out when you're getting married." The Star of David cuff link came out of his sleeve as he bent his arm for a pull at his glass. "By the way, Sophie called me and said you were going to make those fixes in *They Told Me You Were Dead*. I'm glad, Sam. It's a peacherino of a story, it really is, but I felt the apartments, the hero and the heroine living one on top of the other, it sort of cheapened it, and the ending, well, Sophie says you know what to do about it, so I'm not worried. How you going to fix the end?"

Sam, who had no idea and didn't at the moment want to think about it, smiled wisely. "That's telling," he said. "I don't want to spoil it for you."

"Writers, Christ," Bud Bienstock said with an amiable chuckle. "Go ahead, boy. She's around the bend, near the orange and black collage, talking to a guy with one of those beards."

Sam came around the bend and, before Rebecca saw him, he saw at once what Anton had meant. Under the animation with which she was talking to the man with the beard was the look of a well-bred woman, trained to conceal her emotions, waiting for bad news. Then she saw him, and the look vanished in a squeal of almost childish relief, "Oh, Sam!" Recovering at once, she said primly, touching her flushed cheek, "Sam, this is Kurt Schneerboehm."

"How do you do?" Sam said.

The man with the beard, which was half an inch wide and ran like a strap down his face and around the point of his chin from sideburn to sideburn, so that he looked as though his head was encased in a hoop, gave Sam a long, accusing look.

"I possess a conviction that we have encountered each other before," he said.

"That's right," Sam said. "A couple of years before the war. A cocktail party right here in this gallery. I bought one of your paintings. Still have it."

"The abstract over the bar," Rebecca said. "Yes, it's lovely."

Mr. Schneerboehm's glance became more hostile. "You were not alone," he said.

Sam gave Rebecca a short glance and said, "No."

"A dark-haired girl," Kurt Schneerboehm said accusingly. "Small, slender, not beautiful, but with brown eyes of an intense and disturbing nature, so that the effect was more powerful than beauty, and one could not forget."

Sam, who had never forgotten, wished Mr. Schneerboehm had not chosen this particular moment to remember.

"Mr. Silver's wife," Rebecca said quietly.

"You are a fortunate man," Kurt Schneerboehm said. "Is she here with you tonight?"

"She was killed in a plane over ten years ago," Sam said.

Mr. Schneerboehm's Teutonic fierceness disintegrated. He looked as though he was going to burst into tears. He turned his stricken glance from Sam to Rebecca and back to Sam, then bowed his head and hurried away.

"I'm sorry," Sam said. "I didn't mean to bring that on."

"You could have said just no, she's not here tonight," Rebecca said.

"The Germans are a thorough people," Sam said. "Whether they're exterminating a race, or pinning down a fleeting memory, they stop at nothing. Mr. Schneerboehm would have wanted to know where Jennie is."

"Which is what I've been wondering all evening about you," Rebecca said.

"I don't blame you, and there's absolutely no excuse, so I'm not even going to try to apologize," Sam said.

"But I think I'm entitled—" Rebecca stopped and corrected that. "I'd like to know."

"When I stopped in at Sophie Sargent's for a drink, where you reached me on the phone, she gave me a manuscript she and Claude were interested in, and wanted my opinion on. I had no intention of even looking at it until maybe tomorrow, but when I got home, and Billy gave me your message that there was trouble at the printer about your program notes, and I should meet you at Tony's an hour later, I thought I'd fill in the time by taking a look at the manuscript and, well, it turned out to be more than a look. It was almost eight-thirty when I came to, so I dashed to Tony's, but you'd been and gone, so I came up here fast, and here I am, late but devoted, liking the way you look, and wishing we were alone somewhere else, where I could do more than just tell you about it."

She was looking up into his face with the faint, puzzled frown he had come to know so well: she was searching for what she called "the something more" beneath his words.

"It must be quite a story," she said.

"What?" Sam said.

"That manuscript," Rebecca said.

"Yes," Sam said, and he wished he could tell her what he had given his promise to Sophie Sargent not to tell anybody: it was the story of his life. What Kenyon Poole had done, and then locked away in his safe deposit box before he got into that plane with Jennie, was to take the material Sam had used in *Yours Is the Earth* and its sequel, *I'll Make My Heaven,* and retell the two stories as a single unit, not from the viewpoint of the boy, as Sam had done, but from the viewpoint of the girl. The result, which when he put down the last page in his Sutton Crescent study had left Sam almost paralyzed with envy, was the novel that once, when he was young enough to live by an inner fire, Samuel Silver had planned to write. He said to Rebecca, "What was all the trouble down at the printer?"

She sighed, and the frown deepened, and she said, "You're not going to tell me any more, are you?"

"I can't," Sam said. "The thing's not finished."

How could it have been? Kenyon Poole did not know that the girl who, to give him as much of the material as he had managed to get down on paper, must have been his mistress for an even longer period than Sam suspected, was going to die in that plane with him before Poole had a chance to learn the end of the story.

"The good stories are never finished," Rebecca said, and once again Sam looked at her with surprise for a moment of perception. "The good stories are like life," she said. "You just live them. What makes them bad is the writers, trying to tie up all the loose ends to make a neat finish. That's when the reader knows they're no longer good stories, because the reader knows there's only one finish to every story, just as there's only one finish to every life." She paused, and looked steadily at the orange and black collage in front of which they were standing, and then, with a small shake of her head, as though something she had wanted to put in had escaped her, Rebecca said, "The trouble at the printer was they delivered the program notes at five-thirty, as they promised, right after I finished talking to you on the phone at Mrs. Sargent's, and I discovered they'd left out the list of numbers identifying the pictures."

"Did it make that much difference?" Sam said. "After all, the pictures are all identified in that nice big fat shiny catalogue stacked up over there."

"Yes, it made all the difference," Rebecca said. "That's why I started raising hell on the phone and made Ibram meet me at the printer and we stood over him until he did a new batch of these program notes, adding the numbers and the names of the pictures."

Sam took the glossy single-fold she handed him and, with a Bud Bienstock chuckle, said, "Artists, Christ. You mind telling a simple-minded writer just what is the nature of this 'all the difference'?"

"All the difference to me, I meant," Rebecca said. "I knew you might or might not read the catalogue, but since you had read these notes in longhand this morning, I knew you'd read them in print again tonight. You're a writer. You couldn't resist doing that, and when your resistance failed, I wanted you to have the list of numbers in front of you."

Sam saw that she, too, was not going to tell him more, and since his puzzlement was not very deep, he said instead, "Then why the troubled look? When I came in here and saw you talking to Schneerboehm, you were all hunched up and tense, waiting to hear the *Titanic* had gone down."

"Well, it could have," Rebecca said. "What the horoscope said about Gemini this morning was: *Be on guard! Today you might lose the one you love!*"

Sam looked around quickly, saw that for the moment they were alone in the west wing, dipped down, and kissed her.

"Now I guess I've got to tell you about the Second Largest Outdoor Swimming Pool in the East," he said.

Rebecca said, "What?"

"On the phone?" Sam said. "When I was talking to you at five o'clock from Sophie Sargent's apartment? You called me the nicest, most thoughtful, sexiest magazine writer in the Western Hemisphere, and when I said the Second Largest Outdoor Swimming Pool in the East, you said what's that, and I said I'd tell you when you told me what the horoscope said this morning about Gemini."

"And I just have," Rebecca said. "So now you've got to tell me."

Sam nodded and said, "Once, many years ago, when I was a kid of twenty, just before I published my first novel, I was on the train going out to Westport to spend Sunday with Ham Farnsworth, the editor of Trafal-

gar, Singlenight, my publishers. I'd never been to Westport, and I was
staring out the train window, the way you do when you've got nothing to
read, and somewhere up there in Westchester I guess it is, after the train
finished going through the Bronx, I saw this huge billboard advertising an
amusement park, I think, something like that, and among the things it
offered, in addition to surf bathing and roller-coaster rides, were these huge
words, the Second Largest Outdoor Swimming Pool in the East, and they
made me laugh, because you could tell the people who had made up the
sign, because they didn't know how to use words, the sign said just the
opposite of what they wanted to say. Each word, instead of making what
they offered larger, made it smaller. The Second Largest is smaller than
the first largest, and Outdoor means maybe somewhere there could be a
bigger pool but indoors, and in the East means not bigger than maybe a
pool in the West."

Sam paused. The explanation, which he had hoped would sound funny
and ease the odd tension between them, seemed to have done just the
opposite.

"I was trying to say something nice," Rebecca said. "And I kicked you in
the teeth."

"Oh, come on, now, honeybunch."

She dismissed the carefully planted endearment with an impatient gesture. "With every word I intended to make you bigger, I made you
smaller," Rebecca said. "The nicest, most thoughtful, sexiest magazine
writer in the Western Hemisphere."

"Well, aside from the sexy part," Sam said, "Claude and Sophie Sargent
agree with you, so let's forget it and go look at some of these pictures."

"You go look," Rebecca said. "I've got to mingle."

"Can't I mingle with you?"

"No," she said. "I've got a surprise for you in the east wing."

"What kind of surprise?"

"You go look and see," Rebecca said.

She smiled, touched his cheek, and went out into the central gallery,
where, Sam could see through the arch, the male members of her family,
who he guessed must have added up to almost half a ton in their bare
feet, were still standing in a solid, silent, proud, and totally uncompre-
hending group. Sam turned, walked into the east wing, and stopped at
once just inside the arch.

The far wall, facing the arch, was dominated by a single picture. It was
hung high, higher than the pictures on the walls to the left and right,
and that this was not an accident was clear from the way the people in
front of it had to tip their heads back, as though they were looking up at

a stained-glass window in a church. The composition of the picture, which consisted of neatly outlined color masses of varying size and shape set very close together, was not unlike that of a stained-glass window, and the effect, at least on the group in the room at the moment, was not unlike that of a church: the murmurings in the other parts of the gallery were absent here; there was a hushed quality in the east wing.

The effect on Sam was somewhat different. The color patterns made no immediately recognizable impression. Yet he did not feel rising within him that inevitable and intolerably stupid question with which people who ask it shut the door at once on whatever chance they might have to understand abstract art: *"Yes, but what does it mean?"*

Sam knew. Looking at the surprise Rebecca had painted for him, he could hear Kurt Schneerboehm's voice saying: "Small, slender, not beautiful, but with brown eyes of an intense and disturbing nature, so that the effect was more powerful than beauty, and one could not forget." Sam could even understand, as he came forward into the east wing to see the number in the corner of the frame, Schneerboehm's glare and his fiercely accusing voice. "How dare you, a lowly magazine writer," he had meant, "possess such a thing?"

All the people except one woman moved away from the picture, and Sam saw the number. He flipped to the back of the program notes, ran his finger down the list, and next to the number read Rebecca's title for her creation: *My Rival.*

"She's caught me rather well."

Sam looked up, saw that the woman in front of the picture had turned, and he dropped the program notes.

"They told me you were dead," he heard his voice saying.

"Sounds like a title," Jennie said. She stooped, picked up the single-fold, and handed it to him. "Here, and stop looking at me as though I'm Miss Favisham in *Great Expectations*. It's quite simple. Ken and I never even got on that plane. When we learned everybody was assuming we were among those who were killed when it disappeared, we decided to let them continue thinking that. I told you to stop looking at me like that."

"I will, as soon as I'm able to," Sam said. "You're still my wife, legally speaking, so I'm going to have to start asking some questions. Until I can think of what they are, you'd better tell me more. Eleven years are a long time."

"Not for someone determined to write a great novel," Jennie said.

"That's why he did it?" Sam said.

"Mainly, yes," she said. "He'd been sick of writing those Westerns for years. He'd been wanting for a long time to take a crack at a serious novel but he couldn't find a subject, and it was easier to ride along with the big reputation he had and the big money he was making. All the time, though, he'd been getting ready. He bought a farm in Alberta eight years before that plane deal, and he'd been putting money in a Canadian bank steadily, under an assumed name, against the day."

"When was the day?" Sam said. "That time in Westport? When Sophie Sargent asked him to come over from the sanatorium to pull us out of that mess? And you and he saw each other for the first time?"

Jennie smiled, and he held his breath, hoping it wouldn't happen, but it did. His heart moved, and at once so did his brain. Up out of the numbing shock came the warning: unless he handled this better than Buggo Salvemini had handled it, he was lost. She could have come back for only one reason, because she wanted something she had left behind, something only he could give her, and he knew that whatever it was, this time, this last time she could have it only at the cost of his life.

"No, not quite," Jennie said. "Although we both knew, at that moment, it was bound to happen. It happened a year later. After you and I came back from Europe. You were working on a Fourth of July story for Bud Bienstock. He had to have it the next day, so I went alone to the cocktail party Bud was giving for Stephen Wise, and Poole was there. Alison Grimsby introduced us. She'd met him when Mercury bought *The Small Meal*. He asked me to come back to the New Walden, where he stayed when he was in New York, but I said no, I wasn't getting involved in that hotel business, so I asked Alison Grimsby to invite us to her apartment and then go out to the delicatessen for some sandwiches and take in a movie on the way."

"You always had to carry the ball," Sam said. "Even in the sack."

"I've never been much of an enthusiast for the male notion that a woman is an object of, and I quote, sexual gratification. My gratification means more to me than any man's, and what I want out of sex, I arrange to get. If you wait around like a simpering boob hoping some man will come along and give it to you, you'll spend your life having wet dreams and very little else. What most men do to a woman when they get her into a bed is about as close to what a woman wants as Columbus was when he kissed Ferdinand and Isabella good-bye and said wait till you see the spices I bring you back from India."

"Before you got yourself killed in that plane," Sam said, "I thought you were getting what you wanted in the building next to Alison Grimsby's."

"I was, until I met Ken Poole," Jennie said. "I don't know what your sex life is like today, but from the look of that delicately beautiful Mrs. Meissen, my guess is it hasn't changed much. You always had sex all mixed up

with love, and she's got the same kind of look. Only a dame preoccupied
with love could have painted a picture as good as this one of a woman she'd
never seen. When you were doing your best jobs in the sack, you were
always murmuring that kind of dialogue Bud Bienstock feeds his readers
with the mayonnaise substitutes. I didn't mind, because I'd trained myself
to get what I wanted out of those wrestling matches and disregard the
sonnets. The minute I met Ken, as soon as we looked at each other that
day in Westport and then again at that cocktail party for Stephen Wise, I
knew I'd met someone who felt about sex the way I did. When we met
we knew at once we were alike about that, and soon after we proved we
were right, Ken found his subject for the serious book that would get him
out of writing Westerns. The subject was me. So he was impatient to get
going. The other reason we decided the time had come to take a powder
was all that garbage those fascist bastards who run the American press
started spilling on the C.T.D.A.B.C.U.O.O.B.Y. Everybody connected
with it was a communist, they started to scream, and Ken saw at once that
until that hysteria died down, he was finished with the dear old patriotic
public that was Remembering Pearl Harbor, and it didn't have a prayer
of dying down until the end of the war, so we just settled down on his
farm in Alberta, and he started on the novel."

"I can see him doing it, but not you," Sam said. "You're not the farm
type. How did you fill in the time? Aside from that good, workmanlike
sex?"

Jennie smiled. "Living with greatness is a full-time and highly satisfying career," she said.

The smile, Sam realized, and not the words, was what he found disturbing. Probing cautiously for a reason he said, "Why did Poole come
back? The book isn't finished."

"Oh, then you've read it," Jennie said. "Good."

A moment or two went by before he realized what her statement meant.
Trying not to sound astonished, and failing, Sam said, "You *arranged* it?"

"But of course," Jennie said mockingly. "You know how highly Ken
always valued your opinion." She paused, allowing the impact of the shot
to take its full effect, before she said, "Don't look so baffled. It was quite
simple, really. That poor fat boob who is the first Sargent has become even
more simple-minded than he used to be, and that Wilkes-Barre wonder
he's married to is so busy pinning back the ears of stahf, and trying to fit
into her notions about the role of a *grande dame,* that she hasn't got time
to ask the simplest kind of business questions. All Ken did was get in touch
with his daughter, who's just graduated from Sarah Lawrence, and we

turned the manuscript over to her with a cock-and-bull story about a safe deposit box, and I'm sure you know the rest."

"Not all of it," Sam said. He still didn't know why they had wanted him to read it, but he knew he would never get that answer by direct assault, so he said, "I still don't understand why, if what you've told me is true, Poole would come back at this stage, with the book not finished."

"He hasn't come back," Jennie said. "He's still up in Alberta. As you must have seen from the way the manuscript stops, he's having a little trouble with the ending."

"*If you prick us, do we not bleed?*" Sam said. "*If you tickle us, do we not laugh? Fed with the same food, hurt with the same weapons, subject to the same diseases, warmed and cooled by the same winter and summer.*"

Startled, Jennie said, "What the hell is that?"

"Something you said eighteen years ago," Sam said. "From the stage in the Grover Cleveland High School gym on graduation night."

"Oh, I know what it *is*," Jennie said impatiently. "I'm asking what's it got to do with what we're talking about?"

"The great gentile artist who needs eleven years in a Canadian hideaway to produce two hundred and sixty pages for posterity, and the lowly Jewish journeyman who needs only ten weeks to turn out two hundred and forty pages for Bud Bienstock, we both have the same problems," Sam said. "With our endings."

"Well, at least one thing hasn't changed," Jennie said dryly. "You're still a Jew."

In his mind, his mother's bitter words that afternoon suddenly hammered again in his ears. Sam found himself staring at Jennie, examining her mocking statement, and without mockery, with terror for what had vanished without his even knowing when or how it had gone, he was asking himself: *Am I?*

"Another thing I'm still," Sam said, "and that's not clear about what you want. If Poole is still working in Canada, what are you doing here? You've never come to me or to anybody else unless you want something. What do you want now?"

"Billy," Jennie said.

For the third time that day the words which had first erupted there in the dining alcove that morning, went roaring through his head: *thus came the impact of tidal waves and earthquakes, without warning, while peaceful citizens, who thought themselves safe and had every reason to believe they were, sat munching their breakfasts, thinking of crops and jobs and dentists' bills.*

"You can't have him," Sam said.

Unexpectedly, Jennie laughed. "Oh, Christ, you slick fiction writer," she said. "I mean only I've come to *see* him. I suddenly realized last week I miss him. I just want to have a look at him."

She was lying. Sam knew it. He didn't know how he knew it, but he knew it.

"I don't know that that's a good thing," Sam said. "For years he's been thinking you were dead."

"So were you," Jennie said. "I don't see that it's hurt you to find out I'm not."

She was wrong, but he couldn't tell her that, so he said, "We'll have to discuss it. This isn't the time or place."

"Let's go to your place," Jennie said. "If he's asleep, I won't wake him. I just want to look."

He felt the temptation come up and put its hand on him and start to push. Billy was almost certain to be asleep. He could let her have a look, and then get rid of her, and it would all be over. But Sam knew it wouldn't. It couldn't be. Jennie had not come for a look. So he braced himself against the pressure of the temptation, and pushed back.

"No," he said. "I don't want him disturbed. We can discuss it tomorrow."

"I came all the way from Alberta," Jennie said. "If you won't discuss it here, or at your place, come over to mine. The New Walden is just around the corner. Come on."

"No," Sam said again, but she reached out and, right there, in the east wing of the Ibram Moulage Gallery, surrounded by the discreetly appreciative murmurs of the knowing, under the picture Rebecca had painted as a surprise for him, Jennie put her hand where it had not been for eleven years, and Sam Silver, hating himself, went.

*10

Twenty minutes later, in the darkened sitting room, he suddenly knew they were not alone.

Sam pushed her away, sat up on the couch, groped for the light she had snapped out, and snapped it on. In the sudden brightness, which wasn't really very bright, while they were both adjusting their clothes, the inside of Sam's head seemed to be going round and round to the same repeated series of sounds, like a phonograph record on which the needle has been trapped in a single groove, chanting: *No, no, no, it can't be; no, no, no, it can't be; no, no, no, it can't be.*

But of course it was, as Sam knew the moment the small figure in the bathrobe repeated the words Sam Silver had first heard on an unforgettable night in front of a Westport police station, when he was twenty and had just been overwhelmed by the terrifying realization that because he had written forty-seven pages to satisfy a girl with whom he wanted to sleep, already at twenty he would never again be quite so good a writer as he had been at nineteen, the words that lacked the old power but still had a touch of the old sardonic ring: "Why don't you stick to writing, kid?"

"She told me you were in Alberta," Sam said stupidly.

"And you believed her?"

The tone was still sardonic, but the absence of anger, even of irritation, was puzzling. Sam thought of himself, when the situation had been reversed, when he had first learned what Kenyon Poole had now just seen, and he searched for some trace of the emotions that had roared through him then like a wild animal gone crazy in a cage too small for it. There were no traces, but the search revealed the details of the incredible change. The patent-leather hair, still parted neatly in the middle, was yellowish white, like the guardsman's mustache, which, still waxed at the ends, twitched erratically, as though the muscles of the leathery, wrinkled, liver-spotted face no longer responded to their owner's commands but worked away at some humiliating tempo of their own choosing. It did not seem possible that so much disintegration could have taken place in a mere eleven years. Kenyon Poole, who Sam was shocked to realize looked older than his mother, reminded him of a ripe, glossy lemon that had been sucked dry and then tossed away to wither in the sunlight.

"I guess I should have known better," Sam said.

"We all should," Kenyon Poole said. "But we never do."

"I'm sorry," Sam said.

"Don't be," Poole said. "Not about that. I'm not much good to her any more that way, as you can see. And for what little pride I may have left, you're an improvement over our hired hand on the farm. After all, you're still her legal husband."

"And you're drunk, as usual," Jennie said. "Get back to bed."

"Not quite yet," Kenyon Poole said. "I haven't been out of the schoolroom for eleven years. A touch of freedom feels good." He smiled at Sam and said, "How'd you like the book?"

Since he was no longer sure of very much, Sam saw no point in lying about the one thing of which he was certain.

"It's the greatest thing I ever read," he said.

Kenyon Poole put a shaking hand to his twitching face, as though to make sure the smile would not come out a distorted grimace, and he said to Jennie, "You see? Praise from Sam Silver is praise from Sir Hubert."

Remembering that this was what Claude Sargent had said on that first day when he had told Sam that Kenyon Poole admired his story in *Landscape,* Sam wondered if the repetition had been intentional.

"He's a hack who minces artfully arranged garbage for Bud Bienstock," Jennie said.

"He's the only hack I ever heard of who hasn't damaged the tools of his craft, and probably the only one who has honed them to a finer cutting edge than they had when they were first handed to him," Kenyon Poole said, and he turned to Sam. "I've followed your stuff," he said. "It doesn't add up to anything, as you know, but anybody who knows anything knows it's being done by a guy who could make it add up, if he wanted to." He flicked one end of his mustache with a pathetic imitation of the old debonair gesture, and said quietly, "I have a feeling I'm the guy who made you stop wanting it to add up. For that, kid, I'm sorry. I didn't want to do it. It happened. I couldn't stop it." Since there was nothing to say to that, Sam said nothing, and Poole nodded, as though he understood the reason for Sam's silence. "You're the last man in the world I have the right to ask a favor from," Poole said. "But that's all I'm able to do any more. Ask favors. She doesn't grant me many any more. She doesn't have to. She's got everything she can get out of me. You're the only one left now who can give her anything. The favor I ask is don't do it, Sam. You'll be doing yourself a favor as well as doing one for me. Don't give her the end to her story, Sam."

It was like that moment eleven years ago in the apartment on Gramercy Park, when after leaving Alison Grimsby on the sidewalk, he had gone upstairs to tell Jennie of his strange adventure, and, on discovering she was not home, he had bowed his head and even put up his hands to shield it, as though the rockslide of revelation was actually a physical thing.

"*Her* story?" Sam managed to say.

Poole's shattered face reflected surprise, then annoyance, and finally amusement before he said quickly, "What do you think I've been doing up there for eleven years? What do you think she's wanted all her life? Why do you think she did synopses for a movie story department? Why do you think she schemed to get Marshall Umberg's job? Why do you think she slept with Ham Farnsworth? Why do you think she married you? Why do you think she kidnapped me? Why do you think she screws like a machine, coldly, efficiently, to get it out of the way for what really counts? Look what she did to that poor Salvemini kid! Look what she did to you! Look at me! Everything, all of it, her whole life, it's all been just to get closer and closer to what she was never born with, what only the lucky few are handed at birth, what I once had and you've still got, what she's got now by stealing it from me, what you and I were born with."

Sam stood silent, his head bowed, trying to think, hoping that something would come to him, something that would help, and then what came seemed ludicrous: a picture of the scene that morning in Mr. Bronson's office at the Porte School when the English instructor was briskly outlining his and Tom Sacheverell's plans for a correspondence course in writing.

"But it *can't* be taught," Sam said desperately. "You told me that yourself. Years ago, in Top Sargent's office. You said it's either handed to you at birth or it isn't. You said it can't be taught."

"It can't," Kenyon Poole said. "But I've learned something new during these years of my imprisonment: it can be handed on."

He spread his arms wide, as though to give Sam a better view of the withered husk to which the once powerful Mississippi riverboat gambler's body had been reduced.

"Look at me," said the author of *The Small Meal*. "Empty. Finished. It's all gone. She's got it all now. All except the one thing I didn't have to give her. The end of her story. That's what she came down here to get. If you give it to her, there won't be any more reason for me to go on even as I am. Don't kill me, Sam. Don't give her the end of the story."

Into the terrible silence, somehow made more terrible by the muted street noises from Madison Avenue far below, Jennie's low, mocking laughter crashed like a tray of glasses hitting a stone floor.

"It's too late," she said. "He's already given it to me."

"She's lying," Sam said to Kenyon Poole. "I haven't given her anything."

"Yes, you have," Jennie said. "When you wouldn't let me go see Billy tonight. I've just figured out why."

"Why?" Kenyon Poole asked, and the sudden desperation in his voice was as shocking to Sam as his appearance. "Tell me why?"

Jennie laughed again and shook her head. "I don't have to," she said. "I know now how to do it myself," she said. "I don't need your help to write the ending," Jennie said. "You can read it when it's finished. I don't need you any more." She turned to Sam. "I don't need you, either," she said. "I don't need anybody any more."

* 11

"It's going to look awful out there," Sam had said, but Rebecca had insisted.

Sam turned from his father's preparations at the table in the middle of the room to look out the window. Across the heads of the men who were still raking away at the two strips of hard brown earth that ran down from Rigo Park Manor's building "E" to the cracked cement sidewalk, Sam could see the liveried Frenchman seated behind the wheel of the sleek maroon and black Bentley parked at the curb.

"Probably the first time anything like that will have been seen on Sixty-seventh Road," Sam had said to Rebecca. "Or maybe even the entire Borough of Queens."

"I do wish Anton hadn't made the offer," Rebecca had said this morning before Sam had set out for Queens. "If you'd only waited until he walked away when you came back into the gallery and told me what you'd planned, he wouldn't have got in on the act. But you blurted it all out right there in front of him, and Anton's so polite and sensitive, I just couldn't let you say no when he offered the car, and I must say you'll find it a lot more convenient. When it's all over, you and Billy won't have to go through all that mess you always struggle through when you go out to Queens, trying to find a cab to take you back."

"It doesn't matter," Sam had said, but now he wished he could have come out with the taxi driver who had brought him here from the Oatley-Wicke Building after his lunch with Claude Sargent, the man who had said this isn't the town it used to be, but it sure as hell once was. Sam would have liked to tell him that once again a small piece of it was going to be. "But you remind me to thank Anton later," Sam had said. "I was so excited when the idea hit me, I couldn't wait to tell you, and I guess I didn't really see Anton standing there."

"You certainly were, and you certainly didn't," Rebecca had said, and the faint, puzzled, searching-for-something-more frown had come into her face as she added, "What's the rush, Sam?"

The collapse of Kenyon Poole would involve Jennie on at least two fronts: with the doctors, and with the reporters. Sam did not doubt that Jennie would not involve herself very deeply, or for very long. She clearly thought she had finally achieved what for all her life she had schemed to get. It wasn't very likely that she would waste much time on the remains or memories of those who had helped her get it. Sam wanted his own plans finished before she started on hers.

"It's something that's been bothering me for a long time," he had said to Rebecca. "I didn't realize how badly it was bothering me until now. When it hit me, when I realized what it was, I knew at last what was wrong, what I wanted, and what I had to do. So I want to do it fast."

"You sound like Saul on the road to Tarsus," Rebecca said.

"If I do, then I'm making the wrong sounds," Sam had said. "I'm not having a blinding vision. I'm just waking up."

Mrs. Silver came hobbling in from the kitchen, carrying the seven-branched silver candlestick that used to be taken down every Friday night from its resting place on the gas meter in the East Tenth Street kitchen, and she set it on the table where Sam's father was unwrapping a prayer cloth.

"So what are we waiting for, for what?" Sam's mother said as she struck a match and started touching the small flame to the tiny wicks, bent sideways in all directions like the heads of a group of puzzled observers speculating in silence on why their presence had been commanded.

"I want Abe and Hannah to be here," Sam said. "Don't you, Billy?"

"Anything you say, Pops," said Billy from the couch on which he was reading in the *Daily News* what, when Sam was a boy, was known as "the jokes." "As long as you give me a note explaining all this to Mr. Bronson, so he won't hit me with a demerit for playing hooky, I'm at your service, beck and call, and yours to command. You see what Daddy Warbucks ordered Orphan Annie to do with Sandy this morning?"

"Don't worry about Mr. Bronson," Sam said. "I'll go back to school with you and explain in person. Ma, I have a reason for wanting Abe and Hannah to be here, so just relax."

"Always with the relax," Mrs. Silver said. "Whenever I ask him when Billy he'll have his bar mitzvah, he tells me never. This morning on the telephone it's all of a sudden hurry up, we'll make our own bar mitzvah here in the house. Now we're ready to make it, it's wait for Abe and Hannah and relax."

She stepped back, blew out the match, and watched the seven tiny struggling flames suck at the tallow for strength, take shape, and stand proudly upright.

"Hey!" Billy said. "You mean I'm having a bar mitzvah after all?"

"A sort of do-it-yourself version," Sam said. "There's no time for a full-dress affair, but as I'm sure Mr. Bronson would put it, it's the spirit that counts."

Billy's face seemed to change, as though an unexpected thought had made him forget he was supposed to be a character in that *Satevepost* story about the Midwestern scoutmaster and the slum kids. Quietly, the boy said, *"Caesar, I never stood on ceremonies, yet now they fright me."*

Just as quietly, Sam said, "No, not quite. Our ceremonies were old and respected and working honorably for thousands of years before Caesar and his boys started cutting up chickens."

"What are you two talking about?" Mrs. Silver said.

"Faith," Sam said, and the door opened.

Abe Ostreich, on the threshold, paused to make his small courtly bow, and his wife Hannah entered. Then Abe came in, his face bright, eager, and apologetic, the folds of the thigh-length sports coat whipping the air as he struggled out of it, saying, "Excuse us. We hope we're not too late. It's that Mrs. Levine in Two-J. Her and her dishwasher. Honest, before we put in here in Rigo Park Manor dishwashers, my life it was like a vacation. Now it's all the time hurry up come fix, especially that Mrs. Levine. I tell her you have to rinse the dishes before you put them in the machine, otherwise you're washing garbage, and the machine chokes up, as much as to say what am I, a dishwasher or a garbage pail, but she won't listen, that Mrs. Levine, and just as we were leaving the house to come over here, she calls again and she—"

"Abe," Mrs. Silver said coldly, "it's here a bar mitzvah, not a plumbers' convention."

Abe flushed, and bobbed his head, and said, "Ooh. I'm sorry. Hello, Sam. Outside, the car, it's yours?"

"Hello," Sam said. "Abe, Hannah. No, it belongs to Mrs. Meissen. She let me have it for a couple of hours."

"Ooh," Abe said again. "The lady from in Winchell yesterday!"

"Abe," Mrs. Silver said icily.

Abe put his hand over his mouth and stepped toward the couch. Hannah followed.

"No," Mrs. Silver said. "You and Hannah over here." Abe and Hannah moved obediently and took their places as directed. "Sam," Mrs. Silver said. "You a little closer." Sam moved a little closer. "So all right," Mrs. Silver said to her husband. "Begin."

Sam's father, his gentle voice almost inaudible, said, "Billy?"

The boy came forward. Mr. Silver put the yamalke on Billy's head, draped the prayer cloth over the boy's shoulders, stepped back to examine him, then adjusted the folds so the long white tassels hung evenly down the front of the Brooks Brothers jacket that was part of the Porte School lower-classman's uniform. Then Mr. Silver picked up the siddir bound in white plastic, with the brass clasp at the edge, that would belong to Billy after the bar mitzvah ceremony was ended, and he thumbed the pages until he found the right one.

"Hold like this," Sam's father said to Sam's son, handing the boy the open prayer book. Billy took it in both hands, and Sam, seeing that the book was shaking, had a stabbing moment of doubt for what he had set in motion. Then Mr. Silver picked up his own siddir, the old black book with the scuffed cover and the broken spine and the frayed pages that had come with him from Rumania more than half a century ago and was a part of Sam's earliest memories and, in a voice at once stern and gentle, the old man said to the boy, "Me, I'll read in Hebrew. Then you, you read back to me there, on that side, it's in English. All right?"

Billy nodded, and Sam, watching the boy's shaking hands, did not at first see him turn his head. Then Sam saw the look on the boy's face, and his heart swelled, squeezing out the moment of doubt. He was doing the right thing.

"So," Mr. Silver said. "We begin." He cleared his throat and, eyes fixed on the old black siddir, he said, "Today, you, Shloymeh Leib—"

As the gently cadenced Hebrew phrases rolled out, Sam felt the startled glances coming at him from all parts of the room, like a shower of arrows from a circular ambush, and he turned to meet them, smiling at Abe and at Hannah and at his mother, and then, on the next circuit, Sam's eyes recorded the change: the surprise has turned to appreciation; they knew why he had insisted on waiting for Abe and Hannah; and all at once he missed Rebecca. He wanted to tell her that Shloymeh Leib was the name of Abe's youngest brother, who was killed at Dachau. It also happened to be Billy's name in Yiddish.

Sam's father paused and waited.

Billy, his hands still shaking, but his voice steady and clear, read: "Blessed are thou, O Lord our God, King of the universe, who hast chosen us from all peoples, and hast given us the law. Blessed are thou, O Lord, who givest the Law."

Sam could feel something inside him give way, like the unhooking of the buckle of a belt pulled too tight, and the vacuum cleaner of his craft, sucking up the image for future use, left him free to grasp what was happening to him not as a writer but as a human being: Jennie at last no longer mattered. Whatever she did with the ending to her novel that she claimed he had given her inadvertently the night before, it could not affect Sam Silver or his son. He had made it back to where he belonged, and Billy had made it with him—no, it was Billy who had led him back—and they were both safe.

"These are your tvillim," Mr. Silver said, handing Billy the small blue velvet bag embroidered with silver and gold. "With these, every morning, to live in peace with God, you must—"

The voice rolled on, reminding Sam of the sounds his mother used to make when he was very small, and he had whooping cough, and she sang him to sleep every night. He turned to look across the room, and he saw she was looking at him. Their eyes met, and his mother smiled through her tears, and Sam's heart swelled again: he had made it back all the way: to the security of the East Tenth Street kitchen, to the relaxed sense of purpose and the climate of untroubled belief that had been the way of life into which he had been born, and which he was now passing on to his son.

"Amen," Sam said in the deep silence of his heart, and the desire to tell Rebecca became momentarily unbearable. Marriage would be impossible for months, until the divorce from Jennie was arranged, but that was a minor point. The main thing was that what had seemed hopeless yesterday morning in his lime-green study uptown, had been accomplished here, in this equivalent of the East Tenth Street kitchen where his life had begun: Sam Silver had found the end to his story.

"I know how to fix *They Told Me You Were Dead*," he wanted to tell Rebecca, and he wanted even more to have her look at him hard, the way she always did when she was most relentlessly searching for the Truth, but this time, when she found it, Sam knew she would not turn and run. The look would change, perhaps she would smile, as she told him without words that the journeyman she had loved but never understood was comprehensible at last: as one artist to another, Rebecca's eyes would say, she finally did understand.

Of course, Sam told himself, he would never be able to sell the ending to Bud Bienstock. It would make the readers of *American Bride* uneasy. They would not grasp what one of their favorite authors had at last grasped clearly: the answer to why, having been unable for two years to love Rebecca, he now knew he could not live without her. Sam, who had trained himself never to write one, had finally learned his lesson: life, which in the pages of *American Bride* had to be a neatly made package, in the real world could never be anything else but a *come-to-realizer*: having realized at last that it was Jennie who had bound him to the almost forty-year struggle to move forty blocks uptown, he was free at last, now that Jennie was forever out of his life, to marry another woman.

"Today," Billy repeated after Sam's father, "I am a man."

So am I, said Sam in peaceful silence, feeling the glow of the inner flame that had gone out eleven years ago begin to come alive and grow brighter, and as the warmth spread through him, he knew Bud Bienstock and *American Bride* would never again matter. Because for Sam Silver the only way to fix *They Told Me You Were Dead* was to burn it.

The inner flame, lighting up areas that had been dark so long, suddenly made Sam wish impatiently that his father would hurry and finish. All this bar mitzvah stuff was important, and nobody knew it better than Sam Silver, but the thing that had possessed him seventeen years ago, when at his mother's kitchen table he had poured out his first book, was gnawing at him again. There was only one way to ease the irritation: by getting back to his study and starting on the book he had thought he would never write, the book Jennie foolishly thought she had at last written.

She was wrong. So was Kenyon Poole. It could no more be handed on than it could be taught. What none of them had suspected, since they were real people and they knew life could never be a *come-to-realizer*, was that it could be stolen.

In the long run, however, when she came to write a second book, Jennie would find that the theft had done her no good. It could not be repeated. There would be nobody left to steal from. Kenyon Poole and Sam Silver were out of her reach at last: he had succeeded where even the author of *The Small Meal* had failed: Jennie, who had stolen the tools of the great man's trade, had not been able to put so much as a scratch on Sam Silver's set.

From somewhere out in the unreal, shapeless world that would always be run by others and had already begun to slip away from him, Sam could hear faintly the voices of his father and his son. In the real and orderly world of his imagination, where he and only he was always in charge, the opening sentence of the book, for which all of his life had been a preparation, was beginning to take shape.

What took him by surprise, Sam could see the old Parker scrawling on the fresh sheet of foolscap, *was the suggestion about a telephone answering service.*

ABOUT THE AUTHOR

JEROME WEIDMAN, novelist and short-story writer, was born in 1913 on New York's Lower East Side. At the age of twenty-four, he was studying law at New York University when his first novel, *I Can Get It for You Wholesale,* was published in 1937. He quit law school at once to devote all his time to writing, and has been doing so ever since, except during the war, when he served with the Office of War Information in this country and overseas. He has traveled extensively in America and the far corners of the world, from which he has brought back raw material for a dozen novels and approximately two hundred short stories, published in almost every magazine in the United States as well as in Canada, Europe, Australia and Asia. His books have been translated into eight languages. His first play, *Fiorello!,* written in collaboration with George Abbott, was awarded the 1959 Pulitzer Prize. Recently produced was his third musical play, adapted from his own *I Can Get It for You Wholesale.* THE SOUND OF BOW BELLS, his nineteenth book, was finished in New York City, to which Mr. Weidman, his wife and his two sons returned after living in Westport, Connecticut, for a dozen years.